THE SIGNIFICANT

BY
KYRA ANDERSON

For information on future works, please visit:
www.kjamidon.com

Copyright © 2016 by K.J. Amidon

All rights reserved. Except as permitted under the U.S. Copyright Act of 1976, no part of this publication may be reproduced, distributed, or transmitted in any form or by any means, or stored in a database or retrieval system, without prior written permission of the publisher

Website: www.kjamidon.com

Published by K.J. Amidon

ISBN: 978-1522730118

Cover Art by K.J. Amidon

Printed in the United States

Dedicated to:

My friends and family who inspire me every day

The numerous people who would not let me quit, even though it was very tempting

T.L. Coulter—You are the best! Thank you for all your support!

All of the readers who took a leap of faith to read this book. You have no idea what you're in for, do you?

Table of Contents

Dedicated to	v
Chapter One	1
Chapter Two	9
Chapter Three	15
Chapter Four	22
Chapter Five	29
Chapter Six	38
Chapter Seven	45
Chapter Eight	52
Chapter Nine	64
Chapter Ten	74
Chapter Eleven	83
Chapter Twelve	92
Chapter Thirteen	109
Chapter Fourteen	122
Chapter Fifteen	130
Chapter Sixteen	137
Chapter Seventeen	144
Chapter Eighteen	163
Chapter Nineteen	175
Chapter Twenty	195
Chapter Twenty-One	209
Chapter Twenty-Two	219
Chapter Twenty-Three	240
Chapter Twenty-Four	257
Chapter Twenty-Five	274
Chapter Twenty-Six	287
Chapter Twenty-Seven	299
Chapter Twenty-Eight	323
Chapter Twenty-Nine	335
Chapter Thirty	352
Chapter Thirty-One	363
Chapter Thirty-Two	376
Chapter Thirty-Three	396
Chapter Thirty-Four	406
Chapter Thirty-Five	416
Chapter Thirty-Six	435
Chapter Thirty-Seven	446
Chapter Thirty-Eight	453
Chapter Thirty-Nine	462
Chapter Forty	537
Chapter Forty-One	552
Chapter Forty-Two	565
Chapter Forty-Three	573
Epilogue	585

Chapter One

Kailynn had to use all of her self-discipline to get out of bed that morning, scurrying across the room to grab her clothes, cringing when she felt how cold the garments were after being strewn about the floor the entire night. A groan behind her caused her to turn, though she lost her balance as her head spun. She pressed one hand to her face and quietly cursed herself for drinking so heavily the previous night.

"Where ya runnin' off to?" a voice, gravelly with sleep, mumbled from the bed.

"Some of us gotta work," she said, pressing her clothes to her chest in an effort to warm herself. "It's *freezing* in here…"

"Heat's out again. What'd'ya expect? I live in a dump."

"Raffy," Kailynn groaned, "you could get a job and *pay* for stuff to work."

"I work," Raphael defended irritably.

"I wouldn't call lifting credits from tourists work," Kailynn murmured, throwing her clothes on the bed to search for her panties among the tangled mess.

"Got you out of trouble with those loan sharks," Raphael said into his pillow.

"That was my brother's shit deal, not mine," she growled, snatching up her panties and pulling them on hurriedly. "I gotta go home and change," she muttered, pulling her pants on, jumping when she could not get them over her hips. Raphael glanced at her and laughed.

"Jump some more."

"Shut up, prick," she snapped, finally succeeding in donning her pants.

"You're getting a nice ass," Raphael noted, turning on his side and propping himself up to look at her. "I guess all that lifting at work has done some good."

Kailynn pulled her shirt on, leaving her bra slung across the bed.

"I'm so late. Brad's gonna kill me."

"No, he ain't." Raphael shook his head, flopping back to the bed. "He's got the hots for you. Just smile and show some cleavage, and he'll forgive you."

Kailynn grabbed her jacket from the back of the door to the one-room flat and swung it over her shoulders.

"Hey!" Raphael called quickly as she opened the door. "Am I gonna see you tonight?"

"Don't you always?" she chuckled, ducking out the door and closing it behind her, shivering as she huddled into her coat. Winter was having difficulty leaving that year. Tiao was generally a cold planet to begin with, but it had been getting worse the last few years, each winter lasting longer than the one before.

The street became dark in the early morning hours. Every night, the street lit up with neon signs and scrolling advertisements, enticing tourists to the Walking District. Even though the tourists who came physically to Tiao and visited the capital city of Anon were part of high society, there were still few curious enough about the darker neighborhoods, looking for drugs and prostitutes.

The Walking District was known for catering to those with salacious appetites. It was considered part of the slums of Anon. Those with money were very conspicuous and were often the targets of mugging and pickpocketing. Anon residents who frequented the bars and brothels knew how to keep their money safe. Tourists were not as fortunate—Kailynn never cared about the tourists. The money Raphael stole from them had always been welcome.

She left the Walking District, crossing the district border through an alley into the district of Trid—the non-citizen district that Kailynn called home. While Raphael, her close friend from childhood was lucky to live in the Walking District, despite being a non-citizen Trid as well, Kailynn was never able to scrape enough money together to keep rent on a place in the flashy Walking District.

Border Patrol was sleeping, as usual. The one conscious guard, who had likely lost a bet with the others on his shift, was nursing a beer, grumbling about his job and the cold winter. Kailynn slipped by him easily, slinking into the shadows of Trid as naturally as the winter breeze.

She passed a few underground bars where Trids sold products they managed to lift off transport vehicles going in and out of the Walking District. Of course, with the Trids being so broke, nothing was paid for in credits, but in services or sex.

That was the way of Trid.

Kailynn greeted a few friends as they stumbled home, numb from alcohol and drugs. She squeezed through the broken doors of the building she had called home for six years and ascended the stairs, being sure to avoid the large hole in the third step. There were a few others who shared the building with her, but they never spoke to one another. They would look at each other nervously, never sure who was coming into the building and never exchanging words with the other squatters.

Kailynn fought to get the door open that led to her room, where she had an old mattress with every blanket she had ever collected—the number totaled eleven. Kailynn knew that she could always get a warm place to stay and a decent meal by cozying up to someone who clearly had money in the Walking District, but after a childhood friend was killed by Officials fighting arrest for illegal prostitution, Kailynn decided it was not worth the risk.

While prostitution was extremely common in Trid, the Walking District was still part of the illustrious capital, which meant all prostitution had to be regulated. Many Trids had been imprisoned or killed in the Walking District for pretending to be legal prostitutes.

Instead, Kailynn spent her nights with Raphael. He may have lived in a dump, but at least under the covers with him, it was warm.

Kailynn tossed her blankets aside, desperately trying to find the jumpsuit she had to wear to work as well as some clean panties and a bra. She was able to find her stash of clean underwear, but the jumpsuit was not around the bed. Cursing and hoping she was not too late to work, she tore the bed apart one more time, finally finding the jumpsuit tangled around one of her blankets.

She stripped quickly, pulling on the new panties and then grabbing her jumpsuit, shoving her legs in and zipping it up to her waist before trying to find a bra. That was when she remembered that she had a habit of leaving her bras at Raphael's place, because she was always late for work after staying with him.

Kailynn rolled her eyes, and put her jumpsuit on completely.

"Fuck it, bras are stupid."

She dashed out the door, hopping to put her boots on again as she reached the top of the stairs. She ran out into the cold and used the well-known route past another Border Patrol station to return to the Walking District and to the warehouse where she worked.

"Kailynn! You're late, *again*!" a voice bellowed from the check-in desk. She waved briefly before running into the back and finding her supervisor, Brad.

When the tall, brown-haired, green-eyed man saw her, he sighed heavily and shook his head.

"Kailynn…"

"I know, I know."

"…we're working on school rations today. Transports Three, Four, and Five."

"Thanks, Brad," Kailynn said, running to join the rest of her team at the loading bays.

Kailynn had been lucky to get a job at the Hunter & Leo Packing Warehouse. She was not educated enough to work in the actual plant, where they made the food rations, but had managed to talk her way into the distribution center. If a crate would break open, Kailynn would sneak a few of the silver-wrapped bars for herself, even though she hated the chalky taste. She never understood why the Hunter & Leo Rations were distributed so widely over the planet when their ration bars tasted like cement compared to Kieble Rations—of course, those ration bars were more expensive because they used ingredients from the food they harvested in their greenhouses rather than just putting the proteins and nutrients into a mush and heating that into a bar form.

Kailynn hoped that she would get an assignment soon to go with a transport team to another part of the planet. She had never been out of Anon, but had a very strong sense of adventure and had always dreamed of getting out of the capital, or even off of Tiao to visit the other planets of the Altereye System.

She was disappointed that she was, once again, not on a long-distance transport. She had been on the Anon Schools Route at least one hundred times. It was boring.

Kailynn helped move the crates onto the transport vehicles, sorting them based on type and school, working methodically, laughing at Jenn's story about her sister giving a lap dance to a rich tourist and slipping seven hundred credits off his account when he paid for her time. Of course, Jenn's sister also owed a shark nearly three thousand credits, so the seven hundred was only a small dent in the amount keeping her dancing tables in the Walking District's clubs.

As the group was loading the final crates onto the transport vehicles, Brad's voice caught Kailynn's attention.

"Kailynn, you got a visitor!"

"What?" She poked her head out of the transport.

"I said you got a visitor!"

Kailynn was surprised to see a very familiar sandy-haired man standing next to Brad.

"Theo?"

She began walking to her older brother when Brad caught her arm.

"Look, I don't mind if you wanna chat with your friends while you work, but I don't pay you to stand around talking to Johns."

"Lay off, Brad," she groaned, pulling her arm out of his grasp. "He's my brother. I'm gonna take a smoke break."

Brad rolled his eyes and watched her walk to the side door of the warehouse, her brother in tow. When the door closed behind them, Kailynn pushed her hand into her pocket and pulled out a crumpled pack of cigarettes and a lighter.

"What the hell, Theo?"

"Nice to see you, too," Theo teased.

"What do you want?" Kailynn asked. "I'm already on thin ice with this job. I can't have you comin' here and pissing off my boss."

"You keep not wearing a bra and he won't mind," Theo chuckled, nodding to her jumpsuit where her nipples were clearly visible, hard from the cold outside air.

"Don't be an ass. What do you want?"

"Lynni," he smiled excitedly, "we've got a great plan."

"Oh no," Kailynn groaned, rolling her eyes, her entire frame slumping. "*No*. I'm not gonna be part of any of those half-baked schemes you and the Heart of Trid gang come up with. I had to beg Raphael to pay for what happened last time."

"No, this is different!" Theo insisted. "Look at this." He reached into his pocket and pulled out an identification card, handing it to Kailynn. She sighed, holding the cigarette in her lips as she took the card and looked it over. When she saw the emblem on the card, she groaned and tried to hand it back.

"Yeah, right, you got one of the Elite's ID cards." She sighed. "You're a fuckin' moron, Theo. It's fake."

"Did you even see *which* Elite it was?"

"Theo, it's a damn fake!"

"No, it's not!" Theo protested sharply. "You know Liam?"

"The twitchy one?"

"Yeah, he got a temp job working in the Syndicate Building. He was doin' janitorial and workin' in the securities office where they were redistributing Elite ID cards because there was some kind of security breach, or whatever. The point is, he was around when Golden Elite Isa's card was being printed, and he took the new one and swapped it with the old one."

"That's bullshit."

"No, it's not!"

"When was this?"

"Three days ago."

"Well, then, if it was true, you would have been tracked and arrested already," Kailynn said, trying to force the card back into his hands. "They probably have tracers on that."

"Did you see that there's a corner missing?"

Kailynn blinked twice at her brother, silent, feeling the card become heavier in her hand. Slowly, she turned the card toward her, looking over the information, struggling with the words written on the card.

"What does this say?"

"It's Golden Elite Isa's ID card, Lynni."

Kailynn looked up at her brother, feeling the fear swell inside her.

"Are you fucking mental?!" she hissed. "You guys have the ID card of the most powerful Elite in the *entire fucking system*?!"

"Just listen, Lynni—"

"No, I don't want any part in this!"

"Just hear me out, please," Theo said, grabbing her arm as she tried to walk back inside. "We're gonna get her."

"What do you mean you're going to get her?"

"Venus. We're gonna find her, and we're gonna shut her down."

Kailynn was so stunned she could only stare at her brother's enthusiastic green eyes for several long moments, her mouth hanging uselessly open. She glanced once each direction and then leaned closer to her brother.

"You're going to shut down the computer that runs the entire damn planet?"

Theo nodded quickly.

"Davi cracked the codes on the card. He found all the addresses classified under the Syndicate and found one that is completely out of character with the rest of the buildings. Golden Elite Isa is the *only* one who can access Venus, so the card has to open the door where Venus is. We have the location of Venus."

"I find it hard to believe that the Elites would be that careless with information."

"Everything is computerized. It would make sense that there is no way to get to Venus without coming across some electronic lock. We get in there, we unplug Venus, and the Elites fall."

"Along with the rest of the planet," Kailynn growled. "I hate Venus and the Elites as much as you do, but this is *suicidal*."

"Where is your Trid pride?" Theo hissed. "It was those asshole Elites in the Syndicate that kept us from becoming citizens. It's the reason we're all freezing and starving to death, and why the raid teams come and kill anyone they find in the streets of Trid. Don't you see? If we can shut down Venus, everyone else will have to do what we do just to survive! We'll all be equal again."

Kailynn sighed heavily.

"Theo..."

"Please, Kailynn, we could use your help."

"What could *I* do?"

"The gang needs a distraction while we get into the building. There's probably guards, and we just need them to be a little distracted for, like, five minutes."

"C'mon, Theo," Kailynn whined. "I've been working here for seven months. I'm starting to get my life back together. I don't need to remind you that *you're* the reason I fell into such deep shit."

"You think they're going to let you go out of Anon?" Theo hissed, pointing at the door to the warehouse. "I bet, even if you let Brad fuck you, he wouldn't let you go anywhere. You're a Trid. Everyone knows it. You need fucking papers to get out of Anon." Theo shook his head. "This is as far as you're going to get, Lynni. Unless we find a way to tear down the Elite Syndicate and shut down Venus, we're going to die in an alley like Dad."

Kailynn shied away from her brother, her fear turning cold in her belly.

Theo sighed and pulled his sister into a hug, kissing the top of her head.

"I'm going to be with the others tonight," he whispered. "Think about it and let me know tonight if you're going to help us."

■■■

Everyone on the team noticed the change in Kailynn as they drove on their route to the schools in Anon. She was thinking over everything Theo had told her, hating that she saw the truth in his words. She would never get any further than the warehouse. She was a Trid—a non-citizen—one of Anon's Forgotten—the black spot on Tiao's glittering surface.

For the first time in several months, Kailynn stared out the small rectangular window in the side of the transport, watching Anon pass by her. As usual, only transports were on the streets in the middle of the day. There was no reason for a well-off citizen of Anon to leave the house. All work was conducted in NCB chairs, devices that allowed people to have a virtual presence for whatever job they worked. There were some lower-class citizens who had to travel for their jobs, but in the middle of the day, there was no one on the roads.

It was very common for people to go days without seeing another live human, or speaking to another person's face. That was why there were businesses like Companion and Secret Partners Inc. that specialized in providing human interaction—for a price. Kailynn had heard rumors of the companion prostitution in Anon, but she could not tell what rumors had been exaggerated and which were fact. She had heard that those who worked as a Significant—as they were called—were asked to do all sorts of sickening things for the people who paid them, such as acting like the child of their client, or the wife or husband. The work of a Significant was always very secretive, so it was impossible to know what Significants actually did with clients.

When they returned from their run to the schools, Jenn walked up to Kailynn and put a hand on her shoulder.

"Hey, you've been quiet all afternoon. Y'alright?"

"Yeah…"

"Try ta be less enthusiastic," Jenn teased.

"I've just been thinking, that's all," Kailynn murmured. "Do you ever think that…maybe the planet would be better without the Elites? And Venus?"

"That's dangerous talk," Jenn hissed. She glanced around before leaning forward to whisper, "But, I'll tell you, I would give my right arm to see those pampered Elites try and survive like us."

Chapter Two

"You're not even gonna tell me what's wrong?"

Kailynn turned to Raphael, surprised out of her silent stupor and brought back to the loud noises of the club.

"Huh?"

"What's with you?" Raphael asked, wrapping an arm around her shoulders as they sat in a booth in the back corner.

"Yeah, ya been actin' funny all night," Viv said, smiling as she leaned forward. "Ya already take somethin' tonight?"

"No."

"C'mon, Viv," Trey laughed, nudging his girlfriend in the arm, "Kailynn's all about gettin' on the straight n' narrow, now."

"Bullshit," Kailynn huffed. "I don't have money to spend on drugs since my shit brother's fuck up last year."

"Ah, lay off 'im," Oggie said, stubbing out his cigarette in the ashtray on the table. "Theo's doin' Trid proud—always lookin' for ways to screw over the Elites."

"And that does Trid proud when he fucks up and pays for a bomb that doesn't even work?" Kailynn growled. "Then *I'm* stuck payin' for it."

"C'mon," Alyssa said with a smile. "You know those asshole Elites don't give a damn 'bout us. It's about time we give 'em something to give a damn about."

"Ah, Kailynn, remember?" Raphael smiled broadly. "You were so proud of him when he put all of Anon in lockdown as they tried to find the bomb. So what if it didn't work? It scared the hell out of them when they thought they were gonna lose those precious Elites."

Kailynn sighed heavily.

"So what if the Elites die?" she grumbled. "There's a thousand made every year. They probably wouldn't even blink."

"Hey, that's not the Kailynn I know," Oggie said. "When did you get so *boring*? You're the Wild Child of Trid. I mean, no offense to Raffy over there, but we all know yer the brains behind this gang. The one who wanted to see the Elites try n' survive like we do, ya know? Who gives a fuck if a thousand Elites are made all the time? They ain't human. *We* are! Where's your sense of pride? When did you conform so much to what Anon thought of you?"

Kailynn's jaw dropped.

"Boring?" she repeated. "I'm *boring*?" She grabbed her drink. "Fuck that, I'm still Trid's Wild Child!"

"A'ight!" Viv cheered.

"My Trid blood runs thicker than anyone here!" Kailynn laughed. She pulled herself onto the table, lifting her glass high and raising her voice.

"Hey!" she called. "I just wanna say somethin'!" The bar did not completely quiet, but many people turned to her. "I know this is the Walking District of Anon, but I think a lot of you have better blood than that!" Cheers greeted her as other Trids agreed. "So, on behalf of all of us, I would like to turn to the cameras and send a message to our leaders." She lifted her glass higher. "*Fuck*. Venus."

Another round of cheers greeted her as she downed her entire shot and cheered loudly. Raphael laughed and grabbed her leg, pulling her into his lap.

"Alright, that's fine in Trid. You do that too often here and you're going to bring the raids."

The drinking continued late into the night, as always. Kailynn was stumbling, her arm around Raphael's waist to keep her steady when they finally exited the bar. Raphael had stolen a few hundred credits off some oblivious tourists, so the drinking had continued even later, which meant Kailynn had imbibed more alcohol than she considered normal.

Raphael took her back to his place where they climbed under the covers so that the heat from having sex would keep them warm. While Raphael slept, Kailynn watched patterns float over the cracked ceiling, feeling the alcohol slowly wear off as she thought over a million scattered ideas.

It was nearing dawn when she grabbed her clothes, dressed, and walked deep into the Trid district, where an abandoned car garage stood near the lake. The garage was surrounded by junk piles from the landfill around the lake that could not fit within the fenced junkyard.

The Heart of Trid gang had claimed the garage as their base of operations, though they had much territory around the lake. Other gangs had not tried to take the land in over a year, but the Heart of Trid gang never let their guard down. For this reason, Kailynn was sure that, when she entered the garage, she knocked three times slowly, followed by two rapid knocks, signaling that she was an ally.

The back door opened loudly, setting Kailynn's teeth on edge as the sound aggravated her growing headache. She stepped in quietly, wondering why the garage was almost silent. She found the members of the gang unconscious in various areas of the main garage floor, bottles thrown carelessly, likely from celebrating their plan to shut down Venus. It did not bother them that shutting down the supercomputer of the planet would leave the entire planet in a state of chaos. To those who had suffered through growing up in Trid, it was only right that those who lived in grandeur had to struggle to survive.

Stepping cautiously around the sleeping, but armed, figures of the Heart of Trid gang, Kailynn found her brother.

"Theo," she said, shaking her brother's shoulder. Theo groaned and tried to swat Kailynn away. "Theo." The older Evada sibling grit his teeth and turned onto his back, blinking slowly.

"Lynni?" he mumbled, his eyes squinted against his hangover.

"Okay. I'll help you take her down."

■■■

"Now I *know* something is wrong."

Kailynn blinked, startled at the ration bag that was suddenly in front of her face. She stared at it before glancing briefly up at Raphael. She took the bag, but did not take a bite out of the bar inside, her eyes returning to her feet. Raphael sat on the bed with her.

"Did your brother do somethin' again?"

Kailynn turned quickly.

"What?"

"Why are you all the way out in space?" Raphael asked with a smile. "I mean, you've always been a bit of a space cadet, but this is out of character, even for you."

"Don't call me a space cadet," Kailynn sneered. "I'm just thinking. Is that a crime?"

"Lynni, don't be like that." Raphael sighed, rolling his eyes. "I can tell something is bothering you. You didn't even notice that I got the heat working."

Kailynn shook her head, resealing the ration bag and tossing it aside, laying back on Raphael's bed.

"I'm just being stupid today, that's all."

"Today?" Raphael teased.

Kailynn punched him in the thigh. The man laughed and went to his side, looking over Kailynn's troubled features.

"Are you really not gonna talk to me?"

"Why do I have to tell you everything?" Kailynn asked pointedly.

"You don't," Raphael admitted. "I just want to make sure you're not in trouble."

"I'm not," Kailynn said. "I'm just sick of this life, like the rest of Trid. Those dickwads in Anon don't give a shit about us, and we're sitting here celebrating that the heat is back on so we don't freeze."

"You did not know the heat was on until I told you," Raphael pointed out.

"That's not the point, Raffy."

"I know, I know," he tried to appease her. "But, there's nothing we can do about it. You and I were born Trids. There's no way for us to get citizenship. Hell, they've even stopped giving citizenship to those who had to move into Trid because they couldn't afford anywhere else."

"And how is that fair?"

"Life ain't fair."

Kailynn ground her teeth together. She wanted to vent all of her frustrations about the upper classes and how much the Trids suffered in comparison, but she knew that the rant would get her nowhere. Everyone in Trid had the same feelings, but talking about them never resolved the problem. It only worked her up and made her angry for days.

"What do you think the world would be like without Venus?"

Raphael sighed and fell onto his back, staring at the ceiling.

"I don't know," he murmured. "Hard to imagine what things would be like without her. She runs everything." He was quiet for a few moments, thinking about how he wanted to respond. "Maybe it wouldn't be much different. I mean, through history, hasn't there always been a low class and a high class?"

"I guess." Kailynn shrugged. "I don't care about history. I only care about now."

"Me too," Raphael agreed. "Why are you askin' now?"

"I'm just wondering if shutting her down would be a good thing or not."

"Why would it matter?" Raphael chuckled. "It's not like you'll ever get a chance to shut her down."

"I know."

Raphael rolled on top of Kailynn, smiling at her.

"I know the heat is working, but I can still screw you so well that you'll forget about the problems of the world."

Kailynn barked a laugh.

"Don't flatter yourself."

Raphael's jaw dropped and he laughed.

"What? You think I can't?"

"Why don't we find out?" Kailynn challenged with a devilish grin.

Even though Kailynn was exhausted—Raphael gave his best effort, and it did take Kailynn a very long time to regain her train of thought—she went into the cold night air, walking among the neon lights that illuminated the streets. She normally did not pay attention to the prostitutes and drug addicts lingering in the alleys of the Walking District, but she kept a watchful eye on everyone around her that night.

She studied where different alleys led, being sure she knew the area as well as possible, in case anything went wrong with her brother's plan. She wanted to believe that all would go well, but she knew from experience that her brother's plans never worked. She remembered too well the catastrophe of the last one. She did not want to be stuck paying for her brother's mistakes once more.

However, she was also watching the area closely because she was slowly moving out of the Walking District and into Anon. She had never dared to move past the Walking District. She knew how quickly Trids disappeared when they were found in the capital city. There was no way for them to blend in. No one walked in Anon. There was no way to sneak any vehicle past border patrol. Even then, with the electronic roads, Officials were immediately alerted when an unregistered car was being driven.

At four in the morning, Kailynn was sure that she would be safe from the electronic sensors in Anon, but if anyone spotted her or saw her in the cameras, it would not take long for Officials to take her into custody.

There was no tolerance for Trids in Anon.

Kailynn was sure that Raphael had worn himself out enough to sleep for at least seven hours, so she wanted to use the time to her advantage. She did not want Raphael to know about Theo's plan. It would put him in danger and he had already done enough to help Kailynn when it came to Theo's botched plots to destroy the government.

The gang was waiting for her near the side gates of an enormous warehouse complex.

"Finally! Fuck, where have you been?" Jamis growled, his hands shoved deep into his pockets to avoid the blistering cold.

"Fuck off. It's none of your business."

"Don't have that kind of attitude when we do this, Lynni," Theo warned. "Remember, you are a lady of Anon who has been assaulted. You need to be helpless."

"Then why the hell did you choose *me* to play your fucking damsel in distress?" Kailynn murmured.

"I need someone I can trust."

"Yeah, but, who's to say that we can really trust her?" Arina said, glaring at Theo. She had always carried a torch for Theo, and thought it was creepy how much the Evada siblings depended on one another. She wanted to be the center of Theo's world.

"First of all, bitch, I don't give shit if you trust me or not. Second, I was the one who freed him from prison when you sat on your ass and waited. What the fuck were you doing when he was locked up?"

"I sure as hell wasn't whoring myself out so that my boy-toy would pay for his bail."

Kailynn started forward, but Theo held her back as another member of the Heart of Trid put his arm in front of Arina to keep her from attacking Kailynn in turn.

"Don't start this now," Theo growled. "We have two days to figure the rest of this shit out. You two wanna scratch each other's eyes out? Wait until we've shut down Venus."

Arina slowly backed away, but she and Kailynn continued glaring daggers at one another.

"Are we ready to get started?"

Chapter Three

Kailynn was shifting her weight back and forth nervously, her arms crossed tightly over her chest, trying to stay as warm as possible in the tiny dress that had been torn around her belly. The scratches that Kailynn had made on her thighs were stinging in the cold air. Theo stood beside her, glancing around as he waited for the signal that everything was ready.

There were twenty-nine participating. When the others were in their agreed positions, Jamis would flash his light twice to Theo and Kailynn. Theo was watching the ledge of the nearby manufacturing plant, his hands closed around the vile of whiskey he was nursing to steady his nerves.

Kailynn ripped it from his hands and gulped down some of the horrid drink. She needed to calm her nerves as well, but was hoping the alcohol would also warm her frozen limbs.

When Theo snatched the vile back, Kailynn ground her teeth together in frustration.

"I'm fuckin' *freezing*!"

"I know, I'm sorry," Theo breathed, his voice betraying his anxiety. He had concocted grand plans of attacking the Elites and rupturing the class system of Tiao, but the previous plans always concerned taking out the nobles or the Elites. He never thought he would get a shot at attacking the head of the snake—Venus.

When a small light flashed twice from the roof of the manufacturing plant next door, Kailynn's stomach flipped. Theo turned to her, pocketing the flask of whiskey and bending to scoop her up in his arms. Kailynn could not tell if her shaking was due to the cold, or realizing that everyone was in position and they were about to attempt taking down the super-computer that ran the planet.

"Ready?"

Kailynn gave a tight nod, wrapping one arm around herself and curling forward.

Theo took a deep breath and raised his voice.

"Help!" he cried, running forward, holding Kailynn in front of him. "Someone?! Anyone?!"

He darted out of their alleyway and ran the short distance toward the front gate of the warehouse complex they had been scouting for days. Kailynn knew that there were four guards at the front gate and two posted at the other seven gates around the complex. The others were supposed to take care of the other guards—some were being drugged, others were being lured away by members who were trying to appear to be casing the fence, and a few of the guards were meant to remain unharmed. The gang hoped to do their work quietly, and wanted a few of the guards around to take the blame for not stopping the raid of the warehouse compound.

"Help us! Please!!" Theo called, looking around frantically. When he saw the confused guards, he ran to them.

"Please! Please help!!"

The guards watched the man approach, wary. However, when they saw that he was properly dressed in Anon attire for an upper-class citizen—not knowing the garments were stolen—they relaxed slightly.

"What's wrong?" one asked.

Theo ran to them, breathing hard. Kailynn started gasping for breath, cringing, her face contorted in agony. She tried to force some tears out of her eyes, but she was so cold and nervous about the plan, that they would not come.

"I found her in an alley." Theo nodded somewhere with his head while the four guards crowded around them, their faces hidden by dark, protective visors. "She was supposed to be home hours ago and, when she didn't show up, I went searching…and…she-she says…" Theo's voice became choked. "She says she was *raped*," he hissed, "by a gang of filthy *Trids*."

"Trids? In this district?" one of the guards hissed, sharing worried glances with the other guards. "Unlikely."

"Please, can you call help for her?" Theo said frantically. "I don't know how badly she's hurt…She's so *cold*."

"Pat, Boomer," one guard said, turning, "do a precautionary sweep. Make sure there aren't any Trids." He turned to Theo and motioned to him. "Bring her inside."

Theo walked in with the shivering and whimpering Kailynn.

Kailynn was surprised that, so far, the plan was working. She had never expected to be let in the main gate. Yet, the guards were unlocking the door next to the transport gate, ushering both her and Theo into the compound. Once the card swept over the electronic lock, the reader in Theo's pocket copied the code to another gang member's proxy card, allowing them to access the back gate of the facility, which should have been unguarded with the now-drugged guards.

The guards opened the door to the small building where they would take shelter and watch the security monitors. Kailynn spared a glance at the screens as she cringed and groaned in mock-agony. Everything seemed quiet. There was no movement on the cameras that would have caused alert.

Everything seemed to be going according to plan.

"Put her here."

Theo moved to the cleared table and gently set Kailynn down. Kailynn let out a cry of pain when her body was moved out of the position, playing up her fake injuries, her hand reaching out to grab Theo's. Theo took her hand tightly.

"I don't know what to do to help her…" Theo choked. He squeezed her hand once. That was the signal that everything was alright. If he released her hand, that meant that something was wrong and they needed to escape. Two squeezes meant that she needed to play up her injuries even more as a further distraction.

"She's probably freezing," one murmured.

"We'll call for an EMU immediately," the second said, moving to the phone. Kailynn knew that, when the Emergency Medical Unit was called, they would have less than seven minutes to complete their plan. When she got two squeezes from Theo, she bolted upright, screaming.

"No! No! Stay away from me!!" she bellowed, flailing wildly.

"Miss! Miss! You're safe!!"

"Get away from me! I want to go home!!"

The other guard moved away from the phone and went to help hold Kailynn down when one of her flailing hands connected with the first guard's face.

"Mina! Mina! It's alright, it's alright…" Theo said, using the code word of her fake name to tell her that the distraction had worked. She turned to him, her eyes going wide.

"Dale?" she whispered. "Dale!" She lunged forward and hugged him tightly, trying to force tears to her eyes again. "I'm so sorry!!"

"It's okay, it's okay."

Kailynn glanced at the screens around her brother. She caught sight of one of the gang members running down the middle of the warehouses, looking for the one they had found to be linked to Golden Elite Isa's identification card. Her heart raced when she realized that they were caught on camera. She pulled away from Theo and took his face, trying to keep the attention of the guards on them and away from the screens.

"I tried to call you..."

"Miss, can you tell us what happened?"

Kailynn turned to the guards, her eyes wide. She legitimately panicked. She had not come up with a story about her assault.

"I...I was..." She lowered her head and raised a hand to her face. "I was out with some friends...Dale and I had gotten into a fight, and I was drinking..."

"You were in the Walking District?" one guard asked suspiciously. "With friends?"

"Yes," Kailynn said. "And, when we left..."

She could not think of how to continue. Instead, she forced her eyes wider and turned back to Theo, trying to draw attention away from the story so that she would have time to form it.

"Dale...I didn't mean what I said..."

"What started the fight?" the first guard pressed. "Were you yelling at one another?"

"Loud enough for the neighbors to hear, unfortunately," Theo said. "I didn't go after her immediately because I was explaining to them what had happened."

Kailynn was watching the suspicious creases on the guards' faces get deeper the more Theo explained the fake fight. Kailynn knew something was wrong. They did not believe the story.

Kailynn turned back to Theo and removed her hand from his, signaling that something was wrong.

"Dale...we shouldn't so openly discuss our problems..." she tried to get him to stop talking. That was when she realized their mistake. The high-class citizens of Anon did not *speak* to one another as Trids did. Often they rarely saw each other face-to-face. That was why companies that provided Significants existed.

Her heart began climbing into her throat.

"I'm feeling ill...please...I want to go home..."

"Where is the nearest hospital?" Theo asked, turning to the guards.

"I don't think it's safe for you to take her there yourself," the first guard said, walking to the phone. "I'll call the EMU."

Kailynn knew that they were not calling an EMU. They were calling the Officials. They knew something was wrong.

"No!" Kailynn cried. "I don't want to go to the hospital! I just want to go home!"

"You must be seen by a physician," the second guard said, his hands moving to his sides.

Theo quickly realized how out of control things were getting. Both guards were armed and could kill them at any moment, and they appeared to be reaching for their weapons.

"I agree," Theo said with a nod. "Where is the nearest hospital? How long will it take them to get here?"

"No, really, I just want—"

"*E-Team, to eleven!!*" a voice bellowed outside. Kailynn jumped when the sound of orders being barked filled the air. She turned to the screens again and barely caught sight of what seemed to be hundreds of armed Officials running out of various warehouses, surrounding warehouse eleven—where the gang had expected Venus to be located.

But, Kailynn did not have long to study the situation before a gun turned on her. Both guards had drawn their weapons, pointing them at the Evada siblings.

"Stupid Trids," the first guard growled. "Did you think we were morons?"

"We've been waiting for you," the second added.

The two Trids were completely still and silent, not sure how to respond or how to get out of the dangerous situation. Kailynn looked between the two guns, her head trying to wrap around how fast the situation had changed. She had never considered they would get into the warehouse compound. Therefore, she had never thought of an escape plan if they were trapped inside.

The sound of rapid gunfire caught everyone by surprise. Kailynn was sure her heart was about to jump out of her throat. However, she knew her only means to escape was when the guards had their heads turned.

She leapt at one, kicking him in the gut and causing him to lose his balance. Theo jumped on the other one, wrestling with the gun.

"Lynni! Run!!" he bellowed.

Kailynn did not hesitate. She ran for the still-open door, almost colliding with the other two guards who were returning to assist in the capture of those who had raided the compound.

Surprised by her sudden appearance, they watched her turn and run out the closing gate. She managed to slip out of the gap just before the gate shut, stalling the guards for a few further seconds. Kailynn darted into the dark alleyways, trying not to notice that snow had started to fall during the time they were inside the compound.

She heard the guards getting closer as she tried to orient herself to determine the safest escape route. The reason she had evaded capture from Officials so many times was because she knew the streets like the back of her hand. She could easily out-maneuver any Official. She knew the alleys. They did not.

The cold was making it difficult for her to move. She was disoriented and frightened and her frozen muscles were locking.

Kailynn lost one of her shoes as she was running and it caused her to fall to the ground. She kicked off the other one, grabbing it when she saw two guards coming at her.

"We have you, you little bitch!"

She lifted her knee into one of the men's groins, while she shoved the heel of her shoe into the protective visor over the eyes of the other guard, shattering it, though she was not sure if it had actually hurt him.

Then, she ran.

She moved quickly, her breath coming out in puffs of smoke in front of her face as her bare feet carried her through the alleys and streets toward the dark area she knew to be Trid. She did not stop running until she saw something familiar. Hearing voices behind her, she forced her way through a broken window, cutting herself on the glass, and hauling herself up the stairs, too cold to feel the pain. She ascended all the stairs until she reached the door for the roof, shoving it open with her shoulder.

She was still in the Walking District, but she knew the crowds and the neon lights would make it easier for her to escape. She knew she had just enough of a head start on the guards that they likely did not see her jump into the building.

Kailynn ran to the far corner of the roof, finally collapsing, trying to catch her breath, her lungs on fire. She closed her eyes and covered her mouth, trying to stifle the noises of her panting and hide the fogging of her breath. She barely had the strength to lift herself up and peer over the edge of the building.

The guards were just below her, their heated argument too quiet for Kailynn to discern.

Her entire body was locked, cold and pained. The scrapes in her skin from her fall and the slices from the broken glass were numb, and she was worried that they were far worse than she realized.

But, she could not move from her hiding spot. Even if she had the strength, she knew she would have to lay low until the guards had searched everywhere they could.

She could not return to Trid as she was.

Kailynn glanced at the snow that was coming down, seeing it stick to the roof. Knowing that her footprints would give her away to any drones passing over the next day, she forced her frozen limbs into action. She clumsily pulled off the dress from her shivering body, pushing it deep into the corner of the building, hoping to hide it from plain sight. Then, she tried to take big steps toward the door to the roof, leaving as few impressions in the sticking snow as possible.

She slipped through the door and down the dark stairs to the floor below. Shaking and on the verge of unconsciousness, she stumbled into an open, empty room. There were holes in the walls and bottles on the floor, adding to the scenes of graffiti that littered the walls.

Kailynn found a hole in the wall that was large enough for her to fit in and she grabbed a few of the cold bottles, stacking them against the insulation in the hole. She then forced her body to contort between them, hissing through gritted teeth as the cold glass and plastic bit into her bare skin, but she knew she had to be surrounded as much as possible to make the best use of her own body heat to warm her again.

Only when she was curled in a hole in the wall, clad only in her panties, did she break down, stifling her terrified sobs in her hands.

Chapter Four

Isa watched the burgundy wine fall into the wide mouth of the wine glass. She was already on her fourth glass that night, but she was not concerned about the amount of alcohol she had consumed.

"Aha!" a voice sounded from the living room. Isa smiled, amused. "I will have you in two moves!"

"Oh?" she called back, setting the wine bottle down and returning to the living room, seeing the other Elite looking over the holographic chess board intently. When he saw the Golden Elite walk in, he smiled triumphantly.

"I'd like to see you get out of this. I blocked your check and have you set up to fall into my trap," Remus said with a definitive nod.

Isa stood next to her seat, looking over the chessboard briefly. She touched the controls on her side, moving the knight forward.

"Checkmate."

Remus' eyes shot back down to the board as Isa smiled, sitting down and sipping her wine. She watched the Silver Elite look over the pieces on the board, his jaw slowly dropping.

"That was deceptive of you," he laughed. She smiled broadly. "I blocked you from here...but, you already had that planned." He looked up at the Golden Elite. "I don't know why I bother playing strategy games with you. You always win."

"You're a glutton for punishment, apparently," Isa teased.

"Have I ever beaten you?" Remus asked, hitting the reset button on the chessboard, watching the pieces move back into place before the board flashed a goodbye message and powered off.

"A few times."

"When you were sober?" Remus pressed.

"That, I can't answer," Isa said with a chuckle, taking a sip of her wine. Remus watched the action carefully.

"That's your fourth glass," he noted. "Are you alright?"

"Fine," she assured. "It was a difficult day. I'm trying to shake it off."

"Yes, today was trying. I'm pleased that you kept our dinner date, though."

"It's a tradition," Isa said with a smile. "Your new caretaker is quite the chef."

"He is."

"Is that why you chose him?" Isa asked teasingly.

"No," Remus chuckled. "He was highly qualified in many areas. His culinary skills were merely an added appeal." Remus leaned back in his seat, picking up his own almost-empty glass of wine. "Isa, there is something I wanted to ask you." The Golden Elite turned her blue eyes to him. He hesitated for only a moment. "If I went with you, would you start seeing Dr. Arre again?"

Isa sighed heavily, lifting the wine glass to her lips again. Remus watched her, knowing she would not answer.

"I think it would be best," he pressed.

"I'm fine, Remus."

"You might be able to convince everyone else of that," Remus said, "but I know you, Isa. You are not fine."

"What makes you think that I need to start seeing Paul again?" Isa asked, turning back to Remus. Her eyes were not angry, but Remus knew he was walking a fine line. Isa was never one to take care of her health, but he also knew that she only got defensive about seeking treatment when she also knew she needed help.

"To start, you're drinking again," Remus murmured.

"I've had some wine tonight," Isa said, turning to glance at him sideways. "You're right, clearly I'm an alcoholic."

"Isa…"

"I don't mean to snap," Isa said, watching the wine swirl around the glass in her hands. "I am still allowed to enjoy alcohol. That should not raise any alarms about my health."

"I'm concerned that it's in relation to what is happening in the Ninth Circle," Remus continued cautiously. Isa sighed heavily once again, hesitating.

"There is no word yet that there is a problem in the Ninth Circle," she said vaguely.

Remus looked over his Golden Elite, trying not to let his concern show. In the muted light, Isa looked as beautiful as ever, but there was a sadness to her expression that was worrying. He knew Isa was no longer the ambitious young woman he had once known, and he knew that Isa could never return to how she had been before. Her wounds may have healed, but the pain was still fresh.

"I understand," Remus said quietly. "I am just concerned." He watched her every muscle movement as he spoke. "However, if our intelligence agents are correct, we must contain Gihron before they get out of hand."

Isa tensed at the name of the planet, but she tried to hide it with a nod.

"We will address that if it becomes an issue."

"And, in the meantime, you'll return to Paul so that you're better prepared to handle—"

"Remus," Isa said, turning to the Silver Elite, "I thought one rule of our monthly dinner was not to discuss any politics."

The Silver Elite could not help but smile at the playful grin pulling at Isa's lips.

"You're right," he chuckled. "I'm just looking out for you."

"I know," she murmured. "You always do."

"Then, you'll consider seeing him again?"

Isa opened her mouth to speak but stopped, reaching into her pocket and pulling out her buzzing phone, popping the earpiece out and putting it in her ear.

"Elite Isa," she greeted.

"Now look who is breaking the rules of our monthly dinner…" Remus chuckled quietly. Isa ignored him, listening to the person on the other end of the call. After a few moments, she nodded.

"I see, thank you. Send the paperwork to the Syndicate as soon as they are processed." She pulled the earpiece out and slid it into the side of the screen, pocketing the device again.

"What was that?"

"They caught the Heart of Trid gang."

"That was a well-thought plan, Isa." Remus smiled. "What do they plan to do now that they have them?"

"Being non-citizen Trids, they'll likely stick them in cells for a few years until Venus decides if she wants to kill them." Isa took another sip of her wine. "Preliminary punishment for conspiracy and treason is three years before the death sentence for citizens."

"The Trids are becoming a problem," Remus said. "Their numbers are growing daily."

"The economy is still hurting," Isa said with a knowing nod. "We must find a better way to strengthen the middle class," she said seriously. "It's amazing how horrifically Gattriel handled the economy when he was in power."

"Three wars will bankrupt a planet," Remus said knowingly. "Gattriel was a moron. We knew that when we succeeded him."

"That was a mess," Isa chuckled brokenly. "Remember staying at the Syndicate Building for days on end trying to mend everything he destroyed?"

"That was where this dinner tradition started," Remus said with a smile. "It was the only way I could get you away from work." Remus lifted his glass. "And now, seventeen years later, we're still keeping our dinner dates."

Isa's smile widened.

"It's an impressive feat."

Remus met eyes with Isa and the two shared a deep conversation without speaking, their eyes conveying their shared memories of running the Syndicate and trying to repair the damage of inept previous leaders. They had spent so much time together, it was hard to distinguish memories that they did *not* share.

"Isa," Remus started, breaking eye contact and glancing at his glass.

"Are you going to ask me to see Dr. Arre again?" she said lightly. She was not angry at Remus' pestering. She knew he was concerned.

Remus looked at her again, his eyes filled with worry.

"Just promise me you will be careful," he murmured.

Isa's smile was gentle.

"I know you're worried. But there is no need to be. I am alright."

■■■

Kailynn knocked hurriedly on the door of Raphael's apartment. When he did not answer, she knocked louder, glancing around nervously. The sun was rising and most had just gone to sleep in the area, but Kailynn was still nervous about being seen mostly-naked, dirty, and injured.

The door finally opened during her third hurried-knocking frenzy. Kailynn did not wait for Raphael to take in her disheveled state before she forced her way into the room. She saw an unknown woman passed out in the bed, her clothes missing and the sheets covering absolutely nothing. Kailynn paid her no mind. She and Raphael were no longer in a monogamous relationship—or a relationship at all, for that matter.

"Kailynn?" Raphael hissed, his eyes wide, staring at her as she limped in, shivering. "What the fuck happened to you?"

"I'm fucking freezing," she managed through chattering teeth. She pressed herself to him and he wrapped his arms around her. Her skin was cold to the touch. He had so many questions, but he could not voice them, startled and frightened by her state. He took her hand, leading her into the bathroom, grabbing the fallen blanket on the ground as they passed it to wrap around her shoulders.

He sat her on the counter and turned on the faucet, grabbing the cleanest towel he could find. Even though the water would be cold, he knew he had to clean the dirt and grime off and be sure that her wounds were not serious. He was thankful that at least the heat was working in his apartment again. Kailynn's blue lips and pale skin were frightening.

"What the hell happened?" he repeated, gently dabbing the dirt away from her skin. She shook her head quickly, pushing his hand away.

"It's cold."

"I know, sorry."

Deciding she was too cold to be treated immediately, Raphael took off his shirt and grabbed the blanket around Kailynn's shoulders. He pulled her off the counter and they both went to the floor, sitting in a corner with Raphael holding Kailynn tight to him, the blanket surrounding both of them to trap their body heat.

When Kailynn's shivering had finally slowed, Raphael glanced at Kailynn's face. She was still pale, her eyes swollen from crying, but she was sleeping soundly.

"Kailynn..." he called. She slowly stirred, turning to look at him. She was warmer, but did not want to leave Raphael's arms. Her mind was still trying to make sense of what had happened and what it meant for her and her brother.

"Please, tell me what happened."

Kailynn felt the tears return immediately. She closed her eyes against them and lowered her head.

"We fucked up."

"Who?"

"Theo and me," she whispered. She went through the entire plot, telling Raphael what the Heart of Trid gang had done by stealing Golden Elite Isa's card and finding the classified addresses before forming a plan to attack the warehouse and rig it to explode and destroy Venus. Raphael was unable to stop the shocked expression that crossed his features as she explained, but he did not interrupt her.

The tears had taken over by the time she was finished explaining. Raphael held her as she cried, mumbling that she did not know whether Theo was dead or alive, or what she would do now that she was a wanted criminal. She was sure her face had been captured by the security cameras and shown to every Official in Anon.

She knew she was going to prison and likely facing death for conspiracy and treason.

Kailynn cried herself into exhaustion. She was sleeping heavily when Raphael carefully moved from behind her and went back into the flat, seeing the woman he had picked up the previous night still passed out on his bed. He groaned and shook her awake, telling her to find her clothes and leave. She was indignant and angry, but he did not care about preserving her feelings. His thoughts were focused on Kailynn.

The failed plan was no minor occurrence. The Heart of Trid gang and Kailynn were in an enormous amount of danger.

Raphael carried Kailynn to the bed and covered her with all the blankets he could find. Once he was sure that she would be warm, he left the apartment and went to her job, telling Brad that she was very sick and could not work. Brad grumbled, but he must have seen the worried look on Raphael's face because he did not press the Trid with questions. Once Raphael had taken care of that, he ran to the different members of their own gang, telling everyone that the Heart of Trid gang had been captured for a failed attempt to shut down Venus and that they needed to find out what had happened to the members, particularly Theo.

Raphael went to everyone he could think of and asked if they had heard about the warehouse incident the previous night. A few had heard about it through other contacts, and that sent Raphael on a chase for some solid information. He was hearing everything from twelve Officials being killed to the entire Heart of Trid gang being killed in the warehouse and dragged away to become medical subjects in Anon.

Just when he was getting frustrated with the search, Alyssa from his own gang ran up to him and told him that she knew what had happened to the Heart of Trid gang.

One Official had been killed in the struggle—adding another criminal count to the gang's sentence—and seven members of the large Trid gang had died as well. The rest had been taken into custody and were being held at Uren Correctional Facility, the roughest, deadliest prison on the entire planet.

"What about Theo?" he pressed.

"He's alive," Alyssa assured. "He's at Uren with the rest."

Raphael rushed to tell Kailynn the news. He found her in the bathroom, naked, treating her wounds with old antiseptic that she had found under the sink. Raphael explained the situation to Kailynn and gave her the clothes he had picked up at her place.

"Viv said she would dye your hair darker. We can find contacts to change your eye color. We'll have to find a way to keep you hidden."

"For how long?" Kailynn murmured. "And what about Theo? He's on death row. And you know they don't wait to execute Trids."

"I know, but *you* are not on death row, so don't do anything stupid enough to put you there," Raphael said strongly. "You are the one that got away. They will be searching high n' low for you. Stay hidden."

Kailynn lowered her eyes. She could not leave her brother in prison to be killed. He was the only family she had left. She had heard horror stories about Uren. Uren did not waste their lethal serums on Trids. They took them out back and shot them. Kailynn shivered at the thought. It was the same way both her parents died—one by Official fire, the other by Trid fire. She could not risk her brother, her only living family, being killed by a bullet to the head.

Raphael embraced her tightly, trying to convey his worry. For all he said to her, he knew that she would not listen. He just had to keep an eye on her and make sure she did not do anything stupid while trying to save Theo.

"I'll help you however I can. Just tell me what you need."

Chapter Five

Kailynn was bound and determined to help her brother get out of Uren. She had helped Theo get one man in the Heart of Trid gang out of the same prison years before and knew that the guards were willing to look the other way on escapees if they were compensated well. Kailynn never knew where Theo had gotten the money to pay for the escape, but she never asked. She knew the Heart of Trid gang had some nefarious dealings within Trid. Her own gang never dealt in drugs or weapons. They were a small group, more concerned with each other's safety than with gaining money and prestige among those in Trid. Each member did what was necessary to survive and stayed together for protection.

For that reason, Kailynn was a little out of practice in dealing with career criminals in Trid.

She had gone to her brother's contact in Uren and asked what it took to release those in the Heart of Trid gang. The answer was twenty-thousand credits a head with her brother being fifty-five thousand credits. He had not even blinked when he told her the numbers.

Kailynn had almost choked on her tongue. Twenty-two members—the surviving members of the Heart of Trid—were imprisoned, one of which was her brother. That was four-hundred-twenty thousand credits for the basic members of the gang. The grand total was four-hundred, seventy-five thousand credits. Kailynn felt as if the words had physically struck her in the chest, causing her to bleed all over the ground.

However, she put on a brave face, hiding her shock.

"How long before they start executing them?" Kailynn pressed.

"A year, maybe," the patrol officer had said with a shrug. "Apparently, your boys did something that has drawn attention from Venus. Everyone's waitin' for her to make an announcement on their fates."

The fear in Kailynn's belly turned cold.

She left feeling discouraged.

Viv was trimming Kailynn's hair and preparing the dye when she finally asked how much money was needed to free the Heart of Trid. When Kailynn whispered the amount, Viv's hands stilled and her eyes went wide.

"What?"

"Yeah..."

Slowly, Viv resumed trimming Kailynn's hair, trying to get over her shock at the large number.

"Is...can we...I mean, do you have a way to get that money?"

Kailynn sighed and closed her eyes.

"I'm sure there are ways..." Kailynn murmured. "But, even if I were to steal as many credits as I could from the Walking District, I couldn't come close. We'd have to take up the Heart of Trid drug ring and traffic at a higher price. I might have to work at one of the clubs and whore a bit to get some more money. I don't think there is enough money in all of Trid to free them."

"You could free only Theo."

"I could," Kailynn agreed. "But he will need the gang with him. The other gangs are pissed that they brought the Officials down on Trid with this stunt. I saw a bunch of Officials just walking here—thankfully, they didn't see me. Theo will need to be protected when everyone comes after him."

Viv continued snipping the ends of Kailynn's hair, thoughtful.

"But...what happens if you get him out? The Officials will come looking for him again."

"I doubt it," Kailynn said. "I mean, what do they care? They don't want to warehouse him, and they have to wait for Venus to tell them what to do. If he disappears, problem solved."

Viv went silent, running her hands over Kailynn's hair before grabbing the dye, setting it on the makeshift table next to her and putting on gloves. She started to move Kailynn's hair around, preparing to dye it.

"Kailynn," she started slowly.

"Yeah?"

"Why not get work in Anon?"

Kailynn snorted.

"You need papers to work in Anon."

"I know someone who can get you papers."

Kailynn turned to Viv, her eyes narrow.

"You've looked into getting papers?"

"Why the hell not?" Viv asked sharply. "You wanna stay in this shithole all your life?"

"What the fuck are we qualified to do in Anon?" Kailynn challenged.

"Will you turn around?" Viv said, exasperated, pushing Kailynn's shoulders. She started applying the dye, hoping that Kailynn would stay still as she spoke. "I know, we're not really qualified."

"Not *really*?" Kailynn repeated, incredulous. "When the fuck did you learn how to read?"

"Shut up, Kailynn. You can't read, either," Viv snapped. "But, there are ways."

"Enough to get nearly five-hundred thousand?"

"Maybe," Viv said. "As a Significant."

Kailynn groaned, closing her eyes.

"Oh no, Viv. Don't tell me that you're thinking of becoming a Significant."

"Why the hell not? They make a lot more money than those who whore themselves in the Walking District," Viv defended. "They make a lot of money. And, most of the time, all they do is talk to people."

"That's what they want you to believe," Kailynn said. "Significants are asked to do all sorts of sick things for those nobleman assholes."

"For seven grand a pop, I'd do some sick shit, too."

Kailynn was about to snap at Viv again about considering the work, but the number stilled her tongue immediately.

"Seven grand? How do you know?"

"One of the guys I chatted up a few weeks ago," Viv said, continuing to apply the dye to Kailynn's hair, watching the light brown color darken almost immediately. "He was talking about how much money he had lost because he had a partnership with a Significant and he lost seven-thousand credits three times a week to spend a night with her."

"For sex?" Kailynn said, blinking in shock.

"That's the thing. The sex cost extra. Like, five-thousand extra."

Kailynn turned around and stared at Viv, her eyes wide with disbelief.

"You're making this shit up."

"No," Viv said. "The guy was slobbering drunk and was whining about how his wife would divorce him for spending so much of their money on a Significant. He was really upset about it."

"All that over a *Significant*?"

"Guess so."

Even though everything inside Kailynn told her that becoming a Significant was not an option, the prospect of the money to be earned gave her pause. Viv walked to one side of Kailynn, continuing to apply the dye.

"It's not a bad way to make money, you know," she said. "I mean, don't you think that most who work as Significants just need the money? It's something to think about."

"The idea of prostituting fake company to the nobles is more sickening than whoring," Kailynn said slowly, lowering her gaze.

"Kailynn," Viv started, standing in front of her, "who cares if it's fake company they want? They're willing to pay for it. There is no reason for you to not exploit that."

Kailynn stared at Viv. The older Trid woman could see that Kailynn was nervous about going against her beliefs for the sake of money. However, Kailynn was also in a situation where leaving her brother in a prison cell, waiting to be shot and forgotten with the rest of the Trids, was unimaginable.

The thought disturbed Kailynn, but at seven-thousand a visit, she was sure she could raise the money to free her brother and most of the others in the Heart of Trid gang working as a Significant. She would have to be smart about how she dealt with her affairs, since her papers would be fake, and she would have to continue working even after getting the gang out of Uren to ensure suspicions remained low.

But it was the first time that Kailynn believed she *could* make the money to save her brother's life.

"Who was the guy you said could get me papers?"

■■

Kailynn had asked for the five hundred credits from Raphael to pay the man who would provide her with forged papers. Raphael immediately demanded to know what she was planning to do, and she explained truthfully. Raphael was strongly against the idea at first. He did not think of the money Kailynn could make at first—he thought only about the steep punishment of life in prison or death for forging papers to get into the capital city. He had told Kailynn not to do anything that would get her in trouble, but she had already concocted a plan that could easily lead her to death row.

However, Kailynn continued to explain the money that Viv had said she could make. Eventually, the words pushed past Raphael's initial worry.

He gave her the money and went with her to the programmer who had been kicked into Trid after losing all his money to his drug addiction. He still had citizenship, which still allowed him access to duplicate the template for electronic citizenship.

When Raphael and Kailynn met with him, he was thin and sickly, still twitching from his high the previous night.

They sat with him as he shakily discussed all the information she would need to know for her fake citizenship, showing her what her documentation looked like before giving her a fake name.

Jacyleen Lynden.

He then warned her that she needed to carry the papers on her at all times and to avoid getting sick or hurt while in Anon. He explained that everyone in Anon had a PIM chip implanted behind their right ear and he could not give her one because they could only be programmed by a hospital computer connected to Venus directly. If she was found not to have a PIM chip, she could be immediately arrested.

Once she had her papers, copied onto a small drive that she held tightly, terrified she would lose it due to its small size, Kailynn went to a shop in the Walking District, buying clothes that would help her blend into Anon. She only bought one outfit, unable to afford anything else.

She then went back to Raphael's place, showered, shaved, and tried to make herself look as least-Trid-like as possible.

The following day, she dressed in her new clothes and, holding her faked citizenship, cautiously crossed the border into Anon.

Once there, she walked out of the older part of Anon into the clean, bright streets of Tiao's capital. There were towering buildings, clean and bright, made of glass and metal, reflecting light from the sun. The streets were clean as well, which was easy to maintain since there were never people on the walkways. Kailynn knew that there were extensive roadways under the surface of the city where the self-driven cars could move about without detection, but she could not hear noise under her feet.

The city was surprisingly quiet, apart from the dull humming that seemed omnipresent on the planet.

Kailynn wandered around the city, feeling small and out of place among the towering structures. She was starting to get nervous about being caught or lost when she finally saw the round building of sweeping glass with the word "Companion" along the top.

Taking a deep breath, she began walking toward Companion.

She walked around the building twice, trying to find the entrance, not sure if she should walk in where she saw the road raise up in front of the building or not.

Taking a chance, Kailynn walked through the black glass doors that opened for her immediately, leading her to another set of black doors.

When she passed through the second set of doors, she felt like she had stepped into another world. The room was dark and slightly cold, with dark coverings on the walls and floor. There were couches of deep red and black scattered about the large greeting room and, sitting on the couches, talking lightly, were several extremely attractive people.

They all turned when she entered.

"Well, hello, beautiful," one man said, standing and walking to her, his opened shirt exposing his well-defined muscles. "Anything I can help you with today?"

Kailynn was immediately reminded of the prostitutes that tried to pick up tricks in the Walking District.

"Trust me, gorgeous," another man started, also approaching her. He was wearing a tight black sweater and sporting a perfect smile, "you don't want him. I'd be better suited for you, I can tell."

"I think she might be here for another reason, boys," one girl chuckled, joining the group around Kailynn. She was wearing a tight dress that accented every curve. "Isn't that right?"

"Actually," Kailynn started, forcing her voice to strengthen, "I'm here to apply as a Significant."

"Oh," the girl said, her expression changing immediately. The boys started looking her over, as if evaluating if she had what was necessary to be a Significant. "Then you want to talk to Jak."

"Okay, where is he?"

"She's brave," one man laughed. "Look at you, charging in here to talk to him. He'll like that."

"I'm not joking around," Kailynn said strongly. "Where is he? I'll talk to him right now."

The others chuckled and the girl smiled broadly.

"I'll call him for you."

She pressed the area just in front of her right ear. "Jak's office," she started. "Jak, it's Mysty," she said. "There's a pretty little girl who wants to talk to you in the greeting salon."

She tapped the same area of her ear again and turned back to Kailynn.

"He's on his way," she said. "What's your name?"

"Jacyleen," Kailynn tried to say as naturally as possible.

"Hmm, that's a nice name," Mysty said. "And you don't seem too nervous about talking to people. Maybe you would be good here."

"She's pretty, too," one man added. "She could probably become a favorite, if she wanted."

"What do you mean?" Kailynn asked, turning as one man walked behind her to continue his examination. She resisted the urge to punch him in the face for leering at her. She knew that Significants were meant to be pretty and to talk to people, so she had to put up with the examination if she wanted to work as a Significant, but it went against all her self-preservation instincts.

"You're good-looking enough that you could get a lot of partnerships."

"What are those?"

"It's where the same client wants you several times," Mysty explained. "They pay more money to have a scheduled time with you every week or every month. You get more money, basically. But that's only if clients like you enough and have enough money to bid for a time slot."

Kailynn could only blink in surprise and confusion. There was a part of her that was sickened at the thought of having to see the same person multiple times as a Significant, constantly having to act as though they were close with the client and pretend to be whomever, or whatever, they wanted.

"Mysty, you better be telling the truth," a voice said at the back of the room, walking to them. "Who's here to talk to me?"

Kailynn looked over the man. He was older, his hair greying and his skin lightly creased with wrinkles around his eyes. He was not particularly tall, but he had burly shoulders that made him seem bigger.

Mysty pointed at Kailynn and his blue eyes turned to her.

"Who are you?"

"My name is Jacyleen," Kailynn started. "I want to apply as a Significant."

"There's an application through our page," he said, confused. "You should have filled one out."

"I didn't have time," Kailynn said hurriedly. "Look, I'm in hard times, and I want to work here. So, I'm applying in person."

"While that's a cute trick, you can't just—"

A gentle chime sounded and the doors opened as an older woman walked in, dressed in rich Anon clothes with her makeup painted heavily over her skin.

Jak groaned and grabbed Kailynn's arm, pulling her away as the Significants in the greeting salon went forward to greet the customer.

Jak pulled Kailynn to the elevator around the corner and punched a button, waiting for the door to close before turning to Kailynn.

"We'll discuss this in my office."

It was a very short ride in the elevator to Jak's office, which was a glass room that was just as dim as the rest of the building. There was something about the dark coverings on the walls and floor that made Kailynn feel like she could hardly see.

Jak closed the door behind her and sighed heavily, walking to his desk.

"Look, I understand that you are in hard times and you want to apply for a job here, but there is a procedure, okay? You need to fill out the application and then come in for the interview."

"Well, I'm here for the interview," Kailynn said strongly. "I need this job, and I'm willing to work twice as hard as everyone else. I'm good-looking, young, and I can handle anything the customers throw at me."

"I am impressed that you are able to keep eye contact," Jak said, nodding. "Most applicants can barely form a sentence and keep their eyes down the whole time."

"I'm not like the other applicants," Kailynn said. "I'm a quick learner, and I already know how to talk to people." Kailynn leaned across his desk and looked at him seriously. "I promise, I will earn my keep *and* more."

Jak looked her over, heaving a sigh and motioning with his hand.

"Stand in the middle of the room."

Masking her nervousness, she did as he ordered.

He leaned against the front of his desk and looked her over. "Take off the jacket."

Again, she did as she was told.

"Okay," he started, nodding. "You're thin, but that can be fixed. In that time, I'm sure you'll fill out some cleavage, though it's not bad now." He stood straight and walked around her, looking over every inch. "That dye in your hair will have to come out. It's poorly done." He continued to circle her as she tried not to shiver in anger.

She closed her eyes, hating the scrutiny. She felt like something less than a Trid as she stood there, being examined for her worth as a Significant. She was tempted to storm out and never return, but the thought of Theo being executed was enough to make her stay and bear up to the humiliation.

"Not bad at all." Jak finished his circle and walked back to his desk. "I will admit, you do have some potential, and you are a little darker, so you have an exotic look."

He sat down at his desk.

"Why do you think I should hire you?"

Kailynn was thrown off by the question. She hesitated, thinking carefully about what he wanted to hear.

"Because you don't have anyone like me," she finally said.

"How do you know that?"

Kailynn smiled, tossing her jacket over his desk and leaning forward once more.

"Because I'm not like these pretty little bitches you have around here," she said. "You have someone that no one else wants? I'll take them. Someone your little, soft-skin babies can't handle? I can handle them. I'm one tough bitch, and I can handle more than these kids can."

Jak smiled, nodding shallowly.

"How old are you?"

"Twenty-two."

"Let me see your papers."

Chapter Six

The last thing Kailynn expected was to be a natural as a Significant.

Jak had hired her, and immediately put her in classes to learn how to act as a Significant. The class in which everyone else struggled, she excelled—communication.

Since people rarely spoke face-to-face, most applicants and other Significant trainees had to go through schooling to learn the art of conversing with another human, but Kailynn was a natural. Having grown up in Trid, where there was nowhere near the technology available in Anon, Kailynn knew how to hold a conversation, how to read body language, and how to hold eye-contact.

Manners and etiquette, on the other hand, were a struggle.

But, she forced herself to behave in class, trying to learn how best to act like a Significant. She figured the sooner she learned, the sooner she could earn money, and the sooner she could leave Companion and get the hell out of Anon.

But, the classes were difficult for her without the skills of reading or writing. She stumbled through and was teased by the other trainees in the classes until they got to conversation class and she excelled.

It got the attention of everyone at Companion and, before long, she was doing simulations where teachers and evaluators for the company would act as clients and have the students come in with different requests for behaviors and those students had to perform as though they were with a real client as a paid Significant.

At first, Kailynn had trouble with the simulations, since they felt incredibly fake and she had difficulty staying in character, but she disciplined herself to keep a straight face.

It was a small relief that everyone called her Jacyleen rather than Kailynn. It made her feel like someone else was acting as a Significant, not her.

The day that she had her picture taken and her promotional video made for the Companion page, she felt accomplished and disappointed at the same time. She was thrilled that she could now get clients and earn money, but her Trid upbringing made it hard for her to accept that she had pleased those in Anon enough to excel in the job.

Shortly after she was made available on Companion's page, Kailynn met Nyx.

He knocked on her door after her classes one day, since she had been living in the Companion dorms since starting her training.

"Hey," she said, looking over his impressively tall and broad stature.

"Uh, hey," he said awkwardly. "I'm Nyx. I'll be your guard from now on."

"Oh, okay."

"Jak said you have a client tonight. I'll meet you in the greeting salon at 18:30."

"Alright," Kailynn agreed, trying to hide her excitement that she was going to have her first client and, therefore, her first paid job. "See you then."

She closed the door and the nerves overtook her.

She was unsure she could be the proper Significant. Fears of not being paid, or being fired and destroying her chances of getting her brother out of Uren, became stronger with every passing moment. She had invested so much time and taken so many risks to get to that point, she knew she could not screw it up at that stage.

By the time she was expected in the greeting salon, she had worked herself into near-hysteria.

She nervously met Nyx in the greeting salon, where other Significants were waiting, scheduled to handle walk-ins. Nyx led her to the car that was sitting in front of the building. It was growing dark, but the brightness of the outside world compared to the dark atmosphere inside Companion gave her pause.

Kailynn had also never been in a regular car before—only the delivery trucks when working for Brad.

She got into the passenger's seat and looked around the sleek, expensive car. There was no means to steer it, though Nyx got into the driver's seat and entered the address of her client. Once the car started forward, Kailynn watched in fascination as they descended into the underground highways of the city, joining the other self-driving cars.

"Jacyleen," Nyx said, calling her attention. He was holding out a necklace with a large, red pendant. "This is how I'll know if you need help once with the client. Just press the pendant, and I'll immediately be inside."

"Okay," Kailynn said, taking the necklace and fastening it around her neck.

"First client?"

"Yeah."

"You'll do fine," Nyx assured with an awkward smile. "This client just wants to talk with you as a friend. It's only an hour. You'll be done before you know it."

Kailynn took a deep breath and tried to steady herself.

They arrived at the apartment building and took the elevator with the guest key from the Caretaker robot at the front desk. Kailynn tried to keep herself from fidgeting as she watched the numbers ascend on the screen above the door.

The numbers stopped and the doors opened.

Nyx led Kailynn out of the elevator and walked with her to the door of the apartment where her client lived.

"You'll be fine," Nyx reassured, smiling. "I'll be right out here if you need me."

She pressed the bell for the door, waiting for a moment before a young man answered.

"Jacyleen?" he asked. She nodded silently, too nervous to speak. "I'll tell him you're here."

Kailynn was surprised to see a live caretaker at the home of her client—that was an indication of his wealth.

She walked into the living room, surprised to see the stark, black-and-white theme. It hardly looked lived-in. She was afraid to touch anything, seeing the paintings and sculptures throughout the house and knowing immediately they were expensive.

"Jacyleen?" a voice asked. She turned to see an older gentlemen walking into the room, followed by the silent caretaker, who slipped away without speaking. "It is wonderful to see you."

Kailynn prepared herself to put on the act he had requested.

"It's wonderful to see you again, Kris," she said with a smile. "It has been such a long time."

"And a lot has changed recently," Kris said with a small laugh.

He motioned for her to join him on the couch, so she took the seat next to him.

"Tell me how things have been going," she prompted.

He began explaining to her that his son had just graduated from law school and was going to another planet to study for a few years before returning to Tiao to work on inter-planetary law—all of which was far beyond what Kailynn could understand.

But, once he began talking about his wife, the tears came.

He suddenly, almost violently, confessed how he had been unfaithful to his wife while on a trip to see the school where his son would be studying off-planet. When she discovered his infidelity, she immediately filed for divorce, and he was extremely upset because he claimed he still loved her.

Kailynn had to bite back her every instinct to tell him that it was not love if he could cheat on her so casually, but she refrained.

She comforted him and let him complain and cry about his life and the turn it had taken.

The hour was up before Kailynn knew it.

She excused herself tactfully by saying that she forgot she had an appointment and that he could call her if he ever needed to talk to her. He thanked her, his tears causing his face to swell, and bid her goodbye.

And, just like that, her first appointment was over.

"See? Nothing to it," Nyx said with a smile as they returned to the car.

For the following four months, Kailynn met with all kinds of clients, from wealthy men and women who just wanted to pretend to hold a dinner party like they had seen on television, to the middle-class men and women who wanted someone to listen to their problems.

She met with a noble family that wanted to get their son to leave his NGS game and sit with them for a meal. However, when the son came out for dinner, he saw a new person in the house, panicked, and retreated to his room.

Defeated, the parents tried to tell Kailynn that they had bought him an NGS console and had been unable to get him away from it other than for his lessons. When she asked what an NGS was, she found out it was virtual reality gaming console that put the player in the middle of any game they wanted, mimicking smells and sounds as well as the weight of weapons and, occasionally any injuries sustained, though the games were proven harmless.

After spending the rest of the night with the parents, who could do nothing but talk about the stock market and financial trends, Kailynn understood why the kid wanted to be in an alternate life with his NGS console.

Kailynn also ended up taking clients that wanted her to spend the night. At first, having sex with the clients was awkward and left her feeling dirty and disgusting. But, as they all started calling her Jacyleen, she started to adapt more to the name, and decided that Jacyleen was the Significant, leaving Kailynn as the Wild Child of Trid.

For months, she took every client she could, offering to take the jobs no one else would, just for the money. At the end of every week, she would receive a credit chip, the different colors indicating the different amounts on the chip. She would count them on days when her determination would waver, and it would help her realize that she was getting closer and closer to buying her brother's freedom.

Occasionally, Kailynn would return to Trid and spend some time with her gang. They knew that she was trying to gather money for the release of the Heart of Trid gang, but they did not ask how. Only Viv and Raphael knew of her work as a Significant.

On one visit back to Trid, Kailynn went to Raphael's apartment and drank herself into a stupor.

She had just finished with a client, a very wealthy man who had bought time with the Significant to talk to his wife, claiming that she never spoke with him anymore because she was always in her GAL life, which was a challenge-like simulator that was very similar to an NGS console, except it focused more on long-term games that were not meant to be beaten, such as cultivating an island and learning how to survive, or playing puzzle games against the clock.

When the wife found that he had called the Significant for her, she began screaming, telling him that he was also always in his GAL life, where he had several wives and did not need her to keep him happy.

As the yelling match progressed, Kailynn watched the caretaker robot deliver a drink to a young girl in the corner of the room, who was drawing on the interactive coffee table.

Kailynn ignored the parents and went to sit with their daughter, drawing with her on the table.

It broke her heart to leave the child there with such horrific parents, but she could not stay past her appointment time.

With a heavy heart, she left the girl with her bellowing parents.

After that, she had to go into Trid and drink herself silly.

"What the hell's up with you?" Raphael asked, lighting a cigarette and laying on the bed next to her.

"I swear, those shitheads in Anon are fucked up," she groaned, declining when Raphael offered her a cigarette.

"Oh, yeah?" Raphael asked. "Well, you have my attention, tell me."

"These people actually pay me to go over there and act with them. Like, they *know* it's fake. But they sit there and pretend I'm some great friend of theirs, or girlfriend, or sister, or mother, sometimes. It's fuckin' freaky."

"Hey, hookers do the same thing," Raphael said with a shrug.

"Yeah, but that's sex."

"So?"

"Sex is different."

"How?"

"It just is. It's, like, instinct or something. All humans need sex, so that's fine."

"All humans need to talk to someone, too," Raphael pointed out. He sighed heavily and took another puff of his cigarette. "Don't get me wrong, I think those fuckers are messed up. But, like you said, if they're willing to pay for it, you should exploit it."

"You should have seen the little girl today," Kailynn murmured. "She was sitting in the corner, drawing, while her parents screamed at each other how much the other ruined their life. The *robot* was making sure that the child was fed. It was sickening. What kinda parents are those? And this other guy, yesterday, he was so terrified to talk to me, that he just sat there and stared, and then he continued to say sorry because he didn't have anything to talk about."

"Shit, that's fucking stupid. Why would he waste the money, at that point?"

"You should see these people," Kailynn murmured. "Kinda feel sorry for the fuckers, actually."

Raphael immediately turned to her, his brow furrowed.

"What?" he barked a laugh. "You feel *sorry* for the privileged-as-fuck assholes in Anon?"

"I just told you about a fucking kid who never speaks with her parents," Kailynn said sharply. "Don't you feel sorry for her?"

"I never spoke with my parents, either," Raphael said.

"That's because they're dead."

"And so are yours." Raphael turned over and looked at her seriously. "Remember who killed your mom? Anon Officials. And you're sitting here telling me you feel sorry for them?"

"I'm just trying to get Theo and the others out of Uren, and it's fucking depressing to see how desperate they are to talk. Life is fucking depressing, you know?"

Raphael sighed and flopped back down on the bed, lifting the cigarette to his lips.

"Next thing you'll tell me is that you think the Elites are good leaders."

"Fuck that," Kailynn barked a laugh. "As soon as I have enough to get Theo and the others out of Uren, I'll never go back to Anon."

As much as she wanted out of Companion as soon as possible, she had no idea that her status as a Significant would lead her to the job that would change her life forever.

Chapter Seven

Kailynn did not like most of the clients she found herself with, but she tried not to dwell on her disgust. She went through each client, focusing only on the amount of money she was collecting. Every night, she would count up the green, blue, yellow, and white credit chips she had stored away, figuring out how much more money she needed to free Theo. She figured she could free most of them in one payment, and then the remaining members could be released at another time, once Theo had sufficient protection from the gangs that sought to kill him.

She needed a big-paying client to partner with her so that she could get the money quickly. It had already been five months. She was worried she was running out of time. She knew that Venus could decide any day to kill her brother.

After another night of no appointments, Kailynn was staring at the ceiling, her mind fluttering with thoughts and worries. A soft chime at the door alerted her to a visitor.

The door opened and a familiar face entered.

"Jacyleen," Jak greeted, walking into her dorm room.

"Hi," she said slowly, noting the drawn look on his face. "Is everything alright?"

"Yeah," he assured. He grabbed her desk chair and rolled it over, sitting in front of her, resting his head on his hands on the back of the chair. "I need to talk to you about something."

"Okay…"

"This conversation didn't happen, if anyone asks, alright?" Jak looked at her seriously. Kailynn turned and dangled her feet over the edge of the bed, cold fear stabbing her gut.

"Alright, but you're making me nervous."

Jak sighed heavily. "I know that you're taking tougher jobs for the higher pay," he said quietly. "I don't want to know why you need the money, so don't tell me. But…considering you *do* need the money, I think you're the person I can come to for this job." Jak hesitated. "I can't really tell you details, but there is a client, an extremely *wealthy* client, that is asking for a Significant for an entire month."

"A *month?*"

"Yes, but…" Jak stopped, hesitating again. "Basically, this person is paying for a very discreet Significant to be at the home of a friend.

The one paying is not the one who wants to spend time with a Significant."

"Paying for someone else?" Kailynn murmured. "For a *month*? Sounds like this guy has a lot of money to throw around."

"He does," Jak affirmed. "However…he requested that the Significant be a woman, and someone who has not been a Significant for long."

Kailynn raised her eyebrows. "Sounds like a red flag to me…"

"He says that the person he wants to spend time with the Significant doesn't like anyone who is fake, and apparently, they think that all well-trained Significants are fake."

"Sounds about right."

"He requested someone with a bit of an attitude. So, naturally, I thought of you," Jak said. "Are you interested?"

"It's all pretty shady…" Kailynn murmured. "Did he say who the friend was that he's paying for?"

Jak looked at his hands.

"Yes," he muttered. "I trust the client with you, but…" He pinched the bridge of his nose. "Jacyleen, this is a very important job, but it's also very dangerous. This person is not supposed to spend time with Significants."

Kailynn narrowed her eyes. "I thought that only Syndicate Elites—" Her eyes went wide and she gasped. "A *Syndicate Elite?*"

"Shh…" Jak said, motioning her quiet, even though they were already speaking quietly. "Yes, I can't reveal a lot of information to you and, naturally, this can never get out. You would have to remain completely silent about who you are seeing, what you are there for, *everything*. At the end of the month, you would come back and say that you went on some business trip with someone and that was why you were gone. You could not ever tell anyone about this."

"…how much are they going to pay?"

"Fifteen thousand a day."

Kailynn's eyes shot wide and her jaw dropped.

"*Fifteen thousand?*"

"Part of that payment is for discretion," Jak added. "Interested?"

"Hell yeah, I'm interested."

"You need to be very careful," Jak whispered. "It's not completely unheard of that a Syndicate Elite asks for discrete services, but even then there are strict laws. You are not to touch the Elite, and you are *not* to have sex with them. They are bound by law to remain celibate. I don't know the punishment for Elites breaking the law, but anyone who breaks that law with them is executed, *quickly*."

"So basically all of the Elites are forced to be blue-balled their whole lives?" Kailynn laughed. "I guess that means they are dedicated to politics if they are willing to give up sex."

"Jacyleen," Jak sighed, "please, tell me you understand."

"I understand," Kailynn assured with a nod. "Since this is all so discrete, how much of the fee will I get?"

"If you stay discrete, you'll get eighty-percent," Jak said. "We're only going to put on the books what would normally be paid for a nobleman business-trip deal. The rest of the payment is under the table."

"How are the Elites going to keep this hidden from Venus?" Kailynn asked skeptically.

"I don't think they do." Jak shook his head. "I think that Venus allows them time to talk to a Significant as long as it is a rare occurrence and they do not break the rule of celibacy."

"Don't worry," Kailynn laughed, rolling her eyes. "An Elite is the last person I would want sex with, anyway."

Jak sighed heavily and nodded. "Okay. You will not have Nyx for this. The less people that know where you are, the safer it is. Tomorrow, between noon and two, you will take public transportation to Syndicate Central and go to Anon Tower. There is a code that will take you to the level of the Elite you will be seeing."

"What should I pack? Formal? Casual?"

"A small selection of both, just in case," Jak answered, standing. "But no more than that. I'm sure anything you might need while there will be provided for you."

■■

There was a knock on Isa's office as she powered down her NCB chair.

"Come in."

The door slid open and Remus walked into her office.

"That was impressive what you did with the trade embargo," he congratulated. Isa sighed and shook her head, resisting the urge to roll her eyes.

"I have to have an iron fist with those morons," she groaned. She smiled warily at the Silver Elite. "I'm surprised to see you up here so late. Is everything alright?"

Remus nodded, looking at the ground.

"I need to talk to you."

Isa studied the expression on Remus' face, unsure if she should be worried about a massive disaster or if it was a personal problem. It was not traditional for the Golden and Silver Elites to speak face-to-face, but Isa and Remus were hardly traditional. They had been close friends since their time in school together, so they found it easy to approach one another. In fact, most of the Elites in Isa's Syndicate were unusual in that sense. While there were still many conversations that took place through the NCB chairs while working, Isa encouraged all Elites to speak with her face-to-face as often as possible, which was easier with all the Elites having known each other since they were children.

"Where shall we go?"

"Anon Tower?"

Isa spent the entire drive worried about what Remus could possibly have to tell her. She tried not to glance in the mirrors of her vehicle to the car directly behind her, forcing her mind not to jump to the worst conclusions.

When they pulled into the secured, secluded parking garage for Anon Tower, Isa waited for Remus to get out of his car before going to the guest elevator. Using her ID card, the two began the ascent to the top floor. They did not speak, wary of the cameras in the elevator car.

Isa could tell that Remus was tense. Having known him for nearly their entire lives, she could discern that he was not nervous about any disaster or catastrophe that Isa had yet to learn. She knew he was nervous that she would not approve of something he had done.

She would have preferred to handle a catastrophe.

They stepped out of the elevator and went to the front door of Isa's home. After walking in the door, they were both greeted by Tarah, Isa's young caretaker.

"Welcome home," she said, bowing her head.

"Thank you, Tarah," Isa said. "Please bring two glasses of wine to the balcony."

"Yes, Miss," she affirmed, scurrying away.

The two Elites moved through the spacious living area to the balcony, stepping into the dusk air as the sun set and the lights of Anon began to illuminate the city.

"Should I be concerned about something you have done?" Isa asked lightly, glancing at Remus with a teasing smile. The Silver Elite pursed his lips, smiling thinly as he looked to the balcony under his feet.

"You should not be *concerned*...but you will likely not be pleased."

Isa took a deep breath.

"Can you wait to tell me until after I have my wine?"

"I'm probably going to need the wine to get the courage to tell you," Remus admitted with a chuckle.

"Why?" Isa laughed. "Do I frighten you?"

"You can be formidable," Remus played along. "You would never be so angry with me that you wouldn't speak to me, correct?"

Isa smiled gently, an unreadable light in her eyes.

"I have always needed you by my side," she said. "I could not function without you. You know that."

"You would be just fine without me," Remus said, shaking his head. "But that was not my question."

"No, Remus," Isa assured. "I might not speak to you for a day, depending on what you did." She laughed. "Once my wine gets here, I want you to tell me what's worrying you."

Remus took a deep breath, nodding, his expression showing his apprehension. He looked over the growing lights of Anon, watching the darkness creep over the horizon as the city lit up and the nightlife began. Isa also watched the city don the mask of nightly entertainment, tantalizing everyone with bright lights and promises of escape.

The balcony door opened and Tarah came out with two glasses of wine, handing one to each Elite before retreating inside. Isa took a sip of the wine at the same time as Remus. The Silver Elite glanced at the wine, his eyebrows high.

"That's very nice."

"It's one of my new favorites. The ambassador from Kreon gave it to me on his last visit. I will admit to spending some money for more bottles."

"Kreon wine, that *is* expensive," Remus said. He took a larger drink of the burgundy liquid, letting out a long breath when he lowered the glass again. Isa watched him and then took a large gulp of her own drink.

"Alright," she breathed. "Why did you need to talk to me privately?"

Remus hesitated.

"I called Companion and hired a Significant for you for a month," he said, his words a little faster than normal. He did not look at Isa, his eyes focused on the wine. However, he could feel Isa's eyes on him get wider.

"You did *what*?" she hissed. "Remus…"

"Isa, you need to talk to someone," Remus said. "Someone who *isn't* me."

"Remus, you know I severely dislike Significants," Isa groaned, turning away from Remus and walking to one of the benches on the balcony. "I would get rid of the practice all together if I thought the nobles wouldn't assassinate me."

"You refuse to go back to Paul. I needed to do something. You're starting to slip again."

"I am not slipping," Isa said, turning to him before sitting on the bench. "It's been a busy few weeks, so I haven't been particularly pleasant. I may have a glass or two of wine to get my brain to calm down in the evenings, but I'm not being destructive."

"I'm not talking about the drinking," Remus said, sitting next to her. "You're losing weight, and your performance is starting to decline once more. Before things get worse, you should take some time and gather your bearings."

"I have my bearings, Remus."

He hesitated. "It's barely been a year since you last went into the hospital. You have a habit of jumping back into the deep end before you're ready."

"That was a bad mix of medication for the flu and the assassination attempt. That's why I was back in the hospital. That hardly—"

"Isa," Remus said, placing his hand on her shoulder, stopping her, "you can't risk your health. Dr. Busen said that if he saw you in the hospital again within the next eighteen months, he would have you confined to the hospital until you were in the same state as when you were first made Golden Elite."

Isa sighed heavily, closing her eyes.

"I hardly think that's fair," she grumbled. "I don't even think *magic* could get me the way I was when I was seventeen."

"That's why we have science," Remus chuckled. He gently rubbed her shoulder. "The Significant is going to be here for your month leave."

"Month leave?" Isa repeated, turning to her Silver Elite with an incredulous look. "Pardon?"

"I've already informed the other Elites that you are out of the Syndicate for the next month. For the first week you are instructed not to work at all. After that, you can work remotely from home."

"You'll never get this cleared through Venus."

"I already did," Remus said. "She agreed that she needed you healthy. But, because it is Venus, you still have to work after the first week, just remotely. Dr. Busen also agreed that it was important you rest."

"Oh, and Venus wants me to have a Significant?" Isa said skeptically. "The possibility of a scandal would be enough for her to say no."

"Actually, she agreed that you probably needed some form of contact with new people," Remus said. "As long as it was a woman, she agreed."

Isa groaned and rubbed her forehead.

"I can't believe you are doing this to me…"

"Isa," Remus started, his voice pleading, "I'm just worried about you. I let this get out of hand before and I refuse to let it happen again."

"You need to stop beating yourself up about that," Isa murmured, closing her eyes. "You did the best you could." She turned to Remus. "I've been off the medication for nearly seven months. I'm alright."

Remus looked at Isa, his hand still rubbing her shoulder.

"I just want you to have someone to talk to who is outside of the situation," he murmured, his hand stilling. "Please? Humor me?"

Isa sighed and smiled, shaking her head.

"You worry about me too much," she chuckled. Remus' hand tightened on Isa's shoulder as she moved closer, leaning against the Silver Elite. "If everything I've been through in my life hasn't killed me yet, nothing will."

Chapter Eight

Kailynn did as she was told.

She had her small bag with her clothes, but the bag felt surprisingly heavy. Even though she had agreed to meet with the Syndicate Elite as a secret client, as she was standing outside Anon Tower, staring up at the impressive structure of glass and steel, her nerves were getting the best of her.

She steadied herself, remembering of the money promised.

Then, she walked into the front lobby, punching in the five-digit code for guests into the electronic lock.

The building was practically silent. There was the gentle humming of the machines that ran the building, but the foyer was devoid of people. The sounds from Kailynn's shoes echoed in the cavernous space and made her feel even smaller.

She walked toward the elevators, but passed them, as she was told, going to the door marked "Caretaker."

She knocked on the door three times and, no more than two seconds later, the panel on the door lifted, depicting a man with clean-cut, black hair and brown eyes.

"Welcome to Anon Tower. I am Caretaker. How may I assist you?" the robot asked.

"I am a visitor," Kailynn said slowly, trying to strengthen her voice.

"What room are you visiting?"

"Code 7734," Kailynn said nervously.

"Thank you. I shall page that room. Please enter the first elevator."

Kailynn turned to see the first elevator door slide open. She was curious about the secrecy of the code to get to the Elite's level of the building, since she was sure no one would try to storm the tower.

She stepped into the elevator and the doors closed.

As the car of the elevator ascended, almost silent, Kailynn concentrated on her breathing, being sure to keep herself from shaking.

She had never seen an Elite before and was unsure how they differed from humans. They were treated almost as if they were mythical beings, ones only seen in the light of a full double moon. The reality that she was about to meet an Elite—let alone spend a month with said Elite—was overwhelming.

The elevator slowed to a stop and Kailynn's stomach flipped.

When the doors opened, Kailynn was startled to see a young woman standing in the hallway. She was young but she had a very natural and innocent beauty to her. She was dressed in simple clothing, but that did not diminish the brilliance of her smile. Her long, dark blonde hair was pulled into a braid that draped over her shoulder.

"Jacyleen?" the young woman asked.

"Yes."

"Good afternoon," the woman said with a bow of her head. "I am Tarah, the caretaker of the household."

"Tarah...caretaker? Are you old enough to be working as a caretaker?" Kailynn asked.

"Yes," Tarah said, surprised by the question. "I am seventeen." She motioned for Kailynn to follow her. "Please, come with me. I will show you to your room."

Kailynn slowly followed the young woman down the short hallway to the only other door. The door opened automatically and Kailynn had to stand in the doorway for a moment to admire the beautiful home. There was a large sitting area filled with expensive furniture and a table that served as a dining space. The lighting was installed into the white ceiling and a fireplace was on the wall that curved outward into a wall of glass, giving a spectacular view of the city skyline from the large balcony.

"Please, do not be shy, come in."

Kailynn had been to several homes of the nobles of Anon, but the elegance and simplicity of the level at Anon Tower was unlike anything she had seen before.

"Thank you for coming to stay here," Tarah said with a smile. "Please feel free to make yourself at home. If you are in need of anything, do not hesitate to let me know."

"Thank you," Kailynn said nervously. "Um...where is..."

"She'll be out momentarily," Tarah assured, understanding the question. "Allow me to show you to your room."

Kailynn was, once again, surprised to see that, when she rounded the corner, there was a bar with mirrors behind the glasses and bottles of alcohol. She would have commented on the sheer number of bottles, but the bar set up was so beautiful that she was captivated with the way the light reflected off the glasses.

She followed the young caretaker through the door on the other side of the bar. There was another hallway beyond with four doors, two on each side. Tarah turned to the first door on the left and it immediately opened.

"This will be your room."

Kailynn walked in, her eyes captivated by the grandeur of the large bed and desk with computer. She set her bag down on the bed, her eyes wide.

"Please take your time to settle," Tarah said. "Come to the main room whenever you feel comfortable."

Once Tarah left, Kailynn immediately went to the bathroom and splashed her face with water, trying not to notice the luxury of the bathroom as well. She told herself to calm down and that there was nothing to be nervous about. The Elites also had to be careful if they wanted a Significant around. Jak had assured her that they had dealt with Elites before. Kailynn just needed to be careful and discreet and not allow herself to be overwhelmed.

She dried her face and checked herself over once before returning to the main room.

Kailynn was not prepared to be confronted with the most beautiful woman she had ever seen in her life.

The Elite was stunning. She was tall and well-built, lined with lithe muscle. Her hourglass figure was accented by the casual Elite attire, but the dark colors were in sharp contrast to her alabaster skin and light blonde hair. But what took Kailynn's breath away was the vivid blue color of her eyes.

Their eyes met and, for those brief seconds, everything else in the universe disappeared.

"Miss, this is Jacyleen," Tarah introduced, standing across the bar from the Elite.

"Jacyleen," the beautiful woman said with a perfect smile. "Thank you for agreeing to be here."

"It is my pleasure," Kailynn barely managed to utter, still captivated by the blue eyes. "How...how should I address you?"

"Just Isa is fine."

Kailynn's jaw dropped and her eyes shot wide.

"Golden Elite Isa?" she whispered.

"You seem surprised," Isa said gently. "Were you not informed with which Elite you would be spending a month?"

"N-no, it's not that..." Kailynn said quickly, trying to disguise her utter shock. "I-it's just that...I don't think it is appropriate to address you so informally."

Isa's smile widened.

"I would actually prefer casual conversation while you are here."

"Y-yes, of course."

Kailynn could not form any thoughts other than the fact that she was standing in the same room as the most powerful person in the Altereye System. She had only heard of the Golden Elite. She had never seen pictures or video, but she was sure that, even if she had, they would not do justice to the perfection Isa exhibited. Even her blinking seemed to be so perfectly timed that it was hypnotizing. Kailynn wondered if all Elites were so flawless, or if it was only Isa.

"Well, Jacyleen, I do hope you will excuse me, but there are a few matters to which I must attend."

"Oh, yes, sure, okay."

Kailynn's tongue felt useless as she tried to form words.

Isa thanked Tarah and walked past Kailynn toward the hall of Kailynn's room. When the door had closed behind her, Kailynn's entire body went slack. She glanced at Tarah, her eyes wide.

"I did not know I was going to be here with the Golden Elite."

"You didn't?" Tarah asked. "Why wouldn't they tell you that?"

"I assume because they wanted to freak me out as much as possible," Kailynn groaned. She walked closer to Tarah. "That was really Golden Elite Isa?"

"Yes," Tarah said with a confused chuckle. "Why are you so surprised?"

"I have never been around an Elite before..." Kailynn said. "I thought it was one of the lower ranked ones, not the most powerful one in the damn system."

Tarah blinked at Kailynn's tone. She had never known Significants before, but she was sure they were not supposed to act so unprofessionally when it came to their clients. Still, Tarah found herself smiling.

"You are in for quite the month, then, aren't you?"

"I guess."

"If there is anything you need, please let me know. Feel free to explore the level. Isa's office is in the back area. Try not to disturb her when she is working. Otherwise, please make yourself at home."

"Um...what should I do?" Kailynn asked nervously.

"Do?"

"Normally my clients are in the same room with me when they want me over," Kailynn said with a light chuckle.

"Oh," Tarah laughed. "It's very difficult to get Isa to stop working. I'm sure that she'll find you when she's finished with what she's doing. You can do anything you would like until then."

Kailynn was unsure what she possibly *could* do.

"Okay."

"Are you hungry? I can make you something to eat," Tarah said, trying to make the Significant feel more comfortable.

"No, I'm alright." Kailynn sighed heavily, shrugging. "I guess I'll just...look around."

"Okay. Let me know if you need anything."

Kailynn watched the teenager move into the kitchen through the door next to the bar. Kailynn sighed once more and looked around the living room, noting the expensive pieces of art and the beautiful, pristine condition of the furniture. The home hardly appeared to be one that was occupied. It seemed to be for show. She walked around the perimeter of the room and glanced over the paintings and photographs. She noticed that there was no television in the room, and that surprised her.

She went to the other door in the main room and it opened automatically. She was surprised when she was confronted with what she assumed was the Golden Elite's bedroom. There was a large bed, the frame intricate designs of gold, holding the mattress and pillows in a nest form, sunken in the middle and slightly tilted upward. The darker colors of the room gave the bedroom a subdued and calming aura.

Kailynn glanced around nervously before stepping into the bedroom, wondering if there was anything in there that could tell her more about the Golden Elite. There was access to the balcony from the bedroom, but the curtains were pulled closed over the windows to mute the light. There was a large closet with the door open—Kailynn was sure that the closet was the size of Raphael's flat in Walking District. There were racks of shoes and accessories along with clothes of rich fabrics that Kailynn was afraid to touch.

Across the room from the closet was the bathroom, white with marble and silver. Even after the time she had spent in the houses of noblemen, she was not prepared for the luxury of the Golden Elite's home.

She left the bedroom, going back into the guest hallway where her room was located. She assumed that the other three doors led to rooms that looked like hers, so she continued to the door at the other end of the hallway.

The surprises continued.

There was a large pool set into the floor, the pristine waters showing the care put into maintaining it. The windows leading to the balcony allowed light and heat into the room. Kailynn walked around the pool, completely overwhelmed. When she realized that there was a smaller room off of the pool area with a sauna and workout area, she could not help but roll her eyes.

"I don't know what I was expecting..." she grumbled.

As she left the pool area, she found herself feeling indignant. She had to struggle to stay warm in Trid and find a way to feed herself, but the Golden Elite had an entire level of Anon Tower that had a pool and guest rooms for guests that Kailynn was sure Isa never had. The class difference between the two was so apparent it almost physically hurt. Kailynn was wondering why Isa was living in such luxury while there was an entire district of her planet that struggled to survive just beyond the borders of her shining capital city.

Kailynn walked through the other door of the pool area, finding herself traveling further into the Golden Elite's level. She found herself in another hallway with four doors, two on each side. When she got to the first door, it opened for her. Kailynn wondered what the Golden Elite needed with four *additional* guest rooms—except the hallway did not contain guest rooms, but guest *suites*. The rooms were even larger and more lavish than the room Kailynn was staying in, which she found to be incredibly extravagant.

Kailynn followed the bend in the hallway and saw three more doors. She approached one, expecting it to open automatically like the others, but it did not. She turned away from it, not sure how to open it, since there was no handle on the door, and moved to the next one, which did open. There was a smaller room with a billiards table and several plush seats facing a large television—the only one Kailynn had seen in the home.

The Significant went to the last door she had not explored and was confused at the sight when it opened.

There were shelves lining the room in many rows. There were boxes sitting on the shelves with writing along the edges. The boxes were different colors and sizes, filling the shelves entirely. Kailynn stepped further in, the lights flickering on automatically. She approached one of the shelves and gingerly touched one of the boxes. She pulled it off the shelf, looking over the design on the front of the long, thin box.

That was when she realized that the box was not a box at all. It was multiple pages bound together to form a package she had never seen before. She touched the pages, shocked at their texture and thinness.

The sudden stop of a humming and the sound of a door opening caused Kailynn to quickly replace the package and leave the room, intent on coming back at a later time.

She quickly went back to the living room, which was empty, and tried to decide what to do next.

She finally made the decision to go onto the balcony. She walked to the glass wall and one of the panels automatically moved aside for her. The cool air brushed her face and cleared her mind a little. Never in her life did she ever think that she would be standing on the balcony of the Golden Elite's home.

Kailynn was looking out over the buildings, trying not to get too close to the edge of the balcony. She had a fear of heights and did not want to risk the vertigo she normally got looking out her own window on the third floor. Anon Tower was far taller than any building she had ever been inside.

She took a deep breath and carefully stepped forward, putting her foot down lightly and transferring her weight as if the balcony would give way under her. She took another cautious step toward the railing, raising on her toes to look over the edge, even though she was too far away to see the ground.

"This building can withstand earthquakes of nine-point magnitude," a voice said behind her. Kailynn whirled around, startled, and caught sight of Isa's smiling face. Kailynn placed a hand against her chest and let out a shaky breath.

"You scared the shit out of me."

Isa chuckled and walked closer.

"I apologize," she said. "You're acrophobic?"

"What?"

"Afraid of heights," Isa clarified, walking past Kailynn and turning around, taking a few steps back until she could lean against the front rail. The younger woman watched her warily.

"Come closer," Isa urged, extending her hand.

Kailynn hesitated, not sure if she should listen to Isa or decline and go back inside. She looked at Isa's bright blue eyes and found herself taking a step forward before she knew it. She slowly reached out and let Isa take her hand. The Golden Elite gently led the Significant a step closer to the edge.

"You're safe up here," she assured. "There are sensors in the bottom of the balcony. If anything falls, a net extends a few floors down to catch it."

Kailynn blinked and turned to the Golden Elite.

"Sounds like there have been some suicide attempts from this balcony."

"Not since they put the net in," Isa corrected with a laugh. She gently pulled Kailynn a step closer. "The trick is not to look down. Look outward."

Kailynn took another step forward, but her fear got the best of her and she froze one step away from the railing.

She pulled her hand from Isa's and shook her head.

"I'm good here," she said quickly.

"It's closer than where you were before," Isa complimented.

"You're not afraid of heights?"

"No," Isa said with a shake of her head. "I never have been."

Kailynn looked over the Elite carefully, unable to help herself. Everything about the Elite was so perfect, it was hard to comprehend how someone could look completely immaculate. They were silent for several long moments, staring at one another.

"I…I thought you were working…" Kailynn started lamely.

Isa made a face. "I *was*, but Remus remotely shut down my chair." She laughed, shaking her head. "He really does not want me working this week."

"Remus?"

"The one who hired you," Isa said gently. "The Silver Elite of the Syndicate."

"Oh…"

"I do apologize if it seemed that I was distant earlier," Isa said. "I will admit, I do not find the practice of Significants at all appealing."

Kailynn groaned and rolled her eyes.

"Me neither."

"Yet, you do this work?" Isa asked.

"Best way for someone like me to make money," Kailynn said with a shrug.

"Someone like you?"

Kailynn felt her stomach flip, so she pursed her lips and turned away.

"Never mind," she said quickly. "I guess I'm just surprised. Seems like a lot of people really *like* Significants."

"Yes, unfortunately," Isa agreed. "That is why it is still in practice." The Golden Elite turned to Kailynn fully and smiled. "What's your real name?"

"What?"

"Your real name," Isa repeated.

"It's Jacyleen," Kailynn said, startled.

"No." Isa shook her head. "I'm sure you have a name better suited to you."

Kailynn hesitated.

"…Kailynn."

"Much better," Isa agreed with a nod.

"Is your name really Isa?" Kailynn asked. "Is it short for something? What about your last name?"

"No, Isa is my full, and only, name."

"Only?" Kailynn asked, blinking. "You don't have a last name?"

Isa pursed her lips with a smile and shook her head. "No Elite has a last name. We do not have parents from whom to inherit them."

Kailynn's eyebrows furrowed.

"No parents?"

Isa looked confused by Kailynn's confusion.

"What do you know about Elites?"

"You run the Syndicate."

"Yes."

"What else is there to know?"

Isa chuckled at the indignant tone in Kailynn's voice. The Significant cringed.

"Sorry, I didn't—"

"It's alright," Isa said. "May I ask a question? Was there criteria for someone with an attitude to act as my Significant?"

Kailynn laughed. "Actually, yes."

"Remus knows me well," Isa mused. "Please, do not feel that you need to censor yourself. I deal with people who are politically correct and vague all day. I prefer someone honest and straightforward."

Kailynn stared at the Elite for a moment before she found herself smiling sincerely.

"You know, that's amazing that you can just *say* that."

Isa's smile knocked the breath from Kailynn's chest.

"Then, tell me, what else is there to know about Elites?" Kailynn asked, trying to shake off the feeling. "I know you run the Syndicate, and that you can't have sex."

"That's not entirely true," Isa said. "We are not *allowed* to have sexual intercourse. But we do have the physical capabilities."

"That's what I meant."

"To be honest, that's about everything there is to Elites," Isa admitted. "There is nothing more to us. No fear, no emotion, high pain tolerance, low physical needs—"

"Did you say no *emotion*?"

"Elites are made, not born, and I do mean that literally," Isa explained. "We are created in incubational chambers and grown to a certain age. During that process, certain functions of the brain are turned off, such as emotions and the ability to cry."

"You can't cry either?" Kailynn gaped. Isa shook her head.

"Elites were made to work. That's all. A great portion of Elites do not even have personality. They simply move about in life as if they were a machine." Isa walked to Kailynn, motioning her to follow as they went back inside. "I'm sure that's quite different from the people you are normally around in Trid."

Kailynn stopped at the door and blinked in shock at the Golden Elite. Isa walked into the living room as Tarah walked out of the kitchen, wondering if there was anything the Golden Elite needed. The Significant quickly caught up to Isa and stood in front of her, blocking Tarah.

"What did you just say?"

"That I'm sure there are far more colorful people in Trid," Isa said. "Did that upset you?"

Kailynn narrowed her eyes.

"You made it sound as though you were calling *me* a Trid," she said carefully.

"Are you not?" Isa asked, her tone without condescension. Kailynn was about to vehemently deny her true birthplace, but stopped, startled by the tone in the Golden Elite's voice. She hesitated.

"What if I was?"

"Then you were born in Trid," Isa stated matter-of-factly. "I do not see anything wrong with that." The Golden Elite looked around Kailynn to Tarah. "Would you please make some tea?"

"Yes, Miss," Tarah said, bowing her head and returning to the kitchen. Isa was about to sit on the couch when Kailynn stopped her.

"Say I *was* from Trid," she started worriedly. "How did you know?"

"Because you did not know that Elites did not have emotions," she answered. She sat on the couch, turning her bright blue eyes back on Kailynn. "That is something taught in all schools on Tiao. Either you skipped your lessons continuously, or you were born in Trid, where there are no schools. Judging from what you said earlier about someone like you needing to make money, I assumed you were a Trid."

Kailynn remained still, staring at the Golden Elite in shock. She had only spoken to the Elite for less than a half-hour and already the woman knew that she was using a fake name and that she had been born in Trid. It briefly crossed her mind that Isa, being the Golden Elite, would send her back to Trid, or even to prison for faking citizenship to work as a Significant.

"Are...are you going to call Officials on me?"

"Why would I do that?" Isa asked gently. "You knew the risks of faking citizenship and getting work in Anon. I'm sure you would not do so lightly. There is a reason you need the money, and I'm not about to make it more difficult."

Kailynn stared at Isa in surprise. For a few moments, she remained still. Then, she stepped to the couch across the coffee table and sat down heavily, still looking at Isa. Several more seconds passed before she spoke.

"You're...not what I expected."

"I'll take that as a compliment."

"...can I ask a question?"

"Of course."

"Why, exactly, am I here?" Kailynn said carefully. "Why would the Silver Elite pay for me to be here for you? I thought Elites were never supposed to spend time with Significants? Aren't you breaking the law?"

"In a way, I am," Isa agreed. "But Remus is, as well, by paying for you to be here." The Golden Elite took a deep breath. "However, Venus does know you are here."

"She does?" Kailynn gasped.

"There is no reason to be concerned," Isa assured. "Remus cleared the action with Venus before he asked for you. She agreed."

"Why would she agree?" Kailynn asked suspiciously.

Isa's eyes turned to the coffee table between them.

"There are many reasons," Isa started. "But the biggest reason is that both Remus and Venus believe that I need to take time off and talk to someone."

"Why not just go to a therapist?" Kailynn asked. "That's what they're meant for."

"I do not feel the need to harass my Specialist again," Isa laughed lightly. "If I am being honest, I was opposed to having you here. I do not like the practice of Significants, and I do not feel that I need to discuss any personal problems. I might need this month-long break to regain some of my mental energy, but I do not think I need a Significant."

"But I'm here anyway."

"I was outnumbered," Isa admitted. "While you are here, though, please make yourself at home. I know you likely deal with customers who are not great conversationalists, but I enjoy face-to-face conversation greatly."

"That would be a first," Kailynn chuckled.

Chapter Nine

Kailynn had been unable to sleep the previous night. She had sat with Isa for much of the day and spoken to her casually and freely. Only twice did Isa go back to her office to find that Remus was keeping her NCB chair on remote lockdown, preventing her from working. She returned and would ask Kailynn to tell her a little more about what Significants were like when they were not with clients.

Kailynn was only too happy to tell her the stories of the Significant lounges. Isa listened and smiled, rarely contributing to the conversation other than to keep Kailynn talking. Kailynn did not realize how much she had told Isa until she looked at the clock and realized that they had been in conversation for over four hours.

She had stopped when Isa got a phone call. The Elite answered it with her earpiece and began laughing gently at the beginning of the conversation. Kailynn had taken the time of the Elite's distraction to study her, still unable to fully comprehend how the beautiful Elite was real.

After the brief conversation, Isa finished her wine and said that she was going to go to bed. She thanked Kailynn again for being there and said she looked forward to spending the month with her. Kailynn was not sure if she was just being polite, but the words made the younger woman smile, regardless.

Kailynn went to her room, but could not settle down. Her thoughts were practically consumed with her situation and with how different Isa was from how she imagined.

Rumors of the Golden Elite were not common, but there were certain things that were expected when one thought of the most powerful person in the planetary system. Kailynn would have thought that the Golden Elite would be cold and cruel, abiding strictly by the laws and being sure that all under her rule did the same. Isa, however, had a strangely gentle nature about her. Her perfection made her intimidating, and there was an air of authority around her, but she did not appear to be a harsh leader.

Kailynn spent most of the night thinking about Isa.

Therefore, she was tired when she walked out of her room and joined Isa and Tarah for breakfast.

"Did you sleep well?" Isa asked.

"I did, thank you," Kailynn lied. She had always felt that the morning after being with a client was awkward and forced, and this was no exception. She had spent so much of the night thinking about the Elite, she felt awkward as she approached the table. Tarah stood to serve her, but Kailynn smiled and shook her head.

"It's alright, I can serve myself."

"No, Miss Jacyleen, it's quite alright."

"Oh, actually, my name is Kailynn. My real name."

"Oh." Tarah stared at Kailynn, blinking slowly, "Kailynn. I will serve you."

Tarah quickly went into the kitchen before Kailynn could protest further. Isa watched her caretaker leave, her eyes lingering on the door for only a moment before she turned to Kailynn.

"She will be more comfortable serving you. It's what she has been taught to do." Isa motioned to the chair across from her. "Please."

Kailynn sat, her eyes averted from the Elite. Isa was in a heavy robe, but she still appeared to be flawless, even dressed so casually. Her hair fell in natural waves around her face. Kailynn realized quickly that the Elite did not have makeup on, but still looked perfect.

It was then that Kailynn had to remind herself that Isa was not human.

The Golden Elite looked up from a small tablet, where she had been reading the news, and smiled at Kailynn.

"How are you this morning?"

"Okay," Kailynn murmured. "Not used to being served, though."

Isa smiled. "I'm sure it's a big change for you."

"I'm not sure that I'm comfortable with it," Kailynn laughed awkwardly.

"Tarah enjoys her work in the kitchen. Letting her serve you is something that will make her happy. If you feel uncomfortable with any of the other things she does for you, then feel free to tell her to stop."

"Other things?" Kailynn asked nervously. "Are caretakers, like, the *servants* of the Elites?"

"We try to avoid that word," Isa said carefully. "They are paid, and of course they are allowed to resign whenever they wish. But they are responsible for the upkeep of an Elite household, and an Elite."

"Upkeep? What, do you have maintenance or something?" Kailynn laughed. Isa chuckled as well, shaking her head.

"No, mostly they make sure that we eat, keep the house clean, and make sure we have everything we need."

"But caretakers aren't expected to wipe the asses of the Elites, or anything like that, right? They don't have to do everything for you?"

Isa could not help but laugh at Kailynn's vulgarity.

"I would certainly hope that those working with me to run the planet are capable enough to wipe their own asses."

Tarah returned with a plate of food and a cup of coffee, setting it down in front of the Significant.

"If you would prefer tea instead, I still have some warm in the pot."

"No, coffee is fine."

Isa turned back to the tablet with the news while Kailynn ate the most delicious food she was sure she had ever tasted. She remembered her shock the previous night when real, organic food was brought out for dinner as opposed to ration packs, which she had grown up eating. Real food was too expensive. Only the high class society members were able to afford it.

Kailynn almost wished she had never eaten the food because she knew it would be difficult to return to ration packs.

Isa stood when Kailynn was half-way through her breakfast. She walked into her room, the door closing behind her as she continued to read the tablet in her hand.

Kailynn turned to Tarah, who was looking at her food, pushing it around on her plate.

"Hey, are you okay?"

"Huh?" Tarah looked up quickly. "Oh, yeah, I'm fine," she assured. "Are you comfortable in your room?"

"Yeah," Kailynn said. An awkward silence fell over them as Tarah tried to figure out what to say next. "So, how did you come to work here?" Kailynn prompted.

"I took over for Rayal when he resigned," Tarah explained.

"Rayal? Was he the previous caretaker?"

"Mm-hm," Tarah affirmed with a nod. "He put in his resignation three years ago, and then trained me for a year, and then left."

"Why did he quit?"

"I think there was just a lot for Rayal to process after…" Tarah trailed off, her eyes going wide when she remembered who she was talking to and that she should not speak too freely. "Sorry. It's just that…a few years ago, things were a little difficult for the Syndicate and Rayal was having trouble keeping up with Isa's needs. He resigned, saying he wasn't young enough to deal with the stress of handling Isa's care."

"Is she difficult to take care of?" Kailynn asked worriedly. She was suspicious about the way Tarah had quickly caught herself and then began speaking vaguely.

"In a way," Tarah chuckled, rolling her eyes. "You will never meet someone who takes *worse* care of themselves. She never stops working. Some days it's a miracle if I can get her to eat anything. She'll often stay up all night working. I keep having to ask her to sleep and eat."

"Sounds like a predicament," Kailynn chuckled. "Was Rayal not a good caretaker, then?"

"He was the best," Tarah said strongly. "No one could do their job as well as Rayal."

"Well, then, why was he having trouble keeping up with Isa?"

Tarah opened her mouth to speak, but stopped. She looked torn and frantic, as if she was trying to keep something secret. Kailynn watched her struggle, hoping that the teenager would just tell her what had really happened, but when she saw how nervous the younger woman was getting, she took pity upon her.

"I guess I'm just wondering if his resignation was because he and Isa didn't get along."

"Oh no, far from it," Tarah said, shaking her head, relaxing a little. "Rayal still works for Isa as head of her Intelligence Agency."

"Humans are allowed to work for the Syndicate?"

"Most of the basic workers in the Syndicate are human," Tarah explained. "Then there's the Gold, Silver, and Bronze Elites—fifteen in total."

"That's it?"

"That's it."

"And they all have caretakers like you?"

"Yes," Tarah said with a nod. "We're trained by our predecessor for a year before we take the position."

"And how do you get to be trained to be a caretaker?"

"It's who you know," Tarah explained. "I was lucky. Isa took interest in me when I was very young, so she asked me if I would like to take over for Rayal, and I quickly agreed."

"Why? Why did you want this position? Sounds like you're basically Isa's live-in maid."

"I wanted to work for her. I owe her my life."

"Your life? What do you mean?"

"I wouldn't be alive today if it weren't for Isa. Working here was the least I could do to pay her back."

"What happened? How did she save your life?"

"That's not a good story..." Tarah said, shaking her head and smiling nervously. "Maybe some other time."

The caretaker stood and grabbed Isa's plate, as well as her own, and returned them to the kitchen. When she came back out, Kailynn grabbed her arm.

"Tarah, I'm sorry if I upset you," she said sincerely. "This is a very strange world to me. I was just trying to converse."

"I know, I'm alright," Tarah assured with a gentle smile. "I know how much of a shock this is for you. I was born into poverty. It took a long time to get used to this luxury." Tarah's smile widened. "Enjoy it while you're here. There's no reason not to."

■■

Kailynn wandered about the home, not sure what to do with her afternoon. Isa had vanished. *Again.* She had appeared for an hour or so and had another cup of tea while she read her tablet. Then she disappeared for several hours before returning for lunch. Kailynn had to busy herself with trying to help Tarah because she did not know what to do with herself otherwise. After lunch, as Kailynn was helping Tarah with the dishes, Isa disappeared again.

Kailynn was wondering what the Golden Elite was doing that she could breeze about the house like a ghost. She also wondered if that was going to be common through the entire month.

She was being paid far too much to act like a piece of furniture in the house.

Kailynn walked into the pool area and was confronted with the sounds of water splashing. Surprised, she watched Isa swim, ducking underwater and changing direction as the Elite swam laps.

Kailynn walked up to the pool's edge, watching the Elite swim away from her, making the exercise look easy. Kailynn was so caught up with how flawlessly the Elite moved through the water that it took her longer to realize that the Elite was swimming naked.

Startled, but also fascinated, Kailynn watched the Elite change direction again and swim toward her.

On the final few strokes, Isa broke form and went to the side of the pool, smiling at Kailynn as she leaned against the edge.

"Hello."

"Hello," Kailynn said, blinking out of her stupor. "You're a really good swimmer."

"You think so?"

"You made it look easy."

"Thank you," Isa said, pushing some wet tendrils of hair behind her ear. "Care to join me?"

Kailynn looked over the pool and laughed nervously.

"Uh, I don't think so..."

"Why not?"

"I...I don't have a swim suit."

"Neither do I."

"I noticed," Kailynn muttered. "Why *are* you naked?"

Isa shrugged. "It's my own home."

"But...what if another Elite were to come over and ask you about something?" Kailynn said, looking at Isa skeptically. "I mean, if they even do that."

"I would hope that Tarah would give me some notice of that," Isa started. "But otherwise, I wouldn't be bothered. I've had the Elites of the Syndicate join me swimming."

"*Naked?*"

"Yes."

"But what if one of them tried to...you know?"

"I don't think any of the Elites would ever think about doing something to me against my will," Isa assured. "And, if the thought ever did cross their minds, they would know better than to come onto me."

Kailynn groaned and rolled her eyes.

"Do you have any experience with the way men are?"

"I do," Isa laughed. "But the men that you know and associate with are *human*," Isa said, pushing away from the edge of the pool and drifting backward. "Elites are not."

"I'm starting to understand that..."

"So?" Isa said, raising her eyebrows. "Are you going to join me?"

Kailynn looked over Isa's naked form distorted in the water and made a face, feeling nervous about her body for the first time in many years.

"No."

"Come on," Isa said with a grin. "There's no reason to be nervous."

"Well, you *say* that," Kailynn sighed. "But...if I looked like you, I wouldn't be nervous, either."

"If you looked like me?"

"You know, a flawless body."

"Kailynn," Isa said, looking over the younger woman, "you have an incredible body."

Kailynn pursed her lips.

"...I don't know how to swim..."

"Then you better get in the shallow end," Isa laughed, jerking her head to the other side of the pool. She turned away from Kailynn and swam into the shallow end. Kailynn watched the Elite move fluidly, standing in the shallow waters, the water lapping at the slope of her abdomen. Kailynn stared at the curves of the Golden Elite's body, noting the indent of her soft waist and the swell of her perfect breasts, leading up into soft, but strong, shoulders.

Kailynn walked around the pool as Isa turned to her.

"What?" she asked when Kailynn continued to stare.

"You really are perfect."

"No," Isa corrected. "I'm artificial. It's easy to look a certain way when a computer plans every gene."

"Like I said, perfect," Kailynn concluded with a nod, stopping at the edge of the pool.

Isa's eyes changed slightly at the words, a sad look touching her expression. However, she took a deep breath and smiled, motioning Kailynn into the pool. "Come on. I'll teach you how to swim."

Kailynn still hesitated. There were a million different thoughts running through her mind. She knew that, as a Significant, she was supposed to do whatever her client wanted. However, her study of Isa's body was worrying her slightly. She found the Elite extremely beautiful. She was concerned that her staring, coupled with the fact that they would both be naked and in close proximity, would make the Elite uncomfortable.

"There is no need to be so nervous," Isa assured, leaning against the side of the pool near Kailynn's feet. "Don't worry about catering to me. If you really don't want to swim, that's fine."

"No, it's just..." Kailynn trailed off. "I dunno..."

"The decision is yours," the Elite said, backing away. "I know that as a Significant, you are meant to do as I ask, but I'd rather you swim with me as a friend, and only if you want."

Kailynn's eyes met the Golden Elite's once again. She was unsure what it was that she saw in Isa's eyes, but there was a type of pain, like loneliness, only deeper. Kailynn had come to notice the excited and nervous looks on the faces of the clients who were so lonely it had become physically painful. But with Isa, the pain looked different.

She decided that learning how to swim would be a way to keep Isa from trying to work during her leave. It was also a way to keep Kailynn from being completely bored.

"Okay."

Kailynn unzipped her shirt and shrugged it off, placing it on a bench where there were some folded towels next to Isa's robe. She then shimmied out of her pants and placed them on the bench as well. She decided to strip off her bra and panties before she could think better of it, placing them on top of the pile of her clothes.

She turned around, having to make great effort not to cover herself. She put her toe in the water, pleased to find that it was warm. She walked down the smooth steps until she was next to the Golden Elite. She ducked underwater briefly and came back up, rubbing water from her face.

"First things first," Isa said. "Don't panic. If you are having difficulty staying above water, I will pull you up."

"My life is in your hands," Kailynn said with a nervous laugh.

Isa started explaining how to tread water. They stayed in the shallow end of the pool and Kailynn tried to tread water, finding the task more difficult than she expected. However, as she started to get the motions down, Isa told her to move further and further into the pool until she could no longer touch the bottom with her toes. Kailynn tried to tread water again, but it took her a while to get the motions strong enough to keep her head above water.

After she had that, Isa kept them in the deep end of the pool and went over to Kailynn, telling her to straighten her legs before placing her hand under Kailynn's legs and pulling them to the surface, her other hand supporting the Significant's back. She explained to the younger woman how to keep her body afloat, teaching her the breathing techniques she had been taught. She kept her hands under Kailynn. When she tried to remove them, Kailynn glared at her.

"Don't let go!"

Isa chuckled and her hands returned, watching Kailynn as she inhaled and tried to kick her legs gently.

Suddenly, Isa's hands were gone. Kailynn turned quickly to see Isa backing away with a smile. However, the Significant lost focus and her body dipped into the water, effectively scaring her.

"I told you not to let go!" she barked, moving her hand and splashing Isa with water before lunging at her. Isa laughed and swam further into the deep end of the pool, Kailynn struggling against the water to get close enough to exact her revenge. Isa watched her awkwardly swim closer and splash the Elite once more. Isa laughed and ducked underwater, swimming back to the shallow end, watching Kailynn to be sure that she stayed above water.

"Shit, shit, shit, shit…" Kailynn huffed, trying to follow Isa, realizing she was in the deep end of the pool. Isa resurfaced when Kailynn could touch the bottom of the pool with her toes again and she darted at Isa, splashing her once more.

The Elite retaliated and Kailynn lunged at her, grabbing her arm and splashing her directly in the face, being sure her arm was restrained in case of counter-attack.

Instead, Isa grabbed Kailynn's wrist in turn and pulled her into the deep end once more. Kailynn tried to swim backward, but Isa brought her forward.

Clamoring to figure out how to stay afloat with the bottom of the pool suddenly out of reach, she climbed onto Isa's back, wrapping her arms around the Elite's shoulders.

"If I drown, you drown with me!" she declared with a laugh.

Grinning broadly, Isa started to swim back to the shallow end.

"You can swim when you're angry enough," Isa teased.

"You let go of me!"

"I knew you would stay afloat," Isa assured, her feet touching the bottom of the pool as her hands released Kailynn's legs. The Significant unhooked her arms from around Isa's shoulders and moved further into the shallow end.

"But I was in the deep end."

"Have you never heard the saying sink or swim?" Isa asked with a devilish smile.

"And I was *sinking*!" Kailynn said, a wide smile on her face, unable to keep from laughing. "If you ever drop me again, I will kick your ass."

"So it wasn't bad enough that you never want to get back into the pool?" Isa asked. "Must not have been as traumatic as you had me believing."

Kailynn stuck out her chin in an over-exaggerated pout. She turned and started to swim toward the deep end of the pool, her arms and legs flailing underwater as she tried to propel herself forward, just to show Isa. The Elite smiled and watched, but was sure to be prepared to swim to the Significant, if needed. Kailynn struggled against the water in a way that almost made Isa laugh out loud.

When the younger woman reached the other end of the pool, she latched onto the siding and caught her breath. Swimming was a lot more work than she anticipated.

With unnatural grace, Isa swam to the other side of the pool and stopped next to Kailynn.

"This is…a workout…" Kailynn gasped.

"That's enough for today," Isa agreed, pulling herself out of the pool, making it look effortless. Kailynn tried to follow suit, but her arms were shaking from the exertion of her frantic swim across the pool. Isa reached down and helped pull the Significant out of the water.

Chapter Ten

For the following three days, Kailynn was sure that she found Isa and made her go to the pool to teach the Significant how to swim. However, sometimes finding the Elite was a chore. Isa was trying to find ways to override the lock on her NCB chair, but Remus would find out what terminal she was working on and shut that off as well. It was amusing to watch Isa walk around, defeated, not knowing what to do with herself when she was not working.

But that did mean that, when Kailynn was lost in thought, or in the middle of doing something with Tarah, the Elite would appear from nowhere, startling the Significant every time.

Kailynn was no longer concerned about being naked in front of the Elite. The second lesson had helped her get over her self-consciousness. Isa had been focused on teaching Kailynn some swimming techniques, and had been in close proximity to the Significant through the entire lesson. Kailynn was beginning to look forward to the swim lessons every day.

However, the lessons were short and Kailynn was having trouble finding other ways to occupy her time. She would help Tarah as much as the caretaker would allow, but Tarah felt uncomfortable with all the help from the Significant. When Tarah would finally tell Kailynn to go do something else, she would go to the entertainment room next to Isa's office and watch television, but there was little on that was interesting. There were a lot of television shows that were half-way into a story that Kailynn did not bother to learn. She had thought that television was more interactive, where the person could be in the role of a character during the episode, but she came to learn that Isa did not have that television because she only watched the news, if she watched television at all.

The Elite had laughed when Kailynn said that people probably preferred those experiences because it was a way to escape reality. Kailynn suggested it as a means to help Isa escape the stresses of her day.

"Perhaps," she had agreed, "but I spend all day at work as a virtual being. I'd like to be in the real world at least some of the time."

On the sixth day of Kailynn's stay, she wandered back into the room she had made a note to explore.

The lights came on automatically when she walked in and the packages of papers were illuminated for her to see. She walked in, looking among the different words printed on the ends. She continued down the aisle of colors and shelves, looking over them carefully. She desperately wished she could read, curious about what the words said.

When she rounded the corner of the first row of shelves, something else caught her eye immediately. Along the wall was a gallery of paintings. Some were smaller, abstract scenes and others were stunning realistic sceneries. There was a photoset of the city of Anon being built. But scattered among the paintings were four large depictions of naked bodies—two women and two men. The bodies stood out against the solid black backgrounds, their faces not depicted in the paintings. They were all positioned differently, exhibiting a side of the body and the musculature of the frame. One woman's back was turned, one arm extended above her head as her body twisted and curled forward. The other was leaning forward, one arm wrapped around herself as the other wrapped her neck, her body tilted, her ribs protruding slightly in the position. One of the male portraits was extremely muscular, his back turned, one hand grabbing one foot and pulling it up behind his back, leaning back to create an arch with his spine. The final picture, the one that caught Kailynn's attention, was a frontal of another man, his frame built, but not too muscular. He was leaning back, his arms extended out of the frame, his abdomen and chest pulled taught by the stretch as his body twisted slightly.

Kailynn was studying the collection of nude paintings when Isa, once again, startled her.

"I was wondering where you ran off to," the Golden Elite said. Kailynn jumped, trying not to blush at being caught looking at nude artwork.

"You need to stop doing that," she said with a nervous laugh. "I'm going to get you a bell or something."

Isa laughed. "I am sorry. I do not mean to keep startling you." She looked at the paintings behind Kailynn. "What do you think?"

"Huh?"

"Of the artwork," Isa clarified. "You were studying it intensely when I walked in."

"Oh, uh," Kailynn glanced behind her at the two particular images that had captured her attention, "I think they're, uh…" She turned back to Isa. "Why do you have so many pictures of naked people?"

"I have an intense fascination with the body," she admitted, stepping closer. "I think it is incredibly beautiful."

"So you have naked pictures? Wouldn't that be considered...I dunno..."

"Pornographic?" Isa completed. "No, I don't think so." She looked at the male nude directly behind Kailynn, her eyes following the curves in the artwork. "The body is not only about sexual desire. It is incredible to see the design of the human body, the way the male and female bodies differ and the utility of the body in its entirety."

Kailynn turned to Isa, watching the Elite's eyes look over the male body.

"Doesn't it make you curious?" Kailynn asked. "You can't actually have sex. Seeing these pictures," Kailynn looked back at the male nude, "it has to make you wonder what you're missing."

"Which one of the collection is your favorite?" Isa asked, ignoring the comment. The younger woman hesitated and then nodded to the picture Isa had been admiring.

"Mine as well."

"His body seems perfect," Kailynn said.

"I agree." Isa nodded. "Symmetrical, powerful, the angle really accents the musculature."

"...I was talking about something else."

"Oh?" Isa chuckled, looking at Kailynn. "And what would that be?"

"Well...I'm not an expert or anything, but I think he has a nice dick."

Isa let out a bark of laughter, causing Kailynn to smile.

"Oh, come on, don't tell me you never looked at it."

"I have, of course," she admitted.

"He has no insecurities."

"You don't know that," Isa said. "His face isn't shown. It's possible that he only agreed to pose because his identity would not be revealed. He might be extremely self-conscious of his body."

"He *shouldn't* be if he looks like that," Kailynn said.

"I agree."

"Be honest, if he came up to you and told you he wanted to have sex, you would do it, wouldn't you?" Kailynn said, raising her eyebrows suggestively. Isa looked at Kailynn with an unreadable light in her eyes.

"Would *you*?"

"Hell yeah," Kailynn said enthusiastically. "Do you know who this is? Because I'd like to see if he is as perfect as this picture makes him look."

"As a matter of fact, I know the artist and I was there for one session of this painting."

"Then you *do* know who this is," Kailynn said. "And you know he's self-conscious, huh?"

"He is," Isa affirmed. "And he is as perfect as he looks in this picture."

"And, not once, did he ask *you* to sleep with him?"

"No, of course not," Isa said, shaking her head. "Elites are forbidden from the sexual life."

"Why is that? I mean, some of the guys I know, if they *don't* have sex, they can't think of anything other than *having* sex."

"For humans, that is likely true," Isa agreed. "However, for Elites, any physical desire, particularly for the males, is beaten out at a young age."

Kailynn stopped, looking at Isa's veiled expression.

"*Beaten*?"

Isa turned to the Significant.

"Yes."

Kailynn stared at the Golden Elite for several long moments, trying to think of something to say.

"Why?"

"Because Elites are meant to work," Isa explained coolly. It was clear she was reciting things that she had been told at a young age. "Everything else is a distraction."

Kailynn could not think of anything to say in response. She slowly turned back to look at the paintings, trying to think of a way to switch the conversation, but the words sat uneasily in her stomach.

"Do the people know that?" she murmured. "That all the Elites are beaten as children?"

"No, I don't think so," Isa admitted. "Most Elites also learn to keep quiet. As I've told you, Elites rarely even have personality. They don't question why they're being beaten. They learn what brings the beatings and learn to avoid it. It's programming."

"It sounds horrible."

"Yes, the Academy certainly can be brutal."

"Academy?"

"The Elite Academy," Isa clarified. "After Elites are removed from their incubational tanks, they are sent to the Academy for schooling until graduation at age twenty." Isa took a deep breath and slowly let it out, turning back to Kailynn. "I don't mean to drag down the conversation."

"No, it's fine, it's just…I mean, it's *not* fine. They're beating kids."

Isa smiled thinly.

"Only until we learn." She laughed, shaking her head. "Which some of us never do."

"Oh? Like you?" Kailynn asked, finding it hard to believe that the calm Golden Elite had ever had a difficult time with teachers at the Elite Academy.

"Let's just say that I used to be a very slow learner," Isa said mysteriously.

"I think you still are," Kailynn teased. "You're still trying to get the NCB chair to work even though Remus continues to thwart your plans."

Isa laughed richly, the sound making Kailynn's breath catch in her throat. Isa turned her eyes, now bright with amusement, onto Kailynn, making it more difficult for the younger woman to breathe.

"Yes, he does keep catching me," she said. "At this point, I don't care about getting the chair working. I'm just trying to see if there is any way for me to work around his lockdown." She shook her head. "He's amused by it as well. It's been a fun way to pass the time."

"You mean distracting your Silver Elite?" Kailynn laughed, surprised.

"Of course." Isa nodded. "I have to remind him how much he needs me around." She winked at Kailynn, causing heat to rise in the Significant's cheeks. Kailynn chuckled as well, trying to dispel the feelings churning in her belly.

"Sounds to me like you're a slave-driver of a boss."

"I just like to keep him in shape," Isa said, trying to hide her smile.

"That sounds dirty."

"It was intended to," Isa said with a nod. "I may be an Elite, but I can still have a sense of humor."

"Can you not work from another computer, or something?"

"Not in the capacity I need," Isa admitted. "I can send messages from other platforms, but I need the NCB chair to handle most of my affairs."

"And you just sit in that chair and…what?"

"Have you never seen one?"

"No."

Isa motioned Kailynn to follow her. Kailynn fell in step behind the Elite, trying not to watch Isa move. It felt like every move—every step, every strand of hair rustled, every swing of her arms—was a perfectly choreographed dance, captivating and powerful. Kailynn had become increasingly curious about the other Elites. She wondered if they were all perfect. With the way Isa was capturing Kailynn's attention so easily, it was no wonder the Elites were such incredible politicians. They commanded attention and respect by their very being.

Isa led Kailynn to her office, which the Significant had never been in before.

The office was mostly bare with a large desk on one wall that had four large monitors on it, and a sitting area in the far corner with windows looking out over the city. However, most of the room was taken up by the NCB chair.

The chair was big, bolted into the floor and had a large ring around the base and around the headrest.

"This looks terrifying."

"It's quite the machine," Isa said with a nod. She patted the ring around the headrest. "Hop in."

"What?"

"It's on lockdown. It's not going to turn on. Besides, you need training to operate one of these. I would never have you sit in it and turn it on."

"Training? Seriously? To sit in a chair?"

"It's more complicated than that. This chair can put you in the hospital if you're not careful."

"Then why are you asking me to sit in it?"

"To show you what an NCB chair does. If I'm ever here and you need my attention, such as in an emergency, then you need to know how to safely interrupt me."

Kailynn stared at Isa, worried and surprised. She was not sure how the chair could be that dangerous, but Isa did have her curious.

Kailynn ducked her head under the upper ring and went to the chair, sitting in it slowly, her hands resting on the cold metal of the arm rests. The chair's seat was tilted upward, which caused Kailynn to slide back until her body was cradled in position. She tried to pull herself back up, but the chair's position made it very difficult to move.

"I don't know if I'll be able to get out."

"It's meant to keep you as still as possible," Isa said. She tapped Kailynn's leg. "Put your legs in the cradles."

Kailynn kicked one of her legs over the slightly-raised middle section of the chair and placed her foot in the covered area, sliding her other leg into position as well.

"There are a lot of settings on this chair," Isa started. "Push your head back into the cushion."

Kailynn did so and was surprised that her head sank into the cushions as a section above her head protruded and covered her hair, stopping at her forehead. Once the movement above her head stopped, two rounded points protruded just behind her nape and touched softly to her hairline.

"I thought you said this thing wouldn't turn on," Kailynn said quickly.

"It isn't on," Isa assured. "When this mode is activated, it's called BCS—BioCranial Sourcing."

"What does that mean?"

"It's the mode used for filing documents, looking up information, composing messages, receiving messages, etcetera. When this chair is not on lockdown, this ring," she tapped the ring on the headrest, "will glow blue and there will be holograms of codes in the area below it. BCS Mode is dangerous. The chair is connected directly to the brain and, if halted too quickly, can cause severe headaches, concussion, memory loss, and a few other problems. If you see this ring glowing blue, and you need to interrupt me for an emergency, there is a number pad on the back of the chair. The code is 77743. That will start the ten-second emergency shut down."

"When you're in this mode, what does it feel like?"

"It feels like being suspended in weightlessness. This is meant to dull the senses to the body and allow for the brain to process information, which is input through the nodes at the back of your neck. From that point, it's a bit like going through documents on a tablet, only it's in your mind."

"That sounds confusing…"

"That's why training is essential," Isa agreed with a laugh. Her expression fell a little. "Now, if this ring is glowing red, it is far more dangerous to interrupt me. It's the same code to disable the chair, though."

"What mode is red?"

"Off-Planet Mode, notoriously nicknamed Opium." Isa took a deep breath and gently tapped the ring again. "This means that my entire body is dependent on the chair to survive. If interrupted in Opium, it is likely that I will be unconscious upon being released from the chair and I will need to go to the hospital. I strongly discourage ever interrupting me in this mode unless there is immediate danger, such as a fire."

"Noted," Kailynn said, her eyes wide.

"If this ring is not glowing at all, I'm not bound to the chair," Isa said finally. "You can just walk up and talk to me."

"So there is a mode on this chair that won't kill you?" Kailynn said dryly. She tried to sit up, but her head was still stuck to the back cushion of the chair. "Okay, how do I get out of the claw?"

Isa ducked under the ring, leaning forward and pressing her right ring finger to the part of the chair that trapped Kailynn's forehead.

When her fingerprint was recognized, the chair returned to its original position, releasing Kailynn's head. However, Kailynn was startled by the close proximity of the Elite. Even though they had been swimming naked together for the previous several days, the way the Elite was positioned, her hand bracing against the back of the chair and the short distance between her face and Kailynn's made the Significant's cheeks burn hotly.

Her gaze was captured in the stunning blue color of Isa's eyes. There was power and strength in her eyes, but there was also a gentle, warm part of the look, and the combination of the two made the simple moment overwhelming. Isa smiled, causing light to touch her eyes and Kailynn's heart to skip a beat.

"Your eyes are beautiful," Isa murmured.

"R-really?" Kailynn said. Her brain had turned to static. She knew it would be impossible to form coherent sentences. One word was already a struggle.

Isa nodded, offering her hand to the Significant. Kailynn tried to stop the shaking in her hands as her fingers closed around Isa's and the Elite helped her out of the chair.

Kailynn knew, in that moment, that the feelings that had been building in her body when she was around the Elite would not easily be quelled.

She knew.

And, based on the look Kailynn saw in Isa's eyes, the Golden Elite knew, too.

Their fates were already entwined.

Chapter Eleven

There was only one more day of rest for Isa, and then Remus lifted the lockdown on her chair and she was able to work remotely from home.

But, even with Isa working, Kailynn could feel the air between them getting thicker when they were in the same room. After the moment of realization she had in the NCB chair, Kailynn had been trying to spend more time with Tarah and getting to know the caretaker more in order to distract her thoughts from Isa.

Kailynn knew that, no matter what her body told her whenever Isa got close, she could never pursue those feelings. Isa was an Elite, forbidden from sexual relationships. To make matters more complicated, Isa was the Golden Elite—the most powerful person in the planetary system. And, for added severity to the situation, Kailynn was a Trid non-citizen with fake papers who was earning money in an attempt to free her brother and the other Trids who had tried to shut down Venus.

Kailynn spent more time around Tarah than Isa the second week of her stay. The young caretaker never left the house, ordering in everything that they needed and having it delivered by the robots that handled such matters in the capital. Tarah was a very talkative one when the two were alone. She was unwilling to discuss her own life, but she was more than willing to dish on a lot of the society gossip she heard as a caretaker.

"How do you learn about all this?" Kailynn asked when she heard about the nobleman who was arrested for having naked pictures of one of the male Elites, named Aolee, and circulating them for profit, which eventually made it to another planet and sparked rumors about the possible kidnapping of an Elite to determine how they were made. There had been a rumor on that planet that the Elites were entirely robotic, and seeing a creature that appeared human had irked the planetary leaders.

"The caretakers have a gossip network," Tarah answered. "I hear about it from other houses."

"I thought no one spoke to each other in the upper levels of society."

"No, I guess not really," Tarah admitted. "The only other caretaker I've ever met in person is Luska."

"Whose caretaker is that?"

"Remus," Tarah answered.

"Then, if he's the only one you've ever met, how do you get all this other gossip?"

"We have our own communication network through our computers," Tarah explained. "We have to find some way to entertain ourselves when the Elites are working all day."

"Damn, that would be boring..." Kailynn groaned, rolling her eyes. "Then your lives are completely dull. You just sit around here, gossip about others in high society, and wait for the Elites to need something. That sounds horrible."

"It's actually not that bad," Tarah disagreed. "For instance, we know before anyone else when something shady is about to happen in the upper circles of society."

"How does that work?"

"Caretakers aren't just for the Elite. The Elites are the only ones *required* to have caretakers, but—"

"*Required?*" Kailynn gaped.

"Yes. Venus orders that there always be a caretaker in an Elite's house. It's law," Tarah explained. "But, there are many noble men and women who have caretakers as well. Isa asked Rayal when he was caretaker to reach out to other caretakers and keep contact with them so that he knew what was going on in other houses. Since then, other Elite caretakers have done so as well, and it has really expanded the network. This lets everyone be informed. We've helped stop some dangerous deals and illegal activity because we've told the Elites what other caretakers have said."

"Seriously? That's scary. It's like every house has a spy." Kailynn's stomach flipped. "Wait, that means that you could tell people about me being here."

"I guess you have to be nice to me." She giggled, shaking her head. "Don't worry, even if someone found out that you were here, none of the caretakers would betray Isa."

"How can you be so sure?"

"Because Isa is special," Tarah said with a gentle smile. "Everyone loves her. They would never hurt her."

The words made Kailynn pause. Perhaps her attraction to the Golden Elite was just the same thing that everyone else saw. Maybe her feelings were not that crazy or out of the ordinary with those who were near Isa.

Tarah's eyes lowered to the table between them.

"Kailynn..." she started slowly, pulling the Significant's attention back, "I wanted to thank you."

"For what?"

"I'm sure you don't realize it, but Isa has been far happier with you in the house," Tarah explained. "It's not a big change, but there are subtle differences. There's a light back in her eyes that I haven't seen in years."

"That might be just because she hasn't had to work for a week," Kailynn said, waving the comment away. She had just believed that her attraction to the Elite was something that was common and that she did not need to pay attention to it. Hearing that the Elite was somehow different with her, *happier* at that, made Kailynn's heart beat a little faster, no matter how much she told herself to calm down.

"Maybe," Tarah admitted with a small nod, "but I don't think so. It's hard to explain. Isa isn't just special, she's very different from every other Elite. I think she *needs* interaction with people. Most Elites just work and work and that's all they do. Isa needs to interact, she needs to talk to people, and I think she finds that she can't talk to me or Remus or Rayal about everything."

Kailynn was looking at the table, her nerves increasing by the second.

She was unsure what it was, but the words held a lot more meaning than she could comprehend in that moment.

"I have to admit, when I heard that you were coming here, I was nervous," Tarah said with a guilty expression. "And after I looked at your reviews—"

"My reviews?" Kailynn said quickly, her head snapping up to look at the caretaker. "What was wrong with my reviews?"

"Nothing," Tarah said quickly, raising her hands. "You can't always trust the reviews anyway. People exaggerate."

"Tarah, what did my reviews say?"

"No, it was just one review, it's fine," Tarah assured, trying to calm the Significant.

"Who? Who was it and what did they say?"

Tarah was now worried she had truly upset Kailynn.

"Fine, just show me!" Kailynn said, standing. "Where the hell is the computer?"

Tarah quickly stood.

"Kailynn, forget I said anything! I promise, it's fine!"

"Just show me. I need to know what asshole said what shit!"

"That's just going to upset you more!" Tarah said, rushing after the other woman as Kailynn remembered that there was a computer in her room. They both went in, though Tarah continued to tell Kailynn that there was nothing wrong with her reviews and she did not need to worry. Kailynn angrily sat in front of the computer and pushed the power button hard enough to nearly knock the computer over.

"I don't know how to check reviews," Kailynn growled. "Pull them up. I need to see them."

"Kailynn, seriously, I'm sorry. I didn't mean to upset you."

"Tarah, I need to know what's being said about me. It might change the way things are for me when I go back to Companion."

Tarah stared into Kailynn's determined eyes and sighed, nodding once. She typed into the computer and clicked a few things on the screen. When Tarah sighed heavily and backed away, Kailynn looked at the reviews, seeing the letters grouped together to form words that she could not read.

"This is pissing me off," Kailynn groaned. "Will you just read the bad one out loud to me?"

"What?" Tarah said, her eyes going wide. "No."

"Tarah, I can't read it. Will you read it to me?" Kailynn was trying to sound so furious that Tarah would not question Kailynn's request. However, after studying the Significant's eyes, Tarah understood Kailynn's illiteracy immediately.

"Oh..." She looked awkwardly at the screen as Kailynn began pacing. Tarah hesitated, looking between the computer screen and Kailynn before scrolling through the reviews on Kailynn's Significant page. Once she found the one she was looking for, she fully regretted saying anything about Kailynn's reviews.

She took a deep breath, glancing back at the impatient and irritated Kailynn before bracing herself.

"Jacyleen is a pretty, but stupid, girl," she started.

"What?!" Kailynn bellowed. "Who the fuck is this asshole?! How much did he write?!"

Tarah cringed, thinking about the rest of the review.

"Well, keep going!"

Tarah turned back to the screen, rubbing her forehead with her other hand as she continued.

"Jacyleen is not one for conversation. She would much rather let sex do the talking. She has a nice body and is open to sexual favors. However, there is a reason her sex fee is lower than most Significants her age. She is rough around the edges and does not know how to look for her partner's pleasure."

"What the fuck is he talking about?!" Kailynn screeched. "Who is the fucker?!"

"She, however, is into fetishes and other kinks. She is clearly desperate for money, so she will likely work quickly to get on to another appointment to earn even more, so don't expect to see her for very long. Fast, kinky, and stupid, Jacyleen is good in bed, but otherwise, a disappointing Significant."

"What the *fuck*?!" Kailynn screeched. "Can you see who posted this review? Who the fuck does he think he is?!"

"No, the names are always anonymous," Tarah said, getting worried that Kailynn would start throwing things around the room in her rage. "You know, it's just the opinion of one jackass. You can't always trust reviews. All the other ones you have were good."

"That's not the point!" Kailynn growled. "I'm desperate to earn money? I am into kinky shit? What the *fuck*?!"

"Kailynn, I need to start making dinner," Tarah said, standing. "Why don't you help me? It will take your mind off it."

"No, it won't," Kailynn snapped. "Shit, I really want to know who this guy is…"

"It's not worth it to get upset."

Kailynn let out a frustrated sound and stormed from her room, going to the living room and pacing, bellowing about how everyone was a perverted bastard and that she only did what they wanted her to do and she still ended up being called a slut. She continued to scream about it while Tarah stood helplessly to the side, wanting desperately to go into the kitchen and get away from the upset Significant.

Kailynn ground her teeth together and, before she could think better of it, she picked up a pillow off the couch and hurled it at the wall of windows leading out to the balcony. The pillow hit the glass and fell harmlessly to the ground, though the automatic door opened shortly afterward, pushing the pillow aside before closing again.

"Is my living room going to survive the evening?" an amused voice chuckled behind Kailynn.

The Significant turned to see Isa standing in the living room next to Tarah, bemused.

"Isa..." Kailynn murmured, her eyes going wide. She looked at the pillow and then back at the Golden Elite. "I...I mean, I just..."

Isa raised her hand, her smile widening.

"I'm not upset," she assured. "I am, however, concerned. What has you so worked up?"

Kailynn groaned and rolled her eyes, her entire body tensing in preparation for the rant. Isa dismissed Tarah and walked to the fallen pillow, picking it up.

"Have you seen the reviews on me?" Kailynn demanded, watching the Elite.

"Pardon?"

"Have you seen the reviews on me as a Significant? Have you read them?"

"No," Isa said, returning the pillow to its proper place on the couch.

"Are you lying?"

"No."

"Well, they're all lying!" Kailynn barked. "I mean, this one was saying shit about how I'm desperate for money and that I don't care about the person I'm with. Damn right I don't! I'm *paid* to be there! I don't know these people! I don't give a shit about their sob stories! But I sit there and listen and do whatever they want me to do because this society is so fucked up people have to pay other people to talk to them! Do you realize how fucking *demented* that is?!"

Kailynn stopped when her eyes met Isa's. She suddenly realized that she had just blown up at her client—a client who also happened to be the most powerful person in the planetary system. Isa appeared to be amused, but Kailynn still forced herself to calm down before she said something stupid.

"Something I have found," Isa started, when she realized that Kailynn was finished, "is that many who say things in that manner are generally trying to hide their own insecurities. It's a very elaborate, and pathetic, form of making one feel better about oneself. More likely than not, that client had certain inadequacies when he was with you and he decided to blame you for them rather than acknowledge his own faults."

"There was that one idiot who spent the first half hour drinking and then ten minutes pawing at me, trying to figure out what the hell he was doing, and then he was done before he even got to the sex because he got off on me calling him "Baby Johnny." Maybe that was his review. Creepy bastard."

"That sounds like Imothy Rex," Isa said, her eyebrows furrowed in thought.

"What?"

"The man, what you just described. He's a powerful figure in the economy, but a complete bastard," Isa clarified. "His advisors, but only his female ones, call him Baby J." Her eyebrows went high. "He seems incompetent enough to not know a thing about women."

"I don't remember what the idiot's name was," Kailynn groaned, flopping down on the couch opposite of Isa, rubbing her eyes and shaking her head. "I mean, that's out there for anyone to see now! They're going to think I'm into all kinds of kinky shit, and I'm *not*! I mean, everyone's curious, but kink is not the same thing!"

"I can't say I know what qualifies as kink," Isa said with a gentle laugh.

"Ugh, I hate this," Kailynn continued. "This is even worse than whoring. At least there no one pretends that they're there for other reasons. There's all kinds of pretense around Significant work."

"That is true."

"It just pisses me off when people assume shit about me," Kailynn pressed on. "Just because I look and act the way I do, people think that I'm some sort of slutty thug, or something." Isa smiled as she saw Kailynn get more upset, winding herself up again even as she sat still on the couch. "I mean, I *waited*. I was sixteen when I first had sex."

Isa barked a laugh before she could help herself. Kailynn glared at the Golden Elite.

"Oh, to *you*, I'm sure that *is* slutty," she snapped.

Isa shook her head. "I first had sex at a younger age."

The shock of the statement calmed Kailynn down almost immediately. For several long moments, she could only stare into Isa's blue eyes and process the words.

"What?"

"I had barely turned fifteen."

"But…I thought…" Kailynn's brow creased in confusion. "I mean…were you raped? Elites aren't supposed to…"

"I was not raped," Isa said, shaking her head. "Just rebellious."

"*You*? Rebellious?" Kailynn barked a laugh. "How can you be rebellious when you end up leading the government?"

"You rebel intelligently, I suppose."

"Then, you were never caught."

"I was," Isa contradicted. "There were cameras in every room of the Elite Academy. We had guards upon us in no time."

Kailynn studied Isa's expression.

"That explains how you know that sexual desire is beaten out of Elites," Kailynn said with a nervous laugh.

"Indeed," Isa said. "I learned first-hand."

"What happens if an Elite has sex?" Kailynn pressed, her curiosity taking hold.

"I assume it's no different than humans," Isa teased.

"No, I mean, the punishment," Kailynn clarified. "Say one of the Elites were to have sex with someone. Would they be killed?"

Isa sighed heavily, thinking about how to answer.

"Not likely," she admitted. "It would depend on how public the incident became. Should any of my Bronze Elites be caught in a public sex scandal, they would have to be immediately removed from their position. If it was a very public affair, then death would likely be the sentence."

"*Why?*" Kailynn hissed. "Yeah, Elites are supposed to work, but everyone has sex. Literally everyone. What's the big deal if Elites do as well?"

"I have never been able to fully understand why, myself," Isa said. "My assumption is that abstaining from sexual activity creates an image to humans that we are infallible, that we are not controlled by basic human desires and, therefore, we are superior."

"But didn't you prove that that wasn't true when you had sex at fifteen?" Kailynn pressed. "You wanted sex, so you had it."

Isa shrugged.

"I do not know that that is the reason Syndicate Elites are forbidden from sexual relationships," she said. "That is only my hypothesis."

"But, you *do* have sexual desires, right?"

"Yes," Isa admitted, her eyes averting to the coffee table. "Biology is still biology. We can try and cover it up and control it with rules and rationalization as much as we want. That does not change that the body wants what it wants." Isa's expression fell a little further and the change surprised Kailynn. It was not an extremely noticeable difference, but it did catch the Significant's attention. "Of course, Elite's don't *want* anything, so perhaps it is easier for us to forego our desires."

Chapter Twelve

Kailynn was getting more and more nervous around Isa. Everyone in the house could sense it. Tarah would ask her every day if everything was alright. She would mechanically answer yes, but she never meant it.

The look on Isa's face had haunted her. She had seen the pain in the Elite's eyes as she talked about the Elites not having desires. Kailynn was sure she had never thought about a single moment as much as she mulled over the moment Isa's expression changed.

Kailynn did not know what it was, but the look had broken her heart. Kailynn did not get upset or sad over many things. She was not a bleeding heart, something that she was often teased about as a younger girl. However, Isa's pained expression struck a chord deep inside Kailynn's being.

Her strange attraction to the Golden Elite was reaching a dangerous level.

Near the middle of her third week with the Golden Elite, someone came to visit the household.

When the front door opened as Kailynn and Tarah were playing a game on the coffee table's interface, Kailynn was surprised to find herself startled by the visitor.

She had become used to the quiet of the house. To have someone suddenly appear surprised her.

Tarah's face lit up immediately when she saw the man.

"Rayal!" she gasped, her tone raising excitedly as she clamored to her feet and ran to him. Kailynn slowly stood, watching the man smile at Tarah. Kailynn was surprised at how *handsome* Rayal was. He had a defined jaw and defined cheekbones. His brown hair was neatly cut and swept away from his face. He was also tall and broadly built. However, his right eye was a deep, powerful brown color, while his other eye was glassy and grey, surrounded by light scarring that extended into his hairline, showing he was blind in one eye due to injury.

"Tarah," he greeted, smiling gently at her, exposing his perfectly white teeth. "How have you been holding up?"

"Fine," Tarah said with a nervous giggle. "It's actually been nice to have Isa home. I don't worry as much."

"Enjoy it while it lasts," Rayal chuckled. "As soon as the month leave is up, she'll bolt out of here faster than you can blink." The former caretaker to the Golden Elite turned to look at Kailynn, who was standing awkwardly in the sitting area. His warm nature faded quickly, surprising Kailynn. "Are you the Significant?"

Kailynn tried not to be offended by his tone and the way he addressed her, but her indignation came through her voice when she spoke back.

"My name is Kailynn."

"Kailynn," Rayal repeated.

"Rayal, there's no need to be worried," Tarah assured. "Isa has actually been very happy to have her here."

Rayal and Kailynn shared an intense look. Kailynn could not help but be intimidated by his stare. However, she held her ground, staring back at him, waiting for him to look away.

Tarah was the one who broke the staring contest.

"Rayal, please, be nice."

"I'm always nice," he chuckled. Once his gaze was off her, Kailynn relaxed.

"Well, not *always*," Tarah teased.

"Why not *always*?"

"Because you don't come to see me anymore," Tarah pouted. "That's not nice of you at all."

"My apologies, my dear," Rayal said with a bow of his head. "I shall try to be more sociable from now on."

Tarah giggled, her cheeks quickly reddening. Kailynn could not help but laugh at the obvious crush Tarah had on the former caretaker.

"How about we have lunch together sometime in the next few days?" Rayal suggested. "Isa is going to be very busy for a while."

"What? Why? What happened?" Tarah asked worriedly.

Rayal tapped the briefcase he was carrying.

"Emergency came up a couple hours ago," he admitted. "From my understanding, she's already in a conference call to try and deal with these morons, but I have some information she'll want."

"She's in her office," Tarah said.

Seeing the two caretakers walk toward Isa's office and worried about Rayal's serious tone, Kailynn followed them. She watched Rayal carefully, not sure what to make of the former caretaker.

However, her study was halted when Rayal opened the door to Isa's office and the three stepped inside.

Isa was sitting in the NCB chair, but it was sitting upright, not restraining the Golden Elite at all. The upper ring was higher, extended on a stand on the back of the chair. Across from the Golden Elite were four standing holograms. One was in the middle of his sentence when the group walked in.

"—damage dealt. Predicting such a catastrophe would have been almost impossible."

"I find that very difficult to believe, Yurim," Isa said.

Isa's face was very different now that she was working. Her eyes were sharp and powerful, even as she looked at the holograms in the room with her. Her perfect posture accented her power and control while still showing that she was furious at whatever had happened.

"Please, try to understand, Elite Isa—"

"Try to understand what?" Isa challenged coldly. "That I have an entire planet being held hostage by the Ninth Circle?"

"We do not know that the Ninth Circle is involved," one woman said. "They are always warring with one another. I doubt they would come together to take over a single planet."

"Even someone on the outskirts of the Ninth Circle would have the intelligence to know that attacking and occupying a planet of the Crescent Alliance is suicide."

"Caroie is not just a member of the Crescent Alliance," Isa said sharply. "They are also under special protection. For an attack, taking over Caroie is a brilliant move. Or have you forgotten that it provides goods to fifty-four of the sixty-one planets in the Alliance?"

"Yes, the hit to trade could be catastrophic," the final hologram agreed.

"Then, why is it that ships from the Ninth Circle were able to land on Caroie and initiate a planetary take-over without detection?" Isa said, her eyes traveling over the other holograms. "The four of you surround Caroie. There is no reason this should have occurred."

The other four in the meeting were silent.

"I have intelligence that Caroie sent distress signals for nearly twelve days as the capital was being overtaken and thousands of people were being killed. These signals reached three of you. Yet, you chose not to act."

Still, everyone remained silent.

Isa sighed heavily and leaned forward in her chair, putting her hands on the armrests and getting to her feet slowly.

"Let me make sure I understand this," she said, her voice powerful and cold, sending shivers down everyone's spines. "Caroie is under special protection, and therefore, by law, their distress signals are to be met immediately, regardless of confirmation of an emergency. And yet, those closest to the planet ignored these signals that were repeated for *twelve* days before communications were interrupted. According to my intelligence, these signals were not lost, they were deliberately ignored. Now, *I* must come in and not only negotiate with Ninth Circle terrorists, but I must also try and mend my relationship with Caroie so that most of the Crescent Alliance does not fall into depression and famine. And this is all because those sworn to protect Caroie were, not unable to help, but *unwilling* to help." Isa stopped slowly pacing in front of the holograms. "Is that correct? Am I misunderstanding anything?"

"Elite Isa, surely you understand that my planet is in no condition to render help to any planet," one man said nervously.

"Yes, including your own citizens, which is why I have deployed seventeen-thousand of my own troops to maintain what little order is left on your planet after your chancellor tore down the mockery that was your economy," Isa said. "Let me repeat that. Seventeen-thousand of *my* troops are already stationed on Imala. Even if your planet is in disrepair from your civil war, it takes thirty-seven seconds for a transmission to come from your planet to mine. If you had informed me, I would have sent what forces I could to assist Caroie."

"Seventeen thousand would not be enough to handle an invasion of that magnitude," one of the women said incredulously.

"Indeed," Isa said, turning to her. "But an army of Hyunen soldiers, such as the one-hundred ninety thousand in your possession, might have been able to assist my meager seventeen thousand and we could have provided reasonable protection for the capital."

"Where did you obtain those numbers?" the woman asked sharply.

Isa's expression turned dangerous.

"Are those numbers inaccurate?"

"Of course they are!" the woman snapped.

"Then should I expect more?" Isa asked.

"You cannot build any troops in excess of one-hundred and fifty thousand in the Alliance," one man said, turning to the woman. "You are in violation of the law."

"That is several counts against you, Miss Yuta," Isa told her. "Abandoning a special-class planet in need, treason, and violation of the Crescent Alliance Peace Act."

"Those numbers are too high!" Yuta cried, her eyes becoming angry and frantic.

"Are they?" Isa asked. "I have been monitoring the trade routes, Miss Yuta. I know what you have purchased and I know the parts that go into making troops. I did my own calculations based on how many Soldier data chips you bought, and how many parts you obtained to craft your own."

The other three holograms turned to the woman, their eyes worried.

"Care to tell me your exact numbers, Miss Yuta?"

"How dare you accuse me of violating our laws?!" the woman bellowed.

"How dare you think me foolish enough to believe your word when you abandoned Caroie and left them to the mercy of the Ninth Circle?" Isa challenged, her voice even. "Because of your inaction, the death toll is already over eighty thousand civilians, and those numbers continue to rise by the minute as more casualties are discovered."

"I am not alone on Caroie's protection front!" Yuta cried.

"You're correct," Isa said. "However, you are the only one who has met with any member of the Ninth Circle ruling class in the last year, and your troop numbers are soaring, even more so since Colonel Ikan's visit."

"I am not consorting with those barbarians in the Ninth Circle!" Yuta barked.

"We will see if that is true," Isa said. "I am ordering, under Title Four of the Crescent Alliance Peace Act, that an investigation shall take place in order to discover any evidence of treason and consorting to overthrow the Alliance."

"How dare you?!"

"You are innocent until proven guilty. However, under Title Four, trade with your planet will be halted and all transmissions will be monitored. Anything found during conduct of the investigation will be brought to the Courts and will be admitted into evidence without question."

"You cannot do this!"

"I will program your monitoring system and it will go into effect today," Isa completed. "As for the rest of you, I ask that you submit your schedules to me as well as the last three months of your trade numbers, and the number of troops you have in your possession. Should any of these orders be ignored, I have full authority from Venus to place all of your planets under investigation."

"You bitch!" Yuta snarled.

"Good day," Isa said simply, turning to her NCB chair and pressing her right ring finger to the steel ring around the top of the chair.

The holograms vanished and the ring slowly lowered to the resting position Kailynn had seen it in when she had first seen the chair.

Isa took a deep breath, closing her eyes briefly before she turned to the three others in the room.

"Forgive me," she said. "I did not mean to ignore your entrance." Isa smiled at Rayal, her face brightening a little. "Rayal."

"Isa," Rayal greeted, his smile equally warm. "Hyun is going to suffer with their trade being monitored so closely. I'm sure you'll find many things that are against the laws of the Alliance."

"I figured that she was in illegal markets," Isa said with a nod. "At least now I have a reason to bring her under investigation." Her expression dropped. "How many are dead?"

"The final count I received was ninety-thousand and eleven," Rayal said. "The capital was ransacked. Their communications are destroyed."

"I don't understand why no one responded to the distress signals," Isa murmured, shaking her head. "It is very troublesome to think that four of the planets with the largest troop numbers refused to help the planet that provides them with over forty percent of their food." The Elite rubbed her forehead, sighing. "I don't think I ever mended the Alliance as well as I believed."

"That area of the system has always been a mess," Rayal said with a shake of his head. "Pride and greed are the only things that drive those planets."

"I think that Yuta, Shane, and Urya are conspiring with the Ninth Circle," Isa said seriously. "It seems that everywhere I turn, another planet has joined the Ninth Circle to conspire against Tiao."

"Repairing relations with Caroie will be exceptionally difficult," Rayal added, shaking his head. "They will not easily forgive being abandoned and their people being slaughtered."

Isa nodded slowly, her eyes briefly falling to the ground.

"Isa," Rayal started, opening his briefcase and handing her a file, "I'm afraid there is more bad news."

"That's alright," Isa said with a thin smile. "That's all I've received today anyway."

She took the file and clicked the screen into life, looking over the information on the tablet.

"These are the transmissions that we were able to salvage from the security mainframe before the shutdown," Rayal said carefully.

Isa closed her eyes, her expression changing to something between irritation and pain.

"These are in Gihoric," she whispered. She looked at Rayal seriously, something brimming behind her eyes. "Gihron is involved?"

Kailynn noticed the way Tarah tensed, looking between Rayal and Isa.

"It would appear so."

Isa sighed heavily, handing the file back to Rayal.

"That complicates things. Over ninety thousand dead so far, easily over a dozen planetary relations in ruin, and Gihron has decided to rear their ugly head again," Isa muttered. "Have you sent this to Remus?"

"I sent it just before I came here."

"Thank you." Isa said. She rubbed her forehead again. "This is a disaster." She turned back to Rayal and forced a smile. "I assume you have met Kailynn."

"Yes," Rayal said, turning to the Significant. "I hope that you have not been overwhelmed," Rayal said, still addressing Isa.

"No, not at all," Isa assured. "I have quite enjoyed Kailynn's stay."

The smile that was directed at Kailynn sent her heart fluttering in her chest.

Rayal glanced between Kailynn and Isa, his eyes already unnerving because of the mismatched color, but even more so when Kailynn saw that there was a look of acute realization in the former caretaker's expression. He quickly looked between the two again, then turned to Isa.

"I'm happy to hear it," Rayal said. "We won't keep you. Tarah, you and I should plan when to have lunch," he said, placing a hand on Tarah's shoulder and leading her out of the room. Tarah's cheeks were immediately flushed again and she followed his guide without noticing that he was leading her out to discuss something far more important than lunch.

Kailynn's eyes turned back to Isa.

The two were silent for several long moments before Kailynn glanced back at the chair and her expression fell.

"Are…are you okay?" she asked stupidly. Isa smiled thinly, her eyes falling to the ground.

"Not really," she admitted. "This has been a very trying morning, and there is still much about this situation that I do not know."

"…who is Gihron?"

"One of the most powerful planets in the Ninth Circle," Isa said vaguely. "They have been against Tiao for hundreds of years. They do not approve of the Elites or Venus."

Kailynn remained silent, not sure what to say.

"Why was that planet attacked?" Kailynn asked finally.

Isa shook her head. "I'm afraid I don't know," she admitted. "Nor do I know why it took us so long to learn of the attack." Isa took a deep breath. "Questions I will be trying to find answers to all day. Not that it matters."

"Why doesn't it matter?" Kailynn hissed, horrified at the statement.

"Because over ninety thousand civilians have already lost their lives," Isa said quietly. "There is no answer to these questions that will explain away their deaths."

Kailynn was surprised at the Elite's statement. Isa was taking the attack on the people of Caroie as though those people were under her care. The Significant could only stare at the Elite, wondering how someone who had stated that they had no human emotions could care for people they had never met.

"I'm sorry, Isa," Kailynn whispered before she could stop the words or figure out why she had said them.

"There is no reason to be sorry," Isa assured. "I am the one who is sorry."

Isa turned back to her chair to return to work, but Kailynn's voice stopped her.

"Isa."

The Elite turned and was surprised to find Kailynn right in front of her. The Significant wrapped her arms around Isa and hugged her tightly. The Elite was still for several moments, surprised—Kailynn was also surprised at her actions.

"I can tell this attack has upset you," Kailynn murmured. "But the fact that you're angry and hurt over the deaths of the civilians proves that you're more human than those who killed them."

Isa could not move for several moments, stunned into silence as the words sunk into her brain. A small part of her that had been forgotten five years previous slowly pushed closer to the surface.

For the first time in years, Isa felt like herself.

She wrapped her arms around Kailynn, tightening the hug.

∙∙

When Isa came out of her office, she looked older and tired, her face drawn in confusion and irritation. Tarah had prepared dinner, but she had been absent-minded most of the day, which meant dinner was later than usual. Isa did not seem to notice.

The Elite pushed the food around on her plate, her eyes distant. Kailynn stopped eating when she saw the look on Isa's face. She could tell that the Elite was greatly disturbed and upset by what had happened on Caroie.

After dinner, when Isa had barely eaten, Kailynn went with the Elite to the sitting area.

"Do you want to swim for a bit?" she tried to suggest lightly, though the question was clearly forced.

"No, thank you," Isa said. The Elite sat down on the couch and rubbed her forehead, lost in deep thought. Tarah continued to clean up, throwing worried looks at Isa. Kailynn took a deep breath and sat on the arm of the sofa next to the Elite, tapping her arm gently.

"Hey."

The Elite looked up.

"What can I do to help you get your mind off this?"

Isa tried to smile, though her expression just became more tired.

"I don't think anything will help."

"The more you think about it, the more you're going to think yourself in circles," Kailynn said. "You need to step away from work for a while."

"I'm an Elite," Isa pointed out with a smile. "I don't know how."

Kailynn tried to think of something, glancing around the room. When her eyes rested on the bar, she smiled.

"Alcohol helps," she said, standing. "What do you like?" she asked, walking to the bar as the Elite chuckled.

"Anything is fine," she assured. Kailynn grabbed some glasses, trying to remember where everything was from the few times she had seen the Elite help herself to a drink late in the day. Kailynn poured two glasses and picked them up when Isa chuckled.

"You better bring the bottle."

Kailynn laughed, tucking the bottle under her arm and walking over with the two glasses.

"You speak my language."

The two downed several drinks together, Isa silent as Kailynn tried to strike up any conversation. The Elite would answer with a few sentences and then fall silent once more, letting the conversation die. Kailynn would fill the quiet with another drink, causing her head to be spinning by the time Tarah wished them both goodnight. The caretaker was clearly worried about the Elite, but she did not know how to help.

Kailynn was not sure she could help, either.

Isa was leaning against the arm of the couch, her head in one hand as the other lightly held the small, now-empty glass. The Elite's eyes were not closed, but they were half-lidded.

Kailynn took a chance and stood, walking around the coffee table and sitting next to Isa. The Elite turned to her and smiled, leaning to the coffee table and pulling the bottle closer to her, refilling her glass.

"Damn, you're a strong drinker," Kailynn muttered.

Isa smiled in response, but did not speak, bringing the glass to her lips. She took a sip, her eyes going distant again.

Kailynn knew that Isa would not be able to get her mind off the attack, so she no longer avoided the subject.

"Have you ever dealt with a situation like this before?"

Isa tuned to Kailynn, her expression genuinely confused.

"What kind of situation?"

"A planet being taken over," Kailynn clarified.

Isa sighed heavily and rubbed her forehead.

"Yes, this will be my fourth hostage planet negotiation," Isa said. "However, I have never had to negotiate for a special-class planet like Caroie." She groaned and closed her eyes. "Those morons have destroyed a large part of the Alliance."

"I didn't even know we were in an alliance…" Kailynn said slowly, nervous about her ignorance.

"That does not surprise me," Isa said. "You were born in Trid. There would be no reason for you to know." Isa closed her eyes and leaned her head back on the sofa. "The Alliance had disbanded when I came into power. Poor political decisions by my predecessors made the Crescent Alliance collapse. I spent years and years trying to fix the mess they left, but it appears that it was not as strong as I had believed."

"How long have you been in power?"

"Seventeen years," Isa murmured.

Kailynn could not help but gawk at the number.

"How old are you?!" she gasped. Isa turned to the Significant, surprised at the younger woman's shock.

"Thirty-four."

Kailynn's eyes were wide.

"You don't look thirty-four."

"I look older?" Isa chuckled lightly.

"No, you look…I mean, you look amazing…"

Kailynn quickly grabbed her drink again, gulping the strong liquor, hoping to somehow swallow the words that had just escaped her lips.

Isa smiled gently.

"Thank you."

Kailynn let out a long breath, setting her empty glass down, though moving made her feel dizzy. She knew she had had too much three drinks previous. Yet, the Elite seemed to barely be tipsy.

"I wish I knew what to say to help you feel better."

Isa's eyes went distant yet again and a small smile took over her mouth.

"You've done more for me than you realize."

Kailynn found herself staring at the Elite again. Isa's expression was complex, a mixture between pain and happiness, as though she found something that had once filled her with joy, but no longer did so—lost in memories of happier times.

Isa's eyes turned to Kailynn and everything stopped.

Kailynn found herself intrigued by the secrets behind the piercing blue eyes. Kailynn could see that there was pain hidden somewhere deep inside the Golden Elite but, for a being with no emotions, Kailynn was not sure how such pain was possible. Everything she had heard over the previous weeks had only increased her curiosity, seeing the

Elite in a manner that she was sure almost no one else had was an overwhelming realization for Kailynn.

But Isa had told her that she had been happy to have the Significant with her. The words meant something to Kailynn, but she was not sure on what level they resonated.

The words came out before she could stop them. As far as Kailynn was concerned, the alcohol spoke.

"Can I ask something? It's going to sound crazy…"

"What?"

Kailynn leaned forward.

"Can I touch your face?"

"Pardon?"

"I just…I wanna touch you…" Kailynn reached both hands out to Isa, clumsily pressing both her hands to each side of the Elite's face. Her face turned serious as the pads of her fingers moved over the smooth skin, her eyes studying every line in the Elite's face. Kailynn turned her eyes to her fingers, trying to understand the sensation of perfection. The Elite's skin was impossibly smooth.

Kailynn still could not understand how one could be so perfect.

Isa stared calmly back at Kailynn. After a few moments looking at Kailynn's flushed and awe-stricken expression, Isa lifted one hand and gently pushed some hair away from Kailynn's face.

"You're incredible," Kailynn breathed.

Isa hesitated only a moment before she forced what little reason she had left aside and leaned forward, bringing her face closer to Kailynn's. She would let Kailynn close the gap between them if she wanted. She would not force the Significant, knowing the steep punishment for anyone that became intimate with Elites.

However, Kailynn took the opening and her lips locked with Isa's.

Once their lips met, everything became electric. Kailynn's hands wrapped around Isa's head and she pulled the Elite even closer, desperate, her reason gone. Isa allowed Kailynn to control the kiss, not sure that it would last long before Kailynn remembered where she was and who she was with and stop.

Kailynn pulled away far too fast for Isa. But one of her hands swept over Isa's high cheekbones as she stared into the Elite's eyes. Isa studied Kailynn's expression.

She pushed upward slightly and reached out, setting her glass on the coffee table, her hand quickly wrapping around Kailynn's neck and bringing their lips together for another fiery kiss. Kailynn eagerly locked lips with the Golden Elite again, her hands holding Isa, pushing her down so that she was on top of the older woman, kissing her passionately. Isa did not seem to mind their shift of positions.

Kailynn was not sure how long they were kissing, but time had no meaning then. It was only her and Isa. Nothing else existed—including consequences.

Kailynn grabbed the front of Isa's shirt and pulled her upright, her lips never leaving the Elite's, sure that she would collapse and die if she had to part with Isa. Isa followed the Significant's guide and found herself standing, her arms finally free to wrap around the younger woman, allowing her to intensify the kiss.

Kailynn made a sound somewhere between a whimper and a groan when Isa pulled away and the Elite was excited by the noise. Her lips hovered over Kailynn's as she looked over the Significant's expression. Her hand left Kailynn's back and she cradled her jaw tenderly, causing Kailynn's eyes to finally flutter open.

Gently moving her thumb over Kailynn's cheek, Isa went in for another kiss.

Kailynn found her head spinning again. She was not sure if it was the alcohol or the way Isa took her breath away as they kissed.

Isa ended the kiss shortly, backing further away and looking at Kailynn seriously. She did not need to speak for the Significant to understand what she was asking. Kailynn took a deep breath and laced her fingers with Isa's, pulling the Golden Elite behind her to the door she knew led to the Golden Elite's room.

Neither of them spoke.

There were no questions of if the other wanted to do this, or that they could stop at any time, or that what they were about to do was very illegal. They both knew the other had chosen to take the risk.

When the door shut on the rest of the world, Kailynn turned to the Elite again and was immediately met with an enthusiastic kiss.

Kailynn tried to open the front of Isa's uniform—she had *thought* the front just pulled apart. Isa chuckled into their kiss, unhooking the row of hooks and eyes that closed the tunic-like front. Kailynn reached to the bottom of her shirt and pulled it over her head, tossing it to the side before quickly shimmying out of her pants.

She had to hop and find her balance as she freed herself from her pants because she was staring at Isa as the Elite undressed with the grace of a dancer.

Isa also left the uniform on the ground, stepping out of the floor-length skirt and walking to Kailynn again, grabbing her face and pulling her into an intense kiss. Kailynn's hands found Isa's shoulders and, yet again, she was surprised by how smooth the Elite's skin was. It was as if her skin was perfectly polished stone, only warm instead of cold to the touch. The combination of those sensations sent shivers down Kailynn's spine.

Isa guided Kailynn back until her legs hit the bed. She broke the kiss long enough to allow Kailynn to climb into the bed before she climbed on top of the Significant and resumed their frenzied kissing.

Kailynn felt completely overwhelmed by the Elite. Her weight, her warmth, her very being surrounded Kailynn and forced out all the wrong with the world. The warm, safe feeling she felt with the Elite dispelled all negative thoughts.

There was only Isa.

Isa's mouth left Kailynn's and immediately went to her neck. She kissed along the column of flesh, her lips soft and gentle, causing Kailynn to hiss and push her neck closer, desperate for more contact. Her bare breasts came in contact with Isa's bra and her skin sang at the friction. She let out a pleading noise, one hand tangled in Isa's hair as the other reached around to try and unhook Isa's bra.

She suddenly understood why Raphael had always complained about bras.

Frustrated and desperate, Kailynn resorted to grabbing one of the straps and forcing it off Isa's shoulder. The Golden Elite smiled against Kailynn's skin and sat upright, giving Kailynn full view of her perfect form once more. She removed the bra and pecked a quick kiss on Kailynn's lips before her mouth descended. She kissed a path down Kailynn's neck and sternum, her lips lingering at different intervals, setting Kailynn's body on fire.

Isa turned her head and took one of Kailynn's nipples into her mouth, her hand passing over the other one, palming her breast. One of the Significant's hands was employed gripping the sheets tightly while the other held Isa's head to her chest, relishing in the feeling of Isa's warm lips and tongue.

When Isa had paid attention to both nipples, she leaned forward, capturing Kailynn's mouth again, her leg sliding forward and making contact with Kailynn's panties. The younger woman gasped into the kiss and a shiver ran up her body. The keening sound made Isa's blood run hot. She suppressed a shiver of her own and moved down Kailynn's body again, kissing a path down her belly until she reached the top of Kailynn's panties.

Kailynn raised her head to look at Isa and saw that the Elite was watching her face with a look of amazement and lust. The intensity of the expression made Kailynn's head fall back to the pillow, weak. Her entire body was vibrating with a pleasure that she was sure she had never known before.

Isa pressed one kiss to the top hem of Kailynn's panties before sitting up and hooking her fingers in the fabric. Her eyes held Kailynn's as she slowly, agonizingly, moved the fabric down Kailynn's legs, her fingers tantalizing skin as they moved.

Kailynn pulled her legs up to allow the Elite to remove her panties. Isa tossed them aside before taking Kailynn's legs and spreading them slowly. She lowered herself back to the bed, pressing a kiss to Kailynn's navel before turning her head and kissing the inside of both of Kailynn's thighs.

"Isa..." Kailynn gasped.

The Elite moved her head to the apex of Kailynn's legs. Her tongue darted out to gently lick Kailynn's moist womanhood. Kailynn's reaction was almost violent. Her body shuddered and her hands gripped Isa's hair tightly. She let out a choked sound as her back arched. Isa, unbelievably turned on by the reaction, wrapped one arm around Kailynn's leg and pushed her pelvis down to the bed, her mouth returning to Kailynn.

Her tongue and lips worked over Kailynn's clit with delicate, loving care. The tip of her tongue gently opened the soft lips as her hands held Kailynn steady, allowing the Elite to work the sensitive flesh.

Kailynn was sure she had never felt so desperate in her life. She was torn between wanting the torture to end and wanting it to continue into eternity. Her legs quivered in Isa's hold, her hips moving in minimal circles, still held down by the Elite. Isa's lips gently closed around Kailynn's clit and she pulled at it gently.

The cry that tore out of Kailynn's throat startled even her. She panted, her eyes closed, a sheen of sweat beginning to break out over her body as Isa continued the blissful torment.

Isa slowly released her hold on Kailynn's pelvis and brought her fingers to Kailynn's wet entrance. She gently caressed the lips, rubbing her thumb over the clit as she looked up at Kailynn's expression. The Significant was panting, her chest rapidly rising and falling, her entire body trembling with need. Isa thought she was absolutely beautiful.

She delicately pushed her middle finger into Kailynn, reveling at the feeling of the younger woman's muscles clenching down on the digit. Kailynn let out a cry of pleasure, her back bowing off the bed once more.

Isa crooked her finger inside Kailynn, pressing forward and caressing the inner walls as her mouth went back to Kailynn's clit, gently licking and kissing, adding to the intensity of the pleasure.

When Isa added a second finger, Kailynn's hips rolled down, bringing Isa deeper inside. She moaned, one hand moving from the sheets to rest over her chest, gently pinching and pulling at one of her nipples. Her hips continued to grind on Isa's hand as the Elite's mouth worked her clit.

As Isa's fingers crooked and flexed, adding pressure to the front wall, Kailynn's cries changed, becoming more desperate and choked. She began babbling, moaning Isa's name over and over again. She could feel the pleasure building to an unbearable point, but she was sure it had never been so intense before. Her entire body was singing with bliss.

With a cry, her hips snapped and began writhing on Isa's fingers. Her orgasm consumed everything of her being. Every pore of her body was bursting with sheer pleasure. She had never experienced something so intense. Her breaths continued in pants, broken and exhausted as the final waves of her orgasm slowed and settled once more.

Isa's fingers slowly left Kailynn and she crawled back up to capture Kailynn's lips in a kiss.

The Elite's slow, gentle kisses brought Kailynn back to the moment.

Before the Elite could register what had happened, Kailynn flipped them, settling on top of Isa as the Elite stared at her in shock. It was the first time Kailynn had been able to notice the need in Isa's countenance. Her cheeks were flushed, her eyes bright with desire and lust. Her body was barely shaking, trying to stay restrained and in control of her pleasure.

Kailynn's hands went all over Isa's body, massaging the full breasts and following the slope of her waist. She stripped off Isa's panties and her fingers went to the warm, soft flesh she found there.

Isa's eyes closed and a shuddered breath left her lips. Kailynn thought it was the sexiest sound she had ever heard.

With the heel of her hand rubbing across Isa's clit, she slid one finger inside, amazed and flattered at the wetness she found. Isa took in a small gasp of air before her head turned, her eyes tightly closed. Her breathing was causing her breasts to catch Kailynn's attention. She gently kissed the side of one of Isa's breasts and then placed her mouth around the nipple, her tongue pressing down on the nub, moving it inside her mouth.

Isa moaned quietly when Kailynn added another finger and used the same technique Isa had used, crooking her fingers forward and pumping them in and out. Isa bit her lip, her eyes fluttering open to meet Kailynn's.

They quickly snapped shut and Isa's back arched, her release much quieter than Kailynn's. The Significant held Isa, letting the final tremors of her orgasm ebb away before she removed her fingers.

Their eyes met in exhausted rapture.

There was no turning back.

Chapter Thirteen

Even through the fog of her hangover, Kailynn knew she was in danger.

Kailynn slid out of the bed, not putting any thought to where Isa was as she stepped into the Golden Elite's bathroom. Her head was foggy and there was a crippling sense of fear as she recounted everything that had happened the previous night. She walked to the shower and stepped in, pressing whatever buttons she could to get the water running. When the hot water began beating over her head, she lowered herself to the floor of the shower and cradled her aching head in her hands.

Kailynn was not completely inexperienced with women. She had been very drunk one night a year previous and had had a threesome with Raphael and Viv. Raphael had been too drunk to participate as enthusiastically as he would have liked, leaving Kailynn and Viv to play with one another while Raphael watched. That night had felt forbidden in a different sort of light. It had been her first threesome and, at the time, she and Raphael had been in a fairly-monogamous relationship.

But her night with Isa had been an entirely different level of forbidden. She had just put her life on the line. If anyone knew what she and Isa had done, she would be killed swiftly and silently.

Isa held Kailynn's life in her hands. Isa had only to say that Kailynn had forced her into sex and that would be the end of it. In a similar way, Isa could hold that threat over Kailynn's head to get her to do whatever she wanted.

Kailynn had made herself into Isa's slave in one night of drunken abandon.

But she knew *she* had made that decision. Isa did not force her. She was the one who led them both into the bedroom.

Kailynn was becoming more terrified the more she thought about the situation. She tried to relax, closing her eyes and chanting to herself that she needed to calm down and breathe. She took several deep breaths, her heart continuing to race.

The door to the shower opened and Kailynn turned quickly, terrified. Isa stepped into the shower, moving slowly, watching Kailynn.

She knelt next to Kailynn and reached one hand out to her. At first, Kailynn flinched, staring at Isa with wide eyes, fear coursing through her veins. Isa hesitated, but then reached forward further, wrapping her fingers around Kailynn's shoulder and bringing her into a gentle embrace. Kailynn was frozen for several long moments before she relaxed into the hold and closed her eyes.

Isa kissed the top of her head.

The two remained silent, sitting in the shower for an indeterminable amount of time.

Once Kailynn had relaxed completely, Isa turned her head, pressing her lips to Kailynn's temple.

"I want you to know that you're safe," she whispered. Kailynn opened her eyes and backed away from Isa, staring at her worriedly. Sincerity was clear in Isa's bright blue eyes. "What happened last night will go no further than the two of us," Isa said. "I will not report you, nor will I threaten to report you."

Kailynn could only stare at Isa in shock and surprise at the way the Elite seemed to read her mind. She stared at the Golden Elite for what felt like an eternity before she spoke.

"You…you won't…say anything?"

"No."

"But…"

"What?"

"It's just…you know, most of the time, in situations like this, someone says it was just a mistake and we should forget about it…" Kailynn said, turning away. Isa was silent for two long moments.

"Do you want to forget?"

Kailynn turned her eyes back on Isa, surprised by the tone of the Elite's voice.

"I don't think it was a mistake," Isa continued. "And I don't want to forget what happened. But, if that's what you want, I will."

"…n-no, it's not…" Kailynn lifted her hand to her head and cringed. "It's just…it's a lot to think about, I guess…"

"I'm sure you're terrified about this being reported," Isa said. "But I give you my word that I would never do that."

"I believe you."

"Then maybe you don't want to forget about last night."

Kailynn stared at Isa and then pursed her lips, shaking her head.

"No, I don't…"

Isa took a deep breath.

"If you want to leave early, I understand," the Elite said slowly. "Things have become more complicated, and I understand if you feel uncomfortable staying. I will, of course, pay for the entire month, as agreed. And I will pay—"

"No," Kailynn interrupted, surprised how fast the word came out of her mouth. Isa blinked. "I-I mean..." Kailynn turned away. "I'll stay the whole month."

"Don't feel obligated."

"I don't."

Isa looked over Kailynn's confused and worried expression. She hesitated before ignoring her more sensible self once again. She leaned forward and gently cupped Kailynn's cheek, turning her face. She leaned closer, pressing a kiss to Kailynn's lips. The younger woman relaxed, even though there was a part of her brain that reminded her that her situation was becoming more dangerous by the moment.

Isa pulled away from the kiss, but Kailynn grabbed her wrist, leaning forward to follow the Elite, intensifying the kiss.

Isa allowed Kailynn to control what she was willing to do.

The Elite found herself pressed against the wall of the shower, Kailynn kissing her enthusiastically. She tried to decipher the feelings of the kiss, worried that Kailynn was even more terrified of being reported and was just trying to appease the Golden Elite. However, it had been so long since Isa had felt such warmth from another person that she also found herself unable to think.

Kailynn finally parted their lips, her breath fanning over Isa's mouth.

"I'm sorry..." she whispered. "I'm just really confused."

"We don't have to discuss it now," Isa assured, taking Kailynn's face again and locking their lips together.

■■■

Kailynn was feeling a little easier at Isa's promises as she walked out of the master bedroom. However, her fear spiked to an unhealthy level when she saw both Rayal and Tarah standing by the bar, their heated conversation immediately halted.

When Rayal's eyes passed between Isa and Kailynn, sharp with understanding, Kailynn was sure her legs would give out from under her. She tried to appear strong, but she was sure fear was evident on her face.

"That didn't take long..." Isa muttered under her breath.

"Isa," Rayal greeted, his tone even.

"Will you be joining us for breakfast?" Isa asked, walking to the bar to get a glass of water. Kailynn found herself almost *angry* at the Elite for being so calm when they had been caught.

"Perhaps," Rayal said.

"Is there a problem? Any more news on Caroie?"

"Yes," Rayal said, turning to face the Elite fully. "That was the original reason I came over."

"And the reason now?" Isa asked, peering at Rayal as she put ice in her glass.

"Perhaps it is a conversation we should have in private."

Isa glanced at the other two in the room and then turned back to Rayal.

"Is there anyone here *not* involved?"

"No," Rayal admitted. "However, there are some not here who *are* involved."

Isa and Rayal shared a silent conversation before Isa sighed and nodded, picking up her glass.

"We'll go to the balcony."

Isa passed Kailynn, who was sure her heart was about to leap out of her throat. The Elite stopped and turned back to the Significant, wrapping her hand around Kailynn's head. She kissed the younger woman's forehead and nodded to her once with a reassuring smile.

When the Elite and her former caretaker were on the balcony, Kailynn turned to Tarah. She wanted to be angry at the caretaker for obviously telling Rayal about what had happened the previous night. However, she was too terrified, and too curious about how Tarah knew.

Tarah shook her head, her face pale and filled with fear.

"I'm sorry, Kailynn."

"Why did you tell him? How did you even know?"

"I'm sorry, I had to tell him. I didn't know what to do," Tarah said, her voice breaking.

Kailynn walked to the young caretaker and sighed heavily.

"How did you find out?" Kailynn murmured. "You went to bed."

"I came back out to ask Isa something and saw you two..." Tarah whispered. "I meant to keep it a secret, I really did. But when Rayal showed up…it just all spilled out. I was terrified. This is all very illegal as it is, and then you two…"

"I know it's illegal," Kailynn said darkly. "I'm freaking out, too. But you just made it worse for me and Isa because you *told* Rayal."

"Rayal had to know."

"I know you like that guy, but that doesn't mean you have to tell him all the secrets that will get me and Isa into trouble. You know I could be killed for this, right?"

"I know, I know, I'm sorry…" Tarah's eyes were brimming with tears. "But so could Isa. I mean, Venus already forgave her relationship once, but a second time—"

"*Once?*" Kailynn snapped, her eyes going wide. "What the hell are you talking about? Isa's been with someone before?"

On the balcony, Rayal sighed as he walked to the railing with Isa.

"I leave you alone for one day and you get into trouble," he tried to tease. A small smile took Isa's lips, but she was also nervous about the conversation with Rayal.

"What can I say?" Isa tried to play along.

Rayal leaned on the railing next to Isa, looking out over the city.

"I should have said something to you yesterday."

"Why?"

"Because I saw this coming," Rayal murmured, shaking his head, his eyes dropping to his feet. "I saw the way she was looking at you."

"Kailynn isn't responsible for last night."

"No, you both are," Rayal agreed with a nod. "But I still should have said something."

"I don't think I would have listened…"

Rayal studied Isa's expression, trying to discern what the Golden Elite was thinking. After several long moments, Rayal closed his eyes, his expression pained.

"Then you're doing even worse than everyone believes," he murmured.

Isa closed her eyes as well, shaking her head.

"I wish everyone would stop obsessing over my health," she said coldly. "I am capable of taking care of myself. I know the last few years have not been easy on anyone, but I assure you, I am doing far better than before."

"Yet you were upset enough yesterday to risk your life again, *and* Kailynn's life," Rayal said. "I know that this is because of Gihron's involvement in—"

"Rayal," Isa interrupted, turning to her former caretaker, "we both know the reason for my actions. Yes, I was upset yesterday. Being with Kailynn felt natural and it helped me. I know the risks, I've dealt with them before."

"And it led to disaster before," Rayal said coldly.

"Don't say that."

"It *did*," Rayal insisted. "You pushed your luck with Venus' mercy then. She will not be as lenient now. When she finds out, she'll immediately kill Kailynn and likely have you removed from power." Rayal's voice went quiet. "Which means you'll be executed, as well."

Isa lowered her eyes to the railing under her hands.

"You said when, not if."

"You know she'll find out eventually," Rayal said. He heaved a sigh and shook his head. "I will do my best to keep the information from reaching her mainframe, should any evidence of this get out." Rayal hesitated for a brief moment. "However, Venus is not the only one that concerns me."

Isa dropped her gaze further.

"Remus will find out, and probably very soon," Rayal said. He turned to Isa. "What will you say to him?"

Isa took a deep breath, thinking.

"I don't know."

"You should send Kailynn home," Rayal said seriously. "This is far too dangerous." His eyes turned pleading. "I know you, Isa. The longer she's around, the more you'll start to care for her, and it's going to hurt more to let her go. But, for your safety, and for hers, you must send her home."

"I gave her the option this morning," Isa said. "She refused."

Rayal closed his eyes, trying to hide the immediate bolt of fear that went through him at the statement.

"What do you want me to do?"

"Nothing," Isa said, shaking her head. "This is something I must do myself."

Rayal's heart dropped.

"Okay," he murmured.

Rayal returned inside, leaving Isa on the balcony. The Golden Elite closed her eyes and let out a heavy sigh, deciding to stay outside to collect her thoughts.

When Rayal approached Kailynn and Tarah, Kailynn stopped trying to get the caretaker to talk about Isa's previous relationship. Rayal nodded once to Kailynn.

"You and I should talk."

Kailynn, who had worked herself up into a frenzy, tried to calm down. She glanced at Tarah once before following the former caretaker into the guest hallway. When the door closed behind both of them, Rayal turned to her, his expression conflicted.

"Isa said that you wanted to stay here for the rest of the agreed time."

"Yes."

"And do you plan to have sex with her again?" Rayal asked bluntly.

Kailynn faltered for a moment.

"I don't see how that's any of your business."

Rayal took a deep breath, lowering his head.

"You know Isa far too little to understand the severity of the situation," Rayal murmured. "Isa is the Golden Elite."

"I know that," Kailynn bit.

"Yes, but you do not know who Isa is when she is *not* Golden Elite," Rayal told her sharply. "It took five years to get Isa back to this point. She was very sick for a very long time, and we were sure we were going to lose her. Now that she's healthier again, I have been doing my best to make sure she *stays* healthy, both mentally and physically."

"If you're worried, I *am* clean," Kailynn snarled.

"I'm not worried about that," Rayal assured. "Her physical health is easier to care for than her mental health. As an Elite, she processes things differently, and this could end up being a very dangerous situation for the both of you because of that."

"What does that even mean? It's already dangerous."

"It's worse than you think," Rayal said. "I'll tell you the truth. We have had past relations with Gihron that went horribly wrong. They have no qualms about taking the loved one of a leader to bully them into unfair negotiations. If Gihron really is behind this attack on Caroie, then you are a danger to Isa."

Kailynn blinked at the former caretaker, not expecting the explanation.

"Isa is the best Elite this planet has had in hundreds of years. She is actually turning things around in the Altereye System. I cannot allow you to bring her to her knees."

"How dare you say something like that?" Kailynn growled. "Yeah, okay, I don't know her as well as you do, and I don't have any clue what she does for this planet or the system, but to think that I could, let alone *would*, find a way to manipulate Isa—"

"You already have," Rayal snapped. He rubbed his forehead, exasperated. "She's already willing to risk her life, and yours, for this fling."

Kailynn ground her teeth together. "Shut up," she snarled. "Yes, she's risking her life, but I am risking mine. I take responsibility for my part last night. I came onto her. She gave me every opportunity to stop, but I didn't. So, if anyone is responsible for last night, it's *me*."

"And now you understand why you are in a position to manipulate Isa," Rayal said darkly. "She should have been the one to stop you. Instead, she put everything in your hands. She gave control of her life to you."

"I have known her for three weeks. Like hell she's handed her life over to me. It's not like Venus already knows."

"Venus is not the only one you have to worry about," Rayal warned. "I am very protective of Isa, but I am not as protective as Remus. If he discovers what happened, there's no telling what he will do."

"He's the one paying for me to be here," Kailynn growled. "What did he *think* would happen? Clearly you guys haven't been paying close enough attention to her, because she is obviously in pain and she *needs* someone to talk to."

"Don't you *dare* accuse me of not watching out for her," Rayal snarled, leaning forward. "You only know a fraction of the situation. You haven't the slightest fucking clue about how to help her."

"And you do?" Kailynn retorted. "I'm here for her now. I was there for her last night when she was drinking herself into a coma." Kailynn glared at Rayal. "You're right. I don't know everything, clearly, but that's probably why she wants to be with me. You guys are treating her like she's fragile and thinking that every little thing is going to make her pain worse, but do you really think she would do anything like that? She's not that stupid."

Rayal hesitated, staring at the Significant, the words slowly processing in his brain.

"I mean, *fuck*, why are you jumping down her throat about this? She knows how much shit we're in. She doesn't need you to tell her. And yeah, she's in pain. But it seems to me like she's trying to hide it because she doesn't want you worrying over her because that makes her feel worse."

Rayal could do nothing but blink at Kailynn in surprise.

He studied the look in Kailynn's eyes. He had been worried when he heard of the plan to have Isa spend time with a Significant. However, staring at Kailynn, and recalling the way Isa had kissed the younger woman's forehead earlier, had Rayal nervous for a different kind of reason.

Rayal lowered his eyes.

"This is even worse than I thought…"

"How?"

"Because I can see why Isa turned to you," he murmured. "You're right. She wouldn't come to me or Remus. We've spent five years treating her like she's made of glass. I know she's still not healed. And she knows that too, but she would never admit it." The former caretaker looked at Kailynn. "But you don't even need her to tell you that she's in pain. You know it. And you seem to know how to help it."

It was Kailynn's turn to blink in surprise.

"There is nothing I can do to change Isa's mind on the situation. If she wants you to stay, nothing I say or do will change that," he continued. "It would be better for you to leave. She has given you control of the entire situation. You should take it and change things before it gets worse. If you don't, I understand. You're being paid a lot. But Kailynn," Rayal's eyes hardened, "if you do anything to hurt Isa, I will kill you."

Kailynn retreated a step.

"I won't," she said quickly.

The two returned to the living room. Tarah was anxiously waiting for someone to walk back in. Isa was still outside, looking over the city. Rayal smiled thinly at Tarah and nodded once.

"I'm going to take over your kitchen," he said. "I need to distract myself."

Tarah nodded quickly, her eyes dropping to the ground after her gaze met Kailynn's.

Kailynn stood awkwardly where she was, throwing a glance out to the balcony, wondering if she should talk to Isa.

"Kailynn," Tarah said suddenly, causing the Significant to turn back to her. "I'm really sorry."

"I know," Kailynn said, sighing. "I get it. You didn't know what to do."

"I really didn't," Tarah admitted. "I just…I'm scared. I had to tell someone."

"It's alright, Tarah," Kailynn assured, trying to force a smile, though she was not sure it was convincing. She was not angry with the young caretaker. She understood why Tarah had told Rayal. But so much had changed in her life in the previous day that she was disoriented.

Kailynn was about to press Tarah more about Isa's previous relationship, but the balcony doors opened and Isa walked back into the room. The caretaker immediately turned to her and bowed her head.

"Miss, I apologize. I am so sorry."

"There is no need for apologies, Tarah," Isa assured, walking to the bar and placing her empty water glass in the sink. "I understand that what happened last night was a great deal to process."

"I still wish to apologize," Tarah insisted.

"I accept your apology," Isa said. "I apologize as well, for putting you in this difficult position." She glanced around the living room. "Where is Rayal?"

"In the kitchen, Miss," Tarah answered. She bowed her head and turned, knowing that Isa was discreetly asking her to leave the room. She ducked into the kitchen obediently.

Isa's eyes turned to Kailynn, who found herself lost in the blue color more so than she had been before. The color seemed even more stunning that morning.

"Are you alright?" Isa murmured, a comforting smile touching her lips.

"Yeah," Kailynn said too quickly. Isa's smile widened and Kailynn chuckled nervously. "I mean…a lot has happened really suddenly."

"It has."

Kailynn looked at her feet, trying to think of something to say.

"Isa...I—"

The gentle tone of Isa's phone cut Kailynn off. Isa reached into her pocket and pulled out her phone, using the earpiece.

"Remus," she answered. Kailynn's stomach dropped in fear, even though she knew there was no way the Silver Elite could know what had happened the previous night. "Yes, I know, my apologies. Rayal came to see me and I got caught up." Kailynn stood awkwardly, waiting for the conversation to be over. "Thank you," Isa continued. "No, no, I'll do it now. It's alright." Isa nodded. "Very well. Thank you, Remus."

She hung up the phone and removed the earpiece.

Isa glanced at Kailynn.

"I must work," she said quietly.

"Okay."

Isa started toward the guest hall door to go to her office. Even knowing where the Elite was going, Kailynn's heart began racing as Isa drew closer. The Elite passed her and walked to the door that opened automatically. However, she stopped.

"Kailynn."

The Significant turned around quickly.

"No matter what Rayal said, and no matter what I say, the choice is yours."

Kailynn blinked stupidly at the Elite for a moment.

"But doesn't what he say have a lot to do with my decision?" Kailynn pressed.

"If it makes sense to you," she agreed. "But, in the end, no one can make the decision for you. You choose what you want to do and what is right for you."

Isa turned to go through the door when Kailynn stopped her.

"Isa," she started nervously, "when do I have to make the decision by?"

Isa smiled. "There is no timeline," she said. "You make the decision whenever you are ready."

■■■

Kailynn had spent much of the day in silence, wandering around the level of Anon Tower, trying to sort her thoughts. Words and emotions were ricocheting in her head, confusing her. She wanted to go and sit with Isa and discuss everything, but the thought of being in such close proximity to the Golden Elite again made her mind go blank. She was sure she would be unable to communicate anything she wanted to the Golden Elite.

She wanted to stay. She was unsure *why* she wanted to stay. She was trying to convince herself that it was for the money, but she knew that, if that was truly the case, she would have taken Isa's offer to pay her in full even if she left early. There was some other reason that she wanted to stay. Some deep, dark part of her knew that she *needed* to stay, because the thought of leaving Isa without knowing more about her was too painful.

But that was not something she was willing to acknowledge.

She began to remember that she would be returning to real life in just over a week. She would be back to working as a Significant to raise more money for her brother's release.

Kailynn was a Trid. She was a non-citizen with fake papers working to release the man who had tried to shut down Venus and kill the Elites several times in his life. And she was earning most of the money spending time with the Golden Elite herself.

Rayal's words began to haunt her in that moment.

She knew that, from a Trid perspective, she could be a hero. She had the Golden Elite in an extremely delicate situation. She had only to expose the Elite and that could bring down Isa's entire regime. Venus would be compromised with her Golden Elite having to be replaced so suddenly, and it could cause enough upheaval in the people to overthrow the super-computer.

However, Kailynn knew that it was far more complicated than that.

She had always been taught, as a Trid, that the Elites were the enemy. She never really understood *why* the Elites were the enemy. All she knew was that she had to struggle to eat and stay warm and the Elites never had to struggle. She had been told that she struggled because the Elites made it so. That was enough to fuel her hatred toward the Elite Syndicate.

But the previous night had changed that perspective entirely. She had seen how upset Isa was at the attack on Caroie. Isa had been trying to repair the damage that the previous Golden Elites had dealt. Rayal explained that Isa was the best Elite the planet had had in a very long time. Somehow, even without knowing what Isa had done and how the planet had been before Isa took over the Syndicate, Kailynn understood that Isa was very special, even among the Elites.

The sudden change in beliefs, and remembering how she had felt before about Elites, was causing her head to spin.

She did not know what she was supposed to do.

But Isa had given her the decision. She was letting Kailynn choose how she wanted to proceed.

Kailynn was unsure if she was smart enough to make that decision.

Over dinner, both Isa and Kailynn hardly ate, lost in different thoughts. Kailynn was trying to determine her next step while Isa was trying to understand her current situation with the other planets after more information about the attack on Caroie had been uncovered.

Tarah cleaned up the plates, feeling helpless, watching both of them struggle silently.

Isa stood.

"I'm going to bed," she murmured.

"Oh…okay…" Kailynn said, startled out of her thoughts.

Isa walked over to her and placed a hand on hers, squeezing it gently with a knowing smile before walking to her room. Kailynn watched her disappear and the door close behind her.

For over an hour, Kailynn sat at the table, staring at her hands, trying to figure out the tangled mess of her thoughts. Tarah went to bed, worried. There was a part of her that hoped Kailynn would decide to go home so that there was no more danger to either of them. However, there was another part of her that wanted the Significant to stay because of how much happier Isa seemed to be with Kailynn around.

Finally, Kailynn stood, feeling her heart race with every step she took toward the door. When the door opened, Isa sat up, clearly surprised that Kailynn had come into her room. The younger woman walked over to the bed and stood next to it for three long seconds before Isa lifted the covers, inviting her in.

Kailynn shimmied out of her pants and shirt and climbed into bed with the Elite, her arms wrapping around Isa. She closed her eyes and tightened the hug, pressing her face into Isa's neck. The Golden Elite held her, her hand gently stroking Kailynn's hair until they both fell asleep.

Chapter Fourteen

"Isa, there are a few things I wanted to ask you."

"Okay," the Elite said, dressing in her Syndicate uniform. It had been three days since the fated night that had changed their lives, and Kailynn finally felt like she could gather her thoughts enough to ask some of her burning questions.

"Rayal said that you were sick for a long time. That they thought you would die."

Isa turned to Kailynn, surprised that Rayal had revealed that information. Kailynn turned away, hugging her knees as she sat in the bed, still covered in the sheets.

"Is that true? You were that sick?"

Isa hesitated before turning back to the mirror, straightening the collar of her uniform.

"I was very ill, yes," she admitted. "To be honest, I do not remember much of my time in the hospital, but I was there for eight months."

"*Eight months?*" Kailynn gawked.

"The doctors said that I was on the verge of death, but I do not recall anything of my treatment."

"What put you in the hospital?"

"It was a combination of things," Isa admitted, brushing through her hair. "My health was in decline for over a year before I was in the hospital. And then I fainted and fell down the stairs and through some glass at the Syndicate Building."

Kailynn's jaw fell open at the story. She could not respond as Isa turned around.

"But that was almost five years ago," she concluded. "It's ancient history now."

"Are you...I mean, clearly...you're better?"

Isa chuckled lightly.

"I am fine," she assured. "Every now and then, particularly in stressful times, some of the pains return, but they are not serious." Isa walked over to the bed and sat on the frame, smiling gently at Kailynn. "I am a little surprised that Rayal told you that."

"I've actually been hearing a lot of things about you that have me curious..."

"Oh?"

"Like that you've been in a relationship before."

Isa's eyes were unreadable. She stared at Kailynn for a few moments before heaving a sigh and nodding.

"I was."

"How did you even manage that? Was it a short-term thing?"

"No, it was not short-term," Isa admitted. "And I was very careful about it."

"But Venus still found out," Kailynn said knowingly.

"She did."

"But she didn't kill you," Kailynn continued. "Did she kill the person you were with?"

"No."

"She doesn't enforce her own rules?" Kailynn asked skeptically.

"At the time she found out, there was a crisis within the Alliance. The relationship was very secret and she found out while it was a still a secret. Because it was not public, and she still needed me to help with the crisis throughout the system, she did not kill me. She ordered the relationship terminated, and that was all."

Kailynn looked down at the sheets, thinking.

"But, there won't be that kind of reaction if she finds out about us, will there?"

Isa took Kailynn's hand and squeezed it.

"I don't know," she admitted. "But I do not plan to have her find out."

She leaned forward and kissed Kailynn's forehead.

"I must work."

"Okay."

Isa left the room while Kailynn flopped back on the bed and stared at the ceiling. Even though she and Isa had been sleeping together the previous nights and continuing sexual relations, there were several moments where the reality of the situation hit her hard enough to knock the breath out of her. Hearing that Isa had been in a relationship before eased her mind because it meant that Isa did know how to keep their relations secret. However, knowing that Venus had still discovered Isa's prior relationship caused Kailynn to be overcome with anxiety.

Tarah had been her biggest support. When the younger caretaker realized that the Significant would be staying, she seemed relieved and overjoyed. She would talk to Kailynn constantly, trying to get her to stop thinking about the dangerous situation. She knew she only had to distract Kailynn while Isa was working, because the Elite always seemed to calm the anxious Significant when she appeared.

Tarah was very careful not to reveal much more about Isa's past, but she did tell everything she had heard from the other houses about the interesting, and sometimes illegal, things those in the upper class did, which helped ease Kailynn a little bit, but it would also increase her anxiety in other ways.

Rayal stopped by later in the afternoon to discuss information with Isa that their intelligence agents had found. He also stayed for dinner, helping Tarah cook. Kailynn had far too much time to worry as they were cooking, though she was sometimes distracted watching Tarah glance at Rayal with bright stars in her eyes. Kailynn wondered if Rayal noticed Tarah's crush.

During dinner, Kailynn immediately felt more at ease. Whenever she saw Isa, she calmed, feeling safe.

She sat next to Isa at dinner, no longer across from her.

Rayal spent his time watching them at dinner, noting every secret glance and every small smile.

He saw that, somehow, in the three days he had left them, they had become even closer. He could tell from the way Kailynn was acting that she did not entirely understand Isa, or know her secrets. Instead, it was as if the Significant was instinctively gravitating to the Elite, and the Golden Elite was also pulled to the younger woman.

The realization scared Rayal.

Things were getting more dangerous the longer the two women were together.

■■■

Two days after Rayal's visit, a second unexpected visitor appeared.

Kailynn was helping Tarah clean the living room, listening to the caretaker relay a story Rayal had told her. The younger woman had been unable to stop talking about Rayal and Kailynn was starting to get annoyed with the crush. She did not say anything, hoping that thinking about Tarah and Rayal and listening to Tarah's stories would take her mind off her own inner turmoil, but it was still starting to grate her nerves.

The front door opening stopped Tarah's story short as they both turned.

Kailynn did not see the way Tarah's face dropped, but she could feel the shift in the tension of the room when he walked in. The man who entered had dark blonde hair and piercing green eyes. He was tall and broad, built with impressive muscles and an extremely handsome face. From his appearance alone, Kailynn knew he was an Elite. He was dressed in the same Syndicate uniform that Isa wore, but somehow, it made his already-perfect physique seem impossibly perfect.

"Elite Remus," Tarah murmured, quickly running forward to greet the Silver Elite. Kailynn's heart stopped and fell into her stomach. His eyes found her immediately and held her gaze for what felt like days. Kailynn was sure her legs were trembling, because it was difficult to stay standing. His green eyes were sharp and clear, veiled and powerful in their knowledge. "Is there anything I can get for you, sir?"

"No, Tarah," Remus said simply, glancing at the caretaker before his eyes settled on Kailynn again. "Please retrieve Isa for me."

"Yes, sir."

Tarah threw an apologetic look back at Kailynn for leaving her alone with the Silver Elite and then disappeared to find Isa.

Two seconds passed before Kailynn moved. She shifted her legs, trying to brace herself on one to keep from shaking. She crossed her arms over her chest and looked over the Silver Elite, as if Elites were something she came in contact with every day.

"Are you the Significant?" Remus asked.

"I would think that would be obvious," Kailynn said, her voice shaking only a little.

The corners of the Silver Elite's mouth quirked slightly upward.

"I'm glad my instructions were followed to send someone with a little bite."

Kailynn did not respond and forced herself to remain still as Remus approached her.

"Let me ask you something," Remus started, his voice cold. "Were you instructed on what to do while you were here?"

Kailynn said nothing, not sure what the Silver Elite meant.

"You were supposed to sit with her and talk with her, and that was all," Remus explained.

Kailynn's expression faltered, her eyes going wide.

He knew.

The warning from Rayal rattled her skull again.

"I'm guessing from your reaction that you did not follow those instructions," Remus said, his voice growing dark.

Kailynn was already intimidated by how tall Isa was, but Remus towered over her and was broad, which made his looming gaze even more frightening as it was cast down on the Significant.

"I was hoping the information was false," Remus continued.

"How did you find out?" Kailynn asked, putting on her strongest face. "What happens in Isa's private life is none of your business."

Remus' eyes darkened.

"*Everything* to do with Isa is my business," he growled. "And this is something that cannot be ignored."

"Because it's *illegal*?" Kailynn challenged. "We've both heard that argument enough." The Significant sighed, trying to sound indignant as she shifted her weight to brace herself on the other foot, her legs still shaking. "Look, you wanted me to be here to talk to her and comfort her, but when all this shit happened with Caroie, she needed more than someone to talk to."

Remus hesitated, the muscles in his jaw clenching for a brief moment.

"What happened on Caroie shook her up, that is without question," he started, his tone measured. "However, even if she was upset, or drunk, or whatever it was, *you* as a Significant should have known the rules of interactions with Elites and stopped her from making this monumental mistake."

The words cut Kailynn deeper than she anticipated.

"*Mistake*?" she growled. "For your information, *I* was the one who came onto *her*. She did not start anything, I did."

"What you did was illegal," Remus hissed.

"What you did was illegal, too," Kailynn snarled. "But you would know that, already. You're the one paying for me to be here."

"That's right. I am the one paying," Remus repeated darkly, glaring at Kailynn. "But I never paid for you to touch her. Do you have any idea the implications of what you're doing?"

"She needed me," Kailynn said. "That's why you hired me, right? Because she *needed* someone?"

Remus was about to speak when the door opened to the living room and Isa walked out of the guest hall, Tarah behind her.

"Remus," she greeted. "You should have told me you were coming over." She approached the two, looking between them. It was clear she already knew the situation. "Is there a problem?"

Remus turned to Isa fully.

"I was hoping that it wasn't true."

"Rayal told you," Isa said knowingly.

"He's terrified for you," Remus hissed. "When he comes to *me*, I know there is a problem."

"Kailynn is not a problem," Isa said, her tone turning cold.

"You are having sexual relations with a Significant," Remus near-growled. "You have put her life, and your own, at risk."

"I am no stranger to risking my life," Isa said, standing next to Kailynn. "And I will protect Kailynn," her eyes hardened, "even if I have to protect her against you."

Remus shook his head.

"You misunderstand," he assured. "You know I would never report you. However, this is still a problem. Kailynn needs to leave."

"I don't believe that is your decision to make," Isa responded.

"*I'm* the one paying for her to be here," Remus said. "She violated the law. I should have her arrested for even touching you."

Isa's eyes hardened.

"Would her cell be next to yours?"

Remus blinked at the Golden Elite, surprised. Kailynn's eyes shot wide as she connected the pieces, looking between the Elites.

Isa looked at Kailynn. "I was the one who asked Kailynn to be with me. If anyone violated the law, it was me."

"Isa, this is *not* the time to be defiant," Remus growled. "We have half the system breathing down our necks and trying to find a way to tear you down. The Ninth Circle is threatening to destroy the Crescent Alliance. Are you willing to risk that because of this sort of distraction?" Remus motioned to Kailynn. "I think it would be best if she left. She's only here because I'm paying her. If I stop, she has no reason to stay." He turned to Kailynn. "That *is* the reason you're here, right? The money?"

Kailynn hesitated, caught off-guard by the question. She looked at Isa, not sure what to say. The Golden Elite looked at her briefly and then nodded once.

"Fine, I will pay for her," Isa said. She glared at Remus. "You are not the only one with money in this room, Remus. How dare you put her in that position?"

"She's *using* this for money!" Remus snapped. "You're a fucking Elite, no one should *use* you!"

"I'm a fucking Elite," Isa repeated coldly. "I was made to be used." She nodded to the door. "Good day, Remus. We will discuss this at a later time."

Remus ground his teeth together and sighed heavily.

He swept out of the room as Kailynn turned to Isa.

"Isa...I..."

"I don't want to hear your answer," Isa said. "It was not fair of him to ask such a loaded question."

Kailynn glanced at the door.

"He was your previous lover," Kailynn said knowingly.

Isa nodded slowly. "He was."

"Makes sense why Venus didn't kill both of you," Kailynn said. "You were both Elites." She hesitated. "In school, too?"

"Yes," Isa admitted. "We were sexual partners for many years."

"Did you love him?"

Isa's eyes turned sad.

"Elites have no human emotions," she reminded the Significant. "I cannot fall in love."

Kailynn's brow furrowed, the words hurting. She looked at the door once more.

"But he's jealous."

"No, I don't believe so," Isa disagreed. "He's worried. He knows the risks of this sort of relationship."

"Why did you two call it off?" Kailynn asked, confused, turning her eyes back on the Golden Elite. "You could have ignored Venus' order and continued to keep it secret. And you still work together and clearly you still talk to one another."

Isa hesitated, her eyes falling to the ground for a moment as she thought about her answer.

"Things just ended," she said slowly. "I can't say that there was one reason in particular. There were a lot of factors and we decided it was best to comply with Venus' order."

Tarah dropped her eyes to the ground, swallowing hard.

"It is in the past." Isa waved the conversation away. "In a way, I am relieved he knows."

"Why?" Kailynn asked in horror.

"Because it saves me trying to keep it a secret from him." Isa turned to Kailynn and smiled gently, brushing her fingers over the younger woman's cheek. Kailynn's body shuddered as her eyes were captured in Isa's powerful gaze. "I do not want you to worry about him, or about the money," she assured. "I will be sure you are properly paid for your time."

"But...Isa..."

"No, you do not need to answer his question. It does not matter to me if you are here because of the money or not," Isa said. "What matters to me is that you *are* here."

Kailynn blinked at Isa, following the Elite's fingers as they left her cheek. Kailynn almost cried at the loss of contact.

Isa turned to return to work but Kailynn grabbed her arm, turning her around and grabbing her face. She crushed their lips together, hoping that her feelings about Remus and the money were conveyed in the kiss. She knew Isa did not want an answer, but she wanted to give one.

While she was frantic and desperate to convey her emotions to Isa, the Elite was quiet and calm, as usual, slowing the kiss to a gentler pace.

When they parted, Kailynn took a deep breath and swallowed hard.

Isa smiled and ran her fingers over Kailynn's cheek again, leaning down to kiss her once more.

Chapter Fifteen

Kailynn's eyes fluttered open lazily as she slowly came back to reality with the help of Isa stroking her hair. Her throat was dry and her breath came in pants. She was hot and sticky with sweat, which made resting on top of Isa uncomfortable, but she did not want to move.

She propped herself up and glanced at the Golden Elite, who looked amazingly composed for someone post-coitus.

Isa ran her fingers over Kailynn's cheekbone, looking over the younger woman's features. Kailynn turned her head and kissed the Elite's hand before leaning into the touch and turning her eyes back on Isa.

"Isa..."

"You don't need to say anything," she whispered. "I know."

But Kailynn was sure that the Elite did *not* know. How could she know the complex feelings coursing through the Significant when she could not feel human emotions? Kailynn knew that it was her last night with the Elite. The following day, Kailynn would return to Companion and then to Trid with the money she had earned being with the Elite. She would be returning to free some of the criminals who had tried to destroy Venus, the very computer Isa obeyed.

Kailynn leaned down and kissed Isa, her lips hovering over the Golden Elite's when she pulled away.

"Will you be alright?" Kailynn breathed.

Isa's hands tenderly stroked Kailynn's back as she pecked another kiss on the younger woman's lips.

"Yes."

"Are you sure?" Kailynn pressed. "It sounded like things with Caroie really heated up today."

Isa sighed and closed her tired eyes, trying not to recall the difficult preliminary negotiations for Caroie and the number of planets she found trying to thwart her every step.

"This is certainly not an easy situation," she said. "I will have to be very careful how I proceed."

"...I feel like I have only been a distraction," Kailynn murmured. "You've had to handle Remus and Rayal chewing you out because of me, on top of all this shit with Caroie."

"You have been a very welcome and necessary distraction," Isa assured, smiling. "As difficult as it is to turn my brain off, if I don't distract myself from time to time, I do not do my job as well."

"Maybe that has to do with the brain damage from falling down stairs," Kailynn tried to tease, finally swinging her leg over the Golden Elite and taking her place on her side next to Isa. The Golden Elite chuckled.

"Perhaps," Isa agreed. She turned to Kailynn. "May I ask you something personal?"

"Uh oh..." Kailynn laughed nervously.

"Why are you trying to make money as a Significant?"

Kailynn's entire body went rigid. She had not been expecting the question at all.

"Why do you ask?"

"I've noticed that you know more about me than I know about you," Isa murmured. "If you do not want to answer, you are under no obligation. I just want to know if there is any way I can help."

Kailynn was silent for a few moments.

"What?"

"You have done much more for me in the last few weeks than you probably realize," Isa said. "I want to return the favor."

"You mean you just needed to get laid?" Kailynn joked.

"Perhaps," Isa laughed. She turned onto her side and propped her head up with her hand. "But it has also been nice to have someone here who doesn't treat me like I'm made of glass."

"They're just worried about you."

"I know," Isa said, brushing some of Kailynn's hair over her shoulder. "Why are you trying to earn money?"

"...my brother is in trouble," Kailynn answered vaguely.

"Is he ill?"

"Yes," Kailynn lied.

Isa nodded slowly, her eyes going distant, lost in thought.

"How much do you need?"

"No, it's fine," Kailynn assured quickly. "The money from this will be more than enough." She did not know what the average cost of medical treatment was and she did not want to make Isa suspicious.

"If Remus refuses payment, for any reason, let me know and I will take care of it."

Kailynn looked down at the sheets, feeling awkward. There were a lot of feelings coursing through her, including the dread of tomorrow, when she knew she would have to leave the Golden Elite's home. The thought filled her with a sense of emptiness that scared her.

She leaned forward and took Isa's face in her hands, kissing her again.

■■■

The following morning, Kailynn moved slowly, gathering her clothes and placing them in her bag. She had awoken to being alone in Isa's bed. She did not look for the Elite. She did not want the entire morning to be a drawn-out, awkward goodbye. She felt like it was getting harder to breathe as she realized her time to go back to Companion was coming closer.

She brought her bag into the main room, where Tarah was waiting, trying to hide her tears.

"It's going to be so quiet, now," she said slowly.

Kailynn could not imagine how lonely Tarah was, being alone for most of the day with very little human interaction, always around Isa and the other Elites. It was no wonder the younger woman clung to Kailynn and Rayal whenever they were around.

"Are you going to be alright?" Kailynn asked.

"Yeah," Tarah assured. "I'll be fine. It's just…with you gone and Isa going back to the Syndicate Building for work every day, it will be quiet."

Kailynn hesitated. Her immediate reaction was to invite Tarah to spend time with her outside of Anon, but she knew she could not offer any place for the young woman to stay, particularly after the teenager had become accustomed to living in the luxury of the Elite's home.

"I would say you could come spend time with me," Kailynn offered, "but I don't have anywhere to host you."

"That's alright," Tarah said. "I don't really like to leave the tower anyway."

"Never?"

"If I can avoid it."

"Why?"

"I just…it scares me, that's all."

"There's nothing to be afraid of," Kailynn said. "If you ever just want to get out and go on a walk or something, I'll go with you."

"Go on a walk?" Tarah chuckled. "No one does that."

"Exactly," Kailynn agreed. "So it will be just us. No one else to worry about."

Tarah giggled, trying to discreetly wipe away a few tears.

"I might like that."

"I think you should," a voice said behind them. They both jumped and turned to the door to the guest wing. Kailynn shook her head, grinding her teeth together. When Isa saw the expression, she chuckled. "What are you going to do without me sneaking up behind you all the time?"

"I'm getting you a bell," Kailynn said shortly.

Tarah smiled lightly and bowed her head, ducking into the kitchen, understanding that it was time for Isa to say goodbye to the Significant. Kailynn felt her body tremble when she heard Tarah leave. She stared at the Golden Elite as the door to the kitchen closed.

Isa stepped forward, pulling a card out of her pocket and extending it to Kailynn.

"What's this?"

"It's a small gift," Isa said. "Fifty-thousand credits."

Kailynn's eyes shot wide.

"H-How much?"

"It's just a little extra," she continued. "To supplement what you'll be getting for being here."

"I can't accept this," Kailynn said, shaking her head and extending the card back to Isa.

"Then don't use it," the Golden Elite said with a shrug. "But keep that card. It will give you access to this level."

Kailynn had to take several moments to process what that meant.

"...what?" she barely managed to breathe.

"You are welcome here whenever you please." Isa invited. "That card will give you access to the building and to this level."

"But...I..."

"There is no obligation for you to return," Isa continued. "The decision is yours. But you are always welcome."

Kailynn stared at the grey card, surprised beyond words. Isa watched the emotions that passed over the Significant's face. Kailynn finally swallowed hard and shook her head.

"I don't know what to say..."

"You don't need to say anything."

"Thank you," Kailynn whispered.

"You're welcome."

Kailynn walked forward and rose up on her toes to kiss Isa, pulling away while she was still able. Isa took her hand and squeezed it.

"Thank you," she said sincerely.

Kailynn could only nod, trying to swallow the lump in her throat. She turned and picked up her bag, casting one final look around the room as she pocketed the card Isa had given her. She turned back to Isa, trying to push down the lump forming in her throat.

"Goodbye," she murmured.

"Goodbye, Kailynn."

Kailynn began backing away, her eyes unable to leave Isa. After a few paces, she raised her voice.

"Bye, Tarah!" she called.

Tarah poked her head out of the kitchen, trying to mask her tears.

"Bye, Kailynn."

"Tarah," Isa said, motioning the caretaker to her. Tarah walked over, standing next to the Golden Elite as Isa put her hand on Tarah's shoulder. Kailynn looked between the two of them.

"Bye."

Knowing she was seconds away from a breakdown, she turned and half-ran out of the home. The door opened automatically for her and she went to the elevator, waiting for it to arrive, trying to stop the shaking of her body. She forced her feet to move forward when the door to the elevator opened. The descent of the elevator car was too fast, and a type of pain that Kailynn had never known before began to seep into her bones.

When the door to the elevator opened again to let Kailynn into the lobby, she was startled to see Rayal walking toward the elevator. She was still for several seconds as the former caretaker approached. Thousands of thoughts raced through her mind.

"Leaving?" Rayal asked casually, breaking her out of her stupor. She stepped out of the elevator and walked past him.

"Yeah."

"Kailynn," Rayal called. She stopped, but did not turn to him. "If she invited you back, I have some advice. Don't come back."

Kailynn tried not to flinch at the words.

"This was already dangerous. Don't push your luck, or hers."

Kailynn kept walking, keeping her head up, trying to calm the storm of her mind. She left Anon Tower and felt her head spinning. She quickly hurried away from the large building, disoriented and unsure where she was going. She just knew she had to get as far away from the building as possible.

She stumbled toward the center of the city, intent on returning to Companion. She could see the building of the company get larger, but she was unable to get there before her confusion overwhelmed her.

She ducked into the nearest alley and collapsed.

Leaning against the side of the building, she let confused tears overtake her.

■■■

When Rayal walked into the living room, he was alarmed at what he saw.

Isa was standing near the bar, her arms around Tarah as the younger woman cried quietly into the Elite's chest. He walked to the both of them, his footsteps drawing Tarah's attention.

"What happened?"

Tarah hiccupped between her sobs and turned away from both of them, walking into the kitchen quickly. Isa let out a defeated sigh.

"What's going on?" Rayal pressed.

"She's upset over Kailynn leaving," Isa murmured. "I was concerned that having another person here would complicate things for her."

Rayal turned to the kitchen, understanding what Isa meant.

"I'll talk to her," the former caretaker offered.

Isa nodded her thanks as he went into the kitchen. Tarah was in front of the sink, her hands wrapped around the edge of the basin as she crouched in front of it, crying.

"Tarah," he called quietly.

"No, go away," she snapped, her voice breaking.

Rayal walked over to her and grabbed her shoulders, pulling her up and turning her around to hug her. He smoothed over her hair as her arms went around him, her sobbing wracking her entire body. Rayal held her tight, letting her break down.

He kicked himself for not realizing how difficult the situation would become for Tarah. Tarah had thrived with Isa, and he hardly remembered the starved, bruised, terrified child that Isa had brought into the capital. But, as he held her, he remembered how young Tarah was, and how much of her past she had been unable to leave behind.

"I'm sorry…" she choked, shaking as her crying slowly subsided.

"No, I apologize," Rayal murmured. "I didn't realize how difficult this would be for you."

"It *shouldn't* be," Tarah hissed. "She wanted me to go out and see her, but I haven't left this tower in years. But, she…she…she can do whatever she wants, she can *help* Isa. But…I…"

Tarah was overwhelmed and confused, her sentences jumbled.

In those few moments that Tarah buried her face back in Rayal's chest, the former caretaker started to see how complicated the situation was for everyone. Tarah had become attached to Kailynn, who was finally someone that the younger woman could talk to. Tarah had also been able to see that Kailynn was *good* for Isa. The words hurt Rayal, knowing that he had told Kailynn not to come back, even knowing that Isa had already become very fond of the Significant.

"Rayal," Tarah breathed. She glanced up at him, swallowing hard. "I knew her from before."

"What? What do you mean?"

"I remember her from when I was younger," she continued. "She's a Trid."

Rayal was sure that his heart stopped beating for a few seconds as the words processed.

"Are you sure?"

"Yes," she whispered. "We had the same Keeper."

"But she didn't recognize you?"

"No."

Rayal was not sure what to think. The fact that Kailynn was actually an orphan from Trid who must have faked papers to get work as a Significant added even more weight to the situation.

"Rayal," Tarah started, "I'm so confused."

"We all are."

"Will you stay?" Tarah asked. "Not for me, but for Isa?"

"Yes," he assured. "I'll stay for both of you."

Chapter Sixteen

Kailynn paced anxiously by the abandoned car garage. She knew that the members of the Heart of Trid gang had likely already made their escape, but she was still terrified that something would go wrong. She had quickly taken the money from her job with the Golden Elite and paid the guards at Uren to turn away when Theo and the others escaped. It had only been four days since her return to Trid and she had quickly busied herself with the gang's escape, trying to keep her mind off of the perfectly clear blue eyes that haunted her.

"Relax," Raphael chuckled as she continued to pace. "The guards don't give a shit. They'll get out."

"You don't know that."

Raphael walked over and grabbed Kailynn's shoulders, pulling her close and kissing her. She stopped, surprised. When he pulled away, Raphael kept his arms secure around her, smiling.

"It will be alright," he assured. "Theo's smart. He'll be fine."

Kailynn was about to object but Raphael pinned her against the wall of the car garage, capturing her lips in a near-bruising kiss. She was, once again, stunned, but when Raphael's hands went up the front of her shirt to palm her breast, she broke the kiss and pushed him away.

"Not now."

"You have been acting weird since you came back," Raphael said, stepping away. "Are you alright?"

"I'm worried about Theo, alright?" Kailynn groaned. "I risked my fucking life to get this much money, and I want to make sure that this works."

For another two hours they waited, joined by a few other members of their gang. Kailynn was trying not to let herself get too worked up, but her heart was practically in her throat, choking her. She continued to look around for signs of movement, knowing that Theo and the other gang members could come from any direction, depending on how they had managed to escape.

"Alright, spill it," Alyssa finally said as she sat in the shade of the car garage, throwing pebbles and cracked pieces of concrete at one another in boredom. Kailynn turned when she did not continue, surprised to find that Alyssa was speaking to *her*.

"What?"

"Spill," Alyssa repeated. "How d'ya get the money to bust 'em out?"

"Why should I tell you?"

"Because you don't get that kinda money whoring," Alyssa said simply. "How d'ya get it? Stealin' from people in the capital?"

Kailynn was about to deny the accusation, but hesitated. There were only two people in the gang who knew she was working as a Significant. Kailynn did not want anyone else to know. In Trid, pride was everything and rumors could be a death sentence. That was the reason Theo could not be broken out of Uren without others of his gang. The gossip of his failure and the possibility of bringing the Officials into Trid put a target on Theo's head. Kailynn's situation was different, but not drastically so. Faking papers to find work in the capital was not brave or admirable, but cowardly and selfish. If one was born a Trid, they died a Trid. A Trid was never supposed to want to become a citizen of Anon. Trids were proud to be Trids, proud to be rough and strong, and proud to not need the guiding hand of Anon, the Syndicate, or Venus.

Kailynn would be ridiculed for what she was doing, particularly since she was earning money to break out the most-hated gang of Trid.

"I ain't tellin," she said with a cocky smile, turning away. She heard Alyssa and the others laugh behind her.

"That's our girl."

Raphael did not feel the same sort of relief as the others. He saw the brief hesitation that crossed Kailynn's face. With her strange behavior the previous four days, he was sure that something more had happened that she was trying to hide. He wondered if she had gotten into even more trouble. He understood that Kailynn would do anything to help Theo. Theo was her only surviving family, but Raphael knew that Theo was far from the ideal older brother. Raphael did not understand the hold that Theo had over Kailynn.

He was about to ask Kailynn if she wanted to check if her brother had gone to her place, which would give him a chance to talk with her privately, when Viv gasped, pointing.

"There they are!"

Kailynn whirled around to see a group of men and women jogging toward them, waving.

The others of Kailynn's gang called to them, welcoming them and congratulating them on their escape. Kailynn ignored the others, searching the faces for her older brother. When she finally saw him, he smiled and walked over to her.

She let him approach but, before she could help herself, she slapped him across the face.

As soon as he turned back to her, surprised and confused, she threw her arms around his neck and hugged him tightly.

"I guess I deserve that," he chuckled.

"You deserve a helluva lot more than that, you jackass," Kailynn groaned, breaking the hug. "You cannot keep pulling stunts like that."

Theo smiled and ruffled Kailynn's hair playfully.

"Are you kidding? Do you know how close we were?"

"To being *killed*? Yes," she said sharply. "I'm serious, Theo, lay low. More than half the gangs around here want you dead and now you've drawn the attention of the Syndicate. You do anything stupid now and they're going to label you as a KOS."

Theo did not seem worried about being classified as a Kill on Sight target. He just smiled, glancing at the others of his gang, causing them to smile at what they believed to be Kailynn's dramatics.

"Theo!" Kailynn snapped.

"Alright, alright," Theo chuckled, hugging his younger sister again. "It's alright." He rubbed her shoulder. "We're here now. We got out."

Kailynn was about to snap at Theo and tell him that the only reason he was able to escape was because of her bribe money, however, she decided against it. She let her brother hug her and pretend like she was exaggerating.

She knew that she was not overreacting.

■■

While some of the territory of the Heart of Trid gang had been taken by rival gangs, there were still several small areas that belonged to them. Combined with Kailynn's territory, they had a safe place to celebrate the escape from Uren.

Aron, one of the oldest members of the Heart of Trid gang, did not mind having everyone over at his place, as it was the most central in the gang's territory and the largest. The Trids lifted drinks and ration packs from cafes and bars in the Walking District, smuggling them back to Aron's for their celebration. The elation of having booze and several ration packs raised the already-celebratory mood. They did not care about preserving the loot. They were too happy to have most of the Heart of Trid gang free of Uren.

All of them toasted to the safe return of Theo and the others and the drinking began. Alyssa hooked up a speaker to play some grainy music from weak signals in the Walking District. Some Trids played cards and drinking games, feeling safe and secure in the flat.

Kailynn drank and drank but she could not join in the festivities. No one noticed her distant, sad look as she sat against the far wall with a drink in hand. Anyone who looked at her figured she was merely drunk.

When Raphael noticed the look, he crawled to her, heavily inebriated, and sat next to her.

"Hey."

"Hey," she responded.

"You okay?"

"Yeah."

"You don't look okay."

"I'm drunk."

Raphael fell silent. He knew that there was something bothering Kailynn. He tried to think of something to say that would get her to tell him what was wrong, but his mind was foggy with liquor.

"Wanna tell me what's wrong?" he finally said.

"Nothing's wrong," she answered, her eyes never leaving the floor. She was staring at the dirty concrete, lost in thoughts she could not follow. She closed her eyes and ran a hand through her hair, sighing.

"Something is wrong," Raphael disagreed.

Kailynn was still for several moments before she let her head fall onto Raphael's shoulder. Her eyes still closed, she tried to fight the sudden urge to cry in frustration. She did not know what she was upset about, but the alcohol made her emotional and upset.

She had to blame the alcohol.

Raphael decided not to think too much about his next course of action.

He took Kailynn's chin, tilting her head up and capturing her lips in a kiss. He felt her smile against his mouth, so he kissed her again, his lips covering hers in a way that he always enjoyed. Kailynn had been the one who called off their monogamous relationship, saying that he could be with other women if he wanted. Raphael never questioned why she did that, but now that he was kissing her again, he wondered why they were no longer a couple.

Raphael had been attracted to Kailynn from the moment he saw her at the Keeper—the Trid orphanage. The orphans stayed in their groups, never letting in new orphans, which led to four or five newcomers creating a group of their own. Raphael had been with the Keeper since he could remember, having been abandoned as a newborn. When Kailynn came through the door, his eyes were unable to leave her. She was one year younger than him, and had been dropped off by her fifteen-year-old brother because he could not feed her. She had cried when he walked away, never turning back to look at Kailynn, calling over his shoulder that he would be back.

Raphael broke the unspoken rule of the Keeper and immediately took Kailynn into his group. That group eventually became the founding members of their own gang.

It was natural that Raphael and Kailynn would become a couple. They were around each other constantly and there was a definite spark between them. They got together when Kailynn was sixteen and were a committed couple for two years before Kailynn said that they did not need to be monogamous.

And slowly, their intimate relations stopped.

Occasionally, they would have sex, when they were lonely, or cold, or just bored and wanting to pass time, but it had never been with the intent to resume their relationship.

Kissing her then, he wanted her to be with him once more.

He wanted to hold her every night as she drifted off to sleep. He wanted to wake up just before her so he could kiss her awake. The thought of being sappy and romantic did not bother him. She was worth it.

Kailynn broke the kiss and leaned her head against his.

"Do you want to leave?"

She nodded.

He stood and offered his hand to her. He shared a quick glance with a few of the others who saw them move. They waved and nodded, some winking suggestively as the two left.

Raphael had his arm around Kailynn's shoulders as they walked silently back to his flat. He would glance at Kailynn and smile gently.

She never once looked at him.

Kailynn's eyes were focused on the ground, her thoughts elsewhere.

She walked into Raphael's apartment without thinking. She heard the door close and she turned to him. He immediately took her face in his hands, kissing her as he backed her up to the wall.

For several moments, Kailynn was too startled to move. She felt Raphael's lips on hers and they gave her pause. It was not what she had been expecting.

However, he was warm and his weight against her body was comforting. She leaned into him and returned the kiss. She had been so busy the previous days that focusing on the feeling of his warmth was calming and comforting.

Raphael's hands ran up and down her body, his lips working against hers, his tongue ravaging her mouth.

Kailynn closed her eyes and tried to turn off her mind and enjoy the sensations.

However, her mind turned to a pair of stunning blue eyes that made her blood run hot. She thought about those eyes looking into her soul, penetrating everything of her being, while still being gentle. The smile that touched those eyes permeated through her intoxicated mind, causing her to smile as she leaned her head back against the wall.

Raphael's mouth moved over her skin, gently scraping his teeth along her neck, sending shivers up her spine.

He guided her back to the bed, gently pushing her so she was flat on her back before he made work of her clothes, stripping them off slowly and seductively, smiling when Kailynn trembled under his fingers.

But Kailynn could only think of water moving over her skin, warm, as she enjoyed the weightless feeling. She could feel hands pressing into her back, holding her afloat, steady and sure. She could almost see the perfect face over her, smiling.

Raphael draped his body over her, kissing her once more.

Kailynn slowly came back to reality.

She was not with Isa.

She was with Raphael.

Naked and being kissed all over, Kailynn felt exposed and uncomfortable. There was something about the situation that felt...wrong.

But Raphael was safe. There was nothing dangerous about them being together. They had known each other for so long there were no secrets between them. They always supported one another as best they could in their times of need, and loved each other, even if that love was difficult to describe.

Raphael knew exactly where to touch to make her tremble in pleasure. Her body reacted to Raphael.

But that was not enough anymore.

Her mind was elsewhere.

When Raphael entered her, she was almost shocked at the feeling. It was not painful—her body was ready for him—but it felt intrusive, like he was not only penetrating her body, but also her mind, invading an area of her thoughts that she had already dedicated to someone else.

Even as her body bowed and climaxed in pleasure, Kailynn felt as though she was betraying Isa.

Chapter Seventeen

Kailynn felt as though she was living in a dream as she went to the home of her next client. There were still seven members of the Heart of Trid that needed to be broken out, and Kailynn knew that there was no way Theo would be able to come up with the money on his own, so she continued her work as a Significant.

Focusing on releasing the remaining Trids allowed Kailynn to get her mind back in the right place. She had been dwelling on Isa far too much.

Her night with Raphael had made matters worse. She felt guilty, as though she had betrayed and hurt Isa, even though she and Isa were not a couple, technically, and Kailynn was not sure she was ever going to see the Elite again. Being with Raphael was, in many ways, safer than being with Isa. And, she did love Raphael.

She could not name what she felt for Isa.

Going back to work at Companion felt necessary. She needed a distraction. However, she was not called out for a job for nearly four weeks after the Heart of Trid gang escaped, so Kailynn had a lot of time to herself to think.

Her thoughts always went back to Isa.

She approached the door of her first client in a month and was surprised to find herself nervous.

When the caretaker opened the door and let her in without greeting her, she relaxed a little. She found the couple standing awkwardly in the living room, stiff, uneasy about speaking with the Significant.

Kailynn smiled as if she had known them for years. Their request was to host a "dinner party" with a Significant. It was their first time with a Significant and they did not know how to react when she walked up to them and hugged the woman before shaking hands with the man. She commented on how beautiful their home was, even though Kailynn actually found it dark and dull, like most noble homes.

It took the couple a few minutes to relax, but even then, Kailynn had to skillfully ask questions to keep up the charade. She asked them what they had been up to, asked them to explain their jobs as though she was a friend who had forgotten or wanted to know about the promotions they had obtained. The couple was confused by how much Kailynn was talking.

Kailynn felt like she was pulling teeth. The couple wanted her there to talk to through the dinner party, but they were unable to hold up their end of the act. Kailynn forgot how tedious the work could be.

Through dinner they started to relax and speak more. The woman asked Kailynn's opinion about current political affairs and everything happening in the Ninth Circle, which was something that made Kailynn hesitate.

"Oh, politics is such a frightening thing to talk about over dinner," Kailynn tried to laugh. "I have complete faith in Elite Isa and the others of the Syndicate that they will solve the problem efficiently."

She then asked another question, hoping to draw the attention off politics.

Kailynn, for all the free time she had to mull over her own thoughts, had not been keeping up with the current political state of Tiao. Now reminded of the trouble in the Ninth Circle, she wondered if Isa was alright. She wondered if there was any progress with Caroie and if Isa was able to resolve the hostage situation. Kailynn worried that Isa was not taking care of herself, too worried about political problems to think of herself.

Kailynn stumbled her way through the rest of the appointment with her client, her mind focused on Isa.

It had become a warily constant theme in her mind.

When it was finally time for her to say goodbye to the couple that, she had to admit, was very nice, just awkward, Kailynn rushed to the elevator, eager to get out of the building. She met Nyx at the car as he tried to keep up with her, even as she quickly clamored in. When he saw her worried expression, he blinked, staring at her.

"What's wrong? Did they hurt you?"

"No, no, I'm fine," she assured, taking a deep breath.

"Are you sure? You don't look okay."

"I'm just…I have a lot of things on my mind, okay?"

"…are you pregnant or something?"

"Excuse me?!" Kailynn gasped, rounding on Nyx.

"You've been acting weird," Nyx said, shrugging. "I was just asking."

"I can have a lot on my mind without being pregnant, Nyx!" she snapped.

"Fine, sorry I asked. Not like I'm worried about you or anything."

"Don't use that tone," Kailynn groaned. "I know you're worried. I know that's why you asked. I just have a lot bothering me."

"Do you need to talk about it?" Nyx asked, turning the car on and leaving the parking garage. Kailynn sighed and rubbed her face, trying to get her thoughts under control. She felt like she was obsessed with Isa. She had been thinking about the Elite every waking moment for the past month. It was starting to feel like a full-time job.

"Have you ever thought about something for a month non-stop?" she finally asked.

"Yeah," he said with a nod. "Wait, a good thing or a bad thing?"

"...what if you didn't know?"

"Then that's a predicament," Nyx chuckled. "If it's a good thing, then you can say you're thinking about it because it makes you happy, and there is nothing wrong with that. If it's a bad thing, then thinking about it helps you process it and helps you get over it. If you don't know..." Nyx sighed heavily. "I guess you're thinking about it trying to decide what it is."

Kailynn groaned and leaned her head back.

"I feel like I'm obsessed."

"With?"

Kailynn shook her head.

"Too personal."

"Oh? Are you falling in love with someone?"

Kailynn had a strong urge to punch him.

"I doubt it."

"Is it a person you've been thinking about constantly?" he asked, turning to her as the car moved along the tunneled roads under the city.

"So?"

"Maybe you're in love," Nyx suggested. "That's what happens."

"You think about the person so much it might as well be obsessive?"

"Yeah," Nyx chuckled. His face fell quickly. "Wait, did you fall for a client?"

"No!" Kailynn growled. "I haven't *fallen* for anyone."

"Are you sure about that?"

"...no."

Kailynn closed her eyes and lightly hit her head a few times against the window of the car.

"I don't know what to do."

"Maybe talk to the other person?" Nyx suggested. "That might be best."

"Not really possible..."

"Why not?"

"...it's complicated."

The two fell into silence for a several minutes. Kailynn did not notice it, but her body was becoming tenser with every passing second. Nyx tried not to smile, but he knew it was only a matter of time.

"Okay, *fine*, just...exit at the next stop and let me out. I'll walk the rest of the way!"

Nyx chuckled.

"What?"

"Nothing," he assured, touching the screen and programming a new exit for the car.

"Then why are you laughing?" she demanded.

"I had a mental countdown of when you would finally tell me to stop."

Kailynn narrowed her eyes.

"Don't tell anyone about this," she snarled darkly. He raised his hands and shook his head.

"No, my lips are sealed. But what are you going to tell Jak?"

"I'll just tell him that I needed to see my brother in the hospital," she said.

Nyx's expression softened.

"Has he taken a turn for the worst?" he asked gently. Kailynn shook her head.

"No," she said. "He's actually doing better."

"That's a relief," Nyx said with a smile. "And you've fallen in love. Things are looking up."

"I have not fallen in love," Kailynn said quickly, looking around as the car rose up to ground level and sat still, hazard lights flashing, waiting for further instruction.

"There's nothing wrong with it," Nyx assured. "It's a wonderful thing."

"Goodnight, Nyx," Kailynn said, exasperated, getting out of the car and waiting for him to drive away before walking around the buildings of Anon, glancing up at the lit windows and hearing the hum of the machines as the city remained awake late into the night. The city was so devoid of people and noise that Kailynn could hear the commotion of the music in the Walking District, which was a fair distance from where she stood.

She had to look around for several moments, walking a few blocks and looking around again, trying to locate Anon Tower.

When she finally saw it her pace became determined, deciding to push all her thoughts and doubts away. As she got closer, she reached into her bag and shuffled around the contents, being sure to find the small, grey card that she kept on her at all times. She became flustered when she did not find it immediately, but she also did not stop walking, continuing down the walkways toward the building as she searched for the access card.

Kailynn finally found it, holding it tight as her steps hastened.

Entering Anon Tower felt surreal. She remembered her nerves when she first walked into the building to spend a month with an unknown Elite. She also recalled the pain and confusion she felt upon leaving, and Rayal's words came back to haunt her.

"Don't come back."

For a brief moment, Kailynn hesitated.

But she had been thinking about Isa every day since leaving the Elite. She could not turn back now that she was in the lobby.

Taking a deep breath, she stepped into the elevator and swiped the card to go up to the level of the Golden Elite.

Her stomach was tangled with butterflies as the elevator ascended. She wondered if Isa would be there when she opened the door. There was a part of her that wanted to see the Elite's face the moment she walked in, and another part of her that knew she needed time to prepare.

The elevator doors slid open. She stepped out and walked to the door, shaking, though she did not understand why. Nervously, Kailynn stepped in front of the door and it opened. She was immediately greeted by Tarah running to her and hugging her tightly.

"I almost didn't believe it when I saw your picture on the monitor," Tarah gasped, refusing to let go of Kailynn. The older woman laughed and returned the hug.

"Where is the security system?" she asked, confused.

"My room and the kitchen," Tarah answered, finally pulling away from the Significant, her face beaming. "It feels like it's been years since I've seen you."

"How have you been?" Kailynn asked, walking into the main room after Tarah. The younger woman sighed heavily.

"Alright, I guess."

"That wasn't convincing," Kailynn teased. Tarah smiled thinly.

"Things haven't been the same since you left."

Kailynn was not sure what Tarah meant, but it made her concerned. She glanced around the main room, trying to hide her shaking.

"She's not home, yet," Tarah said quietly. "She had a late meeting."

Kailynn was both disappointed and relieved.

"Do you mind if I wait around?" she tried to ask casually. Tarah's smile widened.

"I was hoping you would."

Tarah got Kailynn a drink and then sat with her in the living room, asking her what she had been up to, thrilled to see the older woman again. Kailynn was surprised how easy she found it to talk to the caretaker. She missed the younger, bubbly girl. Her smile was infectious.

However, when the door opened, Kailynn's attention was immediately diverted.

She could feel her entire body react to the Elite when she walked through the door, even though she was talking on the phone.

"—know what else I can do," she said, sighing heavily and shaking her head. She stopped when she saw Kailynn. Tarah stood and dipped her head in a bow to the Golden Elite, but Isa did not notice. She watched as Kailynn slowly stood from her seat, a nervous smile overtaking her face.

Isa smiled as well.

"I'm starting to feel overwhelmed," she murmured, placing her fingers against the earpiece to show she was speaking to someone. "And I think I'm coming down with something." She paused, listening to the other person. "Yes, I think that might be best. I'll work from here tomorrow and try to rest my body a little. I think Opium is starting to take its toll."

Kailynn's heart skipped a beat. She wondered if Isa was actually feeling unwell, or if she was saying that so that she could stay at home—with Kailynn—the following day. Kailynn could feel the heat rising to her cheeks.

"Thank you, Remus," Isa said gently. "Have a good night."

She took out the earpiece and set it with her phone on the bar.

"This is an unexpected surprise."

Kailynn was still overpowered by how beautiful Isa was and the radiance of her smile. No matter how many times she had thought about the Elite's stunning features the previous month, she was still enthralled by Isa.

"Is there anything I can get you, Miss?" Tarah asked. She was trying not to smile at the way Isa and Kailynn had not broken eye contact.

"No, thank you, Tarah. I ate at the Syndicate."

Still, Isa and Kailynn had their gazes locked.

"If that is all, Miss, then I will say goodnight," Tarah said.

"Thank you, Tarah," Isa repeated. "Goodnight."

Tarah bowed her head and started toward her room, allowing the smile to creep over her face when she went into the guest hall.

Kailynn heard the door open to the guest hall, but she did not turn to make sure that Tarah was gone. As the door was sliding shut, she strode quickly over to Isa and grabbed her face, crashing their lips together as if her life depended on it.

The Significant backed the Elite up until she was pressed against the bar, pushing her body against Isa's, her hands holding Isa's face tightly.

Isa smiled into the kiss and her hands went to Kailynn's waist, holding the younger woman to her, reveling in the contact.

Kailynn's entire body was sparking as their lips worked against one another. She felt that she could not get close enough to Isa. She needed to be closer, she needed to feel every inch of Isa's being, even though it was physically impossible. She whined at the longing and broke the kiss.

Both of them were still, their lips barely apart, their breaths mixing between them.

Isa's hand brushed over Kailynn's cheek. The Significant leaned into the touch, her eyes fluttering shut.

Isa swooped down and captured her mouth once more.

■■

"Isa…"

"Hmm?" Isa's eyes opened and she turned her head to look at Kailynn. The younger woman hesitated before turning onto her stomach and crossing her arms to prop herself up on the bed.

"Are you staying home tomorrow?"

"Yes."

"Is it because you're not feeling well?"

Isa chuckled.

"It has more to do with you being here," the Elite admitted.

Kailynn chuckled nervously, dropping her gaze to the bed.

"That's unnerving."

"Why?"

"Because you're the leader of a planet, and I'm distracting you from running that planet," Kailynn explained. There was an underlying question in the jest, and Isa immediately understood. She smiled, running the backs of her fingers tenderly over the Significant's shoulder.

"I have been trained to run the planet since I was ten years old," she whispered. "I am very good at my job."

"I know but…" Kailynn trailed off, hesitant. "I am still distracting you. And I hear that things are getting worse with the Ninth Circle."

Isa's fingers continued trailing over Kailynn's skin lazily.

"I'm a grown woman," she said. "You can't be held responsible for my actions."

"Then I *am* distracting you."

Isa chuckled, closing her eyes.

"You said it yourself when you were here last," she started. "If I don't get my mind off work, I'm going to think myself in circles."

Kailynn looked over Isa's relaxed features. Now that she was studying the Elite, she could see the exhaustion on her face. She still looked perfect, of course, but the skin around her eyes was darker and she had lost weight in the month that Kailynn had been gone.

The Significant crawled closer, drawing Isa's attention and causing her to open her eyes. Kailynn leaned down and kissed the Elite.

"I should probably go."

"I would like you to stay," Isa murmured, her eyes betraying how much she wanted Kailynn's company. "I missed you."

Kailynn's smile widened.

"I missed you, too."

Isa took a deep breath.

"I was actually relieved to see you," she said. "I was concerned you would not come back."

Kailynn swallowed hard and turned away from the Elite's gaze.

"I wasn't sure I was going to come back," she admitted. "I wanted to come back much sooner, but…I thought it was too dangerous for the both of us," she completed. She looked at Isa seriously. "What do you think would happen if Venus found out about this?"

Isa was quiet for a few moments, thinking.

"I truly do not know."

"Can't you convince her that you work better when you're allowed to fuck every once and a while?" Kailynn groaned.

Isa laughed.

"She's a computer," she reminded the Significant. "Her logic is infallible."

"What does that mean?"

"That she's without fault. That she is correct, no matter what she decides."

Kailynn scoffed.

"Really?" she groaned. "So, creating children that she can beat for wanting sex and then forcing them to work themselves to death while she ignores a growing number of Trids isn't the *wrong* decision?"

"To her, no," Isa said. "The Elites garner more respect than she. People like having a person, a living being, to look to when discussing human problems."

"If that is the case, why is everything we do so dependent on technology?" Kailynn asked. "If people want someone to talk to, why don't they talk to one another? The Significants would disappear if people would just talk to one another!"

"I wish that were so," Isa murmured. "But the dependence on technology is so deeply rooted in our society that changing it would be almost impossible."

"Why?"

"It's extremely complicated," Isa said. "If one person wanted to change, wanted to start talking to their husband or their children, both the husband and the children would have no concept of how to react. They have never been exposed to those circumstances before. One person cannot start the change in society just from changing themselves, particularly if that society is set up to stop them at every attempt."

"Couldn't you do something?" Kailynn asked. "I'm sure you heard a while ago that some Trids tried to shut down Venus."

"Yes, I remember."

"Can't you shut her down? *Can* she be shut down?"

Isa hesitated, her eyes looking over Kailynn's face, making the Significant nervous. She realized she was discussing treason with the leader of the planet, but she hoped that Isa would take the question as Kailynn's curiosity, rather than plotting.

"Yes, she can be shut down," the Elite finally murmured. "But it won't work to just go in there and smash her wiring. The problem with shutting down Venus lies in the way she was created."

"She's just like any other computer, though."

"No, no, she is far from," Isa said quickly. "She's is a very advanced artificial intelligence. She was created as an early detection disaster program. When the city was being built, there were fires and earthquakes and violent storms and several other obstacles that continued to set back development of Tiao. Venus was programmed to detect dangers and warn the city before the damage was done. However, that required her to be able to determine when a threat was credible. That artificial intelligence grew quickly, to the point where she was monitoring transmissions from other planets and patterning criminal behavior. It was not long before she was watching every person on the planet. She changed the way the city operated entirely."

"So why would that matter if she was shut down?"

"Because she was wired into the entire planet in order to monitor for disasters," Isa said. "To go in and cut her wires would do nothing. She is everywhere. Her coding and power source is in the entirety of the planet. And even then, she has a secondary backup. If she were to be properly shut down, the entire planet would shut down. Transportation, power, food production, water treatment, heat…no one would be able to survive."

"We have none of that in Trid," Kailynn noted.

"You don't have power, or heat, this is true. But you do not treat your water, or produce your food. You steal what you can from Anon."

Kailynn hesitated, deciding it was best not to respond.

"And, this planet, even the undeveloped parts, is not suitable for producing enough food to feed every inhabitant. That is why we have ration packs. That is why we have to import food from other planets."

"But, you could shut down Venus and then find a way to program everything without her," Kailynn suggested.

"We would have no power to reprogram after she was shut down," Isa explained. "It would take us years and years to get the planet up and running again. In that time, the citizens would starve and die, plague would set in from poor sanitation, wars would break out within the city..." Isa sighed heavily. "Too many would die if she were to be shut down."

"But she's a *dictator*," Kailynn said strongly. "And, in Trid, we're sure that the Elites are running the show and just using Venus as an excuse to do things. People can't see or interact with her, so how can she be expected to lead this planet?"

"She does exist," Isa said. "And the fact that no one can interact with her is the reason she created the Elites. The Elites obey her, and they give a human face to her orders. That's why she won't get rid of the Elites. The data showed that people were more willing to follow the orders when given by Elites rather than Venus."

Kailynn sighed and flopped onto her back, staring up at the ceiling. Isa turned onto her side and looked at Kailynn seriously.

"Did I upset you?"

"No, it's just..." Kailynn groaned. "It's frustrating."

"Yes, it is."

"So, she looks at the Elites as just extensions of herself," Kailynn said. "You're not your own person? You're just part of her?"

Isa hesitated, her eyes showing pain hidden deep below the cool exterior.

"No," Isa said. "I am my own person."

Kailynn looked at Isa, hearing the agony in the Elite's voice.

It was as if Isa was trying to convince herself that she was not merely an extension of Venus.

■■

"I'm really happy you're back," Tarah said with a smile as Kailynn finished her breakfast. Kailynn chuckled nervously at the elated look on Tarah's face.

"Why?"

Tarah shrugged, her smile widening.

"This place just feels different when you're here," she said. "And Isa's happier, too."

Kailynn paused.

"You think so?"

"I know so."

"Tarah," Kailynn started, turning to her almost-empty plate and shifting the remaining pieces of food around, "can I ask you a question?"

"Sure."

"Were you around when Isa and Remus split?"

Tarah's eyes shot wide and she blinked a few times, stunned.

"She told you?"

"She told me she and Remus were partners for a while, and that things just ended between them."

Tarah let out an exasperated chuckle, raising her eyebrows.

"Eight months in the hospital is what ended the relationship," Tarah grumbled. "I was around, yes."

"Were you also around when Venus found out about them?"

"No." Tarah shook her head. "Why?"

"I was trying to figure out how Venus found out about them," Kailynn said. "Are there cameras around the level?"

"Yes." Tarah nodded. "For security reasons, there are cameras everywhere."

"Then Venus probably already knows about us?" Kailynn hissed, horrified.

"If she knew, she would have said something by now," Tarah assured. "I'm sure Rayal is doing a good job keeping the camera feeds from Venus. They don't go directly to her, anyway. They filter through the Intelligence Agency before they are processed into her computers. Rayal is probably deleting them."

"You mean...he can see when Isa and I..." Kailynn stopped, not wanting to continue.

Tarah chuckled.

"I guess so," she said. "There is a camera in Isa's bedroom."

"Does she know that?" Kailynn asked, nodding to the guest hallway to indicate Isa, who had disappeared into her office twenty minutes previous.

"Of course."

"But that's not how Venus found out about them?"

"No." Tarah shook her head. "According to Rayal, someone leaked the information to blackmail Isa."

"I thought you said that no one would harm Isa," Kailynn said quickly.

"This was over five years ago," Tarah murmured. "Politics got ugly. It wasn't a caretaker, it was someone else that had stumbled on the information."

"Was he caught?"

"Yeah," Tarah said, though her voice trembled on the word. "He was punished."

Tarah stood and started collecting the dishes, smiling weakly.

"Are you finished?"

Kailynn wandered around the level of Anon Tower, remembering the month she had stayed and how much the job had changed her life. She had grown up hating Venus and the Syndicate Elites. She never thought that meeting the Golden Elite would change her perception so drastically. It was as if there was some other-worldly power to Isa that drew people closer. It was a feeling of security and strength that was addicting to all that came in contact with the Elite.

Kailynn started watching the clock, waiting for Isa to finish working. She had gone in to see if she could speak with the Elite—she did not have anything in particular she wanted to talk about, she just wanted to be with Isa—however, she found the Elite in BCS mode with the ring glowing blue and a hologram curtain of various-colored boxes slowly rotating around the chair.

The Significant had to wait.

However, when Isa finished up her work, she found Kailynn and asked if she wanted to swim. The two spent nearly two hours in the pool, talking lightly about nothing in particular. At one point, Isa cornered Kailynn and began kissing her passionately. Kailynn's eyes were rolling back into her head as Isa's hand descended into the water to gently touch her when Tarah opened the door to the pool area, startling both of them.

The caretaker turned away, blushing at the scene she had stumbled upon.

"So sorry to disturb you," she said quickly. "Dinner will be ready in about twenty minutes."

"Thank you, Tarah," Isa said with a smile, clearly not as embarrassed as Tarah or Kailynn. When Tarah left, Kailynn let out an exasperated groan.

"How can you be so damn calm about everything?"

Isa chuckled. "Practice." She stepped closer to Kailynn again, her hands gripping the Significant's hips as she smiled. "Where were we?"

Kailynn was a little embarrassed to meet Tarah's eyes at the dinner table, knowing what she had stumbled upon in the pool. She sat down nervously next to Isa, who seemed to not be concerned at being caught earlier.

However, before the Elite could start dinner, her phone chimed and caught her attention.

She stood and grabbed the small device, looking over the screen.

"My apologies," she said, her face creasing with concern. "An emergency. Please continue dinner without me."

Isa made her way into her office once more as Kailynn watched. When the Elite was out of sight, Kailynn turned back to Tarah, worried about the emergency. The younger woman shrugged.

"It happens. She's called away all the time to deal with emergencies."

The two ate their dinner. Tarah brought up conversation to dispel the tension between them. As they were doing dishes together, as they had done during Kailynn's previous stay, Tarah finally brought up what she saw.

"I don't want you to be embarrassed," she said, though it was clear that she was embarrassed herself.

"Oh…" Kailynn dropped her gaze, running her cloth over the already-dry, washed dish. "Yeah…sorry about that."

"Don't be," Tarah assured. "It was just a surprise, that's all."

"You seemed embarrassed about it, though," Kailynn noted.

"It's…it's just strange to see Isa like that, that's all," Tarah murmured. "I was not around when she was with Remus, but Rayal told me that he walked in on them a few times in different rooms."

Kailynn blinked, surprised.

"They had sex that often?"

"From what I heard," Tarah affirmed. "Rayal said he used to call them his teenagers because they could hardly keep their hands to themselves when they were here together."

Kailynn was startled to hear that Isa and Remus had been so sexual with one another. She had always believed that Isa was restrained when it came to their sexual relations. There was another feeling pooling in her gut. She was irritated to hear that Isa and Remus had been so close. It made her feel like she was not as close to the Golden Elite as she believed herself to be.

Tarah glanced at the silent Significant and saw the jealousy written on her face.

"I wouldn't let that get to you," she said quickly. "Just promise me you won't do that to me. I don't know if I could handle finding you two doing it in every room of the house."

Kailynn chuckled.

"Could give you some ideas with Rayal."

Tarah's jaw dropped to her chest and she turned to Kailynn with horrified eyes.

"*What?*"

"Oh, come on, everyone here can see what a crush you have on the guy," Kailynn teased.

"He is *fifteen* years older than me!"

"So? You like the guy, don't you?"

"That's not the point!"

"Why not?"

Tarah's cheeks burned hotly, and she turned back to unloading the dishes from the dishwasher, handing them to Kailynn, her eyes cast down.

Kailynn leaned over and smiled devilishly.

"Why are you pouting?"

"I'm not."

"Yes, you are," Kailynn laughed. "It's not a big deal, you know."

"Yes, it is," Tarah murmured. "I mean…I've never even been kissed before."

Kailynn smiled.

"Not even when you were in school?"

"No," Tarah said quietly, still pouting. "I finished my schooling here in Anon Tower. The three years I went to public school, I never even spoke to my classmates outside of the NCB chairs."

Kailynn tried not to roll her eyes.

"Right, I forgot. No one here talks to one another," she mumbled. "Well, then ask Rayal to take you somewhere. You've been in this tower too long."

"I have been out of the tower. I've been to the Syndicate Building," Tarah defended.

"By highway, I'm sure, which means you were underground. That doesn't count."

"Why not? It was—"

A shrill alarm sounded, causing them both to jump. Kailynn looked around quickly, not sure of the meaning of the alarm.

"Are we under attack?" she asked quickly.

Tarah gasped and ran out of the kitchen, Kailynn following her.

"Tarah? What's wrong?!"

"It's Isa!" she called as she ran through the pool area.

Kailynn did not ask for more explanation. Her heart stopped temporarily in fear before she forced herself to run even faster to the Elite's office.

Tarah opened the door and the loud alarm sounding through the house increased in volume. Kailynn stopped dead in the doorway, terrified at the sight.

Isa was locked into the NCB chair, the ring around it illuminated red, though the color was flashing. The Elite was strapped into the chair, but her body was writhing in spasms against the restraints. There was a trickle of blood coming from her nose and her eyes were rolled back into her head.

"Don't touch her!" Tarah cried as she ran to the back of the chair and quickly put in the override code. An automated voice sounded through the room.

"Emergency Shut Down Initiated. Shutting down in ten seconds."

As the voice counted down to zero, Kailynn waited anxiously by the chair, watching the Elite spasm, fear gripping every cell of her body.

The whirring of the chair stopped as it moved back into the powered-off position and the alarm finally stopped piercing the air. The red color faded and Tarah darted forward. With Kailynn's help, they pulled the still body of the Elite from the chair, putting her on the floor.

"Isa! Isa! Can you hear me?!" Kailynn said, taking the Elite's face. Isa's eyes were half-open, rolled back, her mouth slightly open and a trail of blood from her nose staining her smooth skin.

"The EMU should be here any moment," Tarah said, her voice tight with tears. She reached into her pocket and pulled out a handkerchief, wadding it up and pushing it to the back of the Elite's neck where the nodes from the NCB chair had been.

"She's not breathing!"

"We can't treat her!" Tarah snapped, the tears springing from her eyes.

"She's not breathing, Tarah!" Kailynn cried.

"I know!"

The door to the office opened and several automated robots came into the room. Tarah backed away, but Kailynn refused to move. She had never seen the EMU teams, and was surprised to see that they were all robots. There was not one human.

Tarah grabbed Kailynn and pulled her away, which allowed the robots to grab Isa and put her on the gurney. One of the robots touched Isa's arm as they all moved out of the office.

"No pulse detected," it read. "Heart stopped approximately four minutes, eighteen seconds ago."

"They can save her, can't they?!" Kailynn gasped, turning to Tarah as they followed the team out of the house and to the vehicle elevator door that was open at the far end of the hall. Tarah looked at Kailynn, her eyes filled with fear and tears.

The EMU team rolled Isa into the vehicle and Tarah and Kailynn climbed in, sitting on the two available seats in the back as the doors were closed and the elevator descended.

"Code Red Emergency. Golden Elite Isa in critical condition," the robot said, its hand still on Isa's arm. "Initiating breath and pulse simulation."

One of the other robot's hands went over Isa's nose and mouth and Kailynn watched in shock as Isa's chest began rising and falling.

"Initiating Plug In," another robot said, both hands going under Isa's neck as the screen on the head of the robot lit up with lines that were splayed in jagged spikes.

The first robot, the one with the engraving of Unit Leader on the chest, turned to Kailynn and Tarah.

"Identify."

"Tarah Marxus," Tarah whispered, her voice tight with tears.

"Confirmed. Golden Elite Caretaker." The robot turned the blank screen on its head to Kailynn. "Identify."

Kailynn was too stunned and scared to answer immediately. When Tarah elbowed her, she cleared her throat.

"Kai—Uh, Jacyleen Lynden," she corrected quickly.

The robot took a moment to process the name.

"Confirmed. Significant of Companion Corporation."

Kailynn and Tarah shared a terrified look. It was registered with the Emergency Medical Unit that the Golden Elite had a Significant in her home, and neither of them knew how far that information would travel.

"Transmitting message from Dr. Michael Ren Busen," the robot said. Before Kailynn could begin to wonder what that meant, the screen on the unit leader's face lit up and the face of a frantic man was shown. He was very attractive, with dark brown hair and sharp hazel eyes, but his worried expression concerned the other two in the vehicle with the Elite.

"Dr. Busen," Tarah said.

"Tarah," he greeted. "The EMU is on Code Red Emergency. The roads are clear. You will be at the hospital in under a minute," he explained. "My team is receiving all the needed information. We are prepared to take her."

"What happened?" she whispered, her voice choked.

"It was an assassination attempt," Dr. Busen said seriously. "Somehow, someone got the Pulse Virus into her personal NCB chair."

"Oh no…" Tarah moaned, her hands going up to her face.

"We're prepared to help her," Dr. Busen said. "We've dealt with the Pulse Virus before. We know how to combat it."

"But Isa…" Tarah trailed off.

"Remember everything that Isa has already survived," Dr. Busen said. "She's very strong. She'll be alright."

The vehicle started to slow and one of the robots announced that they were pulling into Bay One of the hospital. Kailynn could only look at Isa, fear twisting her gut into a tense knot. She saw the sharp spikes on the screen of the robots and the way Isa's chest rose and fell. But her body did not move, and Kailynn knew that Isa was in critical condition.

She was legitimately afraid that Isa was dead.

She was so focused on Isa that, when the doors to the vehicle opened, she almost jumped out of her skin.

More robots and a few nurses were there to take Isa into the hospital, orders and codes being yelled around them as Isa was pulled from the car.

In the commotion, one male nurse walked up to Tarah and Kailynn.

"You'll have to wait," he said. "Dr. Busen's team needs to work on her without interruption."

"Okay," Tarah whispered. She turned to Kailynn and grabbed her arm. Kailynn looked around, becoming more nervous by the moment. Somehow, she understood that the information in the EMU had made it to the hospital and everyone wheeling Isa further into the halls of the hospital knew she was a Significant.

"Perhaps it would be best if you returned to Companion," the nurse said to Kailynn. She knew that the suggestion was actually a warning. Fear began tunneling her vision. If it got out to the public that Isa had a Significant in her home, then their relationship would be a public affair, and Isa said that could lead to one or both of them being executed.

"No, wait!" Tarah said. She looked around frantically before turning to Kailynn, her eyes trying to communicate something. "I know that I only asked you to join me for dinner, but…this…" She shook her head. "I'll pay, of course, but could you stay with me until I know for sure that she's better?"

The nurse looked between the two, suspicious.

Kailynn felt relief, and even worse fear, course through her at the same time. She looked at the nurse, trying to keep her expression calm.

"My client wants me to stay," she said.

The nurse did not seem to immediately believe them. He looked between the two, noting the way Tarah was clinging to the Significant's arm.

Finally, he nodded.

"Very well. This way, please."

Chapter Eighteen

Seven agonizing hours passed in the upstairs private hospital waiting room. At first, only Tarah and Kailynn were present. However, within fifteen minutes of being brought into the hospital, Remus showed up.

Remus approached them, his eyes hard and cold with realization.

"Elite Remus," Tarah greeted, standing and bowing. Noticing the nurses and orderlies in the room, Kailynn also stood and bowed her head. Remus' expression caused panic to rattle Kailynn's bones.

"*You...*" he breathed.

"My apologies, Elite Remus," Tarah said quickly. "I know how bad this looks, but I called her for *me*. She's here with me."

Remus looked between the two before casting a careful eye around the room. It was clear he understood that he needed to protect Isa, despite how much his rage was blinding him at realizing Kailynn's visit to the Golden Elite.

"I see," he murmured. He turned to Kailynn. "And your name?"

"...Jacyleen, sir," she whispered, unable to keep the trembling out of her voice.

"Jacyleen," he repeated. "I'm sure you understand the delicate nature of this situation," he started. "Therefore, your extreme discretion is requested."

"Of course, sir."

"Good."

Remus took a seat across from the two woman, crossing his arms over his chest and fixing them both with a purposeful look.

Ten tense minutes passed before Rayal also entered the room. He immediately went to Tarah as she stood, relieved to see the former caretaker.

Even as he hugged Tarah, he glanced at Kailynn, his eyes sharp.

"Any word, yet?"

"None," Tarah said, backing out of the hug and shaking her head. She looked between Rayal and Kailynn, her eyes barely glancing at Remus as well. "Uh, this is the Significant I told you I was calling," she said, motioning to Kailynn.

"Right, of course," Rayal said, his tone slightly clipped. "It was good of you to accompany Tarah here, but I will take care of her now. You may go."

Kailynn stared at Rayal in horror. While she knew it was very dangerous to have her there, everyone already knew she had come in with the Golden Elite and had been with her at the time of the assassination attempt. Since everyone already knew, Kailynn figured she might as well stay until there was news on Isa.

"I am concerned about Elite Isa," Kailynn said carefully.

"I understand, and I thank you for your concern," Rayal said, trying to keep his tone even. "But this is not a matter in which Significants should be party," he continued. "The other Elites will be here soon. She will be well cared for. You should leave."

Kailynn's stomach flipped for the umpteenth time that evening. All of the Syndicate Elites were coming to the hospital.

She felt like all eyes in the hospital were on her, waiting to see her reaction, ready to jump on her and arrest her when they realized she had been with the Golden Elite.

"I…"

Kailynn could not bring herself to leave. She continued to think about Isa writhing in the chair, the way the blood trickled down her face, her still, dead countenance as she was wheeled away by the EMU. She did not know how she was expected to leave when they did not yet know Isa's condition.

Remus sighed heavily.

"There's no point in forcing her to leave," he said. Rayal turned to the Silver Elite, surprised. Remus shared a knowing look with him. "It's already too late. The damage is done." Remus leaned back in his chair, shaking his head. "Let her stay."

Kailynn could only stare at the Silver Elite in shock. She had not expected the Silver Elite to come to her aid and allow her to stay.

"Thank you, Elite Remus," she whispered.

The Silver Elite did not acknowledge that she had spoken.

Rayal turned back to Tarah.

"Are you alright?"

She shook her head. "No, not really…"

"Isa's very strong," Rayal assured. "This is not the first time she's had an attempt on her life."

"It's the first one I've ever seen…" Tarah choked.

"This is the second time Isa has dealt with this sort of attack," Remus reminded both of them. "She came out of a Pulse within a week last time."

"But that was before…" Tarah trailed off, her eyes welling with tears. "She's much weaker now. What if—"

"She may not be as strong, but that does not mean she is weak," Rayal interrupted. "She will be fine. She has the best Elite Specialist with her now. Dr. Busen has treated every injury Isa has ever had. He knows what to do."

Rayal wrapped his arms around Tarah once more and held her tightly.

He stood for several long minutes, holding Tarah as she cried into his chest. She was terrified and tired. She had never been witness to an assassination attempt before, and the terror and stress of the situation was proving to be too much for the seventeen-year-old caretaker.

When Tarah finally sat down, Rayal sat between her and Kailynn, one arm wrapped around Tarah's shoulders.

He turned to Kailynn.

"How are you holding up?"

"Not great," she admitted truthfully.

"Trust me, it will take much more than a basic Pulse Virus to take Isa down," Rayal assured. "She'll be alright."

"But…after she's recovered…" Kailynn decided that the hospital waiting room was not the place to discuss her concerns. Isa was fighting for her life, and Kailynn was worried about what would happen to her after the leaked news that a Significant had been with the Golden Elite during the assassination attempt. She had to make sure that Isa was alright. After that, she could worry about her own situation.

Rayal turned to Remus and the Silver Elite lowered his gaze.

"This is not the first time," he said. When Kailynn turned to him, he looked at her seriously. "For *any* of this. We've dealt with these situations before. And we will do so again," he said. "We will do everything we can to protect Isa."

Kailynn stared at the Silver Elite. As he looked at Kailynn, she could see the depth of his worry. She did not know if the Silver Elite was worried about Isa's health, or the repercussions and rumors that were sure to start, but there was concern in his eyes. Kailynn was about to ask if she could speak to the Silver Elite in private when another person was brought to the waiting room, capturing everyone's attention.

"Anders," Remus greeted, walking to the other Elite.

It was clear that all the Elites were built to be perfect. Even Anders, who was older than Remus and Isa—and currently the oldest Elite in the Syndicate—had stunning features. His dark brown hair was starting to grey at the temples and his dark brown eyes were set into an angular, sharp face. He was tall and well-built with broad shoulders. Kailynn felt herself become nervous once again. She was sure that, by the end of the evening, every Elite in the Syndicate would know the truth about her relations with Isa.

"Everyone is in a panic. There have already been calls asking if she's been killed."

"Dr. Busen is with her," Remus said. "It was a Pulse Virus. She'll be alright."

"How the hell could someone Pulse her private NCB chair?" Anders hissed. "That one has tighter security than the one at the Syndicate."

"I'm not sure," Remus admitted. "Therefore, until we know for sure, all NCB chairs are to be operated in safe-mode. If they got to that chair, then there is no doubt they can get to everyone at the Syndicate. We'll cancel all Opium meetings. We'll run investigations, have her personal chair dismantled, bring in a new one and tighten security."

"Understood," Anders said. "I called Maki and Chronus on the way here. They're already programing traces. The chair must have been in Opium, so we'll have to trace all transmissions and try to locate the one it came in on."

It was only minutes later that two other Elites joined them. At this point, there were guards lining the room. With all the Elites in one place, and the fact that the Golden Elite had been attacked that night, there was a greater need for security. Both live guards and automated ones stood silently around the room as more Elites arrived.

It took over an hour before all thirteen Bronze Elites had joined Remus and the others in the waiting room. Most waited in silence. Kailynn spared glances at them between long periods of keeping her head down. She noticed that, while all the Elites had different hair color and eye color, they all looked about the same. Their skin tone was the same, and their facial structure, even between the men and women, was similar. Their eyes were identical, just different colors, like they had all come out of the exact same mold.

Whenever she looked up, she noticed that one of them, the Elite that had been called Maki, was staring at her. There was something about him that set him apart from the other Elites. His hair was jet-black and his eyes were brown, but they had a lighter hazel color around the pupil. He seemed to look right through her, seeing the secret between her and Isa without inquiring Kailynn's identity.

When she had made eye contact with him for the seventh time that night, he smiled and turned to Remus.

"*This is an interesting turn of events,*" he said in another language. The different language caught the attention of all the Elites. Remus turned to Maki, his face controlled. He had tried to ignore the way Maki was staring at Kailynn. He had known that Maki would be the first to figure it out.

"*What?*"

"*The Significant,*" Maki said. "*I thought she was for Tarah, at first. But, it's very clear to me she's here for Isa.*"

The other Elites glanced at Kailynn and the Significant knew immediately she was the subject of their conversation.

"*Is this true, Remus?*" Anders pressed, his eyes wide with surprise.

"*Venus approved her to meet with a Significant,*" Remus murmured.

"*I thought that was a month ago,*" Chronus said. "*Why is she here now?*"

Remus turned away.

He did not need to say more for the other Elites to understand immediately. Once more, they turned back to the Significant, looking her over. Kailynn shifted uncomfortably in her seat. She considered leaving to avoid the awkward confrontation happening in the waiting room. However, she could not leave without knowing that Isa was alright.

Therefore, she took a deep breath and sat confidently in her chair, lifting her head to look at the Elites. They already knew, clearly. It was time to act like she belonged there.

Tarah fell asleep on Rayal's shoulder as the night progressed. Several Elites took short, five-minute naps. A few of them took phone calls, reaching to their ears to activate their implanted earpieces and walking away from the group, talking quietly.

Remus was the only one who did not sleep or take calls. He remained in his chair, transferring all calls he received to Anders and Maki, who answered them without complaint. They knew that the Silver Elite was very worried about Isa. Even knowing that Isa was very strong and had survived multiple attempts on her life, there was an underlying worry that this was the one that would finally take the Golden Elite down.

When seven hours had passed and Kailynn was falling asleep in her chair, a doctor walked into the waiting room. Rayal spotted him immediately and straightened, grabbing the attention of Remus, who turned.

As Rayal woke Tarah, the Elites stood to surround the doctor that Kailynn recognized.

"Dr. Busen," Remus greeted.

"Remus," he said with a small smile. "She's stable. She'll be fine."

The Elites relaxed and let out relieved chuckles.

"How bad was it?" Remus asked.

"Well," Dr. Busen started, sighing and shaking his head, "I don't feel comfortable letting her leave without surveillance. Her body is not in optimal condition, and I worry that she's declining again."

"Why do you think that?" Maki asked worriedly.

"Her heartbeat is irregular, and her brain activity is…concerning."

"Then it's getting worse?" Remus asked knowingly.

"That's to be expected," Dr. Busen said, his eyes dropping to the ground. "She is prone to illness and deterioration now. That's part of reconstruction. She needs to be on boosters again, and I'll prescribe her some other medication while she's recovering from this. We don't need any more infections setting in."

"She's been overworked. I'm sure her immune system is weak."

"That is not news to me," Dr. Busen chuckled. "I will submit my report to Venus and strongly recommend that she remain *out* of the NCB chair until at least two follow-up appointments." The doctor hesitated. "Until her strength returns, she cannot handle any more risk. She's in delicate condition for the next several days."

"You're going to have to keep her here, then," Remus said strongly. "You know that we can't monitor her properly anywhere else. She needs to be here."

"I agree," Dr. Busen said. "But I need your approval and a ruling majority from the Syndicate to keep her."

"You have my approval," Remus assured.

"And I don't think anyone here is opposed to her being here to recuperate," Chronus said, glancing at the other Bronze Elites. When they all shook their heads, Dr. Busen nodded.

"Good. We'll be sure to keep her quiet and be sure that she follows treatment until she is out of this delicate stage."

"Is there anything that can be done to make her stronger?" Anders asked worriedly. "I understand that what happened five years ago was horrible, but there has to be something you can do to strengthen her body again."

"I'm afraid Elites don't heal the same as humans. Her brain was altered completely from the accident. It doesn't function as it did before and, therefore, there are a lot of signals that are getting lost between her brain and her body, including healing responses. The best we can do is keep an eye on her, and try to translate what we can."

"May we see her?"

"Of course," Dr. Busen said. "But…before I take you there," he glanced at Kailynn, "there is something that needs to be addressed." He lifted a finger and motioned to Kailynn. The Elites turned to the Significant, causing the younger woman to freeze temporarily. However, she forced her feet forward. She stood in front of the doctor, who reached a hand to her face. She backpedaled, confused, but Rayal placed a hand on her back and forced her to stay still.

When Dr. Busen reached for her right ear, another fear gripped Kailynn. He was looking for her PIM chip, which she did not have as a Trid. Dr. Busen's fingers pressed into the skin behind her earlobe and his eyes met hers.

For two tense seconds, they stared at one another.

Dr. Busen smiled and reached for his pocket, pulling out the pen that read PIM chips. He pressed it to her skin, staring at her purposefully. She waited, her heart choking her as it sat in her throat. He pressed a button and it beeped loudly. He pulled it away from her skin and glanced at the small screen.

"Excellent," he murmured. "Follow me."

The entourage that had been waiting for news on the Golden Elite followed Dr. Busen to the elevator and took it to the next floor, walking through the quiet, deserted hallways to one of the larger rooms. Dr. Busen stepped to the side of the door and motioned everyone in. As Kailynn started into the room, the doctor grabbed her arm and pulled her back, allowing the Elites in and then the caretakers before pressing the button to close the door.

Kailynn watched as the doctor turned to her slowly, smiling.

"Don't worry," he assured. "I won't report you."

Kailynn remained silent.

"I'm not an idiot," he said. "I know full well why you were at Anon Tower, and who you were there with."

Kailynn's head dropped and her eyes focused on the ground, her body shaking nervously.

"I want you to know that I have one of the most difficult jobs on the planet," Dr. Busen said. "I have been charged to care for the health of one of the worst patients in history. However, it is my responsibility to watch out for her, and I take that duty very seriously. I cannot tend to her every need, though. And, even working together, her other Specialist and I cannot care for her in every moment. Therefore, I am not surprised to find that someone like you has entered her life."

Kailynn was surprised at the warm tone in his voice.

"Please take good care of her," Dr. Busen murmured. "Isa needs all the support she can get. If you are willing to risk both of your lives, then be sure that you are fully invested in being with her. She has seen enough pain in her life. Don't cause her more."

"…I won't," Kailynn promised, her voice soft.

"And, just one more thing," Dr. Busen said with a nervous chuckle. "I know you get tested at Companion." She nodded slowly. "You're clean, yes?"

"Yes."

"Good." Dr. Busen nodded. "I have to ask. I'm her doctor."

He pressed the button to open the door and motioned for the Significant to enter. Kailynn glanced at the doctor and smiled weakly.

"Thank you."

She walked into the room, but did not get far before her eyes settled on Isa and she had to stop and lock her legs to keep from collapsing.

Isa looked worse than she had when convulsing in the chair. Her face was pale and chalky. There were wires and needles poking into her skin. The light of the room made her look sickly and thin. The Elites were gathered around her but they did not seem as nervous about her condition as Kailynn.

All eyes turned on the Significant. Chronus, Anders and two other Elites—Ainee and Kyrin—stepped aside to allow the Significant through. Kailynn stepped forward, trying to keep her legs strong as she approached the bed. Remus and Rayal were standing beside the Elite, while Tarah was in a chair, holding the Elite's hand, her eyes swollen with frightened tears.

Kailynn walked to Tarah's side, looking over the Elite and swallowing hard to keep her own tears at bay. She was acutely aware of all the eyes on her, but she still could not think past Isa's condition. She stood next to Tarah, placing a hand on the caretaker's shoulder in a small gesture of comfort.

The world narrowed. The only thing Kailynn could see was Isa's ill countenance.

"The hospital always makes everyone look worse," Rayal murmured. "She will be alright."

Kailynn only nodded. She could not bring herself to speak.

She was not sure how long the room remained silent, but when Chronus spoke, she nearly jumped out of her skin.

"What do you want to do, Remus?" Chronus asked.

"How far has the information spread?" Remus asked, turning to Rayal. The former caretaker shook his head.

"I'm afraid I don't know," he admitted. "It was processed through the EMU network. It's probably planet-wide by now."

"Venus has not spoken," another Elite, Hana, murmured. "If she knew she would have said something."

"Not necessarily," Remus whispered. "She's probably processing everyone's reaction. For now, we continue with the original story." Remus turned to look among the Bronze Elites. "The Significant was there for Tarah. No laws were broken. Is that understood?"

"Yes, sir."

"Security is our highest priority. We will direct all questions and conferences to the security breach that happened to get the virus in her chair. I want everyone working in safe-mode, all Opium meetings cancelled, and all speculation that this was the Ninth Circle shot down. We do not know that they were behind this."

"No, but can you think of anyone else that would do this?" Anders challenged.

"No, but until we can confirm it, we don't need the entire Alliance in an uproar. That will lead to war."

"And what of Isa's condition?" Maki asked. "The people will want to know, but others could see it as a sign of weakness and take the opportunity to attack."

"We will just say that she survived an assassination attempt. For safety reasons, she is in hiding. No more details need to be given until she is well again."

"Understood," Maki said with a nod. He turned to the other Elites. "You heard the man, we're on damage control. Hana and Kyrin, you start on security for the NCB chairs. Run every scan possible on the Syndicate Building and get a diagnosis of our security. Chronus, you and I can go to Anon Tower and deal with Isa's chair."

The Elites turned to leave the room, knowing they had to pick up all the work for the Silver and Golden Elites. They did not question it. They knew that it was the Golden Elite's job to take care of the planet, and the Silver Elite's job to take care of the Golden Elite. When the Golden Elite was unwell, the Silver Elite took charge while remaining at the Golden Elite's side. It was part of the framework for the Syndicate.

Maki walked to Remus and put a hand on his shoulder.

"Call me if you need anything."

"Thank you, Maki."

The Bronze Elites filed out of the room, leaving Remus, Rayal, Tarah, and Kailynn with the unconscious Golden Elite.

Kailynn felt even more intimidated. Now, Remus, who Rayal had warned was the most protective of Isa, was staring at the Significant darkly.

"Kailynn," he started. She closed her eyes before turning to him, trying to put up a brave front. "It would be best if you went back to Companion."

"I can't just leave her," Kailynn said strongly.

"It is in everyone's best interest if you leave," Remus said. "This is a very dangerous situation, and you do not know most of it."

"I know that my life is in danger just by being here," Kailynn growled. "I know enough."

"No, you don't," Remus corrected sharply. "There is no doubt in my mind that this attempt on Isa's life was from Gihron. And now the news is likely widespread about a Significant in the home of the Golden Elite. That puts a target on your head."

"Rayal told me that they could take me as a way to get to Isa."

"You have no idea of what they are capable," Remus hissed. "They have done much worse in the past. Isa is not strong enough to handle something of that magnitude."

"I don't see how that is your call to make," Kailynn said. "I don't know how bad her health is, true. But she seems happier when I'm around, and I think that says a lot."

"You're a fool," Remus whispered. "Isa is the Golden Elite of Tiao, and you are a non-citizen Trid with forged papers working as a Significant. Even if we keep this information from Gihron, the others in the Alliance will see this as a weak point in the Syndicate. They will think that Venus is no longer capable of running Tiao, and the other planets in the system will destroy us."

"Isa is strong enough to handle the other planets," Kailynn snapped. "You've all said that she is the best Elite the planet has seen, and you *know* she is damn good at her job. If the other planets doubt Venus, that's one thing, but I don't think anyone would doubt Isa. In fact, if it was discovered that Isa was rebelling against Venus, but was still able to maintain perfect control over Tiao and the Syndicate, then the people will rally behind her as a strong leader."

"That is not the way this works!" Remus said, exasperated. "You have absolutely no concept of politics, so do not pretend that you know how this will play out." The Silver Elite took a deep breath. "Go back to Companion. Keep quiet about what has happened, and do not seek out Isa again. You will only bring harm to her."

Kailynn crossed her arms over her chest.

"Tell me something, Elite Remus," she said, her voice dark and cold. "How much of this is about your jealousy?"

Rayal and Tarah's eyes went wide.

"Jealousy?" Remus barked a laugh. "You may have helped Isa feel better, and you may even share her bed on occasion," he started, stalking forward and looming over Kailynn, "but you will *never* understand her."

Kailynn continued staring defiantly at Remus

"Then this *is* about jealousy." She glanced at Isa. "I don't claim to know anything about her. It's true, you know her better. But when she needed someone, *I* was the one she turned to, not you. And that makes your blood boil, doesn't it?"

Remus' jaw clenched. Rayal started forward, though he was not sure he should get between the two. He knew that this confrontation would have to happen eventually.

"I don't know everything that has happened to her," Kailynn continued. "And that is why I don't treat her like she's fragile. You said it yourself, she has survived worse things than this one attempt on her life. You know what she went through when she was in the hospital for all that time, and I'm sure you can see how strong she is now, even after all that. So why do you treat her like she'll break if the wind blows?"

Remus' eyes changed and the look confused Kailynn.

"Until you have seen the strongest person you ever knew waste away in front of you, and you are forced to realize that *you* were the reason, do not judge my actions regarding Isa."

Rayal walked over to Kailynn and put a hand on her shoulder, slowly pulling her away from Remus.

"That's enough," he whispered. "This is not the time or place."

"What happened to her?" Kailynn asked. "What happened to her that put her in the hospital five years ago?"

Remus' expression hardened.

"Gihron happened," he said darkly.

Kailynn looked at the various faces in the room, understanding that everyone was not entirely worried about Kailynn's proximity to Isa. They remembered what happened to Isa when Gihron was last active, and they did not want to see Isa go through the same hell she had endured before.

"Kailynn," Rayal said, standing between her and Remus, "Isa will be in the hospital for a while so the doctors can be sure she follows her treatment. During that time, she is going to need to stay quiet." He squeezed her shoulder. "When she is out of the hospital, I'm sure she'll call you and let you know that she's alright. Until then, it would be best for you to go back to Companion and let the rumors about a Significant in the Golden Elite's home die."

Kailynn did not want to leave Isa's side, but she understood that it really was for the best. It would save both of them, as well as the rest of the Syndicate, stress.

"Alright," she agreed quietly.

"Thank you," Rayal said, relaxing. "I will call you if anything changes, alright? Do you have a phone?"

"No."

"I'll reach you at Companion, then," Rayal said. "I'll take you there now, okay?"

Kailynn spared another glance at the faces in the room, her eyes finally settling on Isa. Her eyes still locked on the Elite, she nodded.

Chapter Nineteen

When Isa started to wake, she felt several sets of eyes on her. She could also feel the horrendous strain on her ribs as her breathing became heavier, fighting the pain of her body as she was brought back to consciousness.

Her eyes blinked open weakly. She saw a blurry finger move in front of her.

"Isa, focus on my finger," Dr. Busen said, standing over the Golden Elite.

"I...I should pay you...for every time you have...had to say that," Isa chuckled breathlessly.

"Or maybe I should pay you for all the months I *don't* have to say it," Dr. Busen chuckled, moving his finger away. "Maybe that will give you some incentive to stay out of the hospital."

"But it's my second home..." Isa teased with a weak smile.

"How are you feeling, Isa?" Remus asked on her other side.

"I've felt worse."

Remus let out a sigh, picking up Isa's hand.

"You can't keep doing this to me," he said with a wary laugh. "One of these days I will have a heart attack and end up here in the room next to you."

"Do you remember what happened?" Rayal asked.

Isa sighed, cringing as she tried to move. She tried to straighten, but her body protested the movement.

"Just stay quiet," Dr. Busen murmured, placing a gentle hand on Isa's shoulder and pushing her back to the bed. The Golden Elite gave a defeated sigh.

"I can't remember..."

"That's alright," Rayal assured.

Isa's eyes traveled to the quiet young woman standing near the corner of the bed, one arm crossed in front of her chest and her other hand to her mouth as she bit her nails, trying to remain composed.

"Tarah," Isa whispered, reaching out a hand. Tarah walked to the Elite, trying to keep her tears at bay. "I'm alright."

Tarah nodded tightly, swallowing hard. Isa smiled gently and took her hand from Remus to reach out for the caretaker. Tarah took the hand.

"I'm sorry I scared you," Isa murmured.

"Isa," Dr. Busen started, "we're going to keep you here for a few days to continue proper treatment."

"I was afraid you were going to say that," Isa breathed. "I can't, Dr. Busen." She shook her head. "This is no time to have me silent in the Syndicate."

"This is the best time to have you silent," Remus contradicted. "Rumors will happen no matter what, but this was an attempt on your life, and we do not need anyone else trying to kill you while you're weak."

"I won't work in the NCB," Isa assured. "I'll keep all contact through—"

"That won't stop anyone if they truly want to kill you," Rayal interjected. "There have been plenty of attempts on your life from people you've met in person."

"There is less of a chance of them succeeding in person."

"Isa," Dr. Busen called her attention, "I agree that we don't need to put you in any further danger of assassination. The hospital is a protected site. Any attack will result in immediate punishment. They won't risk it. We'll have guards here and we'll keep you safe. If there is a pressing matter, we can bring a terminal to the room and you can use that." Dr. Busen lifted his finger to keep the Golden Elite from speaking. "And," he continued, "this is to be sure you actually stick to treatment. I know you, Isa. Everyone else here may be willing to let you talk them out of enforcing your treatment, but not me."

Isa smiled tiredly.

"I'd rather go home."

"I know," Dr. Busen said. "But this is very important." He sighed heavily. "You're not as strong as before, Isa. We must keep a very close eye on you."

Isa nodded slowly.

"I understand."

"There is something else that I would like to discuss with you," he said, his gaze purposeful. "It's a private matter."

Rayal turned to Tarah, who was still holding Isa's hand tightly.

"I'll take you home."

"I want to stay..." she protested tiredly.

"Tarah," Isa said with a smile and a gentle squeeze of the younger woman's hand, "I'm alright, really. Once Dr. Busen is finished speaking with me, I'm going to get some sleep. You should go home and rest. I know I frightened you, but I am alright. You can come see me at any time. I don't think I'm going anywhere."

Tarah wanted to protest, however, Rayal pulled her shoulders carefully, causing her to step back and her hand to leave Isa's. She managed to utter a choked, "yes, Miss" as she left the room, Rayal bowing his head to the Elites as he walked out. Remus began to leave, but Dr. Busen shook his head, telling the Silver Elite to stay.

When the door closed behind the two caretakers, Dr. Busen sighed heavily and crossed his arms over his chest.

"I was afraid this would happen when Venus approved for you to have a Significant," he mused.

Isa hesitated before speaking.

"I have it under control," she murmured.

"You may have," Dr. Busen agreed. "However, she was identified while in the EMU. It's been leaked that you had a Significant in your home."

"Where is she now?" Isa asked worriedly, starting to sit upright.

"She's fine. She's safe," Dr. Busen assured as Remus gently pushed Isa back to the bed. "We sent her back to Companion. Tarah took the initiative and played like she was the one who called for a Significant. We're trying to make sure that that is the only rumor that spreads."

"Unfortunately, as we have already heard, that is causing some to believe that the Significant is the one who made an attempt on your life," Remus added. "Some believe that she responded to Tarah's call to get close enough to you to kill you."

"She has a name," Isa said sharply. "Call her Kailynn."

"We can't even call her that," Remus said darkly. "Since she has been using a fake name as a non-citizen."

"Isa, this is a very delicate situation," Dr. Busen agreed, his tone even.

"Are you telling me to push her away?" Isa asked, her voice cold.

"I know that, even if I did, you would not listen," Dr. Busen said. "So, no, I am not telling you not to see her."

"Michael—" Remus started, surprised.

"There was a reason we all agreed time with a Significant was the best course of action," Dr. Busen said, interrupting the Silver Elite. "Granted, we did not expect this to take a sexual turn."

"What makes you think it has?" she challenged.

"Past experience," Dr. Busen said, looking between the two Elites in the room. "My point is, if you do plan to continue seeing her, security measures will have to be taken."

"Such as?"

"Such as getting her a PIM chip," the doctor said. "Preferably one similar to yours."

"An emitter?" Isa said. "You'll need her consent, which I doubt she'll give."

"The reason the emitter chip was invented was because of what happened five years ago. After what happened to Remus and Rayal and the Bronze Elites, Venus ordered everyone close to you have an emitter chip. With Gihron involved, we cannot be sure that the same thing will not happen again with Kailynn."

"He's right, Isa," Remus seconded. "If you insist on having Kailynn near you, this is necessary to protect her life."

Isa closed her eyes and took several deep breaths.

"It's not my decision to make. It is hers."

"It is actually yours," Dr. Busen corrected. "If you want to keep her close, if you insist on this relationship, then it is mandated by Venus that she have an emitter."

"Venus does not know about her."

"How can you be opposed to this?" Dr. Busen hissed. "After everything Colonel Amori did to Remus and Rayal? After all the pain he put you through? And all the pain *we* had to endure watching you fall apart?"

"Michael, you *promised*..." Isa said, her eyes closing again as her voice broke in pain. "You promised me you would never bring that up again."

"You know this is a real threat," Remus pressed.

"Do you really want to put Kailynn through what Remus went through?" Dr. Busen asked. "Measures have to be taken for her safety, and for yours."

Isa's face creased in pain and her arms wrapped around her abdomen as she turned on her side.

"Isa, breathe..." Remus said, crouching by her side and taking her hands, pulling them away from her body. "Count your breathing."

"Don't patronize me!" she snapped, pulling her hands sharply from his grasp. She did not open her eyes. "Do you really believe that the thought hasn't crossed my mind every damn day since I met her?

Why do you think I'm…" Isa trailed off, swallowing hard. She shook her head.

"What, Isa?" Dr. Busen pressed. "Why are you shaking your head?"

Isa shook her head again, clenching her jaw tight.

Dr. Busen shared a worried look with Remus and sighed heavily. He grabbed Isa's shoulder, pulling her onto her back.

"Okay, I apologize," Dr. Busen murmured. "I should not have pushed you."

"Stop treating me like I'm made of glass!" she barked.

"Alright, I'm sorry," Dr. Busen said, raising his hands peacefully. "You've just survived an assassination attempt. You need to rest. That was all I meant." He took a deep breath. "But, I'm going to call Paul."

Isa groaned and let her head fall back on the pillow.

"No, don't bother him."

"Bother him?" Remus said, surprised. "Isa, his job is to watch out for you. It's not a bother."

"It's too early in the morning," Isa said, nodding to the clock on the other side of the room. Dr. Busen glanced at it as well.

"He's already awake," he said. "He wakes up earlier than this."

Isa's eyes remained closed.

"I want to sleep," she murmured. "I'm tired."

Both Dr. Busen and Remus shared an exasperated and frustrated look before nodding. Remus squeezed her hand.

"I'll be right here," he said.

The two men waited in the room until Isa was asleep. Dr. Busen continued to watch the monitors and screens, making a few minor adjustments when needed.

When Remus leaned back in the chair he occupied, his hand slowly leaving Isa's, Dr. Busen nodded to the door and they both stepped outside, waiting for the door to Isa's room to close before they spoke.

"It's good to know her stubbornness is still intact," Dr. Busen tried to joke. Remus barked a laugh.

"She's been stubborn her entire life. Nothing will ever change that."

Dr. Busen nodded, his eyes dropping to the floor briefly.

"This is a very dangerous situation," he whispered. "And, I never thought I'd say this, but Venus is the least of their concerns."

"I know," Remus agreed. "I will talk to Rayal. Perhaps he can discuss safety precautions with Kailynn and get her to agree to an emitter chip. I don't think we'll be able to keep Isa away from her."

"I'm going to call Paul," Dr. Busen said. "I don't want her working herself up like that again."

"That reaction surprised me," Remus murmured. "It means she's been thinking about this for quite some time. She's already starting on the spiral that led to what happened five years ago."

"I know," Dr. Busen breathed. "I don't want you to worry, Remus. We'll keep a very close eye on her. And, if we can get Kailynn to be proactive about her own safety in this manner, it will help Isa immensely." Dr. Busen hesitated. "Speaking of which," he started slowly, "this cannot be easy for you, Remus."

"What?"

"Everything," the doctor said. "You were horribly affected by Colonel Amori as well."

"I did not have to go through anything like what she endured," Remus whispered. "And, if you'll remember, I had over a year of weekly sessions with Paul."

"Yes, I do recall," Dr. Busen said. "But now you are having to deal with Isa turning to someone else."

Remus' eyes dropped to the ground.

"This must pain you greatly," Dr. Busen whispered.

"You are confusing me with a human, Michael."

"Forgive me," Dr. Busen said with a knowing smile. "I do forget that I am speaking with an Elite on occasion, since you do not act like a typical Elite. But, then again, you never have."

Remus glanced at the doctor.

"I better call Rayal and talk to him before Isa wakes," he said carefully. "I do not want to leave her for long."

He began to turn when the doctor stopped him.

"Remus," he called, "please impress upon Rayal the severity of the safety concerns with Gihron. We do not understand how they operate."

Remus was silent and still for a few moments before he turned fully and walked back to the doctor.

"When we were at the Academy, and learning about all the planets *not* in the Crescent Alliance, our professors told us that there were two currencies on Gihron—pride and blood. If Gihron pride is hurt, blood will spill. If Gihron blood is spilt, pride will lead to revenge." Remus glanced at the door to Isa's room. "There is no doubt in my mind that Gihron will exact revenge on Isa. Because that is the way they operate."

■■■

Kailynn could do nothing but pace around her room for hours after she returned to Companion. Her mind was frantic. She continued to scold herself, telling herself that she had no idea what she was getting into and there was far more to everyone's actions than she could ever understand.

When her legs were tired, she sat on her bed and found herself asleep almost instantly. She was exhausted, the stress of the night before wearing down her last threads of energy.

She woke near dinner time and decided to venture downstairs to grab something to ease the tight knot in her stomach. When she entered the almost-silent dining hall, the silence became deafening. Everyone turned to her, stopping their quiet conversations or looking up from their tablets. Kailynn was frozen in the doorway, scanning the eyes in the room.

Her heart began pounding. She was sure that everyone knew of the attempt on Isa's life, and it was possible that everyone knew she was in the Elite's home when the attack occurred. But the way they were looking at her made her feel as though they already knew about her relationship with Isa.

She held her head high and walked toward the rations counter, ignoring the whispering that started around her.

When she reached the counter, she looked over the packages, trying to think enough to pick something to eat.

However, a voice startled her.

"Jacyleen."

She turned.

"We're curious about something," Amyn said, smiling darkly, surrounded by her friends. "Why was a fresh-out-of-the-ghetto girl like *you* in the Golden Elite's home when she was attacked?"

"I was there on a job," Kailynn said, her voice dark and strong in an attempt to scare off the other Significants.

"A job, huh?" Brett said, his tone disbelieving. "You weren't booked for anything last night."

"It was a private request," Kailynn growled, "in an attempt to avoid *this* kind of speculation. I was there with Tarah, the caretaker."

"Seems a little suspicious, don't you think?"

Kailynn's heart was starting to climb into her throat again.

"Perhaps, she *wasn't* there with the caretaker," Jyun said, his eyes sharp on her. "Perhaps, you were the reason our Golden Elite was attacked."

Kailynn's eyes shot wide.

"Are you *accusing* me?"

"Hey!" a deep voice said, walking to them. Kailynn turned to Jak, relieved to see him, but also ready to start a fist fight in the dining hall. "What's all this about?"

"Jak, Jacyleen is trying to tell us that she was booked with Golden Elite's caretaker last night."

"She was," Jak said simply. "Because the appointment was in Anon Tower, it was kept off-record for security reasons." He took Kailynn's arm as he glared at the others in the room. "Remember your place."

He pulled Kailynn from the room. Even though he had lied for her, Kailynn could not help but be worried. She thought that no one would pay too much attention to the information that she had been in the Golden Elite's home when the assassination attempt occurred if she said she was there for Tarah, but it only raised more suspicion.

Jak pulled her through the halls of Companion to his office, closing the door and locking it behind them.

"Jak—"

"Quiet," he snapped. "You have put everyone in danger."

"I didn't mean to!"

"What were you doing there?" Jak growled, walking around his desk and grabbing a pack of cigarettes. "Are you *insane*? It was dangerous enough to have you over there when Venus and the Silver Elite were on board. Now you're going over there whenever you fucking please?!"

"No!" Kailynn protested. "Jak, it's not like that."

"You did not check in the night before last, so you were out all night. The next time I hear from you, you are being brought back by the head of Syndicate Intelligence after an assassination attempt on the Golden Elite. What the hell were you doing there?"

"Look," Kailynn said, raising her hands peacefully, though she kept her eyes averted, letting her exhaustion show in an attempt to disguise her lie, "I went and saw my brother," she said. "He was doing better, but it's still difficult to see him like this. So I went to get some air. I was walking around when I got a call from Tarah, the caretaker."

"You shouldn't be walking around," Jak said, rolling his eyes. "It raises suspicion."

"The point is, I went to spend some time with Tarah. She was so good to me when I was staying there that I felt like it would be nice to spend some time with her. We were having dinner when Elite Isa was attacked. I was in the wrong place at the wrong time."

Jak looked her over, unconvinced.

"For your sake, I hope you're telling the truth."

He lit his cigarette and shook his head.

"Somehow, running this company has become more difficult since I acquired you," he murmured. He grabbed a box on his desk and extended it to her. "Here."

"What is it?"

"A package addressed to you," he said, shrugging. "There is no name on it other than yours."

Kailynn carefully took the light, small package.

"It might be best if you stay clear of the others for a while," Jak advised. "I'm going to clear your schedule until this blows over."

Kailynn merely nodded.

"You may go."

Kailynn returned to her room, her hunger forgotten. She opened the package and was surprised to see a phone. She stared at it for several long moments, sure that the phone without a message could only mean something ominous. She picked it up carefully, trying to tell herself that there was no reason to be afraid of something as trivial as a phone, but she was in such a high state of anxiety, she could not help but worry.

She pressed the button on the phone's screen she knew to be the power button and then tried to think of all the times she had seen nobles and Isa use their phones to see if she could figure out how to make it work.

Pressing a mechanism on the side released the tiny disk that acted as the ear piece. With the disk in her hand, the screen lit up with a message.

Call?

Below the question was a name. She kicked herself again for being unable to read. She could not even make out the name on the screen.

Hesitantly, she hit the green button and placed the disk in her ear. A monotone beeping sounded as she struggled to put the earpiece in correctly. A voice came through the phone before she could figure it out and she had to contend with holding the disk as close to her ear as possible.

"Rayal Teleta."

"Rayal?" Kailynn repeated. "It's, uh, it's Kailynn."

"I see you received the phone I sent."

"*You?*"

"Yes," Rayal responded. "I figured it best that we have a way to reach you directly."

"I don't know how this works," Kailynn admitted, pressing the disk into her ear. Rayal chuckled lightly.

"You get used to the discomfort after awhile." He sighed heavily. "Kailynn, you and I need to discuss some things."

"I was worried you were going to say that."

"It's far too late now, and it has been a very trying day," he continued. "Tomorrow morning at ten, I will come by Companion and pick you up."

"…and go where?"

"My office," Rayal said. "You are not in immediate danger. There is no need to be suspicious."

"So you say," Kailynn muttered. "It feels like this is getting out of control."

"No, not yet," Rayal assured. "Everyone who knows is working very hard to keep this a secret. We're doing damage control on what happened last night. I understand that everyone has been warning you about the dangers, and they are right. But we are going to do our best to protect both of you. That is why it is imperative we speak tomorrow."

Kailynn was silent for several long moments.

"Okay," she finally whispered.

She slept in sporadic periods that night, waking up with night terrors of Officials banging down her door, there to kill her. The night terrors took their toll on her sleep, but she was too exhausted from the previous night that she managed to fall immediately back to sleep every time her dreams woke her.

When she did wake and dress for the day, she could only sit on her bed, fiddling with the phone and watching the time pass on her clock.

She did not want to go downstairs, worried that she would be confronted with glares and whispers of other Significants.

As the time drew close, she ventured downstairs, trying to keep her head high. She did not see anyone until she was in the greeting salon, where those who were open for walk-ins were sitting, dressed in their finest attire. Kailynn felt as though she had walked into a brothel, particularly with the glares of superiority she felt from the Significants waiting for clients.

Kailynn sat on an empty couch and waited for Rayal.

After several long moments, one male Significant spoke to the others in the room, raising his voice.

"Who do you think attacked Elite Isa?" he asked, his eyes briefly glancing at Kailynn with a small smile on his face. "I doubt security would be so lax around the leader of our planet."

"It does seem suspicious that there were more people in the home than customary," one woman agreed.

"And what a horrible time for the caretaker," another chimed in. "Could you imagine? Being blamed for not seeing there was a danger to the Golden Elite?"

Kailynn bit her tongue until she could taste blood.

"That caretaker is going to be put under investigation," another man said. "She'll probably get kicked out to Trid for such a failure." The door opened to the greeting salon. "If they don't kill her, I suppose."

"You clearly know nothing about the system of caretakers."

Everyone turned to the door, so immersed in the gossip that they had not seen the man walk into the greeting salon. Kailynn was relieved to see Rayal.

"Forgive us, sir, we did not see you come in," one woman said, walking to him, accenting the swing of her hips. She sidled up to him. "What can we do for you today?"

"You can get your hands off me," Rayal said, pushing her away and turning his eyes around the room. "Perhaps you do not realize that your trivial gossip is being heavily monitored by Syndicate Intelligence. I would be very mindful of what you say."

He looked at Kailynn and nodded once to her, turning to leave. She walked out with him, her eyes low but her head high.

Those left in the greeting salon let out chuckles of disbelief.

"Did she just get hauled away by Syndicate Intelligence?" one woman gasped, her eyes wide but filled with amusement.

"We won't be seeing her again," the man who had started the bullying said with a smile.

Rayal stood by the passenger's door to the car and waited for Kailynn. She climbed into the car and watched Rayal walk to the other side and get in with her, hitting several buttons on the screen before selecting a destination.

Kailynn watched silently, but when the car started the move, she looked at Rayal.

"How is she?"

Rayal gave her a small smile.

"She'll be alright," he answered. "She's tired and weak now, but that is to be expected. She woke up early this morning and was coherent. They're expecting a full recovery in the next few weeks."

Kailynn let out a relieved sigh, turning her eyes to her lap, where she continued to fiddle with the phone. She turned to Rayal.

"I can't figure out how to put the earpiece in," she said suddenly.

Rayal laughed.

"I'll show you."

He showed her the way the disk was supposed to fit in the ear and how to take it out and put it in. She tried to put it in her ear, but it was extremely uncomfortable and she quickly removed it.

"Is there any way to use this without the earpiece?"

"Afraid not," Rayal said. "That's why most have the earpiece implanted."

"That's disturbing," Kailynn groaned. "But Isa doesn't have an implanted one. I've seen her take it out."

"She used to have an implant," Rayal corrected.

"Used to?"

"They had to take it out after the accident, when they were reconstructing half of her face."

"Half of her face?"

"What did you expect when she falls through glass?" Rayal asked. "The entire left side of her face was destroyed. She can't have another implant now, because it has caused infections in the reconstructed part of her face three times."

Kailynn's eyes were wide.

"Did I shock you?"

"Yeah," Kailynn murmured. "I'm starting to understand why everyone is so afraid to talk about five years ago."

Rayal's eyes fell to the floor of the car. He did not care to tell Kailynn that it was far worse than anyone wanted to admit.

"How is Tarah?" Kailynn asked.

"Scared," Rayal said truthfully. "That was the first time she's seen an assassination attempt. She's understandably shaken."

"At least someone is," Kailynn grumbled. "I know everyone rushed to the hospital, but no one seemed really scared that someone had tried to kill the Golden Elite."

"Sadly, everyone is desensitized to it now," Rayal agreed. "There have now been eighteen plots on Isa's life, that we know of."

"*Eighteen*?" Kailynn gasped.

"She's had to deal with assassination attempts since she was seventeen. Even she is desensitized to it," Rayal elaborated. "So, while everyone knows that Isa can survive just about everything, there is an underlying concern that her luck will run out."

"Seventeen years old and someone tried to kill her?"

Rayal looked at Kailynn seriously. "When there's a brand new leader, and one that wishes to change the framework of the entire planet, people get nervous." Rayal leaned back in his seat and his eyes went distant. "The youngest Golden Elite to come into power in the history of the planet…"

Kailynn looked over Rayal's face.

"You love her, don't you?" she whispered.

Rayal nodded.

"I do," he said. "But do not worry," he chuckled turning to Kailynn, "it's not the same kind of love. I admire her greatly, and I would do anything to keep her safe."

Kailynn could not respond. She stared at the floor of the car as it slowed and pulled in front of the underground door for the Syndicate Intelligence Agency. Rayal got out of the car and Kailynn opened her door, looking over the plain door as she climbed out.

Rayal gently tapped the button on the front of the car and it pulled away to park in the garage below the building.

Rayal motioned to the door and walked Kailynn into the building.

The building was surprisingly noisy. Security footage and conversations picked up by Venus' microphones around the planet filled the air. There were several large rooms where monitors were being watched by various people as robots wheeled around and moved cases, taking them out of the room and bringing in new ones.

"Is it normally this busy?" Kailynn asked.

"No," Rayal said. "But there is great cause for concern currently." He led Kailynn through the halls until he reached an elevator. They both walked in and, when the doors closed, the noise abated, leaving them with only the humming of the elevator as it ascended.

Once they reached the desired floor, they both walked a short distance on the very quiet floor to Rayal's office.

Kailynn glanced around the large, mostly-bare office. Rayal had an NCB chair as well and then a separate desk with several monitors on it streaming different cameras in a very familiar home.

Rayal grabbed a chair and put it in front of his desk chair, motioning for Kailynn to sit. She sat slowly, looking over the main room and kitchen of Isa's home on the screen in front of her, imagining seeing herself running across the screen when the alarm sounded through the house two days previous.

Rayal took his seat and typed something, causing the computer monitors to go black.

He then turned to face Kailynn.

"There are a lot of things we need to discuss."

"Are you going to tell me to stay away from her?" Kailynn whispered.

"No, I'm not."

The answer surprised Kailynn.

Rayal rubbed his hands together, trying to think of how to begin.

"Dr. Busen and Dr. Arre have agreed that it would probably be best if you were to continue to see Isa," Rayal started. "I don't know what arrangement you two have, or the reason you went to see her again when you did, but her doctors agree that you two should continue with that arrangement."

"There is no arrangement," Kailynn said. "I have an open invitation."

"I see," Rayal murmured. "Then it is even more imperative that you listen very carefully to what I'm about to tell you." He reached behind him and grabbed a small box on the table. He held it in both hands, tapping his finger against the side. "This is an emitter PIM chip," he explained. "This is a very special class of PIM chip, developed to protect the people closest to Isa. If you consent, I would like you to have one implanted."

"I can't," she whispered. "I'm not a citizen, you know that."

"We're going to grant you citizenship, if you desire to continue this relationship with Isa," Rayal said. "However, if you are using her just to become a citizen and plan to leave her after getting this, then I will be sure to hunt you down and make you suffer."

"You clearly don't know Trids," Kailynn groaned sarcastically. "None of us *want* citizenship."

"I need you to understand that this is not given lightly," Rayal said sharply. "However, this will help everyone if you consent to having it."

"How?"

"First, it will give you citizenship, so that will no longer be an issue."

"Even though I was born a Trid?"

"It has happened before," Rayal said. "As long as you have legal citizenship, it will not be a problem. This will contain your identification, or rather, your identification as Jacyleen Lynden, the Significant, since that is the name on your forged papers. Your medical history, allergies, any other physical things that we need to know about you for treatment will be recorded, and it will also allow us to track you, should it ever be needed."

"I thought all PIM chips did that. Why do I need a special one?"

Rayal looked down at the box.

"Venus has mandated that everyone close to Isa have an emitter chip."

"But Venus doesn't know that I'm still around her."

"No, which is why we need your consent. You are not mandated to have it," Rayal said. "What this chip does is keep a detailed record of your body's rhythm. It monitors when you are healthy, when you have a cold, the flu, or any infections that you may get. And when there is a drastic and sudden change, it immediately lets emergency personnel know your location and what is happening with your health. This chip was the reason the EMU got to Isa so quickly. The chip noticed something was wrong before the NCB chair noticed."

"And these are mandated for everyone in close contact with Isa?"

"Yes," Rayal affirmed. "I have one, every Elite in the Syndicate has one, Tarah has one as well."

"Why should I have one?"

Rayal leaned forward.

"For your well-being, as well as Isa's." Rayal shook his head slowly. "If we had had these five years ago, Isa would not have been in the hospital for eight months."

"I don't understand."

"Remus and I were used in a plot against Isa's life. Rather than abduct us and show the immediate threat to our lives, the ambassador from Gihron tried slowly killing us and using us to control Isa's actions. Had we had these chips, it would have been clear to others what was going on, and we could have avoided that hell entirely."

Kailynn blinked at Rayal, confused.

"No one is going to give me a straight answer about what happened five years ago, are they?" she asked sharply.

"We will tell you what you need to know, when you need to know it. Isa doesn't like to talk about it, so we do our best not to bring it up," Rayal explained. He extended the box to her. "That is what this is. If you want it, we will go to Dr. Busen today and get it implanted."

Kailynn stared at the box worriedly.

"If I agree, that means that I am permitted to be close to her?"

"By those who know of your relationship, but not by Venus. Therefore, you still have to be discreet."

Kailynn continued to stare at the box.

"Then my life is still in danger."

"Yes," Rayal said. "But less so than before," he continued. "You will be a citizen. The fact that you are a born Trid will no longer put you in danger of arrest."

Kailynn nodded slowly, her eyes distant.

"What does Isa think about all this?"

"She does not know that we are discussing this," Rayal admitted. "When asked, she, once again, put the situation entirely in your hands. You need to make the decision based on if you want to stay close to her or not, and if you do want to stay close, how serious you believe the risks to be."

Kailynn stared at the box in Rayal's hands, her mind racing.

"Take it from a veteran," Rayal whispered, extending the box further, "be proactive about your own protection so that Isa does not have yet another thing to worry about."

Kailynn glanced up at Rayal, letting the words sink into her skull. She reached forward and took the box from Rayal's hand.

Kailynn did not understand why, but she felt different after having the chip implanted behind her ear. She would spend extended periods of time staring at her reflection, feeling over the small bump covered in a bandage until the incision healed completely. There was a new weight on her shoulders and a strange feeling of elation.

She was a citizen.

Rayal helped her take care of her paperwork and discarded the forged information to hide the discrepancies. He also told her how to use her phone entirely and gave her special programs to use to learn how to read and write. He then told her to call him if she ever needed anything.

Kailynn remained quiet for several days, listening to the news and waiting to hear about Isa. She tried to call Tarah, but the caretaker did not answer her phone.

Two weeks after the assassination attempt, when most of the rumors had blown over, Kailynn received a call from Rayal.

"Come downstairs," he told her. "Isa is out of the hospital."

Kailynn practically ran to the elevator and then impatiently bounced as the car descended. She gained enough sense when she reached the ground floor to slow down and act like she was not in a hurry. She ignored the calls and jests of the other Significants, as well as their suspicious glances, as she walked calmly out of the greeting salon to the car waiting for her outside.

She got in and turned to Rayal quickly.

"Is she alright? The doctors said everything was alright?"

"They released her," Rayal said with a shrug. "I thought she was fine to leave a few days ago, but Dr. Busen held her just in case. She still needs about a week of downtime and then she'll be back at work."

"Have you told her about the chip?"

"No," Rayal said, shaking his head. "The hospital does strange things to people. They tend to forget everything they're told. I did not want to confuse or frighten her further. You should tell her yourself, anyway."

Kailynn nodded slowly, her stomach fluttering with butterflies at the thought of seeing Isa again. She was worried that Isa would look as she had at the hospital, pale and sick. She had been so concerned over the Elite's health that she had not gone back to Trid to check in with her brother or Raphael, worried she would miss the moment Isa was released from the hospital. She had spent her time worrying over the Elite's condition and fussing over the newly implanted chip.

Now that she was on her way to see Isa, her anxiety was even higher.

Her impatience in the elevator to the top of Anon Tower made Rayal smile.

When the front door opened, Remus and Dr. Busen were talking to Tarah, explaining the final stage of Isa's recovery. Isa was sitting on the couch, clad in her heavy robe, looking tired, but not ill. Kailynn stopped in her tracks when she saw Isa, a wave of relief washing over her.

"Kailynn," Isa greeted, standing.

"No, no, sit down," Kailynn said, rushing over. "You just got out of the hospital."

She took the Elite's shoulders and sat her back down as Isa chuckled.

"I assure you, I am alright."

"She will be fine," Dr. Busen assured. "Just one more week of remaining quiet. I'm going to count on all of you to be sure she does so."

"She can't work from here anyway. Her chair has been dismantled," Remus teased.

"And I'm sure that the *delay* you are all talking about on my new chair will no longer be an issue as soon as this week is over."

"Wouldn't that be a coincidence?" Remus chuckled.

Isa took Kailynn's hand and gently pulled, bringing the Significant to sit beside her on the couch.

"I think they're conspiring against me," she said with a playful smile.

"There, you see?" Rayal said. "She's fine."

"Well, in that case, I am no longer needed here," Dr. Busen said, turning to Isa. "Please, stay quiet for a week. It's just a week, the planet will survive in that time."

"I promise."

"Thank you."

Dr. Busen shook hands with Remus and nodded to Tarah and Rayal, leaving the house. Remus turned to Isa.

"I should go as well."

"Please keep me informed of what is going on," Isa said gently.

Remus narrowed his eyes playfully.

"You made a promise to your doctor."

"I just want to know what is going on," Isa said with a smile. "You know how I am. I'll assume the worst."

Remus walked over to Isa and put a hand on her shoulder.

"Alright," he agreed. "But only if you promise to stay quiet."

"I promise."

Remus squeezed her shoulder and turned his eyes to Kailynn. He was still for only one second before he turned to leave.

"Elite Remus," Kailynn called, standing quickly. He turned to her. "Um...I...about...about what I said at the hospital—"

Remus lifted his hand to stop her, shaking his head silently. He turned and left as Kailynn stared after him.

Isa's hand taking hers caused her to turn back to the Golden Elite.

"Do not let him get to you," Isa said, guiding Kailynn to sit next to her once more. "What did you say to him?"

Kailynn sighed heavily and turned to Isa, hearing the kitchen door close as Rayal and Tarah left the room.

"Nothing, it's just..." She shook her head. "They were telling me to leave the hospital...and I said some things to Remus I probably shouldn't have..."

Isa placed a hand gently on Kailynn's cheek, her thumb moving over the skin slowly. Kailynn's eyes met Isa's.

"Are you alright?"

"Yes, I'm fine," Isa assured. "It's not the first time this has happened."

"Rayal said that you've had someone try to kill you eighteen times."

"He would know," she agreed. "I've stopped keeping track."

Kailynn could only stare at the Elite.

"Does that not scare you?"

Isa shook her head. "No."

Kailynn was still for several long moments before she leaned forward and kissed Isa, wrapping her arms around the Elite and resting her head on Isa's shoulder.

Isa wrapped an arm around Kailynn's shoulders as her other hand went to Kailynn's cheek, holding her tightly, her head resting on Kailynn's.

"You scared me," Kailynn breathed.

"I know," Isa whispered. "I'm sorry."

Kailynn's arms tightened around Isa and she closed her eyes, listening to Isa's quiet, even breathing.

Chapter Twenty

Kailynn took care of Isa, which allowed Rayal time to spend with Tarah. Kailynn would smile whenever she saw the starry look in the younger woman's eyes as she looked at Rayal. Isa appeared not to notice.

Isa was good on her promise and remained quiet for the week. Kailynn spent all day with her, talking lightly about everything they could think of without bringing up the assassination attempt. Isa took frequent naps, and Kailynn often slept at her side. When she finally told Isa that she had the emitter chip implanted, a very serious discussion ensued, and it took a lot of convincing for Isa to believe that Kailynn was not coerced into the decision.

Even though Isa seemed worried about the implant, she was, in fact, relieved.

Kailynn also kept the Elite from any sexual activity. Isa teased that sex would not hurt her, and that it was exercise to help her get stronger. However, she did not push Kailynn. She would touch and kiss the Significant, but when Kailynn told her to stop, she did.

On the fifth day of Isa's rest, when she appeared to be completely recovered, the two went swimming in the pool. They raced and waded around, enjoying the time together. When Kailynn saw the mischievous light in the Elite's eyes, she smiled and backed away slowly. Isa followed, grabbing her hips and pinning her to the side of the pool.

Kailynn closed the gap between them, kissing the Elite passionately, their tongues dancing against each other. The feeling of the Elite's body against hers caused her hair to stand on end and her muscles to quiver. It had been difficult to deny Isa the previous days, but there were new facets of their relationship that made Kailynn nervous. She was no longer a Trid. Those who were close to Isa—aside from Venus—knew of their relationship and were doing their best to protect them.

There was something about the changes that made Kailynn nervous.

However, with her body flush against Isa's, all negative thoughts left her about their situation. It simply did not matter.

Isa was worth the danger.

"Miss," Rayal said, walking into the pool area. He was not in the least bit surprised or embarrassed by what he stumbled upon.

"Yes?" Isa asked, her mouth parting from Kailynn's.

"Elite Maki is here. Shall I show him in?"

"Please do."

As Rayal turned to leave, Kailynn wiggled out of Isa's grasp and clamored out of the pool.

"Are you *insane*?" Kailynn gasped, staring at Isa incredulously.

"What?" she chuckled. "The entire Syndicate knows."

"*So*?" Kailynn hissed, snatching her clothes from the bench. "That doesn't mean that he needs to come in here and *see* us."

"I did not think it would be a problem," Isa said, unable to keep herself from smiling at the frantic look on Kailynn's face as she grabbed a towel.

"Not a problem?" Kailynn snapped. "I'm *naked*."

"As am I."

"Put some clothes on before—"

The door opened and Kailynn darted into the opening in the wall for the spa, nervous about being seen naked. It was true that the entire Syndicate knew about the relationship, and she was sure that Maki had been the first to notice, but she did not want to meet him naked after what had been turning into a very intimate moment.

However, as she stood in the spa area, barely hearing Isa's quiet chuckle, she felt like an idiot for hiding like a child.

Maki smiled as he approached the pool.

"What are you laughing about?"

"Nothing," Isa said, swimming to the other side of the pool and folding her arms over the edge next to Maki's feet. The Bronze Elite sat down next to the pool and took off his boots and socks, pulling up his uniform and sticking his feet in the water.

"How are you feeling?"

"Well," Isa assured. "Much stronger."

"I can see that. You're swimming," Maki said. "Too bad your life was predetermined. You could have continued competing."

"Ah, well," Isa said, shaking her head, "Elites can't compete against humans. We have an unfair advantage."

"I'm still trying to determine that advantage," Maki laughed. "It's not like the Elites are better than humans. We're all made from the same mold." His smile widened. "Except, of course, you and Remus."

Isa laughed lightly, shaking her head.

"It was never a blessing to be labeled a degenerate," she said. She fell silent for several long moments. "How is he?"

"Remus?" Maki hesitated, thinking about how to answer. "…he's trying to process everything."

Isa sighed and closed her eyes.

"I was afraid of that."

"Can you blame him?" Maki asked. "You two were together for, basically, your entire lives. It's going to be difficult for him to accept that you're involved with someone else."

Isa remained silent, her eyes going distant.

"Will you please keep an eye on him?"

"Of course." Maki was quiet for a few moments before turning to her once again. "Has he told you about the rumors?"

"Yes."

"It's not like we haven't dealt with rumors before," Maki reminded her. "It was always speculated that you and Remus were together. But everyone was set on keeping it secret. And we will do so again."

"Even with the threat of war looming?"

"There is always threat of war," Maki said. "If there was no war, humans would die of boredom."

Isa laughed. "Sadly, you are not wrong."

"However, as far as the rumors are concerned, they do know her name and have released her picture. We've done everything we can to remove her picture and keep her safe, but enough people have seen it. If she is spotted anywhere near you, the rumors will spread like wildfire. And you know the damage of gossip."

"I know," Isa assured. "We will have to take extreme precautions. If she quits Companion, it will raise more suspicion. If she quits and then is never seen again, people will think that she was responsible and that we've silently killed her, which will show more weakness than we can afford right now."

"I can hold a press conference and show the proof of where the virus came from."

"No," Isa said. "It was a domestic attack. I cannot have the people worried."

"It was a domestic attack, but it was probably just routed from another chair on Tiao. The virus itself was encrypted in Gihoric," Maki told her.

Isa sighed heavily.

"Regardless, until we have an actual culprit, let's not give away information."

"Understood."

"I will try to think of ways to keep Kailynn out of the spotlight until people find something else of interest."

"Very well," Maki said. He glanced around the pool. "Where is she, anyway? Remus said she was staying with you."

"She's taking a nap," Isa said with a smile.

■■■

Kailynn continued to think over Maki's conversation with Isa about the rumors of her involvement in the plot on Isa's life. Even though Isa assured her over and over again that there was no immediate danger and that she would handle the rumors, Kailynn's worry could not be quelled.

Therefore, on the day that Isa was to return to the Syndicate, Kailynn told her she was going to go back to Companion before people became more suspicious. The Golden Elite smiled gently and told her to come back whenever she wanted and to call her if she needed anything. Rayal also returned to work, leaving Tarah alone in the house. Kailynn promised to be back more often and Tarah just smiled and told her that she looked forward to having her around more.

Then, Kailynn returned to Companion.

So many things had happened so quickly, Kailynn felt disoriented.

Only two days after returning to Companion, Kailynn was thinking about returning to Trid once more when Jak sent her on another job. He told her to be careful and to keep Nyx close. He had seen that her picture was circulating and he was worried, but she had been booked for an appointment and he said she still had to earn her keep.

Kailynn was thrilled to have the appointment. She was close to getting the money she needed for the release of the final members of the Heart of Trid gang. Once she had the money, she had planned to stay at Companion only for a month or two before returning to Trid. However, now, she was not sure that her plans were the same. As a citizen, she did not have to live in fear of being arrested being in Anon. She was able to leave and go wherever she wanted. The thought used to excite her, but now that it was possible, it frightened her.

What scared her more was a thought that had become increasingly prominent—she could stay with Isa.

There were several things about the notion that made her uneasy. She had never been one to be tied down, and she knew that, if she lived with Isa, she would be confined. She would have to be sure it was okay to be seen and when it was important to stay hidden. She would have to know the safety measures of being around the Golden Elite—she knew that there was more to it than just the emitter chip.

Perhaps she could find another job in Anon, and then find a place to live, and then see Isa on occasion.

There were many options open to her now, but so many of her decisions relied on knowing what Isa wanted.

She thought about the possibilities over and over again as Nyx drove her to the home of her client. When Nyx told her that they were close, she finally asked him what the client wanted that night. She hated to hear that he wanted a Significant Other experience, meaning he wanted her to pretend to be his long-time girlfriend. However, Nyx said that he did not book sex. That did not ease Kailynn's mind. She had been in a few appointments where sex was discussed during the appointment and the client agreed to pay more.

The thought of that unsettled her this time.

However, she walked to the door of her client all the same. She took a deep breath and closed her eyes briefly, reminding herself that she did not need to take many more clients. She was close to getting everyone from the Heart of Trid gang out of Uren and being done with work as a Significant.

She rang the alarm bell and waited. A caretaker opened the door. He was an older man with grey hair and wrinkles etched deep into his skin. He nodded once, motioning for her to follow him. She stepped in as Nyx took his position outside the door.

Kailynn followed the silent caretaker into the house, studying the design of the home. The space was gloomy, with dark painted walls and windows covered with heavy drapes. The atmosphere made the area seem smaller and the ceiling lower, making Kailynn claustrophobic.

The caretaker led her into the living room on the other side of the foyer, where her client, a man with black hair and dark eyes, sat on the sofa, waiting. His eyes turned to her and, for the first time in a long time, Kailynn was nervous about being left alone with her client.

The caretaker stood by the door and waited, showing that he planned to be there for the entirety of the appointment.

"Ah, there you are," her client, Rek, said, motioning for her to sit next to him. She forced a smile and walked forward, sitting next to him.

"Sorry to keep you waiting," she said, putting as much tenderness into her voice as she could manage. He put his arm around her and she leaned against him. He smiled at her and put his head against hers, taking a deep breath and closing his eyes.

They sat like that for a very long time. Kailynn began to wonder why she was worried about being with her client in the first place. He had done nothing more than sit with her and rest his head on hers. She figured he was just lonely and he wanted to sit with someone for a while.

Once Kailynn started to relax, he turned his head and kissed her forehead.

"May I ask you a question?" he murmured.

"Of course."

"A few nights ago," he started, his voice quiet and even, "you were with someone."

The hairs on the back of her neck stood up. She could not think of a response that fit with the role he had asked her to play. She hesitated before sitting upright and turning to him, nervous. She forced a smile.

"I don't know what you mean."

"I think you do," he said, a dangerous light in his eyes. She backed away on the couch. "Don't you?"

"No, I don't."

"You were with someone who is very influential in the circles I travel in," he continued, his expression never wavering. Kailynn could feel her heart begin to race in her chest, though she did her best to maintain her impassive expression. She knew that her picture and name had been released to the public through broadcasts about the assassination attempt, but she did not think that would encourage people to become her clients. If anything, she thought it would cause her to lose clientele because no one wanted to be associated with a criminal.

"I'm sorry," she said, trying to keep her voice strong, "I'm afraid I do not understand."

One corner of Rek's mouth curved upward briefly and he leaned forward, touching Kailynn's face.

"Don't be coy," he whispered. "I know the truth."

She backed away, standing.

"Clearly, there has been a misunderstanding."

She knew she was in danger. She could feel it in her bones. Everything inside her was telling her to run as fast as she could.

When a hand latched onto her wrist, forcing her to sit on the couch again, her fear doubled.

"I don't recall saying I was finished with you."

She jerked her hand away, glaring at Rek.

"*I'm* saying that I'm done."

She tried to stand again, but this time, the caretaker stepped forward to stop her.

"Why don't you stay for awhile?" Rek insisted, also standing. "There are some things we need to discuss."

"No," she snapped. "I'm leaving."

"What about your payment?"

"My company will sort that out," she said, walking to the caretaker with the intention of pushing past him. The older man grabbed both of her arms and yanked her to the side, forcing her to the ground. She barely had time to realize that she had fallen before the caretaker had pinned her arms above her head.

She began kicking violently, hoping to connect with something, but Rek's hands grabbed her legs, pinning them as he sat on her knees.

"You misunderstand," Rek said, chuckling. "I won't hurt you."

"Let me go! I will have you arrested!"

"Really?" Rek chuckled. "You think you can do that when you're a criminal yourself?"

"What the hell are you talking about?!"

"After all, you were the one who attempted to kill Elite Isa," Rek said, smiling as he leaned over her. "The Intelligence Agency did not find any evidence against you, but isn't it interesting that you were back at Anon Tower only a few days ago?"

Kailynn blinked in surprise at the man, stilling her struggle. Rek chuckled and tilted his head.

"You think that people don't know?" he murmured. "There are thousands that would pay more than you could ever imagine to have Elite Isa dead." He leaned closer to Kailynn. "And you, my dear, are pivotal in securing the kill."

Kailynn lifted her head quickly and felt her forehead connect with Rek's nose. He let out a startled cry and backed away, getting off Kailynn's legs as he nursed his broken nose. Kailynn thrashed her body, pulling her arms free of the caretaker and punching him in the jaw. However, with her position on the floor, the punch had little strength and did nothing more than stun the caretaker momentarily.

In that moment, Kailynn reached for her necklace and pressed the pendant, alerting Nyx that there was a problem.

The caretaker was on her once more, trying to stop her as she kicked and punched, sometimes hitting him as he made attempts to grab her.

However, Nyx appeared at the caretaker's back, pulling him off Kailynn and putting him on his stomach as Nyx kneeled on his back to keep him down.

Kailynn turned her attention to Rek, seeing that he was trying to get to his feet. She lunged across the floor and grabbed his ankles, toppling him.

"Nyx!" she gasped. "Tie them up! They're plotting against Elite Isa!"

It took Nyx a few moments to process the words before he used the one set of handcuffs he kept on him to restrain the caretaker as Kailynn tried to keep Rek still. Nyx took off his jacket and tied Rek's hands to his feet, remaining on top of him to keep him still as he called the Officials.

Kailynn stayed until the Officials arrived and answered their questions as the two were hauled away. Kailynn could not help but ponder the fact that she was in two situations where there had been attempts or plots on Isa's life. She was sure that the report would bring up many questions and peg her as someone who was a danger to the Elite.

Nyx took her back to Companion, both of them silent. When they got out of the car and were about to head into the building, Nyx took her arm. She whirled around, still on-edge.

Her guard pulled her to him and hugged her tightly.

She did not understand what had prompted him to hug her or why she felt like the hug was exactly what she needed, but she was grateful for the attention.

"Everything will be alright," he whispered.

When Kailynn got to her room again, after a lecture from Jak about how she was getting into trouble so often, she got on her bed and stared at the ceiling, allowing her thoughts to form and vanish as they pleased.

The beeping from her phone caused her to jump out of her stupor. She grabbed the phone from the desk, popping out the earpiece and putting it in place, cringing at the discomfort.

"Hello?" she said when the soft beep told her that the call was connected.

"Good evening," Isa's voice said, her tone worried. "Are you alright?"

"How do you already know what happened?"

"Rayal called and told me about the arrest," Isa answered. "Are you alright?" she repeated.

"I'm fine," Kailynn said. "I'm worried."

"Understandably," Isa said. "Did he hurt you?"

"No," Kailynn assured. "I promise, I'm fine." She heaved a sigh. "Are you going to kill him?"

"No, not yet, at least," Isa admitted. "Rayal and his team will try to get information from him about a plot." Isa hesitated before speaking again. "Kailynn…your account about what he said…"

"I didn't lie," Kailynn murmured when Isa did not continue. "He said I was pivotal." Kailynn opened her eyes. "Does that mean anything to you?"

"Unfortunately, yes," Isa whispered. "Kailynn…I know it's asking a lot, but I would like you to come here. It's safer."

"Isa, he said he saw me in Anon Tower. They can monitor where I am, apparently. Going there would be more dangerous, wouldn't it? They might be waiting until I'm there to attack you."

Isa heaved a sigh on the other end of the call.

"It worries me not having you close," she said gently. "I won't be able to protect you if you need me."

Kailynn could not help but chuckle.

"I broke that asshole's nose," she reminded the Golden Elite. "I'm pretty good about protecting myself."

Isa let out a soft laugh as well, but her tone did not lighten.

"Perhaps in some ways," she agreed. "But, when it comes to politics, things get far more vicious."

The two were quiet for an indeterminable amount of time, acutely aware of the other person on the call, but not sure what to say. Finally, Kailynn spoke.

"I have a few things I need to take care of. I probably won't take my phone with me," she explained. "I'll be alright, I promise."

"Will you let me know when you are back on the radar?" Isa said with a light chuckle. Kailynn smiled.

"Of course I will." She was quiet for several more seconds. "Isa…"

When she did not continue, Isa asked her what was wrong.

"Please be careful."

With those words, Isa understood the intensity of Kailynn's fear. She had been trying to quell Tarah's fears ever since the assassination attempt. The caretaker was constantly terrified that something horrible was going to happen to the Golden Elite. Now that Kailynn had uncovered another person plotting on Isa's life, the Elite was sure that the Significant was nervous.

"I will," Isa whispered. "I promise."

■■■

Kailynn was thoroughly irritated when she was sent to various locations in Trid trying to find her brother. The Heart of Trid gang had been staying quiet since their release, waiting for the worst of the anger to blow over before resuming their normal activities, which included drug trafficking. Kailynn found one member of the gang in one of the exchange alleys who told her that her brother was at Aron's house.

However, Aron told her that Theo had left nearly an hour previous, saying he was going to the car garage to grab a few things.

Kailynn could only roll her eyes when she went to the car garage and no one was there.

As she was walking back to find Raphael and spend some time with him, she ran into another member of the gang, who told her that Theo went to Sonya's house.

She went to the woman's house, recalling that Sonya and Theo were in a difficult-to-define relationship. She kicked herself for not checking there before.

When she knocked on the door, it took several minutes for anyone to answer. Theo pushed the door open, fighting the rusted mechanisms.

He had his shirt off and his pants were undone, causing Kailynn to roll her eyes, already irritated from her searching.

"Lynni," he greeted, surprised. He walked forward and hugged her quickly. "I have been looking everywhere for you."

"You have?"

"You've been gone for *weeks*. I thought you had been killed and dumped somewhere."

"Thanks for having so much faith in my ability to take care of myself," Kailynn groaned, pushing her brother away. She glanced back into the room, seeing Sonya walking around naked, picking up a bottle of alcohol and taking several gulps. Kailynn rolled her eyes again and reached into her pocket, pulling out a card. "Here."

Theo glanced at it, taking it slowly, confused.

"What's this?"

"Thirty thousand credits," she said. "This with your money should allow you to get the other members of the moron committee out of Uren."

"Thirty..." Theo looked between Kailynn and the card several times. "But..."

"Theo," Kailynn said, "don't do anything so fucking stupid again."

"Wait!" Theo said, quickly fastening his pants and closing the door to Sonya's place, stepping into the hallway as Kailynn turned around. "Where did you get this money?" he whispered, stepping close to her.

"None of your business."

"It is!" he hissed, grabbing her arm when she tried to turn away. "Are you whoring?"

"No."

"Does Raphael know?"

"Stop it, Theo!" Kailynn snapped, jerking away from her brother. "I am not whoring, so don't accuse me."

"You have no circles, you have no product, so what the hell else could you exchange for this amount of money?" Theo growled. "I'm not going to accept it if you don't tell me where you got it."

Kailynn rolled her eyes.

"What does it matter how I got it?" she said sharply. "It's sitting there, in your hand. What do you want me to do? Give it back?"

"I want to know where you got it!"

"I *worked* for it," Kailynn said.

Theo looked at the card.

"*Brad?* He pays you this much?"

"I had to pick up some other jobs to pay for this," Kailynn said. "The point is, I worked, and I didn't whore myself in the Walking District. Alright?"

"No, not alright," Theo said. His expression turned suspicious. "You paid for us to be released, didn't you?"

Kailynn quickly saw that the amount of money she would have needed to break them out of Uren would be impossible of obtain outside of Anon. She tried to think of a response, of some job she could tell her brother that would appease him without telling him that she was working as a Significant.

"How did you get all that money?" Theo whispered. "Even if you were a whore, there is no way you could get all this so quickly, and everything you paid to get us out."

Kailynn looked at the ground, trying desperately to come up with something.

"Lynni," Theo breathed, worried, "what have you done? How did you get this?"

"Theo," she started, her voice weak, "it doesn't matter how I got it."

"It does. It matters to me!"

"Why?"

"Because I want to know what my baby sister had to go through to get us out," Theo said. "I want to understand why you have been so absent. And I want to help you out of whatever trouble you are in."

Kailynn could not help but bark a laugh.

"You can't."

"Kailynn, what did you do to get this money?"

Kailynn looked over Theo's worried expression. He was struggling to think of any jobs where she could obtain so much money in such a short amount of time, and his inability to come up with an answer terrified him all the more. He walked forward and took Kailynn's shoulders.

"Please, tell me."

She looked at her older brother, her resolve to keep him in the dark about her job as a Significant chipping away. So much had happened so quickly since she had started working as a Significant that the thought of actually being able to confide in her older brother was too appealing to resist.

She dropped her head and Theo's hands tightened around her shoulders.

"It's alright," he whispered. He pulled her into a tight hug. "It's alright. I'll help however I can."

She braced herself, unsure of her brother's reaction.

"I have been working, Theo," she started, her voice weaker as she pulled out of the hug. "I found work…in Anon."

Theo's eyes shot wide.

"You've been working in Anon?" he hissed. "Do you have any idea how dangerous that is? You could have been caught and killed!"

"I know."

"Who would even hire you? You don't have citizenship."

Kailynn hesitated once more.

"Kailynn," Theo urged.

She took a deep breath to steady herself and closed her eyes.

"I was working at Companion," she whispered. She opened her eyes and spared a glance at her brother. "I am working as a Significant."

Theo was still and silent. She could almost see the words fall into place in his mind.

Suddenly, his hand struck her across the face so hard she saw stars.

"You better be lying," he growled.

"Theo—"

"You were working as a fucking *Significant*?" he growled. "Fuck, even whoring is more honest than that fucking circus."

"You don't understand—"

"How could I not understand?!"

"You were going to be killed!" Kailynn snapped, shoving Theo away. "You are all I have left! I couldn't let you die!"

"But you didn't have to go be a slave to fucking Anon and cater to their sick desires!"

"You don't know anything about it!" Kailynn yelled. "Fuck you, Theo! I did it to save your life so I wouldn't have to hear that you were dead!"

"I know what happened to Father upset you—"

"What the fuck do you know about it?!" Kailynn barked. "*I* found him! You didn't! And you are the only family I have! What the fuck was I supposed to do if you died?!"

The tears were forcing Kailynn's voice to break. She turned away and pressed a hand over her mouth, trying to compose herself. Theo took a deep breath, shaking his head.

"Fuck, Kailynn," he sighed, closing his eyes and pinching the bridge of his nose. "This would have never happened if…"

"If you hadn't had such a shitty plan for shutting down Venus?" Kailynn snarled.

"Yes," he admitted. "If not for Venus, things would be very different."

Kailynn's heart stopped. She recognized the tone of Theo's voice. It bespoke determination and decision.

"Theo, no," she said sharply.

"You know it's true. If it weren't for Venus, the Trids would not have to scrounge for food and shelter. We would not be freezing to death in alleys and being killed by Officials without reason."

"Theo, no, not again," Kailynn pled. "This is how I got stuck in this shit in the first place. There is no way to shut down Venus."

"I know," Theo said, turning to his little sister with a serious expression. "But we don't need to take down Venus. Only her messenger."

Kailynn's eyes shot wide, terrified.

"What?"

Theo took Kailynn's shoulders.

"I was not going to tell you this," he said. "I did not want you in any danger. I know I screwed up last time, but this time is going to be different."

"Theo, what the hell are you talking about?" Kailynn choked.

"We're going to win, Kailynn," he said confidently. "The Golden Elite, the shining star of the Altereye System. We are going to send a message to the entire system that the *people* are the true source of power and that we will not be ruled by some computer and her army of genetically-altered freaks."

Kailynn's breath was caught in her throat and she was sure that she was choking. She could only stare in horror as the words continued to cut through the air and pierce her ears like daggers, their meaning slicing open her chest over and over again.

She backed away from her brother in horror.

He smiled and nodded.

"That's right," he breathed. "We're going to kill Golden Elite Isa."

Chapter Twenty-One

Kailynn wandered around Trid in a daze for over an hour while the words processed. It felt as if there was a knife in her belly that she could not rid herself of and each step and every breath made it dig deeper into her flesh.

She went to her own home, unable to face anyone with the words rattling in her brain. She sat heavily on her bed and stared at the wall.

The conflict within her made her feel ill.

She tried to find her breath, running her hands through her hair and closing her eyes. She focused on calming down and getting her thoughts under control.

She could not.

If she told Isa about yet another plot on her life, then it would go without question that Theo would be arrested and likely killed. It would be the second time that he went against the Syndicate and Venus in such a brazen manner, and she was sure that, this time, there would be no hesitation in killing him.

However, if she said nothing to Isa, it was possible that the Golden Elite would be killed. All she could think about for several hours was the way Isa's body convulsed in the NCB chair when the Pulse Virus hit, and how sickly she looked when she was lying in the hospital. When she thought about the way the Elite looked when she was home once more, tired but smiling, the thoughts of the Elite made her heart skip a beat. She remembered the way Rek whispered to her that she was key in killing Isa.

To have become witness to three plots on Isa's life was enough to make her feel like she was losing her mind.

If she had heard about any of these plots one year previous, she would have laughed and celebrated, excited to think that the Elite Syndicate could be dismantled and the Trids could become equal to those in Anon, even if that meant that the citizens of Anon would be forced to live as the Trids lived.

Now that she had been close to the Elite, her perspective on everything had changed.

Isa was not the enemy.

She still remembered vividly the day that the news of Caroie had been announced. She remembered the pain that creased Isa's face, the way she blamed herself for being unable to maintain peace in the

Crescent Alliance, the way she stared into space, lost in what she believed to be her failure. The look pained Kailynn. That had been the moment she understood that Isa was trying to mend everything broken in the Altereye System and was faced with opposition wherever she turned.

Kailynn did not want Isa to die.

She also did not want to lose her brother, the only family she had left.

She fell sideways on her mattress and cried quietly into the blankets, waiting and praying for sleep to take her to a less-confusing world.

She woke from a gentle shaking of her shoulder. She blinked her eyes several times, forcing her pounding head to focus on Raphael's face above her. He smiled gently, his eyes sad.

"Hey," he whispered.

"Hey…" she responded, her voice cracking.

"I didn't see you all day," he said, running a hand over her hair. "I was worried about you."

"Sorry…"

"Why are you sorry?" he asked lightly. He tucked some hair behind her ear and leaned close. "What's wrong? You're acting like the fate of the world rests on your shoulders."

Kailynn closed her eyes and pressed a hand to her head. She wanted to tell Raphael everything—her relationship with Isa, Theo's plan to kill the Golden Elite, how confused she was at how easily she had changed after meeting Isa—but she knew that he would not understand. She was sure that he would remind her of her Trid heritage and that getting rid of the Elites and Venus would be the best thing for their future.

But Raphael had not spent time with Isa.

He was just as ignorant as Kailynn used to be—ignorant and fueled by anger.

Raphael leaned forward and kissed her.

"Talk to me," he murmured. She turned away, trying to keep him from being able to kiss her again. "You haven't been yourself."

"I have a lot on my mind."

"Kailynn, please, tell me what's wrong," Raphael begged. Kailynn stood, leaving Raphael sitting on the mattress, watching her walk across the room and search through her minimal belongings for different clothes. "I want to help you."

"It's nothing I can't handle, Raffy," Kailynn assured, giving up on the search for clothes, deciding she would go back into Anon and change at Companion. "I just need time to deal with it, alright?"

Raphael searched her expression, worry creasing his face.

"...alright."

"Thank you," Kailynn said. "I'll be back later tonight."

"Where are you going?"

"I have some things to take care of."

Kailynn walked out of her disheveled apartment, knowing exactly where she was going.

■■■

After changing her clothes at Companion and being sure she looked as professional as possible, she hailed a car and went to Syndicate Intelligence, her heart choking her as it threatened to crawl out her mouth.

Kailynn tried to keep calm. She tried to remind herself that she was in a very dangerous world now, where her close proximity to the Golden Elite could mean her death. If she let on that there was a problem to Rayal, she was sure that the former caretaker would take any measure necessary to protect Isa's life without understanding Kailynn's connection to the attacker.

She took a deep breath as the car slowed in front of the door.

The Significant got out of the car and walked to the door of the Intelligence Agency, stepping through the automatic doors to the security desk. The building was far quieter than it had been on her previous visit, and that made her nervous.

"May I help you?" one robot guard asked, rolling in front of her when she tried to walk forward.

"I'm here to see Rayal Teleta."

The robot extended its arm and she had to force herself not to back away when the sensor on the end of the arm pressed into the space at the back of her ear. A few seconds passed before the robot moved its arm away and spoke again.

"Follow me, please."

Kailynn fell into step behind the robot, which rolled slowly through the halls. Already knowing the way to Rayal's office, she was tempted to pass the robot and walk on her own, but she remained behind the robot, her eyes on the ground, focusing on keeping calm.

When they finally reached the door, the robot stood to the side as the door opened. Kailynn walked in, surprised to see Rayal waiting for her.

"Kailynn," he greeted, motioning her in. "I was surprised to hear you were here. I did not expect you."

"Sorry to just drop in," she said, walking forward as the door closed behind her. She took the seat that Rayal motioned to. "I wanted to talk to you."

"What about?"

Kailynn looked at her lap, nervously.

"Nothing discussed here will leave this room, right?"

"No, of course not," Rayal assured. "If there is one thing I pride myself on, it is my discretion."

"You said that Isa has had eighteen attempts on her life," she started. "Why do people want to kill her?"

Rayal sighed heavily, thinking about how to answer.

"Everyone has their own motivation," he started carefully. "When a young leader comes into power with big ideas about change, people get nervous. Change is uncomfortable."

"What has she changed, though? She said herself that she did not think she mended the Alliance."

"She has mended it far more than she will ever take credit for," Rayal corrected, shaking his head. "The Altereye System is in a better state since her rise to power."

"But there are still people who want to kill her."

Rayal took a deep breath, his eyes lowering.

"The reasons have changed over the years," he admitted. "This latest strain of plots is related to Gihron and everything that happened five years ago."

"Why would that make people want to kill her?"

"Because one of the planetary leaders of Gihron died while visiting Tiao," Rayal said. "And Gihron wants revenge."

Kailynn hesitated. "...how did he die?"

"He was assassinated," Rayal said. "But he was under Isa's care as a foreign leader when it happened. Therefore, Gihron blames her for what happened to Colonel Amori. And they want her to pay for their loss."

"Why does Gihron hate this planet so much?"

"The same reasons that the other planets not in the Alliance hate Tiao," Rayal explained. "They hate Venus. They hate the Elites. They think that Elites are dangerous and should be destroyed. They feel the same about Venus. It also has to do with many of these planets being crushed under taxes and trade embargos and all sorts of other economic problems that come from being outside the Alliance. It was better for those planets when the Alliance had disbanded."

"…sounds a bit like the Trids."

Rayal let out a broken chuckle.

"Yes, I suppose it does."

Kailynn sighed heavily, looking at the ground again.

"Finding that man upset you a great deal, didn't it?" Rayal murmured. Kailynn glanced up at him, her mind taking a few moments to realize he was talking about her client, Rek.

"It just kind of seems like everyone is out to kill her, and it's scary."

"I know," Rayal agreed. "And many people are out to kill her. We've found many plots over the years. Most of them do not develop far enough to be considered an attempt on her life, but there are a few that we miss."

"*Miss?*"

"Well, we do our best to monitor everything for the safety of the Elites, but we are only human. We make mistakes. The computers and Venus don't always catch everything, either."

Kailynn was silent for several moments, looking around the office, trying to decide how best to voice her question. When Rayal saw the worried look on her face, he leaned forward.

"Kailynn? Are you alright?"

"Can Venus hear everything we say in this room?"

"No."

"Do you…you were in Isa's service for a long time, right?"

"Yes, since I was fifteen."

"Did you ever…in the time that you were with her….think that, maybe, things would be better without the Elites? Without Venus?"

Rayal was silent for a few moments, looking over Kailynn's expression carefully. He finally took a deep breath and rubbed his hands together, trying to think of how to answer.

"I think that's a normal thought to cross everyone's mind," he said. "Yes, I did occasionally think that things would be better without Venus."

"And the Elites?"

Rayal hesitated. "That's a little more difficult," he said. "The Elites are a complicated system. I'm not sure I can adequately explain. They're not usually dangerous. Most of them are made to obey, and they obey without question."

"Isa doesn't seem to obey," Kailynn murmured.

Rayal laughed. "Isa has always been a special case," he admitted. "According to many, Isa was different from day one. She was the youngest Elite to ever come into power. She's also one of only two Elites to ever jump classes."

"What does that mean?"

"It means that Isa was made to be a Bronze Elite, but she jumped to the position of Golden Elite."

"They even determine the type of Elite before they're born?" Kailynn asked, startled.

"They determine everything before they're born—class, hair color, eye color, height, absolutely everything about the Elite is determined before they are born. That is one of the reasons Isa has always been special. She broke through everything she was made to be and became something far stronger. Because of this, you can imagine, she has seen more pain in her life than most. And that is how she gained so much favor in the inter-galactic community. She may not be able to feel emotion, but she can understand it."

"You spent years with her," Kailynn whispered. "You really think she can't feel emotion?"

Rayal smiled mysteriously.

"Kailynn, I must confess something to you," he started. "I'm sure you recall when I told you to stay away from Isa and to never return after you left."

"Yeah."

"I don't think you fully understand why I said that."

"Because we are risking both of our lives and you want to protect her."

"It's more than that," Rayal admitted. "Apart from Remus, I may know Isa better than anyone. When she first came to power, she was ambitious and driven to change things. She had strength within her that enthralled and empowered everyone. She had such enormous plans, but...time progressed, she got older, and she faced more challenges in her job. Then, when she had the accident five years ago, that strength almost disappeared." He looked down at his hands and took a deep breath, slowly letting it out. "For many years, I truly believed that her relationship with Remus was diminishing her strength. Having to keep that relationship secret from Venus and other planetary leaders and the people...I was sure that that was wearing her down. And when their relationship began to fall apart..."

Rayal trailed off, closing his eyes briefly and shaking his head.

"Anyway, the point is, I was worried that her already-diminished strength would disappear, having to keep you as a secret," he said, looking at her seriously. "Now, I have to apologize for thinking that."

"What do you mean?"

"I believe you give Isa strength," Rayal said. "I think Isa needs people, just as everyone else does, if not more so. You are a Significant, so I'm sure you understand how lonely everyone on this planet is. I think it's far worse for Isa. She has been working herself to death since she was a child, and it has been seared into her very being that she is there only to serve the people and Venus. But, just like everyone else, she needs someone to care for her, and see her as more than just the Golden Elite. She takes care of the planet, but I think you take care of her in a way that no one else can."

Kailynn stared at Rayal, unsure how to respond to the words. They struck a part of her soul that made her mind go blank and her chest tighten.

Rayal smiled gently.

"I'm sorry if that puts some kind of pressure on you," he chuckled. "I know that this is a dangerous relationship for both of you. That is just how I see you and Isa."

Kailynn let out a long breath and closed her eyes.

"I just...I would have never thought that my life would take this kind of turn," she tried to joke.

"I'm sure it's a lot to take in," Rayal said knowingly. "But I think you are very good for Isa."

"And you think Isa is good for the planet?"

"I think she's regaining the strength she needs to change things for the better," Rayal said with a nod. "She can do great things, Kailynn. She just needs the right support."

Kailynn returned to Companion, unable to face returning to Trid immediately after the conversation with Rayal. Even though he had joked about putting pressure on Kailynn, she felt a new weight settle on her shoulders.

She had to choose between what her heart was telling her to do, and the loyalty she felt to her family.

Feeling anxious and a little sick to her stomach, she reached for the phone and told it who she wanted to call. She paced around her room, listening to the monotone beeping sound three times before cutting off.

"Are you back on the radar?" a gentle voice asked.

The tone seemed to soothe Kailynn's fears, if only for that moment when the words washed over her ears. She closed her eyes and let out a long breath.

"Yes."

"Are you alright?" Isa asked, her voice turning worried.

"Yeah, yeah," Kailynn said quickly, closing her eyes and leaning against the wall of her room. "I'm just tired. I didn't really sleep last night."

Isa hesitated, clearly not convinced.

"Am I going to see you soon?" Isa asked, her tone betraying her concern.

"Yeah," Kailynn repeated. "I just have a few things left to do and I'll come see you." She swallowed hard. "Should I call you beforehand or just surprise you?"

"Either way," she said. "You have an open invitation."

Kailynn fell silent, trying to hear Isa's breathing on the other end of the call, but she could not.

"Are you still there?" Isa asked quietly.

"I'm here…"

"Kailynn, what's wrong?" Isa pressed. "You're upset. I can tell."

Kailynn sighed and lifted a hand to her face.

"I'm confused," she admitted. "I feel like my life is spiraling out of control."

"How so?" Isa asked. "What can I do to help?"

Kailynn tried to suppress her confused sob behind her hand. She took several moments to calm down, worried about blurting out the truth to Isa.

"I'm scared..." she choked.

"What are you afraid of?"

Kailynn closed her eyes again.

"I'm afraid of how I feel," she said. "I'm afraid of how you are making me feel. I don't know what to do."

"Would you rather take some time to yourself and think all this over?" Isa asked, her tone light and gentle. "Do you want to not see me for awhile?"

Kailynn's eyes shot wide.

"No, no," she said quickly. "It's not that. I just...I want you to be okay. I want everything to be okay."

"Everything is alright."

"How do you know that for sure?"

Isa was silent on the other end of the line.

"Kailynn, why don't you come here?" she said. "Let's discuss this in person."

"I can't," Kailynn said quickly, almost interrupting the Elite. She knew if she went to Isa, she would immediately tell her the truth about her brother's plot. She did not want to betray her only living family. "I have a client tonight."

"I see," Isa said slowly. "I made a promise to you, remember? I told you I would be safe. And I will be."

"People are trying to kill you, Isa," Kailynn half-sobbed.

"There will always be people who want to remove me," Isa said, her tone even. "But I know how to keep myself safe."

Kailynn leaned her head back on the wall, her eyes closing tight. She remained silent, trying to keep her tears at bay.

"Kailynn, I am very worried about you. Do you want me to come see you before your appointment?"

"No," Kailynn said, shaking her head quickly even though the Golden Elite could not see her. "No, I'm sorry...I'm acting stupid..." She sniffed and cleared her throat. "Just...promise me that you won't leave Anon Tower unless you absolutely have to. And that your guards are always around."

"Kailynn—"

"I have to go," Kailynn said. "I'll call you when I am on my way to see you."

She ended the call before she could say anything else and took the earpiece out of her ear, angrily throwing it across the room. She slowly sank to the floor, leaning against the wall and cradling her head in her hands, breaking down into tears once more.

Chapter Twenty-Two

That night, and the two days after that, Kailynn was in a drunken stupor. She slept in between alcohol binges and got into two physical fights with Raphael when he tried to take the bottles away. They were thrown out of their usual club when Kailynn became too rowdy and tried to pick fights with the tourists, who cowered from her and looked on in fear as she was thrown out with the rest of her gang.

On the third night of her binge, she went to her brother and drunkenly demanded that he tell her the day and time of their plan. Theo took her aside, out of earshot of the rest of the Heart of Trid gang and forced her to drink water. She punched him in the stomach when he called her a drunk and told him that he needed to tell her his plan exactly or she would turn them over to the Officials.

While Theo did not actually believe that she would do that to him, he did tell her that, in four days, they would shoot Isa as she was leaving a charity event.

Armed with the information, Kailynn went to her apartment to get her phone, only to find Raphael there.

"I have been looking everywhere for your drunken ass," he snarled, irritated. "Come on. Let's get you to my place and get you some water."

"Stop it, I have to call someone," she slurred together, trying to walk away from his hands as they reached out to grab her.

"Call someone?" he said, barking a laugh. "You don't have a phone. Come on."

"I do have a phone!"

"Sure," he droned.

"Oh…but it's not here…" she said, her eyes sliding shut in sudden exhaustion.

"Okay, we'll find it when you sober up," Raphael assured. "Come on."

He hauled her to his apartment as she incoherently babbled about needing to call the Syndicate with important information. He humored her until he got her to the apartment, where he forced her to drink water and lie in bed until she fell asleep.

Of course, after several days of drinking, she felt horrible when she woke in the morning.

She spent the entire day snapping at Raphael for being too loud and nursing her pounding headache.

After a day of rest, Kailynn was back on a rampage, only it was of a different sort.

When Raphael woke and saw that Kailynn was gone, he groaned and quickly got dressed, ready to search for her.

He spent half of the day asking everyone he could think of if they had seen Kailynn. They all told him the same thing.

"She's looking for Theo."

Raphael became more frantic as the day wore on.

Finally, he found Kailynn walking angrily down one street, her eyes on the ground.

"Kailynn!" he snapped, darting across the deserted street and grabbing her arm, turning her around. "I have been looking everywhere for you."

"I need to find Theo," she said, yanking her arm out of his grasp.

"Why?"

"Have you heard about his latest shit-brain idea?"

"What?"

"This stupid fucking plan he has to kill the Golden Elite," Kailynn said sharply.

"What the *fuck*—will you keep your voice down?!" Raphael hissed urgently, looking around to be sure that no one heard them. "Are you still drunk? What the hell is wrong with you?!"

"Do you know about his plan?" Kailynn growled.

Raphael looked over Kailynn's expression, trying to figure out why she was upset about Theo's idea. He thought that it was because Kailynn had just gotten him out of one botched plan and he already was concocting another. However, there was a fire in Kailynn's eyes that gave Raphael pause.

"You know, don't you?"

"Yes," Raphael said.

Kailynn shoved him backward.

"Why the hell didn't you try to talk him out of it?!" Kailynn bellowed.

"Kailynn, please, keep your voice down," Raphael said, holding his hands up peacefully. "You know how your brother is. He's set on it."

"Where is he?" Kailynn growled. "We have a few days to try and talk him out of it."

"Why?"

"*Why*?!"

"You know that the only way the Trids will get anywhere is by removing those in power and starting a revolution," Raphael hissed. "We've dreamed about this since we were kids, remember? We were going to start the movement to bring down Anon."

"And it's fucking stupid!" Kailynn snapped. "If we get rid of one Elite, then others will come to take her place. And they won't do nearly as much good as she has!"

"Wait, *what*?" Raphael gasped, his eyes shooting wide. "Are you…you *support* Elite Isa?!"

Kailynn stared at Raphael for several long moments, her eyes showing her turmoil.

"I've just learned enough to realize that we're ignorant of what revolution actually means."

Raphael stared at Kailynn, slowly shaking his head.

"Who *are* you?"

Kailynn began walking away.

"I'm going to find Theo."

"It's too late, Kailynn," Raphael called after her. She stopped and turned around quickly. "Theo lied to you."

"What?" She quickly walked back to him, her heart sinking.

"He didn't want to risk your life again," Raphael said. "They've already left. They're going through with it tonight."

Kailynn's eyes shot wide and she turned once more. This time, Raphael grabbed her wrist and yanked her back.

"No, Kailynn!"

"Let go of me!"

"What are you going to do?!" Raphael barked, yanking her back once more. "You think you can just stroll up to the Elites and tell them what's going on?!"

Kailynn managed to yank her wrist out of Raphael's grasp.

She stared defiantly at her childhood friend for two long seconds before turning and walking quickly along the sidewalks toward the towering structures of Anon.

Raphael did not follow.

■■■

Kailynn rushed to Companion and grabbed her phone, quickly trying to call Isa's phone. However, the Elite did not answer. Her attempt to call Tarah also failed.

She called Rayal's phone, pacing and quietly pleading for him to answer. Her heart was racing and frightened tears were welling in her eyes. She was worried that, if she did not warn them immediately, Isa would be killed.

As Kailynn listened to the beeping, waiting for someone to answer, at the charity event, Isa, Remus, and Rayal were sitting with the other Elites at a large table watching the art auction pieces pass silently as the bids were tracked electronically. The hall was silent, everyone in their respective seats in front of the Elites, bidding on the pieces that were wheeled in front of them.

When Rayal's phone lit up next to Isa, she slowly lowered the wine glass from her lips, turning to look at the screen. Rayal's eyes also fell on the phone before slowly turning to Isa.

They both had been expecting the call.

Isa's eyes lifted to look at Rayal before she reached over and pressed the ignore button on the phone.

"She's trying to warn you," Rayal whispered.

"I don't want her in danger," Isa breathed.

"She knows something," Rayal said. "Let her tell you."

"No," Isa said, shaking her head. "There is a reason she did not tell me earlier." She turned to Remus and nodded once. He nodded in return and stood, walking out of the hall silently.

Kailynn hung up the phone and looked around her room, desperate to find a way to warn Isa.

She ran downstairs to Jak's office and rapidly hit the call button on the outside of the door. When he did not answer, she began furiously pounding on the door with her fist.

Finally, Jak opened the door, taking the earpiece out of his ear and looking at her incredulously as she barged into the office.

"Have you lost your fucking mind?" Jak growled, closing the door immediately.

"We need to get in contact with Syndicate Intelligence, *now*."

"What the hell has gotten into you?"

"There will be an assassination attempt tonight," Kailynn said breathlessly.

"How do you know this?"

"Something I remember from my last client," she lied, pacing, her eyes frantic and her breath caught in her throat. "I didn't think anything of it until I heard there was a charity event today."

"Yeah, it's an annual art auction. They do it every year. Security is ridiculously tight."

"Someone is going to try and kill Elite Isa," Kailynn said seriously.

"Jacyleen, take a deep breath. Explain yourself."

"I can't get in contact with Isa," she said quietly.

"Are you on a first-name basis with her?" Jak said, his eyes wide. "Jacyleen, tell me what the hell is going on."

"I can't," Kailynn said, shaking her head.

"You're scaring the shit out of me," Jak said, placing a hand on her shoulder. "You're *shaking*."

"This is really complicated and I really need you to work with me on this."

"Okay, I will. Just…take a deep breath."

"Call Syndicate Intelligence and tell them that someone will try to shoot Golden Elite Isa when she leaves the auction."

Jak stared at her, a million questions running through his mind. Deciding it was best to do as Kailynn asked in an attempt to calm her, he went to his phone and commanded it to call Syndicate Intelligence. When he was connected to the tip line, he explained that one of his Significants heard from a client that someone would try to shoot Elite Isa when she left the auction. Kailynn listened to him explain, continuing to pace, running her hands through her hair multiple times.

When Jak fell silent, Kailynn turned and watched his expression. He turned to look at Kailynn, but the look confused her.

"I see," he said. "No, that is a relief. Thank you."

He disconnected the call.

"Where did you get this tip?"

"From the last client, the one who was arrested," Kailynn said.

"He must have told them, too," Jak said, looking at her seriously. "He said they already received the tip. They were working on apprehending the group." He walked back around his desk. "Do you want to tell me what the hell is going on? Why are you so frantic?"

"I just realized there was a plot on Elite Isa's life."

"I know, but showing such intense reactions when you would scoff at any Elite a few months ago…" He studied her expression, slowly shaking his head. "Please tell me that you obeyed all the rules when you were there."

"Of course," Kailynn snapped, indignant. "But, she did make me realize that the Elites are not that bad, so I'm worried about her."

Jak stared at her, clearly not convinced.

"Okay, I understand," he finally said. He sighed heavily. "Well, seems like the Intelligence Agency has this under control. You can go."

"Oh, uh…right…"

Kailynn walked out of the office, standing in the hallway for several seconds. She finally turned and half-ran to the elevator to get to the greeting salon.

Ignoring the sneers from the other Significants, she ran outside and pressed the button to hail a taxi. One of the taxis owned by Companion drove to the front of the building. She got in and told the automatic computer to go to the charity art auction. After several failed attempts to get the right location, the taxi asked if she wanted to go to Anon Convention Center for the Annual Charity Auction. She agreed quickly and the taxi began its path.

She sat in her seat, bouncing her legs rapidly and fidgeting. She was terrified. She did not know when the auction would end or when her brother was going to be there to attempt his plan. Being in the dark worsened her anxiety.

She nearly jumped out of her skin when the car's automated voice sounded.

"Apologies. There appears to be damage repair," it said as it slowed and pulled over. "Recalculating route."

Kailynn closed her eyes and let out a pained breath.

Every passing moment was making it more difficult to breathe.

"All routes to Anon Convention Center are showing one hour delays," the car explained. "Do you have another destination?"

"No," Kailynn said quickly, inserting her card into the slot on the dashboard before opening the door and getting out among the other cars pulled over on the highway, the car warning her about the dangers of pedestrians on the road.

She began running along the side of the road, ignoring the strange looks that she was sure other automobile passengers were giving her. At the nearest garage, she darted in and found the elevator, quickly ascending to the street and running along the deserted walkways between the buildings, looking up and hoping to spot the convention center.

When she came across a large, rounded building with several neon holograms flashing around it, she stopped and caught her breath, sure that she had found the convention center.

As she tried to find her way to the front of the building, glancing around for any sign of Theo or the others of the Heart of Trid gang, she could feel eyes on her.

It was then that she realized how suspicious she looked to any security detail that was looking for those plotting against the Golden Elite. She stopped and looked around, trying to spot guards.

A loud clank caused her to jump and turn to the opening door in the parkway in front of the convention center. A car drove out of the opening and pulled in front of the building. As it slowed, Kailynn saw several robots and black-clad guards walking toward the car. Kailynn's heart was in her throat, choking her.

Isa was leaving the convention center.

The moment she spotted the blonde-haired woman walking among the guards next to Rayal, she took a step forward and began to take a breath to yell at Isa, when the ear-piercing sound of a gunshot sounded.

Kailynn watched in horror as Isa's torso was pushed backward with the force of the bullet. Rayal stepped in front of her immediately as the guards and robots closed the area around the Golden Elite, who was crouching on the ground.

Kailynn was barely able to see Isa, her blue eyes scanning the building across the street, one hand clamped over the bullet graze on her shoulder. Rayal lifted his wrist to his mouth.

"Take any shot you can."

The robots lifted their guns to the area where the bullet had originated, some firing when they saw movement in the windows.

Kailynn backed away from the area, ducking around the nearest building and peering out to watch in horror.

When she had heard the first shot fired, her mind went blank. She could not even form the questions of how severely Isa had been injured, or the state of the Heart of Trid gang in the other building.

Bullets were flying in the space between the two buildings, the shots echoing around the structures as Kailynn remained still, watching helplessly. She dared not run to Isa, sure that she would be shot as well. She could only wait for the chaos to abate.

Almost as suddenly as it had begun, it slowed. The bullets were no longer being fired in rapid succession, but in short bursts when movement caught the robots censors or when those shooting from the other building thought they had a clear shot.

It felt like hours to Kailynn, but two minutes after the first shot was fired, the bullets stopped.

When Rayal got the clearance from those in the other building, he stood, as did Isa.

Kailynn was relieved to see the minimal graze on the Golden Elite's left shoulder. The Golden Elite was holding the wound to slow the bleeding, but she was clearly not in severe pain. She looked up at the windows of the other building and told Rayal she wanted to see the attackers.

Rayal ordered the robots and guards to secure the Golden Elite's path through the apartment building.

Kailynn looked around quickly, watching the guards disperse and move across the street. She darted down to the parking garage for the convention center and ran across the empty lanes of the underground highway. She was sure that the Syndicate had purposely closed off the area to contain the danger. Because of that, she was able to run across and find the garage elevator for the apartments across the highway. When she could not access the elevator, she found the emergency stairs and began climbing them two at a time.

Now that she knew Isa was alright, her thoughts turned to her brother.

She did not know if he was alive or dead. She did not even know if he was there or if he had sent others of the gang to shoot the Golden Elite. She had no idea what their punishment would be or if Isa would find out Kailynn's connection to the group that tried to kill her.

Kailynn poked her head out every door she came across, listening for the sounds of orders being barked.

She felt as though she had been searching the doors for hours when she finally heard voices in the hallway. She quickly got out of the stairwell and went toward the noises only to press herself to the wall when she saw the number of guards around the corner, standing post around an open door.

Kailynn listened, every muscle in her body tense.

"Four dead, seven injured," Remus's voice said. "All Trids."

"Fuck off, Elite scum!" Theo's voice bellowed. Kailynn closed her eyes and felt her stomach flip.

"What were you trying to accomplish by killing me?" Isa's calm voice asked.

"You could never understand the pain we feel! You kill us without reason! You force us to live in filth, hungry and dying. We can never climb out of Trid because you won't ever let us!" Sonya's voice screeched.

"See?" Theo growled. "You can't even deny it. You know it's true."

Kailynn took a deep breath and turned the corner, fully expecting another commotion when the guards and robots spotted her. Once she stepped into view, the guns in the hall pointed at her, but, to her fortune, Rayal was also looking in her direction. He quickly lifted his wrist to his mouth.

"Stand down," he ordered quietly.

The guns lowered and Kailynn started forward.

"I wish you had thought more carefully about your actions," Isa's voice said in the apartment that the Heart of Trid gang had broken into for the assassination attempt. "It is true, Anon does not allow for Trids to climb out of poverty. However, you ruined your own chances of changing that by trying to take my life. Now, Venus will be more convinced that the Trids are too dangerous to be assimilated into Anon society. There will be nothing I can do to change her opinion."

"Liar!" Theo bellowed. "Venus does not even exist! We tried to shut her down! There was nothing in the warehouse!"

Isa sighed heavily.

"That is because you had the wrong location," she said simply. "I knew there was a Trid gang that wanted to shut down Venus, so I set a trap. And you played into it. Just as you played into this trap. We knew you would try to kill me today."

"*How?*" another member demanded.

Isa did not respond. Kailynn started forward when the silence became too heavy, worried. However, Rayal held out his hand and shook his head, telling her to stay back. She stared at his hand and then at him, not sure how to respond.

"Miss?" one of the Officials that had helped the Silver Elite storm the apartment asked. "What do you want to do with them?"

"You know the punishment," Remus said darkly. "Execution."

The Official raised his gun, along with three of his comrades, and pointed it at the remaining members of the Heart of Trid gang.

"Wait!" Kailynn cried. Before she had a chance to think of her actions, she pushed past Rayal and ran forward, standing between the guns and the kneeling, bound Trids on the floor of the ransacked living room. Kailynn spread her arms in a sad attempt to shield the Trids and her eyes frantically met with Isa's. "Don't kill them!"

"Kailynn?" Isa hissed, blinking in surprise.

"What is she doing here?" Remus asked coldly.

"Miss?" the Official asked, turning to Isa.

"Kailynn?" the disbelieving voice said behind her. Kailynn chose to ignore it and looked at Isa seriously.

"Isa, please, I'm begging you."

"Who do you think you are?" Remus growled, stalking forward. "This does not concern you!"

"Isa! *Please!* Don't have them killed!" Kailynn cried, backing away from Remus as he approached. "Please!"

"Kailynn, what the hell are you doing?!" Theo snapped behind her.

"You will not interfere in this," Remus growled, seizing Kailynn's arm in a surprising grip and yanking her away from the group of Trids.

"Let go!" Kailynn barked, trying to rip free, the nails of her other hand scraping at him.

"Enough!" Isa ordered, motioning for the Officials to lower their guns. "Remus, release her." Remus hesitated only a split second before letting Kailynn go. Isa turned back to the younger woman. "You want me to spare their lives?"

"Please, Isa…I-I know what they did…" Kailynn said, her voice choked. "But…*please*, don't kill them…"

The two shared an intense, silent conversation before it was broken by Theo.

"Are you fucking for real?" he sneered, glaring. "All the time we spent tearing Trid apart looking for you, and you were kissing up to the fuckin' Elites?!"

"Theo, please, not now."

"Yes! Fucking *now*!"

"You're a damn traitor!"

"We don't need your help!"

"Killing us won't do anything!" Sonya bellowed, spitting at Isa. "We've got power in Trid you could never imagine. Soon, we'll drink and dance on your corpses! We'll overthrow you! You have no power over us!"

"Officers," Isa said coldly. The Officials pulled out their guns and pointed them at the prisoners once more.

"Isa!" Kailynn cried.

"Kailynn, come here," Isa said, extending her hand. Kailynn hesitated, but started toward the Golden Elite, her step slow and weak. She stood next to Isa as the Golden Elite turned to the silent, concerned Trids.

"Cease."

The Officers did not hesitate in lowering their weapons again.

"Remus."

The Silver Elite pulled out his own gun, pointing it at the Trids, forcing them to tense in apprehension again. They remembered when the formidable Elite barged into the room and immediately killed two of the gang, including Austin, the twitchy trigger-finger that had fired the first bullet.

"*I* have the power here," Isa said. "You will do well to remember. Cross me, and it takes only one word to end your lives."

"We'll never bow to you!!" Theo bellowed.

"I don't need you to bow," Isa told him. "You're already kneeling." She looked at the Officials. "Take them into custody, but do not harm or kill them. Instructions will be sent when I better know the situation." Isa turned to Kailynn. The younger woman looked at the ground quickly, trying not to notice the wound on the Golden Elite's shoulder or the concerned look in Isa's eyes.

As the Trids began spitting insults and hateful words, Remus turned to Isa seriously.

"Isa, this is a very bad idea," he whispered.

"I have had them before," Isa said simply.

"You cannot start to go soft because your new toy is concerned for them."

Isa rounded on Remus.

"Call her that again, and you will regret it instantly." Isa turned back to Kailynn and motioned her hand toward the door. Not sure what else to do, Kailynn walked with the Golden Elite and the silent Silver Elite out of the room. Rayal fell into step behind all of them as the robots and guards surrounded the leader of the planet. Kailynn spared a glance back at her struggling brother and the others of the Heart of

Trid gang as they were pushed out of the room and down the other hallway, away from the Elites, to be taken to prison.

Kailynn swallowed back tears, closing her eyes briefly.

Rayal reached forward and gently touched Kailynn's shoulder, offering a comforting squeeze and a soft smile.

"The press is outside, I'm sure," Remus said as the elevator doors opened and the guards stepped back to allow Isa and the others inside. "We better go underground to get to the cars. The roads should still be blocked."

"That sounds best," Isa agreed, sighing heavily. "Let the rumors fly as they will. We will formally address the issue at a later date."

"Venus will want an explanation," Remus murmured.

"I'll give her one."

It was a silent walk through the garage and pedestrian tunnels until they reached the garage of the convention center once more. Isa had to call her car back down, as it was still sitting outside the front door of the convention center.

"Don't come to work tomorrow," Remus said. "It will be best to remain quiet until you can make an official statement. I'll call Dr. Busen and set up an appointment around your schedule. Tarah can probably treat that at home for now."

"Thank you, Remus."

Remus turned to Kailynn, who unwillingly flinched from the glare. The vehicle appeared before them and Isa climbed in, motioning Kailynn to join her. Kailynn spared one final glance at Remus and Rayal and then got in the car with Isa.

Despite all the confused thoughts in Kailynn's head, she could not form any sentences to speak to Isa as they went to Anon Tower.

They were both silent.

However, Isa turned to her. Kailynn could not look back.

Isa reached over and wrapped her fingers around Kailynn's, squeezing them gently.

■■■

Tarah was ready to treat the Golden Elite the moment she walked in the door. She greeted Kailynn as well, but she was far more concerned with Isa's wounded shoulder. The graze from the bullet was minimal. Isa sat patiently while Tarah treated and wrapped the wound.

Kailynn paced slowly near the couch where the Elite sat, biting her nails and feeling exhaustion seep into her bones.

The silence in the house was deafening.

When Tarah was finished, Isa smiled.

"Thank you, Tarah," she said. "Some privacy, please."

"Yes, Miss."

Tarah obediently went into the kitchen as Isa stood, walking to Kailynn and gently taking her shoulders.

Kailynn's eyes raised to Isa's face, watching the Elite's expression as Isa pulled her hand from her mouth, squeezing the Significant's fingers tenderly.

She brought Kailynn to the couch and sat her down, sitting on the coffee table in front of her, holding Kailynn's hand as her other hand went forward and brushed her cheek.

"I'm sorry…" Kailynn choked.

"No need to apologize."

Kailynn pressed a hand to her face, bending her head forward.

"You already knew?" she asked, her voice choked.

"Yes."

"How?"

Isa was still for a moment before she took Kailynn's hand away from her face again.

"You worried me," she said. "When you called and asked me not to leave Anon Tower, I knew something was wrong. Rayal did the rest of the investigation and figured out when an assassination attempt was most likely. We were prepared." Isa leaned forward and pressed a kiss to Kailynn's forehead. "How did you find out about it?"

The tears came on so suddenly that they knocked the breath out of the younger woman. Her face creased in pain and she bent forward again, sobbing quietly.

Isa moved to her knees and wrapped her arms around Kailynn's shoulders, pulling her into a hug as Kailynn pressed her forehead to Isa's shoulder. The Elite rubbed her back, holding her as Kailynn's tears overwhelmed her.

When she finally regained her tongue, she let out a shuddered breath.

"I'm so confused…"

"Help me understand," Isa whispered, leaning her head against Kailynn's. "I want to help."

Kailynn pulled away from the hug, looking over Isa's worried face. She took the Elite's face in both hands and pulled her into a tender kiss. When their lips parted, she still held Isa's face, looking at her through tear-filled eyes.

"I don't understand anything anymore," Kailynn breathed. "I don't understand what you've done to me." She dropped her head, sobs beginning to wrack her body once more. "I betrayed...I betrayed my family for you..." She lifted her head. "Only a few months ago, I would have celebrated their plan...but now..."

Isa thumbed away the tears on the Significant's face.

Kailynn closed her eyes and leaned into the touch.

"I don't want anything to happen to you," she whispered. "I want to keep you safe." She opened her eyes once more. "I saw you almost die once. I couldn't bear seeing it again."

"I'm safe, Kailynn," Isa said gently, her thumb still stroking the Significant's cheek. "As are you."

Kailynn closed her eyes tight.

"Everything is so fucked up..." Kailynn whimpered.

Isa took a deep breath, slowly letting it out before she asked her question.

"Who were they to you?" she murmured. "How were they your family?"

"My brother was the leader of that gang," she said quietly. "He's the only family I have left. My mother was killed when I was only four. My father was killed a few years after that. Then I was sent to a Keeper because my brother did not want me around while he fenced drugs." She sniffed, her face creasing with pain once more. "I became a Significant to get him out of Uren after you caught him. All the money went to him. I couldn't bear the thought of him being executed." Her eyes went back to Isa. "But then you..." She trailed off, looking into the clear, stunning blue of Isa's eyes. "I met you...and now I don't understand myself anymore. The thought of you being killed...it was worse than the thought of my brother dying..."

She choked on the words, her hands dropping from Isa's shoulders, where they had been resting. She cradled her face in her hands, the tears coming once more.

"Isa...please...I'm begging you. Don't have them killed."

Isa leaned forward once more and pressed her lips to the top of Kailynn's head. Kailynn could feel the apology in the action.

She looked up quickly, forcing her tears back as her expression became frantic.

"Please, Isa."

"I'm afraid..." Isa trailed off, looking to the ground and letting out a heavy sigh. "I'm afraid that the decision is currently out of my hands."

Kailynn let the words bounce around her mind, her eyes searching Isa's face for an answer.

"What do you mean?"

"Venus will make the decision. This was a public spectacle. There were cameras around. I'm sure that most of the planet knows by now that there was an attempt on my life. To deter others from trying the same, Venus will want to make an example of them."

"You're just going to prove the Trids right," Kailynn said quickly. "You're going to prove that you are the enemy."

"There are limited actions available to me," Isa tried to explain. "I certainly can't let them go. That would prove weakness, and with the Alliance in the state it is in, I cannot afford to appear weak. If they are not punished, then that won't send a message to Trid, nor to anyone else, that we do not tolerate this behavior."

"Killing them won't stop more from trying, though!" Kailynn gasped. "More Trids will want revenge for the death of a gang that tried to help Trid."

"But they are harming Trid by doing things like what happened tonight," Isa said, her voice remaining calm. "I cannot argue for Trid if they are undermining my work with Venus. If she sees Trid as a threat, there is nothing I can do to change her mind."

"No, you have to convince her," Kailynn said. "You have to tell her that they cannot be killed."

"I cannot simply tell Venus what to do," Isa said. "It doesn't work like that. She tells me what to do."

"You have to do something. They can't die."

"Kailynn, do you understand my position here? Venus will not accept it if I tell her that I do not want them killed. They made an attempt on my life. She'll want them executed. The decision is in her hands."

"They wouldn't have done that if they had any other options!" Kailynn barked. "What else are they supposed to do? They're Trids! I was beyond fucking lucky. And it was all because of you! Why can't you do something to help the district of Trid?"

"It's very complicated, Kailynn."

"How complicated can it be?"

"Trid is essential to Tiao," Isa said.

"*Essential?*" Kailynn said in disbelief. "I thought it was the black spot on Tiao."

"It is," Isa admitted. "And that is why it is essential. The only way to govern people is by proving that you have power over them, and the way you do that is through fear, even if it is surreptitious. Trid instills fear in the classes about what could become of them if they do not do their part in society. Trid gives the others in Anon, and on all of Tiao, something to fear."

Kailynn stared at Isa in disbelief, the words cutting her deeply.

"You won't do anything to help the Trids because you're trying to *control* everyone? You're trying to *scare* them?"

"Humans need a form of governing," Isa said strongly. "Otherwise, what is to stop anyone from doing harm to others?"

"Why would they want to do harm to others if they have access to everything they need?" Kailynn challenged.

"When it comes to the average person, you're right," Isa agreed. "Most humans would not wish harm on others. Many would do anything to help one another. That is the way human beings are made as a species. But not all humans are like that. And when a human manipulates, they gain power over others and then that breeds discontent in other humans. That is why there needs to be a structure to keep everything in line."

"That doesn't make sense," Kailynn said, shaking her head. "Because then *you* are the one breeding discontent, aren't you?"

Isa sighed heavily.

"Society is far more complex than that."

"And I'm just too stupid to understand it?"

"I never said that," Isa defended gently.

"You didn't have to," Kailynn hissed, standing and walking to the guest hall. Her mind was clouded and she needed a few minutes to gather her thoughts before she continued the discussion.

"Where are you going?"

Kailynn did not answer. Isa was immediately on her feet, following the Significant.

"I did not mean to upset you," Isa said. Kailynn almost started jogging when the door to the guest hall opened. She went to the room she had when she stayed there and entered, turning around to press the lock button as it slid shut, barely shutting before Isa's face could be seen on the other side.

Kailynn turned her back to the door and leaned against it, sliding down to sit on the floor, desperately trying to control her tears.

"Kailynn…" Isa said, pressing her forehead to the door. "Please, come out and talk to me."

Kailynn leaned her head against the door, listening to the Golden Elite's voice. She knew she was tired and her tears had upset Isa, but she was also upset and confused. She had never felt so conflicted in her life.

"Kailynn."

"Not now," Kailynn choked. "I can't do this right now."

Isa was silent for a moment.

"What you said earlier," she started, "that you wanted me to be safe, I want the same for you." Isa pressed a hand to the door. "Seeing you in this much pain hurts me greatly, and I want to do whatever I can to help. But you have to understand that politics is a very dangerous and very delicate game. I have to plan every move very carefully."

"Please, Isa," Kailynn pled, "don't make this about politics."

"It *is* politics," Isa insisted. "I can help you, Kailynn. But it would require deception on both our parts. And deceiving Venus is no easy feat, nor is it safe."

Kailynn's brow creased in confusion and she hesitated before speaking.

"Deceiving Venus?" she whispered. "We're already deceiving her."

"I mean lying to her directly," Isa clarified, "not keeping information from her."

Kailynn turned around to face the door. She was silent, trying to understand what the Elite was planning. She stared at the door, her mind going blank.

"What are you talking about?" she finally murmured.

Isa sighed, closing her eyes and bowing her head.

"I will admit that I have been trying to think of ways to keep you close to me without raising suspicion."

"You knew I wouldn't stay all the time," Kailynn said.

"I did," Isa agreed. "Nonetheless, I felt that it was necessary I do everything in my power to keep you safe, and to plan for your safety in future situations."

"What kind of future situations?"

"As many as I can consider," Isa said. "If I were to be killed, or replaced, or if we were to go to war with Gihron." She paused, once again placing her hand on the door. "The fact that you agreed to have an emitter chip tells me that you are willing to stay close to me."

Kailynn hesitated, not sure how to respond.

"Kailynn, please," Isa said. "I do not want to discuss this through the door."

The Significant took a deep breath and closed her eyes, preparing herself. She had no idea what Isa was planning, and the uncertainty made her feel powerless, a sensation that made her uncomfortable.

She unlocked the door and it opened.

Kailynn leaned against the doorframe, sniffing back her tears as she crossed her arms over her chest.

"What do you have in mind?"

"First, I want to tell you that this is not a command, nor an order. You are, of course, free to go as you like. But I will always do what I think is best to keep you safe," Isa started. Kailynn nodded shallowly, her jaw clenching. "You are not the only one who has been confused about what is going on between us. In all honesty, I do not believe I have ever felt this way before, and it perplexes me." Isa's eyes softened. "If it were possible, I would have all of Trid granted citizenship and cleaned up, but I cannot convince Venus. I have tried for many years. She will not be persuaded. The only way she could be swayed is if she came to believe that Trids were a greater danger of social upheaval than as a tactic to keep the classes in place."

"…what does that mean?"

"It means that the Trids would have to spark some discomfort in the classes, particularly in Anon," Isa said. "Venus monitors the population as a whole to monitor stability. If the Trids were to protest, to show the horrid poverty that they are forced to endure, to show the sick and injured and the number of orphaned children, there might be a push to build schools and to assist the district from the upper classes."

"No there wouldn't," Kailynn scoffed. "Everyone looks down on the Trids."

"That is because the Trids have had to resort to criminal behavior," Isa said. "It's a complication in human psychology. There is a sense that anyone who breaks the law, even so much as to steal food, deserves whatever punishment they receive." Isa sighed heavily and shook her head. "It will not be an easy task, nor will it be fast. It will take time and careful persuasion. We would have to start with basics, such as healthcare and schooling."

"*How*, though?" Kailynn pressed. "You expect to get up and make a speech about that?"

"No." Isa shook her head. "I would need your help to play a very dangerous game with Venus."

"Play a game with her?" Kailynn asked incredulously.

"That's all I do every day," Isa said. "I know the rules very well. If you are willing, we can set forth a plan that might help the district as a whole and could, potentially, keep your brother off death row."

"Would it set him free?"

"I doubt it," Isa said honestly. "He will likely spend the rest of his life in prison."

"In Uren?" Kailynn choked.

"No," Isa said, shaking her head. "He was caught in the main Anon district. He'll be sent to Ikurah. There, he will get a cell where he will be fed, kept warm, and perhaps even educated in a trade so that he might be able to work, even though he will not be set free. But, that is only if I can keep him off death row."

"How do we do it?"

"I would take you on as my advisor," Isa said. "You would be employed under Rayal in the Syndicate Intelligence Agency. You would be my authority on Trid."

"How can you get that past Venus?"

"Carefully," Isa said. "I would have to tell Venus that Rayal was the one who scouted you for this project, after the incredible loyalty you showed me during the three plots on my life that you have, unfortunately, endured."

Kailynn dropped her head.

"Then, we would stage an operation that will start the chain of events leading to rallies in Trid. They will have to be peaceful and properly timed," Isa said. "The details will have to be decided, but only if you agree."

Kailynn closed her eyes, remaining silent, her arms crossed over her chest.

"It will save my brother?"

"If you trust me, I will do my best to spare him of the death penalty," Isa said. "You have my word."

Kailynn sighed heavily, looking over Isa's face and shaking her head.

"Why are you doing this for me?" she whispered. "I just…ran to you and begged you not to kill someone who tried to kill you. You have no reason to do it other than…"

"Other than for you?" Isa completed when Kailynn did not continue. "Because I care about you and I don't want to hurt you?"

Kailynn swallowed hard. "I feel like the leader of the planet shouldn't be so easily influenced by one person."

"That is why I was created as an Elite, and not a human," Isa assured.

"You don't act like any other Elite."

"Have you spent time with many?" Isa tried to jest.

"I've heard that statement from a lot of people," Kailynn said, ignoring the joke. Isa smiled.

"It's true," she said. "I've always been different." She took a deep breath. "However, I have also been called the best Elite Tiao has had in three hundred years." She shrugged. "I still don't know who judged that, but," she looked at Kailynn, her smile growing wider, "sometimes, change is the healthiest thing."

Kailynn swallowed hard and stepped forward, grabbing Isa's face and pressing their lips together in a kiss. She felt the heat of the Elite's lips, the softness of her skin under her fingertips, the power that engulfed her whenever she was close to the Golden Elite.

She continued to kiss the Elite whenever she turned to look at Isa as they made their way to Isa's bedroom. When the door closed, Kailynn quickly helped Isa out of her clothes, pushing her gently until the Elite fell back on the bed.

Quickly shimmying out of her pants as Isa backed her way up the bed, Kailynn climbed on top of the Elite and kissed her again, becoming desperate. It was as if the anxiety of the previous days, the fear and worry that consumed her every moment since learning of the plot on Isa's life, rushed forward.

She was desperate for reassurance that Isa was alright. She had spent so much time agonizing over what it would be like if Isa was killed that the reality had not yet hit her that Isa was safe and alive.

Her body blanketed the Golden Elite, her hands running over Isa's body as she kissed her eagerly.

When she felt cloth under her fingers, Kailynn stopped and backed away.

Her fingers lingered on the edges of the bandages around the wound in Isa's shoulder. She stared at the gauze, her mind going blank, thinking about the way Isa's body recoiled from the wound and the horror that ran through her when she thought Isa had been killed in front of her.

Isa stared up at Kailynn, watching the fear and pain cross her eyes. She turned her head and looked at her shoulder, seeing the way Kailynn's fingers rested ever-so-slightly on the edge of the bandages.

She reached up and took Kailynn's hand, bringing it down her chest to rest under her left breast, pressing into her ribcage.

Kailynn felt the warmth of Isa's body, but the strong beat of the Elite's heart seemed to calm the Significant's heart as well. Her body relaxed and she let out a shuddered breath.

Her eyes went to Isa's before she leaned down and kissed the Elite gently.

Chapter Twenty-Three

"Jacyleen, can you hear me?"

Kailynn took a deep, nervous breath and slowly let it out, nodding. "Yes, Rayal, I can hear you."

"Good," his voice said in her ear. "I am connecting with the Syndicate now. Elite Isa?"

"I'm here," Isa said. "The video feed is fuzzy."

"Jacyleen, can you lift your head and blink a few times. I think the contact is out of focus."

Kailynn suppressed her angry muttering as she lifted her head and blinked a few times, trying to ignore the discomfort from the contact.

"It focused," Rayal said. "I know it's uncomfortable, but try to endure it."

"We are connected entirely on our end," Isa said.

Kailynn tried not to let the statement unsettle her. They had been planning this for nearly two months. Isa had discussed the plan with her over and over again. She knew it very well. But it was still terrifying to realize that Venus was currently connected to the camera in her eye and the communication chip in her ear.

"Very good. We'll start then, Jacyleen," Rayal said, breaking her out of her stupor.

Kailynn took a deep breath and turned, getting out of the car and walking through the alleys of the Walking District.

"First, we want to see the areas in the Walking District where the most thefts happen," Rayal explained. "You said that they were closer to the south end of the street?"

"Yes," Kailynn said. She did not actually know which end of the street was south, but she knew where the thefts happened. She began walking through the ramshackle buildings to get to the Walking District. "It's too early in the day, though, for any activity."

"Jacyleen, do the different gangs of Trid have arrangements with the different facilities in the Walking District?"

"...what do you mean?" Kailynn asked, confused by Isa's question.

"For instance, do some gangs have claim over the goods from a particular club or bar? Only one gang can steal from a certain bar?"

"No," Kailynn said, continuing to walk. "When it comes to food, we don't care about territories. The gangs never fight over ration packs."

There was a shrill beeping in Kailynn's ear and she quickly flinched away from the sound, except that it was in her ear and she could not back away from it. She closed her eyes and fell against the side of the nearest building, gritting her teeth.

"I am so sorry," Isa said quickly.

"I still have feedback on my end," Rayal said.

Kailynn opened her eyes and blinked, confused and shocked by the noise.

"Remus, can you redirect?" Isa's voice said.

"Working on it."

"What was that?" Kailynn asked, her ear ringing.

"My sincerest apologies," Isa said. "That was V.E.R., Venus' language."

"What?"

"That was Venus talking," Rayal clarified. "Elite Isa, can you translate?"

"She asked what the gangs *do* fight over, but stay where you are for now, Jacyleen," Isa said. "Remus is redirecting the audio feed through her translator. It will be a moment."

"You can understand that beeping?" Kailynn said, her eyes wide. Isa did not answer.

"Venus, can you direct communication through Syndicate Port Seven?" Isa asked. A moment later, there was a new voice in Kailynn's ear.

"I lowered the decibels," the mechanical female voice said.

"Jacyleen, is that volume alright for you?" Rayal asked.

"Y-yes..." Kailynn murmured.

Even knowing that she was connected to Venus, hearing the voice of the machine, realizing that the computer that ran the entire planet was focused on what she was seeing, there was an instinctive fear in her belly.

"To repeat," Venus said, the grainy voice sharp and harsh, "what is it that the gangs of Trid fight over if not food?"

Kailynn swallowed hard and started walking again.

"Money, drugs, territory, protection..." Kailynn made her way into the Walking District. "Protection is the reason the gangs form."

"The statistics of personal safety do show an increase when an individual is in a group of those with similar goals," Venus said.

"Isa, are you alright?" Remus asked suddenly.

"Fine," Isa said, though there was strain in her voice.

"A-C89072," Venus said, "your blood pressure has risen."

There was a hesitation before Isa spoke.

"The translation is delayed," she explained vaguely. "The feedback is interfering with your other processes, Venus."

Kailynn stopped again, confused and worried about the pain in Isa's voice.

"Isa?" Rayal pressed.

"Venus, with your permission," Remus started, "I will terminate your audio connection and Isa can translate for you."

"Permission not granted."

"I'll be fine," Isa assured, "please continue, Jacyleen."

Confused and worried about Isa, Kailynn hesitated. However, with Venus looming over all of them, she decided it was best to obey the commands.

She peered around the back alleys of the shops, all of which were closed. The dirty alley was littered with trash, but deserted.

"This is where most of the thefts take place. Most gangs take enough to feed their members only. One gang did try to get all the food and sell it to the Trids, but the other gangs quickly killed them. Food is for everyone here, even if you are expected to get it for yourself."

"By that logic, every Trid is a member of a gang," Venus said.

"Yes," Kailynn agreed.

"And how many gangs exist?"

"I don't know."

"What is this illness that you spoke of, A-C89072?" Venus said.

"It's a...Rayal? Please explain." Isa said, her voice now revealing her pain. Kailynn's heart constricted in her chest.

"Uh...it...it was something that Jacyleen told me about. It causes severe dehydration, vomiting, bleeding ulcers, blisters over the skin...it is unclear how it is passed. However, it has killed many Trids. The bodies have not been properly disposed of, either," Rayal explained.

"Take me to one, Significant," Venus ordered.

"E-Elite Isa, are you alright?"

"Her blood pressure is still at a safe level," Venus assured. "Take me to an ill Trid."

Kailynn swallowed hard, but obeyed, walking to the area where she knew the sick Trids to be. When she began to turn down a set of streets she knew to lead to the junkyard at the lake, Isa's voice stopped her.

"Wait," she said quickly, "turn to that building."

Trying to ignore how strained Isa's voice was, Kailynn turned, trying to figure out what Isa was looking at.

"Beyond it, the faded red building," Isa said. "Is that a Keeper?"

Kailynn tried not to let the nausea wash over her, though it was difficult not to with the orphanage where she grew up in front of her.

"Yes."

"Can we get closer?"

Kailynn knew that seeing Trid children was part of their plan to show Venus how horrible the conditions in Trid were, but Kailynn was hoping that they would see the young gang children, not those in possession of a Keeper.

"A-C89072," Venus said, "is this not the same Keeper from which you obtained your caretaker?"

Kailynn's step faltered and a gasp managed to escape her. If the others heard the sound, they did not acknowledge it.

"Yes."

"Significant," Venus said suddenly, "were you ever in care of this Keeper?"

"Yes."

"Were you ever prostituted at that time?"

"*What*? No!" Kailynn gasped.

"But you were aware of the prostitution of orphans that was occurring at this Keeper?" Venus pushed.

"Venus," Isa said strongly, "she was a child."

"I am gathering information."

Kailynn's brain was racing. Her feet continued to carry her to the Keeper from muscle memory. She had long pushed away the few years she had remained in the care of the Keeper. The only Keeper in Trid at that time was a man they called "Sir." He was a thin, tall man with small, beady black eyes and thin, stringy hair that fell over his face and ears. He always left the stench of cheap alcohol in his wake as he stumbled around the halls, grumbling about taking care of all the children and not being paid enough.

The children knew never to go near Sir alone. They always traveled in groups and stayed out of his way.

But one day, a newcomer had appeared at the Keeper. A small, starved girl with bandages around her body. Her father dropped her off without so much as a second glance, walking off with his hundred credits and leaving his daughter at the mercy of Sir. Kailynn never learned the little girl's name. She had been ostracized by the other children, who called her horrible names and threw dirt and garbage at her whenever they saw her.

Kailynn's stomach flipped over as she connected the pieces.

One day, that little girl disappeared, as well. Everyone assumed she had died. Kailynn now understood that she had found her way into the home of the Golden Elite.

"Jacyleen," Rayal said, bringing her back to the present, "are you alright?"

"Significant, answer," Venus ordered.

"Y-yes, I knew…"

"Jacyleen," Isa's voice said gently, "are you alright to continue?"

"I…Elite Isa…" Kailynn wanted to ask a million questions, but she knew she could not with Venus looming over her.

"Look up," Venus commanded. "Let me see the children."

Kailynn was feeling weaker by the moment. She wanted to go somewhere quiet and gather her thoughts. However, she obeyed the order and lifted her head. There were some children of Trid sitting on the steps of the front of the building, talking to one another and playing a courage game where they would try to smack the other child's hands as hard as they could before their opponent pulled away.

"I do not understand," Venus said.

"They're just playing," Kailynn murmured.

"Social interaction is common within Trid," Rayal added.

"Then unity is a possibility," Venus deduced.

"Venus, I must implore you to disconnect your translator," Remus said strongly. "Isa is struggling."

"I'm fine," Isa assured quietly.

"Her blood pressure is still safe, and she is still conscious," Venus said. "I will not cause her permanent harm."

Kailynn was getting worried about Isa. She decided that she needed to take the tour of Trid into her own hands.

"We can't stay," she said quickly, turning around. "I am in enemy territory over here. I'll take you to see some sick Trids."

She walked quickly. Through the silence, she prepared herself. She knew that she had to give the appropriate signal to Rayal so that he could go through with the more dangerous part of the plan. But, as the time was drawing closer, she grew more nervous.

She slipped into one of the alleys and stopped at the corner of the building, pressing her back against the wall.

"Why are you stopping?" Venus demanded.

"I just want to make sure that I'm safe," Kailynn said. She turned and glanced around the corner. She already knew who would be waiting for her, but she allowed time for Rayal to open a virus that Isa had programmed to take down all the blocks on the video feed. This allowed everyone in Syndicate Intelligence to see what Kailynn was seeing, and would, hopefully, spark some controversy. They were sure that the video would quickly spread. She peered around the corner once more.

"Is he a friend?" Rayal asked.

That was her signal.

The virus was working.

"Actually, yes," Kailynn said, trying to sound surprised. "But…I…" She started forward. "Raffy!" she called.

Raphael turned. His face was pale. He was nervous about the plan that Kailynn had explained. Kailynn had not explained why, but she said that they needed to be there at that time on that day and pretend that they had not arranged the meeting. That told Raphael that they were being watched, though he was not sure how. However, he also knew that her plan was to try and save Theo's life, so he decided not to ask questions until afterward. Kailynn was too tense and frantic to explain beforehand. He would have to wait.

"What are you doin' here?"

"I was going to ask you that," Kailynn said, trying to sound confused while communicating with her eyes that they were being watched very closely. "I thought Viv was supposed to bring Amailli her food today."

Raphael swallowed hard and lowered his eyes to the ground.

"Listen, Lynni," he said. Kailynn tried not to show her fear at what he called her, remembering that she had not told him to use her fake name. "Amailli is dead."

Kailynn stopped, legitimately surprised. For several long moments, she could not speak.

Amailli and her two children were under the care and protection of Kailynn's gang. Two years previous, during a dark territory dispute between her gang and another gang that had since been eliminated, Amailli's partner, and father to the two children, had been gunned down, leaving Amailli pregnant and caring for her six-year-old daughter, Emira, alone. Kailynn had seen the bullets tear through Amailli's partner, killing him instantly. Ever since, she had felt a duty to care for the small family, even if it was only providing small amounts of food and clean water when she could.

At the beginning of her care for the three Trids, Kailynn would stay and visit with them, playing with Emira and helping Amailli look after the infant Annette. But, time progressed, Kailynn got a job with Brad, then Theo continued to get into trouble with the authorities. She had delegated the task of caring for Amailli to others of her gang. Even when they got the sickness that was frighteningly common among Trids—nicknamed "Wheezing Death"—Kailynn continued to insist that care was given to the small family.

Suddenly, she believed that she had failed them.

"What?" she hissed. "A-are you sure?"

Raphael nodded and glanced at the door.

"I came here instead of Viv," he said. "When I went in there to check on them…she was dead. Seems like it's been a couple days."

Kailynn was speechless, her jaw opening and closing uselessly.

"Let me see the corpses," Venus said in her ear.

The others watching the video feed did not speak.

Kailynn still could not speak for several long moments. When she did, the words caught in her throat and almost choked her.

"And the kids?"

Raphael hung his head.

"They've both got it," he said. "Annette…probably won't last to tomorrow."

"Show me," Venus ordered.

Kailynn bit her tongue to keep from snapping at the computer to leave her alone. There was a lot for her to process.

"I want to see them," Kailynn muttered, turning and shoving the door open. Raphael glanced around behind her. He was desperate to know what was going on, but he knew that Kailynn was in no position to tell him in that moment. He was worried that Kailynn was in further trouble, and being near Amailli's children, who were extremely ill, he was very concerned for Kailynn's safety on many levels.

Kailynn was sure to keep her eyes up as she climbed the stairs to the flat where Amailli and her children lived so that everyone, Venus included, could see the horrible conditions in which Trids lived. There was a small bite of contempt in her blood as she stepped around a large hole in the stairs, holding the rail tightly, in case more of the staircase collapsed.

Kailynn found the door to the flat open.

She could hear the soft sobbing as she rounded the corner into the dirty, refuse-filled home. There were smashed bottles everywhere, wrappers of rations littering the ground with dirty clothes and rags. The smell was rancid and Kailynn cringed away, covering her face. Raphael came up behind her, holding out a rag that was mostly-clean. Kailynn placed it over her nose and mouth and stepped further into the flat.

Raphael followed nervously, holding his sleeve over his mouth.

Kailynn walked around the half-demolished cabinets that originally made up a functioning kitchen and found Amailli's body curled on her side, facing the cabinets, her eyes wide and glassy and her skin blue, the color only broken by the large, dark, aggravated blisters. Her stiff body was in a disturbing position. Kailynn tried to block out the images of finding her father dead in the alleyway when she was a child. He had also been in a horrifying position, though he had been propped upright against some discarded crates.

"Blue hints in the skin indicate lack of oxygen," Remus said quietly.

"Severe malnutrition," Rayal added.

"Is this spread through air contamination? Or physical contact?" Venus asked Kailynn.

The Significant did not respond.

Unable to look at Amailli's body, she turned her attention to the eight-year-old girl holding a still two-year-old. Emira, Amailli's older daughter, was pale and thin, her eyes sunken into dark sockets as she cried, staring at her mother's body while she clutched desperately to Annette.

Kailynn had made it a point to avoid anyone with Wheezing Death, so the horrifically-ill child caused her stomach to flip and a chill to run through her body. However, she had no concern for her safety. She quickly went to Annette and put a hand on her shoulder, staring at the girl worriedly.

Emira turned her head to Kailynn, shaking.

"She's cold..."

"Please, be careful," Isa said gently.

Kailynn looked down at Annette, seeing the open sores on the girl's skin and the way her chest quickly rose and fell as she tried to breathe. Her eyes were closed, her face contorted in pain.

"She will die tonight," Venus stated simply. "The older girl appears healthier. Take her to the hospital for examination. The bodies will be collected by a HazMat Team and brought in for analysis."

"What?" Kailynn hissed, feeling her anger bubble within her.

"What is it?" Raphael asked, walking over to her.

"I have already contacted the Officials," Venus said. "You can wait with the girl until they arrive or you can take her to the hospital yourself. You will need examination as well. You are not allowed near any member of Syndicate until you are decontaminated."

Kailynn stared with wide eyes at the floor.

"How...how can you..."

"Jacyleen," Rayal said quickly, "it is for the best. The doctors might be able to treat the girl if we get her there in time."

"She just lost her mother, and her sister is dying," Kailynn snapped.

"Kailynn...what..." Raphael trailed off when he saw the distant, angry look in Kailynn's eyes. He realized that she was talking to the person who was watching them. That was when he realized that not only were they being watched, but Kailynn was bugged with some sort of audio feed.

"There is nothing that can be done for the younger girl or the mother," Venus said shortly. "We must gather all information possible for analysis."

"She just lost everything and you want to turn her into a lab rat?!" Kailynn growled darkly.

"She is vital to understanding what illness is plaguing Trid. If we can discern a way to treat it, then we can stop it before it reaches Anon," Venus continued.

"This illness has been killing Trids for years!" Kailynn snapped. "But because it could spread, *now* you pay attention?"

"Kailynn, who the hell are you talking to?" Raphael hissed. Emira's tears began running more freely as she looked around nervously, holding her dying sister tighter.

"Jacyleen," Remus' voice said slowly, "I suggest you let the Officials take the girl to the hospital. You will need to be examined as well."

"I'm not going to leave her," Kailynn said darkly. "She's scared and she's alone, and you want to have her arrested and hauled to a lab for testing like she's some kind of criminal. She has done nothing wrong!"

"She is a Trid," Venus responded. Even though the translation of her voice was even and calm, Kailynn could almost feel anger from the machine. "She is not a citizen."

"So she's going to be arrested?"

"She will be treated," Venus corrected.

"And then turned back here with no family and no protection," Kailynn challenged. "She'll starve to death."

"No, she will not," Venus said. "She will be taken to the Keeper and cared for until the age of fifteen, as is custom."

"The same Keeper that prostituted Tarah?" Kailynn hissed. "Isa, you can't possibly—"

"Learn your place, Jacyleen," Remus said quickly.

"Always address the Elites with their titles," Rayal said, trying to remind Kailynn of the situation.

Kailynn turned to Raphael and, upon seeing his pale countenance, she could feel the color drain from her face as well. She had just said Isa's name in front of him.

He knew they were being watched by the Syndicate.

"If the Officials are coming, we cannot stay," he said quietly.

"Raphael—"

"Are you *insane*?" Raphael hissed.

"Officials?" Emira gasped, her eyes wide. "Am I in trouble?"

"This situation is getting out of hand," Venus said. "Significant, leave the premises at once. Go to the hospital."

"I told you! I'm not leaving her!" Kailynn snapped, closing her eyes and lifting a hand to her head. "This…there has to be another way…"

"She will die if we leave her untreated. She has no one to care for her. She has no citizenship. She will be treated, her treatment will tell us how to keep this from spreading to the public, and then she will be taken to the Keeper where she will be fed until she is fifteen," Venus repeated. "This is a command, Significant."

"This is why the Trids are so desperate to kill the Elites," Kailynn said with an exasperated chuckle. "What choice do we have to change things for ourselves? We are confined to a place where we cannot get medical help, we cannot be taught, we are forced to live in filth and rely on theft just to eat. If you are so desperate to keep your social peace, then why are you letting this happen to us? We're human. We deserve to live, too. Emira has done nothing wrong. Her family was just taken from her, and your solution is to pretend to help by treating her and then tossing her back here? How can you call yourself a ruler?"

"Venus! Venus, there was a meltdown in the security coding," Rayal said quickly. "A virus tore down the blocks. This is being broadcast."

"How far is the reach?" Remus demanded.

"Shut down all feeds," Venus ordered.

Suddenly, everything went very still and silent.

Kailynn stood still, staring at the terrified child holding her dying sister. For several long moments, she could not move. She slowly sank to her knees again, her body shaking.

"Kailynn, what the hell is going on?" Raphael murmured, seeing the terrified look in Kailynn's eyes. "They're going to take her to the hospital and treat her? Are they going to kill her?"

"I don't know. I..."

As Kailynn kneeled on the floor of dirty, rancid-smelling flat, she started to realize how powerless she was. Whenever she had heard her brother talk about how easy it would be for the Trids to rise up and overthrow the Syndicate, she had felt as though she could conquer the planet. She felt powerful and smart, knowing the horrible conditions the Trids lived in and how many Trids were angry with the Syndicate and Venus. She used to believe that if those in Anon could only see the way the Trids lived, they would revolt against the Syndicate and Venus, which would allow the Trids to change their lives and show the power they actually had on the planet.

But in those moments, where an eight-year-old girl, who had done nothing wrong other than be born within the borders of Trid, was about to be hauled away by Officials to a hospital, Kailynn understood what Isa meant by carefully playing a game with Venus. Venus did not have the compassion of a human. She saw everything as a procedure, steps to accomplish a goal. People were not people, they were numbers. Trids were not humans, they were statistics.

Everything was numbers to Venus.

Kailynn did not know how to play the political game. She was worried that she had made things worse. She had forgotten that Rayal had broadcast the feed to the Intelligence Agency, meaning everyone had heard her angry words toward Venus.

There was fear and anxiety coursing through Kailynn like she had never felt before in her life.

"Kailynn," Raphael hissed, "tell me what the fuck is going on."

"I can't..." Kailynn said, shaking her head and swallowing hard. "Not today. They're coming to take her to the hospital. If you want to leave, you should go now."

"What happened?"

"It's too complicated to explain now," Kailynn said, closing her eyes. "Just get out of here. I'll explain another time."

"...I don't even know you anymore," Raphael hissed.

The words hurt Kailynn far more than she should have let them. She flinched away and distracted herself by putting her hand on Emira's shoulder.

"Just get out of here, Raphael," she murmured.

"Next time you want to betray all of us to the fucking Syndicate," Raphael snapped, "leave me out of it."

He turned and left the flat as Kailynn wrapped her arms around Emira and smoothed over her hair.

By the time the Officials arrived to take them to the hospital, Annette had stopped breathing.

■■

Kailynn stayed with Emira through the entire examination. The doctors were stumped at the virus that was slowly killing the child, which made Emira very nervous. Kailynn stayed by her side and held her hand, telling her that everything was going to be alright.

When it seemed like the doctors were getting angry and frustrated with the lack of results and understanding of the Wheezing Death, Kailynn asked if she could see Dr. Busen.

After pointing out, in a condescending tone, that Dr. Busen was head of Elite Special Medicine and, therefore, was too busy to be seeing a low-ranked, new employee of the Intelligence Agency, the doctors told her to be quiet while they continued their examinations.

However, Kailynn insisted that they at least call the doctor and see if he would see her.

One of the doctors used his in-hospital communication piece to page for Dr. Busen to respond. When the other doctor answered the page, the doctor said that there was an Intelligence Agency employee named Jacyleen that wanted to see him.

When he responded that he would be there as soon as he could, the other doctor's face went pale.

Dr. Busen's arrival to the examination room changed the atmosphere drastically. It was clear that he was one of the most respected doctors in the largest hospital in Anon, and his immediate response to the request to see Kailynn caused the other doctors great concern.

He ordered the group of younger doctors out of the room and started doing an examination of his own while he asked Kailynn everything she knew about the illness.

Dr. Busen started talking about tests and large drug names that made her head spin, but she nodded obediently. When he finished speaking, she took a chance. She started to explain the argument with Venus and what was to be done with Emira when Dr. Busen held up his hand with a chuckle.

"No need to explain," he said. "I've already seen the footage."

"How is that possible?"

"Someone at the Intelligence Agency allowed the live feed onto the public broadcasting we have around the hospital to entertain patients. I happened to catch the last five minutes, or so."

Kailynn's eyes were wide as she thought about how many people had probably already seen the footage.

"Well...then...did it...are people angry? What's the response?"

"I'm afraid I'm not a good person to discuss that with," Dr. Busen said, shaking his head.

"...I don't want her to go back to Trid and be with the Keeper. It'd horrible there."

"Yes, I know. I was the one who treated Tarah when she first came to Anon," Dr. Busen said sadly.

"Is there any way we can keep that from happening to her?" Kailynn pled. "Can we keep her in Anon?"

Dr. Busen smiled. "I'll see what I can do. I have some friends in high places." He chuckled lightly. "Don't forget, so do you."

When Kailynn was given a clean bill of health, Rayal came to pick her up.

She got in the car, feeling as though she had been awake for days.

"Why didn't anyone tell me that Tarah was a Trid?" Kailynn asked as the car started forward.

"She's not," Rayal said simply. "She was granted citizenship when she was eight."

Kailynn closed her eyes.

"I knew her in Trid," she said gently. "Well, I knew *of* her."

"I know," Rayal said. "She recognized you. She knew who you were."

Kailynn turned quickly to Rayal, her eyes wide.

"She recognized me?" she hissed. "Why didn't she say anything?"

"She's embarrassed," Rayal said. "You know what happened to her when she was with that Keeper. And she knows that the other children of that Keeper knew what was happening. She is still trying to work through the trauma. She was not about to bring it up to you when she can barely talk about it to anyone."

Kailynn rubbed her face tiredly.

"Then it was all true?" Kailynn asked. "I always thought there was some exaggeration."

Rayal sighed heavily. "When she first came to Anon Tower...she refused to be touched, she could not be left alone, she just clung to Isa. Even when we took her to Dr. Busen, she would not let go of Isa." He looked at Kailynn seriously. "That kind of reaction told me everything I needed to know about the abuse she suffered."

"How did Isa get her right out of Trid?" Kailynn asked, confused.

"Isa was doing something against the rules," Rayal said simply. "She was in Trid, driving around, looking at everything, and she stopped at the Keeper to see the orphaned children. She said she saw Tarah trying to run and a man chasing her. Tarah was naked and had bruises all over her. She was bleeding from her arms and legs. Isa ran to the man and got him away from her before taking Tarah into Anon without permission from Venus. She had Tarah treated, kept her at Anon Tower for several months before granting her citizenship and sending her to school."

"How did Venus allow her to just grant citizenship like that?"

"It was under the guise that Tarah would replace me when I retired," Rayal said. "Just like the reason we were able to give you citizenship was to serve a political agenda." The former caretaker sighed heavily and leaned his head back on the seat. "But, I'm sure you can see why Isa has to be very careful about granting citizenship. She cannot just take a few Trids every month and give them citizenship. Tarah was a special case. As were you."

Kailynn looked down at her feet.

"I don't want Emira to go to the Keeper," she said quietly.

"I doubt Isa will let that happen," Rayal assured.

"Is Isa alright?"

Rayal sighed heavily.

"She's a little weak and tired," he admitted. "It's not normal to have Venus speak through translators like that. Isa has one implanted, which allows her to understand Venus' language. However, the interference between the two translators caused her to get a very nasty migraine. She'll have to go to Dr. Busen just to be sure that she's alright. Headaches are a sign of great concern since five years ago."

Kailynn just nodded.

She did not even have the energy to ask about what happened five years previous.

When they pulled into Anon Tower and took the elevator up to Isa's level, Kailynn was sure she was about to faint. She was exhausted and shaky. She had never felt that way in her life. The stress of that situation, she was sure, would take years off her life.

That is, if Venus did not have her executed for treason after that day.

The two walked into Isa's home and Kailynn saw Isa stand from the couch, where she had been waiting for the Significant.

Kailynn's pace increased as she walked to the Elite. She did not notice Rayal glance into the kitchen before going into the guest hall.

Isa's arms secured Kailynn to the present as she embraced her tightly. Kailynn pressed her face into Isa's shoulder, her eyes closing and her body relaxing.

Even though they remained that way, silent, for what must have been an eternity, it was still too soon that Isa's head moved back and she kissed Kailynn's cheek gently.

"Are you alright?"

"No," Kailynn said quietly.

"I'm so sorry, Kailynn," Isa murmured.

Kailynn's arms tightened around the Elite and Isa's head leaned against the younger woman's.

"I'm sorry," Kailynn said. "I thought I could do it, but…"

"But?" Isa asked. "What do you mean?"

"I screwed it up, didn't I?" Kailynn said, her voice cracking with fear at the end of the sentence.

"No, no," Isa assured, rubbing her back tenderly. "You did not screw anything up." Isa closed her eyes and kissed Kailynn's head. "I'm sorry I put you in that position."

"I can't do this," Kailynn said, shaking her head. "I don't know how to do this political thing."

"You don't have to do the political thing," Isa assured. "I can handle that. I'm sorry that I put such pressure on you. I did not know it would be that bad."

Kailynn swallowed hard and closed her eyes.

"Will you help Emira?" she murmured. "Like you helped me and Tarah?"

"Of course," Isa said without hesitation.

∎∎

A small chime at her door caused Tarah to look up from where she had been reading on her bed. She climbed clumsily off the bed and walked to the door, opening it. When she saw Rayal, she jumped a little.

"Oh," she said, "I didn't realize that you were here."

"Isa let you off early?"

"She didn't feel like eating, so she said I could take the evening for myself," Tarah said. She leaned against the doorframe. "But…I know it was just because she was worried about me."

"Then you saw the broadcast," Rayal said. She nodded slowly. "Are you alright?"

Tarah sighed heavily and crossed her arms over her chest, averting her eyes.

"I think so…"

Rayal did not bother to push Tarah. He could tell just from looking at her that she was upset. He lowered his eyes to the ground and nodded slowly.

"Alright," he murmured. "But, if you ever want to talk about it, or about anything, you know you can call me, right?"

Tarah smiled.

"Do you remember, five years ago, when I had that meltdown and collapsed in the middle of the hospital waiting room?"

"Yes," Rayal said, confused why she would bring that up.

"And you brought me back here, even though you were extremely sick as well, and you sat with me and held my hand as I cried until I finally passed out?"

Rayal nodded slowly.

"I don't think I ever thanked you for that," Tarah said. "Or for everything else you've ever done for me."

"There is no need to thank me," Rayal said.

"There is a lot of reason to thank you," Tarah corrected. She swallowed hard and looked down at her feet, her face flushing. "You always put my comfort and needs before yours. You always made sure that I felt safe, no matter the situation. You always made me feel like I was stronger than I actually am."

"Tarah, you are amazingly strong," Rayal said. "That has nothing to do with me. That's all from within you."

"But I only feel it when you're around," Tarah murmured. She shyly glanced up at the former caretaker. "You make me see it in myself."

Rayal stared at Tarah for a moment, unable to respond. Tarah, nervous and embarrassed, cleared her throat and stood straight.

"Anyway, thank you."

Rayal smiled gently and reached forward, pulling Tarah into a gentle hug. The younger caretaker was startled at first, but then relaxed and hugged Rayal back. The hug only lasted for three seconds, but Tarah's head was still swimming when Rayal pulled away.

"If you need *anything,* just let me know," he murmured. "I'll always be here for you."

Chapter Twenty-Four

Isa took a deep breath and closed her eyes, facing the closed door, gathering herself as best as she was able. No matter how many times she had an audience with Venus, she was never prepared.

Seeking an audience with Venus was very different than communicating to her through the NCB chair or terminal messaging. There was something far more intimidating when staring at the hologram of the machine's persona and discussing delicate topics.

Venus had called her to audience to discuss the protests in Trid and the spread of information about the Wheezing Death Virus and the viral way the video of Emira spread, not only around the planet, but through the entire Altereye System.

Isa reached one hand out and pressed her palm against the orb outside the door. The warmth of the sensor made her skin tingle. A small needle pricked her finger and drew a drop of blood for DNA verification. The door hummed open and Isa stepped in, stopping two steps into the first chamber of Venus' audience hall. When the door closed behind her, Isa closed her eyes and waited for the second verification process.

She could see flashes of green light pass beyond her eyelids and her skin warmed around her chest as beams of light passed over her.

When the lights shut off, the doors in front of Isa opened and the Golden Elite was allowed into the main audience hall. The room was stark and bare with a single ring near the high ceiling of the domed hall allowing for the hologram projection. Venus' computers were hidden under the floor and behind the walls of the room, secured very tightly. Isa had only seen one of her processors when she had to repair it, but the central units that kept Venus running were never accessed, not even by Isa.

But, because of the massive computers and power cores, the audience hall was exceptionally hot. Isa was in full Syndicate uniform, and almost immediately after stepping into the room, she felt sweat break out over her skin.

Alone, five paces into the room, was a single chair—not an NCB chair, just a normal chair with a cushion on the seat and on the back with thick arms and a simple, metal design.

Isa walked to the chair and sat, leaning back and putting her wrists on the edge of the chair arms, activating the hologram.

A whirring of the machines filled the room, and the lights flickered. The composite form of Venus took shape. The image towered into the room, human in appearance, though shrouded by a cloak with the hood pulled over the face. The nose and mouth were visible, though the mouth never moved, as Venus' language was comprised of tones.

"*A-C89072,*" she greeted, using Isa's prototype number.

"Venus."

"*You understand that there are several reasons I called you here,*" Venus started. "*The first of these reasons has to do with the Y-99 Virus that has been in Trid.*"

"I am unfamiliar with the Y-99 Virus."

"*It is the new virus, undocumented. This is the first time that it has been seen. It has been named Y-99.*"

"Is there any treatment?"

"*More research is needed,*" Venus stated simply. "*I have had samples sent off-planet for testing in other areas of the system. Though it has not been documented on any other terminal, it is possible that this virus is in other parts of the system and has gone unnoticed, as it has on Tiao.*"

"I see."

"*However, I noticed that you have put the Trid girl under your protection. She is now listed within your circle. Why?*"

"The girl had very little to begin with, and now she has nothing," Isa stated. "If we are to continue to get samples from her for the virus, she needs to be protected from harm. Very few take kindly to Trids."

"*That is precisely why she needs to be returned to Trid at the nearest possible time,*" Venus said.

"Forgive my defiance, but I disagree," Isa said, shaking her head. "She will die if we return her to Trid. Her face and story are now widespread news, which means that it would be more beneficial to keep her close, as a sign of good faith to the Trids."

"*The Trids want her back,*" Venus said. "*They are protesting at the border, demanding that she be returned.*"

"The sentiment has been noted," Isa admitted. "However, if we were to return her to Trid untreated, there will be no one to care for her. The Trids try to stay away from those who have this virus. She will be isolated and she will either starve or the virus will kill her."

"*Where did you get this information?*"

"From Jacyleen, the Significant, and advisor for the Trid District."

"*I did not approve her as your advisor.*"

"She is the only Trid I have to advise me on matters concerning the district."

"*Your caretaker was once Trid, and has proven her loyalty to you far more than the Significant.*"

"Tarah has been with me longer, it is true," Isa admitted. "But she was a young child when she left. Jacyleen still has contacts in Trid. And she has proven to me, on three occasions, her loyalty."

"*You would keep her close, despite the fact that she forged her citizenship originally to work at Companion Corporation?*"

"Yes," Isa said strongly. "It is as she said in Trid. The Trids have very little means to change their lives. She did what she had to do to survive." Isa leaned back in her chair. "Venus, you have access to all the numbers. Eighty-five percent of incarcerated criminals in this hemisphere are Trids. Their crimes are very often not violent, which is why we imprison them rather than execute them. Two percent of these Trid criminals have been convicted of rape or murder. Seventy-seven percent of Trid criminals are convicted of forgery, falsified documents, and sedition. These numbers speak for themselves. They are willing to risk imprisonment to earn money to survive."

"*You know the Trids are vital to the security of this society.*"

"We can maintain social order with the Trids receiving citizenship."

"*No,*" Venus said, her hologram flickering slightly as a red tinge washed over her figure. "*This is the twenty-ninth time you have suggested the Trids be granted citizenship.*"

"Venus, these are the same people that are willing to kill me to tear down the Syndicate. Compared to that, the risk of granting citizenship would be—"

"*No. If citizenship is granted, then they are given healthcare, sustainable ration numbers, coded housing, and minimum salary unemployment pay. There are no funds to provide these services to the numbers in Trid. And Trids will not obtain jobs upon being granted citizenship. The low-paid workers are now robots. You understand that there is no way for Trid to contribute to society other than to be our low-point scare tactic.*"

"The scare tactic does not work when the Trids grow in number every day," Isa protested. "They are having children of their own because we do not provide birth control and we cannot regulate their numbers with the Child Licensing Board. Soon, those protests at the border are going to turn into an insurrection, and if we try to put them down with force as we have done in the past, they will flood the city and destroy it."

"I will not entertain the notion of Trids being granted citizenship," Venus said, her beeps becoming shrill and causing Isa to cringe. *"You are also to remove the Trid child from your circle. Two Trids close to you is far too many."*

"Alright," Isa said. "She has secondary protection from Dr. Michael Busen, who is keeping her under his protection as a research patient for this new virus. If you wish to remove her from my circle, I will not protest."

"She is removed from your circle."

"Venus, I have been noting the trends in your network and have noticed that many nobles and other citizens of Tiao have put in requests for non-profit fundraising for Trid," Isa started carefully. "If we are unable to grant citizenship, and the public already knows about the Y-99 Virus, then it might be best to allow them to raise the money and put that into a hospital along the Trid border that provides healthcare to Trids and those living in the Walking District."

"We do not need this becoming a larger problem," Venus stated. *"In a few months, this will fade."*

"I do not think it will," Isa disagreed. "We need to assure the people that the virus is being treated. The people are more concerned about the spread of the virus than the Trids themselves. If we allow the citizens to raise money for a hospital, it will be easier to assuage their fears and keep the peace."

Venus was silent for a moment, doing her own calculations and algorithms.

Isa sat in the chair, her expression controlled, though the heat of the room was starting to make her light-headed.

"You have my permission to approve fundraising for a healthcare service building in the Walking District," Venus said. *"Submit a proposal to me by tomorrow."*

"I will."

Isa tried not to show her relief at making small progress.

"Update your investigation on the virus that took down the feed blocks."

Isa tried to hide the deep breath she took to prepare herself, her relief vanishing.

"The virus was an R-type. It was aimed at your security computers. Since you were linked with the feeds, it attacked anything blocking it. Thankfully, Rayal noticed what was happening before more of your security code could be copied for decryption."

"The origin?"

"I have been unable to locate it."

"The timing of this is too close to the attack on Caroie and the various pirating acts that have been occurring along our trade routes," Venus stated. *"Someone is trying to destroy us."*

"I understand."

"You must find the origin of this virus," Venus said. *"There has been another attack on my systems. The coding is in Gihoric."*

Isa straightened, her heart racing suddenly. She was unaware of the second attack, and she knew she could not tell Venus that she was the perpetrator for the first virus.

"Your heartrate escalated," Venus noted.

"When was this attack?"

"Three hours ago," Venus answered. *"It has been blocked and destroyed."* Venus was silent a moment. *"You understand we are on the brink of war with Gihron."*

Isa swallowed hard and tried to gain her bearings.

"Take precaution," Venus said. *"After what you did five years ago, you should have known this war was going to take place."*

■■■

Remus punched in the code for Isa's office door and it opened, allowing him into the locked room. Isa was reclined on the couch, one arm over her eyes, her breathing slow.

"Feeling better?" Remus asked, walking to her NCB chair and leaning against it as he looked her over. He had been sure to let her rest for at least an hour after her meeting with Venus so her headache could subside.

"A bit."

Remus was silent for a few moments before he sighed.

"That was very reckless of you."

"What?"

Remus reached into his pocket and pulled out a small, square device. He put it against the NCB chair and pressed the button. It gave a high whine and the blue and purple lights on the end flickered rapidly. Isa saw the jamming device and her stomach tightened in apprehension.

She had been expecting this confrontation with Remus.

"The stunt you pulled with Kailynn in Trid," Remus clarified. "That was very reckless."

"I got Venus' approval to build a healthcare facility in the Walking District," Isa said, sitting up and swinging her legs off the couch. "You used to support my plan to naturalize Trid."

"And I still do," Remus assured. "Your methods, and motivation, are questionable."

Isa pursed her lips.

"I see…"

Remus looked at his feet.

"Are you sure this is about the good of the planet and not about Kailynn?"

Isa let out an exasperated chuckle.

"Do you really think I would let her use me like that?"

"I think there are many who would take advantage of you," Remus said strongly. Isa groaned and stood, turning away from him.

"I don't need to listen to this lecture."

"Maybe you do," Remus snapped. "Isa, you know better than anyone how quickly a situation can turn bad. The difference is that you've let Kailynn get closer to you than anyone else. She could *destroy* you."

"No, she couldn't," Isa said, turning to look at Remus. "Colonel Amori already did that. I'm never going to be the same."

"You know I hate it when you talk like that."

"Like what?" Isa said sharply. "When I tell you how I feel? When I recall those painful memories? Let me remind you, Remus, that I lived in that hell *every day* for *months*. Every part of who I was was destroyed by him."

"If that were the case, you would not be trying so hard to get the Trid District naturalized," Remus said. "But because of how different you have been since Kailynn came into your life, I can't help but be nervous that she's going to turn around and stab you in the back."

Isa pinched the bridge of her nose.

"You're getting reckless," Remus said again. "And I'm not sure that you're in a state to be handling that sort of pressure."

"What does *that* mean?"

"Dr. Busen and Dr. Arre are worried about your health, as am I. Your latest results show that there has been a decrease in blood flow to your brain. Isa, don't shrug this off!" he snapped when he saw Isa turn away, groaning, irritated. "Stress is going to increase the possibility of seizures and stroke." Isa turned around and fixed Remus with a stern look. However, when she saw his face, her expression softened quickly. His eyes were showing fear, something that he never let show to anyone else.

Remus took a deep breath.

"I don't want you to feel broken," he said. "I wish I could take away the pain he inflicted on you. I wish I had noticed what was going on earlier and maybe I could have done something to change it. I know I wasn't there for you when you needed me." He looked at Isa pleadingly. "But Kailynn is more dangerous than you might realize. She has so easily passed all your barriers, barriers even I couldn't overcome after the accident. And it scares me."

"Remus," Isa murmured, walking to her Silver Elite.

"You know I'm absolutely nothing without you," Remus whispered as Isa stopped in front of him. "I don't care about being your partner again, I just want you to be safe. Seeing you with her, it's like I'm waiting to see you fall apart again, like Kailynn is going to do the same thing Colonel Amori did, and you won't notice it's happening until it's too late." Remus swallowed hard and lowered his gaze to the ground. "If you were to die, I would not be able to live."

Isa placed a hand on Remus' face.

"Remus…" she whispered again. "You can't blame yourself for what happened five years ago."

Remus took her hand.

"Neither can you," he said strongly.

Isa took a deep breath and closed her eyes.

"Remus, you have been, and always will be, my strongest support," she whispered. "You know me better than anyone." She took Remus' face in both hands and smiled at him. "Remember when I was first appointed? You and I had huge dreams about how we would change everything." She closed her eyes and pressed their foreheads together. "The two degenerate Elites revolutionizing the Altereye

System. Every time I became discouraged, you were right there to pick me up and remind me of what we were doing.

"It seems that Colonel Amori also took that fire from you, just as he did from me," Isa murmured. "And maybe, what we *both* need, is a fiery Trid with no manners, but a lot of heart, to come in and remind us of who we really are."

Remus looked at Isa, surprised to see that Isa looked younger, as though she was still the seventeen-year-old Elite that had taken over the Syndicate with passion enough to pull the planet through any ordeal.

"I imagine how painful it is for you to see me with Kailynn," Isa said, one of her thumbs running over Remus' cheek. "And I apologize for the pain I'm inflicting on you." Isa swallowed hard. "But she's helped me feel stronger. She has made me remember who I was, who I *am*." She tightened her fingers on Remus' face to get him to look at her again. "I am the Golden Elite of Tiao," she whispered, "but do you remember what I told Venus when she appointed me?"

Remus looked at Isa and a small smile crept over his face.

"That you wouldn't be Golden Elite," Remus said quietly, "unless I was appointed your Silver Elite."

Isa smiled and nodded.

"And look at where we are now," she said. "You said you're nothing without me, but you were the one who got me to this point. You stood by me through all that shit five years ago, even though I constantly abused you and tried to push you away. *I* am nothing without *you*. I knew I would never have survived as Golden Elite without you by my side."

Remus watched as Isa's smile widened.

"I need you to stand beside me as you did then," she said. "I need Kailynn with me. But I also need you more than you seem to realize. Keep me grounded, and we'll change this planet, and the Altereye System. I promise."

■■

Kailynn was completely unaware of the conversation that Isa and Remus had had when Isa called. When she heard the bright tone of the Elite's voice, she was worried and excited at the same time.

When Isa told Kailynn that she had approval to fund and build a medical care facility in the Walking District that would provide healthcare to Trids, Kailynn thought she was dreaming. She asked Isa where they would get the money and how long it would take and began spewing questions as fast as she could think of them, but Isa just told her that she had to work on all the details and that she would not be home until later.

For some reason, it was very comforting for Kailynn to hear Isa talk to her as though the home was theirs.

Kailynn told her that she would see her "at home," her cheeks flushing, the butterflies jumping in her stomach.

And she had every intention of going back to Anon Tower. However, she had something she needed to handle first.

Walking among the streets of Trid was becoming more and more foreign to her. The dilapidated structures closest to the Walking District were in even worse shape after the protests that had been occurring in Trid. There were different groups demanding different things, such as healthcare, food, and schooling for the children, though some were just yelling and blaming Anon for everything happening in the universe. That was when the Officials would get involved and it normally ended in violence.

Considering the way things had changed after her previous visit, Kailynn knew she had to speak to Raphael.

His words had stung. She had been unable to get them out of her head. They were on constant repeat, getting louder in the quiet hours of the night when she was trying to sleep.

She could not avoid it any longer. She needed to talk to Raphael. She felt she owed him an explanation.

She walked into the bar that her gang frequented and glanced around the tables. She saw a few members of her gang, including Viv and Raphael. Viv was the one who spotted Kailynn. She tapped Raphael's arm and pointed to the door.

Without saying a word to the other members of the gang, Raphael stood and walked out of the bar, finding Kailynn around the corner as she slipped into an alley for some illusion of privacy.

"Hey," she greeted.

"Hey."

An awkward, heavy silence followed the forced greeting. Kailynn shifted her feet nervously back and forth before clearing her throat.

"They're still running tests on Emira," she started. "But she's getting to stay at the hospital under protection of one of the top doctors."

"Really?" Raphael said, unable to keep the bite out of his voice. "Something Isa arranged?"

Kailynn flinched from the words.

"No...actually, I did..."

"*You*?" Raphael said. "Wow. Already a member of high society."

"I want to say I'm sorry, Raffy."

"That's all you want to say?"

"A lot of things happened very quickly," Kailynn said. "I was working as a Significant, and I got caught up in Elite affairs."

"How?" Raphael demanded. "Elites aren't supposed to be with Significants."

"It's really complicated," she said hesitantly. "The point is, I have another job now."

"Which is?"

"Working for Syndicate Intelligence," she murmured, lowering her eyes.

"Oh, it's even better than I expected," Raphael chuckled. "Here I was hoping you had been arrested and this was part of your release program."

"...you were *hoping* I had been arrested?"

"It was the only explanation I could come up with!" Raphael snapped. "You didn't tell me anything. You just said that you needed me to do something for you, and I did it because I always do what you ask. Then you come around, wanting to go into the house of someone with Wheezing Death and then started talking to yourself like a psychotic and *then* you start talking to *Isa*, who is the enemy of all Trids. So yeah, I had hoped that you were arrested and that was the reason for all the madness last week. But, no. Instead, I hear that you have a *job* with Syndicate Intelligence."

Raphael sighed heavily.

"What the fuck has happened to you?" he hissed.

"A lot," she admitted, her voice pained. "Raphael, I don't want this to be the way this conversation goes."

"And how do you want it to go?"

"I want you to understand that a lot of shit is happening in my life, and I don't know how to tell you without pissing you off!" Kailynn snarled. "It's not that I want to lie to you, or keep things from you, but I'm scared you'll hate me."

"Would you rather I make up reasons for what happened?" Raphael asked. "I know something is happening, Lynni. I'm not an idiot. You have been weird ever since you got Theo and the others out of Uren. And now that they're arrested again...it's like you're desperate for them to be released. Look, Lynni. I know he's your brother and you love him, but he has done nothing but *use* you your entire life."

"Raffy, that's not—"

"No, let me say this," Raphael interrupted. "He used you when it was convenient for him. When he needed you, he came to you. And he made sure to tell you that he loved you and wanted what was best for you because he knew that if he was ever in trouble, he needed someone to count on. And you proved time and time again that he could count on you. *Now*, you're working for the fucking Syndicate! How far are you going to sink before you realize that he's not worth it?!"

"Don't talk about my brother like that!" Kailynn barked, shoving Raphael backward. "You know nothing! This isn't about Theo! It started out as a way to get him out, but now...I'm in too deep. I need to find a way to survive and deal with all this shit. My life has been turned upside down...and I don't know that I want to change it."

"...what are you saying?" Raphael whispered.

"I..." The words were trapped in her throat. She opened and closed her mouth several times, trying to decide what to say. "Raffy...My life has changed. *I've* changed. I want different things now. I can't explain how it happened. It just did. I have a chance to shape my life away from Trid, and I want to take it."

"By working for the Syndicate?"

"Yes," Kailynn said. "By working for the Syndicate."

Raphael pursed his lips and shook his head, turning away as if looking at Kailynn would make him sick.

"Raffy..."

"I don't know who you are anymore."

"I'm the one that helped get it approved to have a hospital built in the Walking District for Trids," Kailynn said sharply, walking back into Raphael's field of vision. "I haven't abandoned Trid. I'm trying to help it."

"Wait, what? A hospital?"

"Yes," Kailynn said. "I know that it seems like I'm turning my back on you, but I'm *not*. We can't change things like this. We have to be smarter. If we want to change things for the better we have to try different things until we get the result we want."

"How the hell did you get them to approve a hospital?" Raphael said sharply.

"I had help, of course."

"I'm sure, considering you can't read or write. You would have to."

Kailynn, irritated and angry, slapped Raphael.

"You know what, you're being an asshole!" she snapped. "For fuck's sake. I'm still helping Trid. Now, no Trid can know that I had a part in this, or they'll destroy the project and then there will be no helping the Trid district. And, if this is some sort of way to tell me that I belong here, I will tell you now that I *don't* belong here, and I don't belong in Anon. I don't belong anywhere, which is why I need to do this. I refuse to be one of those people who dies in an alley or in my flat to have other people discover me and dump my body in the landfill. Things have to change, and I'm willing to do it. So if you want to back me up, then back me up. But I will do this with or without your help."

Raphael stared at her, stunned into silence.

"Fine," Kailynn said, walking away. Even though she was upset by the way Raphael had reacted, she was not about to let that get in her way. With Isa's small victory of getting the medical center approved, Kailynn was ready to push harder and do something for the district where she had grown up.

■■

Kailynn made a brief stop at Companion, getting a crazy notion in her head about a way to celebrate with Isa that night. But, when she got to the Elite's level of Anon Tower, there was no noise.

"Hello?" she called.

Since Tarah was almost always in the kitchen, Kailynn poked her head in to see both Tarah and Rayal chatting and cooking. Rayal looked up when she walked in and smiled.

"Hello."

"Hey," she greeted. "What are you doing?"

"Making dinner," Tarah said with a wide smile. "The medical center got approved. That's huge."

"Isa must have sold it just right to Venus," Rayal chuckled. "But that's what she's good at."

"Is she home yet?"

"No, not yet," Tarah said. "She had to work on some things, but she should be back within the hour."

"Okay, need any help?"

"No, we're fine," Tarah said cheerfully. Kailynn glanced at Rayal and saw him smile at the happy tone of Tarah's voice. Kailynn also smiled and excused herself from the kitchen, going to hide the duffel bag she had brought with her in Isa's room.

"Seems like I taught you well," Rayal chuckled, elbowing Tarah lightly when he saw her properly preparing the food.

"You think so?" Tarah challenged with a smile, picking up the sliced carrots and turning to put them in the pan.

"I do," Rayal said.

Tarah glanced down at the oven and stopped.

"You forgot to preheat the oven!" she gasped, laughing.

Rayal turned around and glanced at the oven.

"You didn't tell me to do that," Rayal said, turning back to his task, trying to hide his guilty expression.

Tarah's jaw dropped and she let out a disbelieving chuckle, grabbing a rag from the counter and twisting it, snapping it so that smacked Rayal's rear.

"Hey!" he gasped, jumping away, laughing. "Don't touch the merchandise!"

"Why not? When that merchandise," Tarah snapped the rag again, hitting the side of Rayal's thigh as he tried to awkwardly hop away, his hands raised, covered with flour, "doesn't do what he's supposed to!"

Rayal darted forward and gently patted Tarah's cheek, causing flour to puff up into her eyes and nose. She stopped, coughing and laughing as she tried to wipe the flour from her face.

"Sorry! Did it go up your nose?" Rayal laughed, stepping forward again. He turned sideways. "Here. Use my sleeve."

Tarah shook her head, laughing as she sneezed. She bent down and picked up the rag, using it to wipe her face.

She glanced up at the smiling Rayal and her cheeks flushed again. She averted her eyes quickly and turned away, returning to what she had been doing.

When Isa came home, she seemed tired, but relieved. She kissed Kailynn and over dinner discussed the fundraising and where they were going to build the medical center. She explained the details, though most of it went over Kailynn's head. Still, she watched Isa speak, enthralled by how easily the words flowed from her lips and the brightness in her eyes. She found herself smiling without meaning to.

When everyone went to bed, Kailynn took both Isa's hands and pulled her into the bedroom.

The Elite chuckled and swooped in for a quick kiss.

"I brought us something to celebrate with," Kailynn said.

"Oh?" Isa asked, stepping into the room and hearing the door close behind her as she shrugged off her uniform jacket. Kailynn leaned down and extracted the duffel bag from under the bed, setting it on the frame with a devilish smile.

"Come sit down."

Isa smiled, suspicious. Slowly, she walked forward and sat on the bed, watching Kailynn open the bag. When she got a glance inside, she stopped, blinking a few times.

"What the hell did you bring those for?" Isa laughed.

In the bag was an assortment of dildos.

Kailynn laughed, pulling one out and wiggling it.

"Honestly, I brought them on a whim."

"I fear what your other whims make you do," Isa teased.

"Nothing to worry about. They're all brand new."

"That's hardly the issue…"

Kailynn got a mischievous look on her face.

"I'm curious about something," she started, setting the first dildo down on the bed and picking up another, holding it upright. "How big is Remus?"

Isa's eyes shot wide at the question, startled. Kailynn barked a triumphant laugh and pointed at the Golden Elite with the dildo.

"*Ha*! I broke your poker face! *Finally*!"

"That's because you asked about the penis size of my closest friend!" Isa gasped, picking up the dildo on the bed and playfully smacking Kailynn's arm with it.

"He's also your ex-lover," Kailynn stated, rifling through the bag again. "So you would know the information." She grabbed a smaller dildo. "Is he about this size?"

Isa gave her an exasperated look, but did not answer.

"Or…considering how tall he is…maybe…" Kailynn rifled through the bag again and pulled out the largest dildo she had. "He's closer to this."

Isa's eyes widened further.

"That thing is *horrifying*," she laughed.

"So, he's not this big..."

Isa rolled her eyes and watched Kailynn pull out the various toys she had brought. The Elite did not know what some of them were for, and she glanced over them with startled and confused eyes. As more dildos joined the three on the bed, Isa looked among the various colors and shapes, amused. She finally grabbed one, taking Kailynn's hand and placing the dildo in her palm to stop her from pulling out more sex toys.

"There."

Kailynn's eyes looked at the size of the toy before her eyebrows rose.

"Oh..." she said slowly. "That's...can't really compete with that..."

"Believe me," Isa said, taking the toy from the Significant, "this is no great benefit to males. In fact, it's a hindrance, even to Elites like Remus."

Kailynn laughed and grabbed another toy, raising it.

"But isn't this the reason for everything?" she teased. "I thought, at one time, men ruled everything."

"These things certainly have caused problems in the past," Isa agreed.

"Like war?" Kailynn asked with a laugh, smacking her toy against the one Isa was holding. "It's really just a cock-measuring contest, isn't it?"

"It is," Isa said, also attacking with the dildo she held in her hand, smiling. "It's such a shame that a large army indicates a small dick."

"Oh?" Kailynn asked, playing along with the sword fight as they stood, laughing. "Then shouldn't your army be among the largest?"

"As it would happen, I actually have the largest dick in the system," Isa said, poking Kailynn in the side with the dildo. The Significant yelped in surprise and tried to move away, giggling. "The difference is, I can control mine."

The two leapt about the room in fits of laughter as they smacked the toys against one another in mock-battle. Finally, Kailynn succeeded in toppling them both to the bed. Isa chuckled, reaching under her and pulling the largest toy from under her back.

"We don't really need these, do we?" Kailynn asked with a smile.

Isa glanced at the one in her hand.

"Well, certainly not this one," she laughed.

Kailynn looked over Isa's relaxed face, still finding herself enthralled in everything about the Golden Elite.

However, she was too curious to keep the words from bubbling out of her mouth.

"Was Remus a good partner?"

Isa's face became confused.

"How do you mean?"

Kailynn sighed, tossing the toy aside and resting her body atop Isa's, folding her hands over Isa's belly and resting her chin on them. Isa folded an arm under her head to look at the Significant, puzzled.

"Was he good to you?"

Isa was silent and still for two long seconds. She finally sighed and looked away, pursing her lips.

"Remus has, and always will, support me and protect me to the best of his ability."

"That doesn't answer the question," Kailynn pressed.

"Why are you so interested?" Isa evaded.

"I keep hearing about how horrible things were five years ago, but no one ever tells me what happened," Kailynn said. She could feel Isa's body tense under her, though the Elite's face remained stoic. "I'm not going to ask you to tell me unless you *want* to tell me, but I'm trying to understand how that changed you. Why it changed everything so much, including your relationship with him. I'm trying to figure things out."

Isa sighed heavily and lifted a hand, rubbing it over Kailynn's shoulder tenderly.

"What happened five years ago..." she started slowly, "was extremely difficult, for everyone. I was not the only one changed. Remus has never been the same, neither has Rayal. Every Elite in the Syndicate changed to some degree." Isa closed her eyes and moved her arm back to her side, letting her head fall back to the bed. "If you want to know how it changed *me*..."

Isa hesitated.

"Getting the medical center approved in Trid is something I have wanted since coming to power," she explained. "I always wanted to grant citizenship to Trids and integrate the district into the rest of the planet. For years, I fought against Venus, though she would hear nothing of it. I wanted to do so many things for this planet, and its people, but I had a very large, corrupt mess to clean up when I first came to power. Then, about six years ago, almost seven, I started to gain some ground on cleaning the planet up as I wanted."

The Golden Elite fell silent for several long moments.

"But five years ago...when..." Isa took a deep breath, "when everything happened, I felt like I was the least powerful being in the universe. It felt like everything I was, everything I believed in...was all taken from me. I didn't know who I was...there are many days I still don't know."

Kailynn heard the pain in Isa's voice and lifted her head, shifting to crawl up the Elite's body so that her face was even with the Elite's.

"The hospital is approved in the Walking District," Kailynn said quietly, trying to cheer the Elite up. "It was something you always wanted, right?"

"It was," Isa agreed. "But I did not think I had the strength to fight for it."

"Clearly you did," Kailynn chuckled lightly.

Isa smiled, one hand going up to Kailynn's face and brushing her cheek.

"I have you to thank for that."

Kailynn could only stare at the Elite, trying to figure out how to respond. She was too shocked to think of any words. She was not sure how she felt about the words, either. It was a strange mixture of surprise, embarrassment, and happiness.

Rather than speak, she leaned in for a long, lingering kiss.

Chapter Twenty-Five

Umana had only been in service of Bronze Elite Maki for seven months. He was still in training under Tauren, Maki's retiring caretaker, and even though he knew everything there was to know about caring for an Elite, he was still nervous whenever Elite Maki was around.

His anxiety doubled when any other Elite came to visit.

Therefore, when Tauren was out of the house running errands, and Elite Chronus showed up, Umana was a trembling mess as he opened the door.

He bowed his head deeply.

"Good morning, Elite Chronus," he half-mumbled, his voice breaking at the end of the sentence.

"Good morning."

Umana stared at the brown-haired, blue-eyed Elite for three, very long seconds before he remembered that he needed to step out of the way and let in the Elite.

He hurriedly stepped aside and Elite Chronus entered, the door shutting automatically behind him. Chronus turned his strong eyes onto Umana, who flinched away, trying to still his shaking.

"I'll be right back," he said quickly, keeping his head down and darting into the house, trying to remember where he had last seen Elite Maki.

Chronus sighed and resisted the urge to roll his eyes.

He was not sure how he always managed to make Maki's new caretaker so nervous.

Chronus walked further in, looking around the pristine condition of the living room. Through the open door off the living room, Chronus could see Maki's personal NCB chair.

What confused Chronus was the severe state of disarray in Maki's office. The chair stood untouched in the middle of the room, but around it were books and files and parts of computers scattered on the floor and desk.

Chronus stood in the doorway, looking over the mess, confused.

His office in the Syndicate Building was across from Maki's. He could often see the other Bronze Elite working through the glass walls. Maki was notoriously neat. He did not like things to be disorganized. He had been that way in school and had carried the habit with him into his time at the Syndicate.

Seeing the other Elite's office so disheveled alarmed Chronus.

"Looks like a bomb went off, doesn't it?"

Chronus whirled around, startled. Maki was behind him, smiling at the other Elite's surprise.

"You startled me."

"Sorry about that," Maki said with a teasing laugh. "What did you see in there that had you so focused?"

"Nothing," Chronus said. "It's just a mess in there."

"I know," Maki said with a sigh. "I'll get to it eventually."

The words sat uneasily with Chronus. Decades of knowing Maki would have told him that Maki should have been upset about the mess in his office.

"What brings you here today?"

Chronus reached into his pocket and pulled out a removable drive.

"I ran a few more tests on the power management program in Isa's old NCB chair. I thought you might find some of this interesting."

"Oh," Maki said, taking the drive out of Chronus' hand and walking into the office. "Let's take a look, then."

Chronus followed Maki into the office, his eyes passing over the piles of books and files. As he glanced around, he immediately saw the pattern. The stack on the left side of the desk was on NCB chair programming—which was not alarming, since both Maki and Chronus had been assigned to determine how Isa's chair had been vulnerable to a Pulse Virus. In the middle of the desk was a personal terminal that had been taken apart, different parts scattered by the dismantled casing. On the right side of the desk were medical articles on Elites by Dr. Michael Busen.

On the floor next to the desk was a very tall stack with years etched on the metal casings of the files. Chronus picked up the first file, flipping the protective cover open and tapping the screen to life. Immediately, information on the previous Golden Elite, Gattriel, appeared.

"Chronus?" Maki called.

The other Elite looked up.

"Are you alright?" Maki asked, confused.

"Why do you have this?" Chronus asked, lifting the file.

"I was just curious about something."

"And the other files?" Chronus pressed. "These are not easily accessed. Does Isa know you have these?"

"Remus knows," Maki said, turning back to the NCB chair and plugging the drive into the correct port, tapping a display button on the back of the chair that lifted the panels on the side to make a functioning, interactive screen. "What tests did you run?"

"I ran a few more decryption scans on the coding for the power management. I also ran a few tests on power allotment and priority settings."

"I thought we did that already," Maki said, touching the icons on the screen to pull up Chronus' test reports.

"Yes, but..." Chronus stood next to Maki, touching one of the report files, "those were on all active faces. We didn't run it on background processes."

"Why would we? The chair did not malfunction."

"It had to in some way, otherwise the Pulse Virus would not have been able to get past the security codes," Chronus disagreed.

"You think the hardware and original manufacture coding was corrupt?" Maki asked skeptically. "She had that chair for seven years. The only two that ever do maintenance on it are Isa and Remus. No one else has access."

"I know," Chronus said. "That's why *this*," he motioned to a part of the coding on the screen, "is so disturbing."

Maki read over the lines of code, his eyebrows furrowing as he continued reading.

"This doesn't make any sense," he murmured. "Why are the *outgoing* transmission security codes missing? For an attack, they would need to destroy the security for incoming transmissions. That would be the only way to get a Pulse Virus to the chair."

"That's what I didn't understand, either," Chronus said. "I know you have the log on Isa's chair. I think we need to review all outgoing transmissions from her chair and see when the codes were deleted and how they were able to get into the chair's central processor."

"I agree," Maki said, turning away to search among the stacks of files in his office. "I just don't know how anyone could remotely access it," he muttered. "You have to be physically at the chair to mess with this kind of stuff. Unless you're Venus. But no one knows how to hack her."

"Well, those who have access to the chair are pretty limited. We both know that Remus would sooner shoot himself in the head than cause Isa harm. Rayal, too," Chronus said, looking over the lines of code, his brain trying to create explanations for the problem. "I don't think Isa's trying to kill herself, and Tarah would never hurt her, either." Chronus turned to Maki. "What about the Significant?"

Maki chuckled, turning over his shoulder to look at the other Bronze Elite.

"She's a Trid who can't read or write, yet. Remember?" Maki chuckled. "You expect her to be able to delete a very specific area of security coding in a high-security NCB chair?"

"It's possible," Chronus muttered, his eyes showing his concern.

Maki shook his head, turning back to Chronus as he pulled out another file and a blank drive, transferring the data into the drive to be viewed on the NCB chair.

"No, she wouldn't do that," Maki said gently. "She loves Isa."

"How do you know that?"

"You can see it in her eyes," Maki answered, stopping in front of Chronus, his eyes locked with the other Elite's. Chronus quickly averted his gaze to the file, pointing at it.

"Where is the original drive?"

"I think I left it at the Syndicate."

"Or it's lost in here somewhere," Chronus teased.

"That's a possibility."

Chronus was silent for a moment, watching the transfer complete and Maki put the drive into another port of the NCB chair.

"You don't think the Significant could have done this?"

"Call her Kailynn," Maki said. "That's her name." Maki pressed a button on the NCB chair so a secondary screen would unfold across the back of the chair. "And no, I do not believe she did it."

Maki and Chronus both tried different searches in the log, trying to find anything that would tell them how the chair's security codes had been changed. Before they knew it, three hours had passed. Remus called Chronus when the Bronze Elite did not return to the Syndicate when expected and the other Elite told him that he and Maki were running tests and he would be there until all the scans were completed. Maki told Remus that they would submit anything they found to the Syndicate network to be reviewed.

Chronus rubbed his eyes and turned away from the coding as the third hour wore on.

"I didn't realize that Isa used her home NCB chair so often. These logs are enormous."

"You don't think it's hilarious how many times she tried to contact Remus when she was on leave for a month?" Maki chuckled. "Isa never knows how to stop working, does she?"

"None of us know how to stop working," Chronus laughed brokenly. "Speaking of which, I didn't even ask if you were feeling better."

"I am," Maki said with a nod, still glancing over the log. "I guess I scared a few of you."

"We found you passed out on the floor of your office," Chronus said, his eyebrows high as he turned to face Maki. "It's *Isa* who is expected to pass out and scare us all to death, not you."

"Dr. Busen said it was over exhaustion," Maki said, distracted by the information he was reading.

"You need to be careful," Chronus said. "We can't have you passing out on us all the time."

"I'll be careful."

Chronus went back to Maki's side and looked over the log.

"This is ridiculous," he said. "Three years back in the log, and the codes still aren't there." He sighed heavily. "Maybe it was faulty from manufacturing."

Maki stopped, blinking a few times before turning to Chronus.

"Or maybe we haven't gone back far enough."

"You want to go through all seven years of the log? Are you crazy?"

"No," Maki muttered. "Just the first six months from five years ago."

Chronus stopped immediately, understanding what Maki was thinking.

"You don't actually believe he got into her NCB chair, do you?"

"After everything else he did?" Maki said, typing the query into the computer. "I think he did."

With the narrowed-down log, the two Bronze Elites began scanning the days of coding records.

"Look here," Chronus hissed, pointing. "Right here, the outgoing transmission to Fortunea has the proper security coding with a closed pathway." He pointed to the next outgoing transmission. "Here, on the transmission to Corinne, the pathway is open. The codes are gone a month later."

"This is the entire month before Isa got sick," Maki whispered. He sighed heavily, shaking his head. "He got into her level at Anon Tower and he destroyed the coding of the chair…"

"How could he do that? Rayal was always there."

"I don't know," Maki murmured. "That might have been when he was sick."

"If this was done five years ago, why *now?* And why outgoing?"

"Nothing was logged on the day of the Pulse, right?" Maki murmured.

"Correct."

"A message was sent to Isa on the Altereye Distress Path, which is open to all planets in the Alliance. What if…" he trailed off, thinking. "What if that was just bait to get her into the chair? What if, with the open pathway, they could send the virus to the chair once she sent an outgoing transmission?"

"But she would have received a transmission first."

"Which was the bait," Maki said. "They might have routed the message. They might have had it recorded and then corrupted the data so it was impossible to discern the emergency. Once she was in the chair, they could cut off the transmission, and when she tried to reconnect, they use the open pathway to send the Pulse Virus."

"That would have to be specially programmed. I've never heard of an outgoing transmission causing a virus on the source chair."

"True," Maki said. "But that could explain why they have not done this already. They were programming it, knowing that pathway was open."

Chronus looked at Maki seriously. "You think it was Gihron."

"Colonel Amori is the only one who could have destroyed the security coding. He was the only one outside of Isa's inner circle that *could* have had access to the chair. The timeframe also matches. The codes disappeared during the month that everything started going to hell." Maki took a deep breath, nervous. "What if Colonel Amori told Gihron what he had done? And they have been trying to get a Pulse Virus programmed just for this?"

"Then it's an assassination attempt," Chronus stated. "It's war."

"But they haven't claimed responsibility for the attack. They probably think we don't know."

"We have Gihron heavily monitored," Chronus murmured.

"I don't think we will ever have them monitored enough," Maki said, shaking his head. "I'm going to call Isa and tell her that she needs to build her own central processor for her work NCB chair. Who knows if anyone's gotten to that one…"

Maki tapped his ear and told the implanted phone to call Isa.

"What time is it?" he murmured as Isa's number was dialed. He glanced at the clock and his eyes went wide. "Oh…" He turned to Chronus. "Hey, can you see yourself out? I have a call in five minutes."

"A call?" Chronus asked.

"Isa," Maki said, motioning to his ear to tell Chronus that the Golden Elite had answered. He tried to motion with his hands, asking Chronus to leave, but the other Bronze Elite just looked at Maki, confused.

"Chronus and I just went over the log for your chair to figure out what happened, and we have some information that you might want to know," Maki said. He walked out of the room as Chronus stared after him. "Are you sitting down?" Maki's voice said as he walked out of the office.

Chronus waited until Maki's voice was gone before he sighed heavily and started saving the information on the NCB chair to power it down. There was a lot about Maki's behavior that was concerning. Even if he was expecting a call, he would not have asked Chronus to leave. The two Bronze Elites were very close—they always had been—but Maki had become surprisingly distant and distracted over the previous year. Chronus had noticed the changes more than anyone else in the Syndicate.

He knew Maki was hiding something.

However, he decided to respect Maki's wishes.

Once the NCB chair was properly powered down, Chronus placed the drives on the seat and started to walk to the front door. He did not know where Umana was, but he was relieved he would not have to deal with the nervous, shaky caretaker.

He glanced around, trying to figure out where Maki had gone to talk to Isa. He knew that telling Isa the Pulse Virus was related to Gihron and facilitated by Colonel Amori would upset the Golden Elite. He figured he would stop by Anon Tower on his way home, since Isa was likely at home, and check on her.

He walked to the front door when a high-pitched whine came to his ears.

The sound of the alarm was muffled, but Chronus recognized it immediately. It was the sound of an NCB chair fatal error—the same alarm that would occur if the person sitting in the chair was attacked by a Pulse Virus.

Chronus ran back to the office, knowing that that was the only NCB chair in the home. The chair was still and silent, powered down entirely.

However, the alarm continued to sound.

Chronus started walking through the hallways, following the sound of the alarm until he reached Maki's bedroom. He knocked quietly and opened the door, even though he knew that Maki had gone elsewhere.

The whine of the alarm was much louder in the bedroom. The room was also a horrible mess. There were clothes strewn across the floor with more files and parts of machines. The bed was a tangled mess of sheets, two of the pillows thrown to the floor.

The site terrified and disturbed Chronus greatly. Seeing the office in such a state was shocking enough, but to see that Maki's bedroom was also so disorderly caused Chronus' stomach to flip. It was not uncommon to hear of Elites suffering severe, early-onset dementia and hallucinations. Seeing Maki's room and office in the state they were in made Chronus believe the worst about his closest friend.

What worried him further was the whining emanating from the wall behind Maki's headboard.

Chronus walked to the wall, following the sound, his eyes glancing over the various files and drives littering the floor. When he reached the headboard, he saw there was a very large gap between the headboard and the rest of the bed. Crouching, he found that the headboard had been completely removed from the frame and attached to the wall.

He pushed the pillows aside and ran his hand along the smooth, flat headboard, searching for any sort of opening mechanism.

Along the ridge where the bedframe had once been attached to the headboard, there was a release tab. Pulling it, Chronus saw a panel flip open with a number pad and a screen that was flashing green.

Trying to keep himself from assuming the worst, he typed in the Syndicate passcode. When that was not accepted, he tried Maki's other known passwords. None of the number combinations worked. Chronus stared at the numbers for several long moments, racking his brain for the passcode.

He turned to look at the wall, listening to the NCB chair alarm. Being so close to the noise, there was no mistaking the alarm. He turned his head and glanced among the files around him. One stack of files was annotated as specification sheets for high-power generators.

Chronus knew.

He did not want to believe it, but somehow, he knew immediately what Maki was planning.

For that reason, when he turned back to the number pad, he knew the passcode.

1-7-3-6.

When the light flashed twice and a loud click followed, Chronus felt his heart begin to race.

1736 was a very profound code for everyone in Isa's Syndicate. It was the code they used whenever they discussed Aren, a former Elite Prototype who had died horrifically when they were all in school. Aren's death had hit everyone who knew him very hard, but Isa had always blamed herself for his death. It was when Aren died that Isa truly became the leader everyone in the Syndicate knew her to be.

But, as Chronus pushed the headboard slowly into the wall to reveal the bunker, the name caused his stomach to tie itself in knots.

Aren was synonymous with pain.

Aren was synonymous with *rebellion*.

Chronus walked the short distance to the ajar metal door, allowing the shrill whine of the alarm to echo in the hall. Chronus took a deep breath and pushed the door fully open.

The cavernous bunker was lined with machines and computers, wires haphazardly strewn about the room, connecting different parts. There was an enormous column of hardware that nearly touched the ceiling. It was whirring loudly, the small screen plugged messily into the bottom flashing with the word "error."

In the middle of the mess of cables and hardware was an NCB chair—*Isa's* NCB chair.

Chronus stared, listening to the alarm, unable to process what he was seeing.

He turned to one of the computers and looked at the screen, seeing the log of processes halted with the words "unknown fatal error" at the bottom. Above that line were lines of code about Venus' main security mainframe and power supply.

"Fuck…" Chronus barely managed to whisper.

"Chronus?" Maki called. "Chronus?!" Maki's voice got louder. "Shit!"

Maki ran through his room, tipping over stacks of files, diving into the opening into the bunker and appearing at the door, breathing hard and looking frantically around. Chronus stared at him, shaking his head in disbelief.

"What the fuck are you doing in here?" Maki snapped. "Did you touch anything?!"

"No."

Maki ran to the NCB chair and unplugged one wire before punching a few codes into the back to stop the alarm.

The silence was deafening and heavy.

Maki looked at Chronus, his heart pounding against his ribs.

"What the fuck were you doing in here?!" Maki snapped. "How did you get in?!"

"The alarm was going off," Chronus said, staring at Maki seriously. "How could I ignore it?"

"I closed the door."

"1736," Chronus said. "Do you really think I would forget Aren's code?"

Maki ground his teeth together, walking around the NCB chair and storming over to Chronus.

"You shouldn't have come in here. I told you to leave."

"I knew something was wrong, Maki," Chronus said strongly. "A neat freak like you leaving your office like that? Passing out at work? Tell me what is going on."

"I don't owe you any explanation!" Maki snapped, shoving Chronus angrily backward. Chronus was shocked at the actions, tripping and finding himself on the ground. "You don't know everything about me! You have no right to break into my room!"

Maki pushed Chronus back to the ground, pinning him and grabbing his shoulders in a vice-grip.

"Did you touch *anything*?" he snarled.

Chronus stared at Maki, unable to speak.

"Maki?" he breathed.

Maki continued to glare at Chronus, his breathing labored through his nose, his eyes filled with something Chronus had never seen before.

Suddenly, Maki's face softened. He scrambled to his feet and backed away.

"Chronus...I..."

The other Elite got to his feet, staring at Maki in horror.

"How long?"

Maki lowered his eyes.

"Three years," he muttered. "I think when I got into that crash on Caroie, the head trauma changed things."

"And you never thought to say anything?" Chronus hissed. "That you could feel emotions? Not even to *me*?"

Maki closed his eyes. "What was I supposed to say?" he hissed. "Don't you understand? I'm a degenerate now. If Venus were to find out, she'd have me tested and killed."

It was not until Maki said those words that Chronus suddenly remembered what it meant to be degenerate. He glanced around the room.

"So...all this..."

"It's not for me," Maki whispered.

"You're trying to shut her down?"

Maki did not speak. He merely looked at Chronus, his eyes speaking volumes.

"I'm calling it the Aren System," Maki murmured. "It's a power generator that can operate outside of Venus' control."

"But it doesn't work," Chronus said, nodding to the error messages around the room.

"Uh, no...that's not the generator," he said. "This is the other process...the one that shuts Venus down."

"It can't be done, Maki."

"Do you remember what Isa said in school? All those things that she said needed to change for the planet and the rest of the Altereye System to move forward? She said that Venus needed to be destroyed."

"Until she was made Golden Elite and she *realized* that we can't shut her down."

"That's not the reason she stopped trying," Maki said quietly. "She realized that shutting her down came at a heavier price."

"Of course it does, that's what I meant. Even if you manage to get power to the major cities, communications and defenses would remain down until we could reprogram everything, and that's why we can't shut her down. You know this already."

Maki shook his head.

"We *can* shut her down."

"No, you can't!" Chronus snapped. "She has power sources all over the planet and she can program herself off-planet as well."

"Not without her source coding."

"And you have her source coding?"

"No, of course not," Maki said, shaking his head. He glanced back at the NCB chair. "But I am working on something that will delete her source coding. A virus, actually. So far, nothing has worked."

"How can you test this without Venus noticing?"

"It has taken me *years* to get to this point. Why do you think I'm so tired all the time? Why do you think my house is so disorganized that I barely find my clothes in the morning?"

"You have to stop this," Chronus said.

"No."

"Maki, we're on the brink of war. There are already enough secrets in the Syndicate with Isa and her Significant, we can't—"

"*Kailynn*," Maki snapped. "Call her Kailynn." Maki stared at Chronus seriously. "Isa was right all along. Venus must be shut down. She can't keep up with the evolving society, that's why the Elite generations are getting worse and worse. You remember what a fucking moron Gattriel was, but he was the *best* in that generation. Humans are changing, but Elites and Venus stay the same. On this track, everyone on this planet will die."

Chronus stared at Maki, unable to speak.

"Isa was the first Elite to do anything different in nearly seventeen generations of Golden Elites. She is the one degenerate Elite that could actually change things for the better, but she can't do that if Venus is holding her back."

"Venus would not have allowed Isa to live if Isa was not going to follow the protocol of the Syndicate."

"They almost had her terminated," Maki said seriously.

"*When?*"

"When we were fourteen," Maki murmured. "Venus was sure that she could not be controlled anymore. So she ordered her execution."

"I never heard of this."

"Of course you didn't," Maki whispered. "I looked at the school files. Two days before her execution date, Aren was killed."

That stopped Chronus.

"That subdued all of us," Maki continued. "But it also changed Isa. She knew that she had to change things from a position of power, not from the position of a rebel. So, she played Venus' game. And just when she was getting strong enough to take on Venus, Colonel Amori came and ripped her apart." Maki swallowed hard. "But Kailynn is bringing her back. Kailynn is giving her strength that I haven't seen in her in years."

"…I've noticed, too."

"So, now is the time to change," Maki breathed.

Chronus closed his eyes.

"Maki…" He took a deep breath. "What you're doing…all this…" he motioned to the room, "you'll be killed."

"I'll be killed anyway," Maki whispered. "I'm a degenerate now. That's what happens." He took Chronus' shoulders when the other Elite looked away. "We've talked about the day without Venus for years. We knew that if anyone could find a way to change things, it would be Isa. We wanted this when we were certified Elite prototypes—no emotion, no tears, no weakness, right?" Maki's hands tightened around Chronus' shoulders. "Now that I'm degenerate, I see that we *need* this to happen. The people are disjointed and scared, but no one talks to one another because they are so afraid of what will be overheard, because they are taught not to talk to one another. If we get them talking, Venus holds no power over them."

"And we shut her down?" Chronus asked.

"Yes," Maki said. "For Aren, for Isa, for Remus, for the rest of us, and for everyone who will come after us. We *need* to do this."

Chronus took a deep breath and slowly let it out.

However, he nodded.

Maki let out a breath of relief and relaxed.

"Thank you, my friend."

Outside the opening, Umana's eyes were wide with horror, his hand over his mouth as his stomach turned.

Chapter Twenty-Six

Isa finally came home after a long, exhausting day at the Syndicate. She spent the first part of the morning handling political affairs and the second half of the day building her own central processor for her NCB chair. She had forgotten the harrowing nature of the task.

However, seeing Kailynn's face, creased with concentration as she worked on exercises to learn how to read and write, the Elite's worries seemed to disappear.

She walked to Kailynn and leaned down, kissing her cheek.

Kailynn turned to her.

"Long day," she noted.

"Yes," Isa agreed with a sigh, tucking a tendril of hair behind Kailynn's ear.

"Are you alright?" Kailynn asked, turning to face Isa fully. "You weren't yourself yesterday."

"I'm alright," Isa assured. "Just a lot going on at work right now."

"Rayal said the exact same thing," Kailynn grumbled.

Isa smiled gently, brushing her fingers over Kailynn's cheek.

"I'll tell you everything you want to know, just not tonight. I'm tired."

The night progressed as usual. Rayal, though, did not join them for dinner, and Tarah was clearly disappointed. She barely spoke at all through dinner.

When they went to bed, Kailynn climbed on top of Isa and kissed her passionately, but the Elite smiled and slowly pulled away from the kiss, her eyes closing.

"I'm sorry..." she whispered. "I'm exhausted."

"That's alright," Kailynn said with a gentle smile. She leaned down and kissed the Elite once more. "I just wanted to kiss you goodnight."

She took her place next to Isa and closed her eyes.

Two hours later, a beeping woke both of them. Kailynn groaned, confused and unsure what was making the noise. Isa, however, grabbed her phone, bolting upright.

"Elite Isa," she answered quickly, putting the call on speaker.

"Isa, it's Remus," Remus said quickly. "We have an emergency situation. Venus has ordered Maki's arrest."

"What?" Isa gasped, her eyes going wide.

"Apparently, the caretaker overheard him discussing plans to shut down Venus," Remus said. "The data is unclear right now, but she ordered his arrest. As soon as the Officials appeared, he ran."

Isa was silent, her eyes wide. She stood, grabbing her robe and slipping it on as Kailynn watched, nervous, not entirely understanding what was happening. "Did the caretaker report him?"

"No," Remus said. "Apparently, Umana called Luska on his private phone. Naturally, the call was monitored. When Umana realized the call was on record, he hung up. There's no word on his whereabouts, either."

"And Maki is running?"

"The Officials just called in for a vehicle chase. He put his car on manual and overrode all tracking devices. They're chasing him." Remus hesitated. "They think he's heading to you."

Isa was pacing next to the bed, her eyes on the floor, thinking.

Kailynn could only watch in silence.

"Let him come," Isa said. "I want to talk to him."

"If he really was trying to shut down Venus, he may mean to kill you," Remus pointed out.

"You know Maki would never hurt me."

"...no, he wouldn't," Remus agreed.

"I'll call the Officials now," Isa said. "Thank you, Remus."

"I'm on my way over."

Isa hung up the phone and dialed another number, talking to the Official dispatcher and ordering them to give Maki space and time to get to Anon Tower. When she was met with resistance, she commanded them to do as she bid.

She then called Rayal, asking him for the status on Venus' orders. Kailynn dressed nervously, watching Isa's agitated pacing. Rayal explained that Venus had ordered Maki's arrest on suspicion of treason and degeneration. Isa hesitated, confused.

"Degeneration?"

"That's what it says," Rayal said.

"Does she have a location on him?"

"No," Rayal said. "Two minutes ago she located his car near Grant's Palace Hotel."

"How is he avoiding the cameras?" Isa murmured, snatching up the phone from the bed and walking into the living room, Kailynn close behind. "Even on foot, the cameras should be able to find him."

"I'm not sure."

"Are all of the Syndicate Elites on notice?"

"Yes."

"Tell them to stay away from Anon Tower and not to contact him," Isa ordered, going to the bar and pressing her finger to a sensor under the counter. One metal panel in the bar slid to the side, revealing a control panel for Anon Tower security. "What's the fastest way from Grant's Palace to Anon Tower?"

Rayal was silent as he searched the different routes.

The door to the guest hall opened and Tarah walked out, confused by the noise and tension in the living room. She walked over to Kailynn.

"What's happening?"

"Maki is under arrest," Kailynn relayed quietly. "He's running from the Officials."

"The fastest route on roads is twenty minutes," Rayal answered. "If he was heading to Anon Tower, he would not have driven so far away and gone on foot back to you."

Isa's face lit up in realization.

"He was never in the car," she murmured. "Don't let the Officials open the car. Put them on alert that Maki is armed and dangerous."

"You just said he wasn't in the car," Rayal said, confused.

"I need to buy time," Isa said, punching in codes to the security system.

"Isa, everything in Anon Tower just went down," Rayal gasped.

"That was me," the Golden Elite assured. "They'll only be down for a moment. Can you delay the signal to Venus?"

"For one minute, at most," Rayal said, exasperated.

Isa walked into the kitchen, glancing at the screens on the wall to her right. Her eyes scanned over the various images while Kailynn and Tarah watched from the door.

"He's in," Isa murmured. She went back to the bar while Kailynn and Tarah blinked at the Golden Elite in shock.

"Isa, you're letting him in?" Tarah asked.

"He won't hurt me," Isa said strongly, crouching to the control panel again and bringing everything back online. "Rayal, Maki is here. I'm sure Venus has already dispatched Officials and overridden my command to not pursue him. Please get me as much time as possible."

"Once they are alerted and on their way, I am also coming to Anon Tower," Rayal said.

Isa disconnected the call and closed the cover to the security control panel.

She turned to Kailynn and Tarah.

"Can you give me some time alone with him?"

Tarah nodded obediently, but Kailynn shook her head.

"No, I'm not leaving."

"Kailynn—"

"You think he won't hurt you, but how can you be sure?"

"We've known each other our entire lives," Isa reminded her. "I need to hear what he has to say about this."

"I'm not leaving you alone with him."

"Come on, Kailynn," Tarah said, taking her arm carefully and trying to pull her to the guest hall.

"No!"

The door alarm rang and Isa immediately darted to let in Maki.

"I'm sorry, Isa," Maki said, walking into the living room as Isa followed. "I'm so sorry."

"Tell me what is going on, Maki," Isa said, her voice calm. She glanced at the other two in the room. "Please, give us some privacy."

"It's fine, they should hear this," Maki said. He was breathing hard from running and his face betrayed his panic. He swallowed hard. "It's true."

"Which part is true? Trying to shut her down? Or that you've degenerated?"

"Both."

Isa's face was controlled and calm, but she did not speak for several long seconds.

"You should have told me," she said quietly. "Degeneration is something I can protect you from. Not shutting down Venus."

"You managed to save Remus from a death sentence," Maki said quietly. "But that is because he is your Silver Elite. I am expendable. I'm just a Bronze Elite."

"You should have told me," Isa repeated sharply. "Not try to shut her down."

"I was working on shutting her down before I realized I was degenerate," Maki said. "I started this when you were in the hospital five years ago."

Isa stared at him, thinking over the words carefully.

"Explain yourself."

Maki sighed heavily and lowered his eyes.

"You wanted to shut down Venus when we were in school," he started.

"I was a *child*," Isa said strongly. "She can't be shut down. It will cripple the planet beyond repair."

"No, it won't," Maki said. "Not if we can transfer power sources to new generators."

"There is no such system."

"I made it," Maki explained. "The Aren System."

Isa was about to speak again when the name caused her to stop. She stared at Maki in surprise, unable to form a response. Maki nodded knowingly.

"Isa, I have always stood beside you, and I've always believed in what you could do, and everything you can accomplish. I know that you can change the planet for the better. I know that you can lead the people through this change."

Isa opened her mouth once more and then stopped, closing her eyes and shaking her head.

"No...I can't."

"Maybe not before," Maki admitted. He took a step closer, looking at her with a small smile. "But you *can*."

Isa's brow furrowed as she looked at Maki, trying to figure out the hidden meaning. When the gears in her mind clicked, her eyes shot wide and she covered her mouth, turning away from Maki and walking around him, thinking.

"Isa, you have to believe me," he started. "It's possible."

"Why would you do this?" Isa whispered. "Why would you not tell me that you were doing something that would force me to make this decision? You should have consulted me first."

"I wasn't sure it was even possible," Maki said, walking to her as she leaned on the bar, her eyes distantly staring at the counter in thought. "You were in the hospital, and Dr. Arre explained everything to us about what happened with Colonel Amori. When I realized what he had done to you, I understood that Venus is the source of this planet's power, but it is also the biggest *threat*. All it would take would be someone figuring out how to shut her down or weaponize her, and the entire Altereye System would be doomed. You managed to fend off one person who tried, but he found a way to weaponize your NCB chair and almost kill you."

Isa rubbed her forehead, closing her eyes.

"Venus has to fall," Maki near-growled. "For the good of the people, for you and Kailynn, and for all of us who wish we weren't forbidden from being with someone."

Isa's eyes turned to Kailynn, who was standing in shock to the side of the room, unable to process the situation unfolding before her.

Isa turned back to Maki.

"I was worried about you two for a long time," she murmured. Maki lowered his eyes.

"There's no reason to be worried," he said. "Nothing ever happened between us."

"Did he know?" Isa pressed.

"He found out yesterday," Maki said, his voice quiet and filled with pain. "He had nothing to do with my actions. They were all mine."

Isa cupped her hands over her nose and mouth, leaning on the bar as she took a deep breath and closed her eyes.

"I can't go against the arrest order," she whispered. "Had you not run from the Officials, I could have the treason charges dropped. But you confirmed your own guilt by running."

"I know," Maki said. "And, while the Officials were driving after my programmed car, I hacked and broadcast their radio communications. By the end of day tomorrow, it will be viral that one of the Syndicate Elites wanted to shut down Venus."

"Maki, how could you?" Isa snapped, standing straight. "You are forcing me to deal with this on top of Gihron?"

"I'm forcing you to be who you are," Maki said. He glanced at Kailynn. "You already have the support you needed here, but now, I'm pushing you. You said that you would change everything for the better, then you would find a way to operate the planet without Venus. I'm helping you achieve that goal. You made a promise to us, and you made a promise to Aren."

"Maki..."

The Bronze Elite walked forward and placed his hands on Isa's shoulders.

"Don't be afraid," he said. "You were made to do this. You were the one to break the mold of Elites. You are the one that needs to make this transition. You know no one else will."

He wrapped his arms around her and pulled her close, hugging her tightly.

Isa hugged him back, but pulled away when she felt him drop something into her robe pocket.

Maki nodded to her.

"I believe in you."

A chime sounded from the kitchen and everyone turned.

"It's either Remus or the Officials," Maki said. "There is something I need you to do for me, Isa."

Isa stared at Maki, feeling worry settle into her gut.

"Yes, I have put you in a very difficult position, but I am also going to give you a means to contain it until you are ready to use it to your advantage."

He walked to the bar and opened a drawer, reaching into the back as Isa darted to stop him.

"Maki, no."

"It's going to happen eventually," Maki said, pulling out the gun that he knew was in the drawer. "I'm not as strong as you. You know I would fail the degeneration tests, and I would become a lab rat for months before they finally killed me. They can extract a lot of information from me while I'm alive."

Isa made a grab for the gun as Kailynn started forward, terrified that Maki would turn the weapon on Isa.

Maki moved the gun away for a moment before turning it around in his hand and holding it out for Isa.

She grabbed it quickly and backed away from Maki.

"I don't want to be tortured, Isa," Maki said. "And you need to be the leader of the planet and protect its people from the degenerate Elite that wants to shut down Venus." Maki took a step toward Isa. "You don't have much time."

"I won't do it," Isa said, shaking her head. "I won't kill you."

"Why not?" Maki took another step forward. "I'm very dangerous. I'm a degenerate, and I have information on how to shut down Venus."

"Because I'm not a murderer," Isa said coldly.

Maki let out a dark chuckle.

"Oh, right," he looked at Isa with a twisted smile, "I forgot."

Isa ground her teeth together, her hand tightening on the gun.

"You better hurry," he said. "The Elites might know about you and Kailynn, but the Officials do not."

Isa quickly turned to look at Kailynn, as if it just occurred to her that her relationship with Kailynn was forbidden.

Another soft chime rang through the house, stating that the elevator doors had opened to her floor.

Isa quickly walked around the bar and shot the door controls twice, sealing it temporarily.

"Maki, get out of here. Use the back exit in the entertainment room."

"I'm not running, Isa," Maki said, shaking his head. He turned to look around him. "There is nowhere for me to run."

"We'll figure it out. I'll find a way—"

"Isa," Maki snapped, cutting her off, "you have enough secrets as it is. I've served my purpose and fulfilled my duty to you, both as a colleague and as a friend."

There was rapid knocking on the door and several loud voices yelled Isa's name.

"Maki, we don't have time to argue about this!" Isa walked to Maki and grabbed his wrist, starting to pull him away.

Maki reached to the bar and grabbed a wine glass. He broke the glass against Isa's collarbone, some shards flying to her face and neck, slicing open her skin. She immediately released in him shock as Kailynn darted forward.

However, before Kailynn could get between the two, Isa's other hand lashed out and the gun struck Maki across the face, disorienting him.

Kailynn shoved Maki away, forcing him to the ground and punching him in the jaw.

"Kailynn! Stop!" Isa bellowed.

Maki's hand locked around Kailynn's neck and he lifted the broken stem of the wine glass, slashing her chest enough to draw blood, but not enough to be a fatal injury.

Tarah ran forward when she heard Kailynn's pained yell.

Maki pulled Kailynn down and rolled from under her, forcing her face to the floor as he straddled her back, one of his knees pinning her left arm as her right arm flailed wildly in defense. Maki grabbed her wrist and pinned it to her back as he held the bloodied glass to her neck.

Everything was still as Isa and Tarah stared in horror. The yelling and banging of the Officials was getting louder as they tried to pry open the disabled door.

"Come on, Isa," Maki challenged, pressing the glass deeper into Kailynn's skin, causing her to let out a pained cry. "You want me to kill her?"

Kailynn managed to glance at Maki and saw Isa pointing the gun at him, her eyes hard and dark.

"Don't you dare harm her," she growled.

"Make sure that I can't."

Maki kept his eyes locked with Isa. He quickly pulled the glass across Kailynn's neck and shoulder. Kailynn screamed in pain and a single gunshot sounded, making Kailynn's ears ring before a heavy weight fell on her.

"Elite Isa! Respond!" the Officials yelled on the other side of the door.

"Get out of the way!" Remus' angry voice bellowed.

Kailynn tried rolling out from under Maki, but Tarah had to help her push the Elite off to free her.

"Come on!" Tarah gasped, grabbing Kailynn's arm and hauling her to her feet, pulling her into Isa's room just before Remus forced the door aside with his altered strength and Officials swarmed the living room.

Remus looked at Isa and saw her staring at Maki's lifeless form on the ground, the gun still in her hand.

"Isa."

She quickly lifted her head and the gun, pointing it at Remus, though her hand was shaking. The Officials turned their guns on her, startled and confused.

"It's alright, Isa," Remus assured, lifting his hands peacefully, looking over the cuts on Isa's skin and the blood that stained her robe. "You're safe."

He looked at Maki, trying to keep his mind clear as he took in the situation. Seeing one of his closest friends dead on the ground brought back horrific memories and made his chest tighten.

Isa's eyes also dropped to Maki and the gun lowered.

She dropped the weapon to her feet and let out a long, shaky breath. She backed away from Maki's dead body and Remus ran to her, taking her face in his hands.

"Look at me," he said quickly. Isa's eyes half closed and her body started to relax. "Isa, look at me. Stay here. Stay with me."

Isa's eyes barely opened enough to look at Remus.

"You did not do anything wrong," he said. "You protected yourself."

Isa pushed his hands away and turned around. She walked to the wall and pressed her head against it, taking slow, deep breaths.

The Officials moved forward and looked at the dead Bronze Elite, startled at the accuracy of the single shot to his forehead.

■■■

Tarah had just finished cleaning the large wound on Kailynn's chest as the Significant sat on the vanity in Isa's bathroom when the Golden Elite appeared. Remus followed, though he remained in the doorway, silent.

Kailynn quickly hopped off the vanity and walked to the Elite.

"Kailynn, I still have to wrap those," Tarah said quietly, her eyes resting on the Golden Elite.

Kailynn ignored the caretaker, taking Isa's face in her hands. The Elite's eyes raised to Kailynn's face, but remained half-lidded in exhaustion. Kailynn was surprised at the shut-off look in Isa's eyes. They were darker than she had ever seen them before—the look scared her.

"Miss, I'll clean those wounds," Tarah said slowly, approaching the Golden Elite.

"Kailynn," Remus called, motioning her to him. She glanced at the Silver Elite and then back at Isa. She ran her thumb over the Golden Elite's cheek and then slowly, painfully, pulled away from Isa, walking to Remus, throwing glances back at Isa as Tarah carefully led her toward the vanity.

She finally met Remus' eyes.

"Isa is not going to handle this well," Remus whispered.

"I don't know of anyone that would."

"Any normal Elite would not have a problem moving past this," Remus disagreed. "However, Isa is no normal Elite, and she has been through severe trauma in the past. This is going to be very difficult for her."

Kailynn glanced at Isa once more. The Golden Elite's eyes were lost in the tile on the floor. She did not even flinch as Tarah cleaned the cuts along her neck.

"Do not leave her alone," Remus said strongly, causing the Significant to turn back to him. Remus was also looking at Isa. "It's not safe to leave her by herself."

"What about when she goes to the Syndicate?"

"She's not going to work tomorrow," Remus said. "I've already called Paul. He'll be in touch with her tomorrow and decide her treatment."

"Treatment?"

"Elites aren't like humans," Remus reminded her. "She's going to need immediate attention to process everything that happened here tonight. Paul will help."

Kailynn swallowed hard, letting out a shaky breath.

"I don't understand what happened, either," she admitted. "It happened very fast."

"It did," Remus agreed. He sighed heavily and fixed Kailynn with a stern look. "Swear to me that you will not leave her alone."

"I won't," she assured. "I'll stay with her."

Remus nodded once and approached Isa. He placed a hand on her shoulder and ducked his head down to look Isa in the eye. The Golden Elite did not respond for two seconds. She then turned her head to him, as if just noticing his presence.

"I'm leaving," he said quietly.

Isa's hand latched onto Remus' wrist, her eyes conflicted.

"Do you want me to stay?"

She nodded quickly.

"Alright," he said. "I'll stay in the guest wing." He took her hand and squeezed it. "I'll deal with the Officials, okay? I'll be here in the morning."

He backed away from Isa and Kailynn tried not to be hurt by the way Isa's hand followed his. As Remus left the bathroom, Kailynn walked to Tarah and Isa. She waited for Tarah to finish wiping down the cuts with antiseptic before she placed one hand on Isa's face, turning her head.

Isa's eyes met hers again.

Kailynn's chest tightened in pain.

Isa's eyes dropped to the bandaged wound on Kailynn's shoulder and the uncovered one on her chest. Slowly, as if moving through water, Isa reached up, her fingers hovering over the cut. Kailynn took Isa's fingers in her hand and lifted them to her mouth, kissing the fingertips.

Tarah finished treating Isa's cuts and placing the clear, liquid bandage over the largest wounds. She then turned her attention back to the cut on Kailynn's chest.

When they were both treated to the best of Tarah's ability, she excused herself, trying to keep her tears at bay. When she walked out into the living room, she saw the Officials walking next to the sheet-covered body on the gurney as they left. By the bar, Rayal and Remus were quietly discussing what had happened.

"Tarah," Rayal said when he saw her. He hugged her tightly. She was unable to keep her tears back and began crying into his chest, shaking and shivering. "It's alright. It's over."

Tarah shook her head.

Rayal rubbed Tarah's shoulder and back, trying to comfort her.

Remus stood silently by the bar, his eyes glancing at Isa's bedroom door several times. He had to grip the edge of the bar counter to keep himself from going in to be sure Isa was alright. As much as he wanted to comfort Isa, he knew it was no longer his place. The trauma they shared would make the situation worse, and Remus knew that. The way Isa pushed him away earlier in the evening hurt more than he was willing to admit, but it told him that he was no longer the one Isa needed.

"It's not over…" Tarah hiccupped as she backed away from Rayal. He kept his arms around her, worried about her shaking.

"What do you mean?"

"It's like before…" she choked. "The look in her eyes. She's shut down. Just like with Colonel Amori."

Rayal looked over Tarah's tear-streaked face, his mind turning over the words. Unable to say anything in response, he pulled her back into a hug and turned to Remus. The Silver Elite closed his eyes and dropped his head, unsure what to say, either.

Chapter Twenty-Seven

Kailynn fell asleep again only one hour before the sun rose. Isa had fallen asleep earlier, but Kailynn remained awake, looking over her face, worried about the distant and cold look she had seen on the Golden Elite.

She slept uneasily and woke after sleeping only two hours.

Isa was not in the bed.

Kailynn leapt out of bed and darted into the bathroom. Isa was showering, but she was sitting against the wall under the spray, her head down, her knees tucked into her chest.

Kailynn opened the shower door and walked in, hissing at the scorching temperature. Trying to ignore it, she kneeled next to Isa and pulled some wet hair out of her face. Isa turned her head. Her eyes were still cold and dark, but she was moving at a normal pace, which eased Kailynn's mind a little.

She sat next to the Elite and took her hand, entwining their fingers. They sat in silence for what felt like an eternity.

"I'm sure you have a lot of questions…" Isa finally murmured.

"I do."

"Maki…" Isa trailed off.

"He was trying to shut down Venus," Kailynn completed. "I thought you said it wasn't possible, but it sounds like he made something that could let you do it."

"Just the power supply," Isa said, her eyes distant. "That means we could get power to the cities and shorten the time to reprogram the planet, but only if she were shut down entirely."

"And that's not possible?"

"…anything is possible," she whispered. Kailynn looked at Isa in surprise, trying to discern the Elite's tone.

"You wanted to shut her down when you were in school?" Kailynn asked. Isa nodded slowly.

"The numbers proved that it was the best thing for the planet," Isa said, her voice monotone and even. "Statistics show that the longer she is in power, the bigger the social gap becomes." The Golden Elite sighed heavily. "They make one hundred Elites every six years," she explained. "For the first generations of Elites, it was not uncommon for a Syndicate to remain in power for over a decade. That meant that two generations of Elites were made and not chosen to participate in the

Syndicate. And, of the generations where there was a Syndicate turnover, only fifteen Elites were chosen, leaving eighty-five Elites without Syndicate work."

Isa turned to look at Kailynn seriously.

"These Elites outside of the Syndicate take the highest-paying jobs in society. If an Elite and a human were interviewed for the same job, an Elite would always get the position. They work harder, they are smarter and learn faster, they have no emotions, and they don't exhaust the same as a human. For this reason, the humans moved around the planet in an attempt to get out of the job market where Elites dominated, but the Elites started moving around the planet as well, because Elites don't get fired or replaced the same way humans do."

"But Dr. Busen is a human, isn't he?"

"His father was an Elite," Isa said. "He had connections that allowed him to study and be employed in Elite Specialty Studies."

"I thought Elites couldn't have families."

"Syndicate Elites are forbidden," Isa affirmed. "Even outside of the Syndicate, only male Elites have the ability to have children. Female Elites are barren."

Kailynn was surprised by the news. But, as she thought about it, she had never noticed Isa having a menstrual cycle.

"But the planet became so accustomed to hiring Elites that, now, it's standard to have an Elite employee for positions even if there are human candidates. The problem with that is the same problem with Venus. Humans continue to innovate and change things, it's part of their makeup. They're creative. Technologies are evolving and changing constantly, but none of those technologies are used when creating Elites. Venus has not changed her practices or her methods since she took power. Humans have evolved—Elites and Venus have stayed the same. In the process, the Elites outside of the Syndicate are causing a severe imbalance in the economy, even as the number of degenerate Elites skyrocket. That's forcing humans lower and lower in the classes, until they finally reach Trid."

Isa scoffed quietly, shaking her head.

"And in Trid, it's amazing, but humanity starts to show itself again."

"You clearly haven't spent much time in Trid," Kailynn said.

"You heard what Venus said, when she saw those children playing," Isa said, looking at Kailynn. "*Unity* is possible. Humans communicate in Trid, they form bonds, they help one another, they look out for one another, they fight for one another. That's not how it works in Anon." Isa closed her eyes and leaned her head back on the shower wall. "And Venus doesn't realize that the more she fights against the change, the larger the problem becomes. The Trid population is growing, and it won't be long until the Trid population is large enough to stage a revolution."

"...you really believe that Trid could overthrow Anon?" Kailynn asked skeptically.

"No," Isa said, shaking her head. "Because rebellion is met with violence. It always has been. Revolution has to happen from a much higher position."

They fell silent again as Kailynn thought over Isa's words.

"A position like yours?" Kailynn whispered.

Isa nodded.

Kailynn's fingers tightened on Isa's hand.

"Who was Aren?"

Isa swallowed hard.

"Aren...was a very good friend of mine, of ours, everyone in the Syndicate knew him." Isa took a deep breath. "In school, we were very rebellious. I'm not sure how we managed to survive, to be honest. My execution was ordered, and when I learned of it, I figured I would at least let my death send a message. One night, Aren and I broke into the school's mainframe and began downloading the security tapes of the Elite prototypes being beaten at the Academy. We were about to upload them on a constant broadcast in Anon when we were caught."

Isa lifted a hand to her head, her eyes tightening.

"They began beating us, harder than we had ever been beaten before," she continued, her voice quiet. "But they stopped beating me...to this day I don't understand why. They held me down and forced me to watch Aren be beaten. I remember screaming at them, telling them that they were killing him, but they didn't stop."

Isa paused, her hand dropping from her face.

"When they finally stopped, Aren was..." Isa shook her head. "He was making these horrible sounds...I can't even describe them. All I could do was watch him die."

Kailynn stared in horror at Isa as she recounted the story.

"Needless to say, that changed a lot of things," Isa murmured. "I was afraid to continue rebelling, so I stayed quiet for a while. The death sentence was taken off my head, and I was appointed to the Syndicate. When I was inaugurated, I made a promise to everyone in the Syndicate that we would fight to make the planet better, but we would do it intelligently, never forgetting what happened to Aren, because we never wanted anyone, Elite or human, to be treated like that for standing up for themselves, or for trying to change things for the better."

Kailynn moved away from Isa's side, kneeling in front of her. Isa looked at her, her eyes tired.

"But I never kept that promise," she whispered. "I tried…I really did. But I got tired, and then…"

Her eyes went unfocused.

"Colonel Amori?" Kailynn asked quietly.

Isa nodded slowly.

"What did he do to you?"

Isa shook her head quickly.

"I can't talk about it."

"…okay."

Isa closed her eyes again.

"I don't know what to do," she breathed. "I don't know how to handle what Maki has done…or what I've done…"

Kailynn took Isa's face in her hands, looking at her seriously.

"Maki would not want you backing away from this," she said. "I didn't know him, and I didn't know Aren, or anything that has happened in the past that made you lose sight of what you wanted, but he believed in you enough to go against Venus entirely. Clearly, he knew you would figure out what you needed to do, whatever that was."

Kailynn leaned forward and kissed the Golden Elite gently. She backed away and her thumbs ran over Isa's cheeks.

"You're unlike anything else on this planet," she said with a small smile. "Don't try to change that. Be exactly what you are."

Isa closed her eyes, lowering her head.

"I don't know what that is," she murmured.

Kailynn pushed Isa's head up and looked at her.

"Yes, you do."

■■

The house was quite full that morning. Rayal and Remus had both stayed at Anon Tower—Rayal to watch over Tarah and Remus at Isa's request. Isa seemed surprised when she saw the number of people in the living room. She spared a glance at the floor near the bar, but quickly turned away, relieved that Remus distracted her.

He pulled her into a quick hug that had Kailynn scowling.

"Are you feeling alright?"

"No," Isa said, shaking her head.

"Paul called this morning," Remus said. "He'll be here soon."

Isa could only nod, looking at the worried faces around her.

"Does everyone in the Syndicate know?"

"Don't worry about that right now."

"Then everyone knows," she concluded. "And the people? Have they heard about it?"

"…I'm afraid so," Rayal admitted.

"How viral is it?"

"Considerably," he said. "But the information is splintered and very few reports are remotely close to the truth. Many are saying that he went insane."

"That's the best report for damage control," Remus added. "If we say that he went insane, then we can discount his treason against Venus as mad ravings and that there is no means to shut her down."

Isa took a deep breath.

"You want to lie?"

Remus blinked at the Golden Elite.

"What are you talking about?"

"Maki created a back-up power system," Isa said. "I don't know the details, of course, but he said he created a system—the Aren System."

"…do you think he actually did?" the Silver Elite breathed.

"I don't know," Isa sighed. "I'm not sure I want to know. That's only a small part of attempting to shut down Venus, and you know that."

Remus lowered his head.

"He didn't find a way to save your life?"

"What?" Kailynn said quickly, turning to Isa.

"Isa?" Rayal asked, his eyes wide.

"Well done, Remus," Isa said dryly, turning away from the group and walking into the kitchen. Everyone followed.

"What is he talking about?" Kailynn demanded.

"The reason we never shut down Venus is because we knew she would die," Remus said.

"Are you trying to get a treason charge put on your head as well?" Isa asked sharply, glaring at Remus. "You can't reveal these sorts of things."

"I'm trying to understand how far Maki got in figuring out how to remove her."

"Remus! There is no way to destroy her!" Isa snapped, rounding on him after grabbing a bottle of water. "Accept it!"

Everyone in the doorway of the kitchen went silent, staring at the Golden Elite. Isa sighed heavily and leaned against the counter of the kitchen.

"Look," she said slowly, "I know that we always discussed taking down Venus, but I'm more concerned about Gihron breathing down my neck and threatening war. Taking down Venus when things are this unstable in the Altereye System would be suicidal. No one in the Alliance would come to our aid, not once Venus is shut down. They wouldn't know how to respond. And I doubt that Maki found a way to shut her down without killing me, so you would be the one to lead the people through a war with Gihron and a planetary reform that would likely kill half the population of the planet."

Isa took a deep drink of water, closing her eyes and letting out a long breath.

"That's it, then?" Remus asked.

Isa shrugged, her eyes averted to the floor.

"We have to submit to the reality of the situation."

Remus stared at Isa.

"You're doing it again," he whispered.

"Doing what?" she challenged.

Remus shook his head and turned away, walking out of the kitchen.

Isa sighed heavily and took another drink of water.

"Isa," Kailynn said, stepping forward, "he's just trying to understand. We want to help you, no matter what you decide."

"You can start by getting off my back about making *decisions*," Isa near-growled, walking out of the kitchen, pushing past a surprised Kailynn and speechless Rayal and Tarah.

"Isa," Kailynn called after her, walking back into the living room once more. When the Golden Elite did not answer, continuing to walk toward the balcony doors, Kailynn felt her own anger swell. "Isa!"

"What, Kailynn?" Isa groaned, turning around, her eyes cold.

"How dare you treat us like this?" she snapped. "We're just trying to help!"

"How do you expect to help?" Isa snarled. "What do you know about any of this?"

"I know that there is something about this that you're not telling me, because you are so fucking defensive, it's clear you're hiding something."

Isa spread her arms, her tone going dark.

"But, apparently, you all know more about me than I do, because I'm not acting as I should, or as I once did, or however the *fuck* you think I should act!"

"What the hell is wrong with you?!"

"Kailynn," Remus said, quickly walking up to her, "don't push it. She's impossible to talk to when she's like this."

Isa's arms lowered.

"When I'm like what?"

"When you are trying to act like an Elite," Remus said sharply.

"I *am* an Elite, which is more than I can say for you."

Tarah turned away, lifting her hands to her cover her nose and mouth. Rayal walked over to her and hugged her once more.

"It will be alright," he assured.

"You really are going to let this happen again?" Remus growled. "You're going to start pulling this shit once more? You feel guilty and hurt, so you need to push everyone away? Isa, we're not going anywhere."

"You don't know the first thing about how I feel!"

A chime at the door caused everyone to turn as a man walked into the home.

Kailynn's eyes shot wide and she found herself staring, unable to look away.

The man who walked through the door was the most handsome man she had ever seen in her life. He was tall with thick, wavy brown hair pulled away from his sharp features. His eyes were a stunning dark blue and his jaw was sharp and defined. His well-built frame was accented in just the right way by his professional suit. Kailynn continued to stare, unable to immediately take in the stunning good looks the man possessed.

"Sounds like I arrived just in time," he chuckled, his voice calm, but strong. His white teeth were also perfect as he smiled gently. "Isa, perhaps it would be better if you only spoke to me today."

Isa groaned and turned away, walking out onto the balcony as the man stepped further into the room, setting down his briefcase on the coffee table.

"Paul," Remus greeted, letting out a relieved sigh. He shook the doctor's hand, shaking his head. "She's doing it again. It's the exact same thing she did when Colonel Amori was here."

"Well, the situations are quite similar," Paul said. "She's trying to protect herself."

"They're not similar."

"Yes, they are," Paul disagreed with a gentle smile. "She did something against her duty to protect the few she loves." The doctor turned his vivid blue eyes on Kailynn. She felt weak in the knees, her cheeks flushing. She had to turn away. He was too handsome to bear.

"Yes. Kailynn, this is Dr. Paul Arre, the leading doctor in Elite Psychology," Remus introduced. "Paul, this is Kailynn."

"Yes, I've heard of you," Paul said, extending a hand, his palm up.

Slowly, trying to keep from shaking, she took his hand, but was startled when he leaned down and kissed the back of her hand. When he backed away, Kailynn was worried he would hear her heart pounding.

"You may call me Paul."

"O-okay," she said meekly, her eyes averted.

"Whatever Isa said to you, or if she said anything that hurt you, I want you to try and disregard it," he said. "Elites have a complicated way of defending themselves psychologically. What happened last night opened many wounds from five years ago. You know about that, yes?"

"Uh, no, not exactly," Kailynn said. "A little bit."

"I see," Paul said, his eyes looking over the cuts on Kailynn's shoulder and chest. "Michael really should look at those," he said, motioning to the injuries.

"Tarah treated them," Kailynn said, shaking her head.

"Yes, but I would feel better if he took a look at them."

"You should go see Isa first," Kailynn said quietly, glancing at the balcony where the Elite was leaning against the railing.

Paul glanced at her as he touched his ear to activate his phone.

"She'll need to cool off a bit before she listens to anything I have to say," he said lightly. "Michael Busen." He turned to his briefcase and opened it, revealing a few glass bottles and syringes. "Michael, it's me," he said when the other doctor answered the phone. "What does your schedule look like today?"

He listened to the other man as he pulled out a few bottles, setting them on the table.

"I see, but you're planning to come over here?" He unwrapped a syringe. "Well, Kailynn has a few cuts. I didn't get a good look at Isa's wounds before she stormed out to the balcony." He listened to the other doctor. "About as well as you'd expect," he answered, dipping the syringe into one bottle and pulling back the plunger. "I'm going to give her a mild sedative, so she'll probably be more cooperative when you get here."

He laughed again.

"Okay, thank you. Bye."

He tapped his ear again and unwrapped another syringe.

"You're going to drug her?" Kailynn asked, surprised.

"Do you want to deal with her as she is now?" Paul asked with a smile. "Don't worry, it's just a way to get her to calm down. If we can keep her quiet for a day or so, she'll start to feel better. She's too spun up right now."

He filled the second syringe and returned the bottles to his briefcase.

"I'm going out there," he said. "I don't know how long we'll be, but I suggest you don't come out. I'll bring her in when she's doing a little better. Michael will be coming around in an hour or two to look at both of your wounds."

"Thank you, Paul," Remus said quietly.

The tall, handsome doctor flashed his smile once more and nodded.

"You probably should make an appointment, too," he said with a chuckle. Remus smiled as well.

"Probably."

Paul went out to the balcony, Kailynn's eyes following him.

"*That's* Paul?" she asked, her eyes widening again.

"Yes," Remus said, confused. "Why are you surprised?"

"Hey," Rayal said, snapping his fingers in front of Tarah's face, forcing her to look away from Dr. Arre as he stood next to Isa outside.

"Huh?"

"Why are you staring at him?" Rayal asked.

"Why *wouldn't* I?"

■■

The week after Maki's death was rough on everyone in Isa's home. Dr. Busen had arrived a half-hour after Paul had left and double-checked their wounds, though he said that they were properly treated and complimented Tarah's work. He also gave the sleeping Isa a short medical exam, checking her blood pressure and heart rate—"just to be sure," he said.

Remus stayed for only two days before he returned to the Syndicate. Isa started to come around by the middle of the week, though her eyes still remained dark and she seemed uninterested in eating. Paul came over every day and they went to the balcony and spoke alone, sometimes for hours, while Kailynn waited impatiently inside.

Even though she tried to let go of the way Isa acted the day after Maki's death, Isa's actions startled and confused her so much that Kailynn found herself becoming angrier. On the fourth day of Paul's visit, when Isa came into the living room once more, she sighed heavily and sat on the couch next to Kailynn. Paul excused himself quietly.

"Kailynn," Isa started, turning to face the younger woman. Kailynn looked at the Elite, her jaw clenching to be sure she would not yell at Isa out of frustration. "I want to apologize."

"Good."

"I'm trying to get my thoughts straight," Isa whispered, flinching away from the sharp tone of Kailynn's voice. "I killed one of my best friends four days ago," she murmured, her eyes dropping. "I keep trying to think of ways I could have acted that would have saved his life. I feel so guilty, it physically hurts."

"I thought Elites couldn't feel emotion," Kailynn noted.

"…they can't," Isa affirmed. "When an Elite can, they're considered degenerate. And that's what Maki would have been killed for."

"…are you?"

"According to all the tests I've been through, no, I'm not a degenerate," Isa said. "They can't figure out what's wrong with me." The Golden Elite looked at Kailynn seriously. "I am sorry if I hurt you.

I'm just very confused and worried about everything going on right now. I did not mean to lash out."

Kailynn took a deep breath.

"Don't push me away, Isa," she said. "You and I are both risking everything just by being together. If we can't depend on each other, there is no reason to be risking our lives like this."

Isa sighed, lowering her gaze.

"You're right."

"If you do that to me again, I'm going to call you out on your bullshit," Kailynn warned.

"I would hope so," Isa said with a smile.

The following day, Isa returned to work, as did Rayal and Kailynn.

Kailynn never thought she would enjoy working with the Syndicate Intelligence Agency, and she did struggle with her limited reading and writing abilities, but she was learning quickly, and she started to enjoy working for Rayal, even if most of the time she was only running errands.

Things seemed to be returning to normal, slowly.

Kailynn never asked how the other Elites were handling Maki's death. She did not want to bring up that night. It had frightened her, and she could see the way Isa's eyes darkened whenever it was discussed. The wounds were too fresh to be immediately addressed.

However, a week after Maki was killed, there was a crash reported in Trid that put the entire Syndicate on alert and turned the attention away from Maki.

Kailynn came back from dropping off files at the various desks of the other employees and saw Rayal staring pensively at the screen.

"Everything okay?" she asked.

"Do you know the area around Raizen Lake in Trid?" he asked.

"Yeah, why?"

"There was a drone that crashed there about an hour ago," he said, pointing to the red dot flashing on his screen.

"A drone? Like a spy?"

"Possibly," he admitted. "I need you to come with me. I don't know the area."

"The lake is huge," Kailynn said, walking closer to the screen. "Where is the Walking District on this?"

Rayal pointed.

"So it was close to the Walking District," she noted. "Does that mean it *was* a spy drone?"

"The only way to find out is to retrieve it," Rayal said, standing.

They drove silently to the border of the Walking District, where Rayal parked the car and the two joined the tourists on the streets, walking with their heads down and glasses covering their faces, trying not to be noticed.

Kailynn led the way into Trid, ducking into an alley that allowed them to slip carefully past the border patrol.

Once in Trid, Rayal turned to Kailynn, following her lead.

"Isa apologized?"

Kailynn dropped her gaze and nodded slowly.

"Yeah..."

"You don't seem to have accepted her apology," he noted.

"I have," she said. "I just wish I knew what the hell was going on half the time. I feel like she doesn't trust me."

"She trusts you," Rayal assured.

"Then why won't she tell me what happened with Colonel Amori?" Kailynn snapped. "She's dealing with Gihron again, right? Wasn't he from Gihron?"

"He was," Rayal said with a nod.

"Then I feel like I should know."

"I agree," he murmured. "But I can't tell you everything she endured, because I don't know. She never told me everything. She never told Remus, either. I'm sure Paul and Dr. Busen are the only two who know."

"Then what did he do to *you*?" Kailynn pressed.

Rayal closed his eyes briefly.

"He poisoned me," he said simply.

"*Poisoned* you?"

"Slowly, over the course of four months, or so," Rayal said. "He was trying to take over the planet, and he knew the only way to do that was to have complete control over Isa. So, he made sure to manipulate everything he could to ensnare Isa in a trap. She was being blackmailed by the time she realized what he was doing." Rayal took a deep breath. "I didn't realize what was happening, either. I just started to feel ill and it kept getting worse. I would lose hours of the day. I would just black out. I didn't realize until it was far too late...until the damage was already done."

"What damage?"

"You thought Isa was bad last week?" Rayal said, looking at Kailynn with his eyebrows high. "Imagine her acting like that all day, every day, for months, and you have *no* idea why. You try to ask her what's wrong, and she just…pushes you away. I didn't realize that Colonel Amori was the reason until…"

"Until what?"

"Until I saw him…" Rayal hesitated, "standing behind her as she looked into my hospital room. He was whispering to her, and I had never seen her look so afraid."

Kailynn dropped her eyes to the ground as well, looking up only briefly to be sure that they were going in the right direction.

"You just have to understand that, when she does that, it's because she's trying to protect you, and herself."

"Can Isa feel emotions? Or not?" Kailynn demanded.

"According to the doctors, no, she can't," Rayal said seriously. "She's passed every degenerate test they have. No one has been able to figure out why she acts the way she does, like she's…"

"Human?"

"Yes."

Kailynn sighed heavily and shook her head.

"I just wish she would talk to me," she said. "I'm starting to feel useless, like I'm just around for decoration."

"No, not at all," Rayal said strongly. "I wish I could say something that would make you feel better, because I know how scary and confusing it is when she's like that. But I can only tell you that she cares for you very deeply. And you are the best thing that has happened to her in…who knows how long."

Kailynn sighed once more and dropped the subject.

It was another ten minutes before they reached the general area where the drone crashed. Among the dilapidated buildings with broken windows and crumbling foundations, it was hard to determine where the drone had crashed.

Rayal pulled out a hand-held sensor.

They followed the signal into one building and up three floors, finding the small, round drone sparking sporadically on the ground.

"That's what a drone looks like?" Kailynn asked as Rayal pocketed the sensor again.

"Yes."

"Those things crash here all the time."

"They do?" Rayal asked, turning to Kailynn quickly.

"Yes, at least four times a year, sometimes more."

"For how long?"

"I dunno…at least the last three to four years."

Rayal turned back to the drone, looking it over carefully as he circled it.

"And they look exactly like this one?"

"Yeah," Kailynn said. "Spy drones have been in Trid for years?"

"This isn't a spy drone," Rayal said, crouching on one side of it. "It's a router drone."

"A what?"

"These haven't been in use in decades," Rayal said. "I've never actually seen one operational." He reached into his pocket and pulled out gloves. "They're…something of a transmitter. They pick up a paired signal and move to a location closer to where the owner wants it broadcast. This is ancient technology at this point."

"Could someone change it to do something else?"

"I doubt it," Rayal said, reaching into one of the fractured pieces and pulling out one wire. The small, glowing light faded immediately. "We'll take it back to the office and have it examined. We should also tell Isa once we know for sure what it does."

■■■

Kailynn had never been to the Syndicate Building before, and her eyes continued to wander as she tried to keep up with Rayal. The building was a towering structure of glass and metal, filled with light. The first floor held small offices where robots were taking and directing calls. The second floor, the floor where Rayal and Kailynn got off the elevator, was open and spacious where a hallway led into a cavernous room of computers, with monitors and screens that lined the walls for five stories, different images flashing across different screens. There were three Elites in that room, focused on their tasks as they moved around the different computers.

Kailynn had to jog to catch up with Rayal as he approached an elevator on the other side of the room. Through the glass doors, she looked over the immense control room, seeing the glass-walled offices with walkways overlooking the large room.

They stopped at the top floor of the control room and exited immediately to Isa's office door. It opened automatically for them and Kailynn looked around eagerly.

Isa's office was mostly bare. There were two tables stacked high with files and removable drives. One desk near the balcony doors had a personal terminal on it that was hibernating with the screensaver of the Syndicate crest rotating on it. In the middle of the room was a large NCB chair, even larger than the one Isa had at Anon Tower. Opposite the desk was a small seating area with black couches and a coffee table.

Isa was sitting there, Paul across from her, and a creature Kailynn had never seen before sitting next to Isa, its front legs over her legs. Its head lifted and turned to those who entered the office, ears perking up.

"Kailynn, Rayal," Isa greeted.

"What is that?" Kailynn asked, her eyes fixed on the creature.

"It's a dog," Paul answered with a stunning smile. Kailynn was not sure how one human could be so good-looking. His appearance rivaled that of an Elite. "You probably have never seen one before."

"They're very rare, now," Isa elaborated, motioning Kailynn closer. "They're used for therapy only now, and come at a very high price."

"Is it safe?"

"Very," Paul chuckled. "She's mine. Her name is Tiana."

"Is this the mother of Remus' dog?" Rayal asked, walking forward and extending his hand to the animal.

"She is," Paul affirmed.

Kailynn slowly walked over to the animal, unsure what to do. She had never seen anything like the dog before. Animals were very rare on Tiao—only birds were common. She had never even heard of a dog before.

The animal was very soft, and Kailynn sat down next to it, petting it over and over again. Tiana's tail began wagging and she licked the Significant's hand.

"She likes you," Paul said with a smile.

"Remus has one of these?"

"I prescribed one to him," Paul said, nodding. "Tiana had just had a litter of pups, so I sold him one." His smile widened. "How are you doing, Kailynn?"

"Alright..." Kailynn said, turning away from the handsome doctor.

"Yet another flustered by your stunning good looks, Paul," Isa teased.

"I have to make friends somehow," Paul played along. "Have you two been speaking to one another? Did you apologize, Isa?"

"Of course I did," Isa said, glaring playfully. "I'm not a child. I can admit that I was wrong."

"Did you accept her apology?" Paul asked. "You can be honest with me."

"I told her if she treated me like that again I would call her out on her bullshit."

Paul laughed, looking at Isa.

"She's a good match for you."

"Yes, I think so," Isa said, glancing briefly at Kailynn with a smile.

"We were just finishing up our visit," Paul said. "I hope that you're not here with bad news…"

"Afraid we are," Rayal said, showing him the removable drive in his hand.

"Back to work, then, Isa."

"What are you doing for the rest of the afternoon?" Isa asked as the doctor stood.

"I have an academic paper to finish," Paul said with a heavy sigh. "Doctors are supposed to continue publishing, you know."

"I know," Isa chuckled. "I've read everything you've published."

"What about Michael? His last paper was incredible. I find the genetic reset topic in Elite descendants fascinating."

"I haven't gotten to that one yet," Isa admitted.

"I'm telling on you," Paul teased. "He'll be crushed."

"I think he'll understand," Isa said playfully. "He published that less than six months ago. I've been busy."

"You have," Paul agreed. "But you should read it. Both your doctors are rather brilliant, if you don't mind my saying so."

"How much of that is due to your Elite fathers?" Isa challenged with a smile.

"If you had *read* Michael's last paper, you would realize that we do not owe them much," Paul said with a playful glare. "You have some required reading to do, it would seem."

Isa laughed, standing as Tiana jumped off the couch and trotted to Paul's side, sitting obediently. Kailynn was surprised to find herself upset to have the dog move away. She glanced between Isa and Paul before walking to the dog, crouching next to her while the two continued their conversation.

"I appreciate you coming to see me here, Paul," Isa said. "Things are getting a little hectic. I can't be at home all the time."

"I understand," Paul assured. "If you need me, any time, day or night, you can call. You should know that by now."

"I just hate disturbing you," Isa chuckled nervously.

"You'll never disturb me," Paul said sincerely. "You are very important to me, Isa. I want to make sure you are well."

"You are far too good to me. Thank you."

She glanced at Kailynn, who was petting the dog and smiling. Tiana was clearly enjoying the attention. Paul also glanced down and chuckled.

"She really likes you," he repeated.

"She's beautiful," Kailynn complimented.

"Thank you. Perhaps it wouldn't be a bad idea for Isa to have one from the next litter."

"I shall have to think about it," Isa said. "I do love her, and I love Rio, as well."

Kailynn assumed that was Remus' dog.

"Think about it," Paul said. "She's due for another heat soon, so I'll have pups to train, if you want one."

"I'll consider it," Isa assured, her smile widening when she saw the way Kailynn's face lit up.

"Good," Paul said. "Well, we'll be going now. I'll see you tomorrow."

"Thank you again."

"Kailynn, it was very nice to see you. Rayal, you as well."

"Paul." Rayal nodded back.

"Come, Tiana," he said, motioning to the dog with his hand.

As Paul left the office, the dog trotted along beside him.

"I cannot believe that he's so good-looking," Kailynn said, looking at Isa with an exasperated sigh. Isa chuckled.

"I know," she agreed. "He is exceptionally attractive."

"Thank you, for making me feel self-conscious," Rayal teased.

"He makes Remus self-conscious, too," Isa laughed. She looked between the two. "This is an unexpected surprise, but you said you bring bad news."

"A drone crashed in Trid," Rayal said, holding up the drive once more. "We brought it in for analysis. It was a router drone."

"A router drone?" Isa repeated, taking the drive and moving to the NCB chair. "That makes no sense. Those are obsolete. They were obsolete thirty years ago."

"I know," Rayal said. "We ran all the tests on it, and it's not altered. It's a standard router drone."

"And no viruses?" Isa pressed, plugging the drive into the back of the NCB chair and extending a screen to look at the data.

"None."

"What about the coding?"

"Encrypted, but when we started decryption, it was in English."

"Well, Dover has no reason to spy on us, and we sure as hell aren't spying on ourselves," Isa murmured, scanning through the information. "Router drone…" she repeated, shaking her head, "and there were no files on it? No transmissions?"

"None that we could find," Rayal said, shaking his head.

"What about a manufacture number?"

"Scratched off," Kailynn answered.

Isa's eyebrows furrowed together.

"That doesn't make sense…" she repeated. "If it was unaltered, and it was launched for the purpose of routing something here, then it would have had to originate from somewhere on the planet." She glanced over the information on the screen again. "Looking at the Specs, its range is only forty kilometers."

"Are there any facilities in the immediate area that would be testing with these drones?" Rayal asked. "Kailynn said that those have crashed a few times a year for the last few years in Trid."

"Why haven't those shown up on our scans, but this one did?"

"I don't know," Rayal said, shaking his head. "I'm just as confused."

"This is worrisome," Isa said, turning to look at them. "All eyes of the Alliance are on us now. The news of Maki's death has caused a lot of concern among the members. They are already considering calling for a meeting to discuss the future of our relations."

"And Caroie?" Rayal asked.

"Unfortunately, hostage negotiations have ceased. I sent an ambassador three days ago to see what happened, but no one is responding to any transmissions from any planets in the Alliance. We should know more when they land in two weeks."

"Obviously we have not released information on this drone," Rayal said. "But it seems relatively harmless to me. My question is from where it originated."

"There should be a tracking device on it."

"We looked for it," Kailynn said, shaking her head. "It was either removed or destroyed when it crashed."

"Were it any other type of drone, I would be worried," Rayal added. "But those are harmless."

"They are on their own," Isa agreed. "But it had to come from somewhere with a purpose, as it was emitting some sort of signal to show up on our scans. No tracking device and the manufacture number scratched off…those are red flags."

"Do you think those in the Crescent Alliance would be worried about a router drone crash?" Rayal asked.

"I don't know," Isa admitted, running a hand through her hair, frustrated. "For all I know, it's a distraction. The Alliance is very tense right now, and everyone is waiting for Gihron and the Ninth Circle. We can all feel a war approaching, and fast."

"Gihron wouldn't send a router drone, would they?" Kailynn asked.

"It wouldn't survive entering the atmosphere," Isa said, shaking her head. "And I don't think there are any ships from the Ninth Circle that have come to the planet recently."

"Well, the entire Alliance is nervous. Maybe one of those planets that ignored Caroie's cry had some Gihrons stowed on board when they came here and they're using the router drones from here."

"It's possible," Rayal said.

"I need information on every ship that has been docked near Anon in the last four months. Even if these drones have been crashing in Trid for a while, this is the one that was picked up on our sensors. Something was different."

"Very well," Rayal said with a nod. "I'll also look into all manufacturers of router drones and see if there is anyone who has purchased old models recently."

"Don't extend that search off-planet until you have determined that there was no one on-planet who sold router drones," Isa advised.

"The Alliance is nervous. We don't need them to think we're spying on them. "

"Understood. What about—"

A shrill beep from Isa's NCB chair caused them all to jump and turn to the machine. The ring around the top of the chair was pulsing with a yellow color.

"Emergency Transmission. Origin Unidentified," the mechanical voice of the chair recited.

Isa immediately hit a few buttons on the back of the chair and then pushed her left ring finger to the ring of the chair.

"Display in privacy mode on back screen."

The chair turned slowly in the middle of the room as Isa walked over to her desk and pressed one button on the corner.

"Broadcasting emergency transmission from an unknown location to entire building. Be advised. Remain in privacy mode. Remus, come to my office."

Kailynn turned to the chair when it stopped moving and watched the large screen extend over the back of the chair.

Isa pressed her finger to the ring once more.

"Receive Transmission."

The screen immediately flickered to life.

Isa stood next to Kailynn, who was confused about what she was seeing.

There were four men in black clothes standing in the frame, though their faces were not visible on the screen. Seated in front of them were four children, appearing to be about ten years old. They looked related, with the same face shape and structure, even though their eyes and hair were different colors. They did not appear to be afraid, merely confused, as they sat with their arms bound tightly, folded in front of them, their hands covered in cloth.

It took Kailynn several long moments to realize she was witnessing the unfolding of a hostage situation.

"Tiao Syndicate," a voice started.

"Voice modulator," Isa said immediately. She walked over to the desk and picked up a small metal band, clipping it around her wrist as she turned back to the screen.

"We demand a dismantling of Venus and the Elites of the Syndicate," the man continued. "These terms are non-negotiable."

"Anders," Isa said, speaking into the wristband, "trace this transmission."

"Understood," the voice said through the wristband.

"Hana," Isa said, "contact the Elite Academy immediately. Four missing prototypes in Generation 132. Have them conduct a trace for the prototypes, but do not move in until I give the word."

Kailynn looked at Rayal in horror.

"Those are Elites?" she whispered. He nodded slowly.

"This system can no longer operate under the rule of artificial intelligence, nor will we bow to sub-human Elites. This is no idle threat. As you see," one man grabbed one of the bound prototypes and hauled him to his feet, shoving him close to the camera and tilting his head, pulling his hair from the back of his neck to reveal a white ink tattoo of a number.

"Hana," Isa said into the wristband again, "there's his number, B-Class."

"…we have four of your precious Elite children here. See how they do not cower in fear from us. They do not cry or feel pain."

The man holding the boy close to the camera smashed the gun against the side of the prototypes head, but the boy did not make a sound.

Isa flinched and closed her eyes.

"Isa," Anders' voice said through the wristband, "the signal is being routed from three locations. One of those is at Syndicate Intelligence."

Isa sighed heavily.

"At least now we know why the router drone was sent."

"Isa," Hana said as the men in the video picked the Elite off the ground and put him back in the chair, "they're running searches, but there have been no missing prototypes reported."

"No surprise. They weren't paying attention," Isa groaned. "Keep me updated."

Kailynn was watching the children on the screen as they looked around, confused and worried, but not frightened.

"Our motives are simple and pure," the man continued. "Humans were not made to bow to machines. Venus is the cause of the corruption in the Altereye System. All those not bound to her mainframe are forced to starve and receive no aid unless they agree to become slaves to her whim. We know that you are weaponizing her to destroy all planets that oppose you, disguising her as a protection program as a means to cover the destruction you plan to wreak."

Isa's eyes were sharp on the screen, trying to pick up anything she could about their location. Kailynn's heart was in her throat. Remus walked into Isa's office, slowly approaching the group.

"Our Brother, Colonel Amori, knew the dangers that Venus posed, and he sought to destroy her, but in an attempt to keep yourselves in power, you murdered him while he slept. But he did not die in vain. We have intelligence on you, on your movements, your habits, those you hold dear, and your weaknesses. We will finish what our Brother started. We will annihilate the Elite Syndicate and the Crescent Alliance.

"Golden Elite Isa," the man said, his voice dripping with contempt, "we have a special message for you. We know that you were behind our Brother's assassination, and we failed to avenge him when we Pulsed your chair. But, rest assured, we have other methods. Gihron blood spilt can only be repaid in blood. You are not safe. You never will be. We infiltrated your heavily-guarded Elite Academy, and took these mindless sheep from the confines of those walls. If we can get to them, you know we can get to you."

Kailynn's stomach was twisting sickly.

"Isa," Hana said over the wristband, "their signals are jammed. They're somewhere eighty kilometers away from the docking station."

"Scramble every available military personnel to that area," Isa ordered, her eyes never leaving the screen.

"Everyone should take heed," the man on the screen continued, "this is only the beginning of the revolution. The Syndicate will die and Venus will fall."

The man pointed the gun at the first prototype's temple. The boy looked at the man, his eyes confused. Then, his eyes briefly turned back to the camera and the man pulled the trigger.

Kailynn could not stop the wail of horror when she saw the bullet rip through the Elite prototype's head.

He fell out of his chair and to the floor, dead.

Isa closed her eyes tightly and dropped her head briefly, letting out a shaky breath.

"The Syndicate will all die," the man said, moving to the next prototype as she stared at the dead Elite on the floor, her face filled with confusion. The man put the gun to her head.

"No!" Kailynn screamed.

Her cry was punctuated by the gunshot that killed the next prototype.

Isa grabbed Kailynn and pulled her close, turning her head so her tear-filled eyes were pushed against Isa's uniform, away from the horrible scene playing on the screen.

Rayal lifted a hand to his mouth and turned away, closing his eyes against the tears.

"Elite Isa will die," the man said.

He moved to the third prototype, who tried to move away. One of the other men darted forward and pulled the Elite back to the chair, where the gun was pointed at his head.

"Venus will die," the man continued the gruesome countdown, ending the life of the third prototype. Kailynn jumped at the sound, her hands tightening in Isa's clothes. Isa's arms held Kailynn, though her eyes remained locked on the screen.

"And the Alliance," the man said, pressing his gun to the temple of the last prototype, "will fall."

The fourth gunshot seemed louder than the other three.

Kailynn was shaking violently, terrified as her tears overwhelmed her.

"If you wish to contain this bloodshed," the man concluded, "you will dismantle Venus, you will turn over Golden Elite Isa to face execution for her crimes, and you will disband the Crescent Alliance. Otherwise, you will have a horrible, bloody war and we will kill every citizen of the Alliance. Make your decision."

The transmission cut out and silence fell over the room.

Isa pressed her head to Kailynn's, rubbing her back gently as Kailynn cried.

"This is an open declaration of war on the entire Alliance," Remus said, turning to face Isa. "Not just us."

"Fuck, Remus, they just *murdered* four children to prove their point!" Rayal snapped. "We're past war. This is terrorism. They're threatening the life of our leader and the entire alliance. This is a terrorist cell we're dealing with."

"How did they get them out of the Academy?" Isa asked, turning to look at Remus. The Silver Elite shook his head.

"I don't know," he sighed. "The security is top of the line."

"Then there is concern that they can get to you," Rayal said to Isa. "They can get inside the Syndicate Building if they can get into the Elite Academy."

"The entire building is on biometrics," Isa said, shaking her head. "If they're not in the system, they can't get in."

"They have to get through the docking station, first," Remus pointed out. "We would notice a large group of Gihron citizens arriving on planet."

"Clearly, we wouldn't," Isa disagreed. "This is the only place in the Altereye System with Elites. They're already *on* the planet. And they're ready for war."

Chapter Twenty-Eight

Kailynn was unable to calm down after the terrorists' message. That night, she continued to wake up in cold sweats, shaking, thinking about the kids being killed on the screen. One nightmare, she was sure that Isa was the one sitting in the chair with the gun to her head.

Isa woke up with the Significant each time, soothing her until she went back to sleep.

The next day, she and Isa got into an argument about safety and security before Isa left for the Syndicate. Kailynn was terrified that, the moment she let Isa out of her sight, the Elite would be assassinated. Isa tried to calm her and tell her that there was very heavy security around her and that she would be fine. However, worried about Kailynn's safety, Isa told Kailynn to go back to Companion and keep a low profile.

Kailynn angrily opposed and declared that she was going to quit Companion that day.

She had not been back to Companion in what felt like years, and walking back into the lobby was a surreal experience after the life she had been living in Anon.

As the doors opened for her, she tried to remember how long she had been gone. She had grown accustomed to Anon Tower, to sharing a bed with the Golden Elite, to the comforts provided to her while in Isa's care. Her time at Companion, and her time in Trid before that, seemed like distant memories from decades past.

The stark contrast between the light of the Syndicate and Anon Tower and the darkness of the lobby of Companion was alarming. Kailynn hesitated after her first step into the greeting salon. She felt as though she had entered a place she did not belong.

The Significants in the salon stopped their quiet conversations and turned to her. Kailynn recognized most of them as the highest-earning Significants of Companion. Considering the time of day, it did not surprise her that they were in the greeting salon, but she wished she had remembered the basics of Significant scheduling before storming back into the building.

"Oh my, we have been blessed," Camilla said with a cold laugh, standing from her position and walking forward. "It is Jacyleen, Significant to those in the highest echelons of society, even though she comes from breeding rats in Trid."

Kailynn stopped, looking around as the other seven Significants in the greeting salon stood, surrounding her. She grit her teeth and turned to Camilla.

"Step aside," she said sharply.

"Oh? Are you *commanding* me now? I guess that's what happens when you spend so much time at the Syndicate. You start talking like an Elite."

"I do not work with the Syndicate directly," Kailynn said evenly. "I work for Syndicate Intelligence under Rayal Teleta."

"Do you really believe we are so ignorant?" Harven asked, scoffing. "You forget who you speak to."

"Well, you can't blame her for that," Mika said, her shrill voice setting Kailynn's teeth on edge. "After all, she didn't really spend any time among the Nobel Soirees or with *others* in the higher levels of society."

"Any Significant worth their fee knows that Rayal Teleta is the former caretaker to Golden Elite Isa. And you were spending time with Isa…oh, sorry, I mean *Tarah*, Isa's caretaker, when she was almost assassinated. You were in the house when that happened," Camilla sneered, leaning forward as the circle closed tighter around Kailynn. "You seem to like Elite caretakers. I wonder if you set up that poor boy to turn over his own master to Venus for trying to shut her down."

"What?"

"Umana, Maki's caretaker in training," Myin said, looking at her seriously. "The one who turned Maki over for treason. He was so distraught over it all, they found him with a bullet in his brain and a gun in his right hand. Or have you not heard about that?"

Kailynn blinked, horrified by the news of the caretaker's suicide.

"It would make sense that she did not hear about it," Harven said with a sick smile. "She was probably wrapped up in the much bigger scandal about how Elite Isa's Syndicate is crumbling around her, because we all know that Elite Isa was the one to pull the trigger and kill Maki. Now, the other Bronze Elites are scared of her."

"Trouble in the Elites seems to happen whenever you are close," Camilla noted, her expression filled with mock-confusion. "Isn't that a coincidence?"

"The nobles know that Isa is keeping a Trid near her as an advisor," Myin added.

"Perhaps…it's *more* than that?" Camilla suggested.

Kailynn clenched her fists. She took a deep breath and tried to adapt an air of calm authority.

"You're all morons," she said simply. "I may not have known about Umana, but I did know that Elite Isa killed Maki, because Rayal was there that night, and he saw Maki break a wine glass over Isa's neck. It was self-defense. And, as for the Trid advising her, I have been asked questions about Trid by *Rayal*. Elite Isa has another Trid that has been with her for a very long time. That is who she is getting her advice from," she lied. She took another deep breath and shook her head. "I understand that you're upset that I've managed to pull myself out of whoring my time to rich, entitled perverts, even being a pathetic, rat-bred Trid, but there is no reason to believe that I have any ties to the Elites."

Kailynn tried to step forward, but three Significants held out their hands, pushing her back.

"We know that you're close to Isa," Myin snarled darkly. "We don't give a damn what those fuckers want to do with their free time."

"But when the leader of the planet is so distracted that she allows children to be killed as a declaration of war," Camilla hissed, "then the problem involves all of us."

"How could you think I had *anything* to do with that?" Kailynn asked, horrified.

"You are distracting the Golden Elite. Ever since the Pulse Virus, Elite Isa has not been a proper Golden Elite. You clearly have something to do with that. As soon as the rumors started about a Significant in the home of the Golden Elite, things began to change," Harven said. "Business has been booming, but only because people want to know what Golden Elite Isa's Significant has been doing. They call us to ask about *you*."

"I am not Significant to the Golden Elite," Kailynn growled. "Now get out of my way. I need to speak with Jak."

"We do not answer to you," Camilla snapped, shoving Kailynn backward. "You distracted her, you brought this war on," she said as some of the other Significants grabbed Kailynn's arms, holding her steady as she tried to struggle. "Because of you, four kids are dead. How does that feel? Having that blood on your hands?"

Kailynn lifted her knee into Camilla's stomach, causing a surge of panic and chaos among those in the greeting salon.

Before Camilla could recover from the blow, the others were rounding on Kailynn, lifting their fists and punching her in the stomach and chest, a few blows landing on her face. She flailed against those holding her and kicked her legs, connecting with limbs of unidentified Significants, but in the chaos, there was little else she could do.

She continued to flail and fight back, yelling obscenities as fists and feet rained over her body angrily.

"Knock it off! Break it the *fuck up*!!!" an angry voice bellowed.

The movement ceased around Kailynn and several of the Significants backed away, nursing their own injuries. A few were on the floor, cradling broken fingers or noses that had connected with Kailynn's flailing legs.

Kailynn managed to focus her eyes around the pain and saw Jak approach her quickly, yanking her away from the other Significants.

"Are you all fucking insane?!" Jak yelled. "You decided to attack a *registered Syndicate Intelligence employee?!* Are you so eager to be executed?!"

No one spoke and Jak turned to look at Kailynn.

"You should never have come back here," he said, releasing her and shaking his head. "With everything going on right now, Syndicate employees are under close watch. You're going to make things harder for Rayal by walking around doing whatever the fuck you please. You work for the Syndicate now. There are rules."

"I came here to quit," Kailynn said, trying to breathe around the throbbing of her ribs.

"I accept your resignation," Jak said quickly. "Just get the hell out of here, Jacyleen. And don't ever come back."

■■■

Isa was far more sensitive to things since Maki's death, and her sensitivity concerned her more than anyone else. When she had seen Kailynn's bruises from being jumped at Companion, she became almost-hysterical, silently pacing back and forth behind the couch while Kailynn tried to calm her down, telling her that she was fine and she would never go back there again. Isa continued to run her hands through her hair, trying to think, but nothing came to mind.

Thinking about how easily bad memories were resurfacing, Isa stood anxiously outside the cell door in the maximum security prison, trying to prepare herself for facing the criminal within.

The guards standing around her did not push her to enter the cell, though they did not understand why the Golden Elite was standing, still as a statue, staring at the closed door.

Finally, the Golden Elite nodded to one of the guards and he entered the security code for the door, opening it for the Elite. Isa stepped into the room and waited for the door to close.

The robots stationed around the prisoner turned to Isa and scanned her to be sure she was not a threat. When the screens of their eyes flashed green, Isa knew it was safe to move. However, she did not.

Instead, she looked over the woman in front of her.

The woman, Dienne Marvis, was the reason four Elite prototypes had been taken from the Elite Academy and killed during the broadcast that had become viral. But she looked pathetic, dirty and pale, confined tightly to the wall of her cell, her hair matted over her eyes. She was a heavier woman, but she also had a touch of beauty to her that was indicative of her Elite paternity.

"Golden Elite Isa," Dienne said, her voice dripping with condescension.

"Dienne Marvis," Isa greeted coldly. "Were you informed of the reason for your arrest?"

The woman pretended to think. "I think it has something to do with those four dead prototypes."

"Then you do not deny it."

"No," Dienne snarled. "I don't."

"A guard said that he saw you bartering with someone near the gates of the Academy grounds. Was that for the sale of those four Elite prototypes?"

"Yes," Dienne said, her tone bored and irritated. "Don't you already know about all this? You had all your little birds run off and get information, didn't you?"

"I want to hear you confess."

"Confess…" Dienne chuckled brokenly, shaking her head. "Do you think you hold some sort of power over me?"

"I do," Isa said sharply. "I am the Golden Elite of Tiao."

"You are a degenerate that somehow managed to escape the filtering system," Dienne sneered, pushing against her restraints. "You Elites…you think you're so superior…you spend the first twenty years of your life being kicked around by *humans*, you mindless fuckers!"

"There is no need to raise your voice," Isa said, her voice calm.

"You pretend that you're so high and mighty now that you bow to the great Venus, but I bet if I were to yell "*SIT!*" you would try and find the nearest chair to obey the order!"

Isa stared at Dienne confidently, though her body did tense immediately at the command. Dienne chuckled.

"You never were one for rules, were you?" she said. "I never taught you, of course, and my father was out of the Academy when you were yanked from your incubational tank, but I heard all about you and your gang of merry misfits—destroying school property, organizing rebellions among the prototypes, hacking systems and trying to make yourselves out to be the next revolutionaries. I'm surprised you weren't all taken out back and shot."

"Dienne, I am here to discuss what *you* did, not what I have done in the past."

"Do you know what happens when Elites have children?" Dienne growled. "All that shit, all those beatings, they *continue*. You're programmed. You don't rationalize, and you don't change. You never do."

Isa merely stared at the woman, waiting for the silence to become too heavy for Dienne to bear.

"What do you want from me?" she finally hissed.

"I want to know to whom you sold those prototypes," Isa said coldly. "Each of those B-Class prototypes were worth sixty-eight thousand credits. Collectively, they were two-hundred seventy-two thousand credits."

"Well, then, those bastards certainly got a deal. I only got one hundred thousand out of the exchange," Dienne said, smiling sickly.

"One hundred thousand credits was worth the lives of four children?"

"*Children?*" Dienne snapped. "They were Elite prototypes. They were *machines*. You know better than anyone, Isa. No emotion, no tears, no weakness. We drill that into your brains from the day you turn up at the Academy. You are cold, mechanical, and heartless. That's what you're built for. You can't pretend they're children when it's convenient for you, and then claim that you're superior because you're *not* human. That's not the way it works!"

"Dienne, to me, they were not just machines. I stood on those grounds. I know what it's like."

"*Do* you, though?" Dienne challenged. "You were always treated special. Special Isa, always able to bend the rules. Trying so hard to save everyone in your little group of friends. Still, that little brat, whatever his name was, you got him killed because of your rebellion. Yet, I bet you never cried for him. The rest of the school went on, as if he had never existed. He was just one of many."

"Aren," Isa said darkly. "His name was Aren."

"He got off easy," Dienne said. "In my opinion, I did those brats a favor."

"How do you see that?"

"They are dead. They don't have to deal with the Elite Academy anymore. Is it true that you always hated that place?"

"How could I not?" Isa whispered. "What they made us endure was torture."

Dienne smiled.

"You mean what *Remus*, your lover, endured," she said. "I was wondering why your attack dog wasn't here, but I'm sure you don't want him close to anyone from the academy."

"Was the money worth those children's lives?"

"It was never about the money," Dienne hissed. "I want to see every Elite *dead*. You motherfuckers are not worthy to rule. We teach you, we program you, we build you, and it's time we shut you down."

Isa started forward, grabbing Dienne's throat and pushing her head back against the wall. She glared at the teacher, her fingers tightening around the woman's neck.

"I will not be threatened, and I will not stand by and listen to you speak so lowly of us. We may be programmed and built, but we feel pain, we bleed, and we die. We have a living body, and we deserve more respect than being sold for one-hundred thousand credits."

"*Clearly*...if I lost out on over two-hundred...fifty thousand on those...fuckers..." Dienne choked, cringing against Isa's hand.

"Were the men you sold those prototypes to from Gihron?" Isa growled.

Dienne gasped, her eyes rolling back in her head. Isa ground her teeth together and released the woman's neck, immediately reaching for one of the wall restraints. She released Dienne's right hand and pulled it to her. The teacher struggled, trying to get her hand back from the Elite, or try to strike her, but Isa grabbed her fingers and bent her hand backward, twisting it. Dienne let out a pained cry and tried to move her body to ease the pressure on her hand.

"This is a very simple question, Dienne," Isa said, her tone dangerous. "But I understand if you need to take some time to think about it." She forced Dienne's hand back further, her fingers tightening around the teacher's.

Dienne cringed and ground her teeth against the strain.

"I'm waiting," Isa warned.

"Does it matter?" Dienne growled. "Gihron is not the only planet that hates the Elites and Venus."

"It matters to me," Isa hissed, leaning closer.

"Fuck off!"

Isa's fingers tightened further and four of Dienne's fingers snapped under the strain. She let out a blood-curdling scream and her entire body shook in pain. Isa tightened her fingers further when Dienne tried to get away, causing the teacher's scream to echo again in the cell.

"Why don't we try that again?"

Dienne shuddered, her eyes closed tight. She turned her head to Isa, spitting at her, though she missed the Elite.

Isa smiled and leaned closer, her other hand reaching for Dienne's forearm.

"Allow me to explain something to you," she said quietly. "My patience has been very thin lately, and I am in no mood to play games. This is the only question I have for you, and I am not giving you the option of not answering. Therefore, if I have to, I will break every bone in your body other than your jaw until you answer. The only variable is your schedule this afternoon. Mine's clear, so I have all the time I need."

Dienne stared at Isa in horror, silent.

"No? Not convinced yet?" Isa asked. She began pulling on Dienne's broken fingers, her other hand bracing Dienne's forearm, straining the bone. "I'm sure you know, since, as you have stated, Elites are built, that we have superior physical strength to humans." Isa looked at the teacher's arm. "Would you like me to demonstrate?"

Almost immediately, Isa broke Dienne's wrist.

She screamed and collapsed against her other restraints, her body trembling violently.

"Yes!" she cried. "Yes! They were Gihoric! They were!"

Isa released her arm.

"I'll have you know that, even if I were to let you live, those hundred-thousand credits would not be enough to repair this damage," she said, motioning to Dienne's hand and fingers. "Something to ponder in your final moments when you are dwelling on your hatred for those children."

Isa swept from the cell, leaving the wounded prisoner half-hanging in her restraints, sobbing in agony.

■■■

When Isa returned home from work the next day, she had to search the level for Kailynn. She finally found the younger woman in the entertainment room, watching a news broadcast.

"What are you doing in here?" Isa asked. "You never watch the news."

"There was a lot of talk around the Intelligence Agency today," Kailynn said.

"Talk of what?" Isa asked, sitting next to Kailynn as the Significant muted the sound of the report.

"That the Elite kids were sold by one of the teachers at the Academy," she said. Her eyes turned to Isa. "Isa, you haven't been eating, and you aren't telling me what you're dealing with at work, and that scares me. So, I wanted to see if I could hear anything on the news that would explain what seems to be bothering you."

Isa glanced down, lacing her fingers with Kailynn's.

"Isa, I just want to understand what is going on," Kailynn murmured, squeezing the Elite's hand gently.

"It was a young teacher at the Academy," Isa said. "She harbored an immense hatred for Elites, and she wanted them dead. So she sold them for one hundred thousand credits to some people from Gihron, who killed them to make their statement."

Kailynn sighed heavily.

"The Academy beats the Elites, and even kill them at times, and now have *sold* them to the enemy..." Kailynn shook her head. "And the news said something about it not being the first time that a teacher has done something like this. Is that true?"

"The teachers at the Elite Academy do horrible things to the students," Isa said, her hand dropping as she turned her eyes to the floor.

"They mentioned Remus," Kailynn pressed.

"Yes," Isa said with a nod. "Remus was a spectacle for over a year due to a horrific event that happened between him and a few teachers." Isa said. "Remus…is a degenerate."

"I gathered that, but I don't see how. He seems like he's a normal Elite."

"Well, for the most part, he is," Isa agreed. "Remus has managed to overcome some incredible obstacles, far more than most realize. I'm not sure if you know this, but Elites, when they are created, are already determined to be part of a class."

"Yeah, the Gold, Silver, and Bronze."

"Yes, A, B, and C class," Isa clarified. "But, as always happens, some prototypes do not turn out as expected. There are errors that occur, or spontaneous mutations…in any case, some prototypes that have these problems are killed immediately. Others are tested for degeneration, and if they're degeneration level is deemed safe, they are kept alive for…I guess you could almost call it spare parts for the other prototypes."

"Wait, really?" Kailynn asked, her eyes going wide. Isa nodded.

"Yes," she sighed, "the X-Class. They're the mistakes. And that was Remus' class when we started at the Academy," Isa explained. Kailynn's eyes went wide again, surprised. "His level of degeneration was deemed safe. I have to admit, I do not know exactly how this works, but, apparently, his brain can only react to certain stimuli, which evokes an angry response. His temper is…" Isa shook her head, trying to find a way to explain. "He has worked very hard to keep it under control, but under the right circumstances, he can cause an incredible amount of damage."

Kailynn blinked, surprised that the Elite she had seen remain relatively calm was a degenerate Elite that could feel only anger.

"Remus and I are the only class-jumpers in history," Isa murmured. "But it was a very difficult transition for Remus. To go from X-Class to B-Class was something that no one else in the school deemed acceptable. One of the teachers and his wife, another teacher at the Academy…they believed that Remus needed to be terminated."

"They tried to kill him?"

"No," Isa said, shaking her head. "They tried to break him. They psychologically tortured him for several months in an attempt to reverse the decision that he would jump to the B-Class."

"How?"

"They provoked him intentionally, and then told him he was broken, and wrong, and he would be killed if he continued to act out. Then they would provoke him to act out again as evidence of the severity of his degeneration. They even told him that, if it wasn't for me, he would have already been killed."

"Is that true? That's what Maki said."

Isa sighed heavily. "I guess it is," she said slowly. "I do not like to think of it that way, though."

"What happened with the teachers?"

"They took Remus from his bed one night and locked him in a mechanical room where they..." Isa hesitated. "They beat him, and raped him. They kept him in there for almost three days, continuing the torture."

Kailynn was stunned into silence, the words bouncing around her skull for several long moments before they finally absorbed.

"How did...I mean...did no one else..."

"When it came to the X-Class," Isa said slowly and carefully, "the teachers took it upon themselves to test the level of degeneration in the prototypes. Remus told me, when all that was happening, they continued to tell him that, if he was *really* an Elite, he would take the abuse and rape without complaint and without a fight." Isa closed her eyes. "But how can you ask *anyone* to comply with that?" she whispered.

Kailynn did not respond.

"The incident became very public," Isa continued. "It seemed that the more the school tried to downplay the incident, the more interested the public became. After nearly seven months of constant attention and scrutiny, the two were finally sentenced to death," Isa let out an exasperated chuckle, her face becoming pained, "for sabotage and irreparable damage of government property." Isa looked at Kailynn. "That's all he was—*property*. And they saw him as *damaged*."

Isa leaned her head back on the couch.

"I never understood why everyone was so hateful toward Elites," she whispered. "This whole thing with Gihron...they talk to us like we made the decision to be this way, like we chose how to be born and how to be raised. We're products of the government, the government that humans built. And then, we're raised and damaged by humans, and they still blame us."

Kailynn leaned forward and ran her fingers over Isa's cheek, tucking some hair behind her ear.

"Sounds a little similar to Trid."

Isa smiled slightly.

"You're right," she agreed. "It does."

"So…maybe we're actually not so different."

Chapter Twenty-Nine

Isa tried not to let her feet drag as she walked out of the elevator to her office. The doors opened automatically and the lights came on, but she shied away from them, reaching to shut them off. She stumbled, falling against the wall and resting her hand over the light controls. The lights dimmed immediately.

The Golden Elite put her other hand over her eyes and sighed heavily, gathering her strength to stand straight.

The five-hour meeting with Venus had been brutal. The hot room had dehydrated her considerably, and the tension that always wracked her body when she was in conference with the artificial intelligence had worn down her already-weak body.

She could feel herself slipping back into very destructive habits.

She had been unable to eat, her sleep had been plagued with half-awake hallucinations that had her too terrified to close her eyes at night, and she could feel the tension in her shoulders and belly that she remembered too well from five years previous.

Isa's head began spinning, her world whirling around her. The fuzzy feeling in her head was also very familiar.

She forced herself away from the wall, trying to get to the couches in her office before she passed out.

She only made it half-way.

Remus, in his office one level below Isa's, finished looking over the Intelligence Agency's report on the location of the Gihron men who had killed the Elite prototypes. He ground his teeth together in frustration. They still could not find the men. They managed to find the prototypes, but they were not in the bunker where they had been killed. They were thrown carelessly into a quarry and found by the machines four hours after their disposal.

The attack on the prototypes had hit everyone in Isa's Syndicate far harder than they were willing to admit. Most of them remembered their own beatings, the way the Elites were used and tossed aside carelessly. They recalled what happened to Aren, and they remembered what happened to Remus. With the wound of Maki's death still fresh, they were struggling not to let their past experiences dictate their actions. However, they were working slower than usual, and Chronus had not been to work since the transmission of the prototypes being murdered.

Remus glanced at the schematics of the building, entering his biometrics to see the status of the audience room for Venus. When he saw it marked as inactive, he sighed, rolling his eyes, thrilled that Isa was *finally* out of the meeting.

He got out of the NCB chair and went to Isa's office, only to find the Golden Elite passed out on the floor.

Somewhere nearby, Isa could hear voices. They were muffled and incoherent, but she tried to find them and figure out what they were saying.

"…can't use that as a reason," Remus' voice finally floated to her. "No one else knows what happened to Colonel Amori. The Alliance will not stand behind us if we try to attack Gihron."

"You know that, if they attack, she won't be able to handle it," Dr. Busen's voice responded. "Her body is not able to handle this type of stress anymore."

"Her mind, either," Paul agreed.

Isa's eyes fluttered open. She recognized the ceiling in her office, but it took her a while to focus on the three figures standing next to her in deep discussion.

"She has to handle it," Remus murmured. "She's the Golden Elite. If she's unable to perform her duties, she'll be replaced, which means she'll be killed."

The two doctors remained silent, their heads dropping.

Remus turned his eyes to Isa and saw her conscious.

"Isa," he breathed, stepping forward and kneeling at her side. She moved slowly, her head pounding painfully. She looked around, her eyes meeting those of the three men in the room.

"What happened?"

"I found you passed out on the floor," Remus explained. "You were dehydrated and you're malnourished."

Dr. Busen stepped forward, sitting on the coffee table next to the couch where they had placed the Golden Elite.

"Isa," he started seriously, "we really need to discuss this."

"I'm fine," Isa insisted.

"People who are *fine* do not pass out on the floor like that," Dr. Busen told her.

"I was dehydrated," she said. "I spent five hours in the furnace of the audience hall."

"Five hours is not long enough to starve to the level you are now," the doctor murmured. "You haven't been eating, have you?"

"I have not had an appetite."

"Why not?"

"I don't know."

"Yes, you do," Paul said, standing next to Dr. Busen. Isa sighed and placed her head back on the couch, closing her eyes.

"I've had a lot on my mind," she whispered.

"I'm sure," Paul said quietly. "And I'm sure that everything that has been going on lately has brought up painful memories about Colonel Amori, and the damage he caused."

Isa did not open her eyes, trying to keep her mind from racing at the name.

"Isa," Paul said, crouching next to her, "open your eyes and look at me."

The Golden Elite did not comply.

Paul reached forward and gently placed a hand on Isa's cheek, turning her head to the side.

"You're safe," he assured. "Open your eyes."

Isa took a deep breath and opened her eyes.

"Name every person in this room."

"Remus, Dr. Busen, and you," Isa said quietly.

"And you," Paul added. "No one else is here. He is not coming back, and you are not the same person you were when he was here. You are much stronger now."

"My other doctor would disagree with you," Isa said with a half-hearted chuckle.

Paul smiled, tapping his finger gently against her forehead.

"*This* doctor is talking about up here," he said. "Gihron is threatening you, but Colonel Amori is dead. We know that for a fact. Remember, Michael did the autopsy."

Isa's eyes turned to Dr. Busen, who was looking at her tenderly, though he was clearly concerned.

"He cannot harm you anymore," Paul assured. "He won't harm Rayal, or Remus, or Tarah, or Kailynn. He's gone."

"He'll never be gone, Paul," Isa whispered.

"I suppose that is so," he admitted. "And you can't think of Gihron at all without thinking of him, can you?"

"No."

"And you can't forgive yourself for what happened, can you?" Paul murmured.

"We've been over this thousands of times, Paul," Isa groaned.

"I know," Paul agreed. "And we're going over it again."

"I could never live with myself if I let anything like that happen again," Isa whispered. "To *anyone*. But..."

"What happened to the prototypes reminded you of it all?" Paul asked knowingly.

Isa nodded.

Dr. Busen dropped his head and Remus looked away, both suddenly understanding.

"Isa," Paul started, "you did what you had to do to protect yourself. You were *not* responsible for his actions. You were the victim."

Isa closed her eyes.

"Are you not going to listen to me say this?" he asked. She shook her head quickly. "Okay," he said. "I won't say it, yet, but soon, you're going to have to hear it. For now, I think it would be best if you were to see Michael at least once a week to be sure that you're physically strong enough to endure this stress."

"I don't *want* to endure it," Isa growled. "All I do is *endure* it. I'm *tired*."

"Isa, if you can't perform as Golden Elite..." Remus trailed off. Isa turned to him, her eyes cold.

"Venus will order me dead?" Isa concluded sharply. "I know, but she wouldn't kill me without finding a replacement, and in that time, I'll rip her apart."

"Isa, remember where you are," Paul said, placing his hand on her shoulder. She pushed his hand away and tried to sit up, but Dr. Busen guided her back to the couch.

"You're attached to fluids. Stay put."

"Let go of me," Isa ordered darkly.

Paul backed Dr. Busen away from the agitated Golden Elite, worried about Isa lashing out.

"I don't care if she hears this," Isa snarled. "I am *tired* of having to endure *all* of this. My life was determined to be like this hundreds of years ago. It was never my choice. I was taught to endure the abuse of the teachers, I was taught to endure the threats of Venus. And I was taught to endure this *alone*. I am risking death just by having someone to go home to, someone with whom I don't have to be the Golden Elite.

But because I *am* the damn Golden Elite, everyone around me is in danger, Kailynn especially, if Gihron is so set on revenge for what I did to Colonel Amori."

The others were silent.

"I am sick of my hands being tied no matter what I do," Isa hissed. "After a while, the threat of execution loses its edge. It's been hanging over me my entire life. And every death threat I've ever received, whether it was at the Academy or from fucking Colonel Amori and the rest of Gihron, has been because of *Venus*, so it shouldn't surprise anyone that I want her gone."

"Isa," Dr. Busen said slowly, "you became the Golden Elite because you were very careful and smart about how you rebelled. You have changed a lot on Tiao, and in the Alliance, and I know it's not everything you've wanted to change, but you have accomplished a great deal, even with the horrors of Colonel Amori." The doctor rubbed his forehead. "I guess, what I'm trying to say, is don't throw away all of your hard work. You can still change things, but you are the only one that can at this point. A new Golden Elite will fall right into routine, you know this."

Isa closed her eyes again, going quiet.

Remus rubbed his eyes tiredly, his irritation reaching levels of anger. Paul glanced at him, seeing his agitated state.

"Remus, may I speak with you?" he asked, standing. The Silver Elite nodded quickly, turning and walking out the door of the office. Paul followed him, leaving Dr. Busen and Isa alone in the office.

The doctor reached forward and checked the small screen on the monitor attached to Isa's arm. Content with the knowledge that she was no longer severely dehydrated, he backed away and rubbed his hands together, resting his elbows on his knees.

"I'm not an Elite Psychiatrist," he started quietly, "so I may say the wrong thing here, but I want you to know that I admire you immensely, Isa." She opened her eyes and turned to the doctor. "From the moment I saw you, fifteen and full of fire about changing the entire Altereye System, I knew that, if any Elite were to actually change things, it would be you." Dr. Busen took a deep breath. "There is a fire inside of you still. Colonel Amori did not take it from you, no matter what you think."

"How can you be sure?" Isa whispered.

"Because I see it," Dr. Busen said tenderly. "I see that fire in your eyes again." He looked to the ground, rubbing his hands together once more. "I think...this thing with Gihron has you even more confused than ever before, because you have always wanted to shut down Venus, and they are asking you to do so."

"I can't shut her down, Michael."

The doctor smiled, a mysterious glint in his eyes.

"There it is," he breathed.

"What?"

"There is the Golden Elite," he said. "And I don't mean the A-Class prototype that was appointed from the Academy, I mean the *Golden Elite*, the leader of the planet, the one who knows how to play this bloody game of politics and knows her strengths. You won't shut down Venus because you know it can kill you. And you don't trust anyone else, not even Remus, to implement the changes you want on this planet." He reached forward and took her chin, smiling at her. "That's the fire. You know things have to change, you know how to change things, and you have the confidence and trust in yourself that you are doing right by the people of this planet, which is why you don't trust anyone else to lead this planet through that revolution."

His smile widened.

"*Anything* is possible," he breathed. "We'll always stand behind you. If you want to find a way to shut down Venus, and keep yourself alive, we will find a way."

Isa stared at the doctor for a few moments before clearing her throat and looking at her desk.

"Over there," she said, "bottom left drawer, there is a key secured to the back of the drawer. Take that key and open the hatch on the floor under the desk."

Dr. Busen obeyed, despite his confusion. He found the key, inserted it into the small opening in the floor, and pushed aside the covering of the hatch. In the floor were several electronic files and drives, each marked with a number.

"Which one?"

"Number nine," Isa said.

He sifted through the contents, finally coming across a case marked with the number nine. He pulled it out, closed the hatch, returned the key, and walked back to Isa. She tapped the case and looked at the doctor seriously.

"This is absolutely never to connect to any NCB chair, or any terminal," she hissed. "This computer is wired outside of Venus. It's not connected to her at all."

"How did you manage that?" Dr. Busen hissed.

"It was not easy," she said, "but the information on there is vital." She placed a hand over her heart. "If you want to know anything about how this works," she said, "then carefully look over all that information."

Dr. Busen stared at her, trying to figure out what she was saying. His eyes shot wide when he realized what he was holding in his hands.

"These are the notes—"

"From the very first Golden Elite prototypes," she completed with a nod. "All the failures, all the deaths, everything before they finally figured out how to make it work, all the information is in there."

Dr. Busen looked down at the file, feeling the weight of it in his hands.

"If you really want to help, look over those and see if there is way to keep my heart beating once she's shut down."

∎∎∎

Rayal walked into the kitchen of Isa's level at Anon Tower, following Tarah as the caretaker went to prepare something light for the Golden Elite to eat. Isa had returned home early, pale, shaking, and accompanied by both of her doctors and Remus. Paul told Tarah that Isa was over exhausted and needed to rest and eat, trying not to worry the young caretaker about the Golden Elite's health.

Isa refused to rest, sitting in the living room and working on her personal terminal. Tarah repeatedly asked if she wanted something to eat, but the Golden Elite refused.

When Rayal returned to drop Kailynn off at Anon Tower and saw Isa home so early, he knew something was wrong. There was a look on the Elite's face that worried him. Kailynn went forward immediately and asked if everything was alright. Isa smiled and assured her she was fine and she was just exhausted.

Even though it was clear Kailynn did not believe the Golden Elite, she did not press and sat with Isa.

Tarah came out of the kitchen and asked if they wanted anything, but they both refused.

Standing uselessly in the living room, Rayal finally went into the kitchen after Tarah.

"Hey," he greeted. She turned to him, her face tired and dark circles under her eyes.

"Hey."

"How are you holding up?"

"Isn't it obvious?"

He nodded slowly, his eyes lowering to the ground.

"She collapsed at the Syndicate," Tarah whispered. "She's not eating, she hardly sleeps…" Tarah rubbed her forehead. "I don't know what to do…"

Her voice became choked and she turned her eyes to her feet.

Rayal placed a hand on her shoulder.

"The most you can do is be there for her. She's very stubborn, you know this. You can't do anything about her behavior, but if you show her you care, and that you're worried about her, that will be enough."

"I *am* worried, and I *do* care," Tarah choked. "I can't just sit back and watch her do this. I feel like she's going back to the ways she was when—"

"She's not," Rayal assured quickly. "She's teetering on the edge of it, but she won't do that again. We won't let her. This time, we know what to do when she starts acting like that. Things are already different than they were five years ago. Plus, she has Kailynn, and that has helped immensely."

Tarah nodded, taking a deep breath and slowly letting it out, her hand going over her mouth as her eyes became lost in the floor.

Rayal squeezed her shoulder.

"Hey," he said, ducking his head to look her in the eye. "Remember what I told you when you started training as a caretaker? You can't take everything she does to heart."

"I just don't know how to help," Tarah hissed. "It's so unfair, you know? She has done so much for me. I wouldn't be alive if it wasn't for her. But…I can't do anything to repay her for that."

"Tarah," Rayal caught her attention, "having you alive and well is more than enough to repay her. You don't *owe* her anything."

"It's not about owing her," Tarah said. "It's about…doing something for her…about using this life she gave to me to do something."

Rayal took Tarah's face in both hands, forcing her to look at him.

"You are her caretaker. You are responsible for her home and her safety. You feed her, because you know she won't eat unless the plate is shoved under her nose. You keep her company when she needs it. You are doing something *amazing* with your life. You are helping the leader of a planet. That is nothing meager."

Tarah closed her eyes and sighed, shaking her head.

"It's not enough."

Rayal smiled, grabbing her hand and pulling her out of the kitchen.

"Rayal?" she gasped, confused.

They walked through the living room and to the front door.

"We'll be back," Rayal called over his shoulder to Isa and Kailynn.

He pulled the startled and confused Tarah into the hallway toward the elevator.

"Where are we going?"

"Out," Rayal said. "You have been cooped up in there too long with your thoughts. You need to get out."

"Then shouldn't we get the car?" Tarah asked, pointing to the opposite end of the hallway.

"No."

Rayal stepped into the elevator, pulling Tarah in and pressing the button to go to the lobby.

"Are we getting your car?" she asked, her voice tight with nervousness.

Rayal turned to face her as the elevator descended.

"I have been meaning to tell you this, Tarah," he said with a gentle grin. "You cannot care for Isa when you don't take care of yourself. You can't let yourself go into that dark spiral of thoughts, thinking that you owe Isa something or that you are not doing enough." He took her face again. "Your existence is enough. *You* are enough. Don't think that you need to be anything else to take care of Isa. And you can't put yourself last, because if you do, and she needs you, you won't be able to help her because you'll have no energy left to give her."

"Rayal," Tarah said, "Isa is the leader of the planet. Her problems are significantly more important than mine."

"No, they're not," Rayal said strongly. "There is no difference in your worth versus Isa's."

"Yes, there is," Tarah said, laughing as the doors to the elevator opened.

"No," Rayal repeated. "There is no difference, particularly not to me."

Tarah was surprised by the statement. Rayal walked out of the elevator, taking her hand once more. Tarah had always felt that Isa was more important to Rayal than she. She had not felt jealous about it, because she knew that Isa was the leader of Tiao, and that was the highest position in the entire Altereye System. The statement that Rayal cared about Tarah and Isa equally made her chest bloom with warmth.

However, that quickly changed to fear when she saw they were approaching the doors of the building. The lobby was empty, as usual, and the outside world was beaming with sunlight, but devoid of people.

She stopped walking and pulled against Rayal's insistence.

"No, wait."

"What is it?" Rayal asked

"We can't go out there," she said. "No one walks anymore. It will look suspicious."

Rayal smiled. "No one else is out there, so no one will see," he said. "You're safe with me."

She stared into his mismatched eyes. She had always avoided looking at Rayal's scarred eye, not wanting to make him uncomfortable. Even though Rayal never told her how he received the injury, she had watched the security tapes when she started training as a caretaker. For months after seeing the footage, she thought about the violent fight that broke out in the living room of Isa's home between Rayal and Remus. But even after part of his face had been destroyed, Rayal would not let the Silver Elite get anywhere close to Isa. He stood between them, arms stretched out, face bleeding profusely, trying to protect the Golden Elite.

Perhaps seeing the loyalty he had for Isa was what made Tarah feel so safe with the former caretaker.

With a wobbly smile, she took his hand and followed him into the sunlight.

She had been on the balcony on multiple occasions, but there was something different about being at the base of Anon Tower, staring up at the towering structure among the other sky scrapers in Anon. The sun was bright and hot, but there was something about it that was comforting.

Of course, that might have been the way Rayal held her hand as they walked on the abandoned walkways between the buildings, strolling away from Anon Tower.

Rayal turned to her, walking backward, his hand never leaving hers.

"We have the entire city to ourselves," he joked. She smiled, her cheeks flushing. "Where do you want to go?"

"Anywhere," she murmured. "As long as you're there."

Rayal slowly stopped walking, his hand tightening around Tarah's.

"Tarah," he started quietly, "you know that I'll be here for you. Always."

"I know."

She glanced around the buildings. She felt very small in comparison to the structures of glass and metal, but there was something comforting about the feeling. High in Anon Tower, it felt like everything was so delicate and fragile below. As she stood in the middle of the structures, noticing just how large and beautiful everything was as the sunlight bounced around the angles and facets, things seemed somehow simpler.

"Rayal," she said before she could stop herself, "remember how I told you that you made me realize how strong I was?"

"Yes."

"I'm also feeling pretty brave, right now."

"You are very brave," he agreed. "This is the first time you've been outside in…at least a year."

"It's not only that," she said, looking at him. Her face was burning hot and her stomach was twisting itself into knots, but she took a deep breath and reminded herself of her bravery and her strength.

"What is it?"

Tarah stepped forward, leaning up on her toes and kissing Rayal.

She backed away from the peck and laughed nervously.

"Um, sorry…"

Her hand started to pull out of Rayal's, but his fingers tightened and stopped her from backing away. He took a step toward her, his other hand reaching up to brush over her cheek.

"Don't apologize," he murmured. He leaned closer, but did not kiss her. He waited for her to close the gap between them.

Tarah's entire being felt like it was flying when she kissed Rayal. She had been infatuated with the man for nearly four years, her childhood admiration turning into interest as she grew older. However, she had always been too nervous. Rayal never seemed interested in her.

As she kissed him, she knew that her crush was not just a crush. It was love.

He pulled away from the kiss and smiled.

"Are you alright with this?" he asked quietly.

She nodded quickly, her other hand wrapping around the back of his neck, pulling him back down for another kiss.

Standing among the skyscrapers with the sun's rays embracing them, Tarah and Rayal kissed, alone in the largest city in the Altereye System.

■■■

Kailynn had been too curious about the goofy smile Tarah had on her face and the way she giggled when Rayal said goodbye to leave the young caretaker alone.

As Isa took a nap in the master bedroom, Kailynn went into Tarah's room and asked her what had happened.

She was then launched into a two-hour explanation of what Rayal had done and their first kiss and how it was Tarah's first kiss and how Rayal was the best human being to ever exist…and on…and on…

As happy as Kailynn was that the recently-sulking caretaker was so happy, after the first hour of the rapid explanation, she wanted nothing more than to escape the caretaker's room. However, she sat with Tarah as she explained everything, smiling when she saw the light in Tarah's eyes.

There was something about Tarah's flustered, excited, innocent way of explaining the experience that made the Significant envious.

Obviously, her relationship with Isa was far more complicated.

But, as she left the caretaker's room to check on Isa, she realized that she felt the same flustered excitement with the Elite. She knew how she felt about Isa—that was not complicated. Their relationship itself was not complicated. The society to which they were forced to conform made their relationship confusing and dangerous.

Isa was awake when Kailynn walked into the room. The Significant closed the door and walked to the bed, where the Elite was sitting, her head leaned back on the wall, eyes averted to the ceiling.

When Kailynn climbed into the bed, she wrapped her arms around Isa and rested her head over the Elite's chest.

Isa's arm wrapped around her shoulders and her head rested on Kailynn's.

The two remained silent for a very long time.

"Isa?" Kailynn finally murmured.

"Mm?"

"Why does Gihron want to dismantle Venus?" she asked. "They don't gain anything from it, do they?"

"No," Isa admitted. "Not in reality. But it's the concept. Venus is, more or less, the tyrant of the entire system. She can access information anywhere at any time, even if it's not in her mainframe. She can monitor all transmissions, all trade, all social interactions. She is omnipresent."

"She's what?"

"She's everywhere," Isa clarified.

"There's something else I don't understand about that," Kailynn said, sitting upright. "If she's everywhere, and she can hear and see everything, how do these plots on your life happen? How does she not know about everyone trying to shut her down?"

"She knows," Isa disagreed. "She is just programmed to determine credible threats from false ones. Sometimes, her calculations are wrong."

"I thought she was a computer and, therefore, her calculations could never be wrong."

"Her statistics are never wrong," Isa admitted. "Her calculations on society are correct, but individual people are always unpredictable."

"Then, if she knew that Gihron was trying to destroy her, why doesn't she just kill them?"

"Venus is not a weaponized machine," Isa said, her eyes going distant. "She has certain abilities—she can shut down the planet to its core, but that is not considered weaponized. Because, from that point, humans are the ones that will cause problems, such as sanitation and health concerns, looting, starvation, crime—those are all results of humans, not of Venus." The Elite sighed heavily. "But she cannot shut down other planets, at least not most of them. A few of them she has that control over, but Gihron is not one."

"Can't she, I don't know, hijack their ships and force them to crash, or something?"

"She could, potentially," Isa said with a nod. "But that's where her statistics come into play. Gihron is creating a fuss, it's true. But they have allies that are remaining quiet, for now. If we were to attack, those allies would rear up and fight. She's calculated the risk. The likelihood of them actually doing any damage to her or her system is very minimal."

"But what about you? What about the people of the planet?"

"Those are all things she's considered in her calculations," Isa explained. "For now, she has agreed that keeping the Elites as her ruling Syndicate, and, therefore, risking an attack from Gihron, is less dangerous than removing the Elites from the Syndicate and risking social upheaval."

"Maybe it's because I'm ignorant, but wouldn't social upheaval be easier than war?"

"Not at all," Isa said, shaking her head. "Anything that happens internally is far more devastating than anything that can occur from outside of a society. In war, you can dehumanize the enemy, band together under your leader, your city, your planet, whatever it is you believe in as a collective whole. During a social upheaval, there is no collective belief. Everyone wants something *different*, but they don't know what that is until after they succeed in overturning everything. Then, they have to pick up the broken pieces and try to make a cohesive unit. It's devastating."

"Didn't you say that's what would happen with Trid eventually?" Kailynn pressed.

"Trid is a very good example," Isa said. "Trids protest and fight for rights in Anon, but they do not seem to understand what that really means. They just know that the way they are being treated is wrong, and they want something different. But with the system as it is, the entire social structure would have to be toppled and rebuilt to incorporate Trids as they want. They don't know how they would restructure everything, they just know that it needs to happen."

Kailynn thought over the words, trying to process them fully.

"And, if we were to dismantle Venus, then the planet would be a horrible place to live, and building a new structure would be…"

"Chaotic," Isa completed, turning to look at Kailynn seriously. "When people are desperate for change and don't know what it is that they want to change, or the consequences of that change, corruption sets in and becomes a cancer. Those who have a better understanding of the society, whether that is because of family connections, higher education, or any number of factors, are quick to secure their own wealth and position in such social upheavals. That's why, more often than not, a revolution leaves things more broken than they were before, like what happened to Earth."

"Earth?"

"I guess you wouldn't have heard about Earth before," Isa mused. "Everyone in the Altereye System originated from a planet called Earth, several hundred years ago."

"Where is Earth?" Kailynn asked.

"Far away from here," Isa said, her eyebrows high. "And still not far enough."

"I don't understand…how could all the planets of the Altereye System have origins on the same planet?"

"Earth started out as all these planets started. Humans developed and changed things over time, and the population grew, humans grew stronger, behaved as humans do…" Isa sighed heavily. "Technology developed and allowed further exploration in the universe, which eventually led to the technologies we have today. The entire planet went through many upheavals, each more devastating than the previous. One country had a revolution, and then another, and another, until the entire planet had torn itself apart and tried to rebuild, but it was disastrous. Everything was corrupt. Countries were trading people and weapons without care, killing one another…eventually, it led to a weaponized human."

"What does that mean?"

"A weapon that was born and raised like a human, but had strength like you could not imagine. This weapon was the result of testing on other humans until they created what they believed to be the ultimate weapon." Isa looked at Kailynn, her eyes dark. "And all that testing eventually led," she motioned to herself, "to this."

Kailynn blinked.

"You mean…Elites were the weaponized humans?"

"No, no, not at all," Isa said, shaking her head. "We're far weaker than those weapons, but the research and technology that creates Elites all began with those weapons. But they were as human as possible. When they were traded around, beaten, tortured, forced to fight and kill each other as if they were emotionless machines, they retaliated. They might as well have incinerated the planet. The final reports and explorations of Earth say that the planet was uninhabitable.

"However," Isa continued, "they had found the Altereye System before the bloodshed. And when the weapons began to retaliate, the rich and those in power, who could afford to evacuate Earth, did so. Every country bid and purchased planets based on resources and currency. It was a political blood bath. And then, on top of that, humans were already developed to a certain point, and they decided to develop these planets to that same standard, killing all indigenous species, intelligent or otherwise, and forcing these planets to adapt to what they had been used to on Earth."

"...I've never heard of any of this."

"I know," Isa said. "Many schools learn about Earth, but much of this information is heavily guarded. Obviously, it would raise concerns about the Elites."

Isa sighed heavily.

"So, as you can see, even here and now, these planets were built on corruption from those who could *afford* to leave the destruction of Earth. They left the others to die." Isa leaned her head back on the wall once more. "But, with Earth now a distant memory, more present matters push planets apart that have their roots in the evacuation of Earth. Some planets were less-favorable than others, and poorer countries obtained those planets. These are planets that require more sophisticated tools to cultivate and tame for human habitation. But, often, these planets are also far away from trade routes, which isolates them economically and socially. This breeds discontent. And that is the entirety of the Ninth Circle, Gihron included."

Kailynn took a deep breath, her eyes going wide as she exhaled.

"Wow…" she murmured.

"A lot of information, I know," Isa said, reaching over and running her fingertips over Kailynn's cheek. The Significant turned to look at the Golden Elite.

"Knowing all this, you want to shut down Venus?"

Isa nodded slowly.

"If I could, I would," she said.

"So much for Elites being loyal to Venus," Kailynn tried to joke.

Isa smiled. "I'm not considering myself an Elite anymore," she whispered. She shifted forward, taking Kailynn's face in her hands and kissing her tenderly. "I don't think I ever was. I may have passed the degeneration tests, but I know for sure that I am a degenerate." Isa looked over Kailynn's face. "I've fallen in love with you. An Elite can't be more degenerate than that."

Kailynn looked into the clear blue depths of Isa's eyes, her heart stopping at the words.

"...I love you, too," she breathed.

Isa let out a relieved breath and closed her eyes.

"Can you repeat that?" she asked, the smile touching her eyes when she looked at Kailynn again.

The Significant smiled broadly.

"I love you."

Chapter Thirty

The day was progressing as normal.

Kailynn was picked up by Rayal nearly an hour after Isa left for the Syndicate. They discussed the continuing investigation for the Gihrons that had killed the prototypes and were continuing to send threats to the Syndicate about attacking.

All of the Syndicate Intelligence Agency was on-edge, but it was the environment they were used to working in.

Kailynn went about her normal day, running errands around the office for Rayal and trying to learn as much as she could. She had become much better at reading and writing, partially because Isa's doctors had been worried about her health and continued to send her home hours early to be sure she was well enough to handle the mounting tension. Kailynn was able to spend her evenings with Isa, and the Elite helped her with lessons, finally taking her back into the library where there were electronic book cases and hardcopy books, which Kailynn had never seen in her life.

Kailynn did not mind spending time in the library. Sometimes, it was too much for her to watch the sappy romance unfolding between Tarah and Rayal, so she would escape into the library.

A month had passed since Isa's collapse at the Syndicate Building. While she was not eating as much as she should, she was forcing herself to eat every day, which helped her keep up her strength. This allowed some of the tension to leave the Syndicate.

But on that day, everything would reach a fever pitch.

At 14:36, there was a deep, sonic rumbling that caused everything in the Intelligence Agency to rattle. Kailynn and Rayal both looked up from their tasks, glancing around at the shaking glasses and files on the table.

Before the rattling stopped, every monitor in the room began flashing red and alarms shrieked. Kailynn was immediately on her feet, walking to Rayal as he glanced at the screens, hitting several keys on his keyboard.

"Fuck..." he breathed. He angrily smashed a button on his desk. "Code Red! Scramble detonation control and the military to the Syndicate Building immediately! The Syndicate has been bombed! Initiate emergency response and then evacuate the building!"

Kailynn's hearing had turned to a dull ring as the words bounced around her head.

The Syndicate Building had been bombed.

"Kailynn, we have to evacuate," he said, grabbing her hand.

"What about Isa?!" Kailynn gasped.

"We won't know immediately. Come on!" he snapped, yanking her out of the office. "We'll get as close as we—don't call her!" Rayal snapped when he saw Kailynn reach for her phone.

"What?!"

"If she's in any sort of trouble, you don't want to make it worse!"

At the Syndicate Building, Isa heaved herself out of the small compartment door to escape the audience hall where she had been meeting with Venus. She glanced around the main control room, looking at the flashing lights and warnings as various automated voices in the building recited their programmed words.

"Isa!" Remus yelled. She turned and looked up to the third balcony above her head, where Remus was leaning over the railing. "Are you hurt?"

"No!" she called back over the deafening sounds.

Remus ran down the stairs to get to the main control room as Isa ran to one of the terminals to assess the damage to the building. As she looked over the flashing red sections of the building where the structure had been damaged, a sonic boom sounded and all lights in the building flickered briefly, the sounds distorting as the power began to fail.

"They've hit the central power!" Isa called. Several other Elites had joined her in the control room, also looking over the screens and warnings.

"One more hit like that and they're going to knock out part of our defenses," Hana said.

"All employees to the central control room," Isa said, pressing a broadcast button. "Do not attempt to leave the building."

"The front of the building is completely destroyed," Aolee said, looking over the building schematics.

"…we're about to be ambushed," Isa hissed.

They all rounded on her, their eyes wide.

"Get the employees in here," she said, motioning to the few operators and maintenance employees that were running into the central control room. "Fey, deactivate all of Venus' ports in the building.

Chronus, get a tablet and see what exterior cameras are still operational."

Isa climbed up onto the center platform of the room and walked to one corner, flicking the release switch and typing in several codes.

"Anders! Get the employees down here," she said, motioning to the hatch that opened. "Take them to the far west side of the Pipes. They'll be safe. Stay with them."

Anders nodded, pushing one of the computers to the side and getting up on the center platform with Isa, pulling some employees with him and motioning to the open hatch. Isa watched the first operator go down.

"Hostiles in the building!" Chronus announced. "East entrance."

"Remus, we're going to need protection," Isa said quickly.

The Silver Elite ran to one side of the room to open one of the vaults while Fey turned to Isa.

"I can't deactivate any of Venus' ports," he said quickly. "The mainframe is glitching."

Isa glanced around at the computers in the control room.

"Okay," she said, taking a deep breath, "everyone focus on getting the employees into the Pipes." She climbed off the center platform as more employees quickly ducked into the hatch and disappeared. "Everyone's here, right?"

She got a chorus of affirmatives as she ran to one of the desks and pulled out a communication piece. She shoved it in her ear and placed her pointer finger against the top, going to Chronus and pressing another finger to the edge of the tablet. When the three high beeps sounded, she nodded and looked at him.

"Go into the Pipes and watch them. They're clearly done with bombs or they wouldn't be entering the building. Watch the street. When one minute has passed without a hostile entering, let me know."

"I'm not leaving your side," Chronus said quickly.

"I need you to watch them," she said seriously. "Go. That is an order." She turned to the room. "Okay, everyone, we're going to force shut down the building once they're inside. Stay together. Remember everything we've been taught."

"Isa," Remus said, walking over to her and handing her a gun. She nodded once to him and attached the holster to her waist, pulling the gun out and checking the ammunition as the other Elites were given weapons.

"Wait for me here," she said. "Make sure everyone gets down into the Pipes and then shut the hatch."

She aimed her gun at a small area of the west wall high above their heads. When the bullet connected with the area, sparks flew into the room and rained down on them, continuing for several seconds as the lights flickered and the building groaned.

Isa ran to the same wall, Remus behind her. She shot twice at a handle that was concealed among the monitors to destroy the lock and then she and Remus shoved the heavy door aside.

Isa holstered her gun and ran into the long corridor with the wires and ports for the building.

Remus stood at the door as Isa stopped at the section she knew she needed to rewire. She quickly unplugged all of the ports she knew to belong to Venus' vital information, plugging them into a secondary port that blocked the transmissions to keep them from being copied to any external source.

She was nearly finished when she heard Chronus' voice in her ear.

"I've counted sixty-three," he said. "But they're still coming."

"These cocky bastards…" Isa groaned, running to the end of the corridor and flipping two large switches, typing hurriedly into a computer.

"Isa! They're in the stair corridor! The security robots are down!" Hana called.

Isa continued typing hurriedly. Once she was sure that her coding secured Venus' information, she ran to another, much larger switch. She pulled it down twice, allowing it to snap back into position when the charge had been built.

Isa ran out of the corridor and she and Remus pushed the door shut. Isa pressed her finger to a small touch pad under the desk and the clanking of magnets forced every component in the wall to be completely sealed in emergency lockdown.

"Where are they now?" Isa asked, pulling out her gun again.

"The southeast stairwell."

Isa watched an employee slip into the hatch.

"Is that everyone?" she asked.

"I think so," Remus said, climbing onto the center platform and closing the hatch, securing it correctly.

"Isa," Chronus' voice said in her ear, "I've counted eighty-three. Some were fighterbots, but most were human. All armed. It's been thirty seconds since the last one."

"We've got human and bot," Isa announced, walking back to the center panel and climbing on top of it with Remus. Remus went to one corner and pressed his ring finger to a very small sensor under the lip of the platform. Isa did the same on the opposing corner. A soft beep sounded and a small panel no larger than a phone opened up in the middle of the platform. A touchpad raised up from its fireproof box, exposing the black screen.

Isa and Remus walked to it, glancing at one another.

Isa held out her hand to Remus.

"Stand by me?" she asked.

He took her hand.

"Always."

"Chronus," Isa said. "How long since one has entered the building?"

"Fifty-six seconds."

Isa nodded to Remus and they both went to their knee, pressing their ring fingers into the pad.

Immediately, the building shuttered and groaned, loud gears clacking within the walls to force the building to shut down. Blast doors slammed angrily shut, covering every door and window. The computers went silent, the lack of their humming noticeable to all who worked at the Syndicate day-to-day.

Isa and Remus got down from the center platform and the Bronze Elites began filing out of the room, Isa and Remus following. They were calm and prepared.

"Well, everyone," Isa started as she reached the hallway. She turned around when she was out of the control room and went to a crouch, hitting her fist against one of the floor panels, shattering it. She swept the pieces to the side and turned back to the other Elites.

"They wanted a fight," she continued. "Let's show them exactly who they're picking a fight with."

The Elites backed away from the entrance of the corridor and formed a block in the hallway, the only hallway that allowed anyone to get to the secondary stairwell and, therefore, further into the Syndicate Building. The quiet and the darkness were unnerving, but the Elites fell into formation, three Elites in a crouch, shoulder to shoulder and two

Elites standing directly behind them, all their guns pointed at the only area where the attackers could approach. They quietly crept backward toward the stairwell. Isa was at the back of the group, Remus directly in front of her, both of them with their guns ready.

Isa reached the stairwell and everyone began filing into it. They scaled the steps carefully and quietly, everyone with their guns pointed at any possible direction from which they could be shot. They managed to reach the second floor when they heard the ambush. The footsteps and barked orders echoed in the quiet building. Isa and Remus slipped onto the walkway overlooking the control room, their backs pressed against the wall to stay hidden in the shadows created by the dim, red emergency lights.

Both Elites watched the number of people filing into the room. There were some robots that walked stiffly, carrying their weapons as their mechanical eyes scanned the area. However, their design did not allow them to tilt their heads upward. Isa knew immediately that they were from Gihron, who had not upgraded to the new Soldier robot. Everyone remained still and silent. Two Bronze Elites were positioned at the door of the stairwell, two more along the stairs, their guns pointed at the opening.

When they started speaking Gihoric, Isa had to close her eyes and grit her teeth against the harsh-sounding language.

"*They've probably evacuated.*"

"*No, they're here,*" the man said. Isa immediately opened her eyes and pinpointed his location. "*The lockdown was initiated from the inside. Get a bot plugged in. Get what you can.*"

"*Arna, get in here!*"

Remus nudged Isa gently but she shook her head, craning her neck to look down at the intruders. She held up one finger, reminding him that they only had one shot. A few of the soldiers climbed onto the center platform.

"*Think this is where they are?*" one asked.

"*R-Team,*" the leader ordered. "*Come with me.*" He began to lead some of his men out of the room, calling back orders. "*Get what you can,*" he repeated. "*And see if you can find a panic room. That bitch is in here somewhere.*"

Isa quickly aimed her gun, pointing it at the broken tile on the floor. She took a deep breath, steadying herself.

She fired the gun and everyone turned. The Sergeant was about to go back in the room and see what happened, but he was stopped by the loud humming and cracking of electricity. The robot fighters let out high whines and collapsed, the high-voltage passing through their feet and frying their wires. The humans were unable to make a sound as the electricity passed through them, their expressions lit up by the occasional streak of white energy and sparks that showered over them from the doubly-charged, weaponized floor.

The four soldiers standing on the center platform dropped to a crouch, watching in horror as the others collapsed. They had no idea that the center platform was completely grounded to protect the machines that ran the building in the area the Syndicate called the Pipes.

However, they did not have time to figure out that they were not electrocuted. Remus and Isa both fired shots, taking all four of them out with terrifying accuracy.

"*UP!*" the Sergeant bellowed. A round of cries and whooping followed as the surviving attackers ran toward the stairs. Isa knew they had only killed thirty of them with the electricity, but she was not worried. She knew that they could handle the ambush.

She and Remus moved to the other side of the hall, even though no one was willing to go into the control room to shoot them, not sure if the floor was still live with voltage. The Bronze Elites remained in their formation.

Bullets started firing from both sides. The Elites moved into the walkway, stepping backwards, firing with more accuracy than the human attackers. The Elites were sure to take out all fighter bots first, raining bullets along the front line of ambushers and forcing the ones behind to trip over the fallen bodies, slowing them down as the Elites went into the hallway, two slipping into each alcove that was meant to look like a design choice by the architects, but was actually a tactical point in the building's construction.

Isa and Remus were in the alcove furthest from the stairwell, and Hana remained in the hallway to draw the enemies out. When she saw the first few faces of the ambushers appear, she turned and ran around the corner.

"*There!*" one man bellowed.

Hearing that someone had spotted the Elites, they surged into the hallway and were met with bullets ripping into them. The Elites all had their guns out of the alcoves, peering carefully out as they shot down the next wave of intruders. Their bodies fell heavily to the floor, once again slowing those behind as they tried to navigate around the corpses of their comrades.

Several Elites had to reload, but once the guns were prepare to fire again, Isa called to move once more. They all moved out of their alcoves, the Bronze Elites at the front continuing to shoot at the intruders. Bullets fired back. Isa, at the back of the group, saw two of her Elites sustain small injuries that they ignored as they moved around the hallway to the next tactical part of the building.

However, as they were about to slip into the next alcove set at the pinch point in the hallway, Aolee heard a sound he recognized immediately.

"*Grenade!*"

The Elites darted out of their hiding spots and ran toward the next set of stairs, firing over their shoulders as the bullets chased them.

A concussion through the hallway sent them all reeling, collapsing to the ground as glass shattered and the building groaned once more. Their ears were ringing, and they could not hear the orders of the intruders as they picked themselves up.

Remus hauled Isa to her feet and put her behind him immediately as she tried to orient herself. The other Elites were scrambling to their feet, a few more sustaining injuries that were more serious.

"Go!" Remus snapped, shoving Isa into the next stairwell. When he turned around, gunfire sounded and two bullets struck him, one whizzing past his ear. The bullet in his shoulder was not concerning. The one that lodged into his abdomen, however, caused searing hot pain to blind him temporarily. He pushed past it, raising his gun again and firing multiple times.

"Are you alright?" he called, looking at Isa as the Bronze Elites created their formation once more, climbing into the stairwell.

The Silver Elite stopped at the sight of blood on the stairs.

Isa was holding onto her side, shaking her head.

"I'm fine," she assured through grit teeth. "Broken rib, but lung's fine."

Remus, too, had his hand over the bullet wound in his stomach.

"Come on," he said quickly.

"No, we're not breaking formation," Isa said, steadying her gun once more and firing into the bottom of the stairwell over her Bronze

Elite's heads into the neck of one attacker. She turned the bend in the stairs and leaned over the railing, shooting again.

"*There she is!*" the Sergeant bellowed.

The men who were still alive and fighting leapt at the Elites, bringing them to the ground and breaking their defense line, allowing the Sergeant and two other attackers into the stairwell.

"Go! Go!" Remus barked, shoving Isa up the stairs. He turned and fired several shots, but only managed to take out one of the two grunts. He ran to the top of the stairs where Isa was waiting, her gun drawn.

"Get into the alcove," he said, pushing her once more.

Before his hand left her shoulder, another bullet tore through his body, hitting him just below the shoulder blade on his left side.

Isa steadied her gun and shot the person at the top of the stairs, causing him to fall backward and tumble down the flight.

Remus was on the ground, groaning and holding the wound.

"Stay calm, Remus," Isa whispered, crouching next to him and touching his shoulder. She touched the earpiece quickly. "Chronus, we need the emergency crews ready. Remus has been shot repeatedly."

"They're standing by outside," he assured, his voice betraying his worry.

"Well, well," a voice said, his accent thick and reminiscent of an old adversary. Isa stood immediately and pointed her gun at the Sergeant, "I did not believe them when they said you were more beautiful in person."

His gun was lax at his side as he stood in the stairwell, clearly believing the Golden Elite was not a threat. Isa's eyes were unblinking as she stared at him, her gun aimed at his head.

"And that fire in your eyes, it's so...*arousing*," he said, taking one step forward. Isa tried to hear past him to understand the situation with her Bronze Elites. "I wonder how many men have been fortunate enough to see that look. I guess I should consider myself lucky."

"I can think of one other person," Isa said darkly. "Someone you once knew."

His face fell.

"When you see him in hell, tell him I'm sending more."

She pulled the trigger and watched the bullet rip through his head. He fell backward and tumbled limply down the stairs.

"Isa!" Hana called, darting over the bodies and to Isa.

"Anyone hurt?"

"A couple, none fatal," the Bronze Elite assured.

"Good, we need to get this lockdown lifted," Isa said, tossing the gun to the ground and grabbing the groaning and gasping Remus. "Help me get him to the control room."

Elites who were less injured helped carry Remus to the second floor once more. Isa quickly broke a hole in the wall with her fist and pulled the wires loose so the floor was, once again, safe to tread on. She jumped onto the platform and helped heave Remus toward the touchpad. He groaned in agony, his face contorted.

"Stay with me," Isa said quietly, pulling him to one corner and pulling his finger away from the wound, wiping it on her uniform before pressing it to the sensor. "Stay with me, Remus," she snapped, crawling hurriedly to the other corner and pressing her finger to the sensor. Once again, the panel raised in the center of the platform.

She turned around quickly when she heard the other Elites yell at Remus.

He had gone very still.

"Remus!" Isa cried, crawling over and grabbing him once more, hauling him along the surface of the platform and pressing his finger to the touchpad next to her own. "Don't you dare," she hissed. "You promised me. *Always*. Remember?"

The building clanked once more and a soft humming resumed.

Isa angrily pressed her finger to the communicator.

"Get the EMU in here, *now!*"

She pressed her hand tightly over the wound in Remus' chest and bent her head over his, closing her eyes tightly, every moment passing like an eternity.

■■■

Kailynn ran out of the elevator at the hospital and to the figure standing alone in the hallway.

She wrapped her arms around the Golden Elite as Isa held her tightly, her eyes closing and a shuddered breath leaving her.

"Are you alright?" Kailynn whispered.

"I'm fine," Isa assured, lifting her shirt slowly to show the bandages around her abdomen. "Just a minor wound and a broken rib. Otherwise, I'm fine."

"And everyone else?"

Isa swallowed hard and glanced back at the window in which she had been staring. In the single bed, Remus was still and pale, hooked up to various monitors and machines.

"They said that…" Isa took a deep breath, "another twenty minutes and he could have been beyond help." Her voice shook as she spoke the words. "But Dr. Busen is sure that he'll make a full recovery, with time. Everyone else is fine."

Kailynn ran a hand over Isa's hair, looking over her pale and worn features. The way Isa looked at the sleeping Silver Elite gave Kailynn pause. She blinked at the Elite, her hand slowly dropping to Isa's shoulder.

"You love him," she stated. Isa turned to look at her. "You love him very deeply."

Isa swallowed hard and closed her eyes, nodding slowly.

"I do," she said. "Very much." She wrapped a hand around the back of Kailynn's neck as she pressed her forehead to the younger woman's. "But it's not the same," she continued. "I never felt with Remus what I feel with you."

Kailynn closed her eyes and pecked a kiss on the Elite's lips.

"We both love you," Kailynn murmured. "We'll both stay with you, no matter what."

Isa opened her eyes and backed away from Kailynn.

"Always?"

"Always."

Isa dropped her head, her eyes tired.

"Even through war?"

Kailynn took Isa's face in both hands.

"Look at me," she said. Their eyes met. "*Always.*"

Chapter Thirty-One

War moved much slower than Kailynn anticipated.

After the attack on the Syndicate Building, she was sure they would be bombed every day and have people flooding the city, trying to attack the Syndicate. She was jumpy and nervous, constantly checking every out-of-place noise. It took her a week before she finally started to settle again.

In that week, Isa went from working hard, to being near the point of collapse.

Kailynn returned to Anon Tower a week after the attack on the Syndicate Building with Rayal and they were both surprised to see Dr. Busen punching the entry code into the front door.

"Dr. Busen," Rayal greeted. "Is everything alright?"

"I appear to have an AWOL patient," Dr. Busen chuckled. "I'm trying to track her down."

"She said she had an appointment to see you yesterday," Kailynn said, walking into the home with the doctor.

"She *did*," Dr. Busen affirmed, sighing, "however, she stood me up."

"Things have been crazy lately," Rayal said.

"I know," Dr. Busen said. "But, if she's going to be traveling off-planet, I need to give her a clean bill of health, and I certainly can't do that if I never see her."

As the doctor set his briefcase on the table and opened it, Kailynn's jaw dropped.

"She's going off-planet?"

Dr. Busen turned around, surprised.

"Did you not know?"

"No."

"It was only confirmed today," Rayal interjected. Kailynn rounded on him, glaring at him for not telling her that Isa would be going to another planet. "The Alliance is having a meeting to discuss the attack on the Syndicate and what to do with the Ninth Circle."

"Dr. Busen," Tarah greeted, walking into the living room.

"Hello, Tarah," Dr. Busen said with a smile. "Is she here?"

"She's in the office. I'll show you to her."

"Actually, I would prefer if you would forcefully yank her away from work," Dr. Busen said, sighing and shaking his head. "I swear, these Elites…"

"How is Remus?" Kailynn asked.

"He's doing much better," Dr. Busen assured. "He's healing very nicely. In about two weeks, I'll release him. He's going to have to do some physical therapy and regain his strength, but he'll make a full recovery."

"That's a relief," Kailynn said with a nod.

Dr. Busen smiled. "I'm relieved to hear you say that."

"Why?"

"I was worried that you would be predisposed to *dislike* Remus," Dr. Busen explained. "Considering the situation."

"…oh." Kailynn chose not to tell the doctor about the number of times she was extremely jealous of the bond that Isa and Remus clearly shared.

"Remus is a very good man," Dr. Busen said. Rayal lowered his eyes to the ground. "He has been through much, and he has done a lot of things that are very difficult to forgive, but no one can deny how important he is to Isa and his loyalty to her."

Rayal turned to Tarah.

"Tarah, I'll get her."

He left the living room and Dr. Busen made a face.

"I keep forgetting how much he dislikes Remus."

"He does?"

"Yes," Dr. Busen said. "Anyway, how have you been, Kailynn?"

"Honestly? Not great. I keep expecting the building to explode, or something."

"There is a lot of anticipation in the air," Dr. Busen agreed. "But there is no need to worry. Security around the planet has been tripled and everyone is on alert."

Dr. Busen stood with Tarah and Kailynn in the living room, talking about how he would likely be over every day to be sure that Isa was healthy enough for the meeting with the Alliance. He was discussing how to keep an eye on her when Isa walked into the room, looking pale and tired, though that did nothing to distract from her beauty.

"Dr. Busen," she greeted with a weak smile.

"This is why you cannot skip appointments," Dr. Busen said. He shook his head, walking over to Isa and grabbing her wrist, pinching it as he glanced at his watch. "Isa, I have thousands of hours invested in your health, but you seem to like to challenge me at every turn."

"Admit it," Isa said with a small smile, "if I wasn't such a difficult patient, you would not be so innovative in your treatments."

"You get no credit for that," Dr. Busen chuckled. "Your appearance is worrisome."

"You know, there are several who find me quite attractive," Isa said with mock-hurt.

Dr. Busen chuckled and motioned to the couches in the living room.

"Sit. I'm going to give you a full exam."

"I have an appointment for a full exam next week," Isa reminded him, though she moved to obey.

"Yes, and I'm sure that, when the time comes, you will ditch once more."

Isa sat down heavily on the couch, letting out a long sigh. Kailynn sat next to her.

"Are you really going to another planet?"

"In about a month," Isa said with a nod. "I'm going to Fortunea. The Alliance is meeting to discuss the current state of affairs."

"Why do you have to be there in person if you can just use the Opium mode on the chair?" Kailynn asked, confused.

"With so many members of the Alliance, it becomes extremely difficult to coordinate. Also, having so many planetary leaders in Opium, it's very easy to plan assassinations. It's safer, in situations like this, to meet in person."

"I'm going to ask you to stay out of Opium for awhile," Dr. Busen said, walking to Isa and sitting in front of her on the coffee table, opening his briefcase once more. Kailynn glanced at Tarah and Rayal, who were standing by the bar. Tarah was looking up at Rayal, smiling broadly as he grinned gently back at her. She grabbed the front of his shirt and pulled him down for a kiss, giggling quietly when they parted. She grabbed his hand and pulled him into the kitchen.

Dr. Busen continued with his basic examinations, checking Isa's pulse, blood pressure, and her wound from the ambush of the Syndicate Building. The longer he continued the exam, the more drawn his face became. Kailynn tried not to feel nervous, but she could tell that there was something bothering the doctor.

Dr. Busen sat back, looking over Isa.

"Everything alright?" Isa asked.

"No," he said simply. "Something's not right."

"I feel alright. Tired, but that's it."

"Headaches?"

"I'm bound to get those if I only get an hour of sleep a night," Isa said with a tired laugh.

"Stand up."

The Elite complied and Dr. Busen pushed the coffee table away, turning back to her and holding out his hand.

"Right hand," he said. She lifted it and he gently took her wrist, holding her hand at the level of her belly. "Push up." She did so, fighting against the pressure he put on her arm, familiar with the exercise. He shifted, putting his hand under her wrist. "Push down." He moved her hand and put his fist against her palm. "Push out."

She completed the exercise and he motioned for her other arm.

She was significantly weaker on her left side.

He looked at her, his eyes showing his concern.

"Sit down." When she was seated, he pulled the coffee table back and sat on it, leaning forward and placing a hand on each of her shoulders, feeling around the muscles and collarbone. When he pushed on the left side of her neck near her collarbone, she hissed and backed away. He sighed and continued the examination, finding the painful points on the left side of her neck.

When he reached her jaw, she immediately backed away.

"What?" he asked.

"Nothing."

Dr. Busen looked at her, suspicious.

"Recite your vowels," he said seriously.

She sighed heavily, making a face.

"Michael—"

"Isa," he interrupted quickly, "recite your vowels."

She opened her mouth to enunciate the letter A, and when she shifted her mouth to enunciate E, she flinched and sighed, defeated.

"Okay, remember what I told you?" Dr. Busen said, exasperated.

"Yes."

"Yet, you decide to ignore me?"

He leaned forward and pressed his fingers into her jaw, moving them slowly. "Open your mouth." She slowly did so. "Close."

"What's wrong?" Kailynn asked.

"She's suffering reconstructive deterioration," Dr. Busen murmured, asking her to open her mouth again as he peered inside, feeling along her cheek.

"What's that?"

"When she fell five years ago, she received substantial injuries, particularly to the shoulder, neck and face. I had to reconstruct the entire left side of her face, including the eye, tongue, and nose. But Elites do not react well to reconstruction. For some reason due to their immune system and the way their genes are manipulated, the new tissue breaks down. For some it take several years, for others it takes only a few months."

He sighed and lifted his finger.

"Follow my finger without moving your head."

She did so, but as she turned her gaze to the left, her eyes began closing and she cringed away, dropping her head.

"That's what I was worried about," Dr. Busen said. He reached forward and pressed his fingers carefully around the eye. Isa backed away quickly when he pushed under her eye above her cheekbone.

"Sorry," he said, pressing a little more gently. "No wonder you have a headache. There is a deposit of fluid here."

"Is she going to be alright?"

"Yes, thankfully, since we caught it now," Dr. Busen said. He reached back to his bag and pulled out a syringe. "Isa, lie down. I'm going to drain that."

Kailynn quickly stood and turned away, refusing to watch the process.

When he was finished, he pulled out a bottle of pills and extracted two. As he reached for another bottle, he glanced at Kailynn.

"Could you get her a glass of water?"

"I'm giving you a couple things," he said, grabbing yet another bottle as Kailynn went to the bar. "This is for the headaches. This is to slow the deterioration. In the next few months, I'm going to have to reconstruct everything again."

"…can't you leave it?" Isa asked hopefully.

"Not if you don't want your face to collapse and your skull to deteriorate around your brain," the doctor quipped. "I didn't have you on the table for twenty-seven hours for nothing."

"Twenty-seven hours?" Kailynn gaped.

Dr. Busen nodded.

"The damage was extensive. We thought we were going to lose her."

Isa sighed, too tired to ask the doctor not to say things to scare Kailynn.

"Take all of these," Dr. Busen said, handing the pills over to Isa as Kailynn walked over with the water. "I'm going to monitor you for two weeks. If nothing has improved by then, then I can't sign off on you going off-planet."

"Just tell me how many to take of what and I'll do it," Isa assured, lifting the first pill to her mouth.

"No," Dr. Busen said. "I'll come over and administer them every day."

"Why?" Isa asked, smiling.

"For my own peace of mind," he said. "So I don't lie awake at night agonizing over whether or not you took them."

Dr. Busen concluded his examination and made Isa swear not to work for the rest of the night. He left saying he would be back the following day and that he expected Isa to eat something and sleep for the entire night.

Kailynn extended her hands to Isa.

"What?"

"Let's take a shower," she said. "The hot water will relax you. Then you can eat and we can go to bed."

Isa sighed, but did not protest. She let Kailynn lead her to the shower and they both stepped under the hot spray.

"Have you ever been to Fortunea before?" Kailynn asked as she ran the washrag over Isa's shoulders.

"Yes," Isa said. "It's a beautiful planet. There is a lot more foliage and wildlife than here on Tiao."

"I've never heard of it before."

"It's the third power in the Alliance," Isa explained. "Tiao is the first, and a planet called Kreon is the second."

"What's it like to travel to another planet?"

"Long," Isa chuckled, turning around, her arms wrapping around Kailynn. "We'll be spending a week on the ship alone. Then a few days on the planet just to turn around and spend a week on the ship again."

"I've never been on a ship before."

Isa smiled gently.

"I would say it's nothing special, but that's because I have traveled so many times, I grow weary of the travel." Isa took Kailynn's hands in hers and kissed the fingertips. "With something of this magnitude, it is not uncommon for the leading powers to bring an entourage of people. The entire Syndicate will be going, including the new girl, Tia. And I'll likely have Rayal join me, as well."

"Sounds like quite an ordeal," Kailynn said, trying not to let her disappointment show.

"There are going to be at least twenty-one different planetary leaders there with their entourages. It will be difficult to keep up with everything." Isa glanced down at Kailynn's hands in hers and smiled. "Perhaps it would be best if Rayal had his assistant join him."

Kailynn's face lit up immediately.

"Really?" she gasped. Isa nodded.

"I think an assistant would be necessary for this meeting."

"Thank you!" Kailynn breathed, wrapping her arms around Isa's neck and clashing their lips together. "Thank you! Thank you so much!"

Isa chuckled into the kiss and her arms tightened around Kailynn's waist.

"There is one thing, though."

"What?"

"*We*," she motioned between them, "will have to be twice as careful. The Alliance is shaky, and everyone is nervous. They will look for any means to get to me to tear down my regime. Therefore, we have to be very careful about how we interact."

"I will be on my best behavior," Kailynn said strongly. "I promise."

■■

Kailynn was so excited to travel off-planet that the days were crawling by for her. For everyone in the Syndicate, the days were passing too fast. Trying to repair the Syndicate Building, train a new Elite fresh out of the Academy, and handle the press and other planets when it came to the attack on the Syndicate was causing tension to run high among the Elites.

As promised, Dr. Busen was over every day to check Isa's condition. She seemed to improve under his very careful watch. Similarly, the other Elites healed well from all injuries received during the ambush, and Remus was released from the hospital, though he was asked not to work until traveling off-planet to preserve his strength.

The day to leave the planet came closer and Kailynn could hardly sleep she was so excited. It had always been a dream of hers to leave Tiao and see the other planets in the Altereye System. She had always assumed it would only be a dream that she could never achieve, but it filled her with hope on the days she had needed it. Realizing that the dream was about to become a reality, she could hardly contain herself.

Tarah, on the other hand, was less than enthusiastic.

She had been left alone in the house before when Isa went off-planet on other occasions, but with Rayal leaving, she was disappointed that she could not join them.

Isa apologized that she could not take the caretaker with them, and even though Tarah understood why, she tried not to be hurt that Isa found a way to make Kailynn part of her political entourage, but could not do the same for her.

Rayal did whatever he could to cheer her up, though he knew she was going to be upset for a while.

"I'll be sure to vidcall every day," he said to her when she was pouting about being left alone in the house for a nearly month with Rayal gone.

In the final days before the trip, Kailynn was sure she never slept.

Going to the docking station for the ship was a surreal experience. She was waiting to wake up and realize she had been dreaming.

The security around the Syndicate was extremely intimidating, even for Kailynn who was being protected by the same detail. There were armed robots all around them and the live guards walked around that circle, their guns in front of them, prepared. They spoke quietly to the scouts they had around the entire docking station. All commercial transportation had been halted for that morning, meaning the docking station was mostly-empty, but with the attack on the Syndicate Building, no one wanted to take chances.

Kailynn glanced through the windows at the various ships in the station, enthralled and amazed. She stayed close to Rayal and he constantly had to call to her to remind her that they had to be at the ship at a certain time and they could not linger.

They entered a large hanger where a ship sat idling quietly, being loaded and double-checked by the crew. The ship was black and grey in color, the sleek design accented by the dark colors against the white hanger walls. When the crew saw the Elites walking toward them, they stopped and bowed their heads, waiting for the group to go up the ramp into the ship. The robots would be joining them as security detail for the ship, but the humans stayed behind.

Once inside, several of the small bots that patrolled the ship led various Elites to different areas of the ship. Kailynn and Rayal went one direction while Isa, Remus, and a few other Elites went to the other side of the ship.

The inside of the ship was not at all like what Kailynn pictured. There were long hallways with ornate designs along the walls, and the black panels she had seen on the ship were large, albeit dark, windows. There were several seating areas with interactive coffee tables, like what Isa had at home. There were NCB chairs and NGS chairs in various alcoves of the ship, surrounded by ornate, beautiful dividers that made Kailynn feel like she had stepped into an exclusive club.

The bot stopped in front of one door, turning its wheels so the screen was facing the two passengers.

Rayal pressed the open button on the door and stepped into the room.

There were two beds in the room attached to a bathroom and a sitting area with a large screen. The wall on the far side of the room was made up of dark windows, allowing Kailynn to see the hanger as everyone continued preparations.

"This is amazing…" she whispered.

"You should see some of the big commercial ones," Rayal chuckled, setting both their bags on the floor near the beds.

"There are ships bigger than this?" she gasped.

"Yes," he said. "This is actually a relatively small ship. It's a special class ship, used only for the Syndicate. No markings, no distinguishing features other than the frequency of its communication. For obvious reasons, we don't want to draw attention to the Elites when they're traveling. That's why we don't use the big, lavish resort ships."

"I would like to see those," Kailynn breathed, looking around the comforts of the room, wondering how anything could be more lavish.

"You might be able to, someday," Rayal said with a smile. "This is our room for the week."

"Where will Isa be?"

"In another part of the ship, probably," Rayal said. "Let's go find her."

The two left their room. Kailynn told herself that she needed to pay attention to where they were so that she could find her way back and, therefore, not raise suspicions with the crew about spending time with Isa. However, as they walked through the ship, Kailynn was immediately distracted by how comfortable the ship felt.

Rayal led her down another hallway and knocked on a few of the doors, asking the Elites what room Isa had. Kailynn noticed that the Elites were all paired two to a room, and her stomach began twisting nervously at the thought.

When they came upon the room where Isa would stay, Rayal knocked and opened the door.

Isa was sitting on one of the two beds, leaning back on her hands as Remus stood in front of her. They had obviously been in deep discussion when the two entered.

"Kailynn, Rayal," Isa greeted. "What room number are you in?"

"Fourteen," Rayal answered.

"Why are you sharing a room?" Kailynn asked.

"Safety procedure," Remus answered.

"Everyone on this ship shares a room. It's a means to keep everyone safe and accounted for."

"But why…" Kailynn trailed off, biting her tongue.

"Kailynn, there is no need to worry," Isa assured, looking at Remus. "Remus and I are not engaged sexually anymore. You know that."

Kailynn bowed her head, deciding not to speak. It did not matter that Isa and Remus were no longer in a relationship. There was something about the arrangement that made jealousy bubble in the Significant's blood.

Isa stood and walked to Kailynn.

"Why don't we see the rest of the ship?"

Kailynn and Isa walked around the ship, Isa showing Kailynn the different areas of the Syndicate ship, telling her about the entertainment offered so that the Elites would not go crazy from boredom when traveling. Since they were going to be traveling for a week, Isa was sure the Elites would be getting together for drinks and games—apparently, there was a tradition of a certain betting game that always occurred on the trips with the Syndicate Elites.

When the ship was rolled out of the hanger and to the launch site, Kailynn had her face pressed to the window, eager to see everything she could. The ship hovered, jolting when it was taken off its cable, and then it began soaring into the sky. The feeling was disorienting and Kailynn had to grab onto the nearest seat and hold it as they soared through the atmosphere and into space. Isa sat across from the Significant, watching with mild interest, though she constantly spared glances at Kailynn, smiling at the younger woman's fascination.

Once they were in space, Kailynn felt the ship stabilize and she felt steady enough to let go of the chair.

However, she did not move from her spot at the window, looking over the impressive blue-grey color of Tiao. Her eyes were wide, afraid to blink, should she miss something.

She did not realize it but, for over an hour, she stood at the window and watched Tiao become smaller and smaller.

Finally, around what would be the middle of the day on Tiao, everyone was called into the dining hall for lunch. Kailynn spent most of the time staring at the black sea littered with white dust. She had never thought that space could look so empty and vast, even with all the stars, but there was something about looking into the void of space that had her feeling small. But it was not a frightening feeling—it filled her with peace.

After an afternoon of wandering around the ship with Isa, Kailynn saw the first round of the game called Evolu. It was a speed game, memory game, and a game of chance rolled into one.

Kailynn stood by Isa's side as they started the game at a very large interactive table in the back of the ship. The screen lit up with symbols before shifting into boxes with pictures on them. The pictures were very simple objects and shapes. The electronic table dealt the "cards" to the Elites, each of them getting six different cards. There were thirty different pictures, and the object of the game was to get as many matches as possible, discarding unwanted cards to the person next to them, allowing the cards to make an infinite loop around the table. However, whenever one match was made, a virus card was released and the person who made the match would have to send it to someone else at the table. If they got a virus card and did not make a match in that turn, they would lose a card from their hand.

This was all done at a very fast pace.

Tia, the new Bronze Elite, watched the first game as well, not knowing the rules.

When the game started, Kailynn was surprised at how fast and competitive the Elites became. Whenever one of them was struck by a virus card and lost one of their cards, they would let out agonized groans and make everyone around them laugh.

Not surprisingly, Isa was very good at the game. Her hands moved very fast, swiping the cards around the table that she did not need and quickly matching the ones that she could. When the virus card hit her, she was able to make a match and did not lose a card.

When all cards had been matched or destroyed by the virus card, the points were tallied and the next round began.

The Elites kept their own tally of the points they each received and said they would add them all up at the end of the trip to decide the winner, who would win the sum of the money they each put in the electronic deposit box on the ship. They were required to make at least one bet a day if they wanted to play, so the sum grew very quickly.

As Kailynn watched three rounds of the Elites playing Evolu, she forgot that she was with the Elites of the Syndicate. With the drinks going around the table and the amusing competitive nature of the Elites, the evening felt like one spent among friends.

However, at the end of the night, when most of the Elites were a little tipsy, and Kailynn was very close to being *too* drunk, the Elites retired.

Kailynn went to Isa's room after stumbling, lost, around the ship.

"Kailynn, you need to drink some water and get some sleep," Isa chuckled, sitting in the seating area with Remus as Kailynn clumsily entered the room.

"I wanna drink with you," she slurred, stumbling to Isa and flopping with no grace at all on the couch and across Isa's lap.

"You have had plenty," the Elite laughed. Kailynn sat up, wrapping her arms around Isa's neck and kissing her cheek several times before biting her earlobe teasingly.

"I want you," she cooed.

"Kailynn, Remus is sitting right here," Isa reminded her.

"No, he's not," Remus groaned, standing. "I'll go see if Anders wants to play a game of Evolu. I think he's still awake."

Remus walked out of the room and Isa watched him go apologetically.

"Kailynn..."

"What? He said he wanted to play," Kailynn said, pouting.

"You can't ignore him like that."

"He's not your lover anymore. I am!" Kailynn declared, her words merging as she spoke.

"Yes, you are."

"I want you," Kailynn repeated. "How many people can say they've had sex in space?"

Isa chuckled as Kailynn climbed on her lap.

"Have *you* had sex in space?" she asked, trying to focus on Isa's face.

Isa chose not to speak, but Kailynn knew the answer was yes.

"See! Now you have to have sex with me," Kailynn said. "You did it with Remus, now you have to do it with me."

Twenty minutes later, Kailynn was laying on Isa's bed, trying to catch her breath as Isa settled next to her. The Elite kissed her neck gently and Kailynn turned on her side to look at the Elite, her eyes catching something out the window behind her.

"Whoa! What is that?!" she asked excitedly, scrambling to her feet and darting to the window, not caring about her naked state.

The ship was flying over a long platform of metal on top of a space station. Around the platform were enormous rings, twelve in total, that each rotated in a different direction than the one in front of it. The ship flew slowly through the rings, hovering above the constructed runway.

"We're already at the Gate," Isa noted, joining Kailynn at the windows. "This is the first Gate, Dani-Kahl."

"What's a gate?"

"It's a bit like a jump in space. The gate will launch us into a very fast pace through its route until we reach the other side. Then we'll have to go to the next gate for the next jump."

Kailynn had no idea what Isa was talking about, but she nodded, watching as they flew through another large, rotating ring.

"Is the ship going to jolt?" Kailynn asked.

"No," Isa assured, wrapping her arms around Kailynn's waist and pressing a kiss to her shoulder. "You won't even notice."

The two watched as each ring passed over the ship. When they reached the last one, the stars seen beyond the station were blurred into streaks across the window, shooting by them in the blink of an eye. Kailynn gasped in amazement as Isa leaned her head on the Significant's, both of them watching the stars streak past them.

Chapter Thirty-Two

The thrill of traveling in space lost its effect after the third night in the ship. Kailynn became stir-crazy and bored, as did almost everyone else. The only two who seemed not to be bothered by the long travel time in the ship were Isa and Remus. Most of the time, the two were sleeping or sitting quietly.

At first, Kailynn was irritated by the behavior, until she realized that there was no one to disturb Isa on the long trip, allowing her time to rest.

After that, she left Isa alone until she could no longer stand it.

The sleeping arrangements also got on her nerves. She wanted to continue sleeping next to the Golden Elite, but Rayal refused to share a room with Remus, even when Kailynn begged. Therefore, Kailynn would go to Isa's room and climb into bed with her. When he was too exhausted to put it off any longer, Remus would go back to the room and sleep in his separate bed.

Isa did nothing to change the situation, either.

Therefore, when they finally reached Fortunea, Kailynn was eager to get off the ship.

Once again, Kailynn's face was glued to the window, watching the ship approach the large blue and green planet. The flames that licked the ship as they entered the atmosphere startled her at first, but Isa assured her that everything was alright, which eased Kailynn's mind, but she did not press her face to the glass until the flames were gone.

The ship flew toward a large, grand city, passing over the buildings and streets. There were people walking through the city and the cars were not in underground tunnels, but next to the buildings, causing a lot of movement on the surface of the planet.

Once they landed at the docking station, the entourage was escorted by an enormous security detail to a caravan of cars. Kailynn, Rayal, Remus, and Isa shared a car in the middle of the convoy. As soon as the door closed and they began moving, Kailynn pressed her face to the window and watched the city pass.

Remus reached into his pocket and pulled out a small device, setting it against the side of the car and turning the scrambler on.

"This is not going to be a pleasant meeting," Remus said seriously.

"I am aware," Isa agreed.

"I need to know your intentions."

Every eye in the car turned to the Golden Elite. Isa stared at Remus silently for a few moments before sighing.

"I'm not backing down," she said simply. "I will not submit to threats and terrorism from the Ninth Circle. Anything I do after their threat has been neutralized will be my decision and the Alliance need not know of it."

Kailynn was unsure exactly what Isa was saying, but there was something about the words that caused a feeling of anticipation to pool in her belly.

"You will need their support if you plan to go through with it," Remus corrected.

"There is no reason for them to know about that now," Isa said. "The Ninth Circle is a bigger threat."

The rest of the car ride was silent.

Kailynn was surprisingly tired by the time they got to Leadership Square, which held the heavily-guarded, stunning palace of the Queen of Fortunea. Kailynn's tired eyes tried to take in the stone walls and the incredible carved statues of beasts and humans alike, flanking the large staircase that led up to the columns in front of the grand entrance adorned with gold.

Compared to the metal and glass structures of Tiao, the light stone buildings felt warm and opulent.

Kailynn was swept up with the rest of the crowd, Rayal keeping a close eye on her as the entourage, surrounded by droves of security, were swarmed at the gates of Leadership Square by reporters, cameras, and people curious about the commotion. The Elites did not seem phased, but Kailynn was overwhelmed and tried to hide her face as much as possible, walking quickly to get to the steps of the palace, where security prevented spectators from coming further.

Inside the palace, everyone in the group was scanned for security purposes and then admitted and led toward one of the living quarter areas. As they walked through the marble-floored halls, a woman dressed entirely in black quickly approached the group, walking alongside them until Isa motioned for her to approach.

"Seventeen leaders are here. We are expecting the remaining twelve through the day. The rest will be connecting remotely," she relayed quietly to Isa. "The dinner tonight has been postponed due to an emergency and the meeting is set for tomorrow morning at eleven," she continued.

"Red flags?" Isa asked.

"Several," the woman said. "Orille is here and he brought that Syna with him."

Isa groaned quietly.

"Fine," she said. "What else?"

"Juren was seen speaking with Lynn and Ralphia alone last night at dinner," the informant continued, even as they walked around the corner. "The rumor is that there was an assassination attempt on Kren last night and that is the reason for the emergency postponement. Everyone, of course, suspects Lynn."

"Kren is still breathing though?"

"Barely," the woman groaned. Isa chuckled.

"Alright," she said. "Are there any representatives from Hyun?"

"Yuta is here with some of her advisors."

"She's quite bold," Isa muttered. "Are Shane and Urya here as well?"

"Yes, they arrived late last night."

Isa nodded to the woman. "Thank you."

The woman turned away from the group and walked away. Kailynn took a few quick steps to catch up to Isa.

"Does she work for you?"

"Yes."

"You have a *spy* here?" she hissed.

"Several," Isa confirmed. "Knowledge is power. I must stay informed, or I'll be killed."

"What if the queen finds out?"

"She knows about all but one of them," Isa assured. She smiled. "We may be good friends, but I need to keep an eye on her as well."

Kailynn could only blink at the back of Isa's head as they turned into the wing of the palace dedicated for the entourage from Tiao. For some reason, the former Significant was startled by Isa saying so calmly that she was spying on everyone in the Alliance.

The rooms were divided among the Elites—two to a room, as usual—and Rayal and Kailynn shared a room next to the two other advisors of the Syndicate. Once they were settled, Kailynn poked her head into the hallway to be sure that no one was there and went to Isa's room, Rayal with her.

"—don't trust her," Remus said. "That is an extremely bold move to come here herself."

"It's only going to harm her in the end," Isa assured, turning to Rayal and Kailynn as they closed the door behind them. "We have to be patient. Right now, we have information that gives us power over her. We need to remember that."

"And Shane and Urya? We haven't been watching their planets as we should."

"We have enough," Isa assured gently. "All will be well."

"It is dangerous to have traitors in your midst," Rayal agreed, approaching.

"We have little information on Gihron. You know they abandoned Caroie, which means they're waiting to see what we do. If Yuta is working with Gihron, then she is a very valuable source of information," Isa explained. "We have the upper hand, but we can only keep that if we are very careful about how we proceed. We need to let her convict herself."

"But if you let her get out of hand, then you're going to have a larger war on your hands," Remus warned.

"I agree," Rayal seconded. "The Ninth Circle is using obsolete technology, but if they've managed to swing Hyun, Imala, and Tepian to their side, we are going to be fighting with armies that match our own."

Isa sighed heavily and turned to Kailynn. The Significant was silent, knowing she could not offer any advice to the Elite.

"Let us see how the meeting goes tomorrow," Isa said. "They are not the only planets I am concerned about." She smiled at Kailynn. "What do you think of the palace?"

"It's...huge."

Isa laughed. "It is."

"I didn't know you could make buildings out of rock," Kailynn continued.

"This palace has—"

"Isa," Remus interrupted, "this is a very dangerous situation for us. We do not have time to talk about the palace."

"Remus, you are getting yourself worked up."

"And, for once in your life, you're too damn calm," Remus hissed. "The Alliance is crumbling, and the Ninth Circle has already gotten to Tiao and managed to attack the Syndicate Building. The situation is already out of hand. We need to remind them that we are the hegemon of the system."

"If we start exerting power and dominance over these planets in this fragile state, we will not be hegemon for long," Isa said darkly. "We need to make them feel it on their own. The only way to do that is to remain calm and stay secure in the knowledge that we have the upper hand."

"We *don't*," Remus near-growled.

"They do not need to know that."

"They already know it," Remus said. "They know that our past relations with Gihron are riddled with blood, and anyone who wants to tear you down will use that as a means to pull you out of power and destroy Tiao."

"Only if they gain something out of it," Isa said. "And, as long as Venus is still operational, no one will gain anything from Gihron's victory."

"That is not true. Remember, you—"

A knock from the door stopped him and the door opened as a steward walked into the room and bowed his head.

"I heard that my palace had become infested with Elites," a voice said with a laugh.

Kailynn was surprised to be meeting the queen of the planet in such an informal setting. She was dressed in rich clothes of gold and red, ornaments in her hair and heavy makeup on her face, accenting her soft, dark skin. Despite the incredible difference in her appearance from anyone Kailynn had seen before, she was enthralled by the queen's beauty.

"Glynna," Isa said with a warm smile, walking forward and taking the queen's shoulders as the queen did the same to Isa, both kissing each other's cheeks. "It has been far too long," she said.

"Indeed it has," Glynna agreed. She turned to Remus. "Elite Remus," she said, bowing her head with a teasing smile. He bowed deeply.

"Your Majesty," he said with same teasing tone.

When he straightened, he also kissed both her cheeks. "It is wonderful to see you again," he said, his smile sincere.

"I have missed you both. Isa, Remus, welcome back."

"Thank you," Isa said. "I hope you are well."

"Of course, I always am," Glynna said, glancing at the other two in the room. "You brought your caretakers?" she asked, confused.

"No," Isa said, turning to Kailynn and Rayal. "Rayal works as head of the Intelligence Agency. He's here as an advisor. This is Jacyleen, his assistant."

"Oh, I see." Glynna said.

"I heard there was an emergency that postponed the dinner," Isa asked, her face becoming concerned.

"Ah, did one of your birds already find you?" Glynna asked with a small laugh. "Yes, there was a poison found in the wine. Naturally, everything must be checked, now. As you know, it is terribly bad luck on Fortunea to have a dinner without wine."

"Was it domestic or imported?" Remus asked.

"Both, actually," Glynna answered. "Rest assured, we have the situation under control. There is no need to be concerned. At every summit, there is an assassination attempt. You know this."

"Let us hope that there is only one," Remus said.

"Yes, let's," Glynna chuckled.

Kailynn could not help but wonder how many assassination attempts these leaders had endured to be able to joke about their own murders so lightly.

"I would stay and visit, but I am afraid I have to disappear before the next convoy arrives," Glynna said. She reached forward and took Isa's hand. "I just had to see you. It's been too long."

"It has," Isa agreed, smiling. "We'll catch up sometime after tomorrow."

"Yes," Glynna said. "I will see you both tomorrow."

■■

The Isa that led the Elites into the enormous conference hall of the Fortuean Palace was not the Isa Kailynn knew. Isa was not dressed in her normal uniform. She wore all black, her clothes formfitting and perfectly tailored to her, making her appear far more intimidating. Her hair was pulled away from her face and the look in her eyes changed her entire demeanor from the Isa everyone knew to the Golden Elite of Tiao.

The remaining Elites were dressed in grey dress clothes, all perfect in their appearance, causing everyone's eyes to turn and the conversations around the room to halt as everyone looked at the Elites. Kailynn, Rayal, and the other two advisors were dressed formally, but they were not nearly as impressive as the Elites.

Isa stopped briefly in the doorway as the eyes turned to her. After the two second pause, she barely motioned with her fingers and the Elites began moving around the room, silently following the cue to go around the room and learn what they could.

Isa and Remus walked further into the room, Rayal following them. Kailynn knew that the former caretaker was bugged so he could record every conversation Isa had with the other planetary leaders. There was something about the secrecy of everything happening in the meeting that thrilled, and terrified, Kailynn.

"Golden Elite Isa!" a voice called, walking to her. She smiled graciously and extended her hand, palm down, to the man that approached.

"Juren," Isa greeted. "I have not seen you in years."

"It has been too long," the man said, taking her hand and trying to pull it up to his mouth to kiss, however, she kept her hand low, forcing him to bow down. When he straightened, he released her hand and smiled, trying to hide his irritation.

Kailynn glanced around the room as Isa struck up casual conversation with Juren about his family.

The room was tiered two levels and circular. In the middle, everyone was walking around and mingling, no one interacting with the large, circular table with a hologram of Fortunea's seal in the middle. Around the circular room there were several chairs with glass tables in front of them, a transparent hologram of the planet's name on the front of each table. Kailynn saw a lot of planet's names that she had never heard of, as well as a few that she recognized. She found Tiao's table on the top tier, directly across the room from the golden throne for the Queen with her advisors seated next to her.

Kailynn wondered how they could conduct a meeting in such a large room with so many people.

Another delegation of people walked into the room, quickly assessing the area before walking to the center to mingle with everyone else.

As Isa was finishing the conversation with Juren, one man started toward her. Rayal, spotting him quickly, took Kailynn's arm, turned her to him, and forced her to take a step back from Isa. He glanced sideways, watching Isa, causing Kailynn to watch as well, confused.

"Elite Isa," the man said, smiling broadly and approaching her.

"Habim," Isa greeted with a broad smile.

The man took her extended hand and bent down to kiss it.

"I was hoping to get a chance to say hello before the meeting," he said, straightening. As Isa's hand returned to her side, Kailynn caught the flash of light that reflected off the tiny disk she had between her fingers.

Rayal reached into his pocket slowly.

"Habim!" a man called from across the room.

"Oh, excuse me," he said quickly. "The boss is calling."

The man walked away and Isa turned back to Juren.

"My apologies, please continue," she said.

As the man was about to speak, a soft beeping sounded from Isa's pocket.

"I apologize again, one moment," Isa said, grabbing her phone from her pocket and popping out the earpiece. In the same motion, she slid the disk into the slot in the back of her phone. Kailynn only saw the movement because she was looking for it.

"Your doctors can't figure out how to implant one?" Juren said teasingly.

Isa forced a smile and placed the earpiece in her ear.

"Elite Isa," she greeted.

She turned away from the group and pretended to talk to someone. Rayal extracted his hand from his pocket as Remus took up the conversation with Juren.

Kailynn turned her wide eyes to Rayal.

"Keep your face straight," he said seriously.

Isa took out her earpiece, popping out the disk and slipping it between her fingers as she approached the group again.

"Forgive the interruption."

"Elite Isa," Rayal said walking up to her and pretending to whisper to her. She nodded once and he turned to walk away.

"Oh, Rayal," she said quickly, her hand reaching out and taking his wrist. She slipped the disk into his hand. "Keep an eye on Tia?"

"Yes, Miss," he said with a bow of his head.

Rayal and Kailynn walked away from Isa and moved across the room.

"What the hell just happened?" Kailynn whispered.

"Isa's spies are reporting to her," Rayal whispered back.

"That was…I mean…everything here is so…"

"I know," Rayal said with a nod. "You thought being a Significant had a lot of hidden pretense? Politics is far worse. But Isa's one of the best. Remember, it's all a game of smoke and mirrors as you try to survive those who want to stab you in the back."

Juren excused himself from the conversation and Remus turned to another leader, discussing something trivial. Before the meeting, everyone was catching up and testing the waters, trying to determine the best strategy for each planet depending on the mood of the leader that day. Isa was trying to pay attention, but she continued to glance around the room, seeing who had joined them and who she wanted to talk to in the limited time before the meeting.

"You always did stand out in a crowd," a voice said, suddenly at her ear. She whirled around to face the woman.

The initial surprise of the voice faded and elation filled every part of Isa.

"Vanessa?" she breathed, her eyes going wide.

The woman smiled broadly.

"Hello, Isa."

Isa, unable to help herself, hugged the older woman quickly.

"Sorry," Vanessa said, "I guess I really should call you *Elite* Isa, now."

"I..." Isa looked over the woman and shook her head slowly. "I can't believe you're *here*."

"Ms. Henrick?" Remus asked, also surprised to see the woman as he walked to Isa again.

"Elite Remus," Vanessa greeted. The small group of politicians from the planet Nexia looked over the woman warily. Vanessa Henrick was referred to in the Altereye System as a shadow politician. She was seen at many of the large summits and peace meetings between planets, but no one knew where she had been born or who she truly served, which made her very dangerous.

Isa, however, knew Vanessa as one of the former teachers at the Elite Academy. Vanessa had only been a teacher for half of a year. She was ordered into exile for trying to insight rebellion with Isa and the group that eventually came to run the Syndicate. Isa had not seen the woman in twenty years.

Yet Vanessa looked exactly the same, her red-auburn hair pulled into a loose braid, exposing the piercing hazel eyes. She was extremely beautiful, but unbelievably intimidating.

"What are you doing here?" Isa asked, following Vanessa's lead as they walked away from the group to discuss things on their own.

"Her Majesty Glynna asked me to sit in as advisor for the meeting," Vanessa explained.

"I didn't know that you were in her favor so much," Isa said. "I haven't seen you in twenty years."

"I would have visited, but I was in exile."

"...I thought you had been executed," Isa whispered, her voice straining.

"No, no," Vanessa assured. "Venus could not risk upsetting you further, or you might have caused some damage."

Isa let out a soft bark of laughter.

"Things have been very difficult for you lately," Vanessa noted. "I certainly hope that this meeting does not create more problems."

Isa looked at Vanessa suspiciously. The older woman laughed.

"I keep my finger on the pulse of everything," she said. "I had to watch you from afar."

Isa shook her head again. "I can't quite grasp the fact that you're standing in front of me right now."

"I am sorry for not reaching out to you sooner, but I watched all the reforms you put on Tiao and I've been following your work mending the Alliance. I knew you would do amazing things."

"...not everything I had hoped."

"I wouldn't worry about that," Vanessa said with a gentle smile. "There is still time."

Isa blinked, confused at the tone in the woman's voice.

"Vanessa," she started slowly, "you're here for Glynna, but...it seems strange to me that you are here, yet not a member of her court or council. I have not heard from you in twenty years, and now you're *here*, at this conference, when we are discussing a very severe problem with the Ninth Circle."

Vanessa's smile widened.

"You have learned the game well," she complimented. "I won't try to convince you that I'm on your side, just know that I am. And, if you can handle this problem with the Ninth Circle, I will make sure you have all the support you need, should there be any *other* change in circumstances."

Isa blinked at the woman, surprised and confused. Vanessa glanced at the door and smiled.

"It would appear that Yuta is here. I will go over and say hello," she said, her smile showing her irritation at having to do so.

As she walked away, Isa watched her, concerned.

She was pulled out of her thoughts, however, by a shaky voice.

"*Elite Isa,*" the man said. She turned around and saw Kren, an old, withered man who had been dictator of his planet since he was twenty, standing behind her.

"*Kren,*" she greeted, bowing her head and slipping easily into another language. "*It is a pleasure to see you again. Are you well?*"

As she listened to Kren complain about his old bones and how he wished he was young again, Kailynn and Rayal started walking to the different Elites that were conversing with different planetary leaders. Kailynn could feel the apprehension in the room, and she realized that Rayal was right. There were far more false pleasantries in politics than in work as a Significant.

They had made it back to Remus when Isa was approached by an older, nervous man and a handsome, tall man. Kailynn watched their interaction, seeing the way the younger man leered at the Elite, looking her over appreciatively. Kailynn ground her teeth together.

"What's wrong?" Rayal asked, seeing her expression.

"That asshole," she hissed, nodding.

He looked at the two and sighed.

"That's Orille from Barcel," he said, "and one of his advisors, Syna."

"Look at the way he's looking at her."

She felt even more irritated when Isa looked at him and smiled.

"Don't worry," Rayal said with a small laugh. "Isa can sure as hell handle herself, even with these jackals."

Isa turned and smiled politely as Syna complimented her.

"*I appreciate that you've noticed.*"

"*So confident,*" he said, laughing.

"*I have every reason to be,*" she told him.

"*I do hope we do not offend you,*" Orille said, fidgeting. It was clear he was worried about upsetting Syna. He cleared his throat and laughed worriedly. "*Elite Isa, I do hope you will visit us in the near future. We have developed a ship that—*"

"*I'm sure she's not interested,*" Syna said sharply, glaring at the older man. "*Perhaps you should sit down. You look tired.*"

Isa glanced between the two, seeing the way Orille quickly obeyed, walking away.

"*You have him trained,*" Isa said darkly.

"*Sometimes, even great planetary leaders need to be guided,*" Syna said, standing directly in front of Isa. "*I'm sure you understand my meaning.*"

"*I do,*" she assured, her voice strong and steady.

"*Perhaps you are in need of that sort of guidance?*"

"*No.*"

"*Perhaps…*" he looked over her slowly, his eyes finally meeting hers again, filled with dark fire, "*there are other services that you require.*"

"*I have no need for your services, Syna.*"

"*I hear that often,*" he said confidently. "*But they all come to heel, in the end.*"

"*You think you can bring me to heel?*" Isa challenged. "*You could never control me.*"

"*Everyone in the Alliance calls you the white tiger.*" He gave her a half smile. "*I'm curious if you're like that in all facets of your life.*" Isa stared back, her eyes unblinking and her expression controlled. "*Perhaps I should find out for myself.*"

His hand reached for her waist, but she caught it quickly, smiling.

"*Syna,*" she started, "*if you try to touch me, they will have to amputate after the damage I deal. I promise.*"

Syna laughed quietly, taking his hand back from her.

"*What will they amputate?*"

"*That depends on how insistent you are,*" Isa said, her smile lined with ice. "*Maybe one limb, maybe two.*" She glanced down and her smile widened. "*Or perhaps something you value more.*"

She walked away, her head high.

Syna watched her, his eyes alight with anger.

"*Bitch,*" he grumbled, turning back to his table.

The pleasantries continued with Isa receiving seven secret messages from different people in different forms. Kailynn only saw two of the exchanges and was shocked at how easily Isa managed everyone in the room.

A steward appeared at the door and raised his voice, announcing the arrival of the queen.

Glynna walked into the room, her vestments of gold and red hugging her curvy figure tightly. She wore a headdress that extended down her nose, delicate gold chains brushing across her cheeks. She walked toward the throne as everyone bowed their heads. Once she passed them, they went to their tables, sitting for the start of the meeting. Isa was the only one who remained once Glynna had walked by her. She moved to the center of the room, standing next to the platform and waiting for everyone to take a seat.

Glynna sat in her throne between a young woman who appeared to be her daughter and Vanessa. Kailynn sat in a chair behind the Elites at the table with Rayal, looking at the various faces around the room.

"Your Majesty," Isa started, bowing her head once more. Isa's voice could be heard around the cavernous room, clear and strong. "I offer you my sincerest gratitude for your hospitality to Tiao and the others of this alliance. Your generosity is unparalleled."

"Your gratitude is accepted, Golden Elite Isa," Glynna said with a shallow bow of her head. "You have my permission to command the meeting."

"Thank you." Isa reached into her pocket and pulled out a small disk, placing it on the table. The hologram in the center shifted and, from the center, rose a shrouded figure, the black lines of the cloak sharp, even as they covered the figure's head, exposing only a mouth that did not move.

Kailynn's eyes were wide.

"Is that…"

"That's Venus," Rayal answered with a nod.

"Is she…is she actually here?"

"She is wired into the entire room," Rayal said with a nod. "To every table, every camera, every microphone. She is the cornerstone of the Crescent Alliance. She logs everything about every meeting."

"*Esteemed members of the Crescent Alliance,*" Venus said, her voice reminding Kailynn of the time that she was in Trid with the computer in her ear, "*all interactions will be recorded today. These can be accessed at any time by any member of the Alliance. The meeting will commence now.*"

Isa bowed her head once to Venus, and once again to Glynna before walking to her seat at the table for Tiao, across from the queen.

"This meeting is to discuss the threats of the Ninth Circle," she started once she had sat. "Gihron, in particular, has threatened Tiao several times, and even allied with Jakra and Ulam to attack and occupy Caroie for nearly three months, resulting in nearly two hundred thousand civilian casualties and immense damage to the planet and the trade markets. After the bombing and attack of the Syndicate Building on Tiao, we are here to discuss war preparations."

"You have not made a formal declaration of war," one woman from the table for Nexia noted.

"No, I have not," Isa admitted.

"Yet you prepare for war?"

"The building in which I work every day was bombed and ambushed with every intent to assassinate me," Isa said. "Clearly, there are hostile intentions. I submitted to everyone in the Alliance the threat that Gihron sent where four of the Tiaoian Elite prototypes were murdered and demands to dismantle the Alliance, the Elite Syndicate, and Venus, were put forth. At this point, the attack on my Syndicate was just the first step in a larger plan for the Ninth Circle to dismantle the Crescent Alliance."

"Forgive my ignorance," one man said, "why are they not included in the Alliance?"

"They were extended the invitation to sign with the Alliance and they turned it down upon reading the terms of doing so."

"To what terms did they disagree?"

"The Crescent Alliance Peace Act restrictions on their military and—"

"Gihron's entire hierarchy is military. They are a militaristic society," Yuta said from across the room. "The Alliance would ask them to *destroy* their entire society?"

"We asked them to comply with the terms that all planets have submitted to as a part of this Alliance," Remus stated from Isa's side. "The restrictions on the military are meant to preserve the safety of each planet that *has* conformed to the rules."

"One-hundred fifty thousand is hardly an army," Shane said from the table for Imala. "Perhaps if you had higher numbers of troops, Elite Isa, your building would not have been so severely damaged. Perhaps it is time to rethink some of the terms of the Alliance."

"My troops were not deployed to handle the ambush," Isa said calmly. "They were not needed. And the numbers were carefully calculated based on the average need of each planet for basic protection against civil upheaval and foreign attack."

"Tell that to Caroie," Yuta murmured.

"No, Miss Yuta, I have no need. Your abandonment of their planet when they sounded their distress signals spoke volumes about your beliefs on use of military forces," Isa said sharply. "Do not stress the rules of the Alliance if you are unable to follow them."

Yuta sat back in her seat, glaring, as a few other planetary leaders chuckled.

"I must admit, Elite Isa," Glynna started, "I am concerned about the numbers of our military forces. Should the Ninth Circle choose to attack again, and with more force, one-hundred and fifty thousand troops does not seem to be enough to protect Tiao."

"I agree," Isa said. "Which is why I bring to the rest of the Alliance a proposal of combining forces around Tiao for the duration of the conflict with Gihron."

"I do not see any reason for us to weaken our own forces to protect you, Elite Isa," Syna said from his table lower in the room. "As I understand it, Gihron is threatening to ally with the Ninth Circle and tear apart the Alliance. They have no regulation on their numbers, and with Gihron being a militaristic society, their entire planet is a factory of troops and Soldiers to attack you. This war could last for decades. If we focus our forces on protecting Tiao, we leave ourselves open to attack."

"This is not a command," Isa reminded him. "It is a request."

"It sounds like an order," Syna told her darkly.

"Perhaps that is because you feel inferior to me. How you feel is something I cannot change," Isa said.

"How dare you speak down to me?!" he snapped, standing. "You think you are the only powerful person here?"

"I am the most powerful person in the Altereye System," Isa said simply. "You would do well to remember that."

"We do not have to sacrifice our forces and security to protect you when Gihron wants you dead because you killed their previous ambassador."

"I will not have such disrespect in my palace," Glynna said sharply, glaring at Syna. "Sit down and remember your place. Tiao is the flagship of the Crescent Alliance, and we have a duty to protect one another. Perhaps, Syna, you have forgotten the definition of an *alliance*."

"This is not a war," Syna said. "It's terrorism, directed at Tiao, because of a blood feud. We have no obligation to assist a planet that purposely destroyed relations with a dangerous planet."

"I will not repeat this, Syna, so listen carefully," Isa started darkly. "This is not an order. It is a request."

"I think Barcel has a heightened sense of their own importance," Habim said, sitting next to the leader of Kreon, the second most powerful planet in the Alliance. "If we do not lend aid to the most powerful planet in the Alliance, and they are defeated, then the rest of us appear weak, and Gihron will take us out one by one until they have established control over the entire system."

"They merely want to settle their grudge," Urya said, sitting at the table for Tepian.

"That is not the case," Glynna said strongly. "They would not threaten the Alliance or Venus if this was about a grudge. This is a push to take over the system." She looked around the other tables. "We agreed to this Alliance. For fourteen years, we have lent aid to one another by the rules set forth by Venus, to which we all *agreed.* For this reason, we should be able to provide a strong front against the terrorist actions of the Ninth Circle."

"We do not know the numbers of the Gihron army, or what they have recruited from other planets in the Ninth Circle. The outlier planets are, perhaps, part of this plot as well," Yuta spoke again.

"My intelligence reports that Gihron has a prepared military force of three-hundred eighty-nine thousand troops," Isa said. "They have recruited help from Jakra, Ulam, and Rebma for supplies and troops. Ulam can contribute up to seventy-nine thousand troops, Jakra forty-one, and Rebma eleven. That is a total of five-hundred, twenty thousand troops."

There was outrage around the room as the numbers were recited. Glynna called order several times before the meeting could progress.

"You are certain of these numbers?"

"Yes," Isa said with a nod. "We have been monitoring Gihron for several months."

"We cannot allow them to raise a military that high," one woman said, shaking her head.

"We have no power in the Ninth Circle," the leader of Kreon said. "They are not bound to our rules, and we have no right to attack the planet out of fear. Now, they have attacked the Tiao Syndicate and committed acts of terror in an attempt to strike enough fear in us to dismantle the Alliance, Venus, and the Elite Syndicate. We cannot succumb to such tactics. This alliance must remain strong."

"The Alliance has not been so kind to all of us," one woman said, turning to Isa with a glare. "Our people are still starving, scraping for food and money. Our economy has not benefitted from the so-called aid of the Alliance."

"This is not so much an Alliance as it is an oligarchy," Yuta agreed. "The Elites, Venus, Kreon, Fortunea, and only a few select others rule over the rest of us and use our resources for their needs without regard for our people."

Venus' form flickered and shifted, shifting into a three dimensional rendering of Yuta sitting in an NCB chair.

"We have another thirty thousand Soldier chips coming in from Jakra," a man's voice said. *"But they are demanding payment at the drop-site."*

"Fine," the recording of Yuta said.

"We do not have the funds. Can you get them by tomorrow?"

"Yes. We'll take them from Caroie. They'll be here by tomorrow."

There was shocked mumbling around the room. Isa stared calmly at Yuta, having already seen the footage.

"Won't that add to the deficit? And Caroie is trying to rebuild. What about them?"

"Fuck Caroie, and fuck the deficit. The Alliance doesn't pay attention."

Venus' form shifted back to her figure, but the muttering did not cease. Yuta's breathing was heavy, her eyes alight with fire as she glared at the calm Isa.

"You were so quick to throw the rules in my face," Yuta snarled, "but you cannot spy on a member of the Alliance and blackmail them."

"Under Article Four, I can spy on you, remember?" Isa said. "You will recall, Miss Yuta, that I put you under surveillance after your failure to lend aid to Caroie. If you do not remember, Venus can replay that recorded conversation, as well."

"You filthy bitch!" Yuta snapped, standing angrily. The guards surged forward and grabbed her, restraining her. "I will never bow to you! You cannot control me or my planet! You can kill me, for all I care, but there will be more that will find any way to bring you down!"

"Remove her from the room!" Glynna ordered. "She will face the Courts."

Yuta continued to scream as she was hauled from the room by the guards, her voice becoming incoherent quickly.

"At this time," Isa said, turning to look around the room, "I would like to remind everyone of the terms of the Alliance. If you wish to leave the Alliance, for any reason, you are welcome to do so. However, upon withdrawal, all debts are to be paid with the complete interest, all aid given by other planets will halt, and trade taxes will be raised by one-point-two percent. If more than ten planets wish to withdraw at any time, the rules will be assessed and amendments will be considered. Before we continue this discussion on Gihron and the Ninth Circle, are there any planets that wish to withdraw from the Alliance? Again, if more than ten wish to withdraw, the terms will be revisited and changes can be agreed upon."

Everyone in the room, and those who were in the meeting remotely, remained silent. They knew that it was very dangerous for any planet to admit that they wanted to leave the Alliance. While the terms of leaving had been agreed upon as fair, if the planet wanted to withdraw with the intention of changing the Alliance, and they did not get nine other planets behind them, then they were forever marked as a planet to watch carefully for any attempt to overthrow the Alliance.

Therefore, no one spoke.

"Very well, we will continue."

"*Elite Isa,*" Kren said, his voice shaking as he turned to the Elite, the translations sounding at each table as he spoke, "*during these attacks and terrorist acts, has General Decius of Gihron ever contacted you directly?*"

Isa hesitated for a very brief moment.

"No," she said. "He has not."

"*Have you attempted to contact him to discuss negotiations for a peace agreement?*"

"No, I have not."

"*Perhaps that is the best course of action.*"

Everyone was silent, their eyes falling on Isa. The Golden Elite was silent for a few seconds. In that time, Vanessa leaned over and whispered something to Glynna.

The Queen of Fortunea cleared her throat.

"Under most circumstances, I would agree that extending an olive branch would be the first step, however, Gihron is a militaristic planet," she reminded. "They follow a very strict chain of command. If the lower officers were doing something against the wishes of their General, he would be the first to reprimand them and offer condolences to Tiao. As he has not, it is clear to me that these attacks and acts of terror have been at his behest."

Isa glanced at Vanessa and the other woman offered a small smile, nodding once.

"Kreon will always stand beside Tiao," the leader said strongly. "We lend you our support and aid, however you need it, Elite Isa."

"I thank you, Sebil," she said with a bow of her head.

"I agree with Kreon," another planetary leader said. "Mabira lends her support."

Isa nodded to her as well.

Several other planets seconded. As more planets agreed with the action to engage Gihron in war, several planets remotely attending the meeting also voiced their agreement, their messages appearing on the surfaces of the glass tables for all the leaders to see. Queen Glynna said that she would support the Elite Syndicate, no matter what.

Of the sixty-one planets of the Crescent Alliance, only twelve did not agree to support Tiao.

"For those who have not offered aid, no explanation is required," Isa said when the chorus of support quieted.

"I will also support Tiao, but I have a question I want answered before I do so," Uyra said, leaning back in his chair, cocky. He looked at Isa. "Five, nearly six, years ago, Colonel Amori of Gihron visited Tiao with intentions of coming to a peaceful trade agreement with the Alliance without becoming a part of the Alliance. As we all know, he was assassinated on the planet before an agreement could be made and that has led to a blood feud between Gihron and Tiao." His expression turned pensive. "What I do not understand is why he was on the planet for five and a half months, and you were unable to reach an agreement in that time." He shrugged. "Why such a long negotiation period?"

"As we all know, the Gihron people are very prideful," Remus stated. "He was unwilling to compromise on several key points of the agreement. We would revise, and he would reject, remaining firm in his position of—"

"Silver Elite Remus, if I may interrupt," Urya started. "I was speaking directly to Golden Elite Isa." He turned to her. "You met with him on several occasions, did you not? Why did negotiations take such a long time?"

"We were unable to reach a compromise," Isa said, her voice cold and quiet. "In addition, we were communicating with the Gihron Court for clarifications, and communications were interrupted and delayed considerably. We wanted him to remain on-planet so that we could come to a peaceful agreement. The assassin that killed him, clearly, did not want us to ally with Gihron."

"...I see," Urya murmured. "Well, if that's what you say," he said darkly, "then it must be true."

Chapter Thirty-Three

Kailynn was quiet for their remaining time on Fortunea. Rayal asked her repeatedly what was wrong but she said she was alright and that she was just trying to take in everything.

Isa noticed that something was wrong, but Kailynn did not tell her what was bothering her either.

Their three days on Fortunea passed and they were escorted to the docking station to fly home. It was an ordeal merely to leave the palace. Formalities dictated that everyone needed to bid the leaders farewell as they left. It had eaten up hours the previous days when Isa and the rest of her entourage had to go around and see off other leaders. The queen was the last person they had to see before leaving, and she stood in the marble entrance hall, dressed as opulently as ever. She kissed Isa's cheeks and told her that she would be on Tiao to visit soon.

Isa thanked her for her hospitality and support and turned to lead the Syndicate out of the palace when she caught sight of Vanessa standing by the doors, talking to two other delegates that would be staying for one more day.

Isa turned to Remus.

"I'll be there in a moment."

He nodded, walking out the door and leading everyone to the convoy outside waiting to take them to the docking station.

Isa approached Vanessa and the other two delegates bowed their heads shallowly, walking away as Vanessa turned around.

"Heading home?" she asked.

"Yes," Isa answered. She swallowed hard, her eyes briefly averting to the ground. "I didn't thank you."

"Pardon?"

"For what you said in the meeting," she said. "To Glynna. You turned the direction of the meeting around."

"I was merely stating what I observed," Vanessa said.

"…but you knew that there was no way I would contact General Decius. You got me out of a very difficult situation."

Vanessa's smile widened. "I told you that I would support you."

"Thank you."

The Elite turned to walk to the doors when she stopped.

"Vanessa," she called, walking back to her. She dropped her voice to a whisper. "How much do you know?"

"About?"

"Colonel Amori."

Vanessa sighed heavily, closing her eyes.

"All of it."

"...*everything*?" Isa asked, her voice breaking.

"Yes." Vanessa nodded, knowing what Isa was asking. "I only wish that I had known what was happening sooner. I would have rushed to help you. As such, I only learned of it after you were in the hospital."

Isa lowered her eyes and took a deep breath.

"I don't know how you found out, but thank you for not saying anything," Isa said.

"I wouldn't," she assured. Isa began to walk away once more. "Isa." The Elite turned. "An Elite would have handled the situation with the Colonel differently," she said. "It took a true leader to handle him the way you did."

Isa blinked at Vanessa, surprised.

"Don't think for a moment that you aren't the right leader for this system. You are. You always were."

Isa stared at Vanessa for several long seconds.

"Whenever you can manage, visit me on Tiao. I'll lift your exile status," Isa said.

"I would be honored," Vanessa said with a bow of her head.

Isa left the palace, joining the others.

Everyone was silent as they drove to the docking station. Everyone could feel the seriousness in the air. Even though the meeting with the Alliance had turned in their favor, they knew that they were now, officially, at war with Gihron.

Still silent, they boarded the ship and soared back into space.

Kailynn fell asleep as soon as they started their smooth flying toward their first Gate. She was exhausted from the few short days on Fortunea. The formalities, dinners, meetings, and secret message exchanges were almost impossible to keep up with. Kailynn knew she would never be meant for the political world. She would rather do her job, do it well, and then go home and be with Isa.

Part of her admired the Elite for being able to do what she did, but seeing her in action at the meeting, the way she commanded the room, the secret exchanges, the power play between her and the other politicians, also frightened Kailynn. She had no idea Isa was capable of that behavior.

She was awoken by a gentle hand on her head.

She turned over and saw Isa sitting on the bed next to her, a gentle smile on her face.

"Are you feeling alright?" she asked, pressing the back of her hand against Kailynn's forehead.

"Yeah," the younger woman said, sitting up. "I'm just tired."

"Travel and a quick turnaround like that will do that to you," Isa said knowingly. She ran her hand over Kailynn's hair again. "You've been quiet for a few days. Are you alright?"

"Yeah," Kailynn said. "I'm just…there was a lot for me to think about."

"What do you mean?"

Kailynn shifted on the bed, folding her legs and looking at Isa seriously.

"How many people do you have spying on other planets?"

Isa paused, thinking.

"Over one hundred," she finally answered. "I'm sure you've handled some of their information at the Intelligence Agency."

"Don't you worry that we're being spied on?"

"Absolutely," Isa said with a chuckle. "In fact, Jesmia, the other woman with us, she's a Silver Spoon spy."

"A what?"

"She was approached several years ago by Kren, another planetary leader, who offered to pay her to spy on the Syndicate. However, she is very loyal to me, and I tell her what to tell him. She feeds him information for me, acting as his spy while working for me the entire time."

Kailynn blinked, slowly shaking her head.

"You're different when you're an Elite," she murmured.

"Different?"

"There is something frightening about the fact that you have so many spies around the system," Kailynn said. "I don't know, it just feels scary, like you don't trust anyone."

"I don't," Isa admitted. "I can't afford to. Every politician in the system has an agenda. As Golden Elite of Tiao, the voice of Venus, it is my duty to keep the system as secure as possible. Knowing what everyone is up to is a means to keep control over the Alliance and the Altereye System."

Kailynn looked down at the bed.

"I'm not cut out for this political world," she said. "All the secret notes and messages…it was exhausting to keep up with."

Isa chuckled lightly, reaching forward and resting her hand on Kailynn's.

"It's exhausting for me, too," she said. "But that is how I survive."

"Do you ever get tired of it?"

"All the time," Isa said. "Why do you think I'm so eager to come home and be with you, the one person I don't have to be Golden Elite with?"

Kailynn smiled slightly, her heart skipping a beat at the words.

"This war is going to be bad, isn't it?"

Isa sighed heavily. "I don't know."

"It seemed like there were a lot of planets that weren't keen on supporting you."

"The Ninth Circle makes everyone nervous," Isa said. "They're uncontrollable, and that's frightening for any leader."

"Do they scare you?"

"Yes," Isa said quietly. "They do."

"Did they before Colonel Amori?"

Isa nodded again.

"Yes."

Kailynn averted her eyes, taking a deep breath.

"I wish I understood more about what was going on."

Isa shifted on the bed, facing Kailynn completely.

"The truth is Gihron has always wanted control of the system. They believe that a militaristic approach to society is the best, and that respect should be earned by those who climb through the ranks of service. Those who do not serve the military agenda on Gihron are treated like slaves, forced to live in crowded, unsanitary barracks and make weapons and other goods that keep the Gihron government wealthy enough to raise their troops and build their army. Gihron is a barbaric place. The planet is desert with limited food and water, and the people who do not serve the military do not have access to food or water most days. The way they treat their people is horrific. That is why I invited them to the Alliance, to try and help the people of Gihron. That's why…"

"That's why Colonel Amori wouldn't compromise?" Kailynn asked.

Isa sighed heavily, lowering her gaze.

"Gihrons are very prideful," she continued. "And they believe that an Alliance between the planets destroys the societies of each planet. They say that unity is toxic to civilizations, that everyone should remain separate and out of each other's business."

"Makes sense to me."

"If all planets were like Caroie or Fortunea, I would agree," Isa said with a nod. "But there are many planets that cannot support their own population, mostly due to food supply. Before the Crescent Alliance was formed, those poorer planets attacked larger ones, desperate for something to help their people. When other planets are more fortunate, or wealthier than others, it can breed discontent very quickly. That is why the Alliance is vital. It's the only way some planets can get food to sustain their societies. Gihron, who enslaves their people and lets them die of starvation, believing that food is something that needs to be earned by signing your life away to the ranks of the military, does not believe in giving aid to other planets, like we do."

Kailynn pursed her lips.

"When you explain these things to me," she started slowly, "all I can think about is how Trid is the same way."

"It's the same everywhere," Isa said, nodding. "Humans are the same, no matter what language they speak, or what color their skin is, or who they bow to." Isa's thumb gently rubbed the back of Kailynn's hand. "And we'll work on getting Trid incorporated into Anon. You just have to give me time with Venus."

Kailynn smiled thinly.

"You confuse the hell out of me sometimes," she murmured.

"Why?"

"The way you spoke at the meeting, telling everyone that you were the most powerful person in the room and saying some of the things you did to the other leaders, anyone would think you were a heartless dictator. But then you tell me that you're trying to save the non-citizen criminals of Trid, and that you are trying to keep the Alliance together because the people of the planets should always have food. The two images just don't seem to fit together."

"That's because I have to be a politician with the members of the Alliance," Isa said. "I have to intimidate and flaunt my power with them to serve my agenda. But my agenda has been, and always will be, to be a good leader."

Kailynn smiled and nodded slowly.

"You play the game very well."

"Thank you," Isa said with a quiet laugh. "I hate the game, but I have been well trained in it."

Even though Kailynn felt a little better after talking with Isa about what had happened on Fortunea, there was still something in the back of her mind that refused to be silenced. For three days, she went about partaking in the entertainment on the ship. The Elites played several games of Evolu in an attempt to break the tension of the meeting. It succeeded, particularly when the alcohol started flowing. The pool of money was getting larger and larger, and everyone was trying to gain more points to knock Isa out of the top spot.

On the final day, when they were approaching Tiao behind schedule, Kailynn went to Isa's room, where she found the Elite on a portable terminal, going through her messages. She turned when she heard the door open.

"Sorry, you're busy," Kailynn said, turning to leave, losing her nerve.

"No, please," Isa said, setting the terminal aside and rubbing her eyes, "save me from this. I hate war preparations."

Kailynn closed the door behind her and walked behind Isa. Isa turned over her shoulder to look at the former Significant, but Kailynn took her shoulders, pressing her thumbs into the Elite's tense muscles. Isa relaxed quickly, closing her eyes as Kailynn massaged her shoulders.

After several long minutes, when she could tell the Elite was relaxed, Kailynn leaned down and tilted Isa's head back, kissing her tenderly.

"Thank you," Isa murmured.

Kailynn walked around the couch and sat next to Isa.

"Isa," she started slowly, "I'm sorry, I'm probably going to screw this up," she said, rubbing her forehead, "but this has been bothering me for days."

"What is it?"

"I've tried to tell myself that you'll tell me when you're ready and that I should respect your limits on this, but...I feel like, with this war, and everything going on at home, and the way you've been talking about Venus lately, I should know more about what happened with Colonel Amori."

Isa took a deep breath, lowering her eyes to the couch.

"I know, I shouldn't push you, but I'm scared," Kailynn continued. "I feel like everyone in the Alliance knows something about what happened, and they are trying to use it against you."

"Everyone has their own theories about what happened," Isa admitted. "When a planetary leader, which Colonel Amori was, is killed while in the care of another planetary leader, and, at that, a high-profile one like myself, it makes other leaders extremely nervous."

"Who killed him?" Kailynn asked seriously.

"He was assassinated in the middle of the night."

"Who pulled the trigger?"

Isa stared at Kailynn, silent for several long moments.

"He was stabbed to death," Isa corrected quietly.

"Who was holding the knife?"

Isa's eyes did not leave Kailynn's. The longer the silence continued, the more the truth sank into Kailynn's chest.

"Holy shit…" she breathed, closing her eyes and turning away.

Isa lifted a hand to her mouth, rubbing her face slowly.

"I had to…" she whispered.

"I…" Kailynn shook her head. "I suspected, but…" She turned back to Isa. "How many people know?"

"Rayal, Tarah, Remus, the rest of the Syndicate, with the exception of Tia, Venus, you…"

"And on Gihron?"

"No one," Isa said, shaking her head. "There are rumors and suspicions, saying that we hired someone to kill him when negotiations weren't going the way we wanted."

"Is that what happened?"

"If it was, don't you think I would handle myself better whenever he was mentioned?" Isa asked quietly. "No, that's not why I…" Isa swallowed hard, trailing off.

"Fuck, what did he do to you?" Kailynn hissed, pained by the terror in Isa's eyes.

"…he tore me apart," she choked. "He found every weakness I had and used it against me until he had destroyed me." She swallowed hard again, bowing her head and closing her eyes. "He used me for his own agenda. He blackmailed me, and tortured me…he turned everyone against me and against each other, and mentally abused me for months. There was no other way to escape him…"

Kailynn rubbed her face, standing and pacing by the seating area.

"Kailynn..."

"I...I'm trying to process this," she said. "I believe you, of course, but...I saw the way you handled everyone in the meeting. How could this one guy do so much damage?"

Isa's eyes went distant as she stared at the ground, lost in memories of that time. She let out a shuddered breath and pulled her sleeves down over her hands, her body shaking once.

"It happened very suddenly," she whispered. "Before I knew it, I was trapped."

Kailynn walked back to Isa and sat with her.

"Then this is really for revenge," she hissed. "Gihron wants you to be killed for his death, even though they don't know the truth. Isn't there some way you can convince them that you're innocent and that someone else was responsible? Or just tell them it was self-defense?"

"No," Isa said. "It's more complicated than that."

"Why?"

"Because General Decius, when Colonel Amori was coming to Tiao, contacted me personally and asked me to take care of him. And I didn't."

"Just tell him there was no way you could have predicted what happened."

Isa closed her eyes.

"Colonel Amori was General Decius' younger brother," she said quickly. Kailynn's eyes went wide, her mouth falling open in surprise. Isa sighed heavily. "The betrayal ran far deeper for him than losing a comrade."

Kailynn let out a long breath, her eyes distant as she tried to think over the situation.

"No wonder you're so nervous about Gihron," she whispered. "You really think he'll kill you, don't you?"

"I'm worried he'll do worse."

"What do you mean? What could be worse?"

"Isa," Remus said, walking into the room. They both turned, startled. "We have a problem on the command deck."

Isa sighed heavily and stood, swallowing hard as she walked out of the room. Remus stopped her at the door.

"Are you alright?"

Isa glanced at Kailynn before shaking her head and leaving. Remus rounded on Kailynn.

"What the hell was going on in here?"

"She…" Kailynn hesitated. "She told me the truth about him. About who did it."

She could see Remus' mind working around the words, trying to figure out the meaning. When he realized who she was talking about, his eyes widened.

He fought with himself for several seconds about what to say.

"Just how bad were things when he was around?"

"You can't even imagine," Remus breathed. "If I could kill him a thousand times over, I would, and it wouldn't be enough to pay him back for what he did to her." He stepped closer, looming over Kailynn. "This is a very heavily-guarded secret. You *cannot* speak of this, do you understand?"

"We have to figure something out. This war is all about revenge. She is the sole target."

"Yes, we all know that," Remus said strongly. "And she knows it, too."

Kailynn glanced out the door, frightened and confused tears rising to her eyes.

"Why didn't you protect her?" she asked darkly.

Remus ground his teeth together.

"Do not accuse me," he snarled. "You know nothing about it."

Kailynn pushed past him, hurrying to her room. She closed the door and sat against it, hiding her tears of confusion in her hands.

Remus returned to the command deck and saw Isa near the front windows with the crew.

"You're right," she said.

Remus walked to her side and looked in the same direction as everyone else.

There were several ships docked along the Dani-Kahl Gate. It was not uncommon to see ships docked for repairs or fuel at the Gates, but the ships were very old, and the hulls were marked with a red circle, a twelve-point star in the middle.

"Gihron," Remus murmured.

"Carrier ships," Isa noted. "They're picking up fuel for the war ships."

Isa and Remus both counted the number of carrier ships.

"Considering the amount of fuel each could transport, we're looking at half their army already at our door," Isa stated. She glanced at the other ships that were traveling out of the gate pathway toward Tiao. "Keep a steady speed. Do not activate any stealth or weapons. Let's just quietly pass by." She glanced at Remus as the crew answered with a chorus of "yes, Miss."

"It's begun," he murmured. She nodded.

"I made the first declaration of war five years ago," she said. "It's time we deal with it."

Chapter Thirty-Four

The first three months of the war were the most stressful and terrifying.

Kailynn was extremely tense, worried about every announcement of ships shot down and troops destroyed, terrified that General Decius was going to exact his revenge for his brother's death. Isa was also tense and nervous, partially from the war, but also from the way Kailynn looked at her. The two shared a bed, but never touched one another, their anxieties keeping them apart.

The war took place mostly in the territory above Tiao's atmosphere. Support troops from other members of the Alliance quickly came to Tiao's aid and lessened the burden on the planet's resources.

Gihron retreated into neutral territory when they needed to repair and regroup their forces. Due to the rules of engagement, Tiao could not attack when they were in that space, meaning that, for two weeks, the apprehension of the battles starting again reached a fever pitch.

Isa and Kailynn finally blew up into an argument that ended in a hurried, frantic fuck on the floor of the entertainment room. However, once they had both calmed down, things seemed to lose their urgency. Both of them felt as though they had been holding their breath for months, and they were finally able to take a breath when there was no longer suffocating tension between them. That meant, when Gihron came back into the battle territory, they felt prepared to deal with it.

But the breath of fresh air did not last long.

As the war moved into the fifth month, Rayal pulled Kailynn into his office.

"We have to talk," he said seriously, locking the door and turning on the scrambler to keep anyone from eavesdropping.

"Why? What's wrong?" Kailynn asked hurriedly. "Did we not get the support troops from Kreon?"

"No, no, they showed up late last night," he assured, sitting across from her and sighing heavily. "You have been on edge for months, so I'm a little worried about talking to you."

"We're at war!" Kailynn hissed. "Am I supposed to be at ease?"

"No," Rayal said. "But something's wrong. Something else is bothering you."

Kailynn sighed heavily and rubbed her face, groaning.

"I'm scared, okay?"

"About what?"

"This asshole General Decius."

"He hasn't even entered Tiao territory."

"Yeah, but…" Kailynn closed her eyes. "Isa told me…the truth about how Colonel Amori died."

Rayal's eyes widened.

"She told you?"

"Yeah…" Kailynn groaned again, rubbing her face, trying to focus her thoughts. "I just…how am I supposed to handle that information? I don't know what to do with it."

"It took me a long time to come to terms with it, as well," Rayal said with a knowing nod.

"And she didn't even shoot him," Kailynn whispered. "She *stabbed* him."

"Twenty-four times," Rayal hissed. Kailynn choked hearing the number. "She snapped. Apparently there is a breaking point for Elites, and Colonel Amori found it."

"Fuck…" Kailynn breathed. "She said she was worried that General Decius would do worse than kill her. What did she mean?"

"Probably that he would try to do the same thing Colonel Amori did."

"Take over Tiao?"

Rayal nodded. "Take over Tiao, destroy the Alliance and Venus, enslave half the system…" Rayal sighed heavily. "She's trying to figure out the best way to deal with the war without bringing him close." He closed his eyes. "Which is why…"

"What?"

"Why the last thing I want is for her to be distracted," Rayal said slowly.

"By what?"

"You."

Kailynn blinked in surprise at the former caretaker.

"What the hell are you saying?"

"I need you to remain calm," Rayal started.

"Are you about to tell me to leave again? Because I'm not going anywhere."

"Kailynn," Rayal said sharply. "Just…listen to me."

Kailynn went quiet, her heart beginning to race.

"I screwed up," he said slowly.

"How?"

"We've been working endlessly on this war and monitoring all of our connections and learning what Gihron is doing that I...I fell asleep here last night...as a result of me being unconscious and not paying attention...some footage got into Venus' mainframe."

Kailynn stared at Rayal for a few moments, trying to figure out what he was talking about. He looked at her apologetically.

"I'm sorry, Kailynn. I really am."

Kailynn's stomach turned violently in her abdomen and her heart fell. Fear consumed her entire being. She leaned forward, her world spinning around her.

"Venus knows?" she choked. "About Isa and me?"

"I'm afraid so."

"Does Isa know?"

"I don't know," he said honestly.

Kailynn stood and ran out the door, even as Rayal called to her. However, he did not chase her.

Kailynn did not bother to find a vehicle to get to the Syndicate Building. She climbed to the surface of the city and ran along the walkways toward the Syndicate Building. She barged into the front door and was immediately stopped by the guards. With the repairs done to the building, the security office of the Syndicate Building had grown and the robots would not let her pass through the doors without providing a retinal scan and a blood sample. Her heart was racing in her chest, making it hard to breathe as she pricked her finger on the reader and looked into the retinal scanner.

When she was cleared as having access to the building, she ran through the doors, weaving around the robots and operators, startling everyone she passed.

Ignoring the elevator, Kailynn ran for the stairs, passing Chronus on the way.

"Kailynn?" he called. She ignored him, slipping into the stairway and climbing the steps two at a time. She made it to Isa's office and angrily jabbed the button to open the door.

Isa turned, surprised to see a flushed and flustered Kailynn dart into the room.

"She knows."

"Who knows what?" Isa asked, watching Kailynn pace by the desk, running her hands through her hair quickly, her nails scraping her scalp.

"Venus knows about us," Kailynn panted.

Isa blinked several times, startled by the news.

"Are you sure?"

"Rayal said that some footage of us got into her mainframe last night."

"...oh."

"*Oh*?!" Kailynn snapped. "That's all you can say?!"

"If it's already in her mainframe, then she knows," Isa said simply. "But it's clearly not an urgent matter to her, because she did not contact me."

Kailynn stared at Isa, her mind blank.

"How can you be so *fucking* calm?!" She began pacing again. "Shit, shit, shit. This is really bad. This is *really* fucking bad."

"Kailynn," Isa called, walking to the younger woman.

"Fuck, this is bad," Kailynn muttered, stopping when Isa took her wrists, pulling her hands from her hair. "She's going to have me killed."

Isa squeezed her hands and looked her in the eye.

"No, she won't," she said strongly. "I'm not going to let anything happen to you."

Kailynn shook her head.

"She knows..." she whispered. "She *knows,* Isa."

The Elite leaned forward and kissed Kailynn slowly, holding the younger woman close, trying to keep her still to slow her heartbeat.

When she pulled away, Kailynn's terrified tears started falling down her face.

"Gihron wants you dead, and Venus wants me dead," Kailynn breathed.

Isa kissed Kailynn once more, pushing her back until her hips hit the desk. Isa's lips parted from Kailynn's, her breath fanning over Kailynn's heated mouth.

"I won't let anything happen to you," Isa repeated. "I promise." She captured Kailynn's lips once more. "Gihron wants me dead, but I'm still alive. We're going to win this war. If Venus wants you dead, I'll wage war on her, too."

Kailynn closed her eyes and leaned her head against Isa's.

"I love you," she whispered.

"I love you, too," Isa responded, taking Kailynn's chin and lifting her head once more to kiss her. Kailynn wrapped her arms around Isa's neck as they kissed. Isa's hands dropped to Kailynn's hips and she picked her up, pushing her back to sit on the desk, knocking files aside. Isa pushed her hips between Kailynn's legs, her fingers tight on Kailynn's hips as she held their bodies together.

Kailynn moaned, breaking the kiss as her head fell back, her body shuddering. Isa's lips immediately began working over the flesh of Kailynn's neck, one hand skimming up Kailynn's body to palm her breast.

"Isa…" Kailynn gasped. "We're in your office…"

The Elite chuckled against Kailynn's neck.

"Venus already knows, doesn't she?"

Kailynn smiled at Isa's risky behavior, her body lighting on fire at the danger. Adrenaline was pushing her senses to new heights. Each touch on her body, the gentle tickling of Isa's breath on her skin, the heat of Isa's body as it pressed against her—all of it made Kailynn's head swim with sensation.

Isa's hand dropped down Kailynn's body and her fingers slipped past the waistband of Kailynn's pants, pressing into the warm flesh between her legs. Kailynn gasped and her body bowed, sending more files scattering to the floor. She let out a choked moan as Isa's fingers expertly worked their magic.

Kailynn grabbed the back of Isa's neck and forced the Elite to her, crashing their lips together. Isa's fingers slipped deeper into Kailynn, her thumb pressing into the sensitive clit, slowly moving it under the pad of her finger, varying the pressure.

Kailynn wailed wantonly into Isa's mouth, her hips bucking against the Elite's hand.

All at once, her body snapped and the overwhelming pleasure wracked her nerves. She let out a choked sound and fell back on the desk, shaking and trembling as her muscles sang in bliss. Isa smiled and leaned over Kailynn as she recovered, peppering kisses to her neck.

When she felt Kailynn moving, she backed away.

Kailynn's arm was extended completely, her middle finger high in the air.

"What are you doing?" Isa chuckled, confused, watching Kailynn move the insult around in the air.

"I don't know where the cameras are in here, but I'm letting Venus know exactly what I think of her," Kailynn said, continuing to wave the finger to different portions of the room.

Isa laughed richly, leaning forward and pressing her forehead to Kailynn's.

■■

For all her efforts calming Kailynn down, Isa was extremely worried about Venus finding out about their relationship. The computer contacted her late in the night, telling her to report to the audience hall first thing in the morning.

Isa decided not to tell Kailynn about the upcoming meeting. She spent several hours that evening in her office, working diligently on her computer. Kailynn found her in there past midnight, asking her if she was coming to bed. Isa smiled and said that she would be in shortly, but she was still in her office four hours later.

Isa caught a few hours of rest, but her mind was too busy to be silenced for a restful sleep.

She went to the Syndicate Building early in the morning, but was surprised when she approached the doors of the audience hall and saw Remus waiting for her.

"You're here early," she noted.

Remus sighed heavily, straightening from leaning against the wall and taking a few steps toward her.

"Venus contacted me last night," he said slowly. "She told me to be here early, in case you needed to be contained."

"Contained?"

"Because she's going to discuss your current affair," Remus said. "And, from past experience, she knows how you get when you are ordered to do something you don't want to do."

Isa smiled thinly, her eyes dropping to the ground.

"She clearly doesn't know you well enough," Remus continued. "I don't know what makes her think you would listen to *me*."

"I often do listen to you," she murmured.

Remus pursed his lips.

"I don't want you in danger," he said slowly. "When we were young and stupid, your rebellious spirit was enthralling, but the thought of you gone…it hurts so much I can hardly breathe. I don't know if I could live if I lost you." Remus dropped his eyes to the ground. "But, I always loved you most when you were being exactly who you were meant to be."

Isa stared at Remus, silent for a few seconds.

"Loved?" she whispered.

"Yes," Remus said with a nod. "Everyone knows I'm degenerate. There's no point in trying to pretend like I'm not. I've always loved you, and I still love you. I always will." He smiled, though there was a painful edge to the grin. "I don't want you to be any less than who you are, and if that means you declare war on Venus, then you know I'll stand right beside you."

Isa smiled, taking a deep breath.

"I love you, too, Remus."

"I know you do."

He began walking away from the door to the audience hall when Isa stopped him.

"Remus?" He turned back to her. "Do you think, had Colonel Amori not happened, things would have worked out between us?"

Remus sighed heavily, walking back to her.

"With all my heart, I want to say yes," he started. "But, no. It wouldn't have worked."

"Why not?"

"Because you were never meant to be tethered," Remus told her. "What makes you exceptional is your ability to evolve, to grow stronger, no matter the obstacle. You are creative, and innovative, and brilliant beyond compare. I could never keep up with you, and I would never want to hold you back." He placed his hands on her shoulders. "Everything in your life has been an upheaval, and the reason you and I worked is because I was the only thing in your life that was constant, that *never* changed. I saw you moving away from me long before Colonel Amori came along. You had the stability you needed when you needed it. But you needed something to propel you forward, toward something greater, and that was not me. I was part of the foundation to get you to the top, but you need something else to go farther. I knew, eventually, I would have to let you go."

Isa lowered her gaze.

"You are a powerful creature, Isa," Remus whispered. "You think that Colonel Amori destroyed you, but you took the pieces and you built someone even stronger." His hands moved from her shoulders to her face, turning her head to look at him. "Don't change who you are, who you always were meant to be. Fight for what you want, and what you believe in."

Isa swallowed hard and nodded slowly.

Remus leaned forward briefly and his lips brushed over hers.

The chaste kiss spoke volumes, signifying both the end and the beginning of different stages of their lives.

Remus' thumbs brushed over Isa's cheeks and then slowly left her face.

"Remus," Isa said, her voice quiet. She looked at him apologetically. "I wish that things hadn't ended the way they did between us."

Remus pursed his lips and nodded tightly.

"Me, too."

He walked away and Isa took a deep breath, unable to turn to the doors until the Silver Elite was out of sight.

She performed the proper scans to open the doors and walk into the audience hall.

As usual, the room was unbearably hot and the single chair in the vastness of the room reminded Isa of how small Venus thought her to be.

The computer was already depicted in her hologram form, waiting for the Golden Elite to appear.

Isa walked forward, bowing her head shallowly and sitting in the chair.

"*A-C89072, your rebellion must cease immediately.*"

"My rebellion?"

"*You are in a sexual relationship with the Trid Significant,*" Venus stated. "*I saw a recording of you engaging in sexual activity two nights previous, and then again, brazenly in your office in the Syndicate Building.*"

"Yes," Isa said strongly. "I am in a relationship with Kailynn. As much as you may disapprove, I am in love with her."

"*You cannot comprehend such emotions,*" Venus said. "*This is a temporary rebellion. You are upset by engaging Gihron once more, and you know that I would order your Silver Elite's execution if he were to touch you again. While I commend you for choosing someone you could discreetly dispose of, I cannot condone these actions.*"

"I have no intention of *disposing* of Kailynn," Isa said darkly. "I love her, and I plan to stay with her as long as she'll have me."

"*With the war with Gihron, you should know that they will use her as a means to trap you, just as Colonel Amori used B-X20016 to blackmail you.*"

Isa took a deep breath, but her expression did not change.

"I will be sure to protect her and keep her safe from all harm," Isa's eyes hardened. "Even harm from you. I will rebel against you, Venus, if you order me away from her."

The computer was silent for several seconds.

"*You forget your place,*" Venus said. "*Your priorities need to be reordered. You created conflict between Tiao and Gihron when you killed Colonel Amori. Once he was gone, you were quiet, which allowed things to progress peacefully to this point. What he did to you made you more compliant. That is something to be commended.*"

Isa blinked at Venus.

"You're *commending* that he tortured me?"

"*You inflicted most of the torture on yourself,*" Venus stated. Isa ground her teeth together, biting back the angry words. "*You had become compliant. Now, you are rebelling once more. And I know the reason is the Significant.*"

Isa sat back in her chair, straightening, preparing herself.

"*I will not have you creating another situation with Gihron as you did before,*" Venus said. "*You disobeyed me, you killed thousands of people because you could not be Golden Elite as long as you held irrational attachment to a sexual partner, and you nearly killed yourself in the process while creating the foundations for this war. I will not allow you to fall back into that behavior.*"

"Venus, Colonel Amori killed those people. I was trying—"

"*He would have been unable to do so had you not given him the codes to weaponize my systems.*"

"I did not *give* them to him!" Isa barked. "He *ripped* them out of me!"

"*You should have taken measures to protect yourself,*" Venus said. "*You know the information you hold and how dangerous it is. Since you seem unable to keep yourself safe in such situations, I am ordering the Significant's arrest. I will determine at a later time if execution is warranted.*"

"I will not let you arrest her."

"*I am issuing the order now. The Officials will have apprehended her by the time this meeting has concluded.*"

Isa was silent, her hands folded in front of her, waiting.

After three long, heavy seconds, a high whine wailed through the room and the image of Venus flickered rapidly, distorting and pulsing.

"You will find that order difficult to issue," Isa said coldly. "The information I hold is indeed dangerous. I have programmed your system to respond a certain way to any official order you issue."

The wailing continued, the sound of air being pushed through the room becoming a dull roar as Venus' system attempted to cool down from the virus that surged through her mainframe.

"*I will not allow you to defy me in this manner!*" Venus' tonal language became piercing.

"I have always defied you," Isa told her. "And I will always defy you while you continue dictating to the people of the Altereye System."

Venus' machines whirred, her image flickering. Isa did not move, watching her struggle around the virus she had spent the previous night perfecting. She was not sure how long Venus was silent, but she did not leave the room. The Elite knew that she had to remain strong in her defiance, and watching Venus in those moments was important to show the artificial intelligence how serious she was.

"*You dare to infect me,*" Venus said finally, "*yet, you have neglected to protect yourself once again.*"

In an instant, excruciating pain shot through Isa's body. She doubled forward in the chair, one hand reaching to her chest, her breath knocked out of her. The muscles in her body quivered, straining, tensed in electric agony. Another pulse radiated from her chest, and she let out a choked cry, collapsing out of the chair and onto the hot floor. She gasped, her eyes closing tight as pain exploded behind her eyes. Millions of small sparks danced angrily over her skin and her bones trembled under the flexing of her muscles.

She tried to catch her breath, but it was impossible. Her chest felt as though it was about to explode outwards.

She writhed on the floor, the flickering lights of Venus' hologram disorienting her whenever her eyes fluttered open.

"*You cannot destroy me,*" Venus warned. "*If you shut me down, the entire planet will die, as will you.*"

Isa let out another pained cry, her body convulsing as another painful wave washed over her.

She barely heard Remus' voice yell her name before she fell unconscious.

Chapter Thirty-Five

Isa was very pale when she returned home. She was later than usual, and that worried Kailynn immensely. When she walked through the door, the younger woman immediately ran to Isa and took her face in her hands, looking her over.

"Are you alright?"

"Yes, I'm fine," Isa assured. She leaned forward and gently pecked a kiss on Kailynn's lips. "A rough day at the Syndicate, but I am alright."

"Are you sure?"

"Yes."

Isa was quiet and pensive most of the night. She did not touch her food, staring at the plate distantly. Kailynn finally reached over and took Isa's hand. The Elite jumped, startled out of her thoughts. When she saw Kailynn's comforting smile, she smiled in return, her chest tightening once again.

Kailynn walked with Isa to the bedroom, but stopped at the door.

"Do you think I should stay in another room?"

Isa shook her head.

"No," she said, squeezing Kailynn's hand. "Stay with me tonight."

"What about Venus?"

"Let me handle her," Isa murmured. "I have more power over her than she realizes."

Kailynn was both nervous and relieved to be able to climb into bed with Isa. Isa still wanted her close, even though Venus knew about them. However, she was worried that it was only a matter of time before Venus arrested and killed her.

Isa was different that night. She made love to Kailynn intensely, bringing Kailynn's body to the brink of pleasure over and over again. The former Significant could feel the anxiety and fear in Isa's actions, but the intensity of the Elite's actions told her that being with Kailynn was a means for her to handle her fear. She was trying to lose herself, to focus her thoughts only on being with Kailynn.

However, Kailynn was completely exhausted when Isa finally settled next to her and pulled her into her arms. The Elite's gentle kiss on her forehead and the way her fingers lightly trailed over Kailynn's shoulder guided her into deep sleep, allowing her sated body to rest.

She had no dreams. Everything was dark and quiet.

Until a hand shaking her shoulder disturbed everything.

"Kailynn," Isa hissed. "Kailynn, wake up."

Kailynn groaned, her eyes fluttering open slowly as she tried to clear the fog in her head. Isa's hand became insistent.

"What?" Kailynn mumbled.

"Wake up," Isa whispered. "Quickly, there isn't much time."

Kailynn, remembering that things were actually very dangerous for her lately, clamored out of bed.

"What's wrong? What's happening?"

Isa grabbed a bag from under the bed.

"Get dressed."

Kailynn did not question. She pulled on her clothes as Isa glanced at her phone screen periodically. When Kailynn was dressed, Isa motioned for her to follow and they both went further into the house, finally going to Isa's office. Kailynn thought she was dreaming for a moment, since there was a section of the wall that was missing, but when she stopped, trying to understand why the hole was there, Isa grabbed her wrist and pulled her to it, stepping into the opening with the younger woman.

Isa crouched to the bottom of the hidden elevator and lifted the cover on the control panel, typing in a short code and pressing a button, causing the elevator car to descend.

"What's going on?" Kailynn hissed.

Isa stood and turned to her, extracting an electronic key from her pocket.

"This is the key to a safe house."

"A safe house where?"

"I can't say," Isa said. "I don't know if anyone is listening."

"Did Venus—"

"No," Isa interrupted, shaking her head quickly. "But we can't be too careful."

"Why hasn't she done anything, yet?" Kailynn asked, taking the key. "I thought she would be upset when she found out about us."

"She is," Isa said with a tight nod.

"She said something?"

"Yes. Yesterday."

"What did she say?"

"What I expected her to say," Isa said, turning to the opening as she felt the car slow. When the car stopped, she pulled Kailynn into the underground parking garage. The cars were stacked in rotating columns that held twenty cars each. Isa walked her along the rows of cars for everyone who lived and worked in Anon Tower. "She wanted us to end our relationship and she ordered your arrest."

Kailynn felt her heart trying to climb into her throat.

"Are they coming here now?"

"No," Isa said. "I made sure that the order never made it to the Officials."

Isa pulled Kailynn to one car that was on the bottom of the column, ready to be driven out of the parking system. Isa crouched next to it and reached under the driver's door, feeling along the bottom until she found what she was looking for.

The car clicked, unlocking. Isa hurriedly stood and opened the door, climbing in and using the side of her fist to break one of the panels in the center of the car. Tossing the bag she had carried into the back, she reached inside the hatch she had forced open and pulled out a small, round disk, crushing it in her hand. Kailynn blinked at Isa, startled and confused.

Isa turned to the controls of the car and clicked open the override panel, unplugging two wires and moving a third to a different port. She then popped a small drive out of her phone and slipped it into an almost-impossible-to-see slot under the wiring.

"Okay," she said, getting out and gently, but insistently, pushing Kailynn in. Kailynn sat in the driver's seat, staring at Isa incredulously.

"I can't drive this thing," she hissed. "If they're not coming here now, then what's the hurry? And, if I leave, she can trace me. I have an emitter chip now."

"I disabled the chip, and this is only a temporary solution," Isa told her. "I released a virus in Venus' mainframe. It's going to screw up a lot more than just her ability to issue official orders. Security is going to be compromised with that virus, and I do not know if Gihron can hack any cameras or audio feeds as a means to spy on me." Isa placed her hand on Kailynn's, her expression serious. "I need you to stay at the safe house for awhile, at least until I know the extent of the damage I caused Venus."

Kailynn blinked at Isa, trying to process what the Elite was saying.

"You started destroying her already?"

"No, I weakened her," Isa corrected. "It will take a lot more to shut her down, and I need to buy time so I can figure out how."

"We're at war and you're thinking of shutting her down?"

"No, not until Gihron has been neutralized," Isa said. "But I can't risk your safety in that time."

"I'm not leaving you," Kailynn said, shaking her head and trying to climb out of the car. Isa pushed her back.

"If Gihron finds out about you, I have no doubt that they will use you the way Colonel Amori used Remus to get to me. I cannot risk that. I couldn't do that to you, or to myself. This is the best way to keep you safe for now. Give me time to find another solution."

"Isa, you can't ask me to just watch from afar and hope that you'll be alright," Kailynn said sharply.

"This is a way to be sure that I'll be alright, and you as well." Isa took Kailynn's face in her hands and kissed her quickly. "Please, trust me. I know that this is a horrible solution, but for now, it is the only one I have. Not only have I pissed off Gihron, but I've screwed with Venus. I have two very dangerous enemies that I need to manage, and I can't do that if I am worried about you, or that they'll get to you. As it is, they are both after a way to contain me or kill me, and that's you."

Kailynn swallowed hard. She wanted to scream at the Elite and tell her that she was never going to leave Isa's side, that they would fight the enemies together, but she knew that she did not understand how to fight in these situations. Isa knew how to play this very dangerous game. Kailynn did not.

Tears were welling in her eyes. Isa's thumbs stroked Kailynn's cheeks.

"I am sorry that it's come to this, but I promise," her fingers tightened on Kailynn's jaw, "I will find a way to keep you safe."

"Don't do that if you can't find a way to keep yourself safe, too," Kailynn said darkly. "I swear, Isa, if you try to pull some stupid shit by putting yourself in danger just to protect me, I will never forgive you."

Isa leaned forward, kissing Kailynn again.

"I promise," Isa said. "They call me the best Elite in centuries. It's time to prove them right."

"I'm pretty sure you already have."

Isa kissed Kailynn one more time and then stood, closing the car door.

Once she did, the car turned on and began pulling out of the parking system, turning and heading to the programmed destination. Kailynn watched Isa grow smaller in the distance as the car drove to the street, turning onto the freeway and speeding away as the sun began to rise.

Kailynn tried to pay attention to where she was going, but the car drove out of Anon entirely and for nearly eleven hours, the car did not stop. Kailynn was able to make out some names on signs of areas and cities as she passed, but the names did not allow her to orient herself—she had never heard of most of the places before.

The long drive gave her plenty of time to think over her situation, and the more she thought about it, the more powerless she felt.

She had always felt like a powerful person under repressed circumstances, but she knew now that it had been her ignorance and arrogance that allowed her to feel like that. She wanted to go back to Isa and be there to help the Elite, but she knew that she would not be able to assist other than just being there for support. Isa was the one who knew how to fight and how to protect them, and Kailynn had to trust her to do so.

The matter was entirely out of her hands.

And the feeling of being powerless scared her.

The car finally turned into a garage and slowed, parking in one of the seven empty parking spots. The car turned off and Kailynn sat in silence for several minutes.

She reached into the back and pulled forward the bag Isa had left in there, opening it to see the clothes folded neatly inside under several currency chips, each reading five-thousand credits.

Kailynn swallowed hard and closed the bag, feeling the reality of her separation from Isa settle into her chest. She knew she had not only left the Elite not knowing where she was or how to get back to Isa, but she knew she had to remain quiet and not draw attention to herself. It was as Isa said—she did not know who was watching or listening.

Kailynn stepped out of the car and walked to the only door in front of her, slowly pressing the electronic key to the reader and hearing the door click. She stepped into the elevator, watching the door close as if in a dream. The elevator lifted and stopped only four seconds later, allowing her into the entrance hall leading to the main door of the safe house. She walked in and pressed the electronic key to the lock reader, finally walking into the safe house.

It was small, but clean and comfortable. The living room had a sitting area and a television, and the kitchen was clean and white. There was an open door on the far side of the room that led to a bedroom. Kailynn stood, staring vacantly around the living room.

She dropped the bag heavily to the floor and walked slowly around the safe house, glancing around the walls and furniture, her head in a fog.

Kailynn wandered into the bedroom, turning on the light and staring around the room.

She flopped on the bed and heaved a sigh, letting the frustrated, frightened, and pained tears overtake her.

■■

The moment Isa appeared at the Syndicate Building, she was surrounded by people, operators and Elites alike. Remus pushed through the crowd and put his arm around her shoulder, guiding her through the crowded hallways, barking at everyone to back off. Isa closed her eyes tiredly and let Remus guide her.

"Everyone to the main control room," she said quietly.

Even though there had been a lot of commotion around her, everyone heard the order and obediently followed. Isa stood near the center platform, waiting for everyone to file in around her. Remus stood at her side, his arm around her shoulders until she nodded and gently pushed him back.

She took a deep breath and stood straight. She was trying to mask her weakness and the trembling of her agonized body.

"Good morning, everyone," she greeted. The operators and other human employees of the Syndicate Building heard the shaking in Isa's voice and thought she was merely tired. The Elites who had been in the Syndicate for years knew that Isa was in pain.

"I understand that, when you came in this morning, you were unable to access any information in the mainframe. I already know what happened, and I will work on resolving it. Until then, please respond to messages and orders from Syndicate Elites *only*. Do not respond or process any request or order that appears to be submitted by Venus. A virus was released in the mainframe and is masquerading as Venus."

There was murmuring among the human employees. Tia blinked in surprise. She turned to ask Chronus how they were supposed to know which messages were real and which were the virus, but when she saw the way her mentor was watching the Golden Elite, she hesitated, glancing around the other Elites. They all had a knowing look in their eyes.

That was when she realized Isa was lying.

"I routed all messages from our military and troops through her back-up communications board, which appears to be clean," Isa continued. "Please treat these messages with the highest priority and let me know of anything that needs immediate attention. Until we get her mainframe operating optimally again, we cannot let Gihron, or the military, know that she has been infected."

"Was it Gihron?" one operator asked, hatred in her voice.

"I do not know," Isa said, shaking her head. "Please return to your workstations and access the secondary panel. The instructions on how to do so have been sent to you on your handheld devices," the Golden Elite ordered. "I will keep you updated on the progress in the mainframe."

Hesitantly, the operators left the control room, muttering to one another.

The Elites remained still, staring at their Golden Elite as Isa leaned back against the platform, her eyes sliding shut as she let out a shaky breath.

When the control room had been silent for five seconds, Isa opened her eyes again, though her gaze remained averted to the floor.

"It was you, wasn't it?" Hana breathed.

Isa nodded slowly.

Tia was unable to hide her surprise, but since she was standing in the back of the group, no one reacted to her shock.

"What do you want us to do, Isa?" Anders pressed.

Isa heaved a sigh, her body shuddering.

"We cannot let Gihron know what is going on," she said as strongly as she could manage. "I realize that this was a horrible time to do this, but…" She lifted a hand to her head. "I've made a decision."

Everyone remained quiet, waiting for her to elaborate.

"We will defeat Gihron," she stated. "We will defeat them, we will come to an agreement, and we will deal with the threat they pose with great tact and care. Regardless, we will not bow to the terms that they want Venus dismantled." Isa looked at all of them. "We will dismantle her of our own accord when we reach a peace settlement."

The Elites stared at their Golden Elite, apprehensive, but not surprised.

"You're really going to do it?" Aolee asked.

"I made a promise, didn't I?" she breathed. "I promised you, I promised Aren, I promised Maki…" Her eyes turned to Chronus, who lowered his eyes at the mention of the other Elite's name. "And I intend to fulfill that promise."

"Have you figured out how?" Hana asked.

Isa lifted a hand to her head, closing her eyes.

"No…not exactly…" she said. She cringed. "My apologies for my appearance today…" She took a deep breath and steadied herself. "I have a team working on it," she said. "And I want all of you to join that team."

"How close are you to figuring it out?" Anders pressed.

Isa turned to Chronus.

"How has the work been coming?"

The other Elites turned to him, surprised that he had already been working on dismantling Venus.

"Maki did most of the work," he said. "I think, if we all put our heads together, we can finish it." He looked at Isa. "But…I haven't found a way to keep your heart beating."

The Bronze Elites whirled around to look at Isa, confused and worried by the statement. Only Isa and Remus knew that Isa's life was tethered to Venus in a lethal, one-way bind. If Isa died, Venus would keep operating. If Venus died, she would kill the Golden Elite.

"I have a brilliant doctor working on it," Isa said with a wobbly smile. "If you can figure out how to wire the Aren System to the main areas of the planet where we will need to reprogram everything, and you figure out how to destroy her codes, he'll find a way to keep me alive."

Her eyes caught Tia's surprised and confused ones. She smiled shakily.

"Welcome to the Syndicate, Tia," Isa said with a pained chuckle. "It might not be around much longer, but this is it."

Tia looked at the older Elite and a smile broke over her face. She shook her head.

"I heard all the stories about you," Tia said. "You're a legend at the Academy. The Elites talk about the way you rebelled, how you didn't take the abuse, how all of you started asking questions and realizing that things needed to change." Her smile widened. "Chronus asked me if I would stand by you if Venus were no longer around when he interviewed me to replace Maki. I told him that, if anyone could do it, you could, and I would be honored to assist you however possible."

Isa looked at Chronus, surprised that the Bronze Elite, even after the trauma of having Maki murdered for sedition and treason, would know to find a replacement that was ready to revolutionize the Altereye System.

"I am honored to hear that," Isa said. She took another deep breath, her eyes closing as her body began swaying. Remus stepped up to her and put his arm around her once more. She leaned against him, relieved that she did not have to keep her head up on her own. "Chronus, if you could handle the details…"

"Of course."

"I don't want to worry any of you," Isa started, "but Venus has been attacking me for the last—" she threw a glance at the clock, "—four hours. I'm afraid that I will be unable to operate an NCB chair while like this. I need you to fill in for me as best as possible."

"Honestly, if you tried to climb into an NCB chair right now," Anders chuckled, "I would lock you in the Pipes to be sure you could not access a chair."

Isa laughed with the others, her eyes remaining closed, exhausted.

"I don't think I can be in an NCB chair for awhile anyway," she admitted. "It would be too easy for Venus to access me."

"I'll find a way to rig your chair outside of her mainframe," Remus assured, rubbing her arm.

"What about Kailynn?" Chronus asked. Isa opened her eyes briefly before shaking her head.

"She's in hiding," Isa said. "That is all I'm going to say. I'm not the only one Venus can access."

A loud crack sounded above them and the lights flickered as sparks rained over them. They looked up quickly, hearing the groaning of the control room. Isa flinched, her hand gripping at her uniform at her chest as she curled forward. Remus wrapped both arms around her to keep her upright.

The monitors and screens around the control room changed from their normal monitoring systems to show the image of Venus' head, her cloak covering everything but her nose and hard-set mouth that never moved. The image flickered angrily, trying to find a way to operate correctly around the virus ravaging her system. Some screens went black for several seconds before Venus regained control of them.

A piercing whine surrounded them and caused them to cover their ears, gritting their teeth in pain.

Isa screamed, her body convulsing and falling limply out of Remus' arms.

"*You will yield! You will submit! You will obey!*" Venus' automated voice recited, barely audible with the high-pitch screech in the room.

Isa screamed once more, her back bowing off the floor as she grabbed at her chest.

A few monitors began flashing with the warning code that there was something wrong with the Golden Elite. The emitter chip in her body sent out several calls for help, including to the Syndicate.

The Elites surrounded Isa, trying to keep her still, though it was impossible. They watched in horror, waiting for the EMU team to arrive, though Isa passed out before they made it into the control room.

■■■

When Isa came to, there were three sets of worried eyes on her. It took her several moments to recognize the faces of Paul, Dr. Busen, and Remus. Even when she did, she could not focus on their features with the blinding pain behind her eyes.

One of the machines beeped and Isa groaned as the sound bounced around her skull. The sound of her own voice was also too loud, and the vibration of her voice in her throat felt like thousands of needles piercing her muscles.

Garbled voices sounded around her.

"Look at that activity," Paul said, motioning to the screen that was showing her brain activity in real time. "She has signals misfiring all over the place."

"Her blood pressure is rising," Dr. Busen said. "With that activity, this spike…" He quickly went to the bedside table and grabbed a prepared syringe. "Isa, I'm going to give you something for the pain. Try to stay conscious."

Isa was acutely aware of someone's hand taking hers, and even though it hurt to close her fingers around his, she did so. She tried to focus on her breathing, though each movement was agony.

It seemed to last forever.

The talking continued around her.

"This is only the second day," Remus said, his hand holding hers. "And she's already this bad."

"Stress has lowered a lot of her immune functions," Dr. Busen noted. "And, it would appear, Venus is making the pain even more excruciating than necessary. But we know that, when Isa underwent the pain-resistance degeneration test, she not only passed, she exceeded expectations. She has a higher pain tolerance than the average Elite." He nodded to Isa. "Venus is going to have to deal some severe damage to keep this up."

"It's going to kill her."

"It's not just these kinds of attacks we have to be concerned about," Paul said, shaking his head. "She is suffering reconstruction deterioration, isn't she? Her system is poisoned."

"I can't operate on her if Venus is going to be doing this. It's too dangerous."

"I know," Paul said. "But if she keeps this up, Isa is going to get worse very quickly. And if there is too much deterioration of the skull…" He sighed heavily. "No one, Elite or human, has ever had a skull reconstruction and survived before, so there's no data. I can only hypothesize."

"You don't have to," Remus said, "I can imagine."

"There has to be a way to jam the signals coming from Venus," Paul said, looking at Dr. Busen. "Can you think of anything?"

"I've never seen the processing system she holds," Dr. Busen said, shaking his head and running a hand through his hair, frustrated. "I can't very well look at it. It's in her chest cavity."

"She gave you the information she had," Remus said.

"I would like to remind you that I am a doctor, not a programmer. There is a lot of information I don't understand, and I sure as hell don't understand how they managed to match all this with biometrics as they did." Dr. Busen groaned. "I would have to talk to a doctor that performed the transfer, but there are no names mentioned."

"There wouldn't be," Remus said darkly, shaking his head. "They're killed before they leave the operating room."

Dr. Busen and Dr. Arre both blinked incredulously at Remus, shocked. The Silver Elite glanced back at Isa.

"Venus guides them through the procedure," he continued. "And then she has them killed before they leave the room, along with the previous Golden Elite. That's how she protects the information."

"Then how do you know about it?" Dr. Busen asked.

"Isa told me," Remus murmured. "She saw Gattriel killed, and she saw the bodies of the surgeons when she woke. She couldn't handle that alone."

"Did you know about this?" Dr. Busen asked, turning to Paul.

"If I did, don't you think I would have told you?" Paul said. He sighed heavily and looked over the monitor on Isa's brain. "That processing unit is toxic, the deterioration is releasing toxins, and she's regressing to defensive behaviors she exhibited when Colonel Amori was around—not eating, not sleeping…"

Dr. Busen groaned, once again running his hands through his hair, closing his eyes and trying to think.

"You don't want to medicate her with pain management medication?" Dr. Busen asked, turning to Paul.

"We're going to need to increase the dosage every week," Paul told him. "Her brain adapts too damn quick. That's a big part of the problem. Soon we'll be destroying her liver if we prescribe pain medication regularly to manage this kind of agony."

"There has to be something you two can do," Remus said, worried. "I'll do whatever I can. She can't function when in this pain, and we are at war. We can't afford to have her out of commission like this."

Both doctors went silent for a very long time. Isa slowly felt the pain easing. After thirty minutes of silence from both pensive doctors, she was able to open her eyes and look around the room. Breathing came a little easier, as well. Paul was staring at one of the monitors, his hand over his mouth as he thought. Dr. Busen was pacing at the far end of the room, his head down and his hand raised slightly in the air, moving as he thought through different solutions.

The two doctors did not notice that Isa had awoken.

"Michael," Paul said, not tearing his eyes from the screen he was staring at. The other doctor turned, startled. Paul motioned Dr. Busen over. "Do you notice how all the systems are stressed, but when you did the stress test on her heart, it showed no anomalies?"

Isa glanced at Remus and rolled her eyes with a playful smile at the doctors' discussion. Remus smiled as well, squeezing her hand gently.

The doctors were locked in a heated discussion, pointing to different monitors and test results as Isa and Remus remained silent, listening half-heartedly. Isa closed her eyes, resting as often as she could. She still felt twinges of pain, which caused the doctors to both point and talk about what showed up on the screen. Isa did not understand most of what they were discussing. Even though she had read all of their academic papers, she was in too much pain and too tired to try and follow a language she barely knew.

Suddenly, Dr. Busen's expression lit up and he turned to Paul, saying something that had both Elites looking at one another in intense confusion. Paul asked a clarifying question and Dr. Busen answered. Paul's face also lit up and they both started walking to the door, discussing the technical aspects of the treatment.

Isa chuckled, shaking her head.

"Do they seem a little too excited about the challenge?" she tried to tease.

"They don't want to see you in pain," Remus said, squeezing her hand. "Dr. Busen was frantic trying to find a way to help you."

They both fell silent again for a very long time. Isa fell asleep once more and Remus leaned forward, resting his head on his arm on the bed next to Isa, keeping her hand in his.

A nurse walking into the room stirred both of them.

"My sincerest apologies, Elite Isa, Elite Remus," he said, bowing his head slightly. "Dr. Busen said that he will perform your surgery in about an hour and he would like you prepped." The nurse walked forward slowly. "He...he's not putting this surgery in our computers. Something about Venus' mainframe being locked down?"

"It's locked down for safety," Remus said, quickly making up a plausible lie. "We received threats from Gihron. We took precautions."

"I understand," Isa added. "It's alright. The information will be added later to her mainframe."

The nurse seemed more at ease after hearing the explanation. He approached the Elite and began hooking the Elite up to even more monitors, though it was difficult for him to place them all correctly when there were already so many machines attached to the Elite. Isa did not bother to ask what surgery Dr. Busen wanted to perform. She trusted him entirely.

"You also have someone that wants to see you," the nurse said.

"Who?"

"A woman. She said she's a close friend of yours and the Syndicate sent her over," the nurse elaborated. "Someone named Vanessa Henrick. Does the name sound familiar?"

"Yes," Isa said. "I'll see her. Can you show her up before the surgery?"

"Isa, can you handle that?" Remus asked, worried.

"I don't know what state I will be in when I wake up," Isa said. "But, judging from past experience, I will be nearly incoherent. It won't take long."

"You can see her later."

"Remus," Isa said, looking at him seriously, "I need to speak with her. It concerns this treatment."

Remus blinked at Isa and then sighed heavily, nodding, understanding what the Golden Elite meant.

"Alright, but a *short* visit."

The nurse nodded, lifting his wrist to his mouth.

"Waiting room, send Henricks up to fourth floor security window."

Remus looked at Isa.

"Don't you think it's weird that she just showed up now?"

"I do," Isa agreed with a nod. "But I've been asking around, gathering all information I can on where she's been all these years, and I've noticed that there is a very good trend wherever she appears. She helped guide Kreon through the social upheaval nine years ago. She's been jumping around the smaller planets, negotiating stronger trade routes with the larger planets on their behalf. She's clearly working to strengthen the Alliance." She sighed heavily. "She promised that she would help us, should we ever need it."

"You're going to trust her word on that?"

"Don't you remember what she was like as a teacher?" Isa asked.

"We were children," Remus reminded her. "We were ambitious and more than a little stupid. You know this. Venus had her exiled."

"I lifted her exile status. She was always different from every other teacher we had at the Academy, and Venus was quick to fire her and throw her into exile when we started making some serious headway. Clearly, she understands more than she's letting on."

"And that doesn't concern you?"

"Of course it does," Isa said. "But we should listen to what she has to say. With Gihron attacking and the threat of the rest of the Ninth Circle weighing on us, we need to take a few risks."

Remus sighed heavily, lowering his eyes and shaking his head.

"I'm not sure I have the same faith in her that you clearly do," Remus murmured. "The timing is just too coincidental." He pursed his lips. "But, you know that I will stand by any decision you make."

The two Elites fell silent. The nurse left when he was called by the security office and the two members of the Syndicate waited for Vanessa Henricks to be guided to the room.

When the woman walked in, she looked as she always had—beautiful with the most powerful eyes anyone had ever seen.

"I was worried when the Syndicate said you were in the hospital," Vanessa said, walking forward as the nurse left the room.

Remus backed away from Isa, allowing Vanessa to come forward and sit next to the Golden Elite. He leaned against the wall, watching warily. Vanessa sat next to Isa and looked over her.

"Are you alright?"

"Not really," the Elite chuckled. "But I'm still breathing."

"That's a good start," Vanessa said with a smile. She turned to the Silver Elite. "Hello, Remus. How are you?"

"I'm well, thank you," he said stiffly. He nodded to Isa. "It has been a trying day."

"I can imagine," Vanessa said. She looked back at Isa and took a deep breath, looking over the Golden Elite once more. "How did this happen?"

"Oh, the same way it always does," Isa chuckled. "I was not being as smart as I should be."

Vanessa smiled at the joke. "It does sound familiar," she teased. "Where is your doctor?"

"Prepping for surgery."

"What kind of surgery?"

"I actually don't know," Isa chuckled lightly, cringing at a sharp flare of pain.

"That's a leap of faith, don't you think?" the older woman laughed.

"I trust him immensely," Isa assured. She took a deep breath and shifted in the bed, smiling at her former teacher. "I wasn't aware that you were on-planet."

"I arrived this morning," Vanessa explained. "I came because I have some news for you."

"What kind of news?"

"After some...*heated* negotiation," she started, "I managed to get Ulam to withdraw their support to the Gihron Army. This will drop the Gihoric defenses severely."

Isa's eyes shot wide.

"How did you manage that?"

"It was not easy," Vanessa admitted. "I had to play a card I was trying to avoid."

"What do you mean?"

"I showed them a transmitted discussion between Jakra and Gihron showing that Gihron intended to make Ulam pay all reparations if Gihron lost the war, and that they would be taxed severely if Gihron won."

"How did you get that information?"

"Gihron uses obsolete technology," Vanessa said with a shrug. "I hacked their system."

Both the Elites in the room were staring at the woman with wide eyes.

"How..." Remus trailed off. "Why would you do something like that?"

"Because they were about to launch another thirty-thousand troops to support Gihron, and you would have been overwhelmed."

"How did you get *that* information?" Isa pressed.

"You're not the only one with little birds everywhere," Vanessa said with a mysterious grin. "You could say that knowledge is my trade." She lowered her eyes. "I may not have many eyes on you, but I think I can guess what put you in here." She smiled thinly. "Taking on another enemy?"

"You could say that," Isa said. "I'd say this one is more dangerous than Gihron."

"I would have to agree," Vanessa said. "More at stake with this new enemy than with Gihron."

"Bad timing to focus on both of them at the same time," Isa said with a smile.

"No, no," Vanessa disagreed quickly. "It's a brilliant time, actually."

"How do you figure that?" Remus asked, unconvinced.

"She won't have you killed in the middle of a war with Gihron," Vanessa explained. "You're too important, to her, to the war, to the

Alliance, to the people. She knows that she has no chance of controlling the situation if she does not have the Golden Elite."

"She could use it as propaganda," Isa said, shaking her head. "She could blame it on Gihron."

"That wouldn't serve her agenda," Vanessa said. "You remember the meeting. Others were hesitant to support you because they said that it was a blood feud between Gihron and Tiao. If you were to die in this war, that would show submission to Gihron, who is acting in revenge, and the Alliance would lose faith in the power of Tiao." The former teacher smiled broadly. "She needs you alive. You are far more powerful than you realize."

Isa lowered her eyes to the bedsheets, sighing.

"I have no power over her."

"I can't think of a statement more false," Vanessa said, shaking her head. "You have *all* the power. Every Golden Elite has always had complete power over Venus, but she never allowed them to realize it. Every time any one of them started trouble, she would have them killed. And, if they wanted to shut her down to rebuild everything, she made sure that the Golden Elite would not survive shutting her down. It was a brilliant and very calculated move on her part."

"She can easily have me killed at any time," Isa pointed out. "She controls everything on this planet. The cars, the robots…absolutely everything is under her control."

"Everything that is not human," Vanessa agreed with a nod. "She doesn't control *you*. You know that the times Venus is wrong it is because of *one* individual. And she has always been wrong about you. She believed you could not lead the planet, because you were clearly a degenerate, even if the tests could not determine how. She believed that telling you to stop being with Remus would make you listen, she believed that you were safe as long as you were subdued with the knowledge that rebellion against her would mean death, and she believed that what happened with Colonel Amori would break you and allow her to control you. She's always been wrong about you. So, when she discredits you as a threat, you need to prove her wrong again."

"But how do I know that I can succeed?"

"No one knows that for sure," Vanessa admitted. "But, what makes a great leader is when that leader knows just how much power is at their disposal, and knows when to use it for the good of the people, and when to refrain from using it for the good of society. You clearly have that understanding. You showed that knowledge even in school, with your group of friends, who are now the Elites of the Syndicate. They follow you, even risking death for degeneration and treason, because they know that you are the leader that this planet needs."

"I want to change things," Isa murmured. "But things will get worse before they get better."

"They always do," Vanessa said. She placed her hand on Isa's. "You are an extraordinary being, Isa. You understand the need for change, and you crave something better for the people. That's not a trait one normally sees in anyone, human or Elite. Sometimes, I feel like you are the only hope humanity has left."

Isa chuckled brokenly. "I was *created* by humans. I doubt I can save humanity."

"Often times, what humans create is the thing that saves them."

"But…" Isa hesitated. "What if this isn't the right path?" The Golden Elite looked at her former teacher, her eyes showing her uncertainty. "Venus works for a reason. People need regulation. They can't be governed on their own. Crime is not the same as it was before, and even though there is an enormous social imbalance with Venus and the Elites in power, it has been a stable system for hundreds of years." Isa sighed heavily. "Maybe…maybe Venus is the right way to govern humanity."

"A computer is not a good judge of humanity," Vanessa disagreed, shaking her head. "Humanity is far more than numbers and statistics and death, they are artists and creative vessels for advancement. A computer can replicate art, but it cannot create it. A computer can replicate tones and sounds and words, but it cannot string them together in an original composition, because it cannot determine which sounds are pleasing or which words will evoke emotion in the listener."

"Elites can't do that, either," Isa said. "Well…except Remus."

They both turned to the Silver Elite, who looked between the two of them before slowly lowering his eyes to the ground.

"Correct," Vanessa agreed. "An individual that is degenerate by Venus' standards can create some of the most beautiful music and art that any of us have ever heard or seen." Vanessa turned back to Isa. "There is no standard when it comes to creativity. If there was, there would be no advancement."

Isa's eyes lowered.

"But *I* cannot create art," she murmured.

Vanessa reached forward and lifted Isa's chin, forcing her to look up.

"But you can create *change*," she whispered, smiling. "And I know you will. I've always known you would."

Chapter Thirty-Six

Kailynn was going stir-crazy.

She had never been good at staying inside for days at a time, and now that she had nowhere to go, she was losing her mind. She would spend the days pacing around the safe house, watching the news broadcasts for the tiniest mention of Isa and agonizing over the Elite's safety.

The two and a half weeks were torturous.

She would talk to Isa occasionally on the phone, but the Elite could only call occasionally and only for two minutes. Venus could trace the calls and figure out which of the Syndicate safe houses Kailynn was occupying. Isa would call, make sure Kailynn was alright, assure the former Significant that she was also alright, and then tell her when she would call again.

Kailynn tried to focus on continuing her reading and writing lessons, but she would always break away from them and watch the news for hours on end, learning about the wins and losses of the army fighting in Tiaoian space and the various planets that had lent their support to the Syndicate.

She also learned that the Wheezing Death had been announced to the public upon the opening of the medical center in the Walking District, which officially opened one week after Kailynn left Anon. However, they were so overwhelmed with patients from Trid with the Wheezing Death Virus that they had declared it a regional epidemic and called in doctors from all over the planet to assist Dr. Busen in studying the strange, undocumented illness.

Even though she considered it a victory that the medical center had been opened and allowed health care to Trids, she could hardly celebrate.

She was too worried about the Golden Elite.

Kailynn also received brief, encouraging phone calls from Rayal and Tarah. They both assured her that Isa was, in fact, alright and told her that Dr. Busen had operated on Isa to help with the reconstructive deterioration and the pain from Venus' angry attacks on the Golden Elite.

Due to the limited time allowed on all calls to her, Kailynn had to learn about how Venus was attacking Isa through the course of four days. It caused her anxiety to triple.

Two and a half weeks in the safe house and Kailynn was planning her escape. She could not drive the car, and knew that if it took her eleven hours to get to the safe house from Anon by car, it would take her a week, if not longer, to walk back. She was no further on getting a plan together when she received a phone call.

Since she had been in the bathroom when it rang, she quickly had to scramble out, darting across the living room while she pulled her pants up. She dove for the phone on the coffee table, catching herself precariously on the couch.

"Hello?!" she gasped, trying to catch her balance on the sofa, though she ended up tumbling to the ground. "Hello?"

"Are you alright?" Isa's voice chuckled.

Kailynn let out a relieved breath and smiled.

"Yes, I'm fine," she assured. "I just had to run to the phone and I ended up falling. How are you? Are you alright?"

"I'm fine," Isa assured. "I can't stay on the line long. Venus can still trace it. Just know that in about two minutes, an alarm will sound in the house. Don't worry, you're still safe."

"Wait, why the alarm?" Kailynn asked. There was silence on the other end. "Isa? Hello?"

Kailynn glanced at the screen of the phone and groaned when she saw that the call had ended. She squeezed the phone tight, resisting the urge to throw it against the wall in frustration. She knew if she did not find a way to get out of the safe house and back to Isa soon she would suffer a psychotic breakdown.

She watched the clock anxiously, waiting for the alarm to sound.

Two minutes exactly after the phone call ended, a beeping alarm sounded from various corners of the house. Each alarm site on its own was not loud, however, combined, the noise still caused Kailynn to jump in surprise. She stood, wondering how to stop the alarm before someone heard it, or before the Officials were alerted, but an automated voice, soft and gentle, spoke before she could move from the living room.

"Vehicle parking in bay two. Verified visitor."

Kailynn listened to the voice, thinking over the words as the alarm stopped. She stood still, her breath stuck in her throat. For several seconds, she could hardly breathe.

Her knees shaking and her heart lifting in her throat, nearly choking her, she took careful steps toward the door, listening to every noise. The soft chime of the elevator, followed by the sound of the door opening caused her to still, her eyes fixed on the door.

There were footsteps in the entrance hallway and then the main door opened.

A tall, blonde figure with stunning blue eyes stepped inside, a relieved smile spreading across her face.

Kailynn went forward, her arms wrapping around the Elite's neck and hugging her tightly. Isa's arms went around Kailynn's waist, securing them together, even though Kailynn's momentum caused the Elite to fall back against the closed door.

In those moments, the world stood still.

All that existed was the tight embrace around them both.

Isa let out a long breath and Kailynn remembered that this was not a dream. The Golden Elite was there with her, breathing, smiling, warm and gentle as always.

She backed away from Isa long enough to take her face in her hands and crash their lips together. The touch seemed to break the floodgates, and emotion and anxiety rushed forward. Kailynn let out a primal sound and her mouth worked desperately against Isa's. The Golden Elite was not as frantic, but her hands were shaking as she held Kailynn to her.

Kailynn's hands skirted down Isa's body, quickly shedding the jacket of Isa's uniform, her lips never leaving the Elite's. One of Isa's hands went up to Kailynn's head, her fingers tangling in her hair as they kissed hungrily.

The younger woman's fingers quickly worked at the fastening of Isa's uniform pants and pushed them down sharply, her hands grabbing at Isa's skin desperately, as if worried the Elite would disappear if they were to part.

One of her hands went down to cup Isa, her fingers gently exploring flesh she had not touched in what felt like years.

Isa broke their kiss with a gasp and her head fell back against the door.

She panted as Kailynn kissed her neck, slowly going to her knees, her lips marking a trail down Isa's body.

"Kailynn..." Isa whispered, breathless. "Don't you want to move out of the doorway?"

"No."

Time passed without notice. Kailynn and Isa were both desperate for one another, their hands never leaving the other's body, their lips tangling whenever they were close. It was frenzied, and every action was filled with anxiety that they could not put to words.

Eventually, they found themselves on the couch, sated and calmed. They reveled in the closeness of the other, silent for an indeterminable amount of time.

"…how long can you stay?" Kailynn whispered, her hands drifting over Isa's back as the Elite rested over her like a blanket. Isa sighed and lifted her head, meeting Kailynn's eyes.

"Unfortunately, I have to leave tomorrow afternoon," she murmured. She ran a hand over Kailynn's cheek. "I actually shouldn't be here now, but I had to see you."

Kailynn smiled, lifting her head to kiss Isa.

"Are you alright? Be honest. I'll kick your ass if you lie."

"I'm alright," she assured with a chuckle.

"Rayal said that Venus has been attacking you."

"It's not as bad now," she said.

"How can she attack you? I don't understand."

Isa hesitated, her eyes averting as she tried to find a way to explain. She lowered her head back to Kailynn's chest and sighed once more.

"When I was made Golden Elite," she started slowly, "Venus and I were connected."

"What does that mean?"

"Remember when you were in Trid? And we had to translate Venus' language for you?"

"Yeah, and that hurt you…somehow…"

"I had a few medical procedures when I was inaugurated," the Golden Elite said vaguely. "A tracer chip, a heart monitoring system, a translator, a bunch of other things. This anchors me to Venus. Which means she can send electric pulses to all of these devices and cause a lot of pain."

"…is she attacking you because of me?"

"No," Isa assured. "She's punishing me because of what I have done." She closed her eyes, falling silent for several seconds. "I've disobeyed her. I've incapacitated her in many ways."

"Incapacitated?"

"That virus I released in her system was no simple infection," Isa said. "I made sure to program it so that when she tries to send certain orders, it infects her. The more she tries, the more avenues she tries to work around the infected parts of her mainframe, the worse her system becomes."

"Can you shut her down that way?"

Isa stopped, her eyes opening once more, becoming pensive.

"Isa?"

"That particular virus will not destroy her," Isa said. "However, if we were to find a way to *infect* her main codes, maybe with a virus that would destroy those source codes, it could be possible to shut her down with a virus."

"I thought that was how you were going to shut her down eventually," Kailynn said.

"No, I actually always thought we would have to destroy her source codes through physical force."

"I thought Venus could program herself anywhere."

"As long as she has her complete source coding. She can't exactly move from place to place, since her processors are in various locations throughout the planet. If one of them goes down, or even half of them, she would still function because her source coding, which she uses as a backup, can still be accessed."

"…you lost me."

Isa shifted once more, climbing off of Kailynn to rest next to her, propping her head up in one hand as her other arm draped over Kailynn.

"Venus was created to monitor the planet for disasters," she started. "At the time she was created, she could not monitor the entire planet from one source. There were edges to the areas where she could monitor. Therefore, they built additional processing units and linked them with one another. This gave Venus complete control over every area of the planet. Obviously, as technology advanced, she downloaded more processes and she is not dependent on those processor units around the planet. She used the newer technology to create two backups of her source coding. One of those codes moves around constantly. The other is linked to her first processor."

"Where is the first processor?"

"About a three hour drive from here," Isa explained.

"It's not in Anon?"

"No," Isa said, shaking her head. "Anon is too high-profile for such delicate information. Her first processor is very secluded in a low-profile, low-population area. There are three processors in Anon and the surrounding areas, but if those were attacked or destroyed, her source codes would not be harmed."

"So, if you were to destroy her first processor," Kailynn mused, "she would still have her source codes because of the second backup that keeps moving around." Kailynn's eyebrows furrowed. "How do you know where that is?"

"I can track it," Isa said. "But destroying those source codes...that's far more difficult." Isa closed her eyes, sighing. "Venus' programming is very complex, even more so now than when she was created. She has upgraded herself and downloaded different lines of code from different places to build herself to what she is today. To figure out a virus that could effectively destroy the necessary codes before she finds a means to copy them in another processor..." Isa shook her head. "And both source code backups are never in the same location. So if we destroy one, we would not have the time to destroy the other before she filled in her code again from the secondary backup and we would end up chasing her around the planet until she loaded those codes off-planet."

Kailynn reached up and her fingers brushed over the Elite's cheek.

"How would this affect *you*?" she whispered. Isa blinked at the younger woman, confused. "Remus said that you would die if you tried to shut down Venus."

Isa sighed heavily, leaning into Kailynn's hand.

"One of the procedures I went through when I became Golden Elite was to implant a failsafe into my body," she explained. "If Venus' codes start deteriorating, then the processor inside me will download all the codes into yet another backup, killing me in the process and uploading her to the nearest processor."

"How in hell does *that* work?" Kailynn gasped, her eyes incredulous.

"No one but Venus knows for sure," Isa admitted. "Dr. Busen is trying to figure it out. I've given him as much information as I have. Hopefully, he can figure it out."

Kailynn's eyes averted, her hand dropping to take Isa's, lacing their fingers together.

"If we defeat Gihron," she started. "Sorry, *when* we defeat Gihron," she corrected herself, "if we beat them and *then* shut down Venus, won't they just attack again once the planet is shut down?"

"No, not if I have anything to say about it," Isa said, shaking her head.

"How can you be sure, though?"

"When we defeat them, which we are getting closer to accomplishing, we will discuss a peace treaty. One of my terms will be that Gihron, and Gihron's allies that assisted in this war, will be prohibited from attacking Tiao for the duration of fifty years. If they do attack, the entire Alliance will meet them full-force. Sixty-seven planets against the Ninth Circle is no contest."

"You think they will honor it?" Kailynn asked hesitantly.

"Probably," Isa said. "Of course, nothing is certain."

■■■

Isa was getting tired of the follow-the-finger-without-moving-her-head routine. However, she obeyed Dr. Busen and continued to follow his finger as he moved it around in her field of vision.

"Thankfully, things seem to be holding up," he said, lowering his hand and reaching forward, feeling along her jaw once more. "I replaced the worst of the deterioration, but we will need to completely reconstruct everything within a year."

"Can we do that in increments?" Isa asked hopefully.

"I think so," the doctor said with a nod, dropping his hands and walking over to a cabinet, opening it and pulling out a few monitors. They were in his office, which afforded them more privacy and more tests at Dr. Busen's disposal. "But your headaches have been bad?"

"Some days it's hard to keep my eyes open," Isa said, turning her head as Dr. Busen glanced in her ear. "The light is too much."

"Are you sleeping?"

"Not really."

"Eating?"

"Not much."

"And you wonder why you're getting headaches?" Dr. Busen teased. He backed away and picked up another monitor with a needle on it. He removed the cap and pushed up Isa's sleeve, rubbing down her elbow before inserting the needle and touching a few buttons on the screen.

"How is the research on the virus?" Isa asked, trying to strike up conversation, uncomfortable with the extent of the testing.

"Not well, unfortunately," Dr. Busen admitted, his tone distracted as he looked over the screen. "The virus is resistant to everything we put against it. It's now being classified as a super-virus. We're doing everything we can."

"And the girl? From Trid?"

Dr. Busen sighed, clicking a few buttons before turning his eyes to Isa.

"She's not doing well," he admitted. "The virus is taking hold. The most I can do is try to keep her comfortable."

Isa dropped her gaze to the ground, the words causing a pain in her chest.

Dr. Busen removed the needle from her arm and walked to his desk, grabbing her patient folder and leaning against his desk, scribbling notes.

"Isa, do you think these headaches are at all related to Kailynn going into hiding?"

Isa hesitated, looking at Dr. Busen suspiciously.

"How do you know about that?"

Dr. Busen chuckled lightly, glancing up from his file. "Paul told me."

Isa sighed, though she was smiling. "I thought doctors weren't supposed to discuss their patients."

"You are correct," Dr. Busen said, closing the file and placing it on the desk, walking to Isa and gently taking her head, tilting it up as he looked at her eyes once more. "However, you are not the typical patient." He pulled down her bottom eyelids and studied her eyes briefly before walking back to the cabinet, pulling out yet another examination tool. "You are the leader of the planet. It is critical that your doctors communicate with one another."

Isa laughed quietly as Dr. Busen wrapped the reader around her arm and pressed several buttons on the small screen.

"I must be such a headache for you two," she teased. "What do you do? Meet up every night and go over all of my medical problems?"

Dr. Busen laughed. "Difficult not to when we live together."

It took Isa a few moments to process the words.

"You two live together?"

Dr. Busen nodded, pressing another button and watching the numbers on the screen. When he noticed the silence, he glanced up at Isa briefly.

"What?"

"You two…"

"Are together? Yes."

Isa's eyes remained wide and unblinking. Dr. Busen smiled.

"You didn't know?"

"No," Isa said, shaking her head. "I had no idea."

The Elite Specialist chuckled, removing the reader from her arm and setting it next to her, picking up his file again to enter his notes.

"We met when your personal care team was being assigned," he said. "I thought he was an arrogant asshole and we were in a very intense rivalry for several months when it came to your care. After your first assassination attempt, we had a very intense disagreement about who was responsible for your primary care that ended…in an unexpected way. We've been together ever since."

Isa smiled.

"Sounds intense," she teased. "How could you think he was an arrogant asshole?" she asked. "He's one of the kindest people I know."

"He is very kind. He's also very confident," Dr. Busen said. "Far more than I ever was. And, he's nearly ten years younger than me. It came off as arrogance, not confidence. In any case, I know better now." He sighed and leaned against the desk. "He said that you were reverting back to your behaviors when Colonel Amori was here."

Isa dropped her gaze.

"He said that you subconsciously want to make yourself weaker," he continued, "because that's how you felt when he was around you. You felt weak and powerless, so you made sure you *were* weak." He walked forward, sitting in front of Isa. "I wish I could take away everything he did to you," he said quietly, "but I can't. All I can do is try to keep you from getting that bad again." He hesitated. "I can only assume that you're not eating or sleeping because of Gihron, or Kailynn, or some combination of the two. And I am worried that it's going to get out of hand very quickly."

Isa sighed heavily.

"Now that we're doing better in the war, we're not far from a victory over Gihron. I'm starting to realize that that will force me to meet at the negotiation table with Gihron's leaders."

"You mean General Decius."

Isa nodded slowly.

"I've only spoken with him twice, both over six years ago," Isa said. "But he was Colonel Amori's brother. What if he…"

"You know, if he tries anything like what Colonel Amori did, you can tell us. You can find a way to tell us," he said strongly when Isa started shaking her head.

"No," she said. "If he threatens Kailynn, I won't dare do anything that could risk her life."

"That was exactly how Colonel Amori blackmailed you," Dr. Busen said. "You know, now, what these people are capable of, and you can guard against it."

"No, I can't," Isa said, shaking her head. "I proved that I cannot. If he's just like his brother…"

"Isa," Dr. Busen said, taking her hands in his and looking at her seriously, "you did what you had to do."

Isa looked away, sighing heavily.

"I cannot risk that again."

"What do you want to do, then?"

"I want to have a way to shut down Venus," she said seriously.

"I'm doing all that I can," Dr. Busen said. "There is a lot of information missing. I've looked through all the Syndicate files—"

"No, you haven't," Isa said, shaking her head. "Several files that were highly guarded were seized from Maki's residence when he was killed." She took her hands from Dr. Busen's grasp and pulled the collar of her uniform down. "He did a lot of research on her evolution and the biometrics. He was running tests on whether my heart would stop if he tried several different means of destroying her codes." She reached under the collar of her uniform and to her breast. "Unfortunately, he did not know much medicine, nor did he have time to complete his tests before he was killed."

She extracted her hand from her bra, holding a very small, portable drive. She held it between them.

"He gave me this the night he died," she said. "This is all of the research that he knew would be dangerous if it was seized by the wrong person. I do not have a computer that works away from Venus' systems anymore. You do."

She extended the chip to him and he stared at it before chuckling and taking it.

"That's a safe place for it," he teased.

Isa smiled.

"I've kept it on my person," she explained. "I had to be sure it was safe."

"How was Maki running tests on whether your heart would stop?" Dr. Busen asked, looking at the drive once more.

"He was using my previous NCB chair," she explained. "It used to be linked to my body. It knew my biometric rhythms from Opium mode."

"Where is the NCB chair now?"

"Safely stored in his bunker. Chronus made sure that the area was secure when the Officials seized everything in his home. Chronus and the others are working on getting the NCB chair to a different location so as not to raise suspicion."

"Have him come see me," Dr. Busen said. "I know all calls are being traced and recorded now, so I'll see him face-to-face. We'll figure out a location to move it and I'll run tests. I can handle the medical side if the other Elites can handle the programming side."

"And you'll find a way to shut her down and keep me alive?"

"Yes," Dr. Busen said, nodding. "We will find a way."

"Just promise me something."

"What?"

"If her system gets weaponized again," she started slowly, "don't worry about saving me. I would rather die than witness that again."

Chapter Thirty-Seven

One more month passed and Kailynn was convinced that the world was falling apart. Part of the support for Gihron from the Ninth Circle planets was withdrawn. While everyone was sure that meant there would be a victory for Tiao, it was not easily won. The Gihoric army gave their all in fighting Isa's military. Since there were so many robotic troops in the war, Gihron had no qualms about programming their ships and troops to crash onto the surface of the planet, taking out several large buildings in the process.

When they began attacking the surface of Tiao, the Alliance planets quickly sent aid to Tiao, shocked at the brazen attacks.

Surrounded by the Alliance ships and facing the guns from Tiao, Gihron seemed trapped.

Kailynn was glued to the sofa in the safe house every day. She slept on the couch, ignoring the bedroom entirely, sleeping between news broadcasts. Her two-minute conversations with everyone in close confidence with the Golden Elite were not nearly enough to stay as informed as she wanted, which left her edgy and worried.

For one week, she could not reach anyone. She got through to Rayal for ten seconds, just long enough for him to tell her that things were in a crucial stage with the war and that he would call her as soon as he had more information.

But Rayal never called her back.

Instead, Isa appeared at the safe house one day.

"Why didn't you tell me you were coming?" Kailynn gasped, kissing the Elite as she walked into the safe house.

"I sneaked out of the capital," Isa chuckled, leaning down and kissing Kailynn again. "I got a later start than I wanted," she started, walking further into the safe house, taking Kailynn's hand and leading her to the sofa once more. "There will be a special broadcast today. Come, sit down."

"Special broadcast?" Kailynn repeated.

"Concerning the war."

"Did we win?"

Isa used the remote to click on the television and then took Kailynn's hand, pulling her down to the couch as she nodded with a smile.

Kailynn gasped and quickly joined Isa on the couch, though she ignored the discussions about the upcoming message from the Syndicate. She grabbed Isa's collar and pulled her close, kissing her passionately. She pushed the Elite back to lie on the couch, kissing her tenderly as the Elite held her close.

When the announcer turned the broadcast over to the Syndicate Building, Remus' face appeared on the screen.

"Good afternoon, Tiao," he started. "I am broadcasting to the planet to announce that Gihron has conditionally surrendered to Tiao."

Kailynn felt relieved to hear the words, her body relaxing as she rested over Isa, her eyes closing briefly at the announcement.

"We will be meeting Gihron at the negotiating table to discuss the terms of this surrender," Remus continued. "As always, the terms of this surrender will be made with the well-being of both Tiao and Gihron in mind. These terms will be announced upon agreement."

Remus continued to thank the people who fought for Tiao, as well as the allies that sent aid. While he was talking, Kailynn turned to Isa.

"What terms do they have for surrender? He said it was conditional."

Isa hesitated before speaking.

"All the terms are negotiable, as always."

"What terms?"

"They want us to stop the production of Elites and turn the government over to humans," Isa said quietly.

"Are you going to do that?" Kailynn asked, not sure how she felt about the demand. The Golden Elite sighed heavily.

"I have not yet decided," she admitted. "But I am considering it."

"You are?" Kailynn gasped, shocked.

"The life of an Elite is no type of life," Isa murmured. "And I don't want to put another being through what I went through when I was inaugurated. I don't want another Elite beaten to death because of rebellion. I don't want another Elite to be tortured and tested to prove that they're created properly. It's cruelty at its darkest."

Kailynn pressed her hand to Isa's face.

"What would happen if you stopped Elite production?"

"Hard to say," she admitted. "But I would not completely turn over everything to humans immediately. I would have to create a plan for slow integration to be sure that everything continued running smoothly. However..."

"What?"

"Well, there might be another power shift soon, anyway," Isa said slowly, smiling thinly at Kailynn. The younger woman's eyes went wide once more. "To be honest, Kailynn, with the war over, and being in the negotiation stage now, it's very likely that Venus will focus entirely on bringing me to heel."

"What do you mean?"

"This is going to be a very delicate balancing act," Isa said. "I've also declared war on Venus. She is still heavily-infected, much to the Syndicate's annoyance, since so many things have to be manually computed now. And I plan to make some changes." She took a deep breath and her arms tightened around Kailynn. "Venus is going to do everything in her power to keep me from upsetting the system."

"How can she do that?" Kailynn pressed. "You already have her infected."

"She'll probably try to take me down physically," Isa said. "She'll start attacking with force again. And for all of Dr. Busen's efforts, she has found occasion to work around his work and put me down for a few days." Isa closed her eyes. "I am hoping that you'll support me through this time. It's going to be a very difficult time for all of us. I'm going to need to carefully wrap up everything with Gihron, and then I'm going to turn my attention to taking down Venus."

"…you're really going to do it?" Kailynn breathed.

"Yes." Isa nodded. "It has been too long as it is. It should have been done long ago."

Kailynn stared at Isa, feeling awed anew by her strength and determination. She could hardly remember the time when she blindly hated the Golden Elite and the Syndicate. As she stayed draped over the Elite, looking into her powerful eyes and feeling the words stirring excitement in her belly, she felt as though she had the most powerful being in existence under her, and the thought excited her.

"Why are you staring at me like that?" Isa asked with a small smile.

"I'm just…" Kailynn shook her head, smiling. "You really are amazing, Isa."

Isa tenderly kissed Kailynn, smiling against the younger woman's lips.

"This brings me to my second announcement," Remus started. Kailynn turned to the screen, confused. Isa took a deep breath, preparing herself. She knew, even before the words were spoken, what would happen.

"This war has been very taxing on our planet, on our resources, and on our economy," Remus said. "Due to these difficulties, Golden Elite Isa and the Syndicate have agreed that we must provide every opportunity for our planet to build stronger than before. In order to do so, we need a stronger foundation on which to build. For that reason, we are offering citizenship to all Trids that wish to work with our military building operations and our reparations committee on repairing the damage from the war with Gihron."

Kailynn sat upright, her eyes wide, glued to the screen, her breath caught in her throat.

"Holy shit…" she choked.

"We understand the concerns of the public at allowing Trid non-citizens to become legal citizens of Tiao," Remus continued. "However, all Trids will be afforded a medical exam, given a PIM chip, offered schooling opportunities to reduce the illiteracy rate, and housing within the southern districts of Anon. Other programs will allow for Trids to travel to other portions of the planet to work in these operations."

Kailynn turned to Isa, who was watching Kailynn's reaction with a small smile on her face. Kailynn let out a shuddered breath and leaned back down to Isa, kissing her passionately, small tears gathering on her lashes.

"As Trids become citizens, they will be informed of the laws under Venus and will be expected to conform to those laws. They will be subject to full penalty of the law should they not assimilate into Tiaoian society," Remus concluded. "This program will take effect on the seventeenth of next month. In that time, all of Trid will be informed of this offer."

Isa flinched and backed away from Kailynn, her face twisting slightly as she tried to move out from under the former Significant.

"What is it?" Kailynn asked. When Isa tried to wriggle out from under Kailynn, her face still contorted in discomfort, she stood, allowing the Elite to turn over and go to her hands and knees on the floor. "Isa?"

"Kailynn," Isa started, trying to get to her feet, "I'm sorry."

"What? What are you sorry for?" Kailynn asked quickly, starting toward the Elite, worried. "Are you alright?"

"Don't touch me," Isa said quickly, backing away from Kailynn, her hand over her heart as she continued to cringe. "Shit…" she choked. "You can't touch me, Kailynn. Wait for this to be over."

"For *what* to be over?" Kailynn hissed.

Isa let out a pained groan and sank to her knees. She started curling forward, her hand twisting in the clothing over her heart. Her breath came out in labored pants around clenched teeth. Kailynn watched in horror as Isa curled forward until her forehead was pressed into the floor.

Suddenly, Isa let out a cry of pain, falling to her side and rolling onto her back, her eyes tightly closed and her teeth set against screaming. Her back bowed off the floor and her body began convulsing violently. Isa screamed in agony as she writhed against the cold floor.

"Isa! Isa! What's wrong?!" Kailynn cried. She tried to start forward, but Isa let out another scream and a high, whining feedback sound came from the alarm system in the house. The lights flickered, surging with a buzzing noise. The television flickered on and off rapidly. Kailynn looked around in horror, not sure what was happening.

Isa contorted, freezing in positions occasionally, every muscle in her body tensed, her veins bulging under her skin, her hands clawing at her chest. The Elite let out pained screams in sporadic bursts.

Kailynn started forward once more, kneeling to turn the Elite over, but Isa saw her hands coming closer and she quickly shied away.

"Don't!" she barked.

"What am I supposed to do?!" Kailynn yelled, frightened tears rising to her eyes.

Isa did not respond, her body snapping forward as a choked cry escaped her throat that turned into a loud wail. The lights surged to life, blinding Kailynn briefly until a loud pop cracked the air and sparks flew down from the light fixtures.

Isa screamed, her throat raw and the sound causing her head to nearly explode.

Kailynn crawled over to her phone, grabbing it shakily and, with shaking fingers, pressing the number for Rayal. She shoved the earpiece in, adrenaline coursing through her body angrily.

"Kailynn," Rayal said. "Is she with you? Did you hear—"

"Rayal!" Kailynn cried, the tears choking her. "Something's wrong. I don't know what to do!"

"What do you mean? What's wrong?"

"I don't know!" Kailynn sobbed. "Isa's screaming and having a seizure or something on the floor. The lights are popping, I don't know what the fuck is happening!"

Isa's scream pierced the air again and the tears quickly fell down Kailynn's face. She flinched away from the noise.

"Kailynn," Rayal said quickly, "I'm on my way out to you. I'll get Dr. Busen and Remus, okay? We'll be out there as soon as we can."

"She can't wait that long!" Kailynn screamed.

"Yes, she can," Rayal said. "Even if we were there, there is nothing we can do to stop this. It has to take its course."

"What is it?!" Kailynn wailed.

"Venus is punishing her for granting Trid's citizenship, I'm sure," Rayal said. "I have to hang up, Kailynn. Stay with her. Once she stops moving, you can touch her. Until then, don't move her. Don't do anything other than make sure she doesn't hit any furniture."

"I can't just—"

"You have to, Kailynn!" Rayal barked. "I'm on my way out to you. Just stay with her."

He hung up the phone and Kailynn's heart fell.

Her eyes went to the writhing and screaming Elite on the floor. The feedback on the alarm system was grating to her ears, but she did not care to unplug the system. She could not turn away from Isa.

She could not process what was happening in front of her. Isa was being punished for granting citizenship to Trids. Venus was causing excruciating pain for the Golden Elite, and there was nothing anyone could do to help her.

Isa's scream made thousands of knives pierce Kailynn's chest. She closed her eyes, flinching away from the noise. Isa screamed again, her body snapping fiercely. Kailynn pulled her knees into her chest, her body shaking in fear and pain at seeing Isa suffer.

She watched Isa writhe in agony for six hours, the tears tumbling down her cheeks as Isa's writhing slowed and her screams became quieter with exhaustion. Her body sporadically shook, her eyes fluttering as her breathing became strained.

It seemed to be in slow-motion for Kailynn.

Isa's eyes slipped shut and her body went lax.

For three seconds, Kailynn did not move.

She crawled forward slowly, listening to Isa's exhausted, strained breath. She placed her hand on Isa's shoulder, seeing the sweat gleaming over Isa's skin. The Elite had finally passed out.

Kailynn gathered the Elite in her lap, hugging what she could of Isa, the tears falling faster as the fear slowly abated.

When she felt she could stand again, Kailynn walked around the house, violently unplugging and deactivating everything in the house she could. She did not want Venus finding them, furious at the computer for putting Isa through such torture. Kailynn then ran into the bedroom, pulling all the blankets off the bed and bringing them to where the Elite had fallen unconscious.

She placed a pillow under Isa's head and then piled blankets on top of her to protect her from the chill of the room.

She then wrapped her arms around Isa, pressing her chest to Isa's back, hoping to keep the Elite warm.

She vowed to help Isa take down Venus however she could. She could not bear to see Isa in such agony.

Chapter Thirty-Eight

Kailynn was gently roused by a hand on her shoulder. She opened her eyes and saw Rayal above her. She looked around, feeling uncomfortably hot, and saw Dr. Busen walk forward, Paul behind him, and Remus behind both of them.

Dr. Busen pulled the blanket from them both and Kailynn slowly untangled herself from the unconscious Golden Elite.

Isa's face was pale and there was a sheen of sweat over her skin.

"Let's move her to the bedroom," Dr. Busen murmured. Remus walked forward and scooped Isa up in his arms, walking toward the bedroom as the doctors followed. Kailynn took Rayal's offered hand and pulled herself to her feet. He hugged her before she was hugged tightly by an excited, worried Tarah.

"How are you?" Tarah asked.

"I've been better," Kailynn murmured, glancing in the open bedroom door. "…I've never seen anything like that," she whispered.

"I'm sure that was terrifying," Rayal said. "She must have thought that Isa was at the Syndicate, and was trying to send a message to all the Elites."

"There has to be a way to keep that from happening…" Kailynn said, clearing her throat. She walked into the bedroom, where Dr. Busen was walking around Isa, checking her over carefully, asking Paul to take notes of different things.

Remus turned to Kailynn when she entered the room and nodded once to her.

"Have you seen that happen to her before?" Kailynn asked, crossing her arms over her chest as she stood next to the Silver Elite.

"Yes," he said quietly. "I understand how painful it is to watch that happen and being unable to help." He sighed and closed his eyes. "She was concerned that Venus' reaction would be violent."

"You announced it to the people without her knowing before?" Kailynn murmured, surprised.

"Her system is so clogged with viruses right now that we can actually keep information from her. But anything that is publicly broadcast, she has access to."

They both watched as Dr. Busen undressed Isa's chest, stopping when he opened the front of her uniform, his eyes going wide.

"Holy shit…" he breathed.

"What is it?" Kailynn asked worriedly, starting forward and climbing on the bed next to her. She looked over Isa's chest and saw strange patches of red skin that splayed across her chest in wavy patterns. "What is that?"

"Burns," Paul said quietly, his expression pained. "Michael, we have to find a way to stop this. Venus will destroy her from the inside out."

"Remus," Dr. Busen said, looking at the Silver Elite, "can you jam the signals from this processing unit at all?"

"I can try," Remus said. "I probably won't be able to interfere with all the frequencies," he admitted. "And we'll have to watch her closely to be sure we don't cause arrhythmia in her heart."

"If you can work on a jammer, anything would help," Dr. Busen said, standing straight. "Paul, can you get my bag?" He pointed to the living room and the other doctor went to obey, walking by Rayal and Tarah, who were watching from the doorway.

"Is she going to be alright?"

Dr. Busen sighed and glanced at Kailynn apologetically.

"I have never seen an attack leave her with burns before," he said. "It must have been truly excruciating." He looked back down at the Golden Elite. "She's dehydrated, undernourished, and clearly in pain. But she managed to last a very long time, it would appear."

"Why didn't the EMU come here?" Kailynn pressed. "I'm sure her emitter chip was firing."

"The safe house has been completely blocked from all transmissions," Remus said, shaking his head. "She didn't take any chances with your safety."

"In any case, it's best that this does not get put on record at any hospital. We don't need anyone hearing that the Elite is severely ill when we're heading into negotiations with Gihron."

Paul returned to Michael's side, handing him the bag. The older doctor opened the bag and pulled out various vials and syringes.

"If this is occurring while you are in negotiations with Gihron," Paul started seriously, "we are all going to need to keep a very close eye on her. She'll be weaker, and more susceptible to manipulation."

"You mean like what Colonel Amori did?" Kailynn asked.

"Perhaps," the doctor said with a nod.

Everyone stood around Isa as Dr. Busen treated her as best as he was able. Once he was finished with her treatments, they took various seats around the room, waiting for the Golden Elite to stir. Kailynn sat with her on the bed, holding her hand tightly.

They only had to wait an hour before Isa cringed and opened her eyes. She looked around her, flinching away from the shooting pain that sparked on every moving muscle. When she met eyes with Kailynn, she forced a tired smile and squeezed the former Significant's hand.

When her eyes caught sight of everyone else in the room, her eyes slowly closed.

"I guess I really scared you," she breathed.

"You were like that for six hours," Kailynn choked.

"How are you feeling, Isa?"

"I don't know, yet," she muttered, turning to Dr. Busen. "It's never been that intense before."

"No, I would think not," the doctor agreed. "I've never seen an attack like that leave burns on your body."

Isa lifted her other hand and looked at her arm, seeing the wavy patterns of red and dark brown skin. She sighed heavily again and closed her eyes.

"I'm sorry…" she whispered.

"Don't apologize," Remus said. "You did nothing wrong."

Kailynn gently squeezed Isa's hand, unsure what to say. Isa swallowed hard and cringed, moving her body in an attempt to get comfortable. She let out a short breath, flinching in pain.

"That hurt?" Dr. Busen asked.

"It was less painful to suffer through the Pulse Virus," Isa groaned, her eyes shut tightly.

"Isa, I'm going to work on a transmission jammer," Remus said. "What series transmitter do you think I should use?"

Isa sighed, her eyes remaining closed as she tried to think through her pain.

"Probably a Series Seventeen."

"Not Eighteen?"

"Eighteen has the metered connection rate," Isa reminded him. "It will shut down automatically at these levels." She took a deep breath, opening her eyes. "The car Kailynn had here should have a Series Seventeen transmitter. Use that one."

Remus nodded and left the room. Tarah and Rayal walked in when the Silver Elite left, standing worriedly at the Golden Elite's bedside.

Isa took a deep breath, looking around the room.

"Do you need to go back to the hospital?" Isa asked Dr. Busen. The older doctor chuckled.

"No," he assured. "I'm technically not employed by the hospital. I'm employed by the Syndicate exclusively for your care. I just work at that hospital to keep busy when I'm not working with you."

Isa chuckled, cringing as the action sent pain through her. She turned to Paul, who smiled and pointed at Dr. Busen.

"I just follow him around," he chuckled.

Isa smiled, taking slow, even breaths.

"Isa," Paul started, catching her attention, "when are you starting negotiations with Gihron?"

"Next week," Isa answered. "The diplomatic convoy left Gihron several days ago. They should be here in about six days."

"I'm going to insist that you rest for the entirety of those days," Dr. Busen said strongly. "You need to be as strong as possible for negotiations with Gihron, and I'm sure that Venus will not attack you when you are hosting another diplomat, particularly in this delicate situation."

"We do not know for sure if General Decius is coming to the planet," Rayal said. "It's possible that he will remain on Gihron and send others in his stead."

"Let's hope that he does," Paul said.

"The fact that they're insisting on negotiations on Tiao is a red flag," Dr. Busen mused.

"They want to show us the lengths they are willing to go for a peace agreement," Isa murmured. She let out a strained laugh. "They must think I am an idiot," she groaned. "They came these lengths for war to begin with."

The group let Isa sleep, knowing that they had to return to Anon soon. Kailynn sat with the others in the living room of the safe house, discussing warning signs to look for if Isa was in danger from any of the diplomats from Gihron. Kailynn listened intently. Even though the subject had not yet been raised, she was firm in her decision to return to Anon with Isa.

When the subject did come up, Dr. Busen said that he would have to change her emitter chip, which was still disabled, and make sure that Venus could not locate her. However, no one protested Kailynn's return to Anon.

They knew Isa would need all the support possible.

Late at night, they woke Isa and tried to get her to eat, though the pain in her body made it difficult for her to keep food down.

Kailynn remained in the bed with Isa as the others stayed in various spots throughout the safe house, making up beds with any blankets and pillows they could find.

Remus remained awake the entire night, programming and building a small, box-like device on the table in the living room. He was intensely focused on the jammer, so much so that he did not realize he had spent seventeen hours building it and everyone was waking the next morning when he finally finished.

Kailynn watched in fascination as Dr. Busen and Remus worked together attaching the device directly to Isa's skin, just below her left breast. They inserted nodes into her ribcage, feeding them into position by using a portable scanner to see into her chest cavity. Kailynn watched the process with fascination and horror. She could see that there was a relatively large, metal device in Isa's body, frighteningly close to her heart, and she was concerned that one false move would cause Isa's heart to stop beating.

However, the two finished attaching the jammer to Isa's ribcage and secured it with an adhesive bandage that hardened against her skin.

When Isa dressed again, no one could see the device through her clothing.

They decided to leave the safe house that night. Rayal and Tarah returned first, agreeing to take the shortest route to Anon on the other side of the planet. Remus left three hours after them, taking a different way, a much longer one that would allow him to enter the city from the west. Isa and Kailynn took Isa's car back to the capital the same way Rayal and Tarah had, both of them quiet as they left close to midnight.

Kailynn wanted to sleep through the long, eleven-hour drive back to Anon, but her nerves were too high. She could feel the fear and anticipation in her stomach. She understood that the negotiation stages were far more dangerous than the battles. They did not know who was coming to negotiate on behalf of Gihron, and it could lead to a similar situation to Colonel Amori's manipulation and blackmail of Isa.

Rayal's words many months ago resonated through her skull.

"He poisoned me...slowly...over the course of about four months."

Kailynn had spent many sleepless nights in the safe house wondering how Colonel Amori had managed to poison Rayal, how he had managed to turn the Elites against each other and against Isa, and how it all related to the accident that had caused Isa to have half of her face reconstructed, and end the relationship between her and Remus.

However, she could not come up with any plausible explanations.

She knew Isa was incredibly strong and smart. It seemed impossible to have her so trapped and scared that she felt that she had to kill someone just to escape them.

Then again, Kailynn remembered the incident with Maki, how he provoked Isa into killing him by attacking Kailynn.

Perhaps that was how Colonel Amori controlled Isa. Isa did not care what happened to her, but if anyone she loved was harmed, or threatened, she was willing to do anything to keep them safe.

Kailynn spent a lot of the drive staring at Isa's pale, sleeping face, desperate to understand what had happened six years previous.

They finally made it back into Anon in the late morning. They went to Anon Tower and back to Isa's home, Isa calling the Syndicate and explaining that she was ill and could not go into work that day, but to keep her informed of everything that happened.

She also called Paul and Dr. Busen, being sure that they were traveling safe, since they had left the safe house nearly five hours after she and Kailynn.

Kailynn had only been out of Anon Tower for a month and a half, but she hardly recognized the level when she walked in the door. Nothing had changed, the furniture was exactly where it had always been, but the feeling in the home was entirely different. It was colder, more foreboding, as if reflecting the severity of the situation with Gihron and Venus.

Remus wanted to stay with Isa. His duty as Silver Elite was to protect the Golden Elite, and it was a duty he took very seriously, even more so after previous dealings with Gihron. Isa agreed that he should stay, but Kailynn was not as fond of the idea.

The realization that she knew nothing about what had happened with Colonel Amori other than the fact that he had upset Isa to the point that she had killed him became overwhelming when Isa asked Remus to stay close.

Late in the afternoon, Isa received a call from Anders. He told her that he was directing a video call to her home NCB chair from the Gihron delegate ship.

She went back into the office, taking several deep breaths to steady herself for the conversation.

She sat in the chair, Remus and Kailynn standing near the door as she pressed several buttons, bringing the chair into an upright position for the call. She straightened her shoulders, took another deep breath, and accepted the call.

In front of her, the hologram of a man in a chair appeared. He was wearing a heavy, dark-green military jacket, decorated with various ribbons and metals. His face was thin and angular, with deep-set, narrow, dark eyes and stubble on his jaw and upper lip. His black hair was short, exposing his high forehead.

He had an aura of authority about him, and the way he sat, with his broad shoulders squarely set against his chair, exhibited his power.

"Elite Isa," he greeted, his voice cold and soft.

"General Decius."

Isa's voice was surprisingly steady as she addressed the man—she even managed to smile a little. Kailynn quickly turned to Remus, the question in her eyes of whether or not that was General Decius—the older brother of Colonel Amori. However, the Silver Elite's eyes were fixed on the man's hologram, dark and filled with anger.

"I hope I am not disturbing you," General Decius said.

"No, not at all."

"We are approaching the Dani-Kahl Gate," he announced. "I wanted to let you know that we will be there in approximately three days, but you know how travel like this can be."

"We are, of course, prepared to receive you whenever you arrive," Isa said. "Am I correct in understanding that you are joining your delegation here on Tiao?"

"Yes," General Decius said with a small smile. "I do hope that is not an inconvenience."

"No, no inconvenience," Isa said calmly.

"And we are to stay in Anon Tower?" General Decius said expectantly.

"Yes," Isa said. "I have your delegation accommodated on one level of Anon Tower. However, if you wish to have quarters separate from your men, I will arrange accordingly."

"I do prefer to keep my men at a certain distance," General Decius said. "I'm sure you can understand that. When you let people get too close, the dynamic changes."

"Yes, I do understand," Isa said, a cold edge to her voice. "Very well, I will assure that you have quarters separate from your men."

"You are very generous, Elite Isa," the Gihoric leader said coldly. "I shall not keep you. I will transmit my ship information to the Syndicate so that you will know of our arrival time."

"Thank you, General Decius."

The man's hologram flickered out and Isa quickly climbed out of the chair, darting out of the office, pushing past Kailynn and Remus. However, she did not get far. She collapsed against the wall, breathing hard, one hand over her mouth. Remus and Kailynn quickly went to her side.

"Isa?" Kailynn whispered.

"He looks exactly like him..." Isa gasped, her eyes wide as she shook violently. She whirled around and pressed her back to the wall, shaking her head quickly. "I can't do this," she whispered.

"Yes, you can," Remus said strongly. "You just did. You just spoke to him and you did wonderfully."

"It was a transmission," Isa hissed, her eyes frantic. "How can I do this when he's in the same room? He looks exactly like his brother! He even speaks like him!"

"I know, I know," Remus murmured. Isa lowered her head, her hand covering her mouth once more.

"I can't do this..."

Remus took a step forward and pulled Isa into his arms, securing her in a hug as he rested his head on hers.

"You can do this," he said. "I know you can. You are very strong, Isa."

Kailynn bit her tongue so hard it almost bled.

Isa's hands clenched in the fabric of Remus' uniform and she buried her face in his chest, her body violently shuddering in fear. Kailynn wanted to be worried about General Decius coming to negotiate. She wanted to comfort Isa and tell her that everything would be fine. However, she could only feel the hot fire in her belly burn as she watched Isa turn to Remus for comfort and support.

Remus turned his eyes to Kailynn and motioned with his head for her to follow them.

With his arm secured around Isa's shoulders, he guided her down the hall and into the living room.

"Get her some water," Remus said.

"I need to lie down..." Isa whispered.

Remus guided her into her bedroom as Kailynn bitterly went to the bar and got Isa water. Rayal poked his head out of the kitchen.

"Is everything alright?"

Kailynn shook her head.

"General Decius is coming here himself," she explained. "And apparently, he looks exactly like his brother."

Kailynn turned away from Rayal's stunned and terrified face, walking to the bedroom.

Isa was on the bed, breathing slowly as Remus told her when to inhale and when to exhale. He held her hand, his voice quiet and calm. Kailynn took a deep breath, trying to keep herself calm.

She climbed on the bed with Isa, holding the water out to her.

The Golden Elite slowly sat up and took a small sip of the water, forcing it down with a cringe.

Kailynn set the water aside and watched as Remus continued to count Isa's breathing with her, getting her to calm down from the initial terror of seeing General Decius.

Isa fell asleep for twenty minutes, and in that time Kailynn looked everywhere but at Remus.

Finally, the Silver Elite cleared his throat.

"Do not think much of it, Kailynn," he said quietly. She turned to him, trying not to show her intense anger and jealousy. "She loves you more than she ever loved me. This is just because she is frightened and I know what happened with Colonel Amori."

Isa stirred at the sound of the voices and looked between the two faces above her.

She lifted a hand to her face and groaned slightly.

"Isa," Kailynn murmured. The Golden Elite turned to her. "You are being extremely unfair right now."

The Golden Elite was silent, looking at the former Significant, waiting for her to continue.

"If General Decius is coming here, then I think it's only fair that those who are in danger of being victims of his revenge know exactly what happened six years ago." Kailynn glanced up at Remus. "It hurts to see you turn to Remus just because I don't know what happened."

Isa closed her eyes.

Kailynn pressed a hand to the Elite's face.

"Please," she whispered, "tell me."

Chapter Thirty-Nine

Six years earlier...

"What time is his ship arriving?" Remus asked, leaning against Isa's desk as she looked over several files.

She glanced at the clock.

"In about two hours," she answered. "I have a convoy taking him to his quarters in Anon Tower. We'll meet for dinner tonight."

"You don't think it's suspicious that he reached out to you?"

"No, not really," Isa said, shrugging. "Gihron is struggling. They're at least twenty years behind in technology, they're broke, and their society is unbalanced. They're trying to find a way to stabilize the economy through trade. In the process, we can implement the rules of the Alliance on them, which should make their people happier."

"I don't know," Remus murmured. "The entire Ninth Circle is territory everyone steers clear from for a reason."

Isa chuckled, looking at Remus with a teasing smile.

"Do they scare you?"

Remus smiled.

"No, but you do when you want something," he returned the teasing. Isa's smile widened and she stood in front of him, tapping her finger on the center of his chest.

"Are you coming over tonight?"

"Don't I always?"

Isa and the others of the Syndicate greeted Colonel Amori with a dinner thrown in his honor. He had brought four of his officers on the journey to Tiao, and they all enjoyed the best hospitality the Syndicate could offer. Everyone was aware of Isa's desire to incorporate the Ninth Circle into the Crescent Alliance, so they were all very congenial and showed their interest in learning more about Gihron in order to put the Gihoric delegates at ease.

After the dinner, when they were enjoying drinks around the large dining hall in the Syndicate Building, discussing simple topics, one of the Gihoric delegates went to Remus and asked him to join the conversation he had previously been a part of and explain something the Silver Elite had said over dinner. Remus was led away from Isa, who smiled at the enthusiasm of the delegates who were startled at the kind of technology on Tiao.

Feeling eyes on her, Isa looked around and saw Colonel Amori looking at her over the rim of his drink, ignoring what Anders and Maki were discussing with him.

He excused himself from the conversation and walked to her. Isa watched him approach, a soft smile taking over her face. He was quite handsome in his own way, with a strong air of command to him.

"You have remarkable hospitality, Elite Isa," he said.

"Thank you," Isa said. "I do hope everything is to your liking. Are your quarters acceptable in Anon Tower?"

"Of course," he said. "You are far too kind. I understand that I asked to meet with you on short notice."

"It is no trouble at all," Isa assured, lifting her glass to her mouth and finishing off the wine.

"To be perfectly honest," the man said, "I've never met an Elite before. You are not what I expected."

"What did you expect?"

"Cold," he answered. "Machines, through and through." He looked her over quickly and then shook his head. "But you appear human."

Isa was not sure how to respond, so she remained silent, watching his eyes pass over the other Elites in the room. He turned back to her, extending his hand. "May I?"

Isa hesitated, not sure what the man was asking, but she put her hand in his and his fingers closed around hers. He stared at her hand, his thumb passing over the skin, pressing into the knuckles gently.

"You're warm," he noted. "And you have a pulse, and bones."

"Physiologically, we are human," Isa said. "We have the same organs and bone structure as a human."

"But that does not necessarily make you human, does it?"

"I suppose that depends on how you define human."

"Do *you* think you're human?"

Isa stared at Colonel Amori. His fingers had not released her hand, even as he stared into her eyes. There was something behind the question that concerned Isa, but she merely pulled her hand away carefully.

"I am an Elite," Isa responded.

Colonel Amori smiled broadly. "I see."

The dinner wrapped up late at night and Isa and Remus saw Colonel Amori and his excited, awed delegates to their quarters in Anon

Tower. The lower officers were walking around the rooms, gasping, talking about how amazing the technology was on Tiao in Gihoric, too excited to realize that they were acting like stunned children.

Colonel Amori, however, seemed uninterested in everything except the Golden Elite. He turned to the Golden and Silver Elites after they led him to his quarters.

"I greatly appreciate your hospitality," he said once more. "I believe that Tiao and Gihron can find an agreement that is mutually beneficial."

"I agree," Remus said.

"I do hope that you will be comfortable," Isa added out of courtesy. "Please, do not hesitate to contact the property Caretaker robot should you need anything."

"And we will meet tomorrow at the Syndicate Building?"

"Yes."

"Good night, then." He extended his hand to Remus and shook the Silver Elite's hand. He extended his hand to Isa and bowed to kiss her hand, his lips lingering on the Golden Elite's skin for one second longer than she felt comfortable.

When Isa and Remus entered Isa's level of Anon Tower, the Golden Elite let out a soft groan and rolled her neck.

"The pleasantries do get old after awhile, don't they?" Remus chuckled, following Isa into the living room. "Oh, thank you so much for joining us—no, no, it's our pleasure to have you here—please, tell me again about your planet—we hope the accommodations are to your liking," the Silver Elite said with a mocking tone. "We all know we're trying to manipulate one another to get what we want, but we pretend we're genuinely pleased to see one another."

"Politics," Isa agreed. She grabbed Remus' collar and pulled him down, pressing their lips together. When they parted, she smiled. "In contrast, I am *very* pleased to have you here tonight."

"Not yet," Remus teased as she bit her lip, "but you *will* be."

Remus swooped down for another kiss, breaking the contact only long enough for Isa to lead him into her bedroom.

■■

The three weeks of negotiation were very difficult for Isa and Remus. They were startled that someone who had contacted them to form an agreement refused to bend to any of their terms. Colonel Amori was very eloquent and spoke very well, which meant that he could turn any words the Elites said around, trying to poke holes in the entire structure of the Alliance to justify not joining.

Unfortunately for him, Isa was just as well spoken and, in Remus' opinion, far more brilliant than the Gihoric Colonel.

For three weeks, the negotiations went absolutely nowhere.

On the fourth week, Isa suggested that they include the leader of the planet, Colonel Amori's older brother, General Decius, in the negotiations. However, days passed with all transmissions receiving interference between Tiao and Gihron. Finally, Colonel Amori met with Isa on one of her days off, meeting with her in Anon Tower.

"Apparently our main transmitter suffered a catastrophic failure," he explained. "My brother said that they are working day and night to fix it but, until then, all communications are down."

Isa was irritated, but said she understood.

"Actually, Elite Isa, may I ask you a few things?"

"Of course," Isa said with a nod, motioning for him to sit in her living room.

"I'm trying to understand a few things about how Tiao has managed to stay in power for so long. After all, not twenty-five years ago, everyone was waiting for this planet to collapse. The Crescent Alliance had completely disbanded and everyone was sitting back, watching Tiao destroy itself." He smiled at the Elite as she sat across from him. "And then *you* came along."

"I do not see fit to dictate everything about every planet in the Altereye System," Isa said. "The alliance was meant to provide support to the planets, not change their societies."

"Yet, you would seek to dictate the level of our military if we were to sign even a trade agreement with you," Colonel Amori continued. "Our society is militaristic, which I'm sure you already knew. It is the very foundation of our planet."

"Yes, I understand that," Isa said. "But the Crescent Alliance seeks to put everyone on equal ground when it comes to military force. As soon as one planet has a larger army, fear of invasion begins to take hold. If I were to allow Gihron access to Alliance trade routes without regulating your military force, I would evoke great fear in the other planets."

"You don't seem to understand Gihron's position here," Colonel Amori said. "We are the Tiao of the Ninth Circle. We are the most powerful planet in your so-called outlier planets, and we are the only ones that keep those other planets from waging war on the Alliance."

"I must disagree with you," Isa said. "Jakra attacked Pirian just last year."

Colonel Amori went quiet, staring at the Golden Elite with a cocky expression. He was not thrown off by Isa's information. If anything, it seemed to excite him.

"How powerful do you consider yourself, Elite Isa?"

"As powerful as I need to be for the situation," Isa answered.

"A very good answer," Colonel Amori said, leaning forward. "Gihron is not looking to bow to Venus or the Elites. In fact, if Venus were not the cornerstone of the Crescent Alliance, we would have considered joining decades ago, before your predecessors fucked up everything."

Isa's expression was carefully controlled, veiling her annoyance. She felt that Colonel Amori was in no position to be making demands on her. She was the Golden Elite of Tiao, she was the leader of the Crescent Alliance, and she held more political power than he. She would not give in to his demands. If he was unwilling to yield, she would not allow the trade agreement. She had nothing to lose from not solidifying the agreement.

"But, as such, we are not part of the Alliance," Colonel Amori continued. "Nor will we ever be if Venus is the law of the Alliance."

"Perhaps I have misunderstood you this entire time," Isa said coldly. "I did not realize that you were discussing terms on joining the Crescent Alliance. I have not fully informed you of all the terms for joining, including taxes and war agreements."

Colonel Amori chuckled coldly.

"We are getting off-track, aren't we?"

"Indeed," Isa agreed. "I know that you do not wish to join the Alliance, and as such, it is optional to join for all planets. However, I am bound by the rules of the Alliance as well. These trade routes that you want access to are not mine. They belong to all planets that have signed with, and complied with the terms of, the Alliance. Because I alone do not hold the power to give access to these routes, I must insist you comply with trade and military terms."

"I thought you were as powerful as the situation required?" Colonel Amori challenged.

"I am," Isa agreed. "And I am firm in my position that I will not grant access to the trade routes unless you comply with my terms. I suffer no loss from you walking away from this trade agreement."

Colonel Amori leaned back in his seat, smiling arrogantly.

"You are a force to be reckoned with, aren't you?" he murmured. He sighed heavily, tilting his head. "Why not just allow Gihron to keep its social system in tact?"

"Because it is dangerous to the Alliance."

"What makes it so different from Tiao?"

"I believe my people have the basic right to food and shelter," Isa said darkly. Colonel Amori let out a bark of laughter, shaking his head.

"Is that so?" he challenged. "What about the Trid district?"

"Trid is an entirely different matter," Isa said simply.

Colonel Amori pursed his lips.

"I could say that about our grunts, too," he said. "I could wave the question away and say it was an entirely different matter, and that you couldn't possibly understand, but I'm not afraid of what the lower class represents."

"And what is that?"

"Fear," he answered. "I know that that is what you use Trid for—fear to keep your classes in line and working, keeping the economy running and the planet appearing strong. It's the same with our grunts." He leaned forward once more. "It seems we are not so different after all."

"Politics are politics no matter where you are in the Altereye System," Isa said, her voice cool and calm.

"I'm glad you understand that," he murmured. "Which is why you should understand why I cannot condone tearing apart Gihron's society merely to allow our ships to trade goods."

"If that is the case," Isa started, "then perhaps our negotiations have ended."

"No, Elite Isa, they have not," Colonel Amori said dangerously. "They've only begun."

"I cannot change the rules agreed to by the Alliance. The numbers in military forces were carefully calculated and agreed upon," Isa said strongly. "They are Venus' Law. They are absolute."

Colonel Amori gave her a half smile.

"If you're so keen on the rules, why do you break them yourself?"

Isa stared at the Colonel. After studying the dangerous look in his brown eyes, she started to feel worry settle in her stomach. Her mind raced, trying to think of what he had seen that would make him believe she did not obey Venus.

She did obey the computer.

Apart from being with Remus.

"What do you mean?" Isa asked, keeping her voice steady.

"Nothing, of course." He stood and bowed his head. "I will take my leave now. We will resume our negotiations tomorrow."

"I will not be at the Syndicate tomorrow."

"I know," Colonel Amori said. "But I find your office cold and depressing. I would rather meet with you here."

"It is unprofessional. I will not allow it."

"I will be here tomorrow."

He turned and walked out of the level. Isa groaned and her head fell back on the couch, frustrated.

■■

Even though Isa was sure she had been very careful to keep her relationship with Remus a secret from the Colonel, she was worried that he had found out somehow. The next day, before the Colonel appeared at her house, she called Remus and told him to come over for the negotiations. She said they needed to be firmer in their discussions and that she would rather break ties with Gihron and leave them in their corner of the Altereye System than drag on the negotiations.

The Silver Elite came over and asked her why she was upset, but she did not have time to discuss the possibility of Colonel Amori knowing about their relationship before the Gihron leader appeared at her door.

Rayal answered the door with a bow of his head and then promptly excused himself from the room.

The negotiations that day were very short. Colonel Amori did not seem interested in discussing anything with Remus in the room. Isa, however, refused to speak with the planetary leader alone. He was in her home, a place she preferred to keep free from political matters, and she needed to show that she had the power in that situation.

Once again, Colonel Amori and Isa were in a deadlock with their stances on the trade agreement.

Twice, Isa tried to dismiss the Gihoric Colonel, but he refused. He said he would contact his brother and discuss a course of action with him.

For two weeks, Isa did not see Colonel Amori. Her frustration continued to build, however, when she did not hear from him.

She was also very careful about how she associated with Remus. She had managed to keep their relationship secret for nearly fifteen years, and she was not about to get careless. There was something about the Colonel's demeanor that told her he would resort to dirty tricks to get his way. Therefore, she kept the Silver Elite at a distance, much to Remus' confusion.

Another emergency came up when Kreon sounded a distress signal for the Alliance. One of their power reactors had gone into catastrophic meltdown and Isa's attention was focused entirely on getting the people of her closest ally the assistance they needed. Remus had fallen ill just one day before the emergency occurred, so she was left handling the problem on her own. She deployed her troops to help secure and evacuate the area around the reactor and then sent aid by means of food and supplies for those displaced, as well as four of her most-qualified technicians to organize repairs.

When it seemed the problem was properly contained, Isa had almost forgotten about Colonel Amori. She never saw him, and he had not called her to tell her about his brother's decision.

Remus came to her home when the reactor was reported as stable and shared a drink with her. Her frustrations and stress about Kreon and Colonel Amori caused her to seek Remus intimately. She wanted him to take control of her life, even if it was only within the confines of her bedroom. They had not had sex in weeks, and both were hungry for contact.

She fell into a sound sleep next to Remus, who also slept deeply, still recovering from the strange virus that had taken hold of his system.

As she slept, she dreamt she was swimming in warm, serene waters. The feeling of weightlessness and calm surrounded her, and she allowed herself to enjoy the dream.

Until she felt her limbs become heavy, and she began to slip under the surface of the water. She struggled to breathe as water pressed hard against her nose and mouth. She struggled and flailed violently, panic setting in as she began to drown.

Her eyes snapped open and she realized the drowning feeling had been due to the hand clamped over her nose and mouth.

"Shh, shh…" a dark voice whispered in her ear. "This will be so much easier for you if you don't struggle."

Isa started flailing violently, reaching out to hit Remus, trying to wake up the Silver Elite.

"Don't bruise the poor man, now," the voice laughed. "He's not gonna wake up for awhile."

Isa's eyes focused on the shadowy figure over her and her hand swung, punching him violently in the jaw and rolling her off the bed in the same motion. She quickly turned over and started to stand when the body collided with hers, grabbing her wrists and flipping her over. As she kicked, he pressed his hand deeply into the back of her neck and a pulse of pain shot through her, her muscles freezing in their tensed positions. She could not move. She was paralyzed.

Her eyes moved about the room and she saw the man's face come into her field of vision once more. His bright smile and dark eyes were in contrast with one another, and his cold, dark voice sent a terrible tremor of fear down her spine.

"I told you it would be better if you didn't struggle," he said with a light laugh. He turned her onto her back, her muscles still refusing to move, no matter how she struggled. Once she was on her back, he straddled her, leaning down and crossing his arms over her collarbone, pinning her.

"Allow me to explain how this is going to work," Colonel Amori said darkly. "These terms are non-negotiable, and you *will* obey them."

"The hell I will!" Isa spat, her teeth locked together. "I'll have you executed for this."

"Will you?" he challenged. "My dear Isa, you seem to think that you have the upper hand, when, in reality, I have you completely cornered." He leaned closer to the Elite. "What do you think Venus would do if she knew you were fucking your Silver Elite?"

Isa said nothing. Her mind was working around the situation, trying to figure out how to alert someone that she was in danger and get the Colonel taken into custody for use of force and political coercion.

"No? Is that not enough for you?" Colonel Amori asked. "How about this, then?" He reached into his front coat pocket and pulled out two black devices. One was a portable drive of a sort that Isa had never seen before. The other was a small handle with a button in the middle.

"Do you see this?" He shook the one with the button. "I have two of these. This particular one won't cause as much damage as the other, but I assure you, they will both work."

Isa stared at the device, trying to figure out what it was.

"Your brother seeks war against us?" she growled. "If you harm me, the entire Alliance will destroy your planet without hesitation."

"My dear, you misunderstand me. Decius is not privy to any of this. He never was. And I have no intention of hurting you," he said. "I need you too much."

Isa glared at the other politician, trying to move her arms and legs, but the needle pressing into her neck was effectively keeping her body paralyzed.

"I need you to help me destroy the Alliance and Venus."

Isa stared at Colonel Amori with wide eyes.

"Are you insane?" she hissed. "I would *never* help you. You could threaten me all you want, but you will never destroy Venus, and the Alliance will come to my aid to destroy you."

"Assuming that you call them," he said, shaking the device in his hand. "Do you really think I was sitting around this entire time? I've been hard at work, securing my control over you and Tiao." He put the device in her face. "This holds the life of your Silver Elite, all of your Bronze Elites, and your caretaker."

She looked at the device.

"What have you done to them?"

"I'm sure that you've heard of microbionics?" he asked. "Those tiny little robots used in medical practice?"

"Those were outlawed twenty years ago," Isa said coldly, fear seeping into her gut.

"In the Alliance, yes," Colonel Amori agreed. "But we are not in the Alliance. I happen to be a brilliant programmer. I've developed them to be smart, well, as smart as a machine can be. Certain microbionic cells were injected into each of your colleagues and your caretaker. And this little button," he barely tapped it with his finger, causing Isa to tense, "will activate all of them. First, the ones in your caretaker will eat him alive from the inside out. Some of them have already tried, I suspect, since your caretaker fell ill last week. But the best ones, the microbionic cells I injected into Remus and into your brainless Bronze Elites are far more sophisticated. Those ones will attach to the spinal cord and they will *control* all of them to kill you."

Isa stared at the device.

"I wonder what you would do in that situation," Colonel Amori mused. "Imagine it. You're working in your cold, depressing office and Remus comes into see you, only it's not Remus." He shook the device again. "It's *me*. And he comes after you, with every intention to kill you. Of course, he won't understand why. He'll probably be screaming at you, telling you he doesn't understand what's happening, even as he raises a gun to kill you. I wonder..." Colonel Amori smiled darkly, his face barely parted from Isa's, "how strong are the survival instincts of an Elite? Will you let him kill you? Or will you put a bullet in his brain? Pop!" He tapped the end of the device on Isa's forehead. "Right between the eyes."

Isa stared in horror at the Colonel. She was not sure if the needle in her neck was keeping her paralyzed or if it was her fear at the words.

"But if you kill him, you'll leave the room only to realize that all thirteen of your Bronze Elites are acting the exact same way. They surround you, chase you down, tear you limb from limb, all the while screaming, not sure what they are doing, but fully conscious of the fact that they are murdering their beloved Golden Elite."

"I'll kill you for this," Isa hissed.

"No, darling, you won't." Colonel Amori smiled. "Because there is yet another device, remember? No microbionics, this time. Instead, it's far more primitive. A catastrophic failure of three of your power processors in Anon. I believe they're connected to Venus, too, which is just a bonus for me. Just like Kreon, these processors will go into accelerated failure, and before everyone has time to realize they are in danger, Anon will be erased from the face of the planet." He smiled darkly. "This is your test. If you were a real Elite, you would not bother to worry about your colleagues and your forbidden lover. Instead, you would focus on getting the people to safety, and then you would have me executed, even at the expense of killing your colleagues. That would be the calculated decision. More people saved from danger.

"But you're no ordinary Elite, are you?" he challenged. "The question is, what will you do?"

"I already told you," Isa growled. "I'll kill you."

"Well, before we can get that far," he said, returning the device with the button to his pocket and raising the other one, "there is something I need from you."

He sat up and his hand violently grabbed Isa's left breast, forcing it toward her collarbone before jamming the device against her ribcage, forcing a node deep into her skin until it touched the processor around her heart.

Isa began screaming in pain, and Colonel Amori clamped his hand over her mouth.

"I hate it when women scream. Shut up," he snarled.

Isa continued to scream. The pain forced the noise out of her, cutting it from her lungs and pulling out of her throat. Her body spasmed angrily as shockwaves went through her.

She was not sure how long the pain lasted, but when he ripped the drive from her, she choked and groaned, sure that she had been in agony for days.

"Excellent." Colonel Amori smiled. "Oh, something I forgot to tell you," he said, looking down at Isa. "If you breathe a word of this to anyone and try to get me arrested, I'll pull that trigger and force you to die with me and the rest of the city. And when that happens, my brother will come with the entire planet at his back and destroy everything on Tiao before taking over every planet in the Alliance. You can be sure of that."

Isa tried to move her arms, but she could not. She struggled and groaned, trying to move, her body shaking.

"Oh, right," he chuckled. "It's late. You should get some sleep. After all, this is only the beginning. I need you rested and ready to help me when we move to the next stage."

He leaned forward once more, grabbing a syringe and uncapping the needle. He pushed it into her shoulder and flashed a brilliant smile.

"Isn't it amazing how detailed nightmares can be?"

Isa's eyes slipped shut and she was left at his will.

■■■

When Isa woke, she was immediately terrified, but the pain in her head made it impossible for her to move very fast. She groaned and forced her eyes open. There was no one there with her. She saw the light on to the bathroom and sat up slowly, cradling her pounding head in one hand.

"You feel shitty, too?" Remus chuckled, walking into the room from the bathroom with a package of pills he had rifled from the drawer and a glass of water. "We both drank too much last night and then did too much physical activity," he teased lightly, sitting on the bed next to her and extending the glass and painkillers. "Here."

Isa took them slowly, her mind in a fog.

"I feel like...I don't know..."

"I know, I'm in a fog, too."

"Do you remember anything out of the ordinary last night?"

"No," he said, shaking his head. "Are you alright? You look pale. Are you nauseous?"

"No, that's not..." Isa looked into the water glass. "Look at the back of my neck. Do you see any bruises or cuts?"

"What?"

"Just check, please," Isa said, turning her back to him and lifting her hair. He looked over her skin, but saw nothing.

"No," he said. "Nothing at all."

"And this shoulder?" she asked, turning her shoulder to him. He looked over the area, but shook his head.

"No," he repeated. "Except we better hope that *that* is covered by the uniform," he said, passing his finger gently over a bruise at the base of her neck. She put her hand over his quickly, trying to feel the area.

"What? What is it?"

"That was me, sorry," he said, leaning down and kissing her shoulder. "I got a little carried away last night."

"What do you mean?"

Remus chuckled. "I will try not to be insulted that you don't remember." He stood and nodded to the water. "Take those. You'll start to feel better."

He began walking toward the bathroom once more. Isa sighed heavily and closed her eyes, figuring that it had been an alcohol-induced nightmare. There were no marks on her body from the needles that she remembered penetrating her skin.

But it had felt too real.

She glanced at Remus, about to ask if he had strange dreams as well, when she caught sight of the light bruise across Remus' lower ribcage.

"Don't bruise the poor man, now."

Isa quickly looked down, lifting her breast to look at her ribcage

A small bruise painted her skin, a red dot in the middle showing an entry wound. She climbed out of bed, ignoring her naked state, and walked into the kitchen. Rayal was making breakfast, though he was pale and had large bags under his eyes. He was clearly not feeling any better than he had the previous few days.

"Miss?" Rayal asked, confused by her naked state and the way she immediately went to the security screens. She rewound the recordings, looking for any movement in the hours of the night.

However, there was none.

Two days later, Isa was a nervous wreck. She was trying to determine what of that terrifying night had been real and what had been a dream. She knew that the security footage could be altered, and she knew that it was possible that the needles that had penetrated her skin to paralyze her and knock her unconscious were small enough not to leave noticeable marks. But there was something about the situation that made her question herself.

What made matters worse was that the threat—whether real or a dream—had caused her to ask a very frightening question of herself.

Would she save the people of Anon? Or would she try to find a way to save Rayal, Remus, and the Bronze Elites? Every time she closed her eyes, she thought of Remus coming at her, his eyes wide and terrified, as he screamed at her to kill him to keep him from hurting her.

Because of these images, she had not slept.

She spent her days at the Syndicate Building carefully watching Venus' mainframe for any sign of trouble. If Colonel Amori had stolen codes from Isa's internal processor with the intent of finding a way to shut down Venus, he also held her life in his hands. If Venus' codes started to disappear, Isa's heart would stop immediately.

Occasionally, for no reason she could explain, she would get sharp twinges of fear and her heart would begin racing. In those moments, she was sure that Venus was triggering her failsafe, and Isa's heart was about to stop beating, leaving the other Elites to find her lifeless body.

On the third day after the frightening night, an operator called her office to tell her that Colonel Amori was there to see her.

Nervously, she allowed the Gihoric leader up.

She was expecting the other delegates to be with him when he walked into her office, however they were not. He was alone, and that terrified Isa further.

She stood by her desk, prepared to activate her panic button in her office, if necessary.

"Colonel Amori," she greeted with a bow of her head.

"Elite Isa," he said. "I wanted to let you know that I spoke with my brother and he is asking me to stay until we can reach an agreement. He wants us to come to a compromise."

Isa barely heard him. She was staring at his features, trying to discern any hint of malice.

When she did not respond, he spoke again.

"Elite Isa?" he asked. "Are you alright?"

The Golden Elite walked toward him, her eyes suspicious. He retreated a step, confused. When his back was against the door, Isa patted down the front chest pockets of Colonel Amori's military jacket. He tried to retreat once more, laughing nervously.

"Elite Isa, what are you doing?"

There was nothing in his pockets.

Isa then began patting down his side pockets, once again finding nothing in them. Becoming frantic, worried that she had imagined the entire night, her hands went to his pants pockets.

He grabbed her wrists and gently pushed her away, laughing once more.

"Elite Isa, please don't take this the wrong way," he started. "You are very beautiful, but I am not interested in you that way."

Isa backed away from him, her expression confused.

"My apologies..." she murmured. "I don't know what came over me."

"Are you alright?"

"Yes, I'm fine."

"...good," Colonel Amori said, clearly not convinced. "I'm sorry to have disturbed you. Let's have dinner tonight to discuss what my brother said."

"Yes, let's," Isa said. "My apologies, once again."

"No need to apologize."

Colonel Amori turned and opened the door, walking out into the hallway.

"Oh, Elite Isa?" he called back. She turned around and her heart stopped in panic. "Were you looking for this?"

In his hand, he was holding the device she remembered so vividly from her dream, the small, black handle with a green button in the middle of it, just under his first finger.

However, before she could react to the sight of the device and the sick smile that crossed Colonel Amori's face, the door closed, leaving Isa in the dull buzzing of her office, her stomach doing somersaults.

▪▪

That night, Isa met with Colonel Amori alone in her home, Rayal cooking dinner for the both of them. It was clear that the caretaker was feeling unwell. His hands were shaking and he was very pale. Isa watched him worriedly, telling him to bring the food to the table and then lie down.

Rayal did as instructed, leaving the two alone.

"He seems unwell," Colonel Amori noted.

"Is that because of you?" Isa asked, her food remaining untouched.

"Most likely," Colonel Amori admitted, diving into his full plate. He took a big bite and looked up at Isa. "I will say, I am impressed that you have not tried to have me arrested. I guess you aren't that suicidal." He pointed at her with his fork. "So tell me, are all Elites programmed to do what is needed to survive, or are you just special?"

"What, exactly, are you after?" Isa asked, ignoring the question. "You said you wanted to tear down the Alliance and shut down Venus, but that would do no good for anyone in the system."

"Did you ever learn what happened to Earth?" Colonel Amori asked, turning back to his dinner.

"Yes."

"The *truth* of what happened to Earth?"

"Yes."

Colonel Amori took another bite of his food.

"So why would humans allow themselves to be governed by the same technology that almost killed them?"

"Venus is not built on the technology of those weapons," Isa disagreed. "She has access to some of the genetic information, but the data was mostly destroyed when humans evacuated Earth."

"I was talking about Elites."

Isa sighed heavily.

"We are not weapons," she said. "We are just altered humans meant to obey Venus' command."

"Then Venus has become the weapon and is hiding behind the Elites."

"She's not a weaponized system. She can alert about disasters, but she cannot take action on her own. She is not programmed that way," Isa disagreed. "She is, however, a very powerful monitoring system. She creates a network for all Altereye planets to use and be monitored on."

"And you think that is acceptable?" Isa went silent, staring at Colonel Amori as he looked up from his plate, chewing his food slowly. "No?"

"Everyone can agree that humans are dangerous," Isa said carefully. "Humans need guidance and supervision."

"And you believe that your guidance is better than, say, mine?"

"As I've stated before, Colonel Amori," Isa said, her voice cold, "I believe that humans have the basic right to food and shelter, not forced to slave away until they are near death just to try and ease the pain in their bellies."

"And as *I* have stated before, the grunts are no different on Gihron than the Trids are on Tiao," Colonel Amori reiterated. He leaned back with a heavy sigh, smiling. "You surprise me, Elite Isa." He chuckled, tossing the fork onto the half-eaten plate of food. "You had the opportunity to make good on your promise tonight."

"What promise was that?"

"That you would kill me." Colonel Amori picked some food out of his teeth. "You didn't poison the food."

"I may have promised that I would kill you, but I'm not stupid," Isa growled. "A diplomat in my home, alone, and he's poisoned? Autopsy would show that you ate food that I did not and were poisoned. Then, your brother would have a blood-grudge."

"Seems you do know a little bit about us."

"You seem eager to die, Colonel," Isa noted. "I might have poisoned the food, and you dove right in."

Colonel Amori chuckled.

"Either way, I would have you cornered," he said. "To think, in just one short month, I have brought the greatest Golden Elite in history to heel."

"No, you have not," Isa said strongly.

"We'll see about that," he said. He leaned forward. "And I want to thank you for inviting me to stay in your home while I'm here."

"I've done no such thing," Isa growled. "You are not welcome to stay here."

"I need to keep an eye on you," Colonel Amori said. "I've invested a lot of time, money, and technology into this so far, and I will not have some altruistic Elite fuck it up."

"You've already signed your death sentence," Isa said simply. "*You* were the one who fucked it up."

"Fine," Colonel Amori said, shrugging. "I have camera feeds everywhere in the house, and in the Syndicate Building. Honestly, you should consider increasing your security. It's amazing that no one has done this already. You left yourself open. You can only blame yourself."

■■■

Another sleepless night left Isa was with a splitting headache. She went to the Syndicate Building and passed everyone without greeting them, her head down and her eyes dark with exhaustion. The other Elites figured that she was merely tired from having to handle the stubborn Colonel Amori so soon after the Kreon incident. They let her go to her office without pestering her.

Isa walked to her NCB chair as it greeted her entrance, turning to her. She stopped next to it, putting her hand on the cold metal and staring distantly into the machine.

When her legs began to tire from standing still for so long, she walked to her desk and sat at it, staring at the stacks of files and drives on the surface.

She had spent the entire night and morning thinking about the security in the Syndicate Building and in Anon Tower. While she had not programmed it—the coding had been in place for generations—she knew that it had been updated as necessary by various Elite programmers and engineers. She tried to think of ways that Colonel Amori could get into the building to plant his cameras, or how he could rewire the existing cameras. She was sure he could not access the codes to get into Venus' mainframe and access her cameras.

However, there was a sick feeling in her stomach.

The bruised area where the node had entered her body was evidence that he could have access to Venus' mainframe.

She glanced around the hidden cameras in her office, her body on high alert.

When the soft chime in her ear alerted her to a phone call, she jumped, startled, and then groaned, cradling her head in one hand as she gently tapped the area just in front of her ear.

"Elite Isa."

"Yes, I can see you."

Isa's eyes went wide and she straightened.

"You stood completely still for nearly three hours," Colonel Amori chuckled. "I was beginning to think you had looped the security feed."

"How do I know that you're not just tracking me?" Isa challenged.

"Fine, I'm watching. Do something."

Isa turned to one of the cameras and flipped it off, glaring.

Colonel Amori laughed. "Excellent. Good to see the lack of sleep has not dulled your edge." Isa felt dirty just listening to the way his voice oozed with supremacy, even as she tried to ignore the way he told her he had been watching her sleep—or not sleep—at night. "You flipped me off. To be specific, you flipped off the south-west camera in your office."

Isa lowered her hand.

"What do you want? I need to concentrate."

"I have a task for you," he said. "There is something I'm very interested in. You've managed to terraform part of this planet to grow crops from Earth."

"It's a protected site," Isa said darkly. "If you attack there, you will wage war on every planet in the Altereye System."

"I am merely interested in how it works," Colonel Amori said with a cold laugh. "You're quick to assume that I want to destroy everything."

"I thought you *did*."

"I just want to know how your terraform greenhouses function. Perhaps I can bring the idea back to Gihron and we can produce more food for our people," Colonel Amori said. "I will meet you for dinner, and I expect the information by then."

Isa was about to protest when Colonel Amori disconnected the call.

She groaned and cradled her head in both hands once more.

The door opening caused her to jump, standing up quickly, worried. Remus stopped in the doorway, surprised by her startle.

"Are you alright?" he asked, walking in as Isa let out a shaky breath and sat at her desk again.

"I haven't been sleeping well," she said. "Hard for my brain to settle." She took a deep breath and looked at him. "I had a question for you. What is the status on, uh, what's that one city called with the spire monument to the Alliance?" she asked, her brow furrowing in confusion as she tried to think of the name of the city.

"Dyran?" Remus asked slowly, surprised she did not remember.

"Yes, the name was escaping me," Isa said, forcing a smile.

"You must really be exhausted," Remus noted. "Why don't you go home? Or just sleep for a bit in here?"

"No, I have too much to do," Isa protested. She took a deep breath, rubbing her temples.

"Well, if you want, I can come over later and we can work on getting you to sleep," Remus said with a smile.

Isa smiled as well and shook her head. "As tempting as that is, I must refuse. It's alright. Dr. Busen gave me something to try tonight, so hopefully I'll get some rest."

"You've already spoken to him?" Remus asked. When she nodded, he blinked at her, surprised. "That's not like you," he said teasingly. "You're actually being proactive about your health?"

"Be quiet," Isa said with a strained laugh. "What is the status of the greenhouse project in Dyran?"

"The plans were approved a week ago. Maki is working on coordination and preparation."

"I would like to see those files before he gets too far."

"…alright," Remus said, wondering why she would want to look over the files she had pushed to have approved and acted on as soon as possible. "Are you sure you're alright?"

"Yes, I'm fine."

Remus discussed a few other work-related things with her before leaving her office once more. She leaned back in her chair and took several deep breaths. Dyran was a new terraform development. She did not want to give Colonel Amori information on Saera, the city of engineers, agricultural specialists, and workers that ran the enormous facilities that produced crops from Earth. Most of Tiao's food was grown and distributed from Saera, and because food-related sites were heavily protected, she had never had fear that it would be under attack.

However, she still wanted to keep the city as safe as possible from the dangers of Colonel Amori.

Isa glanced around the office once more, wondering if his eyes were on her in that moment.

She stood and walked to her NCB chair, climbing in and signing into the mainframe. She spent hours going around the mainframe, trying to find weaknesses and trails that would tell her how the Colonel was able to watch her at home and at work. However, even after searching, she could not find anything suggesting Venus' mainframe had been hacked.

Isa was beginning to fear that Colonel Amori was doing his work under her name, using her codes from her internal processor as Golden Elite to grant him access to everything in Venus' mainframe and leave no trace.

The Golden Elite decided to send a very short, simple message into Venus' encrypted archives, hoping that Colonel Amori could not access the area, let alone understand and read the message in Venus' coded language.

Possible breach of security. No information is safe.

■■■

Isa met with the Colonel that night for dinner and gave him the information on Dyran. He took it quietly and then ate the simple dinner that Rayal had cooked before asking to be excused for the night. Isa told herself that she would call a physician for her caretaker the next morning, worried about his declining health.

Colonel Amori did not speak to her over dinner, and when he finished eating—Isa had not touched her food—he took the drive with the information on Dyran and left without a word.

There was something terrifying about the behavior.

For two days, Isa heard nothing from Colonel Amori. Rather than ease her mind, it frightened her more.

She left work one day, exhausted and shaking. She knew that she was weak from not sleeping or eating, but her stomach was constantly twisting inside her and her mind refused to be silent at night to allow her rest. She tried not to notice how pale her face had become, or how dark the circles around her eyes were, or the way her body would fire painful signals randomly in muscle spasms strong enough to knock the breath out of her, but she could feel her body falling apart slowly.

The most she could do was to try and hide it from the Syndicate. She was worried that, if they found out, Colonel Amori, who was watching her constantly, would press the button on his remote and activate the microbionic cells. She knew the threat was not idle—Rayal was getting worse by the day, and she knew it was from the microbionic cells.

She closed her eyes as she sat in the car, feeling the gentle hum of the vehicle as it sped along the highway to its programmed destination.

Isa heard a noise behind her and whirled around in time to see the Colonel's face before a cloth pressed tightly over her nose and mouth and the world fell into black.

When her eyes opened, she spent several minutes staring at the dark grey, metal wall, trying to recall what happened. Her confusion was only enhanced by the drugs still running through her system.

She had to prepare herself to turn over, her body twinging in pain from lying on the cold stone floor. Her eyes scanned the ceiling where the dull lights nearly blinded her tired eyes. With a careful breath, she turned once more and scrutinized the walls. There were no windows on the walls. It appeared to be a solitary confinement cell, with one yellowed window in the door.

In the window of the door was the face of Colonel Amori, twisted in a sick smile.

The screeching of the door opening almost made Isa's head explode in pain. She cringed away, trying to lift her hands to her head, but the sharp tug of restraints on her wrists, waist, neck, and ankles made her realize she was confined like a prisoner in maximum security confinement. She stared at the thick, twisted cables between the cuffs with disbelief.

"As I expected," Colonel Amori chuckled. "You are awake several hours before a normal human. The bio-engineering in Elites is quite remarkable. It's too bad you're all so mindless and stupid. You would be incredibly interesting to study."

"The Syndicate will notice if I'm gone."

"Eventually, yes," Colonel Amori agreed, crouching in front of her. Isa, in her peripheral vision, saw that he had left the door open. She needed only to get her feet under her, stun Colonel Amori briefly, and then lock him in the room. From there, she knew she could find out where she was and get help. However, she did not dare look at the door, not wanting to tip off the Gihoric leader.

"But they won't notice that you're missing for another three hours, when you don't show up for work. Unfortunately, poor Rayal has become so much worse, he didn't notice that you weren't home last night," he said. "And it's such a shame that those blood samples went missing." He wagged a disapproving finger at her with a smile. "Your people clearly aren't as happy as you claim," he stated. "It was so easy to bribe a nurse to *misplace* the blood samples."

"You fucking bastard," Isa growled.

"Name calling is hardly going to help."

"You realize that you've *kidnapped* the leader of Tiao and the Crescent Alliance," Isa snapped. "You are now committing acts of terrorism. You will be killed and your planet will be either destroyed or conquered."

"It's adorable how powerful you think you are," Colonel Amori chided. He stood, walking around her. "You even thought that your little message to Venus would help? Granted, it was brilliant of you to put it in that strange encryption code. I must work on translating that, but I knew it was a warning. It was too short to be anything else. But I guess I didn't give you much time to send something more detailed, since I'm always watching you."

Isa listened to the Colonel's boots as they slowly walked around her, stopping at her back. She kept her eyes forward, on the open door, preparing to fight and escape.

"I was looking into the Elite Academy," Colonel Amori said. "I was trying to figure out why *you* are so different from the others."

"Even the doctors can't understand it, so I doubt you can."

"I've read their reports," he said. "And even with all the trauma you've been through, you seem not to exhibit any traits of mental problems. You saw a classmate killed, your lover was tortured for days, you were beaten probably every other day the entire time you were in school, but still, you march along as though you are *so* powerful."

Isa remained silent, rallying her strength.

"You spent the first seventeen years of your life being beaten and ordered around by *humans*, and you then turn around and think that you can rule them? Does that make sense?"

Still, the Golden Elite was quiet.

Suddenly, Colonel Amori lifted his foot and violently kicked Isa in the back. She let out a surprised cry and her body was forced forward, rolling twice until it came to rest near the door. As she tried to force her lungs to work once more, she pulled her legs under her and tried to get out of the cell.

Colonel Amori's fingers wrapped in her hair and his other hand shoved the door shut as he yanked her backward.

She managed to stumble within her restraints but remain standing. She twisted her body, swinging her restrained hands together to connect with Colonel Amori's face. He quickly regained his balance and grabbed Isa's shoulders, kneeing her in the stomach.

She collapsed to the ground, groaning and gasping in pain.

Colonel Amori smiled, licking the blood from his lips.

"I want to remind you of exactly what you are," he said. He kicked her in the stomach as she started to straighten and she let out a cry of pain, falling to her side. "This is how powerful you are. You are meant to obey, and to *always obey*. Humans, teachers, Venus, it doesn't matter, you are the lowest of the low." He kicked her once more. "And now, you obey *me*."

Isa tried to remain still as the Colonel kicked her. She figured eventually he would get bored and stop. She tried to formulate a plan for what to do when he did stop the beating.

"Don't worry," he chuckled, yanking her up by her hair and smiling sickly. "I'm following the rules of the Academy."

He shoved her back down to the ground and kneeled on her stomach and chest.

"Never hit the face or neck, right?" he asked. "Only the places that are covered by the uniform. That way, you can keep up *appearances*."

Isa struggled to breathe under his weight, her head going light.

Colonel Amori stood only to kick her three more times and then left the cell, not allowing her time to recover before the door screeched shut and the clank of the lock caused even more pain to settle into Isa's chest.

Without windows, there was no concept of time. When the pain in her body became tolerable, Isa stood and clumsily shuffled around the room, looking at every wall, every corner, the hinges on the metal door, and glancing out the window to the empty hallway beyond. The ceiling was solid apart from the lights, and Isa had no way to reach them.

She was trapped.

She pressed her face against the wall, rubbing her cheek back and forth across the surface in an attempt to activate her phone and call for help. When she managed to hear the automatic voice ask who she wanted to call, she said the Syndicate. The automatic voice came back, saying that her location and identity could not be verified, and, therefore, the call could not connect.

Isa barked at the phone to operate on emergency mode, but as it began connecting to emergency operators, the sound warped and eventually turned into a high, painful whine. Isa tried to get away from the noise, but with the implanted earpiece, the sound penetrated into her brain.

She finally conceded to sit in a corner, turning over every possibility of escape.

The Golden Elite did not have much time to think, however. Colonel Amori returned, this time with a tablet and the black handle with the green button.

"You must be feeling alright, trying to put out an emergency call like that," he said with a smile. He closed the door behind him and walked forward, crouching in front of Isa and holding up the tablet. "You seem to need a little more convincing, which is why I brought you here. You will obey me. I have big plans for Tiao, so I would rather *not* destroy everything in the process of conquering it. The faster you cooperate, the fewer lives will be lost."

He tapped the top of the tablet twice and it flickered to life, showing a live video feed from Remus' office at the Syndicate.

"What are you doing?" Isa hissed.

"Showing you that I am not joking about controlling Remus and the others." His other hand lifted the device and he smiled, placing his finger over the trigger. "Just for added assurance that this footage has not been altered or recorded previously, I'm going to have you tell me when to push the button."

"You think that I'll cooperate if you kill them?"

"No, your Elites will survive." He turned his hand to show her how the trigger worked. "If I push this up, it activates the cells. If it's down, however, they return to hibernation."

"I won't do it."

"I didn't give you the option to refuse."

"You said Rayal was worse, I believe you. If you press that button, you might kill him."

Colonel Amori chuckled. "You're more worried about the caretaker than your lover?"

"I don't need to be convinced," Isa said. "You've kidnapped me and beaten me. You have made it abundantly clear that your threats are not idle."

Colonel Amori narrowed his eyes, smiling dangerously.

"All the same—"

He clicked the switch and Isa started forward.

"No, don't!" she cried. "I told you I believed you!"

"Let's solidify that."

Isa's eyes turned back to the monitor and she saw Remus leave his office, the camera switching, locked onto his signature, to him running down the hallway, up the staircase and to her office. Chronus was already there, angrily shoving the door open.

Remus ran into Isa's office and to the NCB chair. He pushed on the machine, his altered strength causing it to snap off the base. Isa watched in horror as three other Bronze Elites stormed into her office, overturning her desk and looking for her. Their faces were frantic and confused, but their actions terrified Isa.

"Stop," she said. When Colonel Amori did not flip the switch down, she turned away from the screen. "I said *stop*!" she barked. "I understand! I'm listening to you!"

He laughed and flicked the switch.

"Finally, some progress," he said. He kept the tablet facing her and she watched as, one by one, the Elites slowed and stopped, breathing hard, turning to one another in confusion.

Before Colonel Amori turned off the tablet, Isa glanced at the clock, seeing that she had already been gone for almost an entire day.

"Now," Colonel Amori started, grabbing the cord between Isa's restraints and hauling her to her feet, "I need to test your obedience."

He yanked her into the dark, short hallway she had seen out the window. She glanced around briefly to spot an exit, but when she could not, she focused entirely on the trigger in Colonel Amori's other hand. She wondered if she could get it and destroy it before he could use it against her once more.

Pushing the door open with his shoulder, Colonel Amori brought her into a room that appeared to be a recreation room of some sort when the facility was in use. There were old tables and chairs and a broken vending machine in one corner. Sitting on one table, in stark contrast to the older furnishings, was a new computer, hooked up to several external drives and two supplemental monitors that were black.

On the computer, Isa could see Venus' mainframe and schematics flashing across the screen with several meters of slowly-ascending numbers.

"How did you access her mainframe?" Isa asked sharply, planting her feet and pulling against his tugging. He let out a bark of laughter, yanking sharply to force her forward.

"That's paltry at this point, I should think," he said. "I told you, I've been able to watch you for some time, all from Venus' mainframe." He turned to her when they were in front of the computer. "And it's all thanks to you." He smiled, gently pulling on the cable between her restraints to bring her two steps closer. "I was going to thank you for the information on Dyran, but you must think I'm a moron. I would think, after everything, you would realize you cannot hide anything from me. I know all about Saera." He nodded to the screen of the computer, so Isa turned her eyes, trying to figure out what she was looking at and how it related to Saera.

"This is your test," he started. "This is a Charge Burst. It's been charging for a while now, just to be safe, but it's currently aimed at the main power generator for Saera. If it hits that generator, it will cause a chain reaction through the rest of the facility and it will destroy the entire city, and all of its inhabitants, as well as decimating your terraform facilities. I'm not sure if anything will grow after something so devastating happens underground and rips apart everything on the surface." He chuckled darkly at Isa's controlled expression, even though her eyes were showing her panic. She watched the numbers increase on the Charge Burst, trying to recall everything she knew about the weapon. It was an old form of warfare, attacking from under the ground. As with microbionics, the Charge Bursts were outlawed in the Alliance with the regulation of military forces.

"Obviously, this provides nearly sixty percent of Tiao's food," Colonel Amori continued. "And I doubt you'll be able to get anyone to eat the native crops of Tiao, since they have no nutritional value to humans. So, if it is destroyed, you're going to be feeding your people chemical rations." He lifted the handle with the green button with his other hand, smiling. "You already know what this does. You have to choose between them. Either kill your caretaker and make your Syndicate of idiots so homicidal, the only thing that will stop them is a bullet to the brain, or destroy the main generator of Saera and annihilate your planet's food source."

"What is the point of making me do this?" Isa growled, glaring at Colonel Amori. "If you destroy the food source of the planet, then Tiao is weakened and not nearly as valuable of a conquest."

"However, if *you* destroy the Syndicate, it will be that much easier for my brother to take over, once I shut down Venus." Colonel Amori smiled. "Quite the conundrum, isn't it?"

"And if I choose neither option?"

"You want to leave it in *my* hands?" Colonel Amori asked. "You and I are far from Anon. I would just destroy the capital and stay with you here while my brother presumed me dead and attacked Tiao. I would force you to watch as your entire planet was conquered and your people slaughtered." His smile widened. "You make the decision, you have three options—destroy your Syndicate, destroy Saera, or destroy Anon."

Isa looked between the screen and Colonel Amori, noting where his hand was on the handle and on the cable restraining her.

In a brief moment of madness, she lunged forward and her head connected with his, stunning him while she tried to reach for the handle. He let out a startled cry of pain and rolled away from her, tugging on the cable and causing her to lose her balance and fall to the ground. His foot connected with her ribs.

"You bitch!" he groaned, holding his bleeding nose. "Have you learned nothing?! Do you want me to destroy all three for you?!"

He kicked her once more. She tried to breathe, but her body was already bruised and beaten from his previous attacks and the pain seared through her.

Colonel Amori pulled out a gun from his jacket and pointed it at her as she tried to catch her breath.

"You have ten seconds to make your decision before I destroy all three."

Isa let out a shaky breath, trying to get to her feet, struggling against the pain. Colonel Amori angrily yanked her upright, holding her steady and pushing the barrel of the gun into her chest sharply.

"Make your choice," he snarled.

He released Isa and backed away one step, keeping the gun pointed at her with one hand raised and his finger on the green trigger.

She stared at him for two long seconds before turning to look at the computer screen, her mind racing, weighing all the options. She fought with the urge to turn around and attack him once again. She was too weak and hurt already to risk not dominating the fight and allowing the Colonel to destroy both cities and her Syndicate.

If the Syndicate were to be controlled to the point of having to be killed to be stopped, leaving only Isa alive, it would leave her without support and would raise suspicions among the Alliance, which would, in turn, cause others to doubt the strength of Tiao. That would limit the amount of aid Isa could get in retaliating against Gihron. However, if Anon was destroyed, millions of lives would be lost, along with the symbol that was the capital of Tiao. The most lives would be lost if she did nothing.

If she were to allow the Charge Burst to destroy Saera, then about one-hundred thousand lives would be lost, and millions of credits that went into developing the greenhouses that developed food. While it would make real food more expensive, there were rations to fall back on, and Dyran was on its way to becoming the next site for terraformed greenhouses.

The gun against her chest pushed hard, breaking her out of her trance.

"Five," Colonel Amori started. "Four."

Isa turned to the computer and looked over the screen, trying to see if there was any way she could minimize the damage. She saw there were seven generators on the screen, the main one, the one that would cause the chain reaction, highlighted and targeted for attack.

"Three."

Isa lifted her hand, allowing her fingers to brush one of the other generators and change the target site before she pressed the launch button.

The numbers on the screen stopped ascending and then went into rapid decline as Colonel Amori let out a triumphant laugh.

"I knew it," he declared. He stepped forward and tapped the top of one of the secondary screens twice to turn it on. "You chose the life of your lover and your Syndicate over the lives of your people." He nodded to the screen that showed a map of the power grid in Saera. "You believe that your rule is better than any humans? You let personal interest guide you to kill over one-hundred thousand people on your planet, as well as doom your people to starve. You even prided yourself on how you believe humans should have basic rights to food, but you destroyed your own food supply to save the man you fuck, and those idiots that do whatever you say."

Isa watched the power grid light up with a red, flashing error symbol and went through a mental map of the city. The generator that had gone into catastrophic failure was on the far north side of the city, a place that was still very under-developed.

The grid beeped several times, and then the generator that had been attacked went completely offline, causing alerts to flash everywhere about an explosion in the city.

"What?!"

Colonel Amori took a step forward and stared at the screen, realizing that the generator that had blown up had not been the one he intended.

He turned to the first screen, seeing which generator was highlighted. He tried to shove Isa out of the way to start another charge when Isa jumped at him, pushing him to the ground and wrapping her bound wrists around his neck, pulling them taught, rolling Colonel Amori on top of her, trying to strangle him. However, Colonel Amori turned over and pulled her with him, angrily jabbing his elbow back into her bruised stomach. She gasped, the breath and strength immediately leaving her.

In that time, Colonel Amori untangled from the cable and went to the computers, starting a second Charge Burst.

Isa turned her body quickly, still on the floor, and kicked his legs, forcing him back to the ground, where she climbed on top of him and tried to smash her restrained fists against his face. He dodged the blow and sat up quickly, grabbing her hair with one hand and shoving his fist deep into her diaphragm. That time, Isa almost passed out from the pain. Her eyes rolled and she let out a pained groan.

Colonel Amori flipped her to her side and banged her head against the floor twice before getting to his feet once more and going to the computer.

Isa did not even have the breath to yell at him to stop.

She watched in horror as the map lit up with warnings and errors, before the central generator went dark and the error reading "Danger! Catastrophic Failure" flashed across the screen.

Three other generators went dark and Isa's eyes slid shut, a different, sharper pain spearing her body.

■■

For two days, Isa was confined to the small cell with a screen secured over the window in the door. The screen played a constant stream of news, discussing the horrors of the destruction in Saera.

The words of the news reports cut into her like knives.

"There has been no word from the Syndicate as to the cause of these horrendous explosions..."

"Over one-hundred thousand workers, engineers, and scientists were killed in the explosions that destroyed Saera..."

The information was painful. She could not sleep around the noise and the pain in her chest. After two days and several runs of the same news with very few developments, Colonel Amori showed up in the cell, turning off the screen.

"I plan to return you to Anon, now," he said darkly, crouching next to her as she remained on the ground, her eyes half-lidded. "Do you want me to drug you to keep you from misbehaving, or will you be a good Elite and come quietly?"

Isa turned her exhausted eyes on him. Slowly, she lifted her wrists and extended them, showing her compliance.

"There's a good girl."

She was silent and cooperative as she was taken back to Anon. She did not bother to note where they had been for four days, or what time they had left and when they finally returned to the capital. Her exhausted eyes projected images of the generators flashing before going blank on the screen. Her ears were ringing with the horrible news on Saera, the number dead, and the silence of Venus and the Syndicate. Her body was pulsing with pain at her bruised and battered ribs and back.

Even if she had the strength to move, she knew she would be unable.

The sun was setting when they pulled into the garage of Anon Tower. The car parked and turned off. Colonel Amori got out immediately. Isa remained still, staring blankly ahead.

Colonel Amori walked around the car and opened her door.

"Come on," he coaxed, his tone annoyed.

Still, Isa did not move.

"I told you to get out of the car," Colonel Amori snapped, grabbing the raw skin of her freed wrist and pulling her out. "You're dead to the fucking world. Go sleep or something."

He shoved her toward the elevators and Isa's legs mechanically carried her.

Colonel Amori saw her to her level of Anon Tower, but then left, going to his own room.

The house was quiet when she walked inside. She stood in the living room for several long moments, trying to process where she was and what she needed to do next.

Her mind remained blank.

Her legs started moving to her bedroom, but she stopped. She went to look in on Rayal, finding the caretaker fast asleep, very pale, and shaking with a sheen of sweat over his face. Isa closed her eyes in pain and turned away, knowing that she was causing the pain to the man who had watched over her for years, the man who had kept her relationship with Remus a secret, and the man she considered a brother.

Isa had to leave his room. She went to her bedroom and collapsed on her bed, shaking uncontrollably.

The next day, she dressed and went to work as though nothing was wrong. When she walked into the building, she passed the frantic operators, her sudden appearance causing them to pause and stare. One of them quickly dialed Remus' office.

"Elite Remus, Elite Isa is here."

Isa barely made it to the control room before she was swarmed by her Elites.

"Where have you been?!" Chronus gasped. "Do you have any idea what's been going on here?!"

"You had us worried!" Anders said quickly. "Where were you?!"

"Saera's generators exploded and destroyed the city," Maki relayed. "It killed almost everyone and the entire area is in ruin."

"I know!" Isa snapped. The Elites stopped immediately, surprised at her tone. "I am fully aware of what happened in Saera."

"Then why didn't you come here for *four* days?" Anders hissed. "Everyone is frantic trying to figure out what happened."

"Generators can go into catastrophic failure," Isa said darkly.

"That's hardly the point," Chronus hissed. "You should have rushed here to help us handle this situation. Everyone is furious that we've been so silent."

"What do they expect us to do?" Isa growled, pushing past them. "Go out there and help with the clean-up?"

Remus stepped in Isa's path, his eyes dark.

"Where the hell have you been?"

"It doesn't matter," Isa said coldly, trying to push past him, but he grabbed her wrist to stop her. She tried not to cringe at the flares of pain that shot through her arm at the contact.

"It *does* matter," he growled. "You have *never* gone missing like that. And for you to ignore a crisis like this is incomprehensible."

"Maybe," she started darkly, angrily yanking her arm from Remus, "I did not ignore it and I wanted you to handle things for a change. Are you all really so incapable of handling things without me?" She glared at all of them. "Perhaps I made the wrong decision about which Elites to appoint to this Syndicate."

The fourteen other Elites in the room were wide-eyed in shock at her words and the cold tone of her voice. They could only watch as she turned away and went to her office. After several long moments, staring in surprise at the empty hall, they turned to one another.

"What the hell just happened?" Hana whispered.

"That…that's not like her at all…" Anders said.

"She's been acting strange for a couple months now," Aolee said slowly. "But that is too drastic of a change."

"She must be pretty upset about Saera," Maki murmured. His brow furrowed. "Maybe she knows something about it."

They all immediately turned back to the direction the Golden Elite had left.

That night, when Isa returned home, she went to Rayal's room and sat on the bed, passing her hand gently over the caretaker's forehead. Rayal stirred, his eyes fluttering open as he let out a strained breath. He slowly turned over in bed and looked at the Elite.

"Isa…" he whispered, trying to sit up.

"Shh, shh," she cooed. "Stay quiet." She sighed heavily. "I'm going to call the hospital and have you admitted," she murmured. "You are getting worse."

"I am so sorry…" Rayal whispered.

"Why are you apologizing?"

"I don't know why I'm not getting better."

"You do not have to apologize for that," she said. "I should apologize for not admitting you sooner."

"Did they call about the blood tests?" Rayal asked, cringing in pain.

"…no," Isa said. "I'll ask them when I call."

She forced a smile and stood, walking out of the caretaker's room and to the main room. She called the hospital and asked them to immediately send someone over to retrieve and admit Rayal. As she was finishing the call, the door alarm rang and Remus walked into the living room.

Isa felt her heart fall into her stomach. She had been hoping that the Syndicate would leave her alone for several days. She needed time to process what had happened, and she did not want Remus or the other Elites pestering her with questions.

She hung up the phone and turned to Remus, preparing herself.

"Is there something you want?"

"Yes," Remus said, his eyes showing his barely-contained anger. "I want to understand what the hell is wrong with you."

"With *me*?" Isa snapped. "There's something wrong with me?"

"Clearly," Remus growled. "You are not acting like yourself at all. You've been distant, absent-minded, even *angry,* it seems. You say you don't sleep, you're losing weight at an alarming rate, and then, in an enormous planetary crisis, you *disappear* for four days."

Isa stared at him before shrugging.

"Okay, and?"

"That's all you're going to say?" Remus snarled.

"There's nothing else to be said."

"Where have you been for the last four days?"

"I needed time to myself, so I left the city," Isa said. "The question *I* have for you, is why you did not come here to find me and see that Rayal is nearly dying?"

"I *did* come here, and I *did* notice," Remus corrected. "I called the hospital yesterday and asked them to take him in. He's still here?"

Isa could not stop the way her eyes widened. It showed her that Colonel Amori had found a way to block the request, forcing Rayal to suffer without the medical care he so clearly needed.

Isa let out a shaky breath and turned away, closing her eyes and trying to remain calm.

"Isa?" Remus asked, his tone changing. "What is it? Is Rayal still here?"

"Yes, he's here. I just called the hospital again." She took a deep breath and slowly let it out, turning around and staring at Remus with a cold expression. "You should go home, Remus."

Remus blinked at her in disbelief.

"I'm not going anywhere until you tell me what's wrong."

"Nothing is wrong."

"The hell nothing is wrong," Remus hissed. "I *know* you, Isa. And you are not the type of leader to run off during something this catastrophic." He stalked forward, fixing her with a serious stare. "You know something about what happened to Saera that you are not telling me."

"What is that supposed to mean?"

"You would not be acting like this if it was a catastrophic failure of the generators. You are acting like this was *planned*, like there was some plot to destroy Saera."

Isa scoffed, trying to hide how much the words hurt.

"I don't need to stand here and listen to your conspiracy theories," she growled, walking away from him and to her bedroom. Remus quickly followed.

"Why won't you just *talk* to me and tell me what is wrong?" he snapped.

"*Nothing* is *wrong*, Remus!" Isa barked, rounding on him.

"I'm not a fucking moron, Isa!" Remus retaliated. "I know that something is wrong!"

"You don't know anything!" Isa growled, shoving him away. "You're not the leader of this planet! You have no right to come in here and accuse me of conspiring to destroy one of the most important areas of this planet!"

"For the past four days, you haven't been the leader of this planet!" Remus retorted. "You ran away from your responsibilities and left your people in fear! How dare you call yourself the Golden Elite after a stunt like that?!"

"Shut the fuck up!" Isa bellowed, shoving Remus away once more. "You know nothing about it! You don't know everything about me, Remus!"

"Clearly, since the Isa I knew would never abandon her people!"

"I did not abandon them!" Isa screeched. "I have done everything in my power to serve this planet and its people! I put myself *after* them! How dare you say that?!"

She tried to shove him once more, but he grabbed her wrists. She tried to free herself, but his grip was firm and the pain that radiated from her wrists caused her to weaken.

"Do you feel how weak you are right now?" Remus hissed. "How can I believe what you're saying when *years* of knowing you and being by your side tells me that your behavior the past few months has been terrifying? You're clearly *lying* to me!"

"Stop accusing me!" Isa bellowed, still trying to free herself from Remus' vice grip. "Let go of me!"

"Not until you tell me what is wrong!"

"I can't!" Isa bellowed.

"Can't or won't?!"

"I can't tell you because, for the last fucking time, *nothing is wrong*!"

"I don't believe you!" Remus snapped, forcing her to take a step backward. She managed to get one arm free and lashed out, slapping him across the face.

"Get your hands off me."

"No. I told you, not until you tell me what is wrong," Remus growled. "I am your Silver Elite. I am supposed to help and protect you, but I can't fucking do that if you're keeping secrets from me and falling apart in front of my eyes."

"I am not falling apart!" Isa snapped. "I am doing what I need to!"

"And what is that?!"

Isa finally got her other hand out of Remus' grip and she tried to slap him again. She knew the situation was spiraling out of control. She wanted to tell Remus what had happened with the Colonel, but the guilt she felt was too intense. She had been the one that had chosen to destroy Saera rather than the Syndicate or Anon. Even though it had been a calculated choice, and she tried to minimize the damage, she felt responsible for what happened to Saera. She felt responsible for not finding a way to deal with the Colonel before things got this out of hand. She felt the weight of the deaths of her people on her chest.

Isa felt like she had failed as a leader, choosing the lives of her Syndicate over the lives of those in Saera. The Colonel's words about letting her personal interest guide her decision to murder one-hundred thousand citizens of Tiao sliced into her like knives.

The pain was becoming too much to bear.

Isa's hands were once again trapped in Remus' and he loomed over her, his eyes dark.

"Fuck you, Remus!" Isa hissed angrily.

She stood still for two long seconds, her breath coming in short pants as her body shook.

Remus lunged forward and kissed her angrily, his weight bearing down on her, his anger and anxiety evident. Isa tried to worm away from him and he released her, but she grabbed the front of his uniform and yanked him closer, craving his contact, his control, his ability to make her forget everything.

His hands immediately went to her uniform, tugging at it sharply and forcing her pants down. With one hand still tangled in the front of Remus' uniform, she clumsily tried to help him, pushing the fabric down.

Remus' hand went up to her jaw and sharply grabbed her, pushing her back and looking into her eyes for a brief moment. He then turned her around, grabbing one of her arms and pulling it behind her back, pushing her to bed.

She fell heavily, her face pressed into the blankets and her back and chest shooting with pain as Remus pushed down on her bruised body.

In the brief, frantic moments before Remus entered her, Isa hoped that he would remove her uniform, that he would see the bruises and realize that there was, actually, something very wrong and it was far worse than they believed. She wanted him to see her injuries and protect her, as he always had, to take the situation out of her hands and keep her safe.

But this was not their normal routine. There would be no gentle removal of clothes, no sensual exploration of each other's bodies. This was a rough, desperate need, something to dispel the tension and frustration they both felt, and Isa did not want it any other way.

Remus kept one hand pinned behind her back, furiously moving behind her as her other hand reached back to hold his hip, keeping him close, quietly urging him to continue.

Between that moment and the moment that Remus collapsed on top of her, gently kissing the shell of her ear, Isa felt herself slip further into darkness.

■■

Isa sat in her NCB chair, trying to concentrate, but she could not focus. The situation with Saera was the main focus of the day, but every time she got new information on what had been found at the site, she felt herself cringe in pain.

She was responsible.

Finally, she turned off the NCB chair and sat upright, cradling her pounding head in her hands.

She was beginning to feel desperate.

A beeping in her ear caused her body to tense quickly. The automatic voice listed the number and she felt sick to her stomach. Slowly, she reached up and pressed the area in front of her ear to activate her phone.

"Yes?"

"I have to express my admiration for you," Colonel Amori said. "Not only did you decide to destroy Saera, but you seem to be destroying your Syndicate without my help."

"Is there a reason you called other than to taunt me?"

"Oh, you are tired today, aren't you?" the Colonel laughed. "Also, I will say how impressed I was at your display last night."

Isa's eyes shot wide, confused and worried.

"You certainly are a capable woman," the Colonel leered. "You can take quite a bit of *abuse*. It's impressive, to say the least."

Isa ground her teeth together.

"I can tell that I've underestimated how much you can *take*," he said, his voice dripping with disgust. "So, let's see how much more you can take, Elite Isa."

"What are you talking about?" Isa demanded, fear coiling around her chest.

"Perhaps you should see what is going on with the other Elites."

Isa's fear doubled, images flashing through her mind of the Elites storming into her office with the intent to kill her. She scrambled out of the chair, the Colonel's sick laugh cutting short as he hung up. She went to the door and opened it just as another Elite called her phone.

"Isa!" Maki said quickly. "You better get to the control room. The Officials are here to arrest Remus."

Isa's vision narrowed, her mind repeating the words over and over again.

She ran down the stairs to the main control room and darted in just as the Officials were turning the Silver Elite around and restraining him.

"What is going on here?" Isa barked.

"Elite Isa," one officer said, approaching her. "We are instructed to take you to the hospital immediately."

"The hospital? What are you talking about? Why?" Isa demanded, backing away from him as he approached. "Under what charges are you arresting him?"

"It is best not to discuss it here," the officer said, glancing at the other Elites in the room.

"You are placing my Silver Elite under arrest, and I demand to know under what charges Venus has ordered this."

The officer sighed, glancing around once more before lowering his voice.

"Elite Remus has been charged with rape of the Golden Elite."

"What?" Isa barked, her brow furrowing, though her eyes had gone wide. "That's preposterous!"

"There is evidence," he said carefully. "Video evidence."

Isa was silent, staring at the Officials in surprise. She turned to the other Elites in the room, who had heard the charges and were looking between their two superiors worriedly. Isa glanced at Remus, who stared back at her, confused.

"I will discuss this with Venus," Isa said sharply. "Release him at once."

"Elite Isa, I follow Venus' orders. I must arrest him. You may discuss this with Venus and, if the charge is removed, we will immediately release him. But you must be seen by your doctor at once."

"I have no need to see a doctor," she snapped. "I am fine."

"Venus insists that you have a medical exam and have a medical professional determine the damage," he said. He glanced around once more and then lowered his voice. "Elite Isa, if I may be so bold, if these charges are not unfounded, do not fight for him to be released."

"Be quiet," Isa hissed. "I will go to my doctor at once."

She left the confused Bronze Elites in the control room as Remus was hauled away, discreetly being taken through the emergency stairs to the garage so rumors would not spread about the Silver Elite's arrest.

Isa was guided by the Officials to the hospital and into a room where Dr. Busen was waiting. He nodded to the Officials to leave the room. They filed out and closed the door behind them.

"Dr. Busen, there has been a misunderstanding," Isa said quickly.

"Has there?"

She swallowed hard, hesitating.

"Venus sent me the security footage," Dr. Busen said. "You do know that it can still be considered rape even if you are in a relationship with your assailant, yes?"

"It was *not* rape, I consented," she said sharply. "I am not lying, Michael."

The doctor sighed heavily and motioned for her to walk to the exam table.

"Isa," he started as she sat down, "is there something that you want to tell me?"

"You, too?" Isa asked with an exasperated sigh. "Dr. Busen, only a few days ago, the largest production area for this planet's food was destroyed. I have been overworked and stressed. I'm sure things looked bad on the footage, but I was consenting and I want my Silver Elite released."

"I'm not talking about last night," Dr. Busen said. "I'm talking about your health in general. I can tell just by looking at you that you have lost a considerable amount of weight, and you look ill."

"I'm fine."

"I would like to do an exam."

"You do not have my permission to do so," Isa said sharply. Dr. Busen straightened, blinking in surprise.

"Why not?"

"You don't need to question why," Isa told him, her eyes dark. "You do not have my permission. It is mine to give for whatever reason I choose."

Dr. Busen stared at the Golden Elite. He was more worried than before.

"I have been ordered by Venus to perform a vaginal inspection to determine the severity of—"

"It *was not* rape."

"I understand that," Dr. Busen said.

"Then put that in the report and tell her to release my Silver Elite."

"Isa—"

"*What?*"

Dr. Busen sighed heavily, briefly pinching the bridge of his nose. "I'm calling Paul, this is beyond my level of expertise."

Isa ground her teeth together.

"What does that mean?"

"Something is wrong, and I am not skilled enough to get it out of you," the doctor said.

"I told you what was wrong," she said. "I've been overworked and stressed. It happens. I have to lead a fucking planet. It can be a little stressful at times."

Dr. Busen stared at Isa for several long moments, trying to let the silence get too heavy for the Golden Elite. However, Isa did not back down, staring back at him with the same intensity.

"I will have to put in my report that there is evidence of sexual intercourse due to the security footage, but no damage to indicate rape," Dr. Busen said quietly. "She will still have him punished."

"I will handle Venus," Isa said, standing. "You just file your report and leave the rest to me."

"Isa," Dr. Busen said, starting after her. She did not turn around, leaving the room. "Isa!"

The Golden Elite left, not once looking back at the worried doctor.

Isa went directly to the jail to pick up Remus only one hour after she left the hospital. Her mind was sharply focused on the task. She already knew how the day was going to go. She knew she had to find a way to protect Remus from Colonel Amori, and that meant keeping him at a distance.

Remus tried to get Isa to tell him what happened, but she only told him that Venus had ordered his arrest because she believed he raped her due to the security footage in her mainframe of the previous night.

"We took care of that years ago," Remus hissed. "Those cameras don't record on her mainframe."

"I am aware."

"Then how did the footage get to her mainframe?"

"I don't know, Remus," Isa growled. "I don't really have time to figure it out. We have to deal with this fucking mess with Saera, and then I have to keep meeting with Colonel Amori because he can't make up his fucking mind about what he wants to do."

Remus stared at Isa, confused and worried.

"Isa—"

"What?" she snapped when he did not continue.

"You're scaring me."

Isa took a deep breath.

"Venus wants to see us immediately," Isa said. "Let's just handle this situation. Alright?"

They were silent for the remainder of the drive back to the Syndicate Building. They walked through the building silently, ignoring the eyes of the other Elites. Remus followed Isa down a hidden stairwell to the audience hall for Venus, which was deep under the Syndicate Building, heavily protected by Venus' most advanced security codes. They both went through the retinal and DNA scans, their bodies checked by sensors for hazardous material before they were let into the audience hall.

The single chair still looked small in comparison to the cavernous room and Venus' enormous hologram. The figure remained still, waiting for Isa and Remus to approach. Isa stood on one side of the chair as Remus stood on the other.

"*I have programmed a visual translator for B-X210016 to understand this conversation*," Venus started, the words appearing across the hologram's front as she spoke. "*The video of what happened between you two last night shows that you have raped your Golden Elite.*"

"Dr. Busen determined that it was not rape," Isa spoke up. "Our relations last night were consensual."

"*Regardless if they were consensual, sexual relations between Syndicate Elites is illegal and punishable by death,*" Venus said. Isa and Remus both tensed. "*You both were engaged sexually at the Academy, as well. Have those relations continued through these years in the Syndicate?*"

"Yes, Venus," Remus answered.

"*As this is still a private matter, and we are in a crisis with Saera being destroyed and Gihron refusing to compromise, I will not order your execution, B-X210016,*" Venus said, addressing Remus. "*However, you are ordered to terminate all sexual relations immediately.*"

"With all due respect, Venus," Remus started, "we—"

"I agree," Isa said. Remus rounded on her, his eyes shooting wide. "I will obey your command, Venus. We will terminate our sexual relationship immediately."

"*I will delete this footage and we will mandate that all Officials who know of the rape allegations remain silent, as well as anyone who has seen the footage.*"

"Isa?" Remus whispered, staring at the Golden Elite in shock.

"As you command," Isa said, bowing her head.

"I will meet with you at a later time when I have completed my diagnostics on Saera," Venus concluded. *"Until then, try to reach a compromise with Gihron. Meet with the Colonel's delegates separately and see if they can convince him to agree to our terms."*

Isa bowed her head and turned to leave. Remus looked between Isa and Venus, confused, surprised, and hurt. He opened his mouth to protest, but decided that trying to convince Venus would be futile. Instead, he bowed his head quickly and hurried after Isa.

"Isa!" he called, running to her. "What the hell was that?"

"What was what?"

"What you said in there!"

"It's for the best, Remus."

She picked up her pace and made her way to the parking garage, Remus close behind.

"Are we even going to discuss this?"

"Remus, it has been a trying day," Isa said, watching her car pull up to the loading area. "Go home."

"No," Remus snapped. "You are not going to push this aside. I deserve an explanation, Isa!"

Isa got into her car, ignoring Remus as he tried to get her to talk to him. She remained sitting upright in her seat, her eyes ahead of her as her car slowly pulled away from the loading area and started toward the street.

Once Remus was out of sight, Isa bent her head forward and pressed it against the front console, her breath leaving her shakily.

She felt so confused and frightened that she did not know how else to react. She had to keep everyone at a distance. If she let them get close, Colonel Amori would harm them, turn them on her…

She closed her eyes tight and her hands went to her head, fisting her hair angrily, her entire body shaking.

She did not want her relationship with Remus to end. He had been her biggest support. Whenever he held her at night, she felt safe, like she could finally be comfortable and not be held to the standards of the Golden Elite. Remus had been the most important part of her success.

It hurt her to say those words, that they would end their relationship.

But Isa could not have Colonel Amori continue to use Remus as motivation. She had broken many rules, but she had always been sure not to cause harm to the people. Seeing the horrors that had befallen

Saera, Isa had been forced to wonder if she had made the wrong decision.

Perhaps she should have chosen to destroy the Syndicate.

Isa was barely composed when she walked into her home. Rayal was setting the table for dinner, his hands shaking.

"Rayal?" she asked, surprised. "I called the hospital to pick you up."

"You did?" Rayal asked. "They never came by."

Isa closed her eyes and let out a defeated sigh, rubbing her forehead.

"I'll call again."

"Is something wrong?" Rayal asked nervously.

"The next person who asks me that is going to end up with two broken arms," Isa growled, walking past him. Rayal watched her, startled by the words.

"I apologize if that was out of line," he whispered.

Isa stopped and took a deep breath, her eyes closing.

She could almost hear the Colonel laughing as he watched her tear her own life apart. She knew she was acting harshly against everyone who had stood by her through the years, and she was hurting her closest support system, but she could not think of a better way to keep them safe. The Colonel watched her. If she told them what was going on, that she was being blackmailed by the leader of Gihron, he would turn them on her, killing Rayal as well. He would then kidnap her once more and force her to watch as Anon was destroyed and Gihron took over her planet.

She tried to think of any way, of any means, to communicate to the Elites, or to Dr. Busen or Paul, that something was wrong. Every form of communication was monitored, cameras set up all over the city and every place she worked. The network was too extensive. It was meant to be extensive to keep her safe, but it had her trapped in a very dangerous situation.

Her head began spinning.

The alarm went off at the door and Remus stormed in, his eyes alight with fury. Isa whirled around.

"You do not get to push this conversation aside," Remus growled, walking to her. "I deserve a fucking explanation."

"It's for the best, Remus," Isa said, retreating.

"*Why?*" he snapped. "*Why* is it for the best?"

"We can't act like this anymore, Remus!" Isa barked. "We were young and stupid when we started this relationship, and we knew that we would be discovered eventually."

"Yes, and you said that when we did, you would fight. You would *fight* for us!" Remus snarled. "You said that we needed to revolutionize the planet, that we had to fight her and her laws against us and humans, and now that this comes up, you just lie down and *take it*!"

"Fuck off, Remus! You don't seem to get how dangerous this is!" Isa bellowed.

Rayal stood to the side, his eyes wide in horror as he watched the fight rapidly unfold.

"I know *exactly* how dangerous this is!" Remus snapped. "I have had to live with it just as you have, but I was always ready to fight for you! I promised I would stand by you, and that I would never let Venus determine our relationship! You do not get to make this decision alone! You owe me more than that!"

"I don't *owe* you anything!" Isa yelled. "*You* are the one who owes *me* for saving your fucking life, or have you forgotten that you're a degenerate?!"

"Who the fuck *are* you?!" Remus snapped, stepping closer. "Anytime anyone said anything like that you would deny it and say that no one owed their life to anyone, and now you're saying that I *owe you*?!"

"I did save your life, didn't I? I told them that if they had you killed, I would rip everything down, and then I even went so far as to help you when you started to class jump, even after all that shit when those teachers—"

"Don't you *dare*!" Remus barked, looming over Isa. "Not you. Don't you even dare."

"It's true, isn't it?" Isa growled. "The truth fucking hurts. You would have been dead if it wasn't for me."

"Maybe it would have been better that way!" Remus bellowed. "At least then I wouldn't have to watch you fall apart in front of me and attack everyone who has ever cared about you. We all know something is wrong, Isa! We're not fucking stupid! And now, you just decide that we need to obey Venus' order? We're ending this relationship we have managed to maintain against all odds for nearly fifteen years?!"

"What do you expect when you pull the shit you pulled last night?!" Isa snapped. She regretted the words the moment they escaped her lips.

"What?" Remus hissed.

"Maybe there was a fucking reason Venus thought you *raped* me!"

Remus' expression changed immediately, his eyes showing his horror. He shook his head, confused and terrified.

"I didn't," Remus murmured. "You never told me to stop, you never said no. You told me to keep going."

Isa shook her head, staring at Remus, trying to show with her eyes how truly sorry she was for what she had said. She swallowed hard and closed her eyes.

"Just leave, Remus."

"No, Isa, you are not going to accuse me of rape and then tell me to leave!" Remus snapped. He loomed over her once more. "Is that what it was to you?"

"Remus, get the fuck out of my house."

"No."

"You asshole, I'm trying to protect you! We're ending this! It's over! Get out!"

"What do you mean you're *protecting* me?!" Remus snapped.

"Get out, Remus!"

"No!" Remus barked. "You can't protect me when you can't even protect yourself! And it's clear you can't protect the people either, since you disappeared on them when Saera was destroyed and one-hundred thousand people were killed!"

Isa's fists balled and she threw a punch at Remus, connecting with his jaw and causing him to stumble. As he straightened, he lifted his hand and struck her across the face with his palm.

"Stop!" Rayal bellowed, running forward.

Remus grabbed Isa's shoulders and pushed her almost violently against the wall.

"You're going to tell me what the fuck is going on, Isa!"

Isa did not have time to register how quickly the situation changed.

Rayal leapt on Remus' back and wrapped his arm around the Elite's neck, pulling him backward quickly, forcing him to release Isa.

"Stop it! Both of you!" Isa cried.

Remus turned around and forced his fist into Rayal's stomach before tossing him carelessly to the ground, looming over him as he coughed, trying to scramble to his feet.

"Remus! Enough!"

The Silver Elite rounded on Isa and was about to push her against the wall once more when Rayal shoved all of his bodyweight into the Silver Elite's side and both sprawled to the ground. The caretaker lifted his fist and punched the Silver Elite twice in the face before Remus' fist raised and he punched Rayal.

Remus felt his fist connect with the high part of Rayal's cheekbone, the bone giving way under his altered strength and collapsing inward, blood immediately erupting from his eye as he let out a pained cry and rolled to the floor, his hands going to his face.

Remus scrambled to his feet, looming over the groaning caretaker, his fists still clenched in anger.

"Stop!" Isa bellowed, leaping at Remus. However, the Silver Elite swept the Golden Elite aside, causing her to collide with the wall with an audible thud, disorienting her.

Seeing Isa hit the wall caused Remus to return to his senses slightly. He turned away from Rayal and went to Isa, fear consuming him.

"Isa!"

However, a figure darted between him and the recovering Golden Elite. Both Isa and Remus stared in surprise at Rayal, who stood on shaky feet, his arms spread to shield the Golden Elite, his breath heaving as he cringed, copious amounts of blood pouring down his face.

"Don't you dare touch her," he growled.

Remus looked over the damage he had caused Rayal and then turned to Isa.

"Isa, I didn't mean—"

"Get out, Remus," Isa said, standing, her expression cold and pale. "Get the fuck out. If you ever touch me again, I will kill you myself."

Isa reached up to her ear and told the phone to call an EMU. Once she had placed the call, she rounded on Remus again.

"I told you to get out!" she bellowed, shoving Remus. "*Get out*!!"

Remus left, though he stood in the hallway for several long moments, his eyes distantly lost in the floor, trying to recall how things had escalated so quickly.

Isa ran back to Rayal, who had collapsed to the floor and pulled him into her lap, holding his head gingerly and trying to assess the damage, pressing her hand over the wound.

"Just hold on," she whispered. "The EMU will be here soon."

■■

Six hours of reconstructive surgery and Isa finally received the news that Rayal was going to survive. They were not sure if the original eye, which they managed to save, would ever be able to function properly again, but they would reconstruct his eye at a later time, if he wished.

The doctors also told her that Rayal's internal organs were under an enormous amount of stress. They were worried that he was suffering from an autoimmune disease and his body was attacking itself, but they had to run more tests before they could determine the problem.

Isa stood outside Rayal's room, watching a nurse take notes on a few of the monitors hooked to the unconscious caretaker through the observation window. It was very early in the morning, so the hallway was deserted apart from the Golden Elite.

When the door opened at the end of the hall, and Isa heard boots approaching, she closed her eyes and suppressed the shiver that ran through her body.

"What an impressive show," his cold voice said in her ear, his breath fanning over her skin. She turned her head away from him, cringing as he stepped behind her.

"How did you get in here?"

"You underestimate me, my dear," he breathed. "He showed such loyalty to you," Colonel Amori said, glancing in the room. Isa turned her eyes back to Rayal. "It is a rare trait to find. Aren't you fortunate." He chuckled. "I wonder what he would do if he realized that *you* were the one who actually put him in the hospital with his face nearly destroyed."

Isa stared at Rayal, recalling all the times that the caretaker cared for her, being sure to pick up the sleeping Elite when she pulled all-nighters at the Syndicate, or bringing food to be sure she ate when she was working. She recalled the late nights when he would just sit with her and talk about mundane things to help her unwind. She remembered the jokes and the shared dinners. Rayal had become a very important part of her life.

"To think," Colonel Amori continued, "had you not upset Remus, this might not have happened."

Isa felt her body tense, but she did not turn to look at the Colonel.

"Of course, we could go so far as to say that, had Remus not been degenerate, he would not have the temper to do so much damage. Oh, but wait," Isa could feel the smile in the Colonel's voice, "you saved his life, didn't you? So, had you let him be executed, he would not have done this, either. It really does come back to you in the end, doesn't it?"

Colonel Amori pressed his cheek to the side of Isa's face.

"You are doing beautifully, my dear," he said. "You're tearing apart the Syndicate without my guidance, and everyone is losing faith in the Elites after the extended period of silence when Saera was destroyed. You are so predictable. Trying to keep up appearances when the truth is, you're no longer running Tiao—*I am*."

Isa closed her eyes, her stomach flipping.

"And I plan to rip this planet apart and show the Altereye System what true power is."

The Golden Elite swallowed hard, staring into the room once more. Colonel Amori, seeing her unwavering gaze, turned to Rayal.

"The poor boy is going to be in pain for months, if not years, after that. And just in time to see you fall as you tear the Syndicate further apart."

"I'll kill you for this," Isa whispered.

"You can try," Colonel Amori said. He pressed his body to her, and she choked back her disgusted response. "You forget who has the power here."

He pressed his hand against her hip, holding the handle that controlled the microbionic cells.

"Should I do it?" he breathed. "Should I save him from suffering?"

Isa did not respond, acutely aware of his hand as he pressed the handle to her buttock.

"No…not yet," Colonel Amori said. He kissed her cheek. "But soon, my dear. Soon."

■■

For three weeks, the Syndicate limped along with Isa not speaking and Remus angrily avoiding everyone. The Bronze Elites did their best to keep the affairs of the planet in order and fend off questions from other planets about Saera and how it would affect trade, taxes, and a slew of other problems.

There were rumors flying around about Isa losing her mind, suffering from dementia or some other mental disorder that had her jumping at every sound, appearing so sickly, and pushing them away whenever they tried to ask what was going on.

But Dr. Busen could not get her to come in for an examination. Nor could Paul.

Instead, the Bronze Elites felt like the planet was entirely on their shoulders. When strange codes and files began appearing in the mainframe, causing viruses to put down the Syndicate for several days, they were sure that things were on the verge of total collapse.

They all knew that Isa was hiding something.

One day, at a meeting, Isa collapsed, which gave the Elites an excuse to call the hospital and have her admitted.

Dr. Busen ran every test he could while she was unconscious, finding her severely malnourished, her heart beating irregularly, and her blood pressure so low she had passed out from staying upright so long.

Once she awoke, she demanded to be let out of the hospital, and despite everyone's protestations, Venus granted her leave from the hospital because another virus had ransacked the Syndicate communications board, making it impossible for them to contact any foreign planet, though other planets could contact Tiao. Venus needed Isa back at the Syndicate to work on fixing the problem.

However, Isa seemed to be unable to figure out the virus.

Rayal was released from the hospital three weeks after his surgery. He was still weak and tests were still being run to determine what illness he had, but he was allowed to return to Isa's service.

When he appeared in the house, he was startled to see Colonel Amori in the living room with Isa.

"Welcome home, Rayal," Isa said, forcing a weak smile.

"Forgive me for disturbing you," Rayal said, glancing at Colonel Amori. There was something about the man that disturbed him greatly, but he could not determine what. He recalled—what he assumed was a hallucination—seeing Colonel Amori standing behind Isa when she was looking in on him at the hospital. Ever since, he could not stop thinking about the cold eyes of the Gihoric leader.

"Are you feeling better?" Colonel Amori asked, as though he had known Rayal for years.

"Yes, thank you," Rayal lied. He bowed his head and walked to his room, but stopped on the other side of the door to the guest hall. Something felt very wrong about having the other planetary leader in the home.

He pressed his ear to the door, but he could not determine their conversation. However, he did hear the tone of Isa's phone. Her muffled voice sounded once more and then the sound of footsteps coming toward the door.

Rayal ducked into his room, glancing at the security monitors as Isa walked out of the living room and down the guest hallway, through the pool area and made her way back to her office to receive a call.

Rayal turned to watch Colonel Amori, who was sitting in the living room, bored. He glanced at his wrist several times and then pulled out his phone, staring at it intensely for several long minutes. Rayal watched every movement, waiting for something, though he did not know what.

For the first time in months, Rayal did not feel like he was walking around in a fog, and even though he was still getting used to barely being able to see out of his left eye, his mind felt clearer.

He watched intently, never tearing his eyes away from the Gihoric leader.

After ten minutes of sitting in the living room, looking at his phone, Colonel Amori groaned and stood.

"Where the fuck is she?"

Rayal tensed.

He watched Colonel Amori walk across the living room toward the guest hall, as though he had lived there his entire life.

Rayal walked out of his room, stepping in front of the Colonel, his eyes sharp.

"Out of my way," Colonel Amori ordered.

"No," Rayal said. "You are not permitted into the rest of the home. It is custom."

"Fuck your custom," Colonel Amori snapped, trying to push past him. Rayal was startled by his demeanor, but he jumped in front of the foreign leader once more.

"I must insist."

"*You?*" Colonel Amori scoffed. "You insist when you couldn't even stand up to Remus?"

Rayal's eyes narrowed. "How do you know about that?"

"Get out of my way."

"No," Rayal snarled. "You stay away from her. You even think about harming her, and I will kill you."

Colonel Amori laughed, the sound sending chills down Rayal's spine.

"That's quite the joke," he said. "Hate to break it to you, kiddo, but it's a few months too late for that." He reached up and pat Rayal's cheek. "But it's cute that you think you can stand up to me."

Rayal smacked his hand away and pushed the foreign leader back.

"You stay the fuck away from her, you asshole."

Colonel Amori reached into his sleeve and pulled out a small blade, grabbing Rayal's shoulder and pulling the caretaker onto the knife.

"I'm sorry, I didn't understand that," Colonel Amori said. He removed the blade and stabbed Rayal again, causing the caretaker's body to slip into shock. There was no pain, yet. Rayal could only take in the situation with wide eyes. "Did you say to stay away from her? You clearly don't know who you're talking to."

He dropped the caretaker unceremoniously to the ground and stood over him with the bloody knife.

Rayal, with one arm wrapped around his stomach, lifted his hand to his ear and pressed for his phone.

"Isa!" he gasped. "Get out of the building! Now! You're in danger!"

Colonel Amori chuckled and crouched next to him.

"You're a bit slow," he said, smiling darkly. "Isa is under *my* control now," he stated. "She listens only to me."

Rayal cringed, trying to stay conscious as his body began tingling. He groaned and closed his eyes, pressing his finger to his phone once more.

"Emergency," he hissed. "Anon Tower…Golden Elite…"

"What a pesky little thing you are," Colonel Amori groaned, lifting his knife again.

The door opened on the other side of the hall and Isa darted forward, immediately grabbing the Colonel and pulling him backward, away from Rayal.

The Colonel turned and his fist and the handle of the knife connected with Isa's cheek. The Elite fell to the ground, the Colonel, kicking her in the stomach again.

"You want a repeat of this? Fine."

He kicked her several times, Rayal's eyelids fluttering violently as he slipped into unconsciousness, the automated voice on the phone telling him that they were locked onto his location and they would be there in three minutes

Isa did not fight back as the Colonel rained blows on her body. She was tired, and merely happy that the Colonel's temper was directed to her and not Rayal. In her mind, she deserved the beating, for not doing her duty and protecting the planet from Colonel Amori. She felt helpless and powerless, unable to help those in her close circle, let alone those who looked to her for guidance and protection, such as those in Saera.

A soft chime went off at the door and Colonel Amori quickly went to his knees next to Isa, placing a hand on her shoulder.

"Elite Isa? Can you hear me?" he called, gently shaking her.

She wanted to spit at him for pulling such an act.

The door to the guest hall opened and Officials and EMU team members swarmed forward.

"Elite Isa? What happened?"

Isa was too tired and in too much pain to answer.

"I found her like this," Colonel Amori said, his eyes wide and frantic. "I don't know what happened. First she walked back here and then Elite Remus, and the caretaker. I heard noises, but…" He shook his head, opening and closing his mouth repeatedly.

"Where is Silver Elite Remus?" one Official asked.

"I don't know," Colonel Amori said, shaking his head.

"Okay, back away from her," the Official ordered. Colonel Amori obeyed and Isa closed her eyes, trying to fall asleep to escape the hell that had become her life.

When the Syndicate was notified of the attack, and the statement from Colonel Amori about what had happened was relayed to them, panic and confusion set in.

Chronus went to Maki's office, finding Anders, Aolee, and Hana already there.

"What the hell is going on these days?" Chronus murmured. "Rayal just got out of the hospital *today*, and now he's back in because of multiple stab wounds?"

"Isa was beaten as well, though it seems the knife wasn't used on her," Maki added. "Colonel Amori found them. He was over there discussing terms."

"Like he's been doing for the last how many months?" Hana groaned.

"He said Remus was there as well," Anders said. "After the rape accusations last month...I'm starting to wonder if they're both losing it."

"You think he did it?" Chronus asked.

"I'm just saying that he was the one to put Rayal in the hospital to begin with, and he and Isa did get into a heated argument to the point where he struck her."

"But it's *Remus*," Aolee murmured. "He would sooner kill himself than beat Isa like that."

"It doesn't make much sense," Maki agreed.

"But you saw the footage from the night Venus said he raped Isa. He hasn't been gentle with her lately," Anders pointed out. "I don't know, I'm just thinking that maybe we shouldn't allow Remus near her for awhile."

"He's the Silver Elite. We can't exactly tell him to stay away," Chronus said.

"Do we have any proof that he was the one who did this?" Maki pressed. "Did we trace him? Where was he when this happened?"

When no one answered, Maki turned to his chair and did a quick search. When he saw the answer, he showed it to everyone else.

"He was *here*..." Aolee murmured.

"Who else has access to that level that could do this?" Hana asked, confused.

Chronus looked thoughtful.

"...maybe they didn't need to have access," he whispered. "Maybe the attacker was already there." He looked at Maki. "What was the date of Colonel Amori's arrival?"

■■

The Elites of the Syndicate were not performing as expected on their work, all distracted by other things. Remus was steering clear of everyone, constantly replaying the night that he had hurt Isa and put Rayal in the hospital. The Bronze Elites were doing intense investigations of their own, looking into the Colonel's arrival on the planet, and when things started getting bad around the Syndicate.

Isa was just trying to hold onto what was left of her sanity.

One day, Maki walked into her office, smiling gently when he saw her sitting at her desk with her head in her hands.

"Still have a headache?" he asked lightly.

She lifted her head, nodding.

"When is your next appointment with Dr. Busen?"

"Next week."

"Do you want me to call and see if we can get you in today or tomorrow?"

"No, it's alright," Isa assured. She forced a smile. "What can I help you with?"

"Well," Maki started, "I wanted to show you something." He walked to Isa's desk, setting his tablet down in front of her and leaning over to point to certain parts of the screen. "Here's what I've been able to find about Saera," he said. "First, this generator was hit, but the damage on the generator showed that it was not an internal problem. It was hit by something from the east side," he motioned with his finger, "which struck it, caused damage to the casing, allowed oxygen in, and caused the first explosion. But the second reaction, the one that hit this central generator, the damage was not as severe to the casing, meaning it wasn't as powerful. It was a Charge Burst, likely fired from the Uran-East Bunker, which is the closest place where a Charge Burst could still be used."

"I see…"

"What is strange is that, when I traced the Charge Burst records from the Uran-East Bunker log, I found that there was an override the day before the explosion that disabled its safety codes. The override was coded in Gihoric."

Isa looked up quickly, her eyes wide. Maki was watching her carefully.

"…what are you trying to say?" Isa whispered.

"That maybe you *didn't* appoint the wrong Elites to your Syndicate," Maki murmured. "And you need us to figure out what is going on so that we can help you."

Isa swallowed hard, a small glimmer of hope sparking in her chest. She let out a shaky breath and closed her eyes.

"I need help, Maki…" she breathed.

"Tell me how to help," Maki said. "Keep researching? Or something more drastic?"

"This is a very dangerous situation," Isa whispered. "Please, keep quiet, but do what you can."

Maki's hands suddenly shoved everything off the desk, grabbing the edge and turning it over.

Isa let out a startled cry, scrambling to her feet and running out of the office.

She knew, immediately, that Colonel Amori had triggered the microbionic cells. Soon, all the Elites would be swarming around her. She knew that the moment she revealed that she needed help, Colonel Amori would remind her how powerless she was.

"Isa! Isa! Wait!" Maki said, his voice betraying his confusion. "I don't know what's going on!"

Isa darted out the door, slamming the close button and going to the staircase. Maki pried his hands into the door and forced it open, bending it with his altered strength.

"Isa!" he bellowed.

Isa tripped half-way down the stairs and tumbled to the stair landing, her breath forced from her as she landed on her back. She tried to get up, but her body was weak and shaking. She forced herself to sit upright, but only had time to back against the wall before Maki's hand grabbed her neck and squeezed.

"I'm sorry…" she whimpered. "I'm sorry…"

Maki's fingers relaxed immediately and he backed away, looking at his hands in horror before looking over his Golden Elite.

"Isa…" he whispered. "Isa…I'm so sorry, I-I don't—"

"Get away from me!!" she bellowed, curling forward and tucking her knees into her chest. The other Elites, who had run toward the stairs to get to her office when the cells were triggered, stood still at the bottom of the landing, watching the Golden Elite sit and shake against the wall while they could only stare and wonder what had possessed them to run to her.

■■

Maki was determined to get an emergency status raised in the Syndicate. He continued to submit reports to Venus stating that there was clearly a problem that needed to be addressed, but the messages were never replied to, and when Maki tried to find them again, he could not. They had been deleted.

Maki rallied the Bronze Elites, telling them that they all needed to try different avenues to get a message to Venus or to other planets for assistance, explaining to anyone that their leader was being held hostage. However, still, they could not send transmissions to other planets.

That was when the Syndicate realized they were being primed for a planetary invasion.

They worked diligently, trying to keep their work secret while still discussing what they had found. The more research they did into the Colonel, the more they believed that he was the culprit. However, they needed proof, and a means to reach Venus.

Isa would walk by the Elites, sharing a silent look with them. Now that they were looking, they could see her silent plea for help.

One day, Isa received a call from the Colonel at her work.

"I've been working very hard on a surprise for you," he said when she answered the phone.

"I hate surprises."

"But this is a very important one," he said. "Your Elites have been trying to order my investigation and arrest. Naturally, I've stopped all their transmissions to her, but their constant attempts have given me much information about the way the Syndicate Building works. It's really an impressive feat of engineering, and it gives Venus a nice base to branch out into the whole city."

"Venus' codes are not here," Isa said darkly. "I have told you a thousand times."

"Yes, you have," he agreed. "But I'm not talking about her codes. Just her network. You know, if properly programmed, she could be quite the weapon."

Isa hesitated, the words causing fear to settle in her gut.

"What?"

"You really should go look downstairs, Isa," Colonel Amori whispered. "Your surprise is waiting for you."

Isa stood, walking out of her office and downstairs to the main control room, not sure what to expect, her anxiety increasing with every step.

However, there was nothing outside the ordinary in the control room. She glanced around, ignoring the eyes of the other Elites on her as they tried to concentrate on their work. Whenever the Golden Elite came around the other Elites, everyone got nervous.

The phone in Isa's ear beeped. She connected the call but said nothing.

"Further down."

Isa walked out of the control room and went to the operator's center.

When she walked in, she immediately noticed how quiet it was.

She descended the final steps, nervous, and looked around slowly. The robots and drones were moving around as normal. But every human was still, slumped over their desk or fallen on the floor, their eyes wide, their faces pale.

Isa let out a choked cry and backed up, her hand covering her mouth as she pressed her body against the wall.

"I wouldn't stay down there too long," Colonel Amori said in her ear. "Carbon monoxide will kill you if you're exposed too long."

"How did you…what…"

"I told Venus that the operators were plotting against her, that they were the reason for all the viruses in her mainframe, and then I gave her the codes to reverse her air filtration system for this level to neutralize the threat."

Isa's heart stopped.

"…you weaponized her…"

"I did," Colonel Amori said. "This is just a little reminder of who you really obey. Don't let your Bronze Elites do anything stupid. Once I have her reprogrammed, this planet will be mine."

Isa quickly ran up the stairs, darting through the control room and to her office. She immediately went to her NCB chair and issued an official order for evacuation of the building due to noxious gas.

As the alarms began sounding, alerting everyone to exit the building in an orderly manner, Isa ran to her desk, her breath short. She grabbed the gun from under her desk and checked the ammunition. Then, she put it under her uniform and ran to the stairs, entering the control room only to take one of the hidden exits before anyone could see her.

She got to her car and anxiously sat in it as it sped toward Anon Tower. She acutely felt the gun at her side, but it solidified her determination. Every time she closed her eyes, she saw the various dead, pale faces of the operators and human employees of the Syndicate. She felt a strong sensation tightening her stomach and chest, making it hard to breathe. Her eyes felt hot as she stared at the road ahead.

When she got to Anon Tower, the car immediately went into her car elevator for her level, and she sat and waited as the car ascended, the door finally opening to the hallway outside her home. She walked out and continued down the hallway until she reached the other elevator, pressing the button for the level she wanted.

By the time the doors to the elevator opened, revealing the hallway of apartments within Anon Tower, Isa's vision had become tunneled.

She walked directly to the door of Colonel Amori's quarters, overriding the lock and walking in, her eyes sharp around the room.

However, he was not there.

She checked every room before moving to the room next door, where his delegates were staying. She had suspected that he had sent the delegates back secretly to Gihron so that they would not interfere with his plans of taking over. She now figured that Colonel Amori was hiding in the other room, always watching her.

She overrode the lock and the door opened.

She was immediately overpowered by the horrific stench. It was thick and heavy, turning her stomach over repeatedly, but it was a stench she knew from her distant times in the lab where Elites were made. It was the smell of death.

She pulled the gun out, preparing to attack as she walked further into the living room.

The horror within was nothing she could have prepared for.

The delegates were dead, all four of them hanging from a beam in the ceiling above overturned furniture and scattered plaster. They were naked, their skin dehydrated and cracked from weeks of decay, their faces contorted in gruesome expressions.

In the skin on their chests were deformed words, carved into the skin.

"Death to Tiao."

One word for each body, the fourth body bearing the planetary symbol for Gihron—a circle with a twelve-pointed star.

Isa retreated behind the corner again, pressing her back to the wall and sliding down, her legs giving out from under her. She closed her eyes tight, but the image was seared into her brain.

She lifted the gun and pressed it to her temple, pushing hard against the skin of her forehead, cringing in a pain she could not describe. She felt the barrel of the gun against her head, her hand shaking as she pushed it harder against her skull.

Her entire being was shaking, sitting in the silence, trying to make sense of what her reality had become.

Isa let out a pained sob and dropped her hand, shaking and choking as her body reacted to the stress without tears.

Isa knew she was breaking apart.

But she could only sit and feel her seams rip open as pain tore through her.

■■

Two nights after the operators were found dead, Isa, who had been mandated to stay away from the Syndicate Building while the final inspections were completed, was called down to the level where Colonel Amori had been staying.

She tried to ignore the shaking of her body as she stood in the elevator while it descended. She contemplated not responding to Colonel Amori's request, but she did not want him in her home again when he came to retrieve her. Therefore, she obeyed, going to him, feeling half-asleep and on the verge of collapse.

She walked into his room, trying not to think of the horrors in the adjacent room. She looked around, unable to find the Colonel, so she walked further back into the apartment, finding him in the bedroom, staring intently at the computer screen as he sat at the desk next to the tousled bed. He did not even turn to acknowledge her.

"You've been moving a lot slower lately," he stated simply.

Isa did not respond.

"At least the evacuation has kept your Bronze Elites from doing anything stupid, but tomorrow will be the real test, won't it? Back to work again?"

"What do you want?" Isa asked tiredly.

Colonel Amori stood and turned to her.

"I almost have all her codes in place to completely weaponize her. Now, not only will she be able to establish "credible" threats, but she'll be able to neutralize them."

"Venus was not created to be a weapon," Isa said. "You've destroyed her."

"You and I have a very different definition of a weapon," Colonel Amori said. "She was already a weapon. Just because she couldn't immediately take human life does not mean she was not a *weapon*." He stopped in front of the Elite, smiling darkly. "But I can't weaponize, or shut her down properly, if I don't have her source coding." His smile widened. "Which you have."

Isa stared at him impassively and he chuckled.

"I've been patient with you. But now, I want those codes."

"I refuse."

"I didn't give you the option to refuse," he said darkly, his eyes turning dangerous. "Or do I need to remind you that I hold the life of your Elites, your caretaker, and all of Anon in my hands?"

"You do not need to remind me," Isa said tiredly.

"Then you will give me those codes now."

"No."

"I will destroy your Syndicate," he warned.

"Go ahead," Isa said, shaking her head. "You've already done most of the damage as it is."

"Oh, what's this? Giving up? Or is this some play for dominance?"

"You can destroy the Syndicate, Anon, the Elite Academy, but I refuse to be aid to you as you morph the artificial intelligence on this planet to be a weapon with which to terrorize the system. Now, you're not only destroying my planet, but the rest of the system, whether the planets are in the Alliance or not." Isa shook her head. "I will not allow you to become the tyrant of the Altereye System."

"This is an interesting change of character," Colonel Amori noted. "I was not expecting this reaction." He looked her over. "You know I can take them by force."

"Try it."

He lunged forward, grabbing her by her neck and throwing her onto the bed. She tried to roll off the bed, but he grabbed her and yanked her back, climbing on top of her and pinning her down, one hand around her throat. Her arms flailed wildly, trying to hit or scratch him, but he backed away, laughing darkly.

"You think I don't have power over you?" he asked. His other hand went down and angrily ripped open her uniform, pressing sharply on the area where he knew the processor was, where he could copy Venus' source codes that were stored within the Golden Elite's body. "You think I couldn't take what I wanted from you?"

Isa kicked her legs, but her body was weak from starvation, lack of sleep and stress. She felt her struggle being easily overpowered and fear began to consume her.

"Remember," he said darkly, moving his hand to reach between her legs, angrily grabbing her, "I own you. *All of you*. And I will take what I want."

Isa's hand fell to the desk next to the bed and found the magnifying lamp used in manufacturing and programming. Her hand closed around the lamp and she brought it, with all her strength, into Colonel Amori's head. The glass shattered, some going into his eye and causing him to yelp and reel backwards. He tried to brace himself on the bed, but his hand went into the glass shards that were still attached to the top of the metal frame.

Isa's arm swung back sharply and slashed the Gihoric ruler across the neck and chest, slicing into his skin and causing blood to soak the front of his shirt. He gasped and rolled away.

"You *bitch*!" he bellowed. "I'll kill you!"

Isa was immediately after him, lifting the sharp broken base of the lamp into the air before angrily plunging it into his side. He yelled and contorted, rolling away once more and onto the hard floor, landing on the open wound and letting out a cry of pain.

Isa leapt on him, raising the broken base of the lamp and repeatedly stabbing his chest and torso. She could not feel the blood that splattered onto her face and neck. Her body was moving as if on instinct, destroying the one who had been torturing her.

When her weak hand released the base of the lamp, her fist still continued the motion, slamming into the corpse of the Gihron leader, breaking a few ribs.

Finally, Isa stopped, her body shuddering violently as she collapsed on the floor, barely finding the strength in her limbs to remain upright next to the body.

She turned her eyes onto her hands, seeing the blood that soaked her skin, dripping down her arms and staining the ripped front of her uniform. Slowly, she lifted her hands to her face and bent forward, her body shaking. She did not care about the blood. She covered her face with her hands, the silence of the room ringing in her ears.

■■

The following day Isa returned to the Syndicate, but her head was low and her body was shaking uncontrollably. She had spent the entire night angrily washing her body over and over again, trying to get rid of the blood under her fingernails and in her hair. She then burned her clothes on the balcony, watching the flames intensely, every muscle tensed.

Then, she paced around her bedroom for five hours before she was expected at work.

But even as she dressed and prepared to go to the Syndicate, she felt no more ready to handle seeing the other Elites.

Isa had no idea how she was going to tell anyone about what happened. There was a part of her that believed she had not killed Colonel Amori, only angered him further to the point where he would flip the switch on the black handle and send all the Elites after her to kill her, forcing her to kill them to save her own life.

She could hardly remember dismantling and destroying the handle the previous night before tearing the room apart to find the second trigger for destroying Anon. She was not sure if it had been a dream, or if she had, in fact, destroyed both triggers.

With her entire body in a high state of stress, she felt as though she was about to break.

She managed to get past the control room without anyone seeing and stopping her, but as she was climbing the stairs, refusing to stand still long enough to use the elevator, she caught Remus on the floor below hers.

"Isa," he said quietly, surprised to see her. She jumped, her eyes wide and frantic as she stared at him. "Are…what is it?"

"Nothing," she said quickly. She turned to walk up the stairs, but Remus called her attention again.

"Isa," he said. She stopped, her shoulders tense as she debated with herself about turning around to talk to him or if she should just run up to her office. She felt as if her world was spinning very fast around her, about ready to collapse into chaos. "I have the reports on what they found for the building."

"Oh?"

"Do you want to see them?"

Isa turned around slowly. That was when Remus noticed that Isa's body was rocking back and forth shallowly, her breathing short. He stepped back, nervous.

"Why don't you come here into the hall and look?" he suggested.

Slowly, Isa walked to him, her steps short and her exhales shaking as she stepped closer. Remus watched her move, terrified.

"Are you…do you need to go to the hospital?"

"No, no, I'm fine," Isa blurted.

"You're clearly not."

"I said I'm fine. Just…just tell me what you want to tell me and then let me go."

Remus blinked, the words frightening him.

"I'm not holding you here, Isa," he said slowly. "You can leave if you really want. You're starting to scare me. What's going on?"

"Nothing is going on," Isa said darkly. "Just, tell me. Okay? I need…"

"What do you need?"

"…I don't know," Isa whispered, her voice breaking. "This needs to be over."

"What needs to be over?"

"…everything…" Isa's voice choked and her body began shaking so violently Remus was about to call an EMU for the Golden Elite. Isa could feel the Colonel watching her. She knew he was waiting for the moment to activate the microbionic cells and send the Elites after her. She could feel the anticipation building and it was choking her.

"Isa," Remus hissed. "Isa, look at me."

"…I can't do this…"

Her legs began giving out from under her and Remus grabbed her arm, pulling her up, his hands gripping her shoulders, trying to keep her standing.

But Isa was sure that Colonel Amori had activated the cells.

"Let go of me!" she screamed, shoving at him weakly and falling to the ground when Remus released her in surprise. She clamored to her feet, turning to run to the stairs, but her legs gave out at the top and she pitched forward, tumbling down the staircase, her left arm slamming against the railing and snapping instantly. She came to an abrupt halt, face down, on the landing.

"Isa!" Remus cried, descending the stairs after her. The commotion was heard by the other Elites, and they quickly went to the staircase.

Isa saw Remus rushing after her and her fear tripled. She forced herself to her feet again and struggled down the next flight of stairs to the next level. She darted onto the walkway but stopped instantly when she saw the gathering of Elites coming to inspect the noise. She let out a pained sound and sank to her knees in the middle of the walkway, looking around frantically as the faces of her Syndicate came closer, their eyes showing their fear and concern, their fast actions terrifying her.

Isa glanced over her shoulder, cradling her broken arm, and saw the control room through the glass railing.

In a terrified daze, Isa moved her legs under her just as the other Elites reached for her and she pushed all of her bodyweight into the glass panel, her body falling with the shattered glass to the floor below, connecting with the computers in the center platform of the control room with an audible crunch.

Her world went black.

••

Nearly twenty-eight hours of agonized waiting passed before the Elites heard anything about Isa. No one slept, sitting around the waiting room, fidgeting uncontrollably and getting up whenever they could not handle sitting.

The nurses and orderlies avoided the room, glancing in every now and then to check on the Elites.

The entire hospital staff was aware that there had been a horrible accident at the Syndicate and that Elite Isa was in critical condition, but no one knew details. However, nurses and other doctors went in and out of the large operating room, relieving one another for sleep as Dr. Busen worked diligently through the entire twenty-seven hour procedure.

As it neared twenty-eight hours since Isa had been rushed to the hospital, another doctor slowly walked into the room, holding her tablet to her chest, worried about breaking the news to the Syndicate.

As she approached, everyone who had been sitting swarmed around her.

"How is she?" Remus asked quickly.

"The damage was very extensive," she said nervously. "Fractured arm, eight broken ribs, a fractured hip, both clavicles shattered, and the left side of her skull was damaged severely." She took a deep breath, closing her eyes and swallowing hard. "Dr. Busen reconstructed everything, but we do not know if she will make it through the night."

All the Elites felt the pain radiate through their bodies.

"The next twenty-four hours are the most critical," the doctor continued. "We will have her on constant watch, and we will let you know of any changes. If she makes it through the night, her chances of recovery greatly increase."

"May we speak with Dr. Busen?" Chronus pressed.

"Not at the moment," she said. "He's sleeping. When he wakes I will let him know that you wish to speak with him. If you would like to return home, we can contact you with any news."

"Thank you," Remus murmured.

The doctor bowed her head and left the room.

The Elites turned to one another.

"What do we do?" Anders asked.

"We'll take shifts being here and being at the Syndicate," Remus said, his eyes distant on the ground. "For now, we just say that she's busy and that is why no one has seen her."

"And if she…"

"We'll prepare a statement if that happens," Remus said shortly. The other Elites dropped their eyes. "It's only one day until we know her chances," he continued. "We'll take shifts being here until we receive news. No one discuss what happened."

"Someone has to tell Rayal," Anders murmured.

"I'll do it," Maki offered.

"Thank you, Maki," Remus said. "Decide among yourselves who will go home and who will stay."

When the Elites had determined their shifts, Maki went to Rayal's room, where the caretaker had been recovering from the stabbing.

"Rayal," Maki greeted, his voice strained.

"Elite Maki…" Rayal said, setting his tablet aside, surprised by the Elite's visit. When he looked over the Bronze Elite's exhausted expression, his heart fell. "What is it?"

"There has been an incident," Maki started slowly, "with Isa."

"What? What happened?" Rayal demanded.

"I think...I think she suffered a psychotic episode," he murmured, his eyes dropping to the ground. "She started running away from everyone, she fell down the stairs and broke her arm. Then, when she stopped in the hallway..." He swallowed hard. "She threw herself through the glass railing into the control room—two stories. She crashed into the center platform."

Rayal let out a shaky breath and lifted a hand to his mouth, his eyes wide.

"Is she...she's not..."

"Dr. Busen just performed extensive surgery to try and repair the damage," Maki continued quietly. "They say that, if she survives the next twenty-four hours, it's more likely that she'll recover."

Rayal felt the tears gathering in his eyes. He tried to swallow them back, but they still spilled down his cheeks, causing his damaged eye to burn, but he did not care.

"It has something to do with that bastard Colonel Amori," Rayal ground out behind his teeth. "It has to."

"Are you sure?"

"I know he had something to do with this," he said, motioning to his stomach. "I can't remember what, but I *know* he was involved. And there is no way he's not involved in this somehow. You have to keep her away from him."

"Okay," Maki said, seeing Rayal working himself up. The Elite reached forward and put a calming hand on Rayal's shoulder. "We will do everything we can to protect her. We'll keep her away from Colonel Amori. I promise."

Rayal nodded slowly, taking a deep breath.

As Maki walked back out to the waiting room, he felt his stomach twisting irritably. He had known that the Colonel was dangerous, particularly with the way Isa reacted when he brought up Saera and Isa tried to plead with him for help. Being in the hospital, now haunted by the image of Isa flying through the glass panel and colliding with center platform, he kicked himself for not noticing the Colonel was a danger much sooner.

He approached Remus, standing in front of the Silver Elite and swallowing hard.

"I need you to come with me to Anon Tower."

"Why?"

"I think I know why this happened."

Remus straightened.

"I think Colonel Amori has been blackmailing Isa somehow, and I think it's finally become too much for her."

"You're on about this again?" the Silver Elite said, groaning and rubbing his forehead.

"The timing is perfect, Remus, and you should have seen the way she acted when I mentioned the Charge Burst on the generators. Don't you think it's strange that they *still* haven't reached settlement and we've heard *nothing* about their negotiations, yet we find Isa beaten in the hallway of her own home and Rayal stabbed next to her? He immediately pointed the finger at *you*. Who's to say that he wasn't the one who changed the cameras in Isa's room so that Venus would see you two? Remus, we need to place him under arrest."

Remus sighed, looking over Maki seriously.

"Let's at least speak to him and see if we notice anything out of the ordinary," he agreed.

"Fine, let's go."

"Right now?" Remus asked.

"Now," Maki said strongly. "If he is the reason she did this, we don't want to give him the chance to run before we can bring him to justice."

Remus was about to protest, feeling like he could not leave the hospital until he was sure that Isa would survive. However, Chronus' hand on his arm stopped him.

"We should probably get out of the hospital for a little bit," he suggested. "For your mental health."

Remus paused, thinking about what Chronus said, before he nodded slowly.

"Let's go."

Maki, Chronus, and Remus went to Anon Tower and made their way to Colonel Amori's quarters. As they approached the door to Colonel Amori's quarters, Chronus stopped and looked at the door where the Gihron delegates were quartered.

"Hey," he started, pointing at the door when the other two turned to him, "did the other delegates leave? I haven't seen them in…over a month."

"I don't recall them leaving," Remus said, shaking his head.

"They must have," Maki said.

Chronus looked at the door and started forward.

"Let's just make sure."

He pressed the alarm on the door, but no one answered. He then knocked, but still there was no answer.

"I guess they did leave," Remus said, stepping forward and pulling out an access card, passing it over the electronic lock to override it. When his identity was confirmed, the door clicked open and all three of them recoiled, backing across the hall, their hands over their mouths as the stench overpowered them.

"What the hell?" Chronus choked.

Remus quickly went forward when he recovered and stepped around the corner into the living room, where he stopped in his tracks and his eyes went wide.

"Remus?" Maki asked, walking in with his sleeve over his nose and mouth. "What—"

When both Bronze Elites saw the bodies strung up on the ceiling with their ominous message, their hearts stopped.

"Fuck..." Remus breathed.

"Do you really think he did this to his own men?" Maki hissed.

"They clearly didn't do it themselves," Remus said, noting the disheveled state of the room, indicating a struggle. "Let's go in there and take this fucker down. I don't care if we have to beat him into unconsciousness. We can't let this psycho run free."

The three left the room, closing the door behind them as they went into the next room. Remus opened the door with the override code and they stepped in quietly, listening for any noise from the Gihoric leader. When they heard nothing, they walked further in. There were files and drives scattered around the room, stacked high, some piles toppled to the ground.

"Where did he get all these?" Chronus whispered.

"What information do they contain?" Maki said, looking at the other Bronze Elite worriedly.

They walked through the living room and kitchen, quiet and vigilant, waiting to hear signs of the Colonel moving.

Remus led them into the hallway leading to the bedrooms and stopped at the door of the Colonel's room. From his vantage point, he could only see one boot on the floor in a huge pool of blood.

He darted in and turned the corner, finding the Colonel's corpse next to the bed, the bloodied lamp next to him. Maki and Chronus followed the Silver Elite, staring in horror at the dead foreign leader, their minds racing with thoughts about Colonel Amori's relation to General Decius, and the pride of the Gihrons. All five of the ambassadors sent to Tiao were dead, killed in gruesome ways.

"Do you think…" Chronus looked at Remus, unable to finish the question.

Maki walked forward carefully, reaching down into Colonel Amori's hand and pulling out some tangled strands of pristine blonde hair from his fingers. He held them up, looking at the other Elites in shock.

Remus lifted a hand to his mouth and closed his eyes tightly.

"She was trying to tell us all along, wasn't she?" Chronus whispered. "And she finally couldn't take it…"

Remus turned away from the body, cringing as he tried to calm his breathing.

"We have to come up with a story," Maki said strongly. "To protect her, to protect our people."

"We don't know the entire story," Chronus said. "We don't know what he did to Isa. If it was self-defense from the ravings of a madman, perhaps—"

"No," Remus said strongly.

"What?"

"This was General Decius' younger brother," he said. "If we say that he was insane, that he attacked Isa, and she killed him in self-defense, then he will deny it. He knew his brother his entire life. He would say that there was no way he was crazy."

"Clearly something was going on!" Chronus snapped. "He killed his own men! Isn't that proof?"

"These are Gihoric leaders we are dealing with, it has nothing to do with the truth or proof or anything like that," Remus said darkly. "General Decius' younger brother was murdered. That is all that matters. The reason is irrelevant."

"We need to cover this up, make it an assassination by someone else. The other delegates need to be dealt with as well, though that's going to be much harder to cover up," Maki mused.

"Do you think this is why she…" Chronus swallowed hard.

The other two Elites fell silent, wondering if Isa threw herself into the control room out of guilt.

■■■

Isa made it through the night and everyone anxiously counted down the hours. Dr. Busen came out and spoke to all of them, exhausted, Paul at his side as he tried to explain what he had done. He was worried, and his voice broke as he discussed the procedure, showing how difficult it had been on the doctor.

"If she survives..." he whispered, his eyes lowering, "there is no guarantee that she will be able to function as she once did."

Isa made it through the first twenty-four hours, but she did not wake, remaining in the coma for nearly two weeks.

During that time, the Elites were informed of the carnage found within the two apartments of the Gihron ambassadors. Each of them did their part in covering up what had happened, making up a story to tell Gihron. When Isa was still not awake after the first week following the incident, Remus broke the news to General Decius. He explained that the cleaning maids had discovered Colonel Amori's body as well as the bodies of the other ambassadors. He said that they were doing everything they could to apprehend the terrorists, a group that, he said, had been sending threatening letters to the Syndicate against allying with Gihron.

General Decius was furious, bellowing at the Elite that he asked Elite Isa to take care of his brother, to which Remus stated that she had also been attacked in the same night and was in critical condition.

The statement seemed to appease the leader, but only slightly.

He angrily demanded that their bodies be returned to Gihron, but Remus reminded him that bodies were not permitted to be transported off-planet without cremation. General Decius demanded a full autopsy report and then to have his brother's ashes returned to the planet.

Remus asked Dr. Busen to do the autopsy, stating that he was sure Isa had been the one to kill the Colonel. The doctor agreed, and did as he was asked, being sure that any evidence that could damn Isa for the crime was destroyed.

He then had the body cremated, watching the flames angrily.

Remus took seven criminals that were already sentenced for execution and pegged them as the terrorist group that had murdered Colonel Amori. He sent the status of the investigation to General Decius and the Gihoric leader demanded the criminals be put to death right away. He was sure to be virtually present for the execution.

During the second week of Isa's coma, Tarah learned of the horrible incident. She had gone to see Isa for their monthly lunch, since

Tarah was at school and could not see the Elite all the time, but she had been told by the other Elites at the Syndicate that Isa was in the hospital.

She quickly rushed there, but Rayal, still extremely ill and recovering from his wounds, kept her in the waiting room, telling her that Isa was very sick and that it was not a good idea for the young girl to see her. Tarah broke down, claiming that she knew Isa had been sick and she did not say anything to anyone.

Rayal took her to Anon Tower and stayed with her until she calmed.

In that time, Dr. Busen sat in the chair in Isa's room and watched the monitors, his chest tight.

At the end of the second week, Rayal was sleeping in the chair in Isa's room, a seat he had been occupying for over a week, while Dr. Busen sat against the wall, his legs tucked into his chest and his head resting on his knees, sleeping.

Paul walked into the room and looked at the silent Isa, watching the monitors document her status. He then saw Rayal and Dr. Busen sleeping and his heart fell. He walked to Dr. Busen and gently shook him.

"Michael."

The other doctor jumped awake, his eyes wide, startled.

"What?"

Paul squeezed his shoulder. "Why don't you come home and get some sleep?"

"No," Dr. Busen said, shaking his head and straightening. "Not until she's out of this coma."

"Michael, you haven't left this hospital in two weeks. It's not—"

"I can't leave her here alone, Paul," Dr. Busen said, his voice straining. "I need to know that she will wake up. I want to be here the moment she does."

Paul let a small, sad smile tug at the corners of his mouth. He sat next to Dr. Busen, putting an arm around his shoulder and pulling him closer. Dr. Busen rested his head on Paul's shoulder, closing his eyes and falling back to sleep immediately.

Four hours later, Rayal shifted in his seat and woke, confused and disoriented for several moments. He glanced at Dr. Busen on the floor with Paul, sleeping against the younger doctor's shoulder while Paul rested his head against Dr. Busen's, sleeping as well.

Rayal shifted as quietly as he could, standing and stretching out the kinks in his body without jarring his abdomen.

He walked to Isa, looking her over, the tears in his eyes.

"Come on, Isa," he breathed. "You can't leave us like this…"

Isa did not move.

For twenty minutes, Rayal paced around the room, timing his steps to the beeps on the heart monitor, his eyes down, his arms crossed over his chest.

Suddenly, the rhythm of the beeping changed and Rayal turned quickly to Isa.

When he saw her eyes opening and closing slowly, he let out choked breath and ran to her side.

"Isa?" he whispered.

Isa's eyes blinked slowly and her breathing changed. One of her fingers twitched and Rayal felt his heart soar.

"Dr. Busen!" he gasped. "Doctor, wake up!"

Both doctors jumped awake, startled. Dr. Busen scrambled to his feet and ran to Isa's other side, looking at her with wide eyes. When he saw her blink the one eye that was not covered with bandages, he put a hand over his mouth and his legs gave out from under him. He sank to his knees at her bedside and took her hand tenderly.

"Isa…Isa, if you can hear me, and understand me, let me know somehow…"

Isa's eyes closed and she let out a shuddered breath, her fingers slowly closing around the doctor's hand.

Dr. Busen let out a sobbed laugh and bent his head forward, pressing Isa's hand to his forehead, breaking down in relief.

■■■

Isa was in the hospital for eight long months. In that time, the people were notified that there had been a horrible accident that had almost killed the Golden Elite, but she was recovering and getting stronger every day.

But Isa got worse before she got better.

Now conscious, Isa could feel the pain of her reconstruction surgery and it was agonizing. She would often cry out in pain merely trying to shift in the bed. She went through physical therapy several times a day. When she was in bed, quiet, Paul would sit next to her and coax out the truth of what happened, Dr. Busen standing quietly behind the younger doctor, listening.

Paul did not relay to anyone what Isa told him until after he had heard the entire story, which it took several weeks to get out of Isa. He explained to the Syndicate the beatings, the microbionics, and what happened with Saera. He told them about Venus being weaponized, and that Isa had been the one to kill Colonel Amori.

The Syndicate went about damage control, all being tested and treated for the microbionic cells. In that time, they also worked on removing the codes that allowed Venus to be weaponized, reprogramming everything they could, though it was a very long process that left most of them frustrated and exhausted.

Isa called the Syndicate to her hospital room three months after the incident.

"There is something very important I want to discuss with all of you," she started quietly. "First of all, I must apologize for the hell I have put all of you through since this started." She swallowed hard. "I should have handled things differently, and I take responsibility for that. I hurt all of you, and I hurt myself in the process. I wish I could take it all back."

She took a deep breath, closing her eyes.

"This incident has proven to me that I am not fit to lead Tiao," she murmured. All the Elites straightened, their eyes widening. "Therefore, I will be stepping down as Golden Elite."

"Don't you dare do that," Chronus hissed. "No, Isa, you did everything in your power to save as many lives as you could. *We* should apologize to you for not understanding that you were asking for help. We learned too late that there was a problem, and because of that…" he trailed off.

"I did not handle the situation appropriately," Isa said slowly. "I let personal interests guide my judgments."

"How can you say that?" Maki whispered. "You took a calculated risk and chose the option best for you and your people at the time."

"That's correct," Anders said strongly. "You saved our lives, you saved the lives of everyone in Anon."

"…not everyone," Isa whispered. "The operators of the Syndicate were killed because of me. And Saera…" She closed her eyes. "I should have contained him the moment I understood he was dangerous. I did not handle the situation as the Golden Elite should have."

"No, you didn't," Remus agreed. He took her hand, squeezing it. "You handled it like a leader. An Elite would have immediately had him executed or arrested and risk war with Gihron, no matter the reason. You tried to keep everything contained to save as many lives as possible while not sparking a war with a very dangerous planet."

"But I have," Isa whispered. "I…I was the one…" She took a sharp breath in and cringed. The other Elites looked at one another before turning back to her.

"Isa, you have always been our leader, friend, and colleague," Hana said. "And you always will be. You cannot step down. We have too much left to do, and you are the only one who can do it."

Isa closed her eyes, leaning her head back against the wall behind her headboard.

"I don't think I can," she murmured.

"We will stand behind you," Anders said strongly.

"You know that we will always be here for you," Aolee seconded.

Remus smiled at her, his eyes showing his own pain.

"If you forget your strength, you can always turn to us for support," he said. "You are still the Golden Elite, and you will remain so, because your Syndicate is standing with you, and we'll remind you of the leader you are."

Isa looked at the gentle smiles and determined eyes around the room. She let out a broken chuckle and shook her head.

"You are all too good to me," she whispered.

The Syndicate Elites smiled wider, ready to stand by their Golden Elite to the end, even knowing that, eventually, Gihron would rear its head again.

Chapter Forty

Tensions were running very high at the Syndicate Building as they prepared for General Decius' arrival. Now knowing what had happened six years previous, Kailynn understood everyone's apprehension and worry. She found herself watching Isa's actions very carefully, looking for anything that would tell her the Elite was struggling to stay strong.

Isa was having difficulty handling the stress. Not only was General Decius coming to the planet himself, meaning that Isa would be confronted with the image of the man who tormented her, but she was also sure that Colonel Amori would be brought up in conversation.

On top of that, she was worried that she was already being spied on by the approaching Gihrons, which meant that every time the Elites would come to her and ask her questions about dismantling Venus, she would quickly quiet them and tell them to figure out a plan on their own and discuss things with Dr. Busen and Paul to be sure they were ready for the plan to move forward.

The day before General Decius was to land on the planet, a strange visitor came to the Syndicate Building.

Kailynn, who had refused to leave the Elite's side and sat in her office while the Golden Elite worked, remembered the woman from their time on Fortunea.

Isa straightened when she saw the woman.

"Vanessa…" she breathed, motioning her hand to close the hologram files she had been looking at on her chair. "I did not realize you were back."

"Only briefly," Vanessa said, hugging the Golden Elite. "I heard that General Decius was coming."

Isa's jaw clenched and she nodded slowly.

"I want you to know that, no matter what, you can ask for my help," Vanessa said. "Even if you think you're overreacting to something he says or does, I want you to call me immediately."

Isa smiled weakly.

"Thank you."

Vanessa turned to Kailynn, who was eyeing the woman cautiously.

"I recall seeing you on Fortunea," she said, walking to Kailynn. "I am Vanessa Henricks, a former professor of Isa's."

Kailynn shook Vanessa's hand, still unsure about the woman and surprised by how *warm* her hand was.

"This is Kailynn," Isa introduced. "One of our Intelligence Agency employees."

"Ah, it would be best to keep your eyes on absolutely everything until Gihron is pushed back to their corner of the system," Vanessa said with a strong nod. "And, also, Isa, *anything* that you need after Gihron is gone, please do not hesitate to ask."

Isa chuckled quietly.

"I'll be sure to keep you informed."

The following day, when General Decius' ship landed on Tiao, everyone was put on high alert and under high security. Everyone understood that the Gihoric leader was dangerous, even if they did not know his grudge against Isa. The Elites of the Syndicate were the most on-alert, constantly monitoring Venus' mainframe to be sure that there were no unexplainable changes. However, monitoring Venus' mainframe was a nearly-impossible task since implementing the various viruses and blocks against the computer's attacks on Isa. There was concern that the viruses slowing down Venus' machines would make her more vulnerable to hacking, but they were not about to expose Isa to the violent, painful attacks from the artificial intelligence.

Therefore, every employee of the Syndicate was told over and over again to keep a sharp eye out for anything out of the ordinary and to immediately report to Rayal or Remus.

Kailynn had special orders to keep a close eye on Isa—orders she took very seriously.

General Decius, Colonel Ikan, and their delegation of seven Gihron officers were brought to the Syndicate in the late afternoon and were led to a large conference room where the entire Syndicate, Rayal, Kailynn, and nine other employees, advisors, military personnel, and intelligence agents were waiting to receive the Gihron politicians.

The moment General Decius walked in the room, everyone felt the tension become nearly unbearable. The General's uncanny resemblance to his brother made many of the Elites question if General Decius was four years older than Colonel Amori, or if they had been twins.

Isa stood when General Decius walked into the room, and the others followed suit.

"General Decius," Isa greeted. "We are honored that you have made the long journey to be here in person to negotiate the peace between our planets."

"It is an honor to finally be on the illustrious Tiao in the presence of the Golden Elite," General Decius said, bowing his head.

Isa motioned for the Gihoric leader to take the seat opposite her on the long conference table. General Decius walked to his seat and stood by the chair, waiting for the rest of the delegation to decide on their seats. Tension was so high that everyone was watching everyone else and it was not until Isa sat that the rustling of chairs being occupied filled the room.

Isa took the brief moment to take a deep breath and prepare herself.

She sat straight in her chair, leaning forward, her shoulders square with General Decius.

"I understand that you have had a very long journey," Isa started, her voice strong and unwavering. "Therefore, I do not want to discuss the entire peace agreement today. I would like to introduce your terms for your conditional surrender and we will discuss them in detail over the following days of your visit."

"Very well," General Decius said, reaching into his breast pocket and pulling out a drive. He placed it on the table and slid it down to Isa. Before it could reach the Golden Elite, Remus grabbed it off the table, looking it over briefly before plugging it into the table and allowing the terms to appear in front of every seat.

At first, Kailynn glanced down at the terms until she realized that everyone's eyes were elsewhere.

Some Elites were staring down other members of the delegation, but Isa and General Decius were locked in an intense staring contest. Isa's eyes were unwavering, her blinking perfectly timed, but she never tore her eyes from General Decius. Likewise, he did not turn away from her. The feeling between the two leaders was growing more intense by the second. Kailynn saw the two of them waiting for the other to back down. General Decius seemed sure that Isa would break the intense gaze first, and Kailynn believed she would, as well, considering her past with Colonel Amori.

However, in the growing silence, General Decius finally turned his eyes to the terms in front of him.

It was only after he looked away that Isa also looked down at the terms.

"I see that you have opened your terms with title one demanding the transfer of all government offices to humans over the next twenty years," Chronus said, turning to the Gihron leader. "If I may be so bold,

General Decius, you were quick to say that the Alliance did not have a right to dictate the way any planet ruled itself or structured its society. Yet, you believe that Elites are unfit to rule over Tiao."

"I do," General Decius said with a strong nod. "Elites are created from the technology that forced humans from Earth. We have studied the trends in your society and have found the frightening pattern in the way the Elites change your society."

"Regardless of any imbalance that the Elites create in our society, I agree that it is a problem for which the Syndicate must determine the appropriate course of action, not Gihron," Isa said strongly, looking back at General Decius.

Several of the human employees of the Syndicate, Kailynn included, were startled by the strength in Isa's voice.

"We will not negotiate on this title," Isa said strongly. "You will strike it from your terms."

General Decius was still for two long moments before his lips pursed briefly and a half-smile took over his face.

"If I recall correctly, Elite Isa," he said, leaning forward in his chair and resting his arms on the table over the terms of surrender, "this was a point that we tried to negotiate six years ago, when my brother was in your care."

Several bodies in the room tensed, from both Gihron and Tiao. However, Isa did not flinch at the words.

"That is correct," she affirmed. "And my stance has not changed in six years. The Syndicate will remain in the hands of the Elites and Venus."

"I wonder," General Decius started, looking at Isa with darkness in his already-dark eyes, "had we come to a compromise on this issue, if my brother's stay would not have been so extended, and he could have returned home *alive*."

Isa's eyes were cold.

"I do not compromise to my planet's disadvantage," she said. "I will not compromise on any of the terms listed in title one. You will strike them."

General Decius' smile widened.

"And if I am unwilling?"

"I did not give you a choice."

The tension was making it difficult for everyone to breathe. While Gihron was getting increasingly nervous, most of the Elites, Isa, and

General Decius were unwilling to back down, making tensions rise higher.

"Then perhaps this negotiation was premature," General Decius said.

"If you wish to return to senselessly destroying all of your technology and killing your men, then we will meet you in battle," Isa said with a shallow nod. "However, considering that *you* were the one to reach out to me with a conditional surrender, I do not believe you have the resources to continue a longer battle. It is for you to decide if you are willing to doom your planet further by straining your assets, or if you are willing to comply with *my* terms and stop this war so we could both get on with leading our planets."

"You were quick to accept my conditional surrender, which tells me you were desperate to end this war."

"As Tiao is not a militaristic society and, therefore, does not believe that war is the only answer, I am quick to stop any war in which I find myself involved."

General Decius chuckled.

"You are not as I remember you, Elite Isa."

"Glad to know that I exceed your expectations, while mine were perfectly met."

Kailynn had to purse her lips and turn away from Gihron's side of the table to hide the laugh threatening to bubble out of her at Isa's sharp words.

"You insolent—"

"Colonel Ikan, sit down," Isa ordered, turning to the second-in-command of Gihron. The man, half-standing from his chair, turned to General Decius, who nodded quietly. He slowly lowered himself to sit, though his eyes were brimming with rage.

"Moving on to title two," Isa continued, "I agree that all those involved in this war shall pay appropriate reparations. From the analysis of the debris collected from the battles, we have determined that two percent of reparations will be paid by Urya, twelve percent by Ulam, twenty percent by Jakra, twenty-nine percent by Hyun, and the remaining thirty-seven percent will be paid by Gihron."

"How did you obtain those numbers?" one delegate asked, confused.

"From all the debris and refuse that we collected after each battle," Isa said. "Tiao was sure to clean the mess made after every fight, as Gihron would not."

"It would appear that Tiao is quite skilled at cleaning up messes," General Decius said darkly.

Kailynn expected to see Isa waver at the words. However, she did not.

She turned back to General Decius. "Pardon, General Decius?"

"I said that Tiao is skilled at cleaning up messes."

"Is that meant to illicit a certain response?" Isa pressed.

Kailynn was having trouble breathing with the tension in the room.

"There was no response sought," General Decius said, his tone clipped. "Merely an observation from our previous dealings, Elite Isa."

Isa took a deep breath and leaned back in her chair.

"I was under the impression that you were here to discuss a peace agreement," she said. "Was I mistaken?"

"No," General Decius assured, "but I believe we all know that there is a topic we are avoiding."

"That topic being?"

"My younger brother's brutal murder six years ago," General Decius said, nearly growling. "As I cannot ask for your execution in peace agreements where I am the losing party, I'll have to settle for demanding that you tell me the truth of what happened."

"The truth was discussed at length in the autopsy and the Official reports," Isa said strongly.

"Do you believe those reports to be the truth?" General Decius challenged.

"I trust in my Intelligence Agency and the medical professionals that performed the autopsy. Therefore, yes, I do believe those reports are the truth."

General Decius stared at the Golden Elite, as if trying to decide if Isa was lying. Tensions were growing in the room. Gihron delegates were watching the Elites' reactions, but all of them were stoic, apart from the uncomfortable shifting when the tensions grew too high. However, their faces never betrayed their discomfort. The human employees were the ones that were showing their worry about the direction of the meeting. Kailynn was sure that none of the humans—other than Rayal and herself—knew the truth of what happened, and she hoped that their confused expressions would assuage the suspicions of the Gihrons.

"Shall we continue?" Isa asked, sitting forward once more.

"Yes."

Isa discussed broad aspects of each of the titles of Gihron's surrender. There were five titles to the surrender, and when they reached number four, Isa paused briefly.

"Title four states that Gihron will join the Crescent Alliance, should an exception be made about the size of military forces for the social preservation of Gihron." Isa looked at General Decius seriously. "The rules of the Alliance cannot be altered or amended without a ruling majority from planets *after* Venus has approved the possibility of an amendment."

"This would not be an amendment," General Decius said. "It would be an exception."

"No."

"No?"

"I will not make an exception for Gihron's military forces," Isa elaborated, her voice clear and strong. "This was a topic discussed in great length years ago."

"Indeed, and I have reason to believe that it was the reason for my brother's death."

"It did appear to be part of the reason, as the assassin group did confess to being concerned about a militaristic change to the Altereye System should Gihron be included on the Alliance trade routes."

"Do you believe, if my brother had not been here so long, he would have returned to me outside of an urn?"

"I do not deal in what-ifs, General Decius," Isa said. "And I do not live in the past. That was six years ago, and currently we are discussing peace agreement terms to end a war that you began upon allowing your men to kidnap and kill four Elite prototypes."

"No, Elite Isa," General Decius corrected. "*You* started this war six years ago when my brother was killed in your care."

"As I just said," Isa said coldly, "we are discussing peace agreement terms to end the war. I will not waste any more of my time, or yours, discussing hypothetical situations. If Gihron wishes to become a part of the Alliance, they will abide by the same rules as all other planets. There is no discussion or negotiation, and certainly no exception."

The meeting continued for another hour, as all major questions were discussed and answered before agreeing to meet the following day to amend terms and find a solution that was beneficial to all planets involved.

Kailynn had to ride back to Anon Tower with Rayal to avoid suspicion, but as she sat in the car, she could only stare blankly at the road. They followed General Decius and his convoy, as they were going to be staying on another level of Anon Tower during the negotiations.

"Isa was very impressive today," Rayal murmured.

Kailynn nodded. "No shit…"

General Decius and the others were shown to their rooms by members of the Intelligence Agency and the security robots for the building, which would be placed along the halls—it was explained to them that it was for their security, considering previous relations with Gihron, and while everyone seemed content with the response, everyone who knew the truth about Colonel Amori knew that the increased security was to watch them for suspicious activity.

When Kailynn finally made it up to the Golden Elite's level with Rayal, Isa had already poured herself a drink and brought the bottle to the coffee table. Rayal went to Tarah, explaining what had happened while Kailynn walked over to Isa after grabbing her own glass.

Isa remained in the living room for hours, silent, her head cradled in one hand as her other hand loosely held an empty liquor glass. Kailynn sat next to her, smiling gently as she leaned her head against the back of the sofa.

"You were amazing today," she finally whispered.

Isa slowly turned her eyes to Kailynn.

"I can hardly remember half of what I said," she murmured. "I went on autopilot."

"It certainly didn't seem like it," Kailynn said, reaching out with one hand and resting it on Isa's, carefully removing the empty glass from her grip. "Why don't we go to bed?"

Isa nodded, her eyes closing. She stood and walked toward her room, but stopped when her eyes lifted to the door. Kailynn stopped next to her.

"What is it?"

Isa did not speak, her eyes locked on the door of her bedroom, though lost somewhere in time. Kailynn looked between the Golden Elite and the door and then carefully took Isa's hand.

"Do you want me to stay in my room?" she asked, understanding that Isa was likely wondering if she was going to be watched once more. Isa's fingers tightened around Kailynn's and she swallowed hard before shaking her head.

"No," she whispered. "I don't want to be alone."

Kailynn also squeezed Isa's hand.

"Why don't we stay in my room, then?"

The Golden Elite nodded quickly and they both turned and walked to the guest hallway.

■■

"I was sure you would not come."

"I feel that it is very important to discuss some of General Decius' terms with you," Isa said. "The past two days of negotiations have been difficult, and I think it is important you review the progress we have made."

"I have reviewed the submitted terms. I agree with all sections under titles two, three, and five. I do not agree with Gihron being brought into the Crescent Alliance as stated in title four, and I do not consent to any of the terms in title one."

Isa took a deep breath and slowly let it out.

"Venus, allowing the humans to take over the Syndicate would take considerable strain off relations between Tiao and the other planets of the Alliance. While Tiao does not teach its population about the fate of those on Earth, most of the other planets in the Alliance learn of the weaponized humans and they know that Elites were created using that technology. It makes many nervous."

"The information from Earth is incomplete."

"That does not appease the other planets," Isa protested. "While I agree that we should not allow this to be a term to which we submit for Gihron's surrender, it is something to consider for the near future."

"Humans are too irrational to rule themselves. They let self-interest guide their actions and their greed dictate their society. As a whole, humans cannot be trusted to govern themselves."

Isa closed her eyes, trying to brace herself. While she did not think it was wise to anger the artificial intelligence while in daily negotiations with Gihron, she knew she had to start moving things in a different direction on her own planet.

"If I can bring Gihron to heel as I hope," she started, "then I think it would be best to implement a system to phase out Elites and have humans take over the Syndicate."

"*That is not your decision to make,*" Venus said sharply. "*When Gihron is brought to heel, you will be submitted to final degeneration testing, and should your levels be found elevated, you will be replaced.*"

The Golden Elite did not flinch at the words. She had been expecting it.

"Gihron is not the only planet discussing that Elites need to be removed from power," Isa continued. "Several planets would be much happier to work with Tiao if the Elites were not involved. You will recall the disastrous state of affairs when Gattriel was in power. I was able to mend these relationships through very careful politics, and the only reason I was able to do so is because I am not a typical Elite, nor is Remus, nor is anyone else in this Syndicate. The planet is stronger now than it has been in over one hundred years and that is because the most human-like Elites have come to power."

"*There is no data to support that that is the reason for the increase in our society's strength.*"

"No data?" Isa asked incredulously. "The data is in front of you."

"*The data in front of me suggests that you let personal interests guide your actions six years ago and, therefore, you started this war with Gihron.*"

Isa bit back the angry growl in her throat.

"Perhaps it is not the Elites, nor the Syndicate, nor the humans that are the problem," Isa started. "Perhaps *you* are the cause of the distress in the Altereye System."

"*While you have done impressive research on the social implications of my rule over the years, compared to previous data on humanity, and the information gathered on planets outside our sphere of control, the data proves that my rule has peacefully run this planet for hundreds of years.*"

"Perhaps that was the case," Isa said, "but that is no longer so. That was not the case when, six years ago, Colonel Amori was able to hack into your system and weaponize you. You have updated your technology to be compatible with the changing times, but humans have changed in ways beyond your comprehension, and things are not as peaceful as you seem to believe."

"*Your evidence?*"

"The Significants," Isa said strongly. "You understand that the greatest threat to our society comes from Trid, where the non-citizens speak to one another, and form friendships and bonds that people in Anon and other areas of the planet do not. Your fear of unity is your biggest weakness," Isa continued. "You want to keep everyone disjointed by not speaking to one another, by being so desperate to feel like they are not alone in this universe that they have to pay other human beings to sit and speak with them because their own families will not do so. This proves that your system is not working. Perhaps there is no unity in the people that will overthrow you, but there is also no unity in the people to stand strong behind you."

"They know that they need me, and they respect me as their leader."

"No, they do not!" Isa snapped. "If they did, the Elites would not have been necessary for you to maintain your power. But the Elites, and you, have not changed while society has. How can you expect to grow stronger if you cannot come back from every challenge different than you were when you started? Every challenge to your authority has been met with violence and death. At the Academy, you almost had me killed because I was getting out of hand, and your response was to exile my professor and kill one of my closest friends, but I have also changed. And I refuse to bow to you when I have been running this planet without your assistance for decades."

The machines in the room began roaring as Venus' machines heated in anger.

"You believe you can defy me?!" she bellowed, her beeps ear-piercing and causing Isa to flinch. *"You bow to me because I created you. I decide if you live or die, and when you will step down as Elite. I will remove you from power now, if you continue with this behavior!"*

"If you do that, you doom your existence," Isa said strongly. "Replace me if you wish, but the new Elite that comes in will be a soft-shelled, obedient child and Gihron will destroy them. General Decius is demanding that you be shut down, or he will find a way to attack your core processors and destroy you."

Venus' hologram was flickering angrily as her computer ran all the algorithms it could, calculating risks and outcomes as Isa straightened.

"Your time has come to an end, Venus," she declared.

Her legs buckled under her as the pain rocketed through her from the processor in her chest reacting to Venus' attack. However, she bit back her cry of pain, her lip bleeding as her teeth sliced into her flesh.

"*You will yield!*" Venus ordered. "*The people see me as their leader, and they will always see me as their leader!*"

■■■

Isa sat in her living room late that night, a cold compress over her eyes as her headache throbbed behind them. Dr. Busen had just left after checking up on her and giving her an update about his research into shutting Venus down and keeping the Golden Elite alive. Remus sat across from the Golden Elite as Kailynn sat next to her.

"You're being extremely reckless about this," he whispered.

"I know."

"It's a miracle that she hasn't killed you yet," Remus continued.

"At this moment, she needs me too much," Isa said. "As soon as this mess with Gihron clears up, I will not be able to keep her at bay. She'll either replace me or kill me and make it look like an accident and then replace me."

"You realize that we can't handle her on top of General Decius, right?"

"We can," Isa assured.

"Isa," Rayal said, poking his head out of the kitchen, "there's a broadcast on all frequencies. It's even on the security monitors. It's from Venus."

Groaning, the Golden Elite stood, walking with her eyes half-closed into the kitchen and seeing the hologram of the computer's face on the twelve screens across the kitchen wall.

"—submit. There are those that would seek to shut me down and destroy me, but I will never yield to such threats or terrorist tactics. I am the life of this planet. If I am destroyed, all communications will go down, defenses as well. All phones, NCB, NGS, and GAL platforms will be rendered useless. The economy will collapse and the planet will starve. Remember this and report all those that claim they will never submit. There are those that would seek to shut me down…"

The computer repeated the message as Remus groaned and rubbed his head.

"She clearly does not care about the delicate nature of having Gihron *on-planet* while she's making this broadcast on *all frequencies*."

He closed his eyes. "We're never going to get them to agree to terms if they think we're fighting with the artificial intelligence we always claim as being our ruler."

"I'm sure Gihron already knows that she's not really our leader," Isa said. She closed her eyes and leaned her head against Kailynn's as the Significant put her arms around the Elite's waist, holding her upright as Isa tried to stay strong from the violent attack from Venus earlier that day. It had now been a pattern for two days—Isa would be in horrendous pain for the day apart from two hours before her scheduled meeting time with Gihron, during the entire meeting with Gihron, and at night when Venus wanted her rested for dealing with Gihron the next day.

They listened to the message several times, thinking over the panic that would probably be running rampant through the people.

Kailynn wondered if people were terrified of losing their NCB, NGS, and GAL platforms because they would not know what to do with themselves, or if they were worried about being unable to produce food or keep the city clean with the incredible number of humans. She wondered if those thoughts were even crossing the minds of the people, or if they were just terrified at the thought of change.

"Come on," Isa said, pulling Kailynn with her as they walked out of the kitchen.

"Where are you going?" Remus asked, following the Golden Elite. Tarah and Rayal followed behind the group, walking with them through the guest hallway, pool area, and into Isa's office.

"Remus, can you piggyback her frequency?" Isa asked.

"Probably."

"Alright, let's record our response."

"We're going to respond?" Kailynn asked, surprised.

"Venus told me that the people see her as the leader, and she's trying to use fear to prove that to me," Isa said, walking to her NCB chair and sitting in it, activating it in safe mode so Venus could not immediately find her. "I'm going to prove to her that the people would rather follow me than her."

"You don't know that, though," Kailynn murmured.

"I know my people," Isa said with a nod. "And I have information she won't like the people knowing."

"I can set you to record on a back-up and work on the piggyback once you are clear of the chair," Remus said, walking to Isa's chair and typing a few things into one of the control panels.

"That will work."

Isa opened up her hologram recording and took a deep breath, preparing herself, forcing her eyes to open past her headache and her face to relax, while her eyes still shone with the intensity of the Golden Elite.

"Start," she commanded.

The chair let out a soft beep and Isa began her message.

"People of Tiao, I come to you in response to the message that has been circulating from Venus, discussing the repercussions of shutting her down. It is true, if she were to be deactivated, the planet would be without power for an unknown period of time. However, Venus has failed to mention that there are many planets of the Crescent Alliance that would support us if we were in need, and there are terms carved out among several planets that, should something occur and Venus was no longer in power, those planets would come to Tiao's aid. Another thing Venus has failed to mention is the dangers of keeping her in power. As she said, she is in control of all our communications, but she also has access to our homes and our businesses, and all electronics on our planet.

"Six years ago, this planet suffered a terrible tragedy," Isa continued. "Saera, our terraformed greenhouse site, was destroyed by catastrophic failures in the generators for the city. These generators were connected to Venus' mainframe, and the catastrophic failures were, in reality, another section of her system attacking and forcing the generators into meltdown, eventually leading to the death of one-hundred thousand citizens and the destruction of our food supply.

"Shortly after the destruction of Saera, Venus was weaponized, and tricked into believing that certain members of the Syndicate staff were a threat—a threat that she neutralized by poisoning those members of her own Syndicate," Isa said, her voice steady even though there was a great deal of pain in her eyes at recalling the memories. "It is possible for Venus to be weaponized. It has happened before, and it can very easily happen again. The attacks six years ago were the result of a madman hacking into an older section of her coding and reprogramming her. The Syndicate has currently dismantled this part of her coding, but it would still be possible for her to weaponize herself now that the codes have been in her system once before.

"Therefore, people of Tiao, I ask for your support in considering shutting down Venus and shifting Tiao into a new future away from artificial intelligence rule," Isa completed. "If you will unite behind me, I will dismantle Venus and help us move forward as a stronger, cohesive Tiao."

She was still for two seconds before she stood carefully, her eyes sliding shut in exhaustion.

"Take it slow…" Kailynn murmured, helping the Elite out of the chair. Isa sighed heavily and swayed a little on her feet. Kailynn took the Elite's shoulders, looking at her incredulously. "Are you crazy?" she chuckled in disbelief. "You just declared war on Venus."

"Yes," Isa said. She leaned her head on Kailynn's. "But this has to happen. The people cannot live under the rule of Venus. She is our greatest weakness, and I won't let anything like what happened to Saera or the Syndicate happen again."

Kailynn smiled and placed her hands on both sides of Isa's face, her eyes welling with tears.

"I love you."

"I love you, too," Isa whispered.

The Elite bent down and gently captured Kailynn's lips in hers, kissing her tenderly before pressing her forehead to Kailynn's again, unaware that Remus had turned the camera on both of them to catch the entire exchange for the broadcast to the people of Tiao.

Chapter Forty-One

Isa was furious when she discovered that Remus had allowed her exchange with Kailynn to be broadcast. They both began arguing in Isa's office at the Syndicate just before meeting with General Decius. Several other Elites were also in the office, listening to the argument, while others were preparing for the Gihron entourage to arrive.

"Do you have any idea of the danger you put her in?!" Isa barked.

"The people are going to need more than your word to stand behind you," Remus said. "You need to relate to them. You said the future would be away from artificial intelligence and the candid moment showed that you were *not* the typical Elite."

"You put a target on her head for Gihron, and for *any* planet that seeks to tear me down."

"You said yourself, we have planets more than willing to help us, planets run by leaders that *know* you. Seeing your defiance to Venus, and knowing what you are capable of, *and* that you have the human compassion and love to fall for someone, you will gain more support."

"She is now a target!" Isa repeated. "How dare you do that to her? To *me*?"

Remus took a deep breath.

"Because you two deserve better than the relationship you had with me," Remus said simply. "You should not have to hide your relationship."

Isa heaved a sigh and turned to Kailynn. Kailynn smiled weakly. She was also nervous about being a political target, particularly with General Decius so near, but she was also a little relieved that their relationship was out in the open.

"I'm sorry, Kailynn."

"Hey," Kailynn started, walking to the Golden Elite, "you may have tamed me a little, but I am still the Wild Child of Trid. I can sure as hell take care of myself if I need to. And I'm not as smart as you, so I won't care if I have to break a few noses if someone's coming after me."

Isa let out a soft chuckle.

"Perhaps it is you who is wise," she murmured.

The chair in Isa's office beeped with an incoming transmission from Fortunea. Isa accepted the message and a brief light passed over the entire room before projecting the Queen of Fortunea, still ornately-dressed, in stunning clarity, two large men behind her in military uniforms, their dark faces half-covered by an ornate black headdress.

"Your Majesty," Isa said, bowing her head.

"Elite Isa," Glynna said, glancing around the room as if she were standing with them. "I see you have many visitors. Did I interrupt a strategy meeting?"

"I suppose you could call it that," Isa said with a smile. "You received my message, I presume."

"Yes," Glynna said. "As I have always stated, I will support you and Tiao to the best of my abilities. Should Gihron get out of hand and try to attack you, I will have troops standing at the ready. Do they have permission to enter your airspace?"

"They do."

"Perhaps I should double my aid?" Glynna asked with a smile. "Considering the message you were sending out after Venus' poor attempt at controlling Tiao's people."

Isa took a deep breath, forcing a smile.

"I assume the entire Altereye System has seen that message by now."

"Indeed," she confirmed. "I cannot tell you the number of calls I have received since last night. Everyone is talking about the renegade Golden Elite declaring war on Venus." Glynna glanced at Kailynn and her smile widened. "You have my full support," she said. "*Both* of you."

Isa visibly relaxed.

"Isa," Glynna said, turning to her, "in celebration of your victory over Gihron, I would like to supply your planet with some of our bountiful crop this year," she said, her smile widening. "My troops will be at Tiao within the week to secure the planet and protect it, and the produce ships will arrive over the next month to be sure that your people are well-cared for."

Isa closed her eyes and swallowed hard, placing her hand over her heart and bowing her head deeply to the queen.

"You are far too generous, Your Majesty."

"I have already spoken with several other members of the Alliance and called on those able to assist to prepare for the change on Tiao. Once you secure peace terms with Gihron, we will immediately declare a State for Relief for Tiao."

"Do you believe that the Alliance can remain strong without its cornerstone?"

"My dear friend," Glynna smiled gently, "everyone is rallying for you. I have never seen the Alliance so united on one issue." She bowed her head. "Golden Elite Isa, Fortunea is at your service."

"I am in your debt, Your Majesty."

Glynna's hologram faded and Isa turned to the Syndicate members in her office. Several of them were staring at Isa in surprise.

"It's really happening," Aolee murmured.

"What is the status on the Aren System?" Isa asked.

"We have seven-hundred generators set up over the planet," Chronus said. "While that will not give us much, it will allow us to start reprogramming in the larger cities, which will get us up and running again quicker than anticipated."

"Has anyone spoken to Dr. Busen?" Isa asked, her voice straining.

"Yes," Anders said. "He believes that, should removal cause problems with the organs, it would be best to be ready to replace it, that includes lung, heart, and esophagus and would mean extensive reconstruction."

"Marvelous," Isa groaned.

"If anyone can do it, he can," Remus said strongly. "After all, he performed your previous reconstruction and you are the only surviving patient with a reconstructed cranium."

Isa took a deep breath, closing her eyes and nodding.

"Alright," she said. "I want everyone prepared to execute Plan Maki at the nearest opportunity. As soon as General Decius has left the planet, we move."

"Understood," Chronus said, followed by several affirmatives.

"Should things with the General take the same turn that they did with his brother, I don't want anyone to hesitate," Isa said strongly. "His delegates are terrified of him, and if we have evidence of any tampering with the Syndicate, we can bring up charges against Gihron through the Alliance. Therefore, if you see anything suspicious, interfere, but not before they successfully incriminate themselves."

■■

Isa did not want Kailynn in the meeting with Gihron, worried that her message that had been playing continuously had given General Decius the idea to use Kailynn as a way to weaken Isa's stance on some of the terms of the peace. However, she opened the cameras from the conference room so that Kailynn could watch what was going on from the Golden Elite's office. While Kailynn was not thrilled about the idea, she did not protest.

She sat nervously, watching the Elites file into the room and prepare for the Gihron delegation.

Remus glanced at Isa and offered a small smile. The Golden Elite took a deep breath and closed her eyes, preparing herself for what she knew would be a very stressful meeting.

When the door opened, Isa opened her eyes and straightened her shoulders.

"Good morning, General Decius."

"Elite Isa," he greeted, walking to his seat. Now on the fifth day of negotiation, the formalities had been dropped on both sides. The tension had been building between Isa and General Decius for days, and they both knew there was no reason to put forth false pleasantries.

General Decius sighed and looked at Isa, his position relaxed, his eyes showing his annoyance.

"I saw your message to your people last night," he said. "As far as I'm aware, it's still on repeat, playing after Venus' message."

Isa did not speak, looking at General Decius with stoic eyes.

The Gihoric leader drummed his fingers along the arm of the chair, glancing around the room.

"There is much about that message that…piques my curiosity." He looked at her seriously. "You said that you wanted to unite your people to take down Venus, but those terms were preposterous six years ago, and I knew that they would not be entertained had I put them in our surrender."

"If we decide to overthrow Venus, it will be a decision made by the people of Tiao and the Syndicate," Isa explained. "I will not be bullied into changing the structure of Tiao's society to end a war where we clearly have the advantage."

General Decius let out an exasperated snort.

"But you would ask me to change the structure of Gihron's society."

"If you wish to have your planet join the Crescent Alliance, then the structure of Gihron's society will be changed," Isa said. "Joining the Alliance was something that you placed in your terms for surrender.

I did not demand that you join. Therefore, it is your choice if you wish to change Gihron's society and join the Alliance."

"There is no choice at all," General Decius scoffed. "With the state of the Altereye System, any planet not in the Alliance is crushed under the weight of having to support their planets without aid from wealthier planets. Gihron's economy cannot hold its own, therefore, I have no choice but to bow to the Alliance."

"No, you have a choice," Isa corrected. "You either change your planet and make it stronger, or you turn your back on your people, choosing to maintain the society that is clearly not working for your planet if it cannot support itself."

While General Decius' eyes narrowed in anger, two of the other delegates blinked, their eyes going distant, thinking over Isa's words.

"Our planet is the strongest in the Ninth Circle," General Decius growled.

"But you are eager for help from the Alliance," Isa pointed out. "General Decius, if the Alliance were to make an exception for Gihron, it would not solve the problems on Gihron, and it would breed discord among the members of the Alliance, weakening it and causing damage to all the planets in the Altereye System." The Golden Elite's gaze was unwavering. "Times are changing, and as leaders, we must change with them."

"Is that what you call your affair? A change for the better?" General Decius challenged.

"My personal life has no bearing on our discussions, General Decius."

"But it does," General Decius corrected. "You are changing things on your planet, and you are breaking the rules set by Venus, rules that you hold to the highest regard, by having a lover. Yet *we* are supposed to herald you as a true leader? You are not human, you cannot have the same compassion as a human, and you will never have the respect of humans. You have no regard for the structure of the way things are. You are a machine. You could never understand."

"Perhaps, it is *you* who misunderstands," Isa said. "Because understanding and respecting a societal structure is one thing, but understanding it and respecting it enough to see where it is weak, and finding a means to strengthen it, *that* is what a leader does, and that is what I have done. I have the respect of my people and of the other planets in the Alliance. I respect that you wish to preserve your planet while still reaping the benefits that come with being part of the Crescent Alliance, but the system works because everyone adheres or they are punished. No exceptions can be made. As a military man, I'm sure you understand that dissent in the ranks is dangerous to the unity of the army."

General Decius' eyes were bright with anger, his hands gripping the arms of the chair.

"I wish to speak with Elite Isa alone," he said darkly.

The shiver that ran through the room was felt by everyone.

"That is out of the question," Remus said strongly. "It is against our customs to leave Elites alone with other planetary leaders."

"No, it is not," General Decius snapped. "My brother was alone with her often."

Remus' nostrils flared and his body tensed. However, Isa quickly put a hand on Remus' arm.

"Wait outside."

Remus hesitated, his eyes locked on General Decius, but he obeyed, standing with the other Elites. General Decius nodded to his men and they, too, walked out the conference room.

When the door was closed, General Decius turned back to Isa, who sat silently at the opposing head of the table, her eyes cold.

"I was raised hating Venus and the Elites," he stated, his eyes dark as he stared at the other leader. "It was something I never questioned. Now that I have had the opportunity to meet with you and work with you in person, I realize that there is a reason for that hatred."

"You hate me because I tell you that you have a choice on how to run your planet?"

"You have no respect for humanity and the way it operates," General Decius growled. He was silent for several long moments, his eyes going to his hand as he drummed his fingers along the arm of the chair. "Let's cut the bullshit right here," he said, leaning forward and clasping his hands on the table as he looked at Isa seriously. "You understand that everything Gihron did to you and your planet was under my order. I was the one who ordered the Pulse Virus be put on your chair, but I was only able to do so once our best coders and programmers were able to discern the information my brother left us about what he had done to your NCB chair."

Isa was able to keep her face straight, staring at General Decius coolly.

"When Amori was murdered, I started to do my research on what was going on here in the months before he died. Your planet was under a great deal of stress, with the catastrophic failures of so many systems that resulted in many deaths. You even were involved in a horrific accident the day my brother was found dead." He raised his eyebrows. "How do you think that looks?"

Isa did not respond.

"It looked to me like you were trying to frame Gihron," General Decius said darkly. "You were trying to bully us into a position where you could impose the Alliance on us and destroy our society so that we would be under your thumb."

Isa could not help but react to the statement in shock.

"Pardon?" she said. "You believe that I was trying to *frame* Colonel Amori? That I ordered him dead?"

"I do," General Decius said. "He was unwilling to yield to your demands, and so you began to frame him. Why else would he want to send an encrypted message to me telling me about how to send a Pulse Virus to your personal NCB chair? He was trying to tell me that he needed help, but I was too late to save him."

"You're wrong, General Decius," Isa told him. "I stood to gain nothing from framing Gihron, and I still gain nothing from allowing Gihron to join the Alliance. I am not in need of Gihron's support or submission, as you seem to believe."

"Then why did you order my brother dead?"

"I did not order your brother dead," Isa said strongly.

"He was trapped on this planet for months, trying to reach me, even though our communications had been knocked out, and every time we spoke, he would tell me these cryptic things that told me that I needed to save him, but I ignored them. He knew his life was in danger."

"His life was in no danger until *he* put it in danger," Isa snapped.

She stopped, forcing herself to control her expression. General Decius also stopped, blinking several times.

"What do you mean?"

"Your brother brought forth radical ideas about changes to the Altereye System. Surely as a politician, he knew the risks of that."

General Decius let out an exasperated laugh.

"You really did have him killed..." he whispered. "I *knew* you were behind his death. How can you call yourself a compassionate leader for your people if you are killing leaders when they do not serve your agenda? You put out this message to your people that you want Venus destroyed when that same desire caused you to kill my brother?"

"Perhaps if you had listened to that message and not let your hatred blind you, you would come to realize that the destruction that occurred on my planet was due to a madman that hacked into Venus' computers and weaponized her." She leaned forward. "Do you want the truth, General Decius? Your brother was the one who hacked into Venus' mainframe, reprogrammed her, threatened the lives of everyone in the Syndicate, destroyed Tiao's food supply, killing one hundred thousand of *my* people, and killed nearly one hundred members of the Syndicate. Had I ordered his execution, I would have had plenty of reason to do so."

General Decius stared at Isa, his brain turning over the words.

"You're lying."

"Your brother kidnapped me, beat me, mentally and physically tortured me, and you have the gall to call me a liar?"

"My brother is dead because of you!"

"Your brother is dead because of himself!" Isa snapped. "Your brother thought that he could control me, but he forgot exactly who he was dealing with, and he brought his fate upon himself when he threatened to rape me and watch my people suffer while he had *you* invade and destroy my planet."

General Decius stared at Isa, silent, surprised.

"You're right, General Decius, I am not human. You cannot intimidate me and you cannot control me. If you try, you will meet the same fate as your brother."

"Admit to me that you ordered his assassination," General Decius hissed.

"I did not order your brother's assassination," Isa growled. "When your brother was beating me and threatening to rape me, I defended myself, and your brother ended up choking on his own blood."

General Decius stared at the Elite's eyes, convinced in those moments that they were not the eyes of a human or an Elite, but the eyes of an animal that had sighted its prey and was circling it with malice.

"My brother would never harm anyone," General Decius breathed.

"You clearly did not know your brother," Isa said sharply. "I believe that I knew him better than anyone, because I saw the side of him that he would never show to anyone other than someone he believed would not survive. His own men probably didn't even suspect him when he murdered them and strung their bodies up to rot in their room for nearly a month before they were discovered. You think you knew this man you called your brother, but he was a monster starving for power, and when he tried to take it from me, he found himself in over his head."

General Decius stood quickly, but stopped, bracing himself on the table, forcing himself not to attack the leader of Tiao in the Syndicate Building. Isa remained seated for several long moments before she stood.

"You wanted the truth of your brother's death," Isa said, "and now you have it. Does that change the terms of your surrender?"

"Yes," General Decius said darkly. "We do not surrender. We will continue this war until I put a bullet in your brain personally." He turned and angrily punched the button to open the conference room doors. He stormed out between the slew of spectators, the others of his delegation following him in confusion, asking what had happened.

The Elites quickly went to Isa who sat heavily in her chair, cradling her head in one hand.

"What happened?" Remus demanded.

"We're still at war," Isa murmured. "He knows the truth now."

"You...you *told him*?" Chronus hissed. Isa nodded.

"He's very much like his brother," she said. "I know that he'll try to take over while on the planet. Our advantage at the moment is that he is furious, and he will act out in anger."

"How is that to our advantage?" Anders asked, exasperated.

"He's more likely to act rashly and make a mistake," Isa said. "Let him make the mistakes."

■■■

Kyle, Rei, and Jamen carefully cut a hole next to the door sensor pad for the Syndicate Building, glancing at the wires within. The three Gihron delegates were hesitant to go through with the plan, feeling that they had not had proper time to develop the technical aspects.

Kyle carefully cut two of the wires, which allowed Rei and Jamen to pry open the doors of the back entrance of the Syndicate Building. The three slipped into the darkened rooms, carefully holding their bags full of explosives that they intended to put around the building. The

General had said that he did not care if they killed any Elites in the Syndicate—though he was partial to killing them off one-by-one to avenge his murdered brother.

Rei was the most opposed to the plans to destroy whatever they could of Isa and her Elites. He was infuriated that Isa had not faced proper charges for killing Colonel Amori, but he knew that General Decius' younger brother had been a horrible ruler that had always blackmailed anyone he could for power. Rei was also haunted by the words of Elite Isa, and wondered why they were holding so close to a system that clearly did not benefit their planet.

However, he had to follow orders.

"Let's tear this motherfucker down," Jamen chuckled. "Fuck these Elites. They think they know war?"

"Let's show them what Gihron can do," Kyle agreed, reaching into his bag and pulling out the explosives he had brought with him.

They spread out to different areas of the room, each preparing to set the first charge when the lights of the building snapped on and blinded them temporarily.

"Freeze! Get on the ground!" several voices bellowed. Officials and police robots swarmed the room, their guns pointed at the Gihoric men.

Slowly, confused and terrified that they had just been caught committing acts of terrorism, the three fell to their knees, their hands extending above their heads. Even as they wondered why their reconnaissance team had not warned them of the Officials in the Syndicate Building, they did not know that the other delegates who had been at Anon Tower to monitor their rash operations were being hauled away by another group of Officials.

At Anon Tower, Colonel Ikan slowly pushed open the disabled door to Elite Isa's home. He glanced around before nodding once to General Decius and walking into the home. General Decius quickly slipped inside, keeping his eyes on every corner as he crept around the living room, slipping into the doorway that led to the guest hall.

He slowly moved through the house, knowing that Isa's office was somewhere in the back of the level, though he did not know where.

As he passed through the pool area, Colonel Ikan entered the guest hall, looking at the doors on each side. He stepped in front of the first one to his right and it slid open, barely making any noise. Keeping his gun drawn, he stepped inside to find the bed neatly made, as though it had never been used.

Colonel Ikan left the room and went across the hall to the first door on his left. It, too, slid open quietly. In the bed, he saw what appeared to be a sleeping figure, back turned to him. With a dark smile, he started forward, moving slowly so that he would not be heard.

He reached out his hand and covered the mouth of the figure, pulling her back quickly as she let out a startled cry.

"Don't you dare scream, you little bitch!" he snarled, pressing the gun to her back. "Get out of the bed."

"What the fuck are you doing?!" she gasped, quickly trying to move away from the gun. She got to her feet and started toward the door, but Colonel Ikan grabbed her arm and violently yanked her back, wrapping his hand around her neck.

"Where the fuck do you think you're going?" he hissed, tightening his hand. She grabbed at his wrist, trying to pull it from her neck.

"Let go of me!"

"Oh, no," Colonel Ikan chuckled. "You, my dear, are very important. You see," he tightened his grip, "you are going to be the best way to get that bitch Isa to comply. Therefore, you will come with me."

He struggled with her as she threw her entire bodyweight into fighting, her elbows flying behind her in an attempt to hit him.

"You are a feisty one, aren't you?" he laughed. "I like them with a little bite. Maybe I'll enjoy you a little before I take you to General Decius."

Kailynn brought her fists together, moving her hips out of the way and angrily jamming her elbow into Colonel Ikan's side. He doubled over and she took the opportunity to grab the gun from his hand, smashing the butt of the gun into his nose.

"Don't you even think about it, you sack of shit!"

As Colonel Ikan held his nose, his eyes tightly shut, Kailynn pointed the gun at him.

"Get on the fucking ground!" she ordered.

"You bitch! Who the fuck do you think you are?!"

"I think I'm the one holding the fucking gun, so get on the fucking ground before I shoot you and put you there myself."

"You think you can kill me, little girl?"

Kailynn dropped the gun down and pulled the trigger, shooting Colonel Ikan in the leg and causing him to crumple to the ground with a shout of pain.

"I told you I would put you on the ground."

From the open bathroom door, Rayal walked out with his gun pointed at Colonel Ikan. He approached him slowly, Tarah peeking out from the bathroom to watch, her own gun lowered at her side.

"Colonel Ikan, you are under arrest, charged with attempted abduction, attempted rape, treason and espionage," Rayal listed. He lifted his wrist to his mouth. "Execute arrest order."

Further into the Golden Elite's level of Anon Tower, General Decius finally found Isa's office, where her NCB chair sat proudly in the center of the room. He climbed into it, pushing his head back into the cradle and tapping twice on the start-up button under his finger.

It took only a few seconds for the chair to boot up and General Decius immediately went into the programming for the Syndicate, choosing to use the chair's credentials to enter Venus' mainframe.

The mainframe began to load when the chair's soft whirring wound down to a dull hum, and the holograms that were beginning to come up from the mainframe disappeared. The upper ring of the chair began glowing red.

General Decius hesitated, his eyes glancing around him as he tried to pull his head out of the cradle. However, he was locked into place.

He urgently tapped the start-up button multiple times, trying to get the chair back online, glancing up occasionally at the red ring, the color causing his heart to race as he realized there was something wrong with the chair.

He glanced up once to see a figure in front of him, her tall frame illuminated in the red light, her hands clasped behind her back.

"What the fuck have you done?" he demanded.

"The chair has a defense mechanism," Isa's calm voice stated as she took a measured step forward. "I programmed it so that, anyone who is in the chair that does not match my DNA, will cause it to go into emergency shut down," Isa's bright blue eyes were unnerving in the red glow of the NCB chair, "and destroy anyone trying to hijack it."

General Decius' eyes went wide.

"That's illegal," he whispered. "You can't weaponize an NCB chair."

"You were about to," Isa pointed out. "You were about to access the mainframe, get what information you could, and then infect the chair so that it would kill me the next time I used it." She shook her head. "You and your brother are very alike, in that respect. Except that your brother managed to briefly weaponize the greatest artificial intelligence that ever came into being."

"You bitch. Are you going to kill me? That won't stop anything. You have already killed my brother, and if you kill me, more Gihrons will come for vengeance."

"You're wrong," Isa murmured. "Your little coup was poorly planned and even more poorly executed. You have just been caught committing acts of terror. You would normally be stripped of your title as leader of your planet, detained on Kreon, and the Alliance would take over your planet in your absence."

"Why are you making this a hypothetical?" General Decius asked darkly. "You said yourself that you do not deal in hypotheticals."

"That would be the situation if you were to survive tonight, General Decius," Isa said darkly. "However, you ordered that my Elites be killed, that the person I love be killed, and you were going to hack Venus and then kill me. I cannot let you survive."

General Decius was about to protest when the chair gave a shudder and electricity pulsed through the Gihoric leader's body. His muscles strained, his skin crackling as the continuous pulsing raced along his nerves. His eyes were wide, focused on Isa as she watched the Gihoric leader shake. He watched as she remained still and unwavering in front of him.

Then his body went slack and the chair immediately turned off, a small chime sounding.

"Unauthorized access to classified information. DNA match possible threat. General Decius Touren of Gihron. Threat neutralized."

Chapter Forty-Two

Isa called Vanessa shortly after the Officials had hauled away Colonel Ikan and the body of General Decius. She asked the older woman to carefully handle the news of what happened between Gihron and Tiao so that Isa could keep as many allies as possible when the truth was discovered.

However, she did not have time to discuss much with Vanessa.

She quickly gathered the bags that they had packed the previous days and hurried to one car with Kailynn while Rayal and Tarah went to another vehicle.

They were executing Plan Maki—go into hiding to shut down Venus.

Kailynn clamored into the car with Isa, who had already altered the car for the journey they would have to take under Venus' radar. Isa got into the driver's seat and inserted the chip she had programmed for their destination. Kailynn did not know where they were going, and when she asked Isa said that she would not say until they were there safely, just to be sure Venus could not find out where they had based their operation.

They pulled out of the garage for Anon Tower and sped toward the rising sun.

"Are you alright?" Isa asked, turning to Kailynn.

"For the moment," Kailynn tried to joke. "I feel like I'm dreaming right now."

"Things did happen very quickly," Isa agreed. She sighed heavily and closed her eyes before turning to Kailynn and taking her hand. "Kailynn," she started slowly, "I want to tell you something."

"You're making me nervous…"

"There is no guarantee that I will survive this," Isa murmured. "As I told you, shutting down Venus requires destroying her source codes, which will kill me. But I was not entirely truthful."

"What do you mean?"

"I hold the other source codes," she said. She placed her hand over her heart. "I already have them. There is the stationary processor that holds her source codes, and I am the back-up. Every Golden Elite before me has held Venus' source codes for the last hundred years or so." She squeezed Kailynn's hand as the former Significant stared at the Elite, trying to understand. "These codes are contained in a processor that is connected to my heart, which is surrounded by a casing in my chest."

"How in the hell…"

"No one knows, except Venus," Isa said. "The doctors that performed the surgery to change these codes from Gattriel to me are all dead." Isa took a deep breath and slowly let it out. "Dr. Busen has done every scan possible and all the research he can, but he does not entirely know what he will be faced with when he tries to remove the processor and casing."

"He's going to operate on you while we're hiding in a bunker in the middle of nowhere?" Kailynn choked.

"Yes," Isa said. "He, Paul, and the other Elites of the Syndicate have been transferring everything to that location for months. They've tried to prepare for everything." She lowered her eyes. "However, there is still a high risk of this killing me."

Kailynn blinked at Isa, trying to let the words sink in, though they continued to bounce around in her brain. She was unable to consider the possibility that Isa could die.

"If you die…" she choked on the words, "what will happen to the planet? Venus might be shut down, but then…"

"Then Remus and the Syndicate will do everything they can to bring the planet back online and move forward," Isa whispered. "I have had threats on my life since I was a child," she murmured. "I had become so desensitized to it, and for a while, I even welcomed the idea of one of the plots succeeding, but now…this is the first time I've ever been truly afraid to die."

She reached forward, resting her hand against Kailynn's cheek.

"I used to be afraid to go through with this plan because I did not want to leave the planet without a leader, and I figured if I was going to fuck up the planet so horrendously, it was my responsibility to repair it. But now," she shook her head, "I know that if I were to die, Remus and the others would do a fine job leading the planet. What I'm afraid of is not being able to be with you."

Kailynn reached up and took Isa's hand, holding it tightly and turning her head to press it to her lips, trying to hold the tears back.

"My life has been dictated by Venus," Isa continued quietly, "and even though I rebelled slightly, I was still a part of her, I was still obedient. Now, I would throw all of that away if it meant I could be with you as I should be, without the fear of death on both of our shoulders."

"Isa," Kailynn whispered, sniffing back her tears and clearing her throat, "you survived your life up to this very moment," she said. "You even managed to bounce back after throwing yourself into the control room of the Syndicate." She tightened her grip on Isa's hand. "Do not let this be the thing that brings you down."

She released Isa's hands and took her face, looking into her eyes.

"You will survive this. I know you will."

Isa closed her eyes and leaned forward, kissing Kailynn gently.

For seventeen hours, the car drove them over the continent, crossing bridges that spanned the seas and going through cities that Kailynn had never heard of. Most of them looked like Anon, clean and white with no one on the surface streets, but cars whizzing around the underground roads.

As they were driving through yet another large city, the windshield of the car darkened and turned into a screen where the word "advisory" flashed on the screen.

In the next moment, the word disappeared and Kailynn's picture flashed on the screen. Next to her picture was the advisory notice. Kailynn was able to read most of the words, but she did not need to read all of them to understand.

Jacyleen Lynden. Height: 170 cm. Weight: 53 kg.
Kill on Sight—by Order of Venus.
Report any information.

Isa stared at the picture and the words next to it as Kailynn gasped, staring at the words that seemed to stab her in the gut.

Kill on Sight.

"Once she is disabled," Isa started, "stay close to me." The Golden Elite turned to Kailynn, her eyes dark with anger. "Until we can get Anon up and running again, you will remain a Kill on Sight target. Once the Official computers are back up and running, we can remove the order."

"How much longer until we get there?"

"Two hours," Isa answered. "We're taking a longer route."

"Can Venus kill you even from here? With the processor and everything? Can she just stop your heart?"

"No," Isa assured. "She has been sending little attacks at me all day. They just haven't been enough to hurt as much as her previous ones. As I continue to move, she has trouble finding a strong signal to the processor in my chest. Once we stop moving, I'm sure the attacks will become severe."

Kailynn took Isa's hand once more.

As the night began darkening the skies, the car slowed and pulled off the road, driving out of the town into barren land where small, sharp brush grew in the fine sand where nothing else could live.

Isa opened the control panel of the car once more and activated manual controls. A joystick protruded from the center console and the car began to slow. Isa moved her foot forward to the front of the car to rest on the sensor that would keep them moving.

"Why are you turning it on manual?"

"Because we're about to leave the road system."

"What?" Kailynn gasped. "You're going to drive this thing over dirt?"

"Yes," Isa said, a small smile taking over her lips.

Isa slowed the car and turned off the road. The car beeped at her twice, telling her there was a problem, but as soon as they were off the road completely, the alarm silenced and the computer for the car shut down, leaving Isa to direct the vehicle over the rough dirt path without interference.

Kailynn, confused and unsure where they were or where they were going and increasingly nervous about the darkening sky, remained quiet. There were no lights so far away from the city, making it very difficult to see.

Isa continued to drive toward a large mound of rocks and finally slowed at the base of it. She tapped the car lights twice and a small red light could be seen in the crevice between two large rocks.

One of the rocks moved backward, showing an underground passage that allowed the car under the rock.

"Where are we?" Kailynn asked as Isa drove forward.

"The outskirts of Saera."

Kailynn turned to Isa quickly, surprised to recognize the name. "Saera?"

"Venus' main processor was placed in a remote location just outside of the city," Isa said with a nod. "Since food production is protected across the Altereye System, previous Golden Elites began projects to terraform Saera into food production." Isa sighed heavily, glancing ahead of her, though she could barely see in the short tunnel that led them to an underground lot where other cars were parked. "That protected Venus' main processor."

"But, when Colonel Amori attacked Saera…"

"The city was leveled," Isa whispered, "because Venus' processor was so close to the generators. The processor was not damaged, it was never in range. However, it provided a lot more power to the Charge Burst that destroyed the city."

Isa got out of the car, Kailynn in tow, and grabbed their bags of food and supplies. Everyone was bringing some rations to hold them through the process of shutting down the super-computer.

Isa typed in a code to the only door in the underground lot and they both walked into the cavernous, hot room. Rayal and Tarah were already there with half the Syndicate, Paul, and Dr. Busen. Tiana, Paul's dog, was also there and ran forward to greet them.

Kailynn was too distracted by the enormous pillar in the room to notice Tiana at first.

Standing in the center of the metal-lined dome was an enormous pillar of light. Small strands of brighter yellow and blue would occasionally flicker in the grooves of the sparse metal casing around the light, but the white light remained constant and unwavering.

"Is that…"

"That's Venus," Isa murmured, stepping forward to greet Dr. Busen.

"Glad to see you're here safely," he murmured.

"You as well," Isa agreed, taking Dr. Busen's hand before hugging him briefly. She also hugged Paul. "How is it going here?"

"They're still trying to disable the monitoring system," Paul explained. "They can't figure out how to turn it off."

Isa walked to the Elites crouched around the base of the pillar as Paul and Dr. Busen turned to Kailynn.

"How are you holding up, Kailynn?" Paul asked.

"I feel like I'm in a dream," she laughed nervously. "I don't know, this seems a bit…"

"Surreal, I'm sure," Dr. Busen said with a nod. He took a deep breath, averting his eyes to the ground. "Did Isa tell you about the procedure?"

"Yeah, sorta," she said, her stomach flipping in fear. "But you managed to help her after everything with Colonel Amori. I'm sure that everything will be fine."

"I promise, I will do everything in my power."

"I know."

Isa and the other Elites were looking over the control panel for Venus that was far more complicated than any of the newer technology to which they were accustomed. They knew they only had once chance to disable the security monitoring system, which would allow them to set up the area where Dr. Busen would perform the surgery. As long as the monitoring system was up, Venus could be notified of any changes in the chamber of the processor, tipping her off to their location when the healthcare machines were plugged in.

Isa carefully moved her finger along the screen, rotating the circle of codes and files represented by small boxes.

"I've never seen one of these before," Aolee whispered.

"I've only dealt with this once," Isa said, her eyes sharp on the screen as she held her finger over one square, seeing the route of the codes listed at the top of the screen. "I had to do repairs on one of her processors, and I know there is a release mechanism for programming somewhere around here."

"This isn't the programming panel?" Hana asked, confused.

"No," Isa said. "Just the control panel."

"What is the difference?"

"Control panel is what you might call the landing page for everything," Isa murmured, turning the circle once more and holding her finger over another box. "Programming panel is what we understand as the control panel."

Isa double tapped the box and a metal panel moved away from under the screen, extending a platform with a touch keyboard.

"There we go," Isa said. She quickly typed in some commands for the processor and opened up the security, disabling the program. She checked once more to be sure that the monitoring was off on all related files and programs and then turned off the programming panel.

"I guess it's safer that her hardware was never upgraded," Anders said, shaking his head. "No one would know how to use it."

The Elites went over to help Dr. Busen and Paul set up the surgical area, while Isa walked back to Kailynn, who was crouched on the ground with Tiana.

The two remained as far away from the surgical bed and monitors as they could, glancing over occasionally and sharing silent conversations with each other in the heat of the humming processor.

Isa began to get nervous when Remus did not arrive at the time he was expected. After three hours of pacing worriedly, the door opened and the Silver Elite walked in, his caretaker, Luska, behind him, and a dog that looked almost exactly like Tiana with them.

Isa ran to him and hugged him tightly.

"You scared me," she whispered.

"I'm fine," he assured, heavily dropping the ration bags and a bag of programming wires and supplies. "Listen, everyone!" he called through the cavern. "Venus has shut down everything on Tiao."

"What?" Isa hissed.

"She's left the Official communications up and planetary communications, as well as her own security monitoring system," Remus continued. "That's why I was late. I had to walk the rest of the way here. The roads were shut down before I could disable the system on the car."

Isa turned to look at the surprised expressions in the room.

"It must be chaos out there," Chronus whispered.

"Dr. Busen, do you have that computer I gave you?" Isa asked. He turned to get it as Isa looked at the other Syndicate members. "This is probably a way to scare the people into believing they need her and cause chaos that will force us out of hiding. She knows if the people cause enough problems that we'll step in because we can't leave them to destroy themselves."

"We have to stay hidden for now," Anders said strongly.

"This is what it will be like when she does shut down," Remus added. "The people know that you're trying to shut her down. Their reaction to this situation will tell us if they support you."

Isa sighed heavily, running her hands through her hair, her stomach tying itself in nervous knots.

Dr. Busen returned with the computer and Isa took it, rifling through one of Remus' bags and pulling out a cord. She went to the processor and connected the computer to it.

"What are you doing?" Tia gasped, horrified. "If you access her mainframe, she'll see it immediately."

"This computer operates outside her sphere," Isa murmured, opening up several windows and typing in codes. "I'm not opening anything she does not already have open. If she has left her security running, then we can just project it onto this screen."

Several codes flashed across the screen before it went temporarily black. Then, the security footage from the Syndicate Building lit up the screen.

Everyone was too stunned to speak.

In Anon, it was the late hours of the night, and the speakers were playing a continuous message, hauntingly echoing through the silent city.

"Without me, this planet will plunge into darkness. Starvation, illness, and war will become rampant. I have kept Tiao strong all these years, and I will show you my power. As the planet sits in darkness, remember the power I hold."

However, the city was not dark. Several small points of light were gathered at the base of the Syndicate Building. As Kailynn looked among the small, floating lights, she realized that each of those points of light were emergency lights, and each was held by a person, pointed upward to the sky.

There were several thousand lights gathered at the base of the Syndicate Building.

The feed switched before they could study it further, and they saw that, throughout the city, there were congregations of lights in the streets.

Beyond the city limits, a gathering of lights and fires could be seen in Trid, contained in the center of the district, near the Keeper's building.

When the feed switched to another city, one where dawn had just begun to lighten the streets, the security cameras showed the citizens gathered in the city center, sitting with one another and chatting lightly, some standing, others by themselves along the edges of the congregation of thousands of citizens.

No one in the processor cavern could believe their eyes.

Yet another city showed gatherings of people in the streets. One city even saw the largest group in the city center, chanting as dusk descended on another area of the planet.

"Isa! Not Venus! Isa! Not Venus!"

Isa placed her hand over her mouth and bowed her head.

Everyone remained silent in awe as they followed Venus while the computer discovered just how much support Isa had across the planet to shut down the artificial intelligence.

Chapter Forty-Three

Kailynn was so overwhelmed by everything she had seen while watching Venus' security mainframe scan the reactions around the planet that, when Paul slipped away to take Tiana for a walk, Kailynn quickly volunteered to go with him and take Remus' dog Rio, allowing Luska to get some sleep.

Kailynn followed Paul to the lot filled with cars and out the direction they came, leading them into the cool morning of the desert.

The former Significant took a deep breath, letting the air fill her lungs and clear her head. She was startled at the difference in the air. The air felt cleaner as it entered and left her lungs, and the cool feeling of the morning relieved her body from the heat of the cavern.

"Amazing how different the air is, isn't it?" Paul said with a chuckle. He also took a deep breath and closed his eyes. "I don't know about you, but I was dying in there."

"It's way too fucking hot in there," Kailynn agreed.

Paul began walking around the rock mound, finding a path that led up the embankment and to the top of the ridge behind the mound of rocks.

"That was incredible," he said.

"What?"

"Seeing the support she has," Paul clarified, leading Kailynn up the path, watching Tiana sniff around the bushes. "Isa is incredible."

"I don't know if that's the word for it," Kailynn whispered. "I'm not sure there *is* a word for what she is."

"No, I don't suppose there is."

"Paul, can I ask you something?"

"Of course."

"Are you and Dr. Busen a couple?"

Paul chuckled. "Yes, we are."

"Dr. Busen is one of the best doctors alive, right?"

"Not one of the best," Paul said, shaking his head. "He is *the* best Elite Specialist alive."

"Does that ever get to you?" Kailynn asked. "Do you ever feel intimidated by him?"

"No," Paul said, shaking his head again. "I'm one of the best, too." He glanced back at Kailynn with a teasing smile. "We're both doctors. Anyone who would listen to our conversations at home would think we were speaking a different language at some of the terms we throw around. Michael astounds me. He's absolutely brilliant, and watching him research this, seeing his dedication and fascination with what we're about to do, it just makes me admire him that much more."

Kailynn lowered her eyes to the ground.

"But it never makes you feel insignificant?"

"No," Paul said. "We're both doctors, so we operate in the same way. You and Isa? You two are extremely similar in many ways, but very different in others." Paul turned around and looked at Kailynn, slowly walking backward up the dirt path. "You should not feel insignificant at all," he said. "I'm sure Isa's power unsettles you. Right now, she has the power to shut down Venus, with help, of course, but that help would have never been available without her power to begin with. That is no small feat, and that would be frightening to anyone."

Paul turned back around and continued walking as Kailynn dropped her eyes to the dirt.

"When this is over," she finally said, "and Venus is gone, Isa will still have that power, though. She'll still be the leader of the planet, and she'll still have the power to affect everyone on the planet."

"She will," Paul agreed. "That's why we should be thankful that Isa is the one who will be doing this, and not Colonel Amori or General Decius."

Paul stopped at the top of the ridge and turned to Kailynn.

"I want to show you something."

Kailynn stepped up beside him and glanced out over the vast area in front of them.

The valley beyond was filled with dilapidated and collapsed buildings. Most of the metal structure still stood, the outer walls outlining the building that had once been there, but the roofs were caved in, the floors sunken in the center, leaving only a destroyed carcass. There were mangled buildings, where the metal of the framework was sharply bent and tangled, protruding from the rubble with malicious appearance, covered in rust.

"Saera," Paul whispered. "At one point, this is where the planet harvested most of its food. Losing it caused significant damage to all of Tiao."

Kailynn stared at the ruins, thinking over the story of Saera's destruction.

"Do you know why it's so difficult to produce our food on this planet?" Paul asked. "There is plenty of food on the planet as it is. Indigenous species would eat the plants and animals here, but humans cannot. Even if we were to, we would starve or poison ourselves, because we were not built to consume them. Our bodies are meant for our origins on Earth. Therefore, we had to produce food from Earth here. But, had we forced people to eat the indigenous plants and animals here, our species would have built up a body that would handle that food. And we would not be struggling to feed the people of this system."

Paul glanced at Kailynn.

"Staying the same is never an option," he murmured. "Just as a person has to change to overcome trials in life, a city, a society, a species, they all must change as well, because that is what nature demands." Paul chuckled. "I used to say this jokingly, but, the truth is, Isa is a force of nature. She had to change to overcome the hardships in her life, and she is changing things for everyone so that this planet and its people may grow stronger. While it's terrifying to stand next to that kind of power, and think of yourself as powerless, it is better to be amazed by that strength and revel in it. Because you are also capable of great change. Just think of the way you clawed your way out of Trid, the way you started reading and writing, the way you came to Isa's aid and helped her strengthen herself. You are just as powerful as Isa. You are anything but insignificant. You gave Isa back to us, and to the planet."

Kailynn could only stare at Paul, letting the words move around her skull slowly.

Paul looked over the ruins and smiled.

"Change can look devastating," he agreed, nodding to the city. "But I see a lot of flowers growing there that would have never grown had a city been there."

Paul walked back down the path, stopping a little further down to wait for Kailynn, who continued to look out over the small splashes of color she had not seen before among the grey concrete and rusted metal rubble.

■■■

Tensions were very high later that day.

Paul and Dr. Busen went to all the monitors in the improvised surgical area, turning them on and preparing the instruments they would need for the surgery. Isa sat against the base of the processor, watching from afar. Kailynn, who had been playing with Rio and Tiana to take her mind off the impending surgery, finally walked to Isa and sat with her. The Golden Elite's eyes did not move from the doctors, so Kailynn wrapped her arm around Isa and rested her head on the Elite's shoulder.

The waiting continued.

Remus and several of the other Elites were setting up the connections between the processor and another machine that Maki had tried to complete on his own to destroy Venus' codes. The Elites of the Syndicate had continued Maki's research and created a computer that would read the codes.

Then, they had built a system that contained the virus to destroy the codes, setting it separate from the other machine and the processor. It was a simple-looking machine with a stand and a handle that would activate the virus and send it to the two processors.

Setting up the three machines was enough to distract them from what was about to happen.

Rayal and Tarah continued to take shifts monitoring the outer areas of the processor's location to be sure they had not been found by Officials. However, they were more interested in checking in with everyone in the cavern.

Finally, Dr. Busen stepped away from the surgery area. He motioned for Paul to follow him and the two left the cavern, everyone watching them.

When the door closed, Kailynn glanced at Isa.

Isa smiled weakly and stroked her cheek before leaning forward and brushing their lips together.

"I love you."

"I love you, too," Kailynn breathed, tears threatening to overtake her, making her voice crack.

The Elites stepped away from their tasks and waited, understanding that Dr. Busen was ready to perform the surgery.

"How much more is left?" Isa asked, looking at Remus.

"Just connecting the final ports to the processor."

"Better do those now," Isa said with a nod.

Remus turned back to the other Elites and they began moving around the processor, plugging in different wires.

Kailynn could hardly breathe.

When the final setup was complete, everyone waited for the doctors to return.

When Dr. Busen walked back in, everyone tensed. Paul and Dr. Busen walked to Isa and crouched in front of her.

"We're ready, Isa," Dr. Busen whispered.

"Okay," the Elite said, taking a deep breath and slowly letting it out to calm herself.

Dr. Busen swallowed hard and looked at the floor.

"Do you want me to tell you what I will be doing?"

She shook her head quickly.

"Tell me afterward."

He chuckled and nodded. "Alright. Let's start, then."

Dr. Busen helped Isa to her feet, and Paul helped Kailynn. Kailynn quickly grabbed Isa's arm and pulled her into a tight hug, the tears falling down her face. She whispered to the Elite that she loved her once again and Isa repeated the sentence.

Then, Isa walked with Dr. Busen to the surgery table.

"Chronus, Anders, Hana," Paul called, motioning them over. "Does someone want to tell Rayal and Tarah?"

Tia left the cavern to get the two caretakers as Kailynn watched the three Elites approach the surgery area, preparing to act as the nurses assisting Dr. Busen and Dr. Arre.

Remus walked to Kailynn and placed a hand on her shoulder. She looked up at him, her hand over her nose and mouth as she fought to contain her tears. Before she thought better of it, she wrapped her arms around him, hugging him tightly. He returned the hug, closing his eyes.

They both remained silent.

Isa removed her shirt and bra and reclined on the table as everyone who would be involved with the surgery washed their hands and covered their clothes. Isa closed her eyes and took several deep, measured breaths.

Dr. Busen started the IV on her and then hooked up her other arm to fluids. He covered her body with a blanket and then the hole in the blanket with another sheet before continuing to attach Isa to different monitors.

Tarah and Rayal walked in, both walking up to Isa and standing in her line of vision as the final preparations were made.

By the time Dr. Busen announced that he would be putting her under to start the procedure, everyone had gathered around the area, watching nervously. Isa turned her head and looked around the cavern, her eyes finally meeting Kailynn's.

The two remained in an eye-lock before Isa's eyes slowly slipped shut, and all the beeping of the monitors evened to a constant, rhythmic sound.

Dr. Busen turned around and looked at the group that had gathered.

"My apologies," he said slowly, "but please give me a little space. This is nerve-wracking enough."

The group not participating in the surgery backed away, going to the opposite side of the cavern. Remus guided Kailynn away, sitting next to her as Rayal and Tarah sat on her other side. They did not bother to watch for Officials finding them. At that point, they could not bear to leave the room, knowing Isa was undergoing surgery.

Kailynn refused to watch the figures on the other side of the cavern. Her eyes were, instead, focused on the machines hooked up to the processor. It was unbearably hot in the cavern, and she was sweating profusely, beads of sweat rolling into her eyes, which she furiously wiped away, refusing to move more.

Some Elites would get up at various times to pace, or walk around the processor to check the connections. Even though they had tested their connections on a processor that had been put out of commission, they had not tried shutting it down. Therefore, they did not know for sure that the virus would work.

They figured that, if Isa could come out of the surgery, and the virus did not work, they would find another way to shut down Venus with the help of the Golden Elite.

Freeing Isa from Venus' grasp was the highest priority.

Even though only two hours had passed, it felt like days for all those watching.

Two hours in, Chronus called Remus over to look at the protective casing they were slowly removing, just to be sure they were removing it correctly and that they would not damage Isa's heart or trigger the processor.

Remus quickly returned to the group when he had finished giving his advice.

"How does she look?" Kailynn demanded.

"As you would expect," Remus said slowly, sitting against the wall once more and loosening the fastenings on his uniform, also sweating. "They're half-way through with the casing. This last panel should reveal the processor and they'll finally be able to see what they're dealing with."

"They don't know for sure?" Kailynn choked.

"No," Remus said, shaking his head. "But have faith in them. Dr. Busen is the best."

Kailynn closed her eyes, unable to look in the direction of the surgery.

Another hour later, after some worried conversations between the two doctors, Dr. Busen told Dr. Arre to prepare for a heart reconstruction. The words caused Kailynn to physically feel pain in her chest. She folded her legs and rested her forehead on her knees, trying to breathe around the fear in her chest and the heat of the cavern.

"It's alright," Remus assured. "Dr. Busen has done this before."

"On a *heart*?" Kailynn snapped.

"Not on Isa's but a heart reconstruction is not uncommon," Remus told her. "They already have one ready for her. They began growing it a week ago."

"*Growing* it?"

"Isa's entire genetic map is documented. She had her tongue and eye regrown for reconstruction when she had the accident," Remus said. "The heart and the reconstruction are not the worry. The concern lies entirely with the processor."

Kailynn felt as though she was about to be sick.

Tarah clung nervously to Rayal, who was also pale and shaking. Everyone was extremely nervous.

With everything prepared for a quick reconstruction, Dr. Busen and Dr. Arre continued working diligently.

At the beginning of the fifth hour, panic set in on the other side of the cavern.

The monitors began sounding alarms and the Elites all jumped, terror bolting through them.

"I clipped it," Dr. Busen hissed.

Kailynn was on her feet, ready to dart forward, but Remus leapt up and grabbed her, getting in front of her and forcing her back.

"Get out of my way!" Kailynn barked.

"Kailynn, keep it down," Remus snapped. "Let him concentrate."

"She's dying!"

Remus wrapped his arms around Kailynn, forcing her to muffle her cries into his uniform, trying to weakly fight him to get to the surgery area, where the monitors continued to beep their warnings. Dr. Busen snapped something at Paul and then told the other Elites to get out of the way. Kailynn did not know what was going on, but she could feel the tension in Remus' body and she knew that everyone had their eyes on Dr. Busen.

After what felt like an eternity listening to the shrill beeping, the warnings stopped and the simple, rhythmic beeping stumbled into a steady beat.

Dr. Busen slowly removed his hand from Isa's chest, shaking.

"Michael, Michael, breathe," Paul said. "Just breathe for a moment."

There was stillness and silence as Dr. Busen took a few moments to collect himself.

When Remus felt Kailynn relax, lulled into a calmer state by the rhythmic beeping of the machines, the Silver Elite released her and guided her back to the spot where they had been sitting.

Two hours later, Chronus called Remus over once more, his voice a little weaker.

Kailynn finally turned her eyes to the surgery area, and saw Chronus holding a bloodied, metal contraption that had everyone standing, their eyes wide.

The former Significant watched, her body locked, as the Silver Elite carefully took the contraption.

It was shaped to be cased around a heart, small needles poking out in different areas to touch the muscle. It was black in color with ridges of gold that made up the pathways of the processor.

The Silver Elite brought it over to everyone else. While the Elites seemed fascinated by the machine itself, Kailynn was focused entirely on the blood that coated it.

"Where did it get its power?" Tia whispered.

"Isa's heart powered it. It's in safe mode," Remus murmured. "We should set it on a circuit before Venus realizes it's in danger."

He walked over to the secondary machine they had set up and two Elites helped to attach the processor to a live circuit to get it out of safe mode and prepare it for shut down.

Kailynn walked around them slowly, approaching the surgery area.

When Anders saw her, he walked over to her, keeping his voice down.

"The processor is out," he assured. "Dr. Busen is just finishing up patching the areas of her heart."

"Then...she's going to be alright?" Kailynn asked, her voice breaking.

"We won't know for sure until she wakes up," he admitted. "We don't entirely know what effect the processor has on her heart and how it will work without the processor. Dr. Busen is doing everything he can."

Kailynn nodded tightly, crossing her arms over her chest and taking a deep breath.

She did not move for the final hour as Dr. Busen finished the surgery and closed Isa's chest once more.

Kailynn had to contend to watching the monitors prove that Isa was alive.

Finally, Dr. Busen backed away from the surgery area, his hands and protective clothing stained with blood and his face pale and covered in sweat.

Everyone surged forward.

"I'm going to let everything stabilize," he said quietly, removing his gloves, his hands shaking. "I'm going to leave her sedated for another hour and see what the monitors say. If everything looks good, we'll stop the drugs and see..."

He did not finish the sentence, but they all knew that there was still some uncertainty.

Dr. Busen and Paul began cleaning the surgery area, continuously looking at the monitors and at Isa. The others did not approach until the doctors were finished cleaning and stood by the machines, watching the lines and numbers move up and down.

Kailynn finally walked up to Isa and looked over the Elite's pale face, terrified that Isa would die the moment they stopped the sedation.

She rested a hand on Isa's hair and let the tears blur her vision.

The hour wait was agonizing, but when it was over, everyone wished they had more time to prepare.

Dr. Busen closed the drip, carefully removing the needle from Isa's arm, though he left her on the fluid monitor.

Then, everyone turned their eyes to the other monitors, waiting, scarcely breathing.

Everything remained stable and normal.

But still, everyone held their breaths, watching the lines and numbers worriedly.

Dr. Busen turned away from the monitors and ran a hand over his face. Paul went up to him and took his shoulders.

"It will be alright," he whispered. "She did not peak, nor drop. She's still stable."

"She might be in a coma," Dr. Busen whispered. "She might not wake up on her own."

"Michael," Paul said strongly, tightening his fingers on the other doctor's shoulders, "look at me." The older doctor looked up, his face creased with anxiety. "This stubborn Elite pulled through a skull reconstruction. This is not going to be the thing that takes her down."

Dr. Busen swallowed hard and closed his eyes, nodding.

Paul pulled Dr. Busen closer and hugged him tightly.

Kailynn watched the time pass on the clock of one of the monitors, one hand still resting on Isa's head. Thirty-three minutes and twenty-seven seconds passed before the monitors changed their tones.

Kailynn looked around quickly as everyone jumped, turning their eyes to Isa.

The Golden Elite slowly blinked her eyes open, opening her mouth to take a pained breath. Kailynn gasped and the tears tumbled down her face as she covered her mouth.

Isa groaned and closed her eyes tightly.

"It's…fucking *hot* in here…"

Everyone in the cavern let out a relieved laugh, a few of them shaking, barely able to keep their legs from giving out on them. Dr. Busen did collapse to his knees, letting out a long breath as Paul went to a crouch next to him and hugged him tightly once more.

Kailynn pressed a kiss to Isa's lips, thrilled to feel that they were warm.

"You have the power to change that," Remus said, walking up to Isa's other side and taking her hand. The Golden Elite looked at the Silver Elite and a small, tired smile came to her lips.

"Then…"

Remus' hand tightened on Isa's.

"He got it out," he said with a nod. "You're free of her."

Isa's smile widened.

"...and you were all so worried..."

Kailynn could not help but laugh, her entire body shaking as she ran her hand several times over Isa's hair.

"The amount of stress I deal with being around you is going to take years off my life," she hiccupped with a teasing smile.

"Mine, too," Dr. Busen groaned, approaching the Golden Elite.

"I knew you could do it," Isa said, looking at Dr. Busen.

"I want you to sit up *very slowly*," he said, taking Isa's other hand.

Everyone watched as Dr. Busen checked the strength of Isa's heart and that she could breathe properly when upright. When everything looked stable, he draped a robe over her shoulders.

Though he did not want her to walk, Isa got to her feet and took a step.

"You need to take it slow," Dr. Busen said. "Just sit for a moment."

"No," Isa said, shaking her head. "There is something that needs to be done."

Everyone turned to look at the two smaller machines hooked up to the large processor. Isa swallowed hard and stumbled slowly to the machines, Dr. Busen and Paul supporting her as she approached. She swayed, the drugs still running through her system.

When she was standing in front of the switch that would release the virus, she slowly pulled her arms away from the two doctors and turned her attention to the switch.

"Is this all I need to do?"

"Yes," Remus answered.

Isa reached out to the switch, but hesitated, feeling the weight of the action even through the fog of painkillers and sedatives still pumping through her veins.

Her hand shook, barely above the switch.

For several long moments in the hot cavern, everyone waited for Isa to move.

But she did not.

Kailynn took a step toward Isa, standing beside her and resting a hand on top of Isa's. She gently pushed the Elite's hand down until it rested on the switch.

Isa turned to Kailynn, seeing the weak, nervous, smile on the younger woman's face. Isa licked her dry lips and turned back to the handle.

A hand rested on her other shoulder and she turned to see Remus behind her, his hand grounding her as he nodded.

Turning a little further, Isa saw the Syndicate members behind her, Rayal and Tarah near the front, their hands clasped tightly together. Paul and Dr. Busen stood there as well, watching her with small smiles that told her they supported her.

Isa turned back to the switch and, with Kailynn's hand on hers, pushed it down.

Two seconds later, the large processor whirred loudly. Sparks flew from the openings in the sparse casing and the colors flickered, the light fading as the machine whirred louder and louder. With a deafening crack, the processor went black, and, for that instant, it was as if the entire universe held its breath.

The darkness and silence of the room remained.

Kailynn felt Isa's fingers move, turning around to clasp her hand.

"We did it," Remus whispered in the darkness.

Epilogue

Compared to the darkness of the cavern, the bright light of the sun blinded everyone. The Bronze Elites had immediately returned to Anon, arriving the day after Venus had been shut down to direct relief parties from Fortunea and to start the programs they had outlined to help rebuild the capital.

However, Remus, Isa, Kailynn, Rayal, Tarah, and the doctors remained in the cavern for two days to be sure that Isa was well enough to return to her duties in Anon.

The reality o what had happened did not hit Kailynn until she and Isa drove out of the cavern into the sunlight. They were the first car out of the remaining members of the group that had taken down Venus, the other cars close behind.

As they approached the road, Kailynn asked Isa to stop. The Golden Elite did so and Kailynn stepped out of the car, inhaling deeply. The air was hot in the middle of the day, but the clear air still refreshed her. She glanced around the desert brush and the blue skies and suddenly realized that everything was different.

Isa also got out of the car as Kailynn walked around and took her hand.

"Walk with me for a moment."

Isa followed Kailynn's lead, hand secured in the younger woman's. With the sun beating down on them and the clean air filling their lungs, they both realized the magnitude of what had happened, but it did not seem as impossible to rebuild now. The entire universe had not fallen into darkness. The sun still shone as the planet rotated around its star, illuminating the surface of Tiao as it always had. However, it felt even more powerful now that they realized that Venus had never controlled the sun.

She had never controlled nature.

"Do you hear that?" Kailynn asked, stopping and turning to Isa.

The Golden Elite closed her eyes and listened.

"Nothing?"

"Exactly," Kailynn said with a smile. "For some reason, I thought everything would be absolute chaos when we walked out of there."

"Admittedly, I did as well," Isa chuckled lightly. She took a deep breath. "Things will not be easy, though."

"They never were meant to be," Kailynn said. "You know, someone once told me that anything that happens from inside a society is more devastating than war," she continued, her smile widening. "We've toppled the society, and now we have to rebuild it." She chuckled. "The easy part is over."

Isa chuckled.

"Shutting down a computer that was hardwired into the entire planet was the easy part…" she murmured. "How does that bode for everything else?"

Kailynn's fingers tightened around Isa's hand.

"With you as the leader, everything will work out," she assured. "You saw it yourself. Everyone supported you. And you succeeded."

Isa looked at their clasped hands.

"I succeeded because everyone supported me," she said. "And because *you* supported me."

She stepped forward and brushed her fingers over Kailynn's cheek, leaning down to kiss her.

"I would not be alive today if not for you," she whispered.

"I think you have Dr. Busen to thank for most of that," she chuckled.

"Living and surviving are not the same thing," Isa said. "I've survived my life thanks to Dr. Busen, Paul, Remus, Rayal, Tarah, and everyone at the Syndicate who has supported me to this point." Isa's hands went up to take Kailynn's face. "But I'm *alive* because of you."

Kailynn's smile widened before she could help it and she took Isa's hands in hers, bringing them to her lips to kiss before she looked at Isa mischievously.

"That was pretty good," she teased. "Have you been practicing that?"

"Maybe," Isa laughed lightly, "but I'll never tell."

Kailynn chuckled and pecked a quick kiss on Isa's lips.

"I do mean it, Kailynn," Isa murmured. "I would not be alive if not for you."

Kailynn took a deep breath and pulled away from Isa, turning to walk past her and back to the car, reaching out as she passed to smack Isa's behind.

"Don't you forget it."

Isa chuckled, walking back to the car even as Kailynn jogged. She kept her eyes on Kailynn, watching her laugh and run back to the group that was waiting for them to return, all standing by their cars, watching silently.

Kailynn bounced around the car and smiled brilliantly at Isa as she opened the door and sat in the vehicle.

Isa approached her car, feeling lighter under the warm sun and surrounded by the fresh air. She suddenly felt her power return to her. She knew that the road ahead would be very difficult, but she understood that it would be better for her, the Syndicate, and all the people on her planet.

She felt ready to face the challenge.

Isa glanced at the others standing by their cars as she opened the door to her car. She winked at them with a smile.

"Try to keep up."

End

More Works by K.J. Amidon | Kyra Anderson

Inside
(Written as Kyra Anderson)
Inside – Pt. 1
Inside – Pt. 2
Inside – Pt. 3
Inside – Alternate Pt. 3
Inside the Commission: Tales from Within
Inside Special Expanded Edition

The Significant
(Written as Kyra Anderson)

The Significant Expanded Story:
(Written as Kyra Anderson)
The Degenerates
The Deserted

The Faith Series:
(Written as Kyra Anderson)
The Faith
The Sacred

The Coalition Series:
(Written as Kyra Anderson)
Forged Under Fire

The Dimension Guardian Series:
The Realm of Beasts – The Guardian Tournament
The Realm of Darkness – Blind Ambitions
The Realm of Humans – Fate
The Realm of Light – Imbalance
The Realm of Demons – Scars in Time
The Realm of Exile – Continuum

The Roadside Paradise Series:
Into Oblivion
Wander the Lost
Until Dawn Breaks

Printed in Great Britain
by Amazon